The Ghosts of Mankind Future

James Bohannon

Cover design and book design by James Bohannon.

Works by Zhuangzi were translated by James Bohannon.

Translated excerpts from works by René Descartes are from Henry Hallam, *Introduction to the Literature of Europe in the 15th, 16th, and 17th Centuries, II (2nd ed.)*, p. 451 (1843) and John Veitch, *The Method, Meditations and Philosophy of Descartes*, pp. 228-229 (1901).

ISBN-13: 979-8842239320

10.12.22.18.45

There are beliefs about beliefs

And there are beliefs about reality

And there is no absolute truth

Contents

The Castellated Mansion

During those months I had the advantage of living in a castellated mansion, in one of the prettiest parts of England, which I shall hate to my dying day, with a constant variety of attendants, who honoured me by sleeping in my room.

It bears so fair an outside that it seems difficult to quarrel with it. Yet the life that it concealed was inconceivably terrible. My head was full of the weakest, the most varying, the most wandering fancies—fancies of sheer and long-continued exhaustion. The parties, games, entertainments, meals, without a friend's face near me, without hope, wish, or volition, with the shouts and cries of the really violent to wake me sometimes at night, with every form of personal affliction to haunt and mock and yet companion me by day, with poor fellows playing all sorts of strange antics round me...the story makes me shrink in the telling, and almost regret that I have undertaken to tell it. But the evil wants cautery to the very core, and I believe that every story of the kind should be told.

Sitting at my desk as I am sitting now, with the comforting pipe and jug of beer by my side (deadly poisons to me, both of them, I have been often assured), and with a profound and grateful sense of extreme physical wellbeing, it is difficult for me to believe that not so long ago I was pronounced to be suffering at different times or all at once from epilepsy, partial paralysis, fits, delusions, suicidal and homicidal mania, 'voices' (a very professional and dangerous piece of humbug, of which I shall have more to say presently), 'visions', and the Lord knows what beside.

I rejoice in agreeing with a friend of mine, who, in talking the thing over, said to me, 'The worst of you is, you are rather brutally sane.'

It's a mad world, my masters.

Herman Charles Merivale
My Experiences in a Lunatic Asylum, 1879

The Cage

Friday, 5 April 2024

"...Russia's Ganymede Lander. The main purpose of the lander is astrobiology, the search for extraterrestrial life. They chose Ganymede, one of Jupiter's moons, because it has a liquid salty ocean beneath its ice surface and a rocky core deep beneath..."

The words filter into Peter Nolen's consciousness, first distant, then closer. The words compete with his dream. The incoherency bothers him as his brain labors to integrate the two. Then the dream evaporates, leaving only the words from the science story, and he is awake.

"...and the Mars rover mission from China, are continuing to build on their successes on the red planet's surface as they prepare us for manned missions in the next decade."

The host responds: "That's fascinating. There's just so much going on out there. Perhaps you could tell us a little about the rovers."

He remains in bed, not moving. His blonde curls frame his face. His eyes stare up at the ceiling, moving only with the occasional subconscious saccade.

"...to get around the long round-trip communication delays which can range from seven to forty-five minutes depending on the exact positions of Earth and Mars in their orbits, the rovers are designed to operate autonomously, like self-driving cars. But of course, they don't have to worry about traffic lights!"

The host laughs at his guest's joke. "It will be a milestone in human history when the first traffic light gets installed on Mars, won't it?"

"You could say we're paving the way." The guest chuckles.

"Do the rovers use some kind of computer vision to get around?"

"Yes, indeed, they do. The US rover, for example, has 3D vision, as well as the ability to see in infrared and other light frequencies, which it uses to identify scientific targets and ..."

After thirty minutes of lying still in bed, he waves his hand across his smartphone to cancel the alarm, turning off the national radio broadcast feed, and the room is silent. He stands up next to his bed and stares blankly. For the next seventeen minutes, he stands as still as a mannequin. He is here, but he's not here. Then, with a jerk, he fixes his gaze on the bedroom window. Rushing over to it, he pulls the blinds apart and peeks out, straining to see in every direction. Then, turning around, he squeezes his head with his hands. He comments to himself: "Gotta get ready. *Focus*."

In the bathroom, he looks at himself in the mirror, then shaves, pausing every minute or two for a minute or two. He cleans the shaver and puts it away. Gazing into the mirror again, he moves in closer, as if to see the details on his own face. "Can you see this? Can you?" Peering into his own eyes, he is angry. "Are you even real?"

Somewhere, a ghost blinks.

He presses hard on his temples to relieve his eye strain, then slides his two index fingers first along the inside of the upper orbits of his eyes, and then along the lower orbits, to massage the muscles around his eye sockets. He massages his head, starting with his forehead and working up over the top.

Standing still for another ten minutes, he gazes into the distance, grimacing. Abruptly, he looks to the right. Then his original blank expression returns and he stands another ten minutes. He uses the toilet, washes his hands, then stands for another several minutes, barely moving.

Gently brushing his forehead with his fingertips, the tension on his face briefly fades. He searches the bathroom for the semaphores of daily life, visual reminders of essential tasks, toothbrush, floss, hand lotion, hand soap, towel, deodorant, bandages, nail clippers, checking that there is nothing more to do.

In the kitchen, he pulls two English muffins out of their package, splits them, and pops them into the toaster. He eats them with butter and gulps down a glass of milk, then washes the glass and puts it away.

He changes out of his sleepwear and into a tight fitting pair of cycling shorts and a bright yellow and gray cycling jersey, then goes back into the refrigerator and pops a pickled pepperoncini into his mouth, which he chews and swallows, producing a pungent shock to his nervous system that helps to prevent muscle cramps in his legs on his daily rides. He's not actually sure how well the peppers work for cramps, but they definitely wake him up and get him going. Gesturing with a pointed finger, he goes through a visual checklist. *Toaster is unplugged... oven is off...nothing else plugged in...fridge is closed...no food left out...*

He puts on cycling shoes, fitted with cleats to lock into the clip-less pedals of his bicycle, then puts on his helmet and cycling gloves. He sets the alarm, and, opening the front door of his Berkeley condo, one of three units in his building, he walks his bicycle, which had been leaning against one wall in the living room, out through the door. He locks the front door. It is now nine o'clock and he is finally on his way, starting his morning ride up into the nearby Berkeley Hills, thankful that the long list of little tasks is complete because his head is killing him.

Once on the road, he and the bicycle are one. The bicycle, made with a carbon fiber frame and high-end components all around, is black, with black-wrapped handlebars. It weighs just fifteen pounds, despite having a large frame to accommodate his height.

His headache dissipates as he rides. No words come to mind. Images of the road enter his mind and transform directly into instructions for his body's muscle-powered motion. Up Marin Avenue, then along Grizzly Peak Boulevard. This section of his daily ride is the steepest, with a grade approaching thirty percent. Sometimes he detours through side streets to reduce the average grade, but today he feels strong and he's going straight up. He is focused, pushing hard, standing on the pedals. All he hears is his own breathing.

Continuing upward, he eventually reaches Central Park Drive and Tilden Park. The hills are still green, they won't turn brown until summer, and the ground is strewn with eucalyptus leaves, scenting the air with the woody camphorous scent of their oils.

With such good weather today, he decides to extend his ride, continuing out past the golf course and then along a higher elevation section of the twisting two-lane mountainous boulevard.

At the apex of his ride, he stops at an overlook. Sweat pours from his forehead. Drinking from his water bottle, he looks out over the Bay Area, the buildings of the UC Berkeley campus at the foot of the hills before him, the Bay Bridge and Yerba Buena Island in the distance, and further out, the skyline of San Francisco, lit by the morning sun. He can barely make out the two towers of the Golden Gate Bridge protruding through the morning fog.

Turning around, he coasts down through the hills, controlling his speed by squeezing the brakes. His leg muscles are large and have grown to accommodate the climb, but his hands always ache on the way down.

The voice in his head is intermittent. He catches individual words, but nothing coherent.

Reaching Virginia Street, he sits up and coasts, resting his hands. It is just a few blocks to his turn on Walnut Street, then another couple of blocks to Peet's Coffee on its peaceful little corner in North Berkeley. He has his usual double espresso, then heads home.

The voice is now speaking continuously, commenting on his parents, and it aggravates him.

He stands in front of the door to his condo, but he doesn't open it, instead yelling "Leave me alone!" But then he regrets it. He doesn't want the neighbors to think he's a wacko. He looks around, but there's no one nearby.

[I'm being a bit of an idiot with you.] Treacher sounds calm and professional. [We're just trying to help.]

He thinks back to Treacher: [You know, that's what it is. You're not trying to help. It's a game to you. You're manipulative. You don't care about people. You jerk them around. How many other people are you doing this to?]

Treacher to Peter: [The thing is, —]

Ignoring Treacher, Peter is reaching for the door handle with his key when he smells a soldering iron melting solder with a bit of flux. An image of a specialized antenna flashes in his head, part of an electronic circuit he designed and built last year. He sees himself sitting in front of a radio device. A data cable connects the device to his laptop.

In a window on his laptop, a frizzly signal pattern repeatedly mutates into different random-looking configurations. Suddenly, the pattern forms into more clearly defined shapes. Noticing that the shapes look similar to audio signals, he isolates that part of the signal and sends it through his laptop speakers as an audio source. He hears people speaking. He doesn't recognize the language. Some Slavic language? Middle-Eastern? It's not Spanish or Chinese.

The scene dissolves, replaced by the view of his condo door. He is still holding his key.

Treacher to Peter: [Why not get this over with? Give it.]

Peter: [Give it?]

Treacher to Peter: [You ground one of your flash drives into powder.]

In fact, he had pulverized it with a hammer. That was many months before, but not long before the voices showed up. It wasn't actually quite powder, but the left-over pieces weren't large.

Treacher to Peter: [Why wouldn't you just erase it?]

Peter: [It's more secure. So what? It was a cheap plastic drive, a throw-away.] *How could they have known about that?*

Treacher to Peter: [What was so important that you needed to be so secure?]

Peter: [Who's asking?]

Treacher to Peter: [Hell. Go clean up.]

Peter enters his condo, disables the alarm, sets his bicycle against the living room wall, closes the door, sets his fanny pack down, takes off his cycling clothes, tosses the clothes into the laundry basket, and gets into the shower. The voice in his head has let up, so this sequence of microtasks is almost as efficient as it would be for other people, taking no more than three minutes. Even so, the process is not automatic. He carries out the sequence deliberately, every microtask a distinct thought, checking that he hasn't overlooked anything. His mind is still not free, and his headache is back.

As he showers, he tries to stay present, taking in the scent of the body wash, cleaning every part of his body and remembering which parts have been cleaned and which haven't yet. He fights to avoid drifting into inner dialog so that he can finish his shower quickly. But Treacher mentions just one word, and he can't help but to reflect further on what had happened. *Radio.*

The signal he had unexpectedly received last year wasn't carried in the usual way. His radio system transmits and receives ultra-wideband signals, signals which are completely unlike the usual radio signals one encounters in AM and FM radio, wireless access points, and cell phones. With ultra-wideband radio, one doesn't tune into a particular frequency to listen. Because of this, he was surprised he had received any intelligible signal at all. There are still no widely used standards for ultra-wideband. Everyone out there has been developing their own formats, usually encrypted. So when his system received the signal, he had been surprised to find it carrying signals in the audio range, wiggling along at the speed of human hearing. He patched the signal into his laptop speakers and he heard a conversation with three, maybe four, people.

He had listened for some twenty minutes, with the voices sometimes suddenly cutting out, then fading back in, as he carried on with software development for his project, before discovering that his system had been reformatting and retransmitting the content the whole time. He had checked, and rechecked, the logic of his code, then searched around for his RF signal power meter and checked near his transmission antenna to be sure. He had a bug. His software wasn't supposed to take the received signal and send it back out. It was supposed to format *his own* signals and send them out. Or send out nothing at all if there's nothing to send. The whole point of receiving signals was to choose codes for his outgoing signals which wouldn't interfere with the signals already out there.

That had been slightly embarrassing. He had assumed he wasn't transmitting anything because he wasn't feeding anything in. So he hadn't bothered to shield his experiment to prevent radio waves from going out. Still, he thought it unlikely that it had caused any problems. The type of signals he transmitted isn't detectable by most radio receivers, anyway. In any case, the whole point of his project was that his signals wouldn't cause interference, so who would care?

That was last year. He had fixed the bug and moved on.

After showering, he tries to make some progress on his project. He gets his laptop out and sets it on the dining room table, then sets a handwritten research journal down next it. It has been a week since he last looked at it. And with all the distractions, the headaches, the mental fog, he can no longer remember the content.

He finds that the thin mental fog which often slows down his thinking and reduces his sense of presence is immediately lifted when he covers his head, and especially his forehead, lightly with his hands. The effect works only for a few seconds before the fog sets in again, but he recovers immediately by shifting the position of his hands. By repeating this procedure, he is able to continue thinking. Which is to say, thinking beyond the minimal level he gets by with when the fog is there.

Deep probes him continuously as he tries to work. His voice is deep. Peter imagines him as a mountain man, barrel chested, with a thick beard. Carrying an ax.

Deep to Peter: [What is compressed sensing?]

Peter: [Go look it up.]

Treacher is no longer talking. They seem to take turns in shifts. The shifts typically last hours, but they turn over without warning. It has occurred to him that it might be a good idea to make a record of when the shifts turn over. Maybe it would give away something about the nature of the voices and the organization behind them. But he'd start looking around for some place to make a note of the time and then he'd get distracted and forget to. Or, by the time it sinks in that a different voice is speaking, he'd have lost track of how much time had already passed. And now, there has just been another shift change. He picks up a pencil and —

Deep to Peter: [I don't get what a fractional Fourier transform is, either.]

He sighs. [Go look it up.]

Deep to Peter: [I did. I still don't get it.]

Peter: [Look, they can explain it to you, but they can't understand it to you.]

Deep to Peter: [Frickin' arrogant.]

Peter: [You're frickin' arrogant. If you don't like it, don't listen. You have no right to listen to my thoughts.]

He figures someone must be burning money doing this to him. Eventually, they have to figure it isn't worth it. Whoever they are.

He sets the pencil down and turns to his journal. But now, his head muscles tighten, distorting his vision. It's almost impossible to read. He squeezes his head for twenty seconds, pushing the skin on his scalp forward and up. The muscles around his eyes relax and he sees better. He returns to his research journal. Gradually, his head muscles clamp down again.

He once considered the old tin-foil hat idea, but even if he could wrap aluminum foil around his thick hair, he already knew it wouldn't work. It wouldn't block any signals. The foil would be too thin, and unless it wrapped all the way around, in a sphere around his head, cutting it off at the neck, the signals could get through anyway. Then he had thought of using a thick steel pot, something heavy that would block anything. Ideally, something with a lot of iron in it, as its magnetic properties are far more effective at absorbing signals than aluminum.

He had pulled a deep four-quart saucepan out from one of the kitchen cabinets, a high-end design made from five fused layers of stainless steel, aluminum, and copper, and placed it over his head, holding its long handle awkwardly off to one side, its flared lip resting on the bridge of his nose. Within seconds, his headache had melted away. The tension released, and his head cleared, and Deep's voice was silenced. He wasn't sure whether it was just because Deep had stopped talking just at that moment, but then Deep's voice started to come through muffled, like Deep had turned up the signal but still couldn't quite break through this new barrier. Then mental exhaustion had set in, along with a reduced sense of presence. Thinking suddenly required enormous effort.

Adjusting the saucepan to try to provide better protection, he had pressed the metal right up against his forehead. It felt cold. Painfully cold. All he could think about was how cold it was. And it didn't warm up. The saucepan had too much thermal mass. He couldn't think with the cold. He had to leave an air gap. Then he tried tilting the saucepan to one side instead, pressing it against his hair, and his head cleared up and he could hear himself think again.

He had walked around in his condo like that, steadying the heavy saucepan with one hand, testing to see whether he could consistently maintain an effective barrier. And then he had suddenly found himself standing there trying to remember what he was doing. For a moment, or more than a moment, he wasn't sure how long, he had gone blank. There was no headache. But there was no thought, either. He couldn't remember why he was standing there.

When he eventually recovered, when he had finally remembered what he was doing, he removed the saucepan. His headache had come back seconds later.

He had thought perhaps he could try to surround his head more completely, cutting off all possible entry paths for signals. Returning to the kitchen and pushing his pots and pans around inside the cabinet, he noticed his set of three stainless steel mixing bowls toward the back. He pulled out one of the pans to make room to slide the bowls out, then turned the entire set upside down over his head, trying to work out how to arrange them. Rotating the bowls this way and that, an unbearable metallic clanking and grinding filled his ears, every little slip sounding like a great sword striking or slicing across a suit of armor.

He headed to the bedroom. There, lying on his bed, he had positioned the mixing bowls around his head to form a large steel bubble, using pillows to hold them in place. It was still awkward, but it gave him shielding down to his neck. As with the saucepan, he noticed a reduction in muscle tension on his head, but it was not as effective, and it quickly became stuffy.

Was he really under attack? Had he imagined it? Perhaps his headache went away because of the weight pressing down on the top of his head, or perhaps because he was holding his arm up, taking the pressure off a pinched nerve or helping to force blood up into his head. On the other hand, perhaps they were just toying with him, turning off the headache when he put on the saucepan to mislead him. He raised his arm up, as if holding the saucepan, but it didn't make any difference at all. Then he repeated the saucepan experiment, with unclear results. The headache stopped *before* the saucepan made it over his head and didn't return.

He had gone in for a physical, mentioning headaches, but his doctor hadn't found anything abnormal, other than elevated blood pressure. The doctor recommended cutting back on caffeine and getting exercise. Not satisfied with this, he then mentioned other problems, like the gestural tics, and smelling things that weren't really there. The doctor had given him a long look, then referred him to a neurologist.

The neurologist had ordered several tests, but the tests also found nothing abnormal. No tumors, no evidence of stroke or seizures. His blood tests came back normal. The neurologist, in turn, referred him to a psychiatrist, but he has not yet followed up.

He squeezes his head again, then re-reads the abstract he had handwritten in his research journal. It dates back almost two years. As he reads, the voice in his head is silent, as if listening.

6/ 2 2/ 22

Ultra-wideband Cognitive Radio Using Compressed Sensing

Abstract: Using compressed sensing,we identify abstract holes in the ~~full range~~ total spectrum of radio communications.We define a cognitive radio system in which wideband symbols for transmission are adaptively defined to achieve non-interference with other ~~transmissions~~ transmitters. These symbols,which may also be described as time-domain signal components covering a variable range of frequencies, are then used for message transmission. To achieve this, the symbols already in use by other transmitters are learned bythe system and a parametrized symbol dictionary for each radio source is thereby constructed and usedfor interference avoidance.

While the abstract still makes sense to him, as soon as he gets to the equations, he bogs down. There's really not that much more work to do on it, but the voices seem determined to grind him down. He has a tension headache. And now, his eyes also hurt, invisible thumbs pressing in. To relieve the pressure, he squeezes his temples just above his cheekbones with his fingertips, stretching the muscles connecting into the orbits of his eyes.

It had taken him a month to figure out the connection between eye pressure pain and the muscles at the temples. Now, it's just one of numerous tricks he has learned to get by with. Like brushing his forehead with his fingertips when it cramps up. Or massaging the top center of his head. There, a band of tough tissue, the epicranial aponeurosis, is pulled tight by muscles at the front and back of the head and in the neck. He had researched it online. Epicranial aponeurosis: a sheet of pearly-white fibrous tissue, one of many layers covering the skull under the skin of the scalp. Every morning when he wakes up, it is already squeezing down over the entire top surface of his head, making it feel like an impatient headhunter is trying to shrink it for later display.

It's a new low-mess process. We get going with it before cutting your head off.

He remembers reading somewhere that one of the goals of a headhunter was to gain control over the murdered person's soul. But why wait until they're dead?

He presses just above his cheekbones one more time. This relieves the pressure on his eyes, if only for a few more seconds. But it's enough. He gets going again. He reads his abstract a third time.

[That's not what we would do,] Deep says.

He shakes his head in disgust, then grabs a sheet of paper and writes out one of the equations, copying it from the notes in his research journal. But he's stuck. He sketches a graph, then pulls some colored pencils out from his laptop bag and uses them to shade in shapes in the graph, one color per symbol. But the next step doesn't come to him.

He puts the pencils down and goes to the kitchen to get a glass of water. The muscle tension fades as he walks. He cracks his neck and briefly feels a sense of relief.

Deep to Peter: [What's it for?]

Peter: [What?]

Deep to Peter: [Cognitive radio. What would you use that for?]

Peter: [What would I use it for?] He tries to think of something sarcastic to say, or rather, to think, and then he notices the irony. [Radio that doesn't interfere. Get it?]

Deep to Peter: [So the symbols don't interfere?]

He's surprised. [Yeah. So the symbols don't interfere. Does that make sense to you?]

Deep to Peter: [So then your partners can transmit, uh, frickin' thing, so how does it help them?]

Peter: [Partners?]

Deep to Peter: [The people you're working with.]

Just like usual, he thinks. Another conversation that doesn't go anywhere. Frustrated, he sits down again at the table and reads his abstract for a fourth time. He tries to exorcise the voices from his mind, replacing them with the logic of signals and the mathematics of information theory. His tension headache replaces the logic with pain.

Deep to Peter: [Frickin' thing about me is I never give up.]

His muscle tension increases further and he goes to lie down. He's wiped. His tension fades, and in a matter of minutes, he's asleep.

An hour later, he wakes up. The headache is gone. But Deep is still there.

Deep to Peter: [Our government's going to frickin' hell, isn't it?]

And the headache is back.

Peter: [That's a weird comment. Don't you have better things to do?] He massages his head.

Deep to Peter: [I'm just saying. There's always somethin'.]

He briefly considers going back into his research, but the headache amps up. He calls his girlfriend instead. The headache disappears. The muscle tension melts away.

Deep to Peter: [That's what I'll be.]

Telling Shasha about his ongoing headaches, she is sympathetic. But he tries to stay positive. Has he seen a doctor? Yes, but they haven't found anything unusual. Maybe it's migraines. He doesn't tell her about the referral to the psychiatrist.

She has been really busy with her PhD research project down in LA. In May, she'll have time for a break. She'll come up to visit then.

Sunday, 7 April 2024

The wind howls outside Peter's bedroom window as he is jolted awake. The voice in his head sounds like an evil villain, deep and resonant. Speaking with passion, the villain warns him not to trust the others.

It sounds like a con. He doesn't buy into it. Anyway, it sounds like a soundtrack from a movie, so he can't take it seriously. It's just too goofy. Amateur acting. He lies back in the dark and studies the sound effects and improv, trying to decide which movie it is most like.

The darkness fades and is replaced with blue. It forms into a blue sky, an innocent blue sky. A blue and white 1967 VW Bus, in spectacularly pristine condition, hovers outside the building, facing the wide floor-to-ceiling window. He is in a high-rise condo, twenty floors up. A flock of snowy egrets flies past behind the VW Bus, their formation like the outline of a drifting cloud. The walls and ceiling of the condo are white and the floor is blonde wood. There is nothing in the room. There is no sound.

Suddenly, he finds himself wading in a large tide pool populated with several giant eel-like fish. Their skins shimmer with fluorescent and supersaturated colors. They writhe and glide near him in the crystal-clear waters. Small sparks jump sporadically from the fish as slowly undulating waves of a glowing blue-green light flow off their bodies into the surrounding water in patterns reminiscent of the aurora borealis.

One of the creatures tries to bite him with its comb of long curving needle-like teeth, its mouth big enough to swallow a leg. He scrambles out of the water onto the rocky bank and then continues to watch from there. The fish writhes, serpent-like, back the other way, ignoring him. In the distance, he sees the ocean. Its gentle roar constantly fills his ears. The scene is both beautiful and frightening to him.

And then it is night and he is in a town by the shore, waiting for Shasha at an exotic restaurant. There are no other guests. No lights are on inside the building, save for a few candles at the entrance ensconced in ornate brass holders. The entrance and halls are draped with intricately patterned fabrics. He waits on the restaurant's second floor balcony, looking out over the town's main street. The town is lit only by the moon. Two-story wooden buildings line the street. They are all dark and seemingly empty.

A circus silently parades by, its performers in full regalia, colors glowing with their own light, not a faded luminescence, but a deeply saturated velvety photonic ink. Fabrics in bitter orange and navy blue, vermillion and gold and moss green. Wispy tentacles of sand in the street swirl around their feet. Marching clowns and gliding horses, parasols held high, large silky flags quivering in the breeze. Wagons roll on well-oiled axles, painted with messages declaring the wonders of the circus. He can hear the ocean in the distance.

It is morning now, the sun rising in the east. Near the beach stands a grove of eucalyptus trees. He flies from tree to tree, searching for Shasha, but he doesn't see her. He stops on a massive rock within the grove and waits for her. He hears children playing nearby. An old couple walks by, pausing to look down at something, then continuing on their way.

Monday, 8 April 2024

Rain pelts the windows hard, the wind whips the trees outside, and the sky is dark. Peeking through the blinds, Peter decides to skip his morning bicycle exercise routine.

After breakfast, he sits down with his laptop at the dining room table and researches his condition. He has gone to the doctors with his symptoms and they've carried out a number of tests, but they haven't found anything wrong with him. The MRI brain scan was clean. His EEG was normal. His blood test indicators all lie within normal ranges. Together with the doctor's physical examination, the tests rule out several of the most obvious explanations for his symptoms. He was given a referral, but he'd like to understand his situation better before following up.

He doesn't remember any head trauma or concussion. Then again, a concussion might have wiped out the memory of it. And the damage can go undetected by a brain scan.

Brain infection is another possibility, either bacterial or parasitic, but he reads that doctors can't easily detect, or rule out, damage from an old infection. Maybe they could see it on an autopsy, cutting into his brain and examining it under a microscope. He doesn't remember any fevers or other symptoms which would likely have accompanied an infection, though.

Withdrawal symptoms from certain prescription medications might have provided another possible explanation for his experiences, but he hadn't taken any.

That leaves him with the psychiatric explanations, anything from anxiety to schizophrenia. He is dismayed by what he reads. With many psychiatric disorders, it seems from what he reads that it's not at all like solving an engineering problem, where one searches for causes. Instead, the diagnosis proceeds by ruling out everything in a given list and then choosing the diagnosis by default, producing what is called a "diagnosis of exclusion". Such diagnoses all involve subjective criteria.

Schizophrenia is one of these. Reading several articles on the subject, he gets the impression that there is no consensus on causes or on the degree to which it is a physical problem with the brain. Another diagnosis of exclusion, somatic symptom disorder, is defined by complaints of symptoms without a medical explanation. The diagnosis includes what used to be called hypochondriasis, or the condition of being a hypochondriac.

"How does that help anyone?" He's baffled. "How could someone define a complaint that lacks a medical explanation as a *medical* diagnosis? And if there's no explanation, how is it a *diagnosis*?" His engineering orientation makes him rebel against the very idea of an illness which is *defined* to be lacking in physical causation. How could there be a problem...and no cause? Or, if there's no actual problem, why give a diagnosis? The problem with a diagnosis which lacks a cause is that there's nothing to fix. The whole concept seems pointless.

He reads about the treatment. Mostly, it's workarounds, like helping a person learn to cope. There's no real fix. Perhaps that's all they can do. They just don't understand the underlying problem well enough. Or at all.

He starts to think it might be a waste of time to visit a psychiatrist.

He takes a break for lunch. He pops a frozen chicken pot pie into his toaster oven, then sets a timer for thirty minutes. While he waits, he peeks out the kitchen window at the large tree in the front yard thrashing in the rain. Then he flips through some news stories on his phone. He eats the chicken pot pie with a glass of milk.

After lunch, he returns to researching his condition. He looks at the characteristics of schizophrenia. Its defining symptoms are grouped into two categories, the positive symptoms and the negative symptoms. The positive symptoms, so-named because they describe additions to the sufferer's behavior, include delusions, paranoia, hallucinations, and disordered or dysfunctional thinking. The negative symptoms include reduced feelings of pleasure in everyday life and reduced emotions in facial expressions and tone of voice.

"I think I'm still pretty expressive," he says to himself. He tries a few facial expressions. They feel disingenuous to him. He returns to reading.

The articles mention paranoid delusions, the feeling that there are people after you. This, apparently, is frequently accompanied by voices in your head. The formal term is auditory hallucinations.

"What if you're not sure whether there are people after you?"

Deep doesn't comment.

Having voices in your head is not necessarily a sign of mental illness, the articles say. A surprisingly large number of people hear voices without any other symptoms at all. More than two percent of the population.

He thinks about that statistic. If you work at a company with a thousand people, maybe twenty of them hear voices, people talking to them who don't really exist. And they're not mentally ill.

One article mentions that a lot of people associate hearing voices in their heads with negative emotions. Fear and anxiety. Depression. But some people who hear voices find them to be supportive.

Peter: [That's definitely not you guys. Losers. You're like irritating children.]

[That's what I'll be to you,] says Deep.

Peter: [Right. That's what you are.]

He feels a beaming smile forced on his face. (-:Beaming smile:-) That's Deep's response.

Or it's his brain making things up.

The article on schizophrenia says it can also be associated with other types of hallucination, such as fake smells, or olfactory hallucinations. The scientific term is phantosmia. He doesn't know how often "normal" people experience olfactory hallucinations without mental illness, but it is dysfunctional nonetheless. The article says that if phantosmia is due to brain damage, it is sometimes due to damage in an area of the brain called the substantia nigra. In that case, it's clearly a physical problem, not a mental illness.

"Can olfactory hallucinations occur *without* a physical cause?" He tries to reason it through, but he still struggles with the idea of problems without physical causes. "Oh, it says here that migraines can also be associated with olfactory hallucinations. That's weird."

He researches migraines. Most of the articles are older and don't provide any real explanation. But then he finds a more recent article that explains it as a kind of rolling black-out in the brain. An electrical problem caused by chemical imbalances. The neurons just aren't working right and this can lead to fake smells and other strange sensations. It's like scrambling the electrons in a computer. Anything could happen.

He takes inventory of his own symptoms. Voices in his head. Fake smells. Headaches. Forced gestures. The forced gestures are literally painful to him. Usually, they occur on his face. A forced smile. A forced blink. But also finger twitches and shoulder shrugs. The medical term is "involuntary movements". He calls them gesticons. They're like emoticons, but with gestures instead. Emoticons you really feel. His own body manipulated to communicate a symbol to him with a kind of remote-controlled sign language.

"What causes involuntary movements?" He reads that they can be a symptom of schizophrenia. But the movements can also be tics. Or they can be due to seizures.

He takes a break from his screen and looks around the room. It's starting to get dark, so he turns on a light. Hours have passed since he started researching his condition. Stretching his arms and legs, he feels his shoulder joints crack. The stiffness which had set in dissipates and he feels a bit better. He goes back to reading.

Another possible cause of involuntary movements, he reads, is a disorder called tardive dyskinesia, whose symptoms can include involuntarily grimacing, smacking the lips, and sticking out the tongue. He never felt his tongue forced out, but who knows? Every month, new gesticons happen to him. Or he experiences them. Or they're *sent* to him.

He sits back and digests all of his reading. It's overwhelming. Diagnosis is hard. Even though he's intimately familiar with his own subjective symptoms, he has a hard time sorting it out.

He figures at least some of his headaches qualify as migraines. It might explain why he hears voices in his head, and it might explain the phantosmia, the fake smells, too. But, supposedly, that's rare. And actually, he hears voices all the time, not just when he's having a headache. So there's got to be something else going on. But his gut feeling is that the schizophrenia hypothesis just doesn't work for him. Choosing that hypothesis would be going down a rabbit hole. He wishes he could announce to the doctor at the beginning of his visit: "Hey, doc. I'll tell you what's going on, let's do some tests, but if you don't find anything, please, don't diagnose anything. It would be *unhelpful*." Maybe other patients would be OK with it, but he'd prefer to have the choice.

Deep to Peter: [Why the boggle would you care?]

Peter: [About what? About getting a *scientific* diagnosis? ... Did you ever get around to telling Treacher he's an idiot? Let him know I said so.]

He tries to ignore Deep as he considers how he might approach a doctor to inquire into checking for the kinds of brain infections that could cause his symptoms. He searches again, but while the search finds a lot of hits, none really match what he's looking for. Then, far down the list, he finds a research paper that might be relevant. It describes muscle-related symptoms such as forced blinks and involuntary movements of the jaw caused by damage to the blood flow and oxygen going to a particular part of the brain. It may even explain the fake smells.

He searches for related articles and finds another one which proposes the same hypothesis. It describes the same parts of the brain and it explains how they relate to the symptoms. Two different articles which give a consistent physical explanation. He finds this promising. Then he notices a mysterious connection. Somehow, involuntary movements and fake smells are caused together. What do they have in common?

Reading the papers, it becomes clear to him that they aren't *functionally* related. It's just a coincidence. The circuitry for them in the brain, the neurons for these two functions, happen to be right next to each other. Damage that general area, and both get hit at the same time. Your muscles don't work right, and you smell things that aren't really there.

He is reassured that there is real logic to the brain. The problems are caused by broken or damaged circuits. So it's a matter of figuring out where the damage is and what kind of damage was done. Then, maybe it can be fixed. But if it's a physical problem with the brain, why visit a psychiatrist?

He returns to the question of what a psychiatrist could do for him. It seems to him that there are no actual cures for many, maybe most, of the psychiatric conditions that could explain his symptoms. Worse yet, many of the medicines used to treat them have potentially serious side effects. He reads stories of patients who have suffered from the side effects. It could be risky just getting a diagnosis. Or a misdiagnosis.

He digs into the question of diagnosis error rates and finds that it isn't one-in-a-million. It's more like one in a hundred. He tries to verify the rate by reading additional papers, but he finds no consensus. It's actually one in five. Or one in twenty-five. Every paper is different. Every study gives different results. And no one knows how many diagnostic errors never get discovered. The one point of consensus is that misdiagnosis is an important and unresolved issue.

Heart surgery patients often completely recover. That's real medicine, he thinks. Scientifically supported and carefully practiced. But in the case of tardive dyskinesia, a condition caused by psychiatric *medications*, patients have a lifetime of suffering. And there are over *half a million* people in the US alone who suffer from it. At least, that's what he reads.

It looks to him like they never figure it out. No cure.

No, it's worse. They don't even know what's broken, much less how to fix it. It's just this-or-that hypothesis.

He sighs. There was once a time when psychiatrists classified being gay as a mental illness. Then they changed their minds. He can't even imagine how much harm had been caused by that kind of misdiagnosis. "What were they thinking? Isn't the point of medicine to help people?"

A voice whispers very quietly in his head, but he can't quite make out what it is saying. "Was that you, Deep?"

He hears only the rain drumming gently on the windows.

"Good. Maybe there's a problem with his volume control." He announces to the room at large: "You should get that fixed, Deep."

Taking a short break, he makes a cup of tea and brings the tea and some cookies back to the table. Returning to his search results as he snacks on the cookies, he finds that the situation with tardive dyskinesia is even worse than his first impression of it. The condition can be misdiagnosed as mental illness instead of what it really is, a neurological disorder. And with the misdiagnosis, patients are given drugs that actually make the problem significantly worse. He's not sure how credible the source is, but it adds to his reluctance to even consider treatments with psychiatric drugs.

He is reluctant to take a psychiatric drug that changes the way his brain works even with a correct diagnosis. He's intelligent. He needs his intellect to live his life. Uninstalling PeterOS to replace it with...what would it be called? He supposes it's something like starting your laptop in safe mode. The downgrade would be unacceptable.

He decides to hold off on the referral.

Deep to Peter: [That's the real you.]

He's back. [The *real* me?] he thinks.

Deep to Peter: [That's what it would be.]

He re-thinks his decision but comes to the same conclusion, then considers reversing it, just to prove Deep wrong. Then he switches again. [Can you shut up?]

Deep to Peter: [That's not the idea. Why not give it?]

[The *real* me?]

[The *real* me?]

[The *real* me?]

[The *real* <*click*>]

Peter is confused. That wasn't him. But it didn't sound like Deep, either. It sounded like his own inner voice.

Deep to Peter: [Frick.]

Peter: [What?]

Deep doesn't respond. Peter hears two more clicks in his head. Then there's just silence...

Peter: [Deep?]

Deep to Peter: [Just give it.]

Peter: [Give it? Give it, give it, give it. Take it, for God's sake, and leave me alone!]

Peter holds his head with his hands briefly, then forces himself to move on with his thoughts. Where was he? ...Psychiatrists. That won't work. But if he's not going to follow up on the doctor's referral, what should he do instead? What's going on with him?

Deep to Peter: [There's nothing wrong with you.]

Peter: [I guess that's why I have symptoms. Right. I can see the clear cause-and-effect relationship between there being nothing wrong with me, and the headaches, and the voices, and...] He sighs. [Never mind.]

He searches for his symptoms again, but now he adds keywords to focus in on external explanations. People doing things to him. Maybe Deep is real. Then he reflects. [Aren't you bored?]

Deep to Peter: (-:Disingenuous smile:-)

The gesticon distorts Peter's face.

He returns to his reading. This time, the search engine brings up blogs written by people who believe they are being attacked with microwave beams. They report the same sorts of symptoms. Their muscles move around involuntarily. They have voices in their heads, and forced blinking, and even electric shocks. But hey sound like nut cases. He doesn't doubt their symptoms. People have been reporting experiences like that for centuries. But their own explanations of their symptoms make no sense to him.

Some of the bloggers mention microwave mind control. Could microwaves be used to manipulate the brain? An online search produces several related topics. Electronic harassment. The microwave auditory effect. Sonic weapons. Attacks on diplomats at the US Embassy in Havana. That was back in 2016. Piercing squeals, buzzing and humming sounds, nausea and dizziness, intense head pressure, and headaches that lasted for months. Mental fog. Memory problems. Some of the diplomats noted that the noises persisted without any reduction in loudness even when they covered their ears. The articles quote experts pitching their favorite explanations for what had happened while discounting alternative explanations from other experts. No one has the definitive story. By 2019, the media was attacking earlier reports, alleging there was no support for what came to be called Havana Syndrome. At least one expert attributed the whole thing to mass hysteria. Having failed to come to any definite conclusion, in 2021, the U.S. State Department reiterated its commitment to continuing the investigation and a CIA task force was formed to expand the search for the true cause.

The microwave auditory effect catches his attention. The effect was first noticed by radar operators in World War II who reported hearing buzzing sounds and feeling pinpricks when they would pass in front of the transmitter. The effects were later investigated in more detail and reproduced in the lab. The bloggers claim the same effect was used to produce the sounds of words in their heads, but he can't find any report of a device that actually does that. Noting the amount of power that would have to be transmitted to make it work, it would hardly be practical. It wouldn't stimulate the brain. It would cook it.

"So it's just pinpricks and buzzing. There's no device to transmit voices. Although... Yeah, hold on. There's another place to check."

As he pulls up the US patent database, a prickly sensation spreads over his face. Slowly, the sensation converges around his mouth, like an effervescent beard. He swipes his hand across his mouth and down his chin in an attempt to wipe the feeling away, but it comes right back. Then a pin pricks him in the left index finger, right at the tip. Then the right index finger gets pricked. Then the left finger gets pricked again.

"Is that you, Deep?"

The beard disappears and his mouth deforms against his will into a smirk. It hurts.

"Right." He sighs. His mouth relaxes back into its natural neutral expression and his headache amps up. He rubs the top of his head, and this produces some relief.

Now he smells grilled steak. A fabulously perfect, juicy grilled steak. The fat floats on the air and melts into it. Then a whiff of black pepper crackles through the fat, a perfect balance of buttery smoothness and piquant accentuation.

"Now you're just showing off."

He really should get dinner soon, but he's not going to be thrown off track. He pushes food out of his mind. He's got work to do. "Forget the patents. I've got a better idea."

The aroma of the steak disappears.

He hauls his radio spectrum analyzer out of a bedroom closet and sets it on the dining room table. Returning to the closet, he brings out a cable and an omnidirectional antenna. He doesn't know how strong the signals he is searching for might be. If he doesn't find anything with that antenna, he'll bring out his horn antenna, with its rectangular flare that gathers radio signals like a large telescope collects light, so that he can see weaker, more distant signals. Since the horn antenna is directional, he'll mount it on a tripod with a swivel to aim it in different directions.

For two hours, he searches for unusual microwave activity. As expected, there are plenty of microwave sources. Nearby cell towers. His wireless access point. His neighbors' wireless access points. No cell phones nearby, except for his. The neighbors must be out somewhere. Weaker cell phone signals come in from further out. Even weaker satellite signals. An occasional radar reflection from aircraft taking off from Oakland International. In the end, he finds nothing unusual. Nothing stands out. He has searched all the microwave bands up through

40 GHz, and the signal formats all conform to standard protocols on the expected frequencies.

He's not surprised. It's hard to see how the microwave auditory effect would work without killing him slowly over time. The diplomats in Cuba had brain trauma from a single exposure. And despite the headaches, he doesn't have any sense of permanent damage. Nor did his doctor find anything to report. The microwave beam explanation has an urban myth feel to it. It's the go-to explanation when something weird happens. No one ever proves it.

"That's only half the problem, though. They can read my mind. It's a full round-trip communication. How would that work? Deep, how would that work?"

No response.

"So much for full round-trip communication."

He switches search terms. Just what is the state of the art in mind reading? He is shocked to discover that there has already been experimentation with interfacing to the mind with wires that pass through the skull and into the tissue of the brain. In one research project, electrodes which had already been implanted to monitor epileptic seizures were used to identify the words the patient was thinking, though the number of words the mind-reading system could identify was small. Mind-reading consumer headset products are also for sale, each one designed to feed your thoughts into your home computer, but the product descriptions are so vague that it's hard to take them seriously. Improve your meditation skills! Float a ball in the air! He rolls his eyes. Then again, what could you expect for a hundred bucks?

Then he runs into a surprise. Researchers at UC Berkeley, his alma mater, reported being able to use an fMRI machine to create video from thought imagery alone. The image quality was low, and the technique requires a giant machine wrapped around the subject's head, a machine which uses magnetism to watch the blood flowing in the brain, but it worked. Real mind reading. Right here in Berkeley.

When he searches for more related results, it appears to him that similar research is being carried out at several institutions around the world. "It's the real thing. Huh." He calculates the dates in his head. "They've been doing that for thirteen years already."

Still, all of the technology he finds for mind reading works up close. There's nothing for reading the mind from a distance. Maybe it's already here, but the people doing it aren't talking about it.

Or they are, but only to him. No press releases.

Tuesday, 9 April 2024

The storm has passed. Patches of white clouds drift in the blue sky and the air is scented with eucalyptus oil. A VW Bus drives by as Peter rides toward the Berkeley Hills. Judging by the hubcaps and a few other design details, he figures it dates back to the 60s.

At the top of his ride, he pushes himself at a steady rate along Wildcat Canyon Road, which skirts the boundary of Tilden Park, sweat dripping from his forehead. His eyes sting and he wipes the sweat away. Sitting up and freewheeling on a downhill section of road, he takes a swig of water from his bottle before returning to a steady pace, watching for areas made slippery by damp fallen debris.

The fresh weather has put him in a good mood and he decides to hang out for a bit at Peet's before heading home. After locking his bicycle out front, he clacks inside, takes off his helmet and sets it on a table, wipes his forehead and face with a towel from his fanny pack, and walks on his heels over to the counter to order a latte, trying not to make too much noise with the cleats of his cycling shoes.

Before picking up his latte, he decides to use the restroom, leaving his helmet on the table. *Nobody's going to steal it.* [Who would bother?]

Deep to Peter: [Bother about what?]

Peter finds this revealing. [He didn't understand.] *Nobody's going to steal it* was an abstract thought, an idea he had in mind. Deep wouldn't have heard it.

In the restroom, Deep continues. [You're not a frickin' hell.]

Peter: [What's wrong with you? Pervert.]

Deep to Peter: [I'm... Frickin' thing.]

Peter: [Stop following me around. You're like a little puppy dog. Woof woof.]

His eyelids are forced to flutter three times together with a slight forced smile. (-:My my:-) Another gesticon. Deep's response.

He rolls his eyes in disgust, then washes his hands. Exiting the restroom, he heels over to the bar to pick up his latte, then sits down at his table. He notices the helmet is still there. He doesn't think that in words. It's just an idea.

He used to get the urge to run around the block looking for the voices. It has been a month since he last tried. He never finds anyone. The weird thing about the situation is that they seem to have become like bad roommates, constantly nagging, providing unnecessary commentary on his life. Wherever he goes, they float right along with him. They pass right through the door and keep on yacking, oblivious to his human functions and uncaring of his need for privacy.

Deep to Peter: [But we're just trying to help.]

That again. [Nonsense. You're not trying to help.] Peter drinks down a quarter of his latte in one go, licks the foam off his mouth, and wipes the remaining residue with the back of his hand. Looking at the residue, he fetches a napkin and returns to his table.

Deep to Peter: [We can help. Just tell us what you're working on.]

Peter laughs to himself, then feels a little embarrassed. He looks around, but no one seems to have noticed. [You think you can help?] *Ridiculous.* He keeps the sentiment to himself. [Let's start here. Look this up on the Internet. Read me the definition of *linear operator*.]

Deep to Peter: [I don't do look-ups.]

Peter: [Right. You don't do look-ups.] *What does he mean by* help? [All right, then try this. You do know math, right?]

Deep to Peter: [Sure. I'll help with the math. What's it for?]

He drinks a bit more of his latte. [Just try it. Here's —]

Another customer approaches and puts his hand on a chair next to Peter, asking him a question, but Peter misses it. Refocusing himself on the world around him, he sees the customer's hand on the chair and nods. The customer takes the chair away.

He returns to thinking to Deep. [Here's a test. An easy question first.] He feels another gesticon, a forced facial expression, half anticipatory, half doubtful. He gives Deep a question that his dad had challenged him with when he was still in middle school. [If you have a rational number written in one base, say base 10, and you convert it to another base, say base 2, is it guaranteed to stay rational?]

Deep to Peter: [It's...of course, it issss...] Deep probes Peter's reaction, waiting, but Peter doesn't show his cards, keeping his mind blank. [...n't.]

Peter rolls his eyes. [Go get an education, then get a real job. You guys are wasting your time. And time is money. Think about it. I still go around doing things, but you, you're trapped there, wherever you are. Chained to your microphone. For how long? Sure, *just* eight hours at a time, but for how many years? Doing *nothing*. Is that a life? Is that a career?]

Deep to Peter: [You're a frickin' hell.]

Peter takes another sip of his latte.

Deep to Peter: [I'm the one who gave you that math problem.]

Peter doesn't get it. [Sure you did.]

He hears a text message arrive. The sound is right in front of him, but there's no phone there. There's nothing on the table but his bicycle helmet and his latte. He looks around, then gets his own phone out to check. Indeed, no message had arrived.

Peter: [Heh. That's your phone, isn't it? You have the same brand.]

Treacher to Peter: [You're not boring.]

Peter: [Treacher? What happened to Deep?]

A gesticon forces a facial expression on him. (-:Displeasure:-) He looks down to avoid giving anyone the impression that it's his own expression.

Treacher to Peter: [Hell. Just give it.]

He tenses up. *Just give it.* He tries to relax. They're probably not even real people.

He drinks down the rest of his latte as an old couple shuffles past his table on their way out, the wife crouched over slightly with a walking cane and the husband holding her around her shoulders. The old man recognizes him, as both are frequent customers of this Peet's store.

"You OK?"

Peter looks up at him. "What?"

The old man's expression shows his concern. "You looked uncomfortable there."

"Oh. No, I'm fine. Thanks."

The old man looks carefully at his face, then tells him: "Take care, young man. See you tomorrow."

The old man gives him a light pat on the shoulder and smiles at him. Peter acknowledges with a head nod and a quick smile. The old man shuffles off, guiding his wife to the door.

The old man recently told to him that he's 86 years old, and that his wife is 90. He told Peter that he's impressed with his wife, that she could keep coming into Peet's daily like this, even at that age. Peter had asked how long he has been coming to Peet's, and the old man told him he's been coming here since they first opened back in 1966, though, he said, back then it was just to buy beans, adding that at the time, he was a grad student at Cal studying biochemistry.

On another occasion, the old man had brought along shiny black-and-white pictures, slightly curled, to show him. "I still remember when that Savio fellow made his big speech on campus," he said. "It was a big deal at the time, all over the news. I called my girlfriend from a pay phone to tell her to come and then snapped these photos of the crowd. That was back in '64." He pointed out Savio in one of the photos. Peter was already aware of Mario Savio's fame as an activist and member of the Berkeley Free Speech Movement and was impressed with the photo. "That was sixty years ago," he said. The old man had nodded.

As the door closes behind the old couple, Peter thinks about his parents. They didn't get old. He wishes they were still here. He'd have so much to tell them. He reminisces about them.

His dad had taught him all the math he knew until he reached high school, years beyond his grade level. Basic algebra in third grade.

Trigonometry in fourth. A picture flashes into his head of his dad giving him a little math lesson back in sixth grade. His dad had asked him: "Do you think numbers are real? One, two, three? The square root of two? Pi? Are they real like rocks and trees?" He remembers saying: "I think so."

His dad loved all aspects of math, everything from the practical to the theoretical, even the philosophical. And with this little lesson, his dad had given him his first exposure to the deeper mysteries of the universe. "You might find this strange," his dad said, "but there are *more* than an infinite number of numbers. There's no way to write them all down, and you can't count them all. *Not even if you go on forever.*" His dad then showed him the proof. It was the first time he had ever heard of the idea that there were distinct things you couldn't count.

They had these little math discussions all the time. It was what made him truly competent in math. It was fun, strange, exciting. "So then is the universe bigger than infinity?" he had asked. "If there can be more than an infinite number of things in the universe, then the universe must be bigger than infinity. Right?"

His dad had laughed hard at this. "Good question!"

Back at home, he tries again to research his symptoms online. This is the umpteenth time he has tried, but he uses different search terms this time. He finds an article about TMS, or transcranial magnetic stimulation. It says magnetic stimulation of the brain can cause changes to how it operates. The explanation seems vague to him, but the phenomenon it describes is a revelation. Stimulate the brain from the outside, and it can be made to perceive things that are not there. Not only that, muscles can be moved involuntarily with the stimulation. It's not a question of whether it can be done, but from how far away.

TMS uses a pair of wire coils to produce a magnetic field in the brain. Depending on what part of the head the coils are placed on, a different part of the brain is affected. He reads that if it is applied to the primary motor cortex, the part of the brain that runs left to right in a strip through the middle of the top part of the head, the patient's muscles will move. If the wire coils are placed instead on the occipital cortex, the part of the brain at the back of the head which connects to the optic nerve from the eyes and handles vision, the patient will see phosphenes, little flashes of light. These are the kind of flashes you might see, for example, if you sneeze too hard. Astronauts have seen phosphenes in space when high energy particles from space hit that part of their brains.

With enough knowledge and computational power, it might be possible to create visual patterns in the brain by sending some sort of energy into it, as happens with TMS or with particles from space, but when he carries out a search for this idea, he can't find anyone doing research with experiments like that.

Following links from the article, he reads about low field magnetic stimulation, electroconvulsive therapy, and a number of other methods of stimulating the brain. It reminds him of an exhibit at a science and technology museum he once saw, back when he was in college. The exhibit, which provided an exploration of mental illness in the 19th and 20th centuries, showed a life-sized model of a person being treated with electroshock therapy. Nearby sat a long, thin wooden cage of the type used for restraining psychiatric patients. It looked to him like a slatted coffin. He was so repulsed by what he saw that he left the exhibit after just a few minutes.

Surprisingly, electroconvulsive therapy, which works by intentionally inducing seizures in the brain, is still in use. The idea of inducing seizures as a form of treatment doesn't make sense to him. Some forms of the treatment give the brain a good hard kick while others are gentler and use a number of small kicks spread out over time, but either way, it is hard for him to believe that would fix brain problems. He views electronic systems as delicate. You don't fix them with jolts. How many times has anyone ever fixed a smartphone by dropping it? And if the brain is a system, it is one of the most delicate and complex systems there is.

The articles he reads claim that the therapies are based on evidence. [Evidence? Evidence isn't enough. What ever happened to proof? How is that science?] It strikes him that 21st century therapeutic knowledge of the brain is alchemy, not science. Like trying to understand life without knowing what DNA is. Or figuring out what's wrong with a computer without ever looking inside.

[It would be like that to you,] Treacher says.

"Yes - it - would - be." Annoyed, Peter speaks out loud, for more emphasis. "They try stuff and look for effects. But there's no real understanding. The galling thing is that the articles claim there's no brain damage with the therapy. It's just the ongoing psychiatric symptoms, they say. They kick the TV to fix it, breaking a wire inside, then say it's just the TV still not working. Billions of neurons, and somehow they know they didn't break anything."

Treacher to Peter: [That's a hell for you.]

"It really is ridiculous," Peter says. "A jolt has no subtlety. By definition. It's a hammer. If you have a complex system like the brain, you need a complex interaction with it to accomplish anything."

Clicking around, he reads a bit more. "It's 86 billion neurons. Although neurons are slow, so..." He checks a couple of statistics, then makes a calculation in his head. "Yeah, like a billion times slower than transistors." He explores a bit further and discovers that while the brain has 100 trillion synapses, which is to say, 100 million million connections between the neurons, a modern-day laptop can easily store over 50 terabytes, which is 400 trillion bits of information. "OK, so it's really no more powerful than a laptop. Still, it's not a *small* system."

He sits up and looks away from the screen. "But this isn't explaining how voices get into my head."

Treacher to Peter: [That's not our —]

"So if the voices are created inside the head, if they don't come from outside, there must be calculations of some kind, inside my head, figuring out what to say. The words aren't random. The calculations figure out what to say, somehow. At the same time, there's no software in the brain. It's all hardware. It's all wires and electrical activity. The neurons are kind of like the transistors in a computer chip. So the problem must be wherever those calculations take place, the place where the brain figures out how to make sentences. Right. There's hardware in the brain and it's making up sentences."

"But wait. I have control of my sentences. I'm talking to myself with perfectly formed sentences. Right now. It's working just fine. There's nothing wrong with my brain's calculations."

Treacher to Peter: [That's a brill —]

"And that's what —"

He's lost. He expected a reaction from Treacher. But did that expectation kick off calculations in his brain, generating the sentence "[That's a brill —]", until he cut it off? He was able to cut it off in the middle. It's as if he were controlling the sentence. But he has no idea what sentences he is going to hear from the voices before he hears them. He has no ideas in mind that the sentences from the voices are expressing. The content of the sentences aren't from his own thinking.

Then again, he's not sure. Sometimes he speaks and meaningful sentences come out of his mouth, even though he doesn't explicitly have any clear idea in mind before speaking. Or so it seems.

"I suppose if the voices were coming in from outside the brain, someone transmitting words to my head with some sort of advanced technology, it would induce activity in the part of the brain that deals with sounds, but it wouldn't create activity in the part of the brain that generates sentences. Those are two different parts of the brain. There's the —" He goes back onto his laptop and navigates to a website that describes the brain and language. "It's right here. There's Wernicke's area and Broca's area and some kind of connection between them. Those are the areas involved with sentences. One for creating sentences and the other for understanding them. And the sound comes in from a different area..." He clicks a link. "Here. It's called a tone map, in the auditory cortex." The page has a little diagram showing a range of sound frequencies laid out neatly in a little section on a map of the brain. "It says that's the area of the brain where you hear ringing in the ear. The ringing isn't actually in the ear at all. It's only there, in the tone map."

Treacher offers no comment.

"Yeah, so that makes sense. If the voices come in from outside, the brain doesn't need to make up the sentence. It hears sounds, so it *hears* the sentence, but it doesn't have to *create* the sentence. And hearing and creating are in different parts of the brain. There must be a way for some sort of brain scan to see the difference." He's impressed with his own idea. "That would be fascinating. Nothing coming out of the sentence creation part of the brain, and at the same time, sounds in the brain which sound like meaningful sentences. The doctor'd have a hard time explaining that!"

He notices his tension headache has gone away. Are they still there? He hasn't heard any comments from the voices for a while now.

Clicking through on another link, he reads about the auditory cortex, the part of the brain which processes sounds. One claim he finds striking is that a person isn't consciously aware of a sound unless nerve signals travel all the way from the ear to this particular part of the brain. "So consciousness, at least for sound, happens right there, in that bit of circuitry." He touches the labeled image of the brain on his laptop screen as he talks to himself. "If someone could put data directly into the circuits there, making the neurons turn on, like, say, with radio signaling, somehow, you'd hear sound. Even if the ears don't hear anything. It would be sound from nothing at all."

He marvels at the idea that consciousness, indeed, one's very being, could come from nothing more than putting data through a circuit. He mulls over this idea. "Robots will probably be conscious someday."

He switches focus. If it's his brain making up the voices, how could he lie to them? The brain would already know everything. But he finds that he can successfully lie to the voices in his head, despite the continuous mind reading. They hear the words in his head, but they don't seem to be able to read his abstract thoughts or ideas. So if it's the brain making up sentences on its own, there's something inconsistent about it.

Since he *can* lie to the voices in his head, they are probably real people. But even if they're real people, there are layers to his thinking and they've only breached the outermost layer. Still, that's a massive intrusion into his privacy and personal security.

"That's a problem," he concludes.

Treacher to Peter: [It's not a problem.]

A deep realization hits Peter. "Oh my God! Every time I use an ATM, you're —"

Bad habit. People will think he's strange talking to no one. He switches to inner dialog. [Every time I use an ATM, you hear every thought. And when I changed my alarm code, too. And my passwords. That's what it is. It would be all of my accounts. That's what this is all about. You're all identity thieves. I get it.]

A feeling of dread fills the pit of his stomach. It's the ultimate identity theft technology. Every PIN code. Every password. Every time he reviews his finances, they're listening. His social security number. His birthdate. All of his social contacts. In no time, they'd have it all.

Except that it's not necessarily true. He can think more carefully. Maybe. He pokes at the table, tapping out the pattern of his ATM PIN code. No words come to mind. It's just a pattern of finger motions. They might not know the code. But can they see what he sees? Does he have to avoid looking when he punches in the code?

He notices something similar with his online passwords. He types them in but doesn't think of each and every character out loud in his head as he does so. The same goes for the alarm code for his condo. What a burden! He has some privacy, but only if he is careful not to let something slip.

Treacher to Peter: [If I were you, I'd just not think.]

[Not think?] He has hardly been thinking anyway, with all the distractions in his head. Now he has to think without thinking? To protect his privacy, he has to know what not to think about with words in his head, before he thinks them. He needs *wordless thinking*. He tries, but he can't do it. Maybe there's some truth to the idea that you need language to think.

He tries an experiment. Grabbing a sheet of paper and a pen, he writes down some dollar figures and tries adding them up without thinking in words, but the numbers pop into his head as words. He can't help it.

It's tough keeping track of what words he uses in his head while trying to get something done. He might have already given away some of his passwords without realizing it. Then he realizes this thought came to him without forming a complete sentence in his head. Intuitively, without syntax, without grammar. A combination of concepts connected together without words.

Treacher to Peter: [I'm not going to help you.]

His headache returns. Grabbing his head with his hands, he feels a slight relief, but the headache still grinds him down. He tries to remember whether he had ever, even once, thought about any of his account passwords in words since the voices started listening months ago. He must have. He must have been checking his accounts every month. He just doesn't remember the experience. And they probably record everything he thinks. It would take only one slip to give it away. His stress builds.

He experiments, trying to invent passwords without thinking about them with words. "[Sn0wboard*(333)$]" comes out as "[Cap-S - n - zero - w - board - star - paren - three-three-three - paren - dollar]". It's clearly enunciated in his head. Or inunciated. As in inner-voice-enunciated. It's in the head, not spoken out loud.

He tries one more time. A random sequence. [g, cap-Q, 5.] He sighs. He has to write it down or repeat it to himself several times to remember it, and that gives it away.

Then he gets smart and tries using software that makes up random passwords for him so he doesn't have to think about it. He figures he'll cut-and-paste it when he needs to use it. He could keep it in the keychain app on his computer, protected with encryption. But he needs his sign-in password to get into his computer at all, and that's one he can't keep in the keychain. He can't cut-and-paste it. He has to remember it. And if they know that password, they can get into his keychain, too. He could change it, but they'd definitely hear him practicing the new one.

He decides not to worry about that. So long as they don't take the computer, or hack into it over the Internet, they can't get to his keychain. Maybe it's good enough.

But they would know the WiFi password, too. They could still potentially get to his computer when he's online. Worse yet, when he opens the keychain, he sees the password. Even if they can't see what he sees, he has to be careful not to read it to himself. It's a real mind game.

It occurs to him that even two factor authentication, where the bank requires your password to sign in and also sends you a text message with a code, isn't safe from mind-reading identity thieves. They would hear it in his thoughts when he reads it. But at least he'd know about it if they try to use it. Indeed, it would be an opportunity to go after them. Finally, there would be a real-world hook to grab onto.

Treacher to Peter: [It's not about the money.]

Peter: [Yeah. It's not about the money.]

Treacher doesn't respond. Peter listens in his head. He waits, but still, no sentence is generated. Or at least, he doesn't hear one. He can't force a comment in his head merely by expecting one.

Peter: [OK, then what is it about?]

Treacher to Peter: [That's the boggle.]

Peter: [Who are you? Government?]

Treacher to Peter: [That's the thing we're not.]

Peter: [Russian spies?] *Who else would read people's minds?*

Treacher to Peter: [Why would the Russians —]

Peter: [It's just interference. Just like the meddling in the elections. Except now, it's targeting American engineers.]

Treacher to Peter: [Do I sound to you like I have a Russian accent?]

Peter: [Maybe you went to school in the U.S.]

Treacher to Peter: [Maybe I did.]

Peter: [OK. I'm being dumb. You're a government contractor.]

Treacher to Peter: [That's not what I would do.]

Peter: [That's ambiguous. You mean you wouldn't be a contractor? Or you wouldn't keep trying to figure out who the voices are?]

Treacher to Peter: (-:Contemptuous smile:-) [Why would I be doing this?]

Peter: [The government wouldn't do this. And neither would their contractors. They'd go to jail if they did. It really is just identity theft.]

Treacher to Peter: [That's not it. Why don't you get it over with. Give it.]

It used to be that pure memorization was the best way to keep something secret, but no longer. When your mind is open to the world, you have to rely on physical security. But even that isn't enough if a hacker, a *neurohacker*, knows everything about you and can use what they know to carry out a social engineering attack.

So it's actually much worse. They might hijack his phone account. They'd know his name, his social security number, his PINs, everything. What good is two factor authentication if they can get into *everything*?

Treacher to Peter: [We're not a bother to you.]

Peter: [You're a *hell* of a bother! Why don't you give up? You'll never get away with it. Whatever you're trying to do.]

Treacher to Peter: [But that's the marvel of it.] (-:Beaming Smile:-)

Marvel? Or atrocity?

Where was he? Security. Threat models. For each type of threat, there is a threat model that helps you understand how information can be stolen and how it can be protected. Computer viruses. Phishing attacks. Card skimmers. Pick-pockets who get your credit cards and leave you without ID. But this is a completely new threat, and a completely new model is required. The *mind reading threat model.* There has never been anything like it.

He decides to keep a closer relationship with his financial advisors. He reflects on this. The oldest and most basic form of security may turn out to be the best: Service by professionals who maintain personal knowledge of their clients. People you can trust. A society in which everyone knows you and you know everyone.

If only we all lived in a village.

But that's not going to be enough. He still has to operate safely on a day-to-day basis. How can he protect his PINs and passwords? If he changes one, the voices will immediately know what the new one is. And how can the bank help? If he tells the bank his password has been compromised, they'll just tell him to change it, but what good would that do? It aggravates him to be trapped like this.

An idea now comes to him, a trick for memorizing a password or a PIN without thinking about it in words. To create a new PIN code, rather than saying "[five, two, seven, three]" in his head, he touches each key and says a sequence number or letter. Pointing to the "5" key on the keypad, he thinks “a”. Next is the “2” key. For that, he thinks “b”. Practicing a few times, he develops the habit of thinking “abcd” as he presses the keys for “5273”. The idea works. He makes a note to change his PINs and his alarm code.

He tries using this new idea to create a password for his laptop. But it doesn’t work. It’s confusing. With a PIN code on a keypad, there are just a few places to press, a small number of choices on a simple rectangular grid. What he did, on reflection, was to associate “abcd” with a pattern of finger movements. But a good laptop password uses keys all over the place.

He’s pretty sure he hasn’t signed into one of his accounts since before the voices started, so leaving that password alone would be better than changing it. It’s an old account he still gets paper statements for. He doesn’t need to see it online. Still, he’s uncertain about the other accounts. He checks each one to consider how to protect it.

“And that’s that,” he says at length. He sighs. “I’ve just give away a thorough analysis of my accounts and passwords.”

How do you protect yourself if merely thinking about it gives it away? It’s a paradox. You have to be prepared before they show up. When you start hearing voices, it’s already too late.

He lies down to nap, burned out by the futility of it all.

Saturday, 11 May 2024

Having finished a key part of her PhD project, Shasha has time for a short break. Keeping her promise to visit Peter, she has come up to Berkeley to visit for a couple of days. She will be returning to Los Angeles tomorrow night.

The weather in Berkeley is perfect. Blue skies, 70 degrees, with a slight breeze. They are on an outing to Pier 39 and Fisherman’s Wharf in San Francisco. Their walk from Peter’s condo to the Downtown Berkeley BART subway station takes them through the UC Berkeley campus, down alongside Strawberry Creek under oak trees, past the towering trees of Eucalyptus Grove, and past massive redwoods. Crossing Oxford Street and continuing down Center, the Berkeley Art Museum & Pacific Film Archive is on the right. On the left is a Tibetan souvenir shop selling scarves and handmade jewelry and singing bowls, and also Indian print cotton bedspreads, and inspirational hanging banners. The rest of the street is a restaurant row. Persian food. Chinese food. An atmospheric Japanese yakitori dinner restaurant and izakaya-style bar.

Burgers. A hot dog and sausages place that has been around for almost sixty years, serving every kind of link. A Mexican-Korean fusion place that serves tacos with Korean-style fillings, or what Peter calls Korean food in a Mexican configuration. A new Tibetan-Naxi restaurant with red lanterns hanging out in front. An even newer place painted in bright colors with a beach theme that sells nothing but hot dogs and ice cream cones. Mostly ice cream cones. It's still early, so most of the restaurants aren't open yet, though there's a smell of something unidentifiable cooking in the air.

Last night, they walked from Peter's place to the Tibetan-Naxi restaurant for dinner. The red lanterns hanging outside glowed with a warm light. It was quite romantic, with rough-hewn logs serving as ceiling supports and their rough lumber table lit with a yak butter candle. They had left civilization and were deposited into a secluded mountain village in China's Frontier.

The owner, a short but strong, trim woman, with a slightly weathered face and jet black hair tipped with pink highlights, barely spoke English. But she could speak Chinese and, speaking to Shasha, she told them her story.

As it turns out, her son got an opportunity to study at Berkeley. When he graduated, he stayed to work in the Bay Area and his mother decided to move here to be near him. Her own mother is from Tibet, and her father, a member of the Naxi Chinese minority group, is from Shangri-La, a small city in Yunnan Province, where she grew up and eventually ran her own inn and restaurant.

They had ordered Yunnan ham, morels with asparagus, fried potato cake, and a sampler of three different spicy Naxi dishes. For dessert, they nibbled on bits of yak cheese and grapes. The owner had said that she imports the yak cheese directly from a small producer she knows in Lijiang, a beautiful town in Yunnan crisscrossed with little granite waterways which is popular with Chinese tourists.

Shasha told Peter that, from what she has heard, Lijiang is like a little paradise, though it's extremely crowded with tourists, primarily Chinese tourists, these days. She'd like to visit someday. She mentioned that her parents went once, years ago, before she was born.

Focused on Shasha and their dining experience, Peter had been able to relax. The voices had receded into the background. But that didn't last. A voice in his head had started up again after they returned to his condo and his headache returned. But the headache this time was different. Usually, the headaches are muscle tension headaches, sometimes migraines, but this headache felt like pressure from the inside pushing outward. The constant awareness of being watched had also inhibited him, ruining the romantic mood. Shasha could sense his distraction, but

Peter said nothing about the voice, saying only that he had a headache and wasn't sure why.

Reaching the intersection of Shattuck and Center, they cross the street to the BART subway station entrance. A young man is playing a Bach flute sonata on the sidewalk in front of the entrance, perhaps testing out the acoustics of its glass arch. The couple looks for a box to toss some coins into, but there isn't one.

In the BART tube, crossing the bay, the train's wheels grind against the curved sections of track. Their screeching is amplified by echoes between the train's metal body and the concrete walls of the tunnel.

Peter can faintly hear a voice in his head. How could a transmitted signal penetrate so deeply into the tunnel? They must be on the train with him. He wants to walk the length of the train to take a look, but Shasha would find that strange, so he suppresses the urge. Instead, he furtively glances around and down through the train. There are only a few people on the train, some with backpacks, one man with luggage, but it looks as though no one is speaking. Then, with all the train noise, he wonders whether the voice in his head can hear his thoughts.

Shasha loudly asks him, over the roar of the BART tunnel transit, if anything is bothering him. He seems moody to her. "Ever since dinner last night, you seem distracted. Is something wrong?"

He gives her a warm hug. "I've been a bit under the weather I guess. It's probably just the headaches."

"Do you take something for them?"

"I try to avoid headache pills. You can't take them too often or they'll make the problem worse."

She urges him to see a doctor again.

Emerging from Embarcadero Station, the weather is typical for San Francisco. Windy, and colder than one might expect for this time of year. They walk along The Embarcadero toward Pier 39, passing the Ferry Building as they go. Palm trees line the plaza in front. Further along, they pass a science museum and several nice restaurants. In the distance, off to the right, the West Span of the Oakland Bay Bridge arches out over two miles to Yerba Buena Island which sits in the middle of the bay.

Reaching Pier 39, they explore the little neighboring harbor filled with sailboats, taking selfies with sea lions resting on floats in the background, then watching street performers banging on drums and posing as statues.

While walking west from Pier 39 toward Fisherman's Wharf, Peter notices a World War II submarine on exhibit and suggests they take the tour, but Shasha prefers to stay outdoors in the fresh air.

As they walk and chat, the image of the sub remains in his mind, and it dawns on him that the sub is a giant Faraday cage. It would never have occurred to him in the past, but now, his mind is primed.

Any completely sealed metal box or room can be a Faraday cage. The metal absorbs electrical signals and radio waves, preventing them from passing either into or out from the box. He has a Faraday cage at home that he has used for his cognitive radio research, to shield his experiments. He can fit a small amount of electronics equipment inside, but it's not big enough for him to crawl inside. He wonders what would happen to the voices if he could hide inside a Faraday cage. Would they disappear? If only he could find a large, heavy-duty Faraday cage he could just walk into. And here it is, a giant, thick metal sheet, wrapped around a space open to him for nothing more than a small fee. Over 1500 tons of steel, a 311 foot long cylinder snugly suspended in sea water.

His radio engineering mind turns on. If the voices enter his head as radio signals, then there are limits on how it can be done. To transmit audible sounds as radio waves, there is a minimum frequency that the radio waves must use. And that allows him to work out how thick the metal would have to be to block the radio waves.

He carries out a quick skin depth calculation in his head. The steel hull, almost an inch thick, would block even very low frequency signals, lower than five cycles per second. That's slower than any signals which might interact with the brain, he figures, and certainly too slow to carry voices. It wouldn't matter whether the signals are carried on a telephone wire, transmitted by cell phones, or beamed to his head. Regardless of the technology, if signals down to five cycles per second are blocked, voices can't get through.

Old Man to Peter: [That's not it.] Old Man's voice always sounds hoarse and raspy, perhaps from years of smoking.

Peter: [What's not it?]

Old Man to Peter: [That's not it.]

Peter: [The sub? It's great!]

Old Man to Peter: [Helluva...]

Peter squeezes his head briefly with both hands, then turns to his girlfriend to focus on her.

Old Man to Peter: [...bottle.]

"So you said your mom, uh, your mom is...?" Peter drops his hands down as Shasha turns to him.

"Weren't you listening at all? She wants to meet you and she's going to be out here from Vancouver next month."

"Oh."

The sea air catches his attention, a wispy chaos of dried seaweed, brine, organic decay, and a faint but rich cabbagy tinge of dimethyl sulfide, the chemical that gives the sea a characteristic smell, carried in on erratic gusts from phytoplankton in the bay. A bakery nearby contributes hints of yeast to the mix.

Off in the distance is Alcatraz island. A big sign advertises cruises out to it, a giant red and white model of a ferry sitting on top of a pole that towers over the ticket office. People are milling about everywhere. But Peter doesn't see Alcatraz, nor does he see the people milling about.

"You're so distracted these days," Shasha says.

They continue their slow walk, holding hands. She looks back up at him, catching a glimpse of his face, which is clearly stressed, muscles tightened, eyes distant as if inwardly focused. She worries about him. "Is something wrong? Is it really just headaches?"

"I guess I have been distracted. The headache doesn't help, but it's... it is hard to focus. I'm not sure." He smiles to comfort her. "Should be fine, though!" They walk a bit further, still holding hands. "Oh, did I mention? Ethan has been teaching me a little Chinese."

"How is he?"

"Seems to be busy. Running around doing interviews, I guess, and writing articles."

"OK, try out some Chinese on me."

"Um... Wo ai ni". *I love you.* He says it just right, including the tones. It sounds like *whoa? aye! knee?*

"Very good! So Ethan was willing to teach you how to say *love* in Chinese? What a guy!"

"Actually, I looked that one up."

"Well, you should keep going. Jia you!"

"Jeeya yo?"

"Perfect!"

"Perfect? Oh, my pronunciation. What does it mean?"

"Pedal to the metal. Keep up the good work."

"Jeeya yo." Peter smiles. "Ethan also started to show me how to write Chinese characters. I know, like, three characters so far."

Shasha laughs. "It's not easy! But it's easier than you might think. On your smartphone, you can use the Chinese keyboard to type in the pronunciation with English letters, and the Chinese characters will pop onto the screen."

"Oh, that's how you do it." It was a mystery to him. How could a Chinese keyboard hold thousands of characters?

"Let me show you."

They sit down together on a nearby bench and Shasha pulls out her phone. She selects one of several different types of Chinese-input keyboards and then spells out a few characters. The characters pop up onto her screen: 程莎莎. She sends the characters as a text message to Peter's phone.

"That looks pretty easy. But it looks like a bunch of different characters pop up when you type."

"That's right. You type in how to say the character, but you still have to know what the characters look like, and you pick which one you want. But at least you can be lazy about learning how to write them. In fact, I read it's a big problem in China these days. Everyone is getting so lazy, they can't even remember how to write some of them unless they use their phone or their computer."

Peter pulls out his phone to check Shasha's text message. "Wow. I had no idea my phone could show Chinese characters. It just works. Just like that."

Shasha gives him a "you're so innocent" kind of look and then laughs sweetly. "Yes, just like that!"

"So, what does it mean?"

"It's my name! The first character is my last name, Cheng. The other two characters are Sha-Sha."

"I've always liked the repeated sound. It's cute."

"A lot of Chinese people have what we call little names. Sometimes, they literally have the word *little* in them, like Little Red or Little Tiger. Other little names use repetition, just because it sounds cute. Binbin. Jiajia. Shasha. But, actually, Shasha isn't my little name. It's my real name. You *could* say it's naturally cute!"

Old Man to Peter: [She's a darling.] (-:Laugh:-)

Peter feels the forced laugh in his belly but manages to suppress an actual laugh from his mouth. [None of your business. Keep quiet. What's wrong with you people?]

Old Man to Peter: (-:Chagrined smile:-)

The smile is forced onto Peter's face, muscles tight, lips sealed straight across. He turns away from Shasha so she doesn't think he's doing that to her. After it passes, he turns back to her and gives her a warm smile.

Old Man to Peter: [I'm frickin' not...] Old Man's voice fades out as he speaks.

Peter and Shasha glimpse a large shadow in the sky and look up to see a murmuration of starlings. They hold each other, not speaking, as they watch their mesmerizing flight patterns.

As they sit there, it occurs to Peter that when he is around other people he cares about, he feels much better. In an analytical sort of way. The headache is still there; it just doesn't matter as much.

Old Man says to Peter, in a rather calm sounding voice: [We're not a bother to you. We just listen.]

Monday, 13 May 2024

Peter opens the door of his white all-electric McAvie Lore, and as he gets in, the baldachin, a kind of built-in awning unique to McAvie automobiles that covers the car from front to back when parked, rolls itself back into its enclosure within the back bumper. The sun screens on the insides of the side windows all retract down into the doors.

Driving slowly through the streets of Berkeley, heading down University Avenue, then getting onto Highway 80 going west, he is on his way to San Francisco. To visit the submarine.

If there are people beaming signals at him, he's not sure what they're hitting him with. Could be microwaves, or maybe some sort of particle beam. But the submarine pretty much covers anything practical that they could be using. If the beam could get through the inch-thick hull of a steel submarine, headaches would be the least of his worries. More likely, it would kill him.

But he has never heard of using particles for communications. Maybe someone has figured out how to use some exotic type of beam to interface with the brain, but he doubts it. If he were hit with charged particles, his hair would stand on end. And neutral particles, neutrons, say, wouldn't interact with the brain electrically. The physics wouldn't make sense.

Radio waves might interact with the brain, though. There's no question that brainwaves go out as radio waves. And it is a well-known phenomenon in radio engineering theory that if something can act as a transmitting antenna, sending out radio waves, it can also act as a receiving antenna. That brainwaves go out into the air is evidence that radio waves could potentially be received in the brain. And if this is how the voices are getting into his head, all he needs to stop them is a well-constructed Faraday cage, a shield that stops radio waves in both directions.

Last night, after seeing Shasha off at the airport, he thought through how to use the submarine to test this theory. He would have to figure out some way to seal himself in. To this end, he had gone online to study the submarine, looking at pictures and reading about its specifications.

The only way for anything or anyone to enter a submarine is through the hatches. Or through the torpedo tube doors, but they'd be closed at one end or the other at any given time. So the obvious way to seal himself off from the voices would be to go down into the sub and close the hatches. Except that they might well follow him down. Maybe they'd already be there in the sub, waiting for him, hanging out at the far end, inside with him but out of visual range. The sub is 311 feet long, and the main passageway doesn't run in a straight line. You can't see all the way from one end to the other. Anyway, he doubts the docent on the sub would close the hatches for him. It would be a strange request. Why would anyone ask the docent to do that?

He noticed in his research, though, that different sections of the submarine can be sealed off from one another by closing thick metal bulkhead doors. So he decided to try to seal himself inside one of these sections, isolating himself from everyone else in the sub. If it's all in his head, he'll still hear the voices and he'll still have a headache. Nothing would change.

Why don't neurologists have rooms like this to rule out external influences, if for no other reason than to satisfy people like him? It would be another standard test, like a blood test or an MRI scan, he thought. But then it occurred to him that the doctors would probably say that any changes in symptoms would be due to the placebo effect.

This realization at first had disheartened Peter. Then he thought through the logic of the situation more carefully. If the voices *don't* stop when he seals himself in, it would be safe to conclude that it's just him, not someone transmitting signals to his head. The test would still be useful in that case because it would allow him to rule out the external influence theory. He could stop worrying about identity theft. And he would no longer feel like he was under attack. It would relieve a lot of his stress. For that reason alone, it would be a useful test. It wouldn't just be diagnostic. It would be therapeutic.

One detail that caught his attention while studying the submarine online last night was that the bulkhead doors have little round glass windows in them. At first he wasn't sure why it would matter, but he later realized it bothered him because they're not made of metal. Radio waves might still penetrate. To eliminate this problem, he visited a hardware store this morning and bought a small sheet of steel, eight inches square, to press against the inside of the bulkhead door's window.

It's a weekday morning, so there are few tourists in the area when he arrives carrying the steel sheet and a bottle of water in a touristy canvas tote bag with *San Francisco* ornately printed on it. He buys a ticket for the self-guided tour at a small kiosk on the dock. He's the only one that goes down the hatch.

The only other person on the sub, as far as he can tell, is the docent, who is sitting in the dining area, half-way between the main and forward hatches, waiting to answer visitors' questions.

As he moves through the sub, he notices that his cell phone reception drops, until at one point, it reaches zero bars. Even here, he still hears a faint voice in his head. Looking for an isolated room that he can duck into, he turns around and walks past the main hatch toward the rear of the sub, eventually reaching the sub's aft torpedo room. There is only one way in and out of the room, and this can be sealed off with its own door.

Peeking down the passageway to make sure no one else is around, he quickly releases the latch at the top of the torpedo room's heavy metal bulkhead door and carefully swings it closed, being careful not to create a loud bang. He then spins the handwheel tight. As the final touch, he presses the small sheet of steel that he brought with him over the viewing window inset in the door.

He quiets his breathing in the silence and listens. And he hears nothing. The voice has disappeared. And so has his headache. He feels completely normal.

His heart jumps as he realizes the implication of this. *They're real.*

And now he is alone.

Thinking of nothing in particular, he savors the quietude in his mind. His muscles relax. It feels to him like working in an office when the power goes out and the air conditioning and office equipment all shut down, the weight of its roar lifts, and the body tension he didn't even know he had just fades away.

Less than a minute passes when suddenly, a distant clanking jerks him out of his tranquil state. He quickly slides the steel sheet back into his tote and swings the door open until it latches.

Making his way back toward the center of the sub, he sees a tourist coming his direction as he peers down the passageway and through a distant bulkhead doorway. Faintly, he can hear a voice in his head again, though he can't quite make out what the voice is saying. He hears something like "[It's the frickin' thing you do...]". The voice cuts in and out.

Later in the afternoon, on his way home, he calls Ethan to tell him about his experience with the sub. Ethan is skeptical. "Maybe you just felt more secure after you closed the door. Psychologically, you felt more in control, and with your anxieties gone, your symptoms disappeared."

He reviews with Ethan the other hints that the voices are real people. The voices would sometimes use words that he didn't know and that he had to look up. Conversely, the voices would sometimes not know words that he knows, such as specialized math terminology. "If it's my own head making this stuff up, how could they not know those words? It would just be me, after all." Despite his analysis, Ethan doesn't buy into his theory. He doesn't push it.

Driving over the Bay Bridge on the way back to Berkeley, the voice hammering him all the way in an apparent attempt to distract him from his thoughts, he notices something odd. As he passes over the hump on the lower deck of the West Span, his head muscles relax and the voice sounds more distant. A quarter mile further along the span, his head muscles tighten up again, well before entering the tunnel through Yerba Buena Island. If they're beaming radio energy at him, this would be the expected result. The beam would travel more or less in a straight line, and if they were trailing him by a half mile or so, they'd still be on the rising part of the bridge as he drives down the other side of the hump in the middle of the West Span. At that high point along the span is a supporting column of concrete, one of the most massive blocks of concrete ever constructed. It soars 300 feet up from the water, supported by another 180 feet of concrete under the water down to bedrock, a veritable skyscraper in its own right, holding up the center of the bridge. The approach to it along the bridge rises up toward it and then drops down over the other side, with the span draped over it on either side. Radio energy would have to pass through that massive block of concrete to reach him during the time that he and the voice following him are on opposite sides, but it wouldn't be able to. Concrete absorbs radio energy like a San Francisco fog absorbs the morning light.

Furthermore, any beamed energy reflecting from the roadway would be directed upward, toward the bottom of the upper deck of the West Span. While theoretically the beam could then bounce back down and over the hump, the upper deck's 24 inch high steel cross-girders would instead reflect it back toward the direction from which it came. Once his stalkers had reached the center of the span, they would have been on top of the concrete support block heading down the back side, behind him, and the beam would no longer be blocked. As a consequence, he senses an opportunity to catch his stalkers.

[Tunnel's ahead. Where's the exit? Can't remember, after the tunnel or before. Shoot, it's right there.] Despite being two lanes over, he quickly swerves left, tires squealing, just as he reaches the exit for Treasure Island, which is just before the entrance to the tunnel through the middle of Yerba Buena Island. The exit is narrow and has a very tight turn, so he brakes hard as he goes around.

Heart racing, he pulls over to the left shoulder and parks, expecting his stalkers to follow. Assuming they're driving 50 mph, he figures they're about a half mile back. At this time of day, traffic is light. He calculates in his head, estimating how long it'll take for them to show up. [36 seconds. 38. They've got to slow down for the exit.] He watches the seconds tick by on the McAvie's dash clock.

He listens inside his head, but there's nothing but an unusual silence. In preparation for video-recording any cars which catch up with him, he pulls out his smartphone.

Fifteen seconds later, a single car goes by, an old silver Honda Civic. He ignores it.

For the next thirty-three seconds, no other cars pass. But there's no other way to go. If they'd kept going, they'd be forced to continue all the way to Oakland, three miles further along the East Span of the Bay Bridge, before they could turn around. Maybe they missed the turn. They should have passed ten seconds ago.

A few seconds later, three more vehicles drive past him: a pickup truck, an old green Toyota Camry, and a newer white Ford. He doesn't recognize the model of the Ford. Because of the flickering of light reflections and shadows on the vehicles' windshields as they go by, he can't see any of the drivers clearly as they pass.

He takes off after the three vehicles, following the Ford. The road curves to the right, following the hill which is Yerba Buena Island and descending as it goes, with San Francisco Bay off to the left and a steep drop down a rocky cliff to the water.

He hears a honk inside his head, just as the Camry starts to pass the truck up ahead. A fraction of a second later, he hears a honk in front of him, like an echo, coming from up ahead, from the Camry, while it is still passing the truck.

"That was strange," he says to himself. "How the...?"

The white Ford falls behind the other two vehicles as he follows it around the curve of the road toward Treasure Island. He considers passing the Ford, but visibility is poor.

Coming out of the curve, he reaches the short land bridge to Treasure Island and drives across, passing the Treasure Isle Marina which is off to the right, neat rows of small yachts moored to its three docks, their masts swaying and halyards clanging in the wind. Looking out past the masts, he spots the white sail-like tower of the East Span of the Bay Bridge which rises up from the bay to the east of Yerba Buena Island.

He slows down and searches, peering out in every direction through the windows of his McAvie. The green Camry has disappeared. Up ahead, the white Ford is pulling into a parking place in a lot on the right side of the road. Beyond the lot, further to the right, is a lawn and a fenced-off construction site. A half-built skyscraper towers from behind the fence. The building is eerily quiet, with no evidence of activity. To his left, a walking path follows a rock breakwater, and beyond that, to the west, is the bay, with downtown San Francisco visible two miles across the water. Immediately to his right, down another road bordering Clipper Cove and Treasure Isle Marina, he catches site of the pickup truck just as it turns left and disappears into the construction site.

He comes to a stop in the roadway and considers what to do. The main question is which vehicle to chase after. Would his stalkers be more likely to drive a pickup? Is the pickup ducking into the construction site to hide from him? The Camry, on the other hand, has completely disappeared. Maybe it's the Camry and his stalkers have already hidden themselves. Or maybe the Camry is gone because it's completely unrelated.

The honk he heard in his head must have been picked up by a mic in one of the vehicles. But which vehicle was the mic in? The pickup and the Camry were a little further ahead than the Ford, but all three were out in front of him. It could have been any of them.

The driver of the Ford gets out of his vehicle. He looks like a maintenance worker, judging by the way he's dressed. Leather gloves hang from his back pocket. The worker walks across a lawn and passes through a gate in the fence which surrounds the construction site, oblivious to Peter. Peter sees nothing special at all about the car or the driver.

He listens for the voice in his head. [You're out there somewhere. Where'd you go?]

Treacher to Peter: [That's a beer! We're ev **n** er **ot** y whe **any** re **where**.] (-:Belly laugh:-)

Everywhere. Not anywhere. He tries to replay the sound of the concurrent phrases in his head, but he can't. How could his own brain make that up?

He pulls into a parking place and gets out, then walks over to the Ford to take a picture of its license plate. Then he peers inside, trying to spot anything suspicious.

It was a nice day earlier when he was visiting the sub, but now, the wind is starting to pick up. Dark clouds are moving in from the west and the steel gray water of the bay is becoming choppy. Shafts of sunlight pierce the clouds at a steep angle. The sky directly overhead has become a misty blue.

He can see San Francisco across the water, distant, dark, hazy, silent except for the wind. He feels utterly alone. There is not a single soul in sight. All he hears is the wind.

He shifts his gaze from the distant city to the left, to Yerba Buena Island, then he turns to look at the construction site. Finally, coming full circle, he gazes again at the city. He says nothing but thinks in a fury. [You're giving away your technology by using it on me. Why would you do that? Of all people to attack, you pick an expert in signal processing!]

He hears nothing in response.

San Francisco's skyline is a shadow as the clouds open up and the sun shines through from the west. Then the sun disappears again. It is too far to see anyone in the shadows across the water.

He spins around again, looking in every direction, yelling: "Who are you?!"

He still hears no response. They've disappeared, if they were ever there.

He returns to his car and drives around through the streets of both of the two connected islands, looking for the pickup and the green Camry. He doesn't find either one. Looping back up and around Yerba Buena Island, which rises high next to flat Treasure Island, he heads east over the East Span of the bridge, toward Oakland. The voice in his head returns briefly and then disappears again. Speculating that he has left them behind, he accelerates.

When he reaches the eastern end of the East Span, another voice starts talking in his head. It's a voice he doesn't usually hear. He drives north on Highway 80, then exits onto University Avenue, and after a short drive through Berkeley, he's home.

As he gets out of his car, he smells the ozone of the approaching storm. A lightning flash strikes deep in the Berkeley hills to the east, followed two seconds later by a loud thunderclap. He rushes into his condo just as a downpour begins. The clouds have caught up with him.

At home, the voice continues to speak in his head. He figures they can't be far. Brain signals are extremely weak. Then again, they don't have to be nearby. They could have left a signal repeater of some kind close by. Maybe inside a parked car. Some kind of transceiver which would relay signals back and forth between his brain and their equipment.

He runs back outside, into the downpour, checking to see if any of the vehicles from Treasure Island showed up. He runs for several blocks, completely circling his condo, but doesn't see them.

Back in his condo, dripping and panting, he grabs a towel from the bathroom and dries off his hair. He stares into the reflection of his eyes in the mirror. The voice says nothing.

Now he smells hot cocoa. But it's not real. All the windows are closed. And the smell wasn't there a moment ago. Stranger still, he hadn't even been breathing in when the smell started. He was on the exhale part of the cycle. It couldn't have been anything in the air.

Why don't you have some hot cocoa? they seem to be saying.

He tries to remember whether he has any cocoa powder in the kitchen. He's annoyed by this manipulation, but then reconsiders. *Sure, why not?*

He changes into dry clothes and then looks for the cocoa powder. It's already expired, but he shrugs and uses it anyway, then settles into the living room couch, warming his hands with the mug. He takes a sip.

He gets back up to retrieve his smartphone from the dining room table and, sitting back down on the couch, he reviews the video he recorded earlier on Yerba Buena Island as the three vehicles passed by. Pausing the video and stepping back and forth, frame by frame, he tries to get a clear picture of the faces of the people in the vehicles, panning and zooming in each frame, but only a few frames have any faces at all in them and they're blurry and mottled with shadows and glare. He scrutinizes one of the frames more carefully. *Are you one of them?* Carefully panning back and forth, and adjusting the brightness of the image, he notes that the shape of the front passenger head rest in the green Camry doesn't look right. He still can't make out a face, but he concludes there must have been two people in it.

Setting his phone aside, he tries to think of ways to defend himself. They're real people. What can he do? He is seemingly powerless. Invisible and untouchable, they do whatever they want.

In a sudden stroke of inspiration, he realizes that he does have at least one resource, one which is hidden in plain view. He has a communication channel. He brainstorms what he can do with it. Maybe he can establish rapport and try to get their empathy. Maybe they'll treat him more like a human being and change their minds about what they're doing.

Good luck with that, he thinks to himself.

Maybe he can make them distrust each other. Somehow play them off against one another. The more he can learn about them, the more successful that strategy might be. He might try to build a profile of the personality of each voice, then leverage that.

Then he doubts he'll get anywhere. It's like a mental illness, but actually, it's worse. It's a thinking enemy who knows everything he thinks and everything he is planning.

For now, the voice has stopped talking. He can't tell whether anyone is listening to his thoughts. His mind is empty.

A loud plonk, plonk, plonk, plonk, plonk now attracts his attention from one corner of the living room, just outside the wall. Probably the downspout, he thinks.

He sips some cocoa, then gets up from the couch and turns to the window to move the blinds aside. He jumps when he sees his reflection, then moves in closer to peer through it. Giving up on the darkness outside, he paces the room, holding his mug of cocoa.

Peter: [What are you guys going to put on your resumes? Stalked some guy with mind reading for a year? Losers!]

Old Man to Peter: [Why don't you give it?]

Peter: [Give it? Why don't I? Why don't you go to —]

Suddenly, he smells a soldering iron. An image of his radio circuit board briefly flashes into his mind. [What's that supposed to mean?]

Old Man to Peter: (-:Smile:-)

Even as he is forced into a smile, he feels an intense headache come on. He sets his mug down and holds his head in his hands. The incongruity of the smile and the headache is so unbearable that he can't even wallow in the pain. It's plain madness.

In the fog of his suffering, he imagines a wrinkly weak old man listening to his thoughts through wireless earbuds, an extended finger poised over a tablet device running some app with an array of colorful buttons, sending phantom smells, headaches, and forced facial expressions, and transmitting his voice whenever he feels like it. The room is dark except for a small circle of light cast from a nearby floor lamp. Off to the side, a glass of water sits on a small table, and next to it, an ashtray with a cigarette the old man occasionally takes puffs from, a habit he hasn't kicked in fifty years, explaining the raspiness in his voice.

The app is exquisitely delicate in its effect. As a weapon in the hands of its user, it's not a cruise missile, destroying the target from afar in an instant. Nor is it a pointed gun, an obvious and immediate threat. Instead, it lingers, it distracts, it frustrates. It wears you down until —

[You're a bore,] Old Man says calmly.

Thunder rumbles in the distance.

Peter: [I'll see you in court someday. Imagine yourselves in prison.]

Old Man to Peter: [It's not a bother to you.]

Peter: [Hell it isn't.]

[Then why don't you give it and we'll be done,] Old Man replies. He is eerily calm.

Peter: [Why don't *you* give it. What the hell is this about?]

Old Man is quiet for a moment, then replies: [You're free to do as you please. It's not a bother to you.]

Peter paces the living room, trying to decide what to do next, but nothing comes to mind. He stops to check his mug and notices that it is now empty, then returns to pacing.

They'd have to be psychopaths to do this to him. Why wouldn't they care about him as a human being? Is this an experiment? Or is it some kind of dark humor?

Then he remembers the sub. The voices are gods making pronouncements from the heavens and sending down lightning bolts. But he can build a shield. These gods use technology, and he can use technology to fight back.

"I'M GOING TO BUILD A FARADAY CAGE. GET IT? GET IT?! Losers."

Old Man scowls: [Hell.]

Rain pounds hard on the windows. A brief flash illuminates the room and a low rumble of thunder reverberates through the nearby hills seconds later.

It is late in the night when Peter suddenly wakes up in bed. Listening to the rain gently drumming on the windows, he feels unsettled.

Then he remembers that earlier, he had gotten out some radio test equipment and wire mesh shielding material and had set it up on the dining room table to test a small Faraday cage design. Just as a way of getting warmed up to building a big one, one he might be able to live in. But he hadn't put away the equipment. After finishing his small experiment, he realized he was hungry and had fixed himself dinner, then had gone right to bed. He really should put it away. It could get damaged if it were to fall in an earthquake.

[We're not going to have an earthquake.] It's Old Man again.

[*We're* not going to have an earthquake?] He remembers what he read in the blogs of people claiming that they're victims of electronic harassment. Satellites reading your mind from thousands of miles away, giant antenna arrays in Alaska, and other similar nonsense. *Not it.* They're *here*. Nearby. A local crime ring, perhaps. He visualizes their location in a position relative to his own body, in polar coordinate form. A radius of two or three blocks in an unspecified direction.

Peter: [They made you take the graveyard shift? It must be, like, three in the morning.]

Old Man to Peter: [Not a bother. And it's four, actually.] Old Man sounds calm, as usual.

Peter reaches over to his smartphone to wake it up. The screen shows 4:02 AM. [Treacher's an idiot. Let him know.]

Old Man grumbles: [That's a hell.]

Peter fluffs his pillow, then blanks his mind and returns to sleep.

One thing, at least, has improved. They don't badger him all night like they did at first. For the first couple of months, he was sure he was suffering from sleep deprivation.

Even so, he has found that they're always there, 24x7. Only once did he ever wake up without a voice in his head since the voices started. He had lain there in bed, talking to himself in his head, and no one responded. There was complete silence, and it was great. He had joked to himself: "[Your expected hold time is: five minutes. Do you wish to continue?]", imagining the message as a woman's voice. He had laughed out loud.

Tuesday, 14 May 2024

[Whaa!

Whaaaaa!

WHAAAAAA! Uh. Uh.

Whaaa! Mluh mluh. Ah.

Ah.]

Peter bolts upright in bed. *What the...a baby?* He wakes his smartphone to check the time. It's still a little early. The alarm hasn't gone off yet.

[Ding ding ding ding DING! Whoosh.] It sounds to him like a bicycle going by. [Follow me! Yaaaay!] There are more sounds all around him. A young boy yelling cheerfully, playing. He can hear other children's voices in the background, yelling back.

He's stunned. The sounds seem to be coming from outside his head, nearby somewhere, but not from outside the room. He looks around the room and sees nothing out of the ordinary. He gets up to look out the window. No one's there.

The young boy's voice, seemingly right in front of him now, asks: [You want some ice cream?] and a girl's voice responds: [OK, where can we get it? Let's go get it right now!] Peter hears light footsteps on pavement running off. He is absorbed into this soundscape, immersed in the space, listening, having nothing to think back to anyone. He just stands there in his bedroom, listening, listening, listening.

[Who are you?] asks an old man. Peter wonders whether the question is directed to him and stiffens upright, but he thinks nothing in response. An old woman then speaks. [Let's go, dear. He's no one we need care about.] The old man responds in turn with an indistinct grumble as he follows the woman away.

Now, in the distance, the ocean drones and whispers.

Am I going crazy?

What led up to this? What was he doing yesterday?

[They're real people. This must be a trick.]

[We're - real - people! Da di doh di doo! Fire-spitting flesh and blood, weapons drawn, and we're after you. We're not your i - ma - gi - nation, so listen up, we're after you.] Drums hammer the inside of his head. An electric guitar amps up. Then the barrage of sound stutters, it flickers on and off repeatedly, finally cutting out altogether.

I am going nuts.

He tries to rationalize his experience. Maybe thinking "real people" triggered a memory. But the music doesn't sound familiar.

Now, he hears a different voice, speaking in a mysterious language. Then he hears yet another voice speaking, again in some language he doesn't recognize. The same thing happens twice more, for a total of four different voices and what seem to be four different languages.

Peter: [Blah blah blah. What the heck?]

Voice to Peter: [Blah blah blah! Yoo-hoo!]

He asks out loud: "Yoo-hoo?"

Voice to Peter: [Who?]

He responds: "Huh?"

Voice to Peter: [Huh?]

"Who is this?"

Voice to Peter: [Who?]

"Who *are* you?"

Voice to Peter: [You *are* who?]

"Stop it!"

Voice to Peter: [How?]

He stops the "dialog" in a Zen-like moment of soundless thought. *But they were real people. The submarine. I was followed across the Bay Bridge.*

Voice to Peter: [And how!]

He covers his head with his hands.

Voice to Peter: [Tick, tick, tick, tick…]

Just then, his alarm goes off and a story on national radio starts playing on his smartphone. This gives him enough of a return to reality to get moving. He waves the alarm off, then, repeatedly covering and uncovering his head, he goes through his morning routine, downing a pepperoncini and getting out on his bicycle.

As he rides, unintelligible murmuring surrounds him on all sides. He thinks he hears someone say "people hate you", but the words are muffled. He hears more murmuring, and then: "Why did you do it? *Why?*" Then he hears only the sound of his own heavy breathing. Sweat pours from his forehead as he leans over the handlebars and forces his way up the steep incline. He stands on the pedals. The wheels crunch and hum on the pavement with every stroke. A litter of leaves scatters on a gust of wind. Patterns of light filter down through the eucalyptus trees.

An hour later, back down at lower elevations, he stops in at Peet's for his morning espresso. He hears a voice, now inside his head. It's Deep. Maybe. It sounds like him. But he's not talking. He's babbling. [Ooo ooo.] [Dum-de-dum-de-dum yum.]

Peter: [It's you. You're pretending.]

Voice to Peter: [Boohoo. The not. Bot. Tot.]

Peter downs his espresso, then, as he clacks back outside, the baby's cry returns. [**Whaaaaaah!**] He immediately gets a tension headache. He stops to massage his head, then puts his helmet on, sighs, and gets on his bicycle.

He thinks it over as he rides home. *There were voices, real people saying real things. For months. What happened?* He considers revisiting the submarine to re-check the situation. Would the sounds in his head go away again? He feels a (-:Belly laugh:-). [OK, right, it's a big joke,] he thinks.

(-:Wink:-) His left eyelid is forcibly blinked. He swerves slightly to the left, just in time to avoid swiping a parked car. *Stay present. Dangerous.* He stops peddling and coasts, the freewheel making a rapid ratcheting sound, then glances back to appraise the situation.

At home, he puts the bicycle away as he thinks things over. *There's no reason to go back to the sub. I'm sure that I was sure.* [I'm going to build the Faraday cage. No matter what.] "NO MATTER WHAT!" he finally yells out loud.

Deep to Peter: [What matters not? Does not the matter matter? Frickin' the matter is not the alma mater, nor is the matter the terra mater. Matterhorn and its twin. Duel the dual. Mind over...]

Deep's voice sounds like it is far away, deep inside a large cave, reverberating, and yet, not out in the world, but inside his head. Deep takes his time, belting out the words phrase by phrase.

Deep to Peter: [...mutter. Murmur on. Babble. Babylon. That's what we do. But the others, they speak in tongues. How about you?]

[You *are* real! You've just been goofing around all morning.] Waiting for a response, Peter hears only the echoes in the cave dying out. Then the ambience of the sound shifts. It's no longer a cave. It's a small room.

Deep to Peter: [I was an English major. Frickin' math problems.]

Deep is back to normal. Just the frickin' normal way he is, normally. He asks impatiently: [Frickin' hell, do you frickin' speak Spanish? Or what?]

[Spanish? Why would you care about Spanish?] Peter screws up his face, then gestures with his hands, surprised Deep would care. [Took three years of it. Forgot everything. I'm not good at languages.]

Deep to Peter: [That's frickin' the *it*. Jeezus Kee-*riste*.]

Phenomenological warfare

Peter had long ago learned to put his arms up around the sides and top of his head to reduce his headaches and clear his mental fog. He makes do in this way when he is out and about and needs to think with less interference. But he isn't going to make serious progress in his fight with the voices unless he shields himself. He needs to think freely to develop a strategy, and he needs privacy so that they don't work around his implementation.

The submarine is a Faraday cage, providing a shield that blocks radio waves. What is a Faraday cage? Simply put, it can be any electrically conductive enclosure. A metal box with no holes in it would work. Or at least, no holes that are too big, depending on the radio frequencies you need to block. And it works only if it goes all the way around, completely boxing in whatever needs to be protected. There can't be any large holes anywhere at all. It doesn't shield in the same way an umbrella shields you from the rain. If there is hole somewhere, anywhere, front, back, or underneath, radio signals can leak through. And the leakage goes both ways. His brainwaves can leak out through the same hole that allows radio waves to get in.

He considers another idea for shielding himself. He could use a special type of sheeted material that absorbs radio energy. The way it provides shielding is not like being boxed in, as with a Faraday cage, forcing the energy to flow around you instead of through you. Nor is it like an umbrella, merely deflecting it from its path. It acts more like a sponge. If you shoot a beam of radio energy at it, it absorbs the energy rather than reflecting it around the room. Even a little bit of the sheeting material placed in the right places helps. The more material you have around you, the more radio waves that will be absorbed and the less effect they'll have.

Absorption material comes in a variety of shapes and sizes depending on the radio frequencies involved and what you're going to use the material for. Some types of material are made with soft foam, with spikes that protrude several inches, while others are formed into heavy flat sheets.

It occurs to Peter that flat sheets might be fashioned into a helmet. It would make a lot more sense than a tin foil hat. Still, it wouldn't wrap all around the head. The neck, the eyes, and the mouth, at least, would have to remain exposed. And he worries his head would overheat if wrapped with the material. He briefly considers how he might provide ventilation inside such a helmet, but he puts this idea aside for now. It's too complicated to build while he is under attack.

Then he considers making a tent with the absorption material. Searching online, he finds a wide range of products, varying greatly in their absorption capability, the frequency ranges they are effective for, and their pricing.

The most effective sheeting is expensive, but it would be the easiest to experiment with. He orders several large rolls totaling a couple of hundred square feet and weighing over two hundred pounds. It's heavy because of the magnetic particles embedded in the sheets that provide the shielding effect. Because he doesn't know what radio frequency ranges are being used against him, he orders two different materials, covering two different ranges. The order costs him several thousand dollars.

When the material arrives, he tries propping up the sheets in the living room in the shape of a tent. He searches for any stick-like object that he can find in the condo and eventually pulls the broom out of the front closet. Unrolling one of the sheets, he jams the broom up underneath it. Then he drapes another two sheets over the first sheet. But it doesn't hold up well, collapsing with the slightest jostling.

He gives up on the broom, but even as he struggles with an ever-intensifying headache, he gets a better idea. He lays a sheet of the material on the living room carpet, then moves the dining table's chairs out of the way and drags the table over the material, so that it provides shielding underneath the table. He then drapes additional sheets of material over the top of the table, ensuring that the two different types of material, one for low frequency radio waves and the other for high frequencies, each cover the whole table, including the space around the sides, creating a tiny shielded room. He doesn't bother fastening the sheets to one another, ensuring only that the sheets overlap near their edges.

Sliding between the draped sheets, he sits cross-legged under the table, in the dark, and listens to his inner voice. And he hears nothing. The grip on his epicranial aponeurosis is released.

Peter: [It works...]

He sits in the silence for a few minutes. It's like he has slipped into a cozy bed in a mountain cabin in winter. The windows are dark and the snow, falling gently outside, muffles the sounds of the forest. He starts to feel sleepy.

But then he feels increasingly disoriented. His sense of presence dissipates with the sensory deprivation. He has no sense of how fast time is passing. The faintest sense of dread fills the enclosure, a dark evil invading the dark space.

Now he hears a voice, but it's faint. Maybe they turned up their signal. Or maybe it's him. He may have become too sensitized from hearing the voices for months on end. The brain is like that. It gets better and better at hearing things. It's like when you get used to every little noise your car makes. The wind whistling past the windows, the hum of the tires on the road, the rattle that the glove box door makes. The exact sound of the engine. You know when a new noise shows up, something that wasn't there before. With time, you can hear every little thing, even the tiniest noise. Perhaps if he hadn't become so sensitized to the voices, he wouldn't hear them at all. But now, it's hard not to, even with shielding.

Or, with the months of exposure to hearing voices, he is now hallucinating them. Like when you feel your smartphone buzz in your pocket, but it's not there.

He starts to feel dizzy. To compensate, he deliberately controls his breathing, but he becomes even dizzier and he starts to feel nauseous.

Crawling out from under the table, he feels a sense of relief as he breathes the fresh air outside his refuge. He is surprised at how much warmer the air had become under the table in the short time he was there.

Treacher to Peter: [That's what I'd —]

Peter: [It kind of works.]

Treacher to Peter: [That's the bit.]

Peter: [But it's not going to work. I can't stay in there long.]

Treacher to Peter: [That'd be about right.]

Peter: [I still don't get what he means by "the bit".]

Treacher to Peter: [That's not really the thing.]

The vague sense of dread which had permeated his psyche now reverses direction, but it is replaced with a muscle tension headache.

The shielding is still not enough. He needs something better. But it's hard to think. It's like he's in a foxhole, and every time he pokes his head up, they start shooting. But it's not bullets. It's fog. Their weapon is a fog machine, but it's fog that only blinds him. They see just fine.

Taking a break from his shielding experiment, he fixes himself a snack of cheese and crackers and some tea. Like magic, his headache disappears. His feet and legs warm up, then the muscles all over his body relax. Taking advantage of this comfortable feeling, he returns to thinking about the shielding, but his headache returns and the mental fog descends. When he stops thinking, the headache again disappears. He lets his mind go blank as he finishes his snack.

Returning to the problem of shielding, he is barraged by the voices. Every thought is questioned. Every decision is challenged, ridiculed even. The dissonance drains his intellectual energy. *[There's not going to be enough air in there.] [It'll look stupid and it won't work, anyway.] [Not bad, but that isn't it. Go back to the sub and take a look.] [That's a hell, you'll need more layers. Order some more.] [You got the wrong material. It needs to be solid metal.] [What a waste of money. Why not aluminum foil?] [What you really need is concrete.]*

Worse yet is the ambiguous commentary. *[That's not the helluva.] [You're an it.] [Do you, the frickin' thing is, not.] [You may not, but hell, that's not the, for real.]* The language center of his brain runs hot, burning energy trying to decode the grammar. And then there's no meaning.

And then, unexpectedly, the nagging stops and the voices tell him not to worry. *[Take your time. It's fine.] [It's what you need to do.]*

The routine is mentally tiring. He repeatedly reminds himself not to think about the voices. They never say anything real. They said so themselves. But sometimes they do. They get his interest with something, it could be anything, trying to engage him in any distraction that gets his attention.

During this time, a new voice shows up. He doesn't have a nickname for him. They must have hired someone new. He's too tired to care. [Losers,] he declares to them.

It becomes clear to him that he needs something better than radio absorption sheeting. He goes back to the Faraday cage idea. It has to be something *like* that. A big metal box, but with extra shielding. Or maybe concrete. Maybe the voices were right. Or better yet, granite. He knows that granite absorbs a wide range of radio waves. It's dense. It soaks up their energy like a sponge. Put granite in a microwave oven and it heats right up. What he needs is a cave, buried deep in granite rock. But he needs it in his living room. He needs to build a cave in his living room, a granite room.

But then he reconsiders. Granite is heavy. He figures he'd need walls at least six inches thick. Not just the walls, but the roof and floor, too. He grabs a scrap of paper and scribbles a calculation. Sixteen *tons* at least. Concrete would be cheaper and a little lighter, and it would also absorb the signals. Then he remembers reading about through-the-wall radar technology that can "see" through twelve inch thick concrete walls. An ordinary concrete bunker might still not be enough to shield him. Certainly not, if it has windows or large ventilation holes. Radio waves don't need to go in straight lines. It's ironic, he thinks, that such a massive structure is required to keep out such an ethereal threat.

He's an expert in radio engineering. Designing effective shielding without unnecessary bulk and expense wouldn't be a problem if he knew something about the signals the voices are transmitting. But he can't think well enough and long enough to figure that out. The headaches ramp up whenever he starts to focus on signals analysis, to the point where they become debilitating and he has to go lie down. He thinks in little bursts.

The conclusion he finally comes to is simple. For now, he can't build something from scratch. He needs a brute force solution. Something off-the-shelf that he can just buy.

Researching the issue online, he runs across a concept called a SCIF. His problem turns out to be similar to one that comes up frequently - the need to protect computer equipment and people from being spied on electronically. SCIFs provide the standard solution. What he hadn't realized until looking into it is that Washington DC, with its need for secrecy, is covered with SCIF rooms. They're everywhere.

If it works for computers, it should work for his brain. The brain is just another system, after all. An information processing unit. They're trying to hack in to get the data.

He needs a SCIF.

SCIF stands for Sensitive Compartmented Information Facility. It's a kind of secured room used for carrying out sensitive work. Indeed, it is often *required* for sensitive work, to protect classified work being done for the military or other parts of the government. If a Faraday cage is a bird cage, and indeed, some Faraday cages look just like bird cages, a SCIF is a bunker. It's that different.

A SCIF is built with several layers of material, to absorb and block radio signals, microwaves, magnetic fields, sounds, and potentially anything else that might penetrate. Some include internal air supplies, like submarines, while others use a specially designed pair of vents to allow air to flow through, bringing in fresh air and preventing the SCIF from overheating inside.

The vents for the models Peter is considering are built with layers of metal mesh and sound-absorbing foam and baffles, and large, slowly-turning steel fan blades, specially coated for low friction, providing a silent multistage air exchange that also blocks radio waves. The entrance would be the same way, with an airlock built with two doors to prevent both the sounds of discussions and radio waves from leaking out when people enter or exit, but with all the layers and detailing, even a small SCIF is an expensive product, on par with a luxury automobile, and he orders the cheapest model the manufacturer sells, a prefabricated SCIF with only a single door, no airlock, that is assembled on-site, with just a few add-ons: a built-in table, pre-installed lighting, an audible alarm for loss of power or ventilation, and prewiring for external Internet connections.

This last feature, an Internet connection, is technically forbidden in SCIF designs because it potentially compromises the security of the equipment inside. Bringing portable electronics into a SCIF, such as a smartphone, would also violate the usual rules for SCIFs. But Peter needs to connect with the real world. His equipment isn't the problem. What he needs a SCIF for is to *think* securely. He is apparently not the first one with this need, though. The prewiring is a standard feature. Just another checkbox on the options list.

He's lucky, the salesman says, explaining that for reasons he's not sure of, the demand for SCIFs has increased greatly over the past few years, and customers frequently have an immediate demand. With the brisk business, they've really ramped up production and streamlined operations. Just a few years ago, the lead time for installation would have been weeks, not days.

The field technicians show up a week later with the SCIF in pieces for assembly. Peter shows them in and points out the masking tape crosses he made on the floor marking where to install it.

The living room and dining room form one undivided space, and the SCIF will occupy a large part of the living room. The front door opens onto this reduced living area, with the entrance to the kitchen a U-turn off to the left, around the small front closet, and the door to the two bedrooms directly ahead, past the dining room. The SCIF will be to the right upon entering the condo. A bookcase sits along the back wall of the dining room, just to the left of the door leading to the two bedrooms. He has relocated the small couch along the same wall, to the right of the door.

Using hand trucks to cart in several large panels and latching the sections together to form a large box, the technicians quickly put the basic structure together, soon moving on to taping seams and layering additional panels. Meanwhile, working at the dining room table, Peter reviews his accounts online. Finding an unexpected charge, he calls his Internet service provider. The voice prompt asks him to say or enter his account number.

Technician 1 calls out to Technician 2: "Did you bring in the tool bag already?"

Treacher to Peter: [Don't forget to tell the technicians that you want it moved.]

Voice prompt: "How may we assist you? You may select…"

Technician 2: "Tool bag's here. But…"

Peter: "Moved?" *Focus!*

Technician 2: "where is the…"

Treacher to Peter: [Screwdriver. Tell the technicians.]

Voice prompt: "I'm sorry, I didn't understand that. You may select..."

Peter tries to remember what he was calling about.

Treacher to Peter: [You canceled it.]

Technician 1: "...copper foil tape. It's still out in the truck."

Treacher to Peter: [Tell them you changed your mind. Look at the shoddy work.]

Peter: "Stop that."

Voice prompt: "I'm sorry, I didn't understand that. You may select..."

Technician 2: "What?" The technician looks right at Peter and waits for a response.

Peter turns his head away and says: "Billing."

Voice prompt: "Billing. All representatives are busy. Would you like to hold?"

Peter turns back to look at the technician. Technician 1 has gone outside and Technician 2 is pulling out his phone. He glances at Peter.

Treacher to Peter: (-:Anger:-)

Peter quickly turns away from the technician again. The technician gives him a strange look, but Peter doesn't see the his reaction. And now, Peter's head muscles contract, tighter, and tighter still.

Treacher to Peter: [Hold on. I've changed my mind.]

Voice prompt: "Your hold time is expected to be: 12 minutes. Press one if you would like to continue to hold. Press two if you would ..."

Peter turns back to face Technician 2. Unexpectedly, he smells whiskey on his breath. He didn't notice that earlier. He starts to have doubts about the installation.

Treacher to Peter: [Tell them to come back later. Give yourself some time to think.]

Peter is wearing down and becoming disoriented. His headache has become unbearable and his eyes are repeatedly forced to blink. The blinks are quick but strong, one every half second. Blink...blink...blink... blink...blink... Voices enter from every direction. The walls of an invisible room close in on him, a room within the room. It isn't light inside, nor is it dark.

Technician 1 calls to Technician 2 from outside: "Can you come out here and help me carry this in?" Technician 2 looks up from his phone, glances at Peter who is now facing away and is still waiting on hold, then heads outside. Peter hangs up and lowers his smartphone, floats into his bedroom, and lies down, mentally exhausted.

An hour later, he wakes up and gradually recovers his memory. *The field techs...are they still here?*

Returning to the living room, he sees a large metal box, perfectly aligned with his tape marks and reaching nearly to the ceiling. The whole thing has a finished look to it, with clean-looking ivory white enameled panels, a perfectly fitting door, and a tidy connections panel down in one corner for electricity and Internet.

He has won this battle. The war is not yet lost. His SCIF has come to life.

In the past, he frequently experienced discomforts making it difficult to fall asleep. Sometimes, he would suddenly wake up, wide awake in an instant, like someone turned off sleep mode, and the voices would get going with a discussion of some kind. He'd desperately want to fall asleep again, but the voices wouldn't let up. And if he did start to drift off again, his arm would jerk and he'd feel an adrenaline rush and he'd be wide awake again.

Why would anyone do that to him? Perhaps to cause sleep deprivation. But why? Just to drag him down? Eventually, he convinced himself that it may just be a problem with his own body. It just wasn't working right. Maybe it was the stress of the situation. Then he wasn't sure whether it was a physical problem with his body or whether it was the voices. How could he tell the difference?

When he'd visit a doctor, his symptoms always disappeared. His blood pressure would still be up, but the doctors never saw his other symptoms. He didn't appear distracted or inattentive. And his muscles were his own. No twitches. No gesticons. And no tension. Not even a trace of stiffness. That was a hint of its own. His symptoms were not persistent. They could disappear.

On two other occasions, all the muscles on his head had unexpectedly relaxed and his head suddenly cleared up, and the voices went silent. He felt completely normal. Good, in fact. A sense of well-being took over. The difference was startling. It was hard to believe there was anything wrong with him at all.

The first time this happened, he was out shopping for groceries. But only a few minutes had passed before the muscle tension returned, and with it, the mental fog. When it did return, it hit suddenly. All at once, he was back in the grip of evil.

The second time lasted longer, some twenty minutes. He was at home at the time and had taken a jog down the block and back because he felt so good, just for the joy of it. It was just one more clue that the problem wasn't him after all. It was their voodoo doll. And for twenty minutes, he had escaped its spell. Maybe it was rebooting after a crash. Or the battery had died.

After dinner, he moves some blankets and his pillow into the SCIF, carefully laying them out on the floor, then closes the SCIF door. It is heavy, like the bulkhead door he closed in the submarine. The interior is quiet, with acoustic foam panels mounted on the interior surfaces to absorb echoes. To test the acoustics, he claps a few times. It's nicely muffled. He is further relieved to discover that the large diameter ventilation fans, which turn slowly, are practically silent. It would have been frustrating to try to work and sleep inside with a constant hum.

Lying down, he closes his eyes and in no time is fast asleep. He has no dreams at all.

The subjective experience

of structure

Today, he continues furnishing his SCIF, bringing in a chair, a lamp, and a few other items. The SCIF already has a built-in table with LED lighting above it, so the lamp would seem to be superfluous, but he likes the look of it. It gives the interior of the SCIF a warmer feeling.

Then it dawns on him that he can't hear a thing outside the SCIF. If someone were to knock on the front door to the condo, he wouldn't hear it. But after a moment's thought, he has a simple solution. He drives out to buy two webcams with sound, the kind people use for home security, first trying an office supply store, then striking out there, driving further out to a big box electronics store. An hour later, he is back home with his webcams. He mounts one webcam outside the condo, near the front door, and the other, he mounts on the outside of the SCIF, facing toward the inside of the front door. Since the webcams have wide-angle views, he'll be able see the kitchen, the dining room, and the living room from the webcam on the SCIF.

He configures both webcams to connect to a wireless access point in the living room, then connects the access point to a network connection on the outside panel of the SCIF. He sets up a second WiFi device inside the SCIF. He needs both, as WiFi signals, which are radio signals, can't pass through the walls of the SCIF. For the same reason, his smartphone doesn't work inside the SCIF as a phone. Cell tower signals cannot reach into the SCIF. But his phone can use WiFi inside the SCIF for calling.

With WiFi set up, he brings up the webcam video feeds on his laptop. He places a framed portrait of his girlfriend next to the laptop. He takes a sip of the Earl Grey tea he has been carrying around, then sets the cup down and returns to the living room to pull down the taped-up print-out of Shasha's name in Chinese characters which he made after their walk in San Francisco, taping it back up on a wall in the SCIF.

He closes the SCIF door, sits down, and leans back, putting his hands up behind his head. His tension melts away. He listens to his hard-won silence.

As he relaxes in his chair, he gradually becomes aware of a faint ticking sound coming from his laptop speakers. Scrutinizing the webcam video feed, he tries to work out what the sound is, until he realizes that it is the battery-powered clock in the kitchen. This provides him with an unexpected source of comfort. Bringing the sound in from outside reduces the sense of isolation inside. But it's more than that. It's a familiar sound. It's the sound of a quiet and comfortable home in a quiet and comfortable neighborhood.

He takes another sip of his Earl Grey tea. Then, inspired by the idea of the SCIF as a modern day bunker, he uses his laptop to design and print a poster to hang inside, taping several pages together. It says:

REMEMBER THE ENEMY IS LISTENING

As he admires his poster, he comments to himself: "Not that they'd ever let you forget it."

With his decorating complete, and in a very good mood now, he celebrates with a video call to Shasha.

"Peter!" She's in her room at the university. "I've been meaning to call you. My mom says she's coming down to visit soon and I thought maybe we could all get together. What do you think?"

"Sure. What did you have in mind?"

"I was thinking maybe we could all go to Yosemite."

"Yosemite. Well... Sure. But it's almost impossible to get reservations on short notice."

"It's not that far. Why don't we go for a long day trip?"

Peter doesn't feel very enthusiastic about a day trip. He calculates the round-trip driving time in his head, then adds on time for hiking or some other activity. They'd have to leave really early and they'd still get back late at night. "It would take..." Taking notice of the beautiful apparition that is Shasha inside the smartphone's 3D display, he updates his calculation mid-sentence. "I can do that." He looks right into her eyes.

"I'm sure you can!" She giggles.

The two coordinate the details for the trip, setting a date and agreeing on some logistics.

Feeling in a rather good mood, he teases her. "So I made up a riddle for you. Ready?"

Shasha nods.

"OK. There are three types of people in the world. The first type consists of those who cannot extrapolate from incomplete information. What type are you?"

"That's it?"

"That's it."

Shasha gives it a little thought, then reasons out loud as she goes. "Obviously, the second type would be those who can."

She continues. "But then, what's the third type?! Is this an impossible riddle?" Her eyes display a mix of determination and suspicion.

Peter laughs. Earnestly, she thinks some more. "Well..." She shifts into super-analytical mode. That's what Peter calls it. Her face is serene and her eyes look into the distance. "OK, we have to use all the information in the problem. We know from the problem statement that there are three types. Not just two, and not four or more. I had originally assumed that when someone isn't the first type, they'd have to be the second type, because that would have to cover everyone else. But since there are three different types, and since I am able to extrapolate from incomplete information..." She lights up. "Oh, I see! A type two person sees how there are two types but can't extrapolate well enough to see how there are three. And a type three person can." She giggles. "So I'm a type three."

Peter is impressed. "Indeed! And well done!"

Shasha feels rather pleased. "Cute riddle!" She smiles at him.

Peter smiles back, appreciating her intelligence. She has always been smart. And cute.

"There are too many people in this world who are type twos," she says, "jumping at the obvious and failing to see the complete picture."

"Agreed. I suppose scientists are better than most."

"Hmm. Probably. But not always."

"What do you think of science? In general? As a budding scientist?"

"I love science!"

"So, if someone from a science talk show were to interview you, what would you say?"

"Good question. Well... Science is learning and exploring. But it's a bit too grandiose sometimes. At least, I think so. People seem to think they've discovered a theory of everything. Like they know how the whole universe works. I don't think about it that way. For me, it's part of being human, an extension of what we've always been doing since even before we had rigorous science."

She takes her time. Peter, for his part, enjoys hearing her talk. And with the SCIF shielding him, he can really enjoy it. He is relaxed.

"We observe some interesting phenomenon and then we try to explain it and make predictions with it; we try to live with it. So a theory involves data, but it also needs the stories that go with it. You see? We need stories so that we can tell each other what we know and how we figure things out." As is usual for her, Shasha sits very still as she talks. She lets the words communicate rather than her body language.

"It's just stories? Like myths or romance stories?" *How could science be described as stories?*

"Ha ha! Well, why not? Like that! All kinds of stories tell us things. Science is good at making stories, but of course it's not the only way we make stories! If you hear a story about the neighbors, it tells you something. It helps you learn about the world, about the kinds of things that can happen and the way they affect people. Stories are how we think, even in science."

"Makes sense."

"But you have to be careful. Stories are not absolute truths of the universe. They're not about the way the universe is. They're about the way mankind sees things."

"But wait. I thought the whole point of *some* stories, at least, is to reveal some profound truth."

"*Profound* just means it matters to *people*. But as soon as you think you've got the Truth, you know, with a capital-T, you stop thinking. You should never stop thinking. There is always doubt. There is always more to find out. And maybe what you think you know is actually wrong. Sometimes, at least. You get locked into a set of stories and you can't move on to create new ones, better ones, unless you keep an open mind. Look at how many people are locked into stories created hundreds, even thousands of years ago, long before we had rigorous science. It's easy to get stuck. And the same thing happens in science, too."

Watching her as she explains, he admires her passion. Shasha, the scientist and teacher. "That's profound! You have to keep thinking to find the truth. So that's what science is: searching for the stories which are really true and not giving up until you find them."

Shasha gazes steadily right at the screen, right at Peter. "But don't you see?"

"What?"

"That's the whole point. There aren't any absolute truths to find."

"But...even so, what you said was really profound. And true. I think so, anyway."

Shasha's face goes blank. She's not sure what to make of this apparent paradox. Her eyes move back and forth as she thinks, trying to resolve her confusion. Then her face lights up. "Oh! You're right!"

Now it's Peter who's confused. "I am?"

"I mean I'm right. So you're right. You see?"

Peter is still puzzled.

"There are two different things. Something can be *profound* while still not being *true*."

Now Peter laughs. "Right. So *that's* what I meant. Um..."

"So as I said, *profound* just means people care about it. They think it's deep and meaningful. We often put the two words together, saying profound *truth*. But it doesn't really matter that much whether it is actually true to be profound."

"I...you know, that's really not obvious."

Shasha laughs. "My original point was that there are no *absolute* truths. After all, every truth depends on assumptions and intuition. Sometimes, assumptions are hidden, or they're so obvious that you don't realize you're making the assumptions, but they're always there. And without intuition, there is no meaning to the stories."

"Okay...but —"

"But that's OK, you can still believe in something," she says without even the tiniest hesitation. "You have to. You make your assumptions and then you believe in something. Some *profound* truth. It's just the way it is. You can't do science any other way."

"Oh..." He kind of gets it. Then he really gets it. "So it might not be right. But if I believe in it, and you believe...you see, that's the kind of thing you can do, Shasha. That's profound."

"Though even this point is not necessarily right. And that's OK, too."

"Huh. I guess religion can be like that. Profound stories from hundreds or thousands of years ago."

"We even have our own modern creation myths and stories. The Big Bang, that sort of thing."

"Myth? The Big Bang? But wait, —"

"Myths and stories. Can we call it a Creation *story*? I think that's the right way to look at it. The best Creation story written so far. It didn't come out all at once, you know. It evolved. The truth is, most people don't know the real story. For example, did you know it started with a proposal by a Belgian Catholic priest?"

"I didn't know that. But what about —"

She cuts him off. "You're thinking of the popularized version."

"Aha. I guess I am."

"It actually has a long history, with a lot of errors and corrections. It's complicated."

Peter nods. "Do you think they finally have it figured out?"

"We'll see. But you see, that's the point. That's what science is like. The stories keep changing. When we find reasons to doubt a theory, we change the story. And sometimes we come up with entirely new stories."

Peter nods again.

Shasha tilts her head. "Maybe, someday, there'll be a better Creation story. Science moves on and what was once Truth later becomes *an earlier theory*. Science stories are the ones most likely to be overturned. Or at least, corrected. Religious stories last forever." She holds the pose.

"That's profound."

She snaps out of her pose and refocuses on Peter through the video interface. "Maybe. Could be." She smiles at him and gazes into his eyes. Peter smiles back. And, unbelievably, she has run out of things to say. She just looks at him, smiling. "You seem to be in such a good mood today."

"Yeah. I am." What should he say? The peanut gallery is not chiming in, of course. He's shielded now. But that's not something he wants to talk about with her. "I actually feel much better today. And so I've been able to start making some progress on my project again. I can get back into the math. I'm…happy." He grins.

"That's great!"

"You know, I like your stories, Shasha. You're going to be a great storyteller. Someday, you should write a book about your views on science. A story about stories."

He decides he'd better say something about his SCIF. He doesn't want to creep her out by telling her he hears voices in his head all the time. But she'll be here next month and she's going to be curious about it.

"Hey, check this out." He turns his smartphone around and shows the view from inside. "I had it installed to run my cognitive radio experiments, to shield all the signals." A feeling of shame overcomes him for not sharing the truth about the voices.

"It's a small room. Where are you?"

He turns his phone back around. "It's inside my living room. It's a Faraday cage for shielding. Well, kind of a high-end Faraday cage."

"Wasn't your equipment already shielded? I thought you showed me once."

"This is a lot more convenient. It blocks out all signals coming in so I can control the entire situation, and I don't have to keep opening and closing a small cage to work. It's actually quite cosy in here." He continues to feel a mixture of shame and elation. In fact, he hasn't felt this good in a long time. It really is cosy without the voices, the headaches, the unwanted gesticons. But now, he is conflicted. *What am I going to tell her? I still don't really understand it. Who are they, the voices? The attack isn't over. It's just that now I have a fortress.*

"Haha! You have a man-cave. Well, is my picture in there? Or some other girl's?"

Peter points his phone at her picture sitting on the table.

"Good. Take a selfie in the man-cave and send it to me."

He looks for a good angle and takes his picture with the poster behind him. REMEMBER THE ENEMY IS LISTENING. He texts it through the call and a couple of seconds later he hears a notification from her smartphone on his own smartphone's speaker.

"Got it! Oh...nice poster. What does that mean?"

"It's a famous phrase from World War II. From England. To remind people to be careful of what they say because the Germans might be spying. It's kind of a joke. I'm shielded. No one is listening."

"But I'm listening," she says.

"Right! Heh. I actually have WiFi in here. It goes to my wired Internet connection."

"Man-cave. That's amazing." She shakes her head in disbelief. "Oh!" She glances down at a notification on her phone. "I'd better get going. I'm going to be late for a meeting with my advisor. Talk to you later!"

"Later!"

Shasha's face fades out, replaced with his own face watching back.

Setting his phone aside, he switches his attention to the problem of finding the voices. At this point, though, he has no idea what kind of radio signals can interact directly with the human brain. He's not sure what to look for. But he experiences the effects of their attacks. He knows what it is like, and that is what will have to guide him in his search.

He gets to work bringing specialized radio and electronics equipment into the SCIF from the closet where he usually keeps it. Some of the equipment is quite expensive. Not the kind of equipment a hobbyist would typically have. He mounts four pieces of equipment in a rack at the end opposite the SCIF door and stacks up the rest nearby. Next, he organizes printed documents and handwritten journals, his electronics tools, and a materials bin, gradually turning the SCIF into something more deserving of the term man-cave.

As he goes in and out of the SCIF, he hears the voices come and go. Almost as soon as he opens the door, they start up, stopping only when he shuts himself inside again. They inquire about each piece of equipment. "[How much did that cost?]" "[What are the specs on the transmitter?]"

Oddly, they also say "[They may be bugged.]" He ignores this at first, but then he can't. What was bugged, the equipment? Did they tamper with it? He considers opening up the case for each piece of equipment to check. But then giving it some more thought, he realizes it's actually a pretty hard problem to deal with. They might have modified the firmware or software inside the equipment. He has no good way of checking that. Worse yet, they might have swapped a chip on one of the circuit boards with a fake look-alike.

Or maybe it's just a ruse to slow him down. Taking a deep breath, he sighs. Later. Not now. One thing at a time.

Slowly, he gets into a zone, moving equipment and not really thinking about anything at all.

Sunday, 16 June 2024

Shasha's mother Joyce, whose Chinese name is He Yue, last name first as is the Chinese custom, retains a decently-slim-but-noticeably-middle-aged figure by walking three miles every day. She flew down to LA from Vancouver a couple of days ago to meet up with Shasha and is looking forward to hiking in Yosemite.

Her father, Samuel Cheng, has stayed behind because he is busy with his work and can't break free any time soon, with a project deadline coming up, and in any case, thought it was great that mother and daughter have some time together without having to worry about him, that is, without having to entertain him or to care whatsoever about his needs.

Yesterday afternoon, Shasha and Joyce drove up to Berkeley, catching up on the details of their lives as they drove, but mostly listening to music. Arriving late in the evening, the two had dinner at a restaurant, then stayed in a hotel. This morning, very early, they have driven over to meet Peter. They don't go in. Peter is already outside, standing by the McAvie Lore where it is parked next to its wall charger, backpack on the ground by his side, waiting to take them to Yosemite.

Joyce wears white khakis and a floral rayon print blouse. Peter and Shasha both wear shorts and T-shirts. Anticipating a hot sun later in the day, Joyce brings along a wide-brimmed white canvas hat. At this hour, though, the air is still and a thin fog mutes the colors and sounds of the city, and all three of them are wearing sweaters.

Shasha introduces her mother to Peter, and then the three of them fetch items from Shasha's car for the trip. Peter pulls the driver's door handle on the Lore and the car unlocks. The baldachin starts to roll itself up, the morning dew wiped off to the side by the brushing mechanism along the rear bumper slot. Shasha transfers items from her car into the Lore even as the side window sun screens are still retracting on the inside. Peter waits until the baldachin has completely retracted before opening the trunk and placing his backpack inside.

Joyce has never seen a McAvie before, and certainly never a car with a baldachin. "Oh! That's unusual!" She walks around the Lore. "Your car is cute, Peter."

Peter smiles, ignoring his mild headache and trying to be cheerful. He has been sleeping well these days, protected in the SCIF nightly, but he's still under attack. One of the voices is yacking in his head. He quickly massages his forehead.

"How do you pronounce it?" Joyce points at the metal logo on the front, with McAvie spelled out with letters like those on an old British shop sign.

Shasha responds cheerfully before Peter has a chance to. She absolutely loves this car. Especially the treated denim seats with brown leather trim. "It's a MAC-a-vee, mom."

"Oh, how nice." Her mother squeezes into the back seat. There's not really a lot of room. "I have never seen ... what you call it?"

Shasha leans in through the passenger door. "What, mom?"

"The thing on the, the, ... *chepeng*." Joyce points up to the ceiling inside the car, then uses the Chinese word for *car awning*.

"Oh, the baldachin," Shasha replies.

"Balachin."

"Bal - de - kin," Shasha says.

"Baldachin. Is that English?" Joyce asks.

Peter, the engineer, takes this opportunity to explain it. He bought the car in large part because of its quirky features, one of them being the baldachin. It is made from an incredibly strong rip-resistant and mildew-resistant superhydrophobic polymer material, printed with the McAvie logo, with quarter-inch diameter rods spanning the width of the sheet every foot or so to give it stability and to provide an air gap for better insulation from the sun, stretched over the top of the vehicle from the back bumper to the front bumper. A push of a button brings it up and over the vehicle after parking, pulled by two nickel-titanium alloy wires running through narrow channels along each side of the roof, with little posts rising up from the wires that raise the baldachin off the roof just enough to keep it from dragging. Since it doesn't cover the sides of the car, passengers can get in and out even with the baldachin deployed. The baldachin not only provides shade on hot days, it also prevents tree sap or other droppings from reaching the vehicle and is easily rinsed off. It's practically non-stick.

"Very nice," Joyce says.

Peter is slightly disappointed that she didn't have any questions, but Shasha admires Peter's technical eloquence and gives him a smile.

Shasha puts two small backpacks, one with their lunch and the other with beach towels and other sundries, in the back seat next to her mother, and then she puts her hand purse and a few snacks into the *cabinet*, a four inch wide, twelve inch deep storage box, leather wrapped, which runs along the right side of the center console and continues under the dash next to the front passenger's seat. A small umbrella lies at the bottom of the cabinet, left there since the last rainstorm a month ago. Finally, she puts two small water bottles into the cup holders and hands her mother a third bottle. "How long will we be driving for?" she asks.

Peter checks the route on his smartphone. "There isn't much traffic, not at this time of the morning. Probably four hours."

Mandopop plays the whole way out, streaming from Shasha's smartphone. G.E.M., Jay Chou, Joker Xue, JJ Lin, and others. Mostly love songs. That's all Shasha listens to these days. She tells Peter there are pop artists from all over the Chinese-speaking world - Hong Kong, Taiwan, and China, Malaysia, Singapore, and also Vancouver and New York City.

Shasha and Joyce speak together in Chinese as they continue to catch up on the family news, news of aunts, uncles, and cousins living in China, with Shasha occasionally translating some of this into English for Peter. She hardly notices the scenery. Deep also speaks occasionally to Peter. But for the most part, for Peter, the drive is a visual experience. The Lore's tires hum along the rural two-lane Highway 120 as austere two-line telephone poles measure their progress past miles of almond orchards, then dry grasslands and scattered oaks. The flats give way to hills and the soil turns red, and pines increasingly fill in as they rise in elevation. Reaching Yosemite's Big Oak Flat entrance, Peter pays the entrance fee, then drives a winding 24 miles down into Yosemite Valley.

While charging the Lore at one of the charging stations in Yosemite Village, the three take restroom breaks, then relax while admiring the scenery nearby. Granite peaks rise up behind the forest that surrounds the village. Park visitors meander here and there, no one in a hurry, all of them wearing jeans or shorts, sandals or running shoes or sturdier hiking boots. Many of the visitors also wear backpacks and baseball caps and carry selfie sticks.

After charging, Peter parks nearby and deploys the baldachin to keep the car cool. The three of them, wearing their backpacks, then ride a shuttle over to the start of the Mist Trail and begin their walk up.

The Merced river flows over rocks and boulders off to the side of the trail. The river babbles and roars in turn as it rumbles along its run. The three take their time, stopping here and there to stand by the stone wall that runs along the trail, looking down at the water and up at the mountains. They stop a passing hiker to ask for a group photo.

After an hour's hike, they have rounded the base of Grizzly Peak and crossed a footbridge over the river, reaching the steep granite steps that will take them to Vernal Fall. Sequoias and pines and oaks cover the terrain.

It is quickly becoming a hot day. For another hour and a half, they sweat as they hike until they finally reach the fall, where the air is cooled by the evaporation of its mists. A moderate amount of water is coming down despite last year's drought, due to the brief storms earlier this year. The water falls as several ribbons swaying across the face of the sheer granite cliff, a drop of 317 feet.

Going off trail, the three of them clamber over large granite boulders, soon reaching the pool of water at the base of the fall. At the bottom, the ribbons of water scatter on the rocks. A large flat rock sits in the middle of the pool, almost completely submerged, its shape apparent just beneath the surface. The water is a deep jade green. Here, they are surrounded on three sides by granite cliffs and on the fourth side by the granite boulders they just crossed. The boulders are mottled brown, gray, and rust, the sides wetted by the mist having particularly rich hues.

Along their hike, something amazing has happened, though only Peter noticed. Deep's voice has faded away, as has Peter's headache. Peter's mood lightens. He surmises that Deep's radio signals don't carry well here, with all the granite. Granite is a good absorber of radio signals, and the radio energy which isn't absorbed by the granite is reflected out into the atmosphere by the rock surfaces. Perhaps Deep can't get a signal through without getting close enough to be seen.

He looks up at the fall and the cliff, studying the configuration of the terrain. He imagines a pursuit up the cliff and an encounter at the top with the people behind the voices, but then pushes it out of his mind. He turns his attention back to Shasha. "Let's go down to the pool!"

The two leave their backpacks with Joyce up on the rocks overlooking the pool, far enough away from the mist of the fall for Joyce to stay dry. They then hike down and take their shoes off, cooling their feet in the water. The fall soaks their clothes and hair. The water is alpine cold. Shasha leans back and splashes Peter with her foot, laughing.

After a short time, shivering with cold, they make their way back to rejoin Joyce, who has been sitting on a boulder watching Peter and Shasha from the slope overlooking the pool. They put on sunglasses now, as the sun silently glides west, past the top of the fall, the fall being to their east, its shadow painted over with light.

Finding a large flat rock amongst the jumble of boulders set in the steep grassy slope, close to the hiking trail but some distance away from the fall, they spread out their towels and, lying side by side, they dry off in the sun. Shasha applies suntan lotion over her face and neck, arms and legs. She offers the lotion to Peter, but he waves it away. Freed from watching their things now, Joyce tells them she's going for a walk.

Lying there, Peter feels utterly at peace. The voices in his head are gone, but it's not merely the quietude that gives him this sense of peace. It's more like the feeling one gets when a threat disappears and you no longer have to be on guard. The tension in your muscles is how you know this. It's how you know you have to be on guard. And his tension has disappeared.

Turning to her side, Shasha smoothes her hair, squeezing out the excess moisture and dotting the rock surface with liquid lenses marked by brilliant caustics of sunshine. A butterfly flutters past, catching her attention. Following it with her gaze, she asks Peter whether he has ever heard of Zhuangzi's Butterfly Dream. He hasn't, so she recites the story.

"Once upon a time, I, Zhuang Zhou, dreamt I was a butterfly, quite vividly a butterfly, with aspirations suitable to butterflies. I did not know I was Zhou. Then suddenly, I awoke, and I was unmistakably Zhou. But now, I do not know whether I was Zhou dreaming I was a butterfly, or whether I am now a butterfly dreaming that I am Zhou. Zhou, or butterfly? There must be a way to distinguish! This is called *transformation*."

"That's a nice story."

"Zhuangzi is an important figure in Taoist philosophy. His real name was Zhuang Zhou, but we call him Zhuangzi. A lot of the great ancients have been given names like that, with zi at the end. It kind-of means that he's *the* Zhuang. You know, like maybe they'll call you Peter the Great some day, except that one's already taken."

Peter chuckles.

Shasha uses a stick to write out two Chinese characters in the dirt next to their boulder: 庄子. "This is his name in Chinese. He lived in the fourth century B.C." She looks over at her mother in the distance and sees that she is taking pictures of the scenery with her smartphone, then looks back at Peter. "He wrote one of China's most famous books of philosophy."

Another butterfly flutters by. Shasha turns her head to follow it. "There's Zhuangzi again!"

Peter jokes: "Heh. Maybe. But he hardly seems to be in a position to write when he's like that."

Shasha gives a false pout. "No, of course not. He's collecting data for his next project."

They give each other meaningful looks.

They relax in silence for a while, and then Peter asks Shasha to tell him more about Zhuangzi.

"Well...Zhuangzi gave us his philosophical beliefs by telling stories - made-up stories about animals and about doing crazy things like conversing with a skull. But what do his stories really mean? They're about the nature of life. I read somewhere that the stories are about Man measuring the world by defining classes of objects and giving them names, and by naming their relationships. Like, what is the self?" She adds: "Well, they're about Woman, too, of course!"

"Of course," Peter says.

"The Chinese word for mankind is better, I think. *Renlei.* The characters mean people-kind."

Peter nods and she continues with her explanation of Zhuangzi's philosophy.

"Definitions distinguish objects from the whole. The way we define things makes those things seem special, but this is not necessarily the case, he wrote. It's just the way we happen to see the world."

"But you're a scientist," Peter says. "At least, a scientist in the making. Don't you believe in finding out actual truths?"

"As a scientist, you need both views. Think about what measurement is. Comparisons to...something. But to what? To our representations of the world! We make measurements, and sometimes we need to invent a new kind of quantity to represent what we find. These days, we measure things inconceivable just fifty years ago. Like, for example, the cognitive states of butterflies!"

Peter doesn't get that. "That's a measurement?"

"We get data about it and we find out what value it has. That's a measurement."

Peter's mind goes blank. "OK, I'll bite. What's an example of a butterfly's cognitive state? And how do you measure that?"

"You know how doctors record your EEG? They attach electrodes to your head and they look at the pattern of electrical activity. The different patterns have different names, like alpha waves and mu waves and theta waves. It's kind of like that, but more complicated."

"Keep going."

"OK, so on one hand, measurement is the basis of all science. But on the other hand, what we can measure is defined by whatever experiences we have. And we don't all have the same experiences. Our brains take these experiences and they, well, they make measurements, don't they? We perceive things in the world and we classify them and then we define properties for them. And these things can be very abstract. For example, think about measuring things like social and emotional relationships between people. While we may think that we are reducing everything scientifically to objective quantities, we always leave some things undefined. And those undefined things are what we call intuitions."

"I always thought intuition was a vague kind of thing. Sure, you can use intuition to figure things out, but in the end, the intuition isn't the result." Peter lies back and looks up at the blue sky bordered by granite cliffs.

"Let me give you an example of my point. You are going to be surprised!"

"Please, do continue."

"First, tell me. Is your math good, my dear Peter?"

"Sure..." He senses a trick.

"It's just that a lot of people who are good at math have such good intuition that they don't even know they're using it. They don't think about it."

Peter likes listening to Shasha. You have to be a high-bandwidth person to keep up with her, that's for sure. The ideas just rush out, densely packed. But if you can keep up, she has a lot of interesting things to say. He really likes that about her. She never runs out of interesting things to say.

"So, it's about Euclid," she says. "He lived at the same time as Zhuangzi, but on the other side of the world, in Egypt. Euclid wrote a book about geometry called Elements, around, um, 300 BC. OK, don't quote me on that. It was around then. Anyway, it is one of the first examples of anyone trying to write down all the rules for math. And he revealed something which I think was really important, not only for math, but for everything. He figured out that there was no way to define everything. At least, not completely. For some things, you have to use intuition. My favorite math example is that there is no definition for a point. He described it as not having parts, but what kind of thing doesn't have parts? How can that be a definition?"

Peter sits up. "Right. Yeah. That makes sense. What is a point? Calling it a dot just changes the name. It's..." He tilts his head slightly, with a thoughtful look on his face, then tilts his head back. "...not obvious."

Shasha sits up straighter and leans toward him a little. "Somewhere in our brains, we know what it is. But we can't write down what it is. At least, not exactly. Not with the rigor that we think mathematics should have."

He smells the suntan lotion on her skin, mixed with her natural skin oils, and these, in turn, pass through his senses and into his intuitive understanding.

"Wait. Let me check something." He tries to look up the definition of *point* in Euclidean geometry using his smartphone. Vernal Fall now sprays them gently from the distance, tossing the tiniest drops with its random sway and froth.

"No signal. Anyway, why wouldn't we define a point as a place or a location?"

"Then how do we define what location means?" she asks.

Peter thinks a bit more deeply about it. Then it seems obvious to him. "OK, so we have a plane and that's the set of all the locations we can have. That was René Descartes' invention. Cartesian coordinates and all that. Every point has its own x and y coordinates. He may have been a philosopher, but he knew his math."

Shasha disagrees. "That's a circular definition! How do you get one location all by itself? You can't say there are many locations and each one is a point, so one of them is a point. That's just saying that a point is one of the points."

"Hm." He gives it some more thought. "I suppose we could define it by how it relates to other things, like where two lines intersect, or like the end point of a line segment."

Shasha crinkles her forehead and then responds again: "But what is a line, then? And what do you mean by the end *point* of a line segment?"

"You're right. I get it. It's impossible to define things without referring to other things. It ends up being circular one way or another." He thinks some more. It intrigues him. She has handed him a paradox. "But somehow, we know the meaning anyway."

"Yes! That's the intuition we get from experience. The brain is able to create some kind of definition from experience. But then it is not really completely objective, is it?"

"I'm, ...hmm, maybe. Can't we make intuitions into objectively defined things? In the end, there must be a way to define everything concretely. I guess if we could do that, we could teach robots to have intuitions, too. If we could, wouldn't that make everything perfectly well defined? It would all have to be there, in the data and in the software."

"But what is it like to be a robot? Would it have the same intuitions as people? The experience of one human being differs from another, and their experiences differ from those of butterflies. So...well, for example, butterflies can sense the earth's magnetic field. You don't have that experience, do you?"

"Right. OK, right. So intuition depends on what kinds of experience you can have. And that makes all of our definitions depend on experience. And, so, they're...relative."

"They're relative," she says. "They're comparisons, and that's what measurement is. Comparisons. So, measurement is the basis of all science. But measurements depend on definitions, and those depend on intuition, and that depends in turn on experience, and...you see? So that's what Zhuangzi was getting at. There is no absolute truth. It depends on your experiences."

"I get it. Yeah, you mentioned before that stories describe human experiences. It's not about what the universe is like, but how we see it. ... Wait. So how can science be objective and also depend on your, well, your subjective experiences? It can't be objective if it's subjective, too. Can it?"

"That's why they call it philosophy." She giggles. "It must be that way, even if we don't understand it yet." She brushes away some of the sand on the boulder and lies back. Peter looks over at her and then also lies back. They gaze up at the sky together.

"Where did you learn all that stuff?"

"I read a lot. And I think a lot. It's my hobby."

The two lie in the sun, not talking, and not thinking, their skin darkening imperceptibly from one minute to the next. The white noise of Vernal Fall masks the sounds of other hikers, a hissing turbulence like a radio set tuned into the cosmos.

Now Peter thinks back to Zhuangzi's butterfly story. "In reality," he says, "the butterfly used to be a caterpillar, not a man. Which makes me wonder: Does the butterfly remember being a caterpillar?"

"We're not completely sure, actually! But, let's see...I think it was 2008. Yes. A paper was published which reported that butterflies do remember some of what they learned as caterpillars. They found that caterpillars can be trained to avoid a specific chemical. And when they turn into butterflies, they remember to avoid that chemical. Another example is that the part of the butterfly's brain that controls its muscles is preserved during the transformation from a caterpillar, even though most of the other parts of the caterpillar disappear. So it does keep some memories." She grins. "Ha ha. Muscle memory, you see?!"

"Well that's good. All those years spent practicing piano as a caterpillar won't be lost." He tries to imagine a butterfly bulking up. It never occurred to him that butterflies *have* muscles. Though in retrospect, it's obvious. How else could they move around?

"So you *can* still be funny." She laughs, then puts a slightly more serious look on her face. "I'm glad you're more relaxed. You seem to be doing better now, Peter."

"There's something about Yosemite. It's nice here." His muscles are relaxed. His head is relaxed. Lying there, his whole nervous system is in a relaxed state.

He turns on his side and props his head up with his arm so he can see her lying on the boulder beside him. Then he lies back down again and asks: "How's it going with the research?"

"Dissecting butterfly brains gets to be a bore after a while. But the thesis seems to be holding up."

"How do you dissect something as tiny as a butterfly brain? Actually, why would you need to? I thought you were focused on their behavior."

"Another good question!" she says. "Did you know that monarch butterflies can actually detect the earth's magnetic field? That's how they navigate. They migrate hundreds or even thousands of miles and manage to follow the same routes each time. One group migrates back and forth between the Nevada desert and eucalyptus groves along the California coast. How do you think they do it?"

"Let me guess. They follow the earth's magnetic field." He read something about this once, but he doesn't remember anything about it.

"Yes! But it's more complicated than that," she says.

Sucked in. Once Shasha gets going, she's totally obsessed. He figures that's what it takes to get through a PhD program. So here it goes...it's complicated.

Actually, he enjoys listening for a change, rather than having to be the one who does all the thinking. For several years at the start-up company where he worked, he would think all day, think all night, think in his sleep. Then write code. Think some more. Code some more. Damn, it doesn't work, it runs too slow. Back to the whiteboard. Think some more, there must be a better way. He was the architect of their product, but everyone coded.

"The butterflies that return on a migration are not the ones who left," she says. "So the mystery is: How do the descendants of the original butterflies find their way back to where their ancestors came from? It takes generations of butterflies to make their way back and forth just once."

"So you mean Zhuangzi decides to head south for the winter, but he doesn't make it back the next year. It's his grandkid that makes it back."

"Silly! But not silly. That's the idea."

"OK, it's simple. The butterfly mom and dad teach the kids how to get around."

"How could they?"

Peter's confused. "What do you mean, how could they?"

"They never meet them!"

Peter considers this point. He feels dumb. [They never meet them. How does that work?]

"They make caterpillars, not butterflies!" she finally explains.

Right. The kids aren't butterflies. Although...he has a different question and he feels smart again. "Hold on. I asked you earlier whether butterflies remember being caterpillars. And you said that part of the caterpillar brain survives to become part of the butterfly brain. And so, is there some kind of information which is transferred from the mom and dad butterfly? Is that what you call them, mom and dad? I mean, do they, ah, well, do they mate?"

"That's what butterflies do! The caterpillars eat and the butterflies mate. And *that* is a complex behavior of major interest." She laughs.

"Got it. So there's a mom butterfly and a dad butterfly, and they get together, and they —"

"Lay fertilized eggs. And these hatch into caterpillars."

"And the caterpillars grow their own brains, but, I'm guessing, by that time, mom and dad are long gone."

"That's right!"

"So the caterpillar's on its own," he says, "and it turns into a butterfly. And the butterfly's brain doesn't know anything about how to migrate back to where mom and dad came from. Mom and dad aren't around any more to show the kid the way. And so...right. But I remember you said they use the earth's magnetic field."

"There was one theory that the migration of butterflies is instinctual, built into their genetics. Maybe that's one kind of intuition. But there was another theory that they follow the position of the sun. And yet another theory says that they use the earth's magnetic field. Which one is right?"

"How could the butterfly's brain detect such a weak magnetic field? Is there iron in their brains or something?"

"Not a bad guess, but no. The real answer requires quantum mechanics," she says. "It's an example of quantum biology."

"Of course." He was wondering whether quantum mechanics was going to show up in this conversation. It's complicated...

He notices Shasha's mother off in the distance enjoying the scenery. The way she lingers makes him think she's giving them their space.

Shasha dives into the details. "There are special chemicals in an organ that connects to the butterfly's brain, protein molecules called cryptochrome. They're kind of like the proteins in the retina of your eye that can sense different colors of light. When blue light shines on them, electrons in the cryptochrome molecules change into an activated state, and then after a short time, they go back to normal. How long it takes the electrons to go back to normal depends on the magnetic field, and the butterfly's brain can sense this."

"So in fact, they can't navigate in the dark. They need blue light. To activate electrons."

"Yes. They're not looking at the blue light. It's just that the light makes the built-in magnetic compass work. You know, the cryptochromes. It kind-of powers the process."

"That's weird. Do other animals have something like that?" he asks.

"Yes, many! European robins, for example. The magnetic sensing in their eyes uses cryptochrome 4."

"Four?"

"Oh, right, I should explain. Cryptochrome isn't just one protein. There are several of them. Each one has its own gene. CRY1, CRY2, CRY4. Robins use cryptochrome 4 for magnetic sensing, but monarch butterflies use cryptochrome 1."

"Got it."

"You might be surprised to learn that people have cryptochrome, too. For example, the CRY2 gene is on chromosome 11 in humans. Cryptochrome is expressed in almost every cell in the body, from muscles to neurons, but it has a special function in the retina, in the eyes. Cryptochrome makes sleep cycles work."

"Oh. Does that have something to do with tinting glasses to block out blue light from computer screens? I heard that's supposed to help you sleep better."

Shasha gets an apple out of her backpack. She talks between bites. "Blue light does affect people. It might help, I suppose."

"So the same process that makes people's sleep patterns work is also used by butterflies to navigate?" He tries to work out some kind of logical connection. "Why would it be like that?"

"Nature often re-uses tricks to do different things. But here's a point to think about: The best time for the butterfly to sleep is when it can't use the magnetic compass. So it makes sense to coordinate sleep and migration."

Peter thinks about this. "Huh." He thinks back to what she said earlier. "So where is the cryptochrome magnetic compass in the butterfly?"

Shasha raises her two hands to her forehead and wiggles her index fingers at him. "It's in the antennae. Well, and in the eyes, too. They work together."

He lies back, bathed in the sunlight, and closes his eyes behind his sunglasses, absorbing their conversation. Then he tunes into the distant splash of Vernal Fall. Shasha finishes her apple and puts the core in a small trash bag.

A few minutes later, Peter comments: "Butterfly cognition and neurobiology. Who would've thought?"

"World's most knowledgeable person on this particular subject! I've always loved butterflies, and now I get to take them apart and see how they work!" She tilts her head and smiles. Then her expression is more serious. "Or I should say, *we* get to. The project I joined for my PhD work is huge."

Peter turns and peers over his sunglasses at her.

"We look at every little detail," she says, "at a microscopic level. Every neuron. There's a million of them, more or less. We've created a detailed three-dimensional digital model of the butterfly. Every system. Brain. Heart. Muscles. Everything." She smiles again.

"Oh. That's different." He had imagined her tearing off the wings and the legs. But no, it's not like that.

The two lie back on their towels. A group of teen hikers joke with each other in the distance as they climb the stone steps to the waterfall. A minute later, they hear only the waterfall.

Opening her eyes after a short rest, the first thing Shasha sees is her mother, seated beside her reading a book of true stories about Canadians, the wide brim of her hat shading the pages. Shasha sits up, and Joyce puts her book away.

"You're awake now. Shall we have lunch?"

"Mm." Shasha turns to Peter, who is still lying on his towel, telling him it's time for lunch, then digs into her backpack to pull out an insulated container of tea eggs and some napkins. She and Joyce peel the shells from the eggs, putting the pieces in the napkins as they go. The hard-boiled eggs look like marble, with crackly brown lines where tea and soy sauce and spices had penetrated their cracked shells while being cooked a second time after being boiled.

Up and about now, Peter gets out a stainless steel thermal food jar of his homemade stew and a set of three plastic bowls and a bag of dinner rolls. He hands out plastic spoons, then dishes the stew into the bowls and hands them out. He asks Joyce whether she and Shasha talk about science.

"Oh no. I studied finance and work in banking. Her father is an engineer and sometimes they talk about science."

"How do you like Yosemite?"

"It is beautiful here. But the waterfall is too tall. It gives me a neck ache just looking up at it."

Peter suggests that they could hike up to the top of the fall. "I've been up there before and the view is amazing."

"That would be quite a hike," Joyce says. "Maybe next time we could have more time."

After finishing the eggs and stew, Peter reaches into his backpack and produces an insulated lunch bag packed with an ice pack and dark chocolate peanut clusters. He passes the bag to Shasha. Noticing that a rainbow has just formed, though, Shasha becomes excited and sets the bag down, getting everyone to pose for a group selfie. Afterwards, they eat the chocolate while watching the rainbow dance across the erratic flurries of mist that drift off from the ribbons of the fall.

Hiking back down to the car, Peter and Shasha walk side by side, continuing their conversation, occasionally holding each other's hands. Joyce follows along slightly behind them. It is much warmer now compared with their hike in and the air here is stiller than it was near the fall.

"Do butterflies actually think about where they're going? I mean, from minute to minute, not necessarily on some big migration. Or are they just attracted, sort of like robots, to bright lights or the smell of fruit or something?"

"They are attracted to fruit," Shasha says.

"They seem kind of random when they flutter around."

"They're not random at all! I like to think of them as beautiful dancers. It's actually quite practical, you know. Predators have a hard time chasing after them."

"They don't talk or chirp, so how do they communicate?"

"One way is by chemical scents that they release into the air. But another way is by the way they fly. You see? Their dance can be a kind of communication."

"What would they have to say to each other?"

"How about: Go away, this is my tree!" She stops in the path and turns to Peter, waving her arms in the air, the butterfly guarding her tree.

Peter chuckles at this. "That makes sense."

They walk for a while longer in silence, looking at the scenery and listening to the wash of the river below.

"All your detailed neurobiology study of butterflies... What would one do with that kind of knowledge?"

"For one thing, it's just cool," she says. "*Hen ku.*"

"OK. Yes. Definitely cool." He chuckles. "What's *hen ku*?" He copies her pronunciation, which sounds like *hun coo*.

"That's Chinese. It means very cool. They borrowed the sound of *cool* from English." She thinks for a moment. "All right, I know you. You always think like an engineer."

"Sometimes. Yeah. Maybe always." He smiles.

"Here's one cool thing that someone's working on. Remote-controlled moths. OK, so that's not butterflies. But no one's doing remote-controlled butterflies. Not yet, anyway."

"Remote controlled moths. That could be useful, I guess." He chuckles again. "OK, so how does that work?"

"They attach electrodes to the moth's muscles so they can control them electronically. Then they wirelessly record signals from the moth's muscles while it's flying so they can capture data to send back to them to make them fly a particular way."

"So that would bypass the moth's brain, right?"

"Yes, it does. Soooo... wouldn't it be cool if you could read the moth's *brain* signals to see what the moth is thinking while it's flying, and then send *those* signals back to its brain to make it fly the way you want?" Shasha seems unnaturally excited about this idea.

Peter hesitates before responding: "And what if the moth doesn't want to go that way?"

Without hesitation, Shasha replies: "But that's what's so interesting about it. It would actually think it really wants to go that way."

"You're kidding."

"We can't do that yet. But it looks like it should be possible. After all, it makes up its mind to go one way or the other when navigating. We just have to give it the information it needs to make that decision the way we want it to." She repeats herself for emphasis: "It just might be possible."

Peter contemplates this news. He hadn't heard about remote-controlled moths before. But the idea that the moth would *want* to do something, just because you send a wireless signal to its brain... He has to think that over. It's not the kind of engineering problem he studied at Cal. *Is it an engineering problem at all,* he wonders.

He thinks it over to himself as they approach the shuttle stop in the valley. [The moth. It would actually think it really wants to go that way.] Then he thinks again. [What does it mean to *want* to do something?]

Treacher to Peter: [Helluva thing about that...]

Peter feels the muscles around his head tighten up. His headache is back.

Tuesday, 18 June 2024

Shasha has returned to Los Angeles and Joyce has returned with her to stay for a couple of more days before she flies back home to Vancouver.

Since finishing his exercise routine this morning, Peter has been tinkering with his equipment, dragging out various items from the SCIF, one by one, assembling them into working configurations, covering the dining room table with electronics and cabling. It has been months since he made any serious use of the equipment. He has stayed indoors at home all day, stopping only for a few food and restroom breaks.

Having put his own cognitive radio project on the back burner, he devotes himself to tracking down the voices. They must be sending signals to his brain to make him hear their voices, and they're almost certainly using some sort of radio transmissions. His first goal is to find a way to identify the source of those transmissions.

While he would prefer to work in the SCIF to avoid the headaches and mental fog that they throw at him, and indeed, that is where he does his heavy thinking, he has been forced to do battle out in the open. To find them, he must find their transmitter, and to do that, he is going to use their own signals to track them down. Initially, he thought he'd set up an antenna outside the SCIF, keeping his radio equipment inside, so he could search for their signals while shielded. But they may not be transmitting while he is inside. There would be nothing to search for. He has to be the bait.

It is slow going, with Treacher constantly distracting him with questions, but he remains focused. He doesn't allow himself to answer any questions. Mostly, he works intuitively, avoiding the use of words in his head as he sets up the equipment and carries out his search. In a way, while out in the open, he is learning to work in radio silence mode. Or at least, the closest cognitive equivalent to it, keeping his true thoughts hidden, inaccessible to the enemy's radio receivers.

He uses his spectrum analyzer to check signals at each radio frequency in the room. The spectrum analyzer, a box seventeen inches wide and nineteen deep and seven inches high, with a small screen and an array of buttons and a few knobs on the front, is connected to a radio receiver with a cable, providing the data that the analyzer needs to operate. He has also connected his laptop to the analyzer to record data for further analysis.

His radio receiver is specialized. It doesn't tune in to any particular frequency. Instead, it brings in a wide range of frequencies all at once so that the spectrum analyzer can see it all. An antenna, connected by a cable to the receiver, is mounted on a tall tripod standing next to the table. Other smaller antennas lie scattered on the table.

It's tricky using a spectrum analyzer to hunt for unknown signals. He knows there's a signal, but he doesn't know what it looks like, and he doesn't know where it is coming from. The radio spectrum is huge, covering billions of separate frequencies, each one potentially carrying a separate signal. Searching for one particular signal is like searching the twinkling stars in the night sky. If one of the dimmer stars is flashing a signal at you, how would you find it? What makes it different from all the others?

He builds up a list of frequencies to ignore so that he can focus on unusual or unexplained signals. Some of the information comes from public sources, like a list of all the known radio broadcast stations in the area. He can also exclude anything that looks like a cell phone or cell tower signal or a wireless access point. Those signals have well-known patterns to them. It's also pretty easy to exclude other well-known sources of radio waves, such as, say, small amounts of leakage from a microwave oven or the signals emitted by automobile key fobs and garage door openers.

Not all of the activity out there in radio space is easily identified. Systematically, he works through the entire space, keeping lists of suspect signals. Last April, he only searched microwave frequencies. This time, he has expanded his search to include lower frequencies as well. But by the time he is done, he still fails to find anything which could explain the voices.

The signals carrying the voices might yet be there, but they may be jumping around, changing frequencies using a technique called frequency hopping. That would be a way to hide transmissions if someone is trying to avoid getting caught. If he's looking at one frequency, and they're transmitting at a different frequency, he wouldn't see their signal. And since frequency hopping involves constantly changing what frequency is used, possibly many times a second, it is hard to identify it. He'd have to know how it hops to follow it around.

Is this a serious possibility? He thinks so. It's possible that his brain would "hear" the shapes of the signals regardless of the exact frequencies carrying them. If so, the voices could be transmitted at any of a broad range of frequencies, jumping around at random, and the brain wouldn't notice the difference.

His spectrum analyzer has a feature to search for frequency-hopping signals, but when he uses this feature to search, he still finds nothing of interest. He makes some notes in his project notebook about his findings, mainly things he has ruled out.

He considers how he would look for signals based on their shapes instead of their frequencies. A spectrum analyzer can't search for a signal shape, meaning the shape of a signal as it changes in intensity over time, like the shape of a function in algebra. Like, say, x-squared or the shape of the top half of an ellipse. The analyzer only understands signals that oscillate. So he pulls out another piece of equipment from the SCIF, a device he built himself for his own research, and he continues his search. He unplugs the spectrum analyzer data cable from his laptop and plugs in his own device in its place. Then he launches a signal analysis software tool that he created for working with the device.

But what is he searching for? Finding shapes in radio waves is a bit like searching for an ancient wreck in the ocean. The ocean is vast, and so is the world of radio waves. But it's worse than that. He has no idea of what shape to search for. At least with a wreck, you know the outline on the ocean floor will look something like a ship.

No simple shapes immediately present themselves in his search, so he retreats back into the SCIF to brainstorm, writing out his ideas in his project notebook. Anything that might help. What would the signals look like? If they interact with the brain, perhaps the radio wave shapes look similar to brainwaves. He writes *antenna reciprocity* in his notebook. This is the concept, well known to radio engineers, that the pattern of radio waves received on an antenna looks the same as the pattern of radio waves on the transmitter's antenna. But that's true only if the transmitting antenna and the receiving antenna also have the same shape. But if his brain is the receiving antenna, what would the transmitting antenna look like? It's hard to imagine. Would it be an antenna in the shape of the brain's neurons? The brain has 86 billion neurons. Would the antenna need billions of tiny pieces? He writes the idea down in his notebook, as improbable as it seems.

He tries to view the situation from a more general point of view. What is it that makes it possible for his brain to receive radio signals? He thinks it through. The neurons in the brain operate through electrical activity. Somehow, there is an interaction. Electrical activity created in the neurons by the radio waves. Somehow.

But he knows nothing about neurobiology. It's something Shasha may be able to help with, but he's not sure what question he would ask her. He'd be starting from scratch going down that path. He'd have to learn cell biology and go from there. It could take years to figure things out that way.

He takes another tack. From a mathematical point of view, what makes the signals special? Nothing comes to mind at first. They're just patterns. Shapes of electromagnetic waves propagating through the air. And yet, radio stations and cell phone transmissions have no effect on the brain. At least, they have no obvious effect. You can't hear them in your head. So what's different about the signals carrying the voices?

There must be some kind of compatibility thing. With just the right pattern of radio waves, the neurons in his brain are triggered into action and he hears something. With the wrong pattern, nothing happens.

Maybe it's like writing in sand with a stick. If you move the sand around at random, there's nothing there. Just sand. And if you move it around some more, it's still just sand. But if you carefully trace out the right pattern, you see a word. The shape in the sand has to match a shape your mind can recognize. Only then will you see something.

He remembers Shasha tracing out Zhuangzi's name in the dirt in Yosemite. He had never seen Zhuangzi's name in Chinese before. He doesn't read Chinese at all, in fact. But he could still see that there was something there in the dirt. Some pattern. It was no longer just dirt. It was a symbol.

He jots down some more ideas in his notebook, but they're vague. It gets him to thinking about his own project with cognitive radio. He paces back and forth in the SCIF, allowing his intuition to work.

Cognitive radio, his own specialty within the field of radio engineering, has nothing to do with cognition. Not literally. While cognitive radio is about sending signals, it isn't about sending signals to brains, nor does it have anything to do with thinking. It's just a way for radios to operate without interfering with each other, by listening to what other radios are transmitting and taking that into account, providing a more efficient way to use the radio spectrum.

His own cognitive radio project involves sending and receiving symbols as patterns of radio waves, shapes in the ethereal mist, invisible to the naked eye, but easily viewed by a compatible receiver. But the shapes that his project works with are not designed for the brain. It had never occurred to him during the development of his project that some radio wave shapes could make you hear something in your head.

He needs to figure out what shapes the voices are sending. If only he could find a compatible receiver, he'd see the symbols.

And then it hits him. "That is just so...I'm stupid." He's too excited to write anything. He jumps up, quickly paces back and forth a couple of times, then sits back down on his chair, leans back and closes his eyes, resting before his next sprint.

Opening his eyes, he writes in his notebook: *The brain is the receiver.*

He writes out his approach. Whenever his brain detects something from "outside", like a voice or a fake smell, he'll record the radio waves that come in using a radio receiver. So he actually has two receivers: his brain, and his radio receiver. And he has what each one "hears" at the same time. The idea is to match them up.

If he hears "frickin'" in his head right now, then somewhere in the radio waves he is recording with the receiver, the shape for "frickin'" will be there, too. If he hears "frickin'" a second time, that will give him another recording of radio waves with the same shape buried somewhere in them. The idea is to search through the recorded radio waves to find all the shapes that are the same in both recordings. One of the shapes will be the shape that creates the sound in his head.

If he has more recordings of the same thing, he can narrow down the shapes even further. If he hears "frickin'" four times and records the radio waves four times, then he'll search for the shapes that show up in all four radio wave recordings. The more examples he has, the more information he will have on just what shape makes that sound. It's like learning the shape of anything, like learning how to write a Chinese character, for example. You need several examples so you can see how they vary and how they're the same, what parts of the shape matter and what parts don't. It's also how machine learning works, the type of software that lets a computer learn to recognize shapes. Feed in enough examples of what a cat looks like, and the computer learns to recognize cats and to distinguish them from other things.

There will be a different shape for each word he hears in his head, each fake smell he experiences, each gesticon that is forced on him. He'll take notes when each one occurs while recording all of the radio waves. And then he'll hunt down the shapes in those radio waves.

Once he knows what shapes to search for, he can find them again, using his radio receiver. He won't need to listen with his brain. And *that* is what will allow him to track down where the signals are coming from. He can program his radio receiver to listen for the same shapes and to identify where they are coming from, using signal processing techniques. Or more simply put, using math.

"OK, this is a good start," he says to himself. He feels like he has gotten somewhere. It's still a huge task, even with his new idea, though. *All* radio waves means everything from a hundred cycles per second up to hundred billion cycles per second. It's a massive amount of data, like streaming 240,000 movies *simultaneously*.

Recording absolutely everything in the entire spectrum of radio waves would require him to store a huge amount of data, like a billion gigabytes. He'd need enough storage to save 170 million movies. But for his problem, it actually won't be that bad. If you're just looking for shapes in the signals, there's math that cuts it down dramatically. Even so, he doesn't have quite enough storage, so he'll order some more today.

Luckily, he won't have to process most of the data he plans to capture. The calculations would take forever. The main thing is to capture the data he might need. Then he can go back to specific time periods in the recordings where the voices, smells and gesticons show up. Especially the frickin' ones that show up repeatedly.

So that's half of the problem. He has focused so far only on how the voices get into his brain. But how do they read his mind? The brain has electrical activity in it. That's how neurons work, after all. And any electrical activity produces radio signals. But, so far as he knows, the signals that emanate from a brain aren't detectable with a radio receiver. He still has to think that through.

The good thing about working in the SCIF is that his intellect is back. No headaches. No mental fog. He feels normal inside. And productive.

But that's the problem. He feels normal *inside*. Outside, he's still under attack. The enemy hasn't withdrawn. They lie in wait. And when he goes out, they attack from the shadows. They *are* the shadows. They're still there, everywhere and not anywhere.

Even now, no one helps him. He is still on his own, fighting an invisible battle. He complains about headaches, but a lot of people do. There is never any objective evidence of a problem. It never occurs to anyone when he is out and about that he is not the highly intelligent person he used to be. Not his friends, and certainly not the doctors. They see a *normal* level of intelligence and assume he's fine. And yet, without his former high level of intellect, it would be hopeless to track down his adversaries.

He shudders at the perfection of the attack. It's insidious. It takes down an opponent just far enough to keep them from defending themselves, but not so far down that anyone would suspect there's anything wrong.

He suspects his headaches aren't just muscle tension. It goes deeper, as a kind of muscle tension inside the head, the arteries squeezing down and restricting the blood supply just enough to dumb him down. Squeezed hard enough, it would produce a stroke. But it's not *that* bad. There's just an *inefficient distribution* of blood flow. Not enough for permanent damage, at least, not in the short term, though maybe his brain would atrophy over time for lack of use. And that's what's so insidious about it. It wears him down and slows him down, but when he goes in to have the doctor check what's wrong, there isn't anything to see. The attack stops and his symptoms disappear, and he's his normal, intelligent self. It's maddening.

He's got a bunker now. And inside, he's got his intellect back. But that's not enough. He's pinned down. Outside the SCIF, he still lives in a fog. And he's still on his own.

Brain sea

Burned out after hours of research, sitting in his SCIF brainstorming, sketching out diagrams, looking up things on the Internet, and placing orders for new equipment, he takes a break. Going out to the kitchen to make himself a cup of Earl Grey milk tea, he taunts the voices in passing, just because it makes him feel more in control, and then he shuts them out again, pulling back into his SCIF, closing the door with its satisfying *thud*.

He takes a sip from his tea and sets it down. Leaning back in his chair, he lets his mind relax, the silence in his head like a comforting blanket, cozy and private.

Then a text message from Shasha announces itself on his smartphone. It is written in both Chinese characters and romanized Chinese pronunciation.

Shasha: 你在我的腦海里。 Ni zai wode naohai li.

Peter: What does naohai mean?

Shasha: Nao means brain and hai means sea. Brain sea. That means the mind.

Peter: That's poetic.

Shasha: The whole sentence means you are in my brain sea. You see? That means in my thoughts.

Peter: Wo ai ni. *I love you.*

A minute later, reminded of her research, he is curious and texts her a question.

Peter: What was that molecule you talked about? The one that lets butterflies sense the earth's magnetic field.

Shasha: Cryptochrome.

He texts her a heart emoticon, then looks up cryptochrome on the Internet.

Shasha's own work isn't out there yet, but he runs across something written by one of her Ph.D. advisors that makes a passing mention of her project as a future research area. There are several articles about bird navigation, especially pigeons. He finds older articles on butterflies. And then he runs into something about magnetic sensing by members of the dog family. As he searches, he finds more and more examples. Fruit flies. Cockroaches. Whales.

"Huh." He leans forward into his laptop, reading article after article. He hadn't expected so much information. Before today, he had only heard of Shasha's work. But it is clear that it is a big field. His cryptochrome search finds tens of thousands of scientific articles.

Cryptochrome is actually a protein, and its design, if you will, is coded into DNA. A conglomeration of several thousand atoms, the molecule is large, with a small pocket in the middle. Another molecule called FAD, short for flavin adenine dinucleotide, is created by cells from the flavin part of the vitamin B2 molecule riboflavin. FAD fits snugly into that little pocket in cryptochrome.

Flavin is what gives vitamin B2 its intense yellow color. And the flavin part of the FAD molecule is also what gives cryptochrome its yellow color when the FAD molecule locks into its place in the cryptochrome pocket. When cryptochrome absorbs blue light, it is actually this hidden molecule, the FAD molecule, that absorbs the light for the two-molecule combination. It is by absorbing blue light that it takes on its strong yellow color.

A drawing in one article of the cryptochrome-FAD molecule combination looks to Peter like a dirt clod with a little golden nugget buried in it. The article explains that due to cryptochrome's particular shape, it is highly functional, allowing cells to carry out several important biological functions.

"Ugly, but functional. Been there, done that." *Whatever works.*

As he continues to poke around on the Internet, he runs across a patent for submarine detection. This really gets his attention. Submarines? What possible connection could there be between cryptochrome and submarines?

He drinks down the remainder of his tea, though by this time, it has become cold. He considers going back out to the kitchen to make another cup, but then changes his mind. Enough caffeine for one day. Pushing his cup toward the back of the table, he glances at Shasha's framed photo sitting nearby, then starts reading the patent.

The patent's summary explains that the submarine detection technique is based on an effect discovered in quantum biology. Blue laser pulses are sent down from an airplane to the ocean's surface in a scanning pattern. The pulses need to be powerful but short, the shorter, the better.

As each pulse penetrates the ocean, diatoms, highly abundant microscopic organisms living almost everywhere in the ocean, absorb the blue laser light and then re-emit green and yellow light in response. Diatoms are transparent, with bodies of crystal-clear glass, the very same kind of glass that windows are made of, so the light easily goes in and out. It's the cryptochrome-FAD molecule combination inside the diatoms which absorbs the blue light and sends out the green and yellow light.

Each cubic meter of water, the patent explains, may contain thousands, even millions, of individual diatoms, each acting as a tiny but sensitive magnetic field sensor when the right light stimulus hits it. When a burst of light is sent to a patch of ocean, the diatoms all respond together and send back a burst of light in return. Two bursts, in fact. First green, then yellow, in quick succession, just a tiny fraction of a second apart.

Detection equipment on the airplane measures how much longer it takes for the yellow burst of light to return to the airplane compared with the green light, watching through a telescope aimed at the point where the laser pulse hits the water. The longer it takes, the more distorted the magnetic field is in that part of the ocean. It works because large metal objects like submarines bend and concentrate the earth's magnetic field. How long it takes yellow light to come out of diatoms depends on the shape and strength of the magnetic field, but the green light, which doesn't depend on the magnetic field, just comes out right away. So the time difference is what counts. That's what tells you about the magnetic field, and this information can tell you whether there's a submarine nearby. The invention explains how to map out the magnetic field on the surface of the ocean, revealing the submarine's outline. With additional calculations, the size, depth, and direction of travel of the submarine can be worked out.

According to the patent, this is much better than older aircraft-borne methods which only measure the magnetic field way up in the air near the airplane itself, where the submarine has much less of an effect on the earth's magnetic field.

Peter notices a comment in the patent pointing out that diatoms are unable to grow without sufficient vitamin B, which, as the patent points out, "could limit the method's applicability in some regions of the ocean". The patent goes on to discuss methods to work around the limitation.

He chuckles to himself. "Sorry, sir. We lost track of the submarine!" "What happened?" "Not enough vitamin B down there."

He bookmarks the patent on his laptop, then gets ready for bed, unfolding the futons he bought yesterday and laying out blankets and a pillow. He leaves the empty tea cup on the table.

As he drifts off to sleep, his mind becomes a vast and deep ocean, its surface shimmering with sunlight, its depths dark and mysterious, and within this ocean, the SCIF becomes a submarine, hatch closed.

Wednesday, 26 June 2024

On the drive over to meet Ethan for dinner, Peter gets a call from Shasha. She has exciting news to share. Using blue light, she is now able to control the flight of a butterfly.

Peter is not sure what to make of this. "But in Yosemite, I thought you said the blue light doesn't steer the butterfly. It just provides the energy to sense the earth's magnetic field. Or, maybe I'm remembering it wrong."

"No, that's right. The blue light just activates cryptochrome molecules. It doesn't tell the butterfly to go one way or the other. Normally."

"And....?"

"I know this sounds a little confusing, but... It's like this. The cryptochrome molecules it uses for sensing the earth's magnetic field are in the antennae. Of course if we change the direction of the magnetic field, the butterfly will change directions, too. But this other effect is different. Instead of affecting the antennae, the blue light is penetrating into the butterfly's brain and into its neurons. This wouldn't matter if the blue light were steady, the way it is when the sun shines. But we rapidly varied the intensity of the light, as part of testing the butterfly's behavior, and...well, wouldn't you be surprised, too, if you saw the butterfly change direction?"

"So that's...hah! It's a remote-controlled butterfly!"

"Better than that," she says. "We can tell which direction it wants to fly by getting information *from* its brain, too. *Before* it changes direction, we know. We know what it's going to do, just before it does it."

Peter reflects on this as he pulls to a stop at a red light. "You can read its mind?"

Shasha enthusiastically responds: "Yes!"

"Just by shining blue light on it?" *That's weird,* he thinks.

The light turns green.

"Yes. Although we also have to get a signal back from the butterfly's brain. So we modulate the blue light and sense the timing pattern of photon emissions of two particular frequencies of light, one which is due to the quantum spin of the electrons in the cryptochromes in the butterfly's brain decaying back to their base state with a rate that depends on local changes in the magnetic fields in different parts of the brain's neural —"

"Wait, wait." He can't keep up.

"Yes?"

"Um. That was a bit... Yeah. Quantum spin?" He stops at a stop sign.

Shasha laughs out loud. "Sorry. That was probably too —"

"Hold on." He waits for traffic, then turns left. "OK. So, you were saying?"

"So it's like this. There are tiny magnetic fields in the butterfly's brain and these change whenever the butterfly thinks."

"OK."

"And the brain cells, the neurons, have cryptochrome molecules in them."

"OK."

"And when the blue light in our experiment enters the butterfly's brain cells, the cryptochrome molecules inside send a tiny amount of light back out again. Green and yellow light. Timed with our blue light pulses. That's what makes it work."

"Green and yellow light. Right. Oh, right!" [The sub. The whole green and yellow light thing again.]

Deep to Peter: [There weren't any yellow or green lights in the sub.]

"That tells us what the butterfly is thinking. Of course you can't see this light. It's a very tiny amount. But we have a clever sensing device to see it."

"And so the green and yellow light doesn't come out until you send the blue light?"

"Actually, cells are always sending some light out, due to their normal biological activity. It's just that when we send a blue light pulse, the amount of light increases, and it's synchronized with our light pulse."

"Right. That makes sense. After our Yosemite trip, I read up on cryptochrome. It seems like a lot of animals have that. Pigeons, dogs. Butterflies."

Shasha laughs again. She's in a really good mood. "Smart guy. In fact, it's one of the most fundamental structures in life."

"So this whole light-based thing works with..."

"*Everything*. All living things glow. Plants. Animals. People. Even bacteria."

"But, it's, OK. How come we never see that? I mean, I don't see myself glowing in the dark." The instrument panel in the McAvie glows with several indicators, creating a silhouette of his hand as he holds it up to look at it.

"It's a very, very faint glow. Much too faint to see with your eyes. But it's there. All you see with your eyes is the light reflecting from living things. You don't see their glow. But it's always there," she says.

"Sort of a universal indicator of life, then." He tries to put it all together. "So you have some sort of special instrument that detects the glow. And magnetism changes the light in the glow. And so you can detect the magnetism changing inside the butterfly's brain cells. And that tells you what it's thinking."

"You got it!"

"Huh." He wonders what sorts of things you could do with that. As an engineer. Still, something bothers him about it. "The glow...it comes from the butterfly's brain cells. It's not just on the surface. So how does the light get out?"

"Most of it doesn't. But enough does. Have you ever put a flashlight under your fingertip and seen the red glow through your finger?"

"Oh, yeah. I've done that! Science class. The teacher went around with her smartphone flashlight turned on and we put our fingers on it. You can actually see the light pulse with your heartbeat, right through your fingernail."

He waits behind someone trying to parallel park, then signals and goes around.

"Is cryptochrome Greek?" he asks. "It sounds like it."

"Kind of. It's a compound of two Greek words. Crypto means hidden and chrome means color. It's because of the yellow color from flavin."

"Flavin. That's vitamin B2, right?"

"Vitamin B2 is riboflavin. That's where the flavin comes from. Riboflavin is ribose and flavin. The ribose part is just a kind of sugar."

"Why does the color matter?" he asks.

"The color of the light is the frequency of the light. It has to have just the right frequency to have the right amount of energy for the quantum mechanics to work."

Peter is finally able to put it together. "So you need vitamin B2 to make the quantum mechanics work?"

"That's right. Smart guy!"

Deep to Peter: [I still don't get it. What's the sub got to do with butterflies?]

Peter: [Magnetism.]

Deep to Peter: (-:Clueless:-)

Peter comes to another stop as the signal is changing from yellow to red. "So, just to check my understanding, you don't attach anything to the butterfly at all? No electrodes?"

"No electrodes," she says. "Just blue light."

"Wow!"

Deep to Peter: [For real.]

Peter: [What the hell do you know?]

The light turns green.

"We think we can use the same basic process to collect more information about what the butterfly is thinking. This is just the beginning. The really interesting thing is that by varying the pattern of the blue light, you get different results. That seems to be a general pattern. So that's what we're looking at next. And not just with one protein like cryptochrome, but a number of other molecules like it."

"When I was reading about cryptochrome, I ran across a patent related to submarine detection. Using lasers."

Shasha is as surprised at this as Peter had been. "Submarine detection?"

Deep to Peter: [Submarine detection?] Deep speaks over Shasha.

"Yeah...something about diatoms. They use a blue laser and it does something to them, and green and yellow light comes out. And how long it takes depends on the magnetism near the submarine. Or something like that."

Shasha doesn't respond immediately.

"Are you still there, Shasha?"

"Yes. That makes sense. As I said, cryptochrome and similar molecules are present in almost all living cells. And the effect does depend on the nearby magnetic field. Hm. So that's interesting. It involves diatoms. I like diatoms. Besides butterflies, they're probably the most beautiful living things. But you have to use a microscope to see them."

"Ah. I'll have to look up some pictures."

"That's pretty cool, using cryptochrome like that."

"So is that the same effect used by butterflies to navigate?"

"Same idea. The magnetic field affects the cryptochrome."

Peter laughs. "Maybe someday, someone will patent a way to use a butterfly as a submarine detector."

He's just joking, but Shasha responds: "That might work. Reading the butterfly's sense of the magnetic field could give you what you need."

"Um." He thinks back over their conversation. "That's not what you've been working on, is it? Some kind of secret government project?"

Shasha laughs. "It is! And we have special spy equipment to keep track of you. We're watching you right now in fact!" She laughs again.

Deep to Peter: (-:Belly laugh:-) [She's for you.]

Peter turns right at a stop sign, then realizes he went the wrong way and works out a route correction in his head.

"Cool. You know, I'd better focus on my driving. I'll call you back later tonight if I get back early enough. I'm actually on my way over to meet Ethan for dinner."

"OK. Say congratulations to me."

"Congratulations!"

"Thank you! And say hi to Ethan for me."

Peter feels happy for Shasha, but his mental energy starts to fade. He feels muscle tension building up around the perimeter of his head. Sinking back into his former mental state, his conversation with Shasha rapidly recedes, then disappears from his awareness.

Deep to Peter: [Not bad. For you.]

Peter drives for another minute in silence before Deep comments again. [Treacher is NOT an idiot.]

Peter feels he just got a small win. *They cared.* [But he is.]

Deep to Peter: [Frickin' hell not.]

Peter shrugs. [You're all idiots. Why are you wasting your lives doing this? Seriously.]

Deep is silent as a gesticon distorts Peter's face into an enigmatic expression. Then his headache fades.

They were far away

inside my head

Peter finds Ethan in the waiting area of the restaurant as he enters and they are seated right away. It's a small place, quiet, with subdued lighting and clear wood. A shelf of sake bottles, blue and brown and green, their brand names written in Japanese calligraphy, lines the back wall behind the sushi chef. Oil-paper umbrellas hang from the ceiling, decorated with many colors and designs.

Ethan is wearing a dark grey business suit and a light blue shirt, typical attire for him. He has just returned from interviewing a C-level executive of a consumer electronics company for a tech media article he is writing. He has removed his tie for the evening.

At their table, they make small talk while they wait for the waitress, then order a plate of hamachi sashimi and two pairs of saba nigiri, a plate of grilled shishamo and a couple of beers.

Peter mentions his trip to Yosemite with Shasha and her mother, then comments on Shasha's research, explaining that she has made a breakthrough with her butterfly research, but he doesn't go into it. Then he talks about his SCIF.

"You remember what a Faraday cage is? From physics class?"

"Vaguely. Electrical shielding." Ethan adjusts his black-rimmed glasses.

"And you remember what I said on the phone about the submarine? How the voices in my head disappeared when I was inside? So, the submarine is a Faraday cage. A really good one, with inch-thick steel. When I discovered the submarine blocked the voices, I figured it would be worth putting together a Faraday cage at home."

"You built a Faraday cage?"

"I built a Faraday cage. Or, I had it built. And actually, it's a SCIF. But basically, it's a Faraday cage. Big enough to work inside. It takes up a pretty good portion of the living room."

Ethan looks at Peter with slight amusement. "Does it work?"

"It does!"

Their waitress arrives with their beers and a bowl of edamame. Ethan picks up his glass of beer and holds it up, waiting for Peter to do the same. "Cheers." They clink their glasses and drink, not saying anything. Shortly afterwards, the hamachi sashimi shows up. Ethan takes the first piece.

"I was losing my mind. Not to dementia, but to hostile takeover. And now, with the SCIF, I'm not just standing out in the open taking hits."

"It's great that you found something that helps you. But, ...OK. You're not the paranoid type. But it doesn't make sense. It would be incredibly expensive to follow someone around 24 hours a day. How could that be worth it to anyone?"

"I don't know. Maybe it's identity theft."

Old Man to Peter: [You're not thinking.]

"Why would they talk to you, then? Why not just listen?"

Old Man to Peter: [We'll just listen.]

Why wouldn't they just listen? Why would Old Man say *he'll just listen?* "I think it goes beyond just picking up minimal information," Peter says at length. "They provoke thoughts. They seem to be trying to dig into things I wouldn't otherwise think about much. Family relationships. Finances. Stuff I worked on in the past. More so at the beginning of this whole thing."

Ethan does a quick calculation in his head. Assuming someone is paid minimum wage to follow a person around, three shifts a day, and adding in employment taxes and other costs, he estimates it would cost $130,000 a year. Minimum. But there would have to be more people than that, just to coordinate, and then there's the sophistication of the technology, if it exists. It just doesn't make sense. Still, Peter's not poor. Ethan recalls when the company Peter worked at went public. He made over seven million dollars. Though that was before tax. Peter had invited him for sushi to celebrate. Some sort of criminal organization might find him a worthwhile target.

"You know," Peter says, "maybe it's a good thing they talk in my head. If it was just the headaches, the mental fog, and the other stuff, fake smells, that kind of thing, I'd probably never have figured it out. It would just feel like my brain wasn't working right."

The saba nigiri and the grilled shishamo are delivered to the table and they each take a piece with their chopsticks.

"I invited them for dinner once."

Ethan raises his eyebrows.

"They thought it was the weirdest idea. They never showed up of course. But I tried."

"Why would you?"

"How could I lose?"

Ethan is on the verge of blurting something out, but he restrains himself. He feels sorry for Peter. But then he understands Peter's real meaning. "So if they were to show up, they'd be real."

"Not just that."

"Of course. Keep your enemies close."

"Exactly," Peter says.

"But they're probably not real. They're *not* real. It really doesn't make sense that anyone would bother to follow you around."

"I can see why you'd think that. But if you knew the story of how this all happened, you'd have to agree that it's pretty suspicious."

"How is it even possible? Brainwaves are incredibly weak, aren't they?"

"That's a good point. But you know how it is. Technology keeps advancing."

"Still, I've never heard of anything like that."

"Let me tell you what happened. Then see what you think."

Ethan sips his beer, then picks up another piece of grilled shishamo.

"So there I was, cruising along the freeway. I was headed down to San Jose to meet some guys for lunch. And there was nothing. Just pure silence. Except, well, the usual."

Ethan looks up at Peter: "The usual?"

"Highway noise."

Ethan sips his beer again.

"But it was, you know, quiet. And then, out of the blue, they just started talking."

Peter sips from his own beer.

"They? The voices."

"Yeah. Just to the left. It actually said [This is outside the left ear.]" Peter uses a fake accent when he speaks as the voice. "It was weird. The voice was telling me where it was. Except that it wasn't. There was just my window, like, six inches away. And it was closed."

"Hm."

"The next thing it said was [This is outside the right ear]. And that's where I heard it. It was just so weird. To be clear, I heard the voice *outside* of my head, but it was close by. A few inches away from my ears, on one side or the other. Up close, but not quite breathing in my ears. Ever since this all started happening, the voices always speak in exactly the same spot in my head. Very consistently. Like, almost all the time. But it wasn't like that right at the beginning. It was like they were trying out different spots in my head. They were all over. Then it became consistent like, maybe a week later. Just one spot in my head, all the time."

"Maybe you weren't sure what you were hearing," Ethan offers. "Some noise in your car just sounded like words and you weren't paying careful attention."

"Just the opposite. The voice had a higher fidelity than any phone call I've ever received. Actually, it was clearer than someone sitting right next to me in the car and talking. The voice cut right through the highway noise. Like they put noise-canceling headphones on me." He looks down at the table, remembering the experience. "The quality has gone down since then. It's like they used a high power transmitter at first and then turned down the power later."

Peter says he was surprised, but kept his eyes on the road while driving down the freeway. "I glanced at the radio, but it was off, and like I said, the windows were closed."

"So what happened next?"

"It just kept going. The voice said [This is inside the head, on the left] and then [This is inside the head, on the right]. And it really did sound like it was *inside* my head. Like it was my own thought. But I wasn't the one thinking it. Then it said [This is inside the head, in the middle], which is where it really sounded like it was coming from. Right in the middle of my head, like someone had drilled a hole in it and inserted a little speaker."

Ethan imagines it must have sounded just like one's own inner speech. Maybe Peter was just thinking to himself. But Peter says he wasn't the one thinking it. Now that he considers the point, though, it seems to him that he never actually pays attention to whether he's the one thinking in his head. It's a peculiar idea to him.

"But then the voice did something completely unexpected, something I hadn't imagined possible. It said [This is inside the head, far away]. That blew me away. It sounded like the voice came from a distance. But it didn't sound like it was far away *outside* my head, but rather, like it was far away, but still *inside* my head. Like my head was a giant auditorium, with the voice still inside but not nearby. Or, like I was suddenly, only in my imagination, in a giant auditorium and I was hearing the voice far away. Which was really confusing, because in my imagined location in the auditorium, the voice was outside of my imagined head, but at the same time, the whole imagined situation was *inside* of my *actual* head."

"And then it stopped. And that was all there was to it." He says he thought back to the voice, trying to communicate with it, assuming it was a real person, maybe someone transmitting his voice to his brain with some kind of machine. "It was almost like they started out with a signal check. Just to make sure the system was working." He says he tried communicating with the voice by thinking "[Who are you?]", and after a short pause, "[Can you do that again?]". But there was no answer.

Nothing further happened. He had met his acquaintances for lunch and everything had been completely normal. No voices in his head.

"Were you tired? Maybe you were sleep deprived."

"It was lunch time. Sometimes my sleep wasn't great, but it wasn't bad. I just slept in if I needed it."

"Any other symptoms? Headache? Fever?"

"No. Nothing. I felt completely normal. It just came in out of the blue, and then it stopped." He thinks about his own point some more. "I have headaches all the time, but that didn't start until later. Like maybe a month later. I can't remember exactly when, but it was later."

"It sounds..." Ethan is not sure what to say. "You called it a *signal check*?"

"That's what it seemed like. Like someone was testing a wireless microphone. Checking to see how it sounded in different places. You know, testing...1...2...3."

"You never heard voices in your head before that?"

"That's the weird thing about it. It just started all of a sudden. And it was all the more weird because it really did sound like someone testing the sounds. I figured if it were schizophrenia, it would be more random or bizarre."

Ethan studies him carefully. He figures Peter looks sincere. He's not making it up. Still, he reserves judgment. It could be the way a signal processing genius would experience hallucinations. One tends to explain things in accordance with one's world view. To a psychiatrist, it's coping behavior. To a signal processing engineer, it's a signal. In his own world view, it's his friend sharing something important. He just doesn't know what it is.

"OK. Then what?"

"Well, the next night, I went out to get some fresh air. I think it was the next night. It's been a while. Everything was quiet. It was a nice night, actually. Clear sky. You could see the stars really well. So I was just standing there, looking up at the sky and trying to pick out some constellations, when the voices started up again in my head. But this time, it was bizarre, psychotic chanting, words rapidly repeating in my head, over and over. And my brain responded, or at least, that's what it felt like. Repeating the words I heard in my own head, faster and faster, like my brain was being forced to take turns in some kind of game. It lasted about fifteen minutes. I think. I really wasn't able to keep track of time with all that going on. And then it just stopped."

Late that same night, he says, a voice woke him up from a sound sleep, announcing itself at a leisurely pace, saying: "[I'm from *The Lab*.]" He reacted by thinking: "[What lab? Berkeley?]" and wondering *who'd have technology like that?*

The voice had responded: "[That ain't it.]"

Peter says the voice was silent for a moment, then said: "[Tell me everything you ever did wrong.]" The only thing he could think of at the time, lying there half awake, was that he may have peed in a swimming pool as a kid. Maybe. He couldn't remember. At three in the morning, what can you say? Except that he didn't say it. He just thought it in his head, and the voice had laughed at him. "[You're f---ing kidding me.]" and then "[Well ain't you a goody two-shoes.]"

Ethan laughs at this. "Crude."

"Indeed."

Ethan smirks, asking: "Then what?"

"The voice asked: [Have you ever killed anyone?]"

"Killed anyone?"

"That's what he said." Peter says he was stunned, still lying in his bed, wide awake but eyes closed. "No one had ever asked me a question like that before." He says he replied, thinking in his head: "[Who are you?]" and that the voice responded: "[You really are a f---ing moron.]"

"They were pretty rough in the early days. They called me bastard, repeatedly. For whatever reason, they don't do that any more."

Old Man to Peter: [Tell him what you were planning.]

Peter ignores Old Man, but a thought flits through his mind: Old Man never talked like that first voice, the one who called him a f---ing moron.

Suddenly, Peter smells the odor of a soldering iron. Again. He glances around the restaurant but sees nothing to explain the smell. It disappears a moment later. Then the memories come back again - his ultra-wideband cognitive radio work, the accidental retransmission of voices in some language he didn't know from some source he never identified, voices he listened to through an audio speaker for quite a while before turning it off to figure out what happened. He eventually found the bug and fixed it and never thought about it again, not until after the voices started in his head.

He snaps back to the present. The smell of beer registers with him and he takes a swig. Then he picks up a slice of shashimi with his chopsticks and transfers it to his plate. Ethan takes a slice as well.

Peter holds his head with his hands again, reloading context so he can continue. What was he talking about? Then he remembers the guy from *The Lab*. He explains to Ethan that the nocturnal "visit" had continued for an hour or more before the voice finally relented and he was able to fall back asleep. But it continued again the following night, and it went on, night after night, for quite a while, before the voice backed off and would rarely wake him up in the middle of the night any more.

Nighttime voices stopped altogether once Peter started sleeping in the SCIF. That said, they have still been hounding him all day long, to varying degrees. The topics have ranged all over the map, but if there's a pattern to it, it's almost as though they've been using the seven deadly sins as a guide. Would he like to go to Vegas? Does he like other beverages besides beer? They wanted to know whether he took software from his previous employer to start his current project. Does he go to church? Is he a racist? And on and on. Most of the questions were roundabout. They didn't just come out and ask them. It took a while, but slowly, he had built up a picture of what they might be doing. Some sort of profiling.

Ethan isn't sure what to say. "Were you feeling guilty about something?" He wants to help, but he doesn't want to pry.

Their waitress checks on them and they order a chef's variety plate of nigiri before returning to Peter's story.

"I think the main thing is to establish whether they're even real," Peter says. "And that's what I've been working on." He gives Ethan a list of reasons for believing the voices are real people. One, the experience in the submarine. Two, the fact that the SCIF really works. Three, vocabulary differences, comparing words he knows with words they know. Words like *bugaboo,* which sounds like a children's word to him. They once said *Brigadoon*, but he had never heard that word before. He had to look it up. They use the word *moniker*. He would say name or nickname, never *moniker*. Maybe they're from a different part of the country where they use different words, though he's not sure where. Who in California would ever use the word *moniker*?

Continuing, he gives point four, which is that he has found correlations between his experiences, such as forced blinks and fake smells, and the signals he recorded with his cognitive radio equipment. There are patterns in the signals that match up with the timing of his experiences. That's the big one, he says. It's objective evidence. Finally, five, he mentions his experience in Yosemite with Shasha by Vernal Fall, surrounded by granite out in the middle of nowhere. There was no cell reception, and for a reason. Signals don't propagate well there with all the massive granite cliffs and boulders.

"OK, I'm not sure about this last point," he says. "Maybe they just didn't keep up with us. But they weren't there. I didn't hear any voices. And if the problem is really just in my head, why would it completely disappear for hours while we were there in Yosemite?"

Ethan responds, as he has in the past, that maybe Peter just felt better when he isolated himself in the sub and in the SCIF. Same thing with Yosemite, relaxing with his girlfriend. As to the vocabulary words, who knows? He probably heard *Brigadoon* somewhere and just didn't remember it.

"It's weirder than that, though. When I made a note to myself about these unusual words, they started tossing other rare words at me. Like they went out of their way to look them up, words maybe even they didn't know. *Prurient*, for example. I still don't know what that means."

"Prurient?" Ethan laughs. "So you don't know that word."

"I never looked it up. Is it something funny? Sounds like a stuffy vocabulary word to me."

"I suppose that depends on the context." He smiles in good humor.

Peter finishes his beer and considers whether to order another, but then another thought occurs to him. "Come to think of it, one of them told me he was an English major. Still, he wasn't particularly eloquent."

Ethan's smartphone vibrates in his pocket. He pulls it out to check the notification as Peter takes another piece of sushi.

"Maybe you should keep a journal. Keep track of everything that happens. It could give you an outlet for your frustrations."

Their waitress drops off the chef's plate and they start working their way through it, eating and not talking.

After a period of silence, Old Man starts talking in Peter's head, making it difficult for him to think. But finally, with only two pieces of sushi left, Peter shuts Old Man out of his mind and refocuses his mental energy. "I'm working on tracking down their signals," he says.

Ethan takes one of the two pieces of sushi with his chopsticks and dips it in soy sauce.

"It's not working yet, but I have a device." Peter immediately regrets saying this. "I shouldn't talk about it. At least, not here. They're listening."

Finishing the bite of sushi, Ethan tells Peter that he probably just needs to relax. He positions his chopsticks over the final piece of sushi as he comments: "Maybe you've been pushing yourself too hard." He looks at Peter who passes on the final piece, which Ethan then takes.

Peter takes a copy of his condo key out of his pocket to give to Ethan. "If anything happens to me, could you take care of things for me? I don't have any close family members that could do it. Just in case."

Ethan hesitates, then takes the key. He studies Peter's face, then puts the key in his pocket. "Sure. But I think you'll be fine. Really. Just relax."

Old Man to Peter: [That'd be about right.]

Peter: [Why are you saying anything at all? Why not just listen?]

Old Man to Peter: [That's a hell. That's what we frickin' do.]

Voice to Peter: [That's not a thing you're doing.] (-:Belly laugh:-) (-:Middle finger twitch:-)

The gesticons jerk Peter around like a puppet. [What the hell is that supposed to be about?] he thinks. The only response he gets is another gesticon. (-:Big grin:-)

The voice, after a long pause, responds: [Did it ever occur to you we're just bored? Do you know how long I've been sitting here waiting for you to come out of your rat cage?]

Peter lets that sink in. [Right. It would be boring, wouldn't it? Go get a real job.]

Voice to Peter: (-:Belly laugh:-) [We're freakin' the *it*.]

Peter is physically tired from all the gesticon activity. His muscles are being worked, not by his own will, but by the forced expressions. He tries to relax his facial muscles. They've been overworked to the point of fatigue and it hurts.

He came out of the SCIF earlier today, taking a break from his usual routine, not wanting to feel cooped up all day long. Interested in doing some more research on electronic harassment, thinking that perhaps it would give him some insight into who might be attacking him and why, he has been sitting at the dining room table, laptop open, searching the Internet, trying to identify other people who may be under the same kind of attack.

While he has found plenty of people talking about electronic harassment, none of them sound credible. They might just be people suffering from delusions. None of them provide any tangible evidence that they are suffering from external attacks. No technical investigation, no scientific data, nothing definitive, nothing helpful that he could use in his own investigation. At the same time, other organizations are dismissive of the very possibility of the existence or use of such technology. And yet, he has found several examples of actual mind-reading technology in development at universities and by corporations. They aren't sophisticated enough to explain what is happening to him. Then again, that doesn't rule out the secret development and use of more sophisticated technology.

These ideas have inspired him to write a novel. A message in a bottle, documenting his own situation, but in a fictional format. And he'll send it out into the world to be discovered. If he's wrong, it's just a novel. No big deal. But if he's right...

In his own novel, which he is basing on the experiences he has been having, the protagonist will also write a novel about his experiences. And that protagonist will use his knowledge of technology and science to search for clues. It'll be a kind of a science-based crime novel where the victim-protagonist, technically capable but under the duress of a continuous attack by invisible but all-seeing adversaries, tries to solve the crime and identify the perpetrators.

Maybe there's a large but well-hidden organization behind the perpetrators. Perhaps some insider will be inspired to blow the whistle, someone who knows what is going on at a high level but doesn't realize how abusive it is. Not just in his novel, but out there in the real world. He's hoping that someone will notice the parallels.

He's not sure who or what the insiders might be, what roles they may play, or who is watching who. But with publication, his novel can reach thousands of people. With luck, millions. Someone out there must be able to connect the dots. And even if no one comes to his rescue, perhaps someday the world will at least understand what had happened to him.

He thinks back to the giant breaches in years past which had exposed thousands of documents about the internal operations of secretive government agencies, sometimes by insiders, sometimes by outside hackers. He recalls news stories of organizations hacking into people's cell phones, of eavesdropping through television sets, of bypassing encryption on laptops by going right to the keyboard and the computer display to get the data.

The amazing thing is that those are true stories. They're in the news, fact-checked by the largest news organizations and later, written up in historical accounts. There's no question that those kinds of things happen. But if you tell someone it's happening to you, you're a nutcase. You think someone stuck a GPS tracking device on your car? Get a life. Why would they? You probably think the NSA's listening to your phone calls, too. Who are you that they'd care?

He thinks fiction is the right way to go. The true account will come out after he solves the crime.

[There are no secrets,] he thinks. [You *will* eventually get caught.]

He gets another (-:Belly laugh:-) in response, followed by irritating comments. The voice chatters away, but he relaxes his mind, letting the words flow through without registering any meaning. In short order, the voice stops and his mind is free again to think.

He is acting on Ethan's advice. Writing as an outlet. Don't interact with the voices, just write. But rather than writing in a journal, he has decided to put his thoughts into the form of a novel. This is a better approach. A journal would be about him, whereas the novel distances himself from it. By writing a novel, he can stay above it all. It's not about him. It's about the idea of it.

Positioning his laptop and opening an editing tool, he starts capturing the mental dialog. The voice in his head comments: [That's not something you're doing.]

Peter notices that the nature of the dialog changes when he shifts into this "meta" mode. The voice tries to feed him empty meaningless dialog. Things like "[That's a bit.]" or "[You're not a nada.]" The phrases sound prerecorded, like someone is just pressing buttons to send sound bites. Maybe it's the intonation. Or the pacing. They don't flow naturally from the earlier dialog. When he points this out, the voice says: "[Blah!]"

Peter writes that down. "[Blah!]" The voice sends him a (-:Belly laugh:-), and he writes that down, too. The voice forces another laugh on him. "[That would be about right for you,]" the voice says, and then, "[That's what I'm going to *let* you do]". As if the voice had a choice. Maybe the voice is trying to sabotage his attempt to capture what the dialog is really like. But he persists. It doesn't really matter. This *is* how it really is.

An outside observer watching the room all this time would not hear anything but the ticking of the clock in the kitchen and the occasional high-speed burst of keystrokes on a laptop. Peter is utterly alone. Hours go by.

The door of his SCIF remains partway open.

Tick... Tick... Tick... Tick... Tick... Tick... Tick...

Peter: [Folktronica.]

Voice to Peter: [What the...?]

Peter: [Have you ever listened to folktronica?]

Voice to Peter: [I'm not going to tell you a freakin' thing.] (-:Gut punch:-) (-:Middle finger twitch:-)

The punch to his abdominal muscles has a real kick to it. He gasps.

Peter: [I love you, too, jerk.]

He feels it again. (-:Gut punch:-) (-:Belly laugh:-) He has to catch his breath. He glances over at the SCIF. His *rat cage*. He considers retreating, but then changes his mind. [Why are you doing this?]

Voice to Peter: (-:Hearty laugh:-)

Peter searches the music on his smartphone and finds a heavy metal track. [Listen to this.] Touching play, heavily distorted electric guitar music blasts out, almost pure noise. He holds the phone up to his right ear. It is about as loud as he can tolerate without damaging his hearing. Then he quickly retracts it.

Voice to Peter: [Ack! Freakin' hell.] (-:Gut punch:-)

The punch makes Peter cough.

Voice to Peter: [Hell with that. I can just torq the volume.]

Peter mutes the music, then starts whispering to himself. Then he does it again, un-muting the music and holding the phone right by his ear.

The voice responds with a (-:Belly laugh:-).

Peter turns off the music. Setting the smartphone aside, he continues writing from his experience. Then he reviews his notes, trying to visualize possible scenes for his novel, but nothing clear comes to mind other than a literal portrayal. How should he expose the crime being committed against him? He gets up to look through his bookcase for examples of writing.

He has quite a number of math and engineering books, mostly textbooks and other reference materials from university...*Applied Partial Differential Equations*, *Applications of Fractal Analysis*, a textbook on signal processing, two volumes on spectrum management in cognitive radio. In a small section on the bottom shelf, he keeps a collection of novels. Mostly sci-fi. The whole Philip K. Dick collection. One volume by Iain Banks. A recent book by Charles Isbouts that he never got around to reading. And a strange and not-very-popular little volume called *Law and Partial Order* written by "A set of authors, with group actions on the left and the right", a story of life in a world in which the members of society who, despite being described by mathematical relationships, are surprising unpredictable and provably so. The book is a satirical novella, like *Flatland* by Edwin Abbott Abbott, which it sits next to on the shelf. His dad had given him the pair of books as a Christmas gift.

Mainly because he hasn't read it yet, he selects the Charles Isbouts book and brings it over to the couch and starts skimming it, studying the writing style. After a short while, he fetches his laptop and sits on the couch with it on his lap, alternating between taking notes and reading in the book.

Encryption plays a big role in the Charles Isbouts book. But for him, it's a post-encryption world. What good does encryption do? With a mind-reading machine, identity thieves, spies, the government, potentially anyone can watch either end of a communication and get it all. They don't need to hack his laptop or smartphone. They can just go to the source. Capture whatever he thinks, as he thinks it. Whatever he writes. Whatever he reads. Whatever he hears.

The voice continually interferes with his reading, but damn it all if he's going to be a prisoner in his own SCIF. He stops taking notes, switching his focus back to the voice, asking: [Are you moral? Are any of you moral? Why are you doing this?]

Voice to Peter: [We're not immoral. We're *indifferent*.]

Peter: [Indifferent? Is that how you'd live your life? Hours at a time hounding me and you're INDIFFERENT? Anyway, I'm writing about you. You'll be in my book. Are you indifferent to that?]

The voice laughs inside his head. A sound, not a gesticon. This is unlike the other voices. The others never laugh. [I'm *indifferent* to books,] he says, [but what the torq is folktronica?]

[Folktronica?] The comment seems to come from out of the blue, but then he remembers his earlier comment. [Oh...] *How to react to that?* [Music. Like electronica, but more real. Acoustic instruments. Real rhythm. Sounds of the real world.] His head feels like it clears up, just a little. [The Books. Four Tet. A few Icelandic artists.] He puts his hands back on his laptop keyboard, poised to take more notes. [So I need a nickname for you. Or as Treacher calls it, a *moniker*. For the novel. You get to pick.]

Voice to Peter: [I'm not going to be some kind of celebrity.]

Peter: [Come on!]

Voice to Peter: (-:Belly laugh:-)

Peter's diaphragm heaves several times against his will while his mouth also widens.

Voice to Peter: [Hell if I'm going to play your game.]

Peter: [I'm taking notes. And thanks for playing.]

Voice to Peter: (-:Left wrist pain:-)

Peter is surprised by the pain. Shouting "ouch!", he quickly pulls his left hand back away the keyboard. Endorphins then slowly diffuse through his left wrist, cooling the heat of the pain.

Tired of the game, he closes his laptop and retreats to the SCIF to get some real work done. The last thing he hears in his head, as he is closing the SCIF door, is the gentle singing, sotto voce, breathy and sometimes warbling, almost a lullaby, of "A Little Longing Goes Away" by The Books. He hesitates for just a few moments, then shuts the door tight.

Friday, 12 July 2024

Ethan enters Peter's condo as the fading evening sunlight filters in through the leaves of the large plane tree behind him. He is wearing a light grey business suit with a blue knit shirt and a skinny dark blue and white polka dot tie.

"Thanks for coming. You want anything to drink?" Peter is dressed casually, as usual. Dark gray jeans and a brown-colored brand-name T-shirt.

"I'm fine, thanks." Ethan turns to the right to inspect the large enameled metal box that occupies some two-thirds of Peter's living room.

"So that's it." He pokes his head behind the back side of the box, which runs along one side of the living room with just enough room to squeeze by if you had to. Then he slowly walks around the corner and along the side that is easier to access, inspecting its features. "Impressive."

"Let me show you around."

He invites Ethan into the SCIF and then closes the heavy door behind them. The door makes a click and a muffled thud, making Ethan look back around.

A narrow table runs along one inside wall in the SCIF, with two simple chairs tucked underneath. Folded up in a box under the table is a futon, a blanket, and a pillow. Several pieces of equipment are mounted in a rack at the opposite end of the SCIF, cables hanging out the back. A utility box protrudes from the wall above the table, providing a pair of electrical outlets and two network connections, marked with different colors. Next to the laptop sits a printer. A technical manual, a notebook, several loose papers and pens and a variety of data cables and other electronics components and devices are scattered across the table.

Ethan notices the poster on the wall. REMEMBER THE ENEMY IS LISTENING. "That's a watchword from World War II."

"Yeah. This is my fortress. My center of operations."

"What operations?"

"I'm a radio engineer, right? So I'd feel stupid if I couldn't track these guys down. You know, the voices in my head." Peter points to the electronics equipment and notes he has been writing up. "One of the biggest issues is just figuring out how it works."

Peter pulls out the two chairs and sits down, offering one to Ethan.

"The Faraday cage has made a big difference. I sleep soundly at night now. I actually sleep in here. No more being woken up in the middle of the night for *questioning*. And I'm finally getting my thoughts back together again, getting my engineering self back."

"You said *Faraday cage*?"

"Sorry. SCIF. More layers, more protection. Basically, it's a Faraday cage for electrical shielding, with additional layers for blocking magnetism and absorbing radio signals and sounds inside the SCIF. I think they use fiber optics to pass through the layers to electrically isolate the signals going in and out to the Internet, too."

Peter explains that he had to assume the voices were using radio signals rather than some other form of signaling. If they were doing something else, he wouldn't know where to begin. Perhaps someone has discovered some wild idea for mind reading using neutron beams or x-rays. But he knows nothing about neutron beams and figured they wouldn't dare to use x-rays for fear of slowly killing their target...and perhaps the neighbors as well. It wouldn't be so good for their own health either, sitting next to an x-ray machine all day long. So he ruled out those sorts of explanations for practical reasons.

The next problem, he explains, was to discover what frequency or frequencies they transmit on. The radio spectrum is huge. He tells Ethan to imagine a single photograph of the entire population of the planet. A satellite image of everyone standing out in a giant field, all crowded together, looking up at the heavens. Then he says to imagine searching for his own face hidden within it. It's in plain view, he says, but then again, it isn't. Not really. "You could pore over that picture for years on end and never find yourself in it," he says. Ethan nods.

Actually, he says, there's already software that does just that. They call it automatic crowd analysis from high-resolution satellite images. But just imagine doing that with your own eyes. So it's that kind of thing, he says. You have to be clever, then automate it.

He did have a clue to go on. The brain has to be able to perceive the signals, whatever they are. He explains what he read about radar operators in World War II, about how they would hear whooshing sounds in their heads when they would walk past the front of the radar transmitters, and how they would feel pins and needles sensations. He mentions the research in the 1960s which studied the effect in more detail and how it led to conspiracy theories about the government transmitting voices to people's heads.

"It would be dangerous to transmit microwave beams that powerful around the city," he says. "In any case, I don't think that's how they're doing it. I did a search for unusual sources of microwaves a while back, and...nothing. Besides, when I hear the voices and I'm sitting right next to you, you don't hear a thing. So there's something else going on. Well, I assume you never hear voices, even when you're with me."

Ethan is puzzled at the very idea. "No."

"Anyway, so that's part of the question. How are they doing that? The irony is that I get better reception in my head than my cell phone does from the towers. And while that may just sound funny, it's a technical clue. The voices are always there. In building basements. In elevators. And the reason for that turns out to be simple. They're using much lower frequencies than cell phones do. They're not microwaves. They're down below where FM radio stations transmit at. Lower frequencies travel through obstructions much better than higher frequencies do. Remember all the coverage issues with the 5G roll-out? That's because 5G uses higher frequencies."

"I do remember that."

"So how is it that I get great reception in my head, and you sit right next to me and hear nothing? There's got to be some sort of protocol thing going on, like the way cell phones keep their own signals from getting mixed up."

Ethan understands Peter's point. Cell phones share the airwaves without interference in part by cooperatively taking turns. A cell phone transmits a small burst of information, then waits for its turn to transmit the next burst. Similarly, it only listens for the tower when its turn arrives. This turn-taking happens so quickly that when you are talking on the phone, you don't notice. But Ethan doesn't get where Peter is going with this line of thinking. The human brain doesn't do anything like that.

"Putting that issue aside, though, the trickier part is reading someone's mind."

Ethan blinks. Then he remembers their discussion over sushi. With another moment's thought, the point sinks in. Peter is trying to figure out how the voices communicate in a full round-trip discussion in his head. The voices speak in his head. And the voices hear what he thinks. But there isn't just a single explanation. There are two parts to it. And how they read his mind is the trickier part.

"Brainwaves are so weak, a radio receiver can't detect them from a distance. Or at least, so it seems when one first looks at the problem. As it is, EEG devices that doctors use for recording brainwaves use probes that stick right onto your head, and even then, the signal they get doesn't have a lot of detail."

"Oh. If you're talking about something on the head for mind reading, there are already products on the market that do that. I know some people in China who are working on virtual reality and they're trying to use mind-reading headsets like that. I went to high school with one of them."

"Right," Peter says. "There is some work on headsets. I'd guess they can't hear the words in someone's head, though. Right?"

"I think it is pretty limited." Ethan sits up in his chair, then adjusts the position of his glasses on his face. "They're trying to make it possible for a game player to move an animated character around on the screen just by thinking."

"There are some tricks which they may not be using yet. And if you're going to spy on people, you need to do it at a distance. And here's where I was going with that. What you'd really need, to read such a weak signal from a distance, because brain signals are so weak, is a good signal to noise ratio."

Peter is getting visibly excited. He's in his element now. "The big idea," he says, "is that mind reading is practical from a distance only if you can break the Nyquist limit. In 1928, Harry Nyquist proved that if you want to accurately receive a signal, you have to record enough values from the signal to get the whole thing. That's the Nyquist limit, the number of values you need to record. There's a simple formula for it. It was actually quite a breakthrough in signal processing theory. His real point was that even if the signal is changing constantly, you don't need to record values continuously. So long as you record enough values each second, it's enough to record the signal perfectly. And I mean perfectly. Not just pretty well. It's kind of a weird idea, if you think about it. You've got this signal wiggling along, like a curvy line on a graph, and you can reproduce it perfectly even if you only check it at a few points here and there. He proved that."

Ethan smiles, then resumes his attentive listening expression. Most of the people he interviews for tech media articles don't take this long to explain their projects. But this is just the way it is with Peter. When he has something to say, there's a lot of detail to it. And Peter is just not the two-minute-elevator-pitch kind of guy. He's the guy in the back room who really makes things work but who you would never put in front of a customer, or the press.

"So what's the issue, then?" Peter asks. "So as I said, it's all about signal-to-noise ratios. Brainwaves send out radio signals, but they're weak, and they're mixed in with a ton of noise. They're *buried* in the noise. Radio broadcasts. Electrical noise from appliances and motors and fluorescent lights and...everything. It's like trying to hear someone whispering from across the room at a noisy party. How do you do that?"

Ethan nods.

"It would be extremely difficult, maybe impossible, to pick up every little wiggle in someone's brainwaves from a quarter mile away with mind-reading equipment."

"A quarter of a mile?" Ethan is incredulous.

Peter raises his hand. "I know. Hard to believe. The fact is, even today, there isn't any medical technology that can accurately read your brainwaves from more than a quarter of an inch away. I checked. There just isn't anything like that. A quarter of a mile? Forget it."

"So it can't be real," Ethan says.

"There's certainly good reason to believe it's not."

Ethan's not sure how to respond to this. "So there really isn't any —"

"Bear with me. Drum roll please. And here it is: The trick is that you don't need get the entire signal. You only need the part you care about."

He pauses for dramatic effect, but this has no effect on Ethan, whose expression remains unchanged.

"I dumbed it down to make it obvious. And you still...OK, so it's not. Look at it this way: If you don't need the whole signal, you don't need to record as much data. All those radio waves coming out of the brain are complicated. There's the visual data of what you see with your eyes, and the sensations you feel on your skin. There's all that activity keeping your balance. And, well, the brain has billions of neurons. The signals they create are complicated. But out of all that activity in the brain, all you want is to hear the sounds in someone's head. You can throw everything else away. The brain may be complicated, but you really don't need more than just a little data from it."

"OK, that makes sense."

"But hold on. It gets better. The formula that Harry Nyquist came up with in 1928 doesn't always apply. It's just the worst case. And if the shapes you're looking for in your signal are simple, and if you can find a way to use sparse coding for the signals, you can do much, much better. So there are these two ideas: simple shapes, and sparse coding. It's the same kind of thing I was working on with my project before the voices showed up."

"I've never heard of sparse coding," Ethan says.

Peter tries to think of a good example.

"OK. Suppose you want to identify some object which is really far away. Say its a junkyard with all kinds of random stuff piled up, and you're trying to figure out what's there from a thousand miles away. I mean, like looking at it through a telescope. Maybe from up in a satellite. You're collecting intelligence data or something. Worse yet, there's smog and airplanes flying around and clouds and...lots of noise, things that block your view. No way, right? But if it's simple, say it's just a giant disk, it would be easy. We look at the moon all the time with our naked eyes and we instantly know what it is. And yet, it's a quarter *million* miles away. That's because the shape of the moon is *simple*. Clouds may come and go, and maybe it's glowing behind the clouds, and we still know it's the moon."

"So the shapes in the signal have to be simple," Ethan says.

"Right. And then there's sparse coding, which just means you're not looking for a lot of different signal shapes. In my example, I explained how the moon is easy to see. Its shape is simple. But if you see something bright and glowing behind the clouds, it might be the sun. Still, there are only two things it could be. It's going to be either the sun, or the moon, and the sun is much brighter. So there it is. Simple shapes with sparse coding."

"How does that help you read minds?" Ethan doesn't see the connection.

"Words. The sounds a mind reader is looking for in your head are word sounds. There aren't really that many words that they can search for in your head. And most radio signals don't look anything like word sounds. Their software can just throw out all those other signals. Less junk, less noise, better signal-to-noise ratio. And *that's* the real trick." Peter gestures with finality.

"You said signals have shapes. But we can't see brainwaves."

"A radio receiver can, if you use the right math with it. There's a technique called compressed sensing that's been around since 2004.

Before then, it probably wouldn't have been possible. The math just wasn't there yet."

Peter stretches his neck, twisting it to the left, then to the right, then stretches his arms out, being careful not to bump into Ethan. Space is tight in the SCIF.

"I've only been talking about word sounds going back and forth. But they also transmit smells and other things to my head. This may sound weird, but if your brain receives the right radio signal shape, you'll smell something. That seems to be how it works. So you've got the same technique being used for different things. It's just different shapes. Some shapes give you word sounds. Other shapes give you smells."

Ethan's not sure he heard right. "*Smells* have shapes?"

"Um. Let's just say that from a mathematical point of view, they do. I guess that wouldn't be obvious to most people. Let's hold that thought. I have something to show you later and you can judge for yourself."

Ethan is starting to tire. "Peter, this just doesn't jive with what I know about technology."

"The technology is definitely possible. The hard part is that it takes a huge amount of calculation. But that's the other thing that has changed in recent years. GPU processors accelerate the calculations and they're in everything. Laptops. Smartphones. They started out in video cards for video games to work at full speed, but these days, GPUs are used for all kinds of things. Speech recognition. Face recognition. Artificial intelligence. Under the hood, it's all just number crunching. It doesn't really matter what it's for. So you've got the math, and you've got the processing power. Someone just had to put it all together."

Peter asks Ethan whether he wants anything to drink. "Water? Anything else? I've got an espresso maker. Tea?"

"No, I'm fine. Thanks."

"I'll be right back."

Ethan adjusts himself in his seat and looks around as Peter goes out to the kitchen and then returns with a cup of water, closing the SCIF door behind himself, cutting off Old Man mid-sentence. Back in the SCIF, he drinks down a quarter of the cup, then sets it down.

"I suspected they're actually transmitting ultra-wideband signals," Peter says.

Ethan is hit with yet another jargon word he's never heard of.

"And using time domain analysis for the mind reading."

Ethan smiles briefly, then pulls his smartphone out to check the time.

Seeing this, Peter feels a bit embarrassed holding his friend captive. "Sorry this is taking so long. Time domain just means the receiver directly reads the signal level changing over time. It's not tuned to a carrier frequency like you would, say, to receive a radio station broadcast.

You know, like tuning into 88.5 on FM. But enough of the technical background. The reason I invited you here is because I found what I was looking for."

"You have proof there's someone out there reading your mind."

Peter smiles and replies "Yep" as he picks up one of the electronic devices from the table to show to Ethan. It doesn't look like much. It's just a black plastic box with a cable coming out of it and two round metal coax connectors for antennas. "I step out of the SCIF and this thing picks up a signal. I don't have a way to get direction or range to the signal source yet, but there's a definite relationship between the experiences I have in my head and the signal shapes that I pick up with this."

He pulls up an image on his laptop showing a multicolored pattern with arrows pointing here and there, annotated with comments. "This is a graph of the signals that my receiver picked up. I marked places where I experienced specific things. Here, for example, is a range of time where the voices are talking in my head. Notice how the pattern looks different from the region around it?" He points to the screen. "And here are several other places with voices."

Ethan peers more closely at the image. It's not obvious to him. "You mean that..." He's not sure how to ask the question. "Keep going."

"I recorded radio signals, and at the same time, I made notes of the times I heard voices, experienced gesticons, or noticed fake smells. It's hard to do. There's no way to automate it. But I quickly scribbled down what I could."

Peter then points out several places on the image where he had experienced phantosmia, or what he calls fake smells. "Look here. The very same smell. See? Three places, three times."

This time, Ethan sees that the patterns in the image indeed do look similar. The pattern stands out against the rest of the image.

"*That* is the shape of a smell," Peter says. "I recorded my own brainwaves, too. Right here in the SCIF." He shows Ethan the notebook, including the screenshot of his brainwave patterns that he had printed out and stapled to a page inside.

Ethan peers at the print-out. It's obvious that there are larger cycles of activity, but within each cycle, the graph looks almost random to him.

"It's the real thing," Peter says. "There is someone out there doing this to me."

Ethan looks back at Peter. "Why would anyone bother? You said the voices talk 24 hours a day. That's an awful lot of effort, and for what?"

"I have no idea. You're right, why would they? Maybe my bank accounts? It's sort of like cyberstalking, I guess. Except that the intimidation, the stalking and the identity theft is all hidden from view. There's no trace of evidence to bring to the police." He thinks it over. "It's a new version of the same old crime. Maybe it should be called neurostalking."

"But with a technology like that, the inventors would be billionaires if they'd productize it for legitimate uses. Why waste the time and take the risk of being caught just to steal a few million?"

"Well, that brings me to the other reason I invited you over. My novel. I've been working on it ever since you suggested keeping a journal. As an alternative."

"What?"

"If there are real people doing this, I need to track them down. But proving that they did this to me will be hard. If I can ever gather convincing factual evidence, I'll take them to court. But short of that, I want to at least provide some form of documentation of what I went through. Someday, people will look back and understand. It's kind of a back-up plan."

"Why not just keep a journal?"

"You should see what people write in their blogs online. I don't want to look like some kind of conspiracy nut. Worse yet, if they're real people, keeping a journal could be a way for them to get their victims to write things down. The last thing I'd do is let them manipulate me, making it seem as though the things they said in my head were actually my own ideas. Just imagine if I were to write…I don't know. *The voices said such-and-such.* Maybe it's designed to help cover up their crime. Or to make me look like a crackpot that no one should listen to."

Ethan doesn't know what to say to this. Peter's point has a certain logic to it. And yet, it does sound just like the kind of thing a conspiracy nut might say.

"The voices actually told me to leave certain things out of my novel. I wrote them down anyway."

"I don't see how that helps anything," Ethan says. "Anyway, you're not a writer. Why a novel? That's a major project."

"It may not be a great novel. But it is just a project. It's engineering. You know, you work out a plot, you make sure the logic makes sense. Fill in the plot details. Layer on character personalities and ambience. You can approach it with the same techniques used in software development, where you write down a bunch of little stories and you put the big story together around the little stories. Divide and conquer. Incremental progress. The usual."

"I doubt novelists… Are you going to take a writing class?"

"I look up things sometimes, but I probably won't take a class. Anyway, it's not really important." He regrets bringing up the novel. The main thing is building his device to track down the signals from the voices. "I can't publish anything factual, that's all. Not yet. It has to be presented as fiction." Peter's mood shifts. "It's not just that, though. If anything happens to me, I want Shasha to have it. If you ever read it, you'll understand."

Peter tries to get Ethan to promise that if something happens to him before he gets it all figured out, his friend will continue the work on it. Take the signal tracker he will be building, and his notes. Whatever he needs. He should take a copy of the novel, too. It may give him context to understand what his attackers are doing.

But Ethan says he can't see how he could help. How could he?

Peter adds that getting the novel published may help. He still has hopes that some reader out there will recognize his situation. Someone with the power to do something about it. Even if it doesn't end up helping him personally, it may help humanity at large.

Ethan checks his smartphone for the time again. "Hey, I've got an early morning meeting to get to, so I'd better head out."

And with that, the two get up and, slowly pushing open the SCIF's heavy door, they return to Peter's living room. Peter sees Ethan to the front door and thanks him for coming over.

The voice in his head doesn't fail to comment. "[So that's Ethan Chen,]" it says. Being preoccupied with seeing Ethan off, he's not sure which voice it is.

Wednesday, 17 July 2024

Peter wakes up in the SCIF to the national radio program on the feed to his smartphone alarm. The guest on the show is explaining that despite years of development work, delivery drones that carry your packages through the air and drop them on your front lawn are likely to become a passing fad. Adverse weather limits their use, and they're also limited in the amount of weight they can carry. Just picture two bags of groceries flying past overhead and you get what what I mean, he says.

Sidewalk delivery robots, by comparison, have numerous advantages, the guest says. Either way, though, in comparison with large, heavy delivery trucks, for conveying small items to homes, the smaller vehicles are more time and energy efficient. And with the bots themselves serving as the delivery packaging, say goodbye to all those wasteful cardboard boxes.

The host asks about warehouses and the so-called dark stores that have been popping up in cities around the world to serve online-only orders, mentioning that in Europe, the proliferation of dark stores in residential neighborhoods has led to complaints of excess noise and round-the-clock traffic.

Not a problem, the guest responds. The robots only cover the last mile or two of the delivery, so you'd think you'd need little warehouses all over the place. But you really can't stock a lot of different items in every little warehouse. So what they're doing instead now is managing a large warehouse which may be more distant and loading up the sidewalk robots onto self-driving trucks which drop off ten, maybe twenty robots at a time to complete that last leg of the trip, with the trucks returning an hour later to pick them up again at the drop-off points. In many cases, he says, they've been partnering with supermarkets and using their parking lots or the receiving areas in the backs of the stores as drop-off points. The robots are preloaded with purchases in the warehouse, so when they're dropped off, they roll down a ramp at the back of the truck and head right out.

Surprisingly, to Peter, the guest mentions that this new delivery option is already available right here in Berkeley. It boosts his mood. Things are going well with the world. He considers ordering something just to see it in action. But there's something more important to attend to. He is going on a hunting expedition.

We live in an ocean of radio waves. And lurking deep beneath its surface are the torpedoes being fired at Peter. To identify, in that vast ocean, which signals to track down, Peter had recorded *all* of the radio signals around him, using math tricks to make it more efficient. And as he recorded the radio signals, he made notes of what he was experiencing at each point in time so he could figure out what shapes in the signals produced each of his experiences. The sounds of specific words in his head. Gesticons. Specific fake smells. In the end, he had it worked out. The radio signals that produced smells are all similar. Small differences between them result in different smells. It was similar for the sounds in his head. There was a pattern to it. And with this pattern, his new signal tracker will recognize the enemy's signals even when they transmit something new, like a smell he hasn't experienced before.

The signal tracker uses an array of antennas, arranged inside a plastic box. The tracker matches up the shapes of the signals coming from *each* antenna into the receiver. If one antenna is closer to the transmitter than another, even by a tiny bit, then the signal picked up by that antenna gets fed into the receiver a little earlier. And this timing difference helps the tracker calculate the direction to the transmitter. At the same time, all those antennas work together to get more signal, making the received signal stronger.

The software knows how to keep track of the motion of the antenna box, too, using the same technology that smartphones do when you move them. So, just as your smartphone camera knows which way is up, even when you turn the phone upside-down, Peter's signal tracker knows which way the antenna box is facing as it receives signals, so it can make sense of the directions they are coming from.

Moving the antenna box around, rotating it back and forth, actually makes the tracker more accurate. It's similar to the way a person rotates their head back and forth while trying to work out where some distant sound is coming from. The auricle, the curly part of the ear that funnels sound into the eardrum, forms fleshy notches, and these notches filter out some frequencies of sound but not others. The effect of the notches depends on which way they are facing. As you rotate your head, the notches change direction, and the sound changes. Peter's antenna design was inspired by this feature of human hearing. Just as the sounds you hear change when you rotate your head slightly, the signals received by his antenna box change when it is rotated slightly, and this change can be used to help calculate the direction to the signal. It works particularly well with ultra-wideband signals because they have a lot of different frequencies in them. Single-frequency signals, for example, radio station broadcasts, wouldn't be affected by the notches. Since he's not interested in single-frequency signals, the software will throw those signals away while tracking, keeping only the signals which have shapes that change as the antenna is rotated. That cuts out a lot of signals, making the analysis much, much simpler.

So that's what's involved in figuring out the *direction* to the transmitter. To determine how far way the transmitter is, and more precisely *where* it is on a map, Peter relies on a different technique. His adversaries' radio signals pass through buildings and other structures, but some of their energy also bounces off those structures. The key is that his tracker receives *all* of these signals, including the reflections. They look like echoes. Each echo has almost the same shape as the original signal, and this makes it possible to match them up and figure out how much longer it takes each echo to reach Peter. And knowing that, the tracker can calculate the distance between the transmitter and each place the echoes come from. Zipping along at some fraction of the speed of light, the radio signals take a predictable amount of time to travel to those places. And because the tracker can also see the direction each echo comes from, it is able to work out a complete pattern of reflections, with the transmitter in the center somewhere lighting up the neighborhood around it like a radar system. Finally, his tracker compares the pattern of reflections to a map of building structures on the Internet, lining up the reflections with the buildings to obtain an accurate location for the transmitter.

There is another method, well-known to signal processing engineers, to locate a transmitter. The first step is to figure out the direction to it from several different places. Next, if you draw a line on a map in the direction of the transmitter from each place you check, the lines will intersect somewhere. That's where the transmitter is. But that works only if the transmitter isn't moving around while you're doing this. Peter doesn't hold out much hope for using this approach, though. The voices follow him around all over the Bay Area. When he moves, they move. He doesn't know how to outmaneuver them.

Excited to try it out, he carries his new signal tracker, which consists of a small stack of equipment, out of the SCIF and plugs it all in. It is still early in the morning.

[Where - are - you?] His inner voice is tauntingly sing-songy.

The voices don't comment. He tries again: [Where - *are* - you?] He slowly rotates the antenna box.

He still doesn't hear any voices, but he smells a bagel toasting. He looks around but can't find the source of the smell. [Oh. It's supposed to be breakfast time. Cute. Haha.]

Old Man retorts: [People need to eat.]

Their exchange is as private as ever. No one standing nearby would have heard the words. But now, Peter is able to record the words radioed to him.

Or, more accurately, he can record radio signals with the signal shapes of the words in them. He still can't play them back on audio speakers because the shapes are not sound shapes like those found in a sound recording. The sounds are encoded in some mysterious way. He doesn't recognize the code. Not yet, anyway. The signal tracker sees only the codes, not the sounds they make.

He carries his equipment back into the SCIF and closes the door. Sitting down and looking at the data collected on his laptop, he sees the signal shapes for the words "[People need to eat.]" He had been rotating the antenna box back and forth while Old Man was speaking in his head, and on his screen, he can see that the shape of the signal was distorted by the motion as the antennas picked up the signal from different directions. The software calculates that the signal originated southeast of his location, almost half a mile away.

"Hell yeah!" he exclaims. It's an exciting result. For the first time, he has pinned the ghosts down to a GPS coordinate, an actual place here on earth.

Pulling up a map on the Internet, he looks up the coordinates, identifying the nearest intersection. Rushing out of the SCIF, he gets into the McAvie and drives as quickly as he can to the intersection. He wants to bring the tracker with him, but it's not portable. It has to be plugged in. So he has to get to the transmitter quickly, before they move. He has no way to chase after them with his tracker.

Half way there, he smells burning oil. Instinctively, he looks down at the dash to check the warning lights, to see if there's a problem with the engine, but there aren't any warnings.

"No. It's all electric." Looking around inside the interior, he tries to identify where the smell is coming from. He looks up just in time to see a stop sign at an intersection and hits the brakes with a quick motion. His heart beats fast.

The smell disappears.

He takes a deep breath, then continues on. In a minute, he arrives at the transmitter's coordinates. But there's no one else there.

He pulls over to the curb and parks the car. Without warning, all the locks pop open.

"Is that you, Old Man?"

Sitting behind the wheel, he tries to understand how the locks popped open. Sensor malfunction? Or the voices. Radio signals can interfere with electronics. It's a well-documented phenomenon. Cities all across the U.S. and Canada have been hit at various times with radio interference problems, affecting cell phones and automobiles and even garage door openers.

There was the incident in 2019, for example, at the grocery store up in the town of Carstairs, Alberta, population 4,077. It's the kind of place defined by its oil and gas fields, its wheat and barley fields, and its cattle, but most importantly by the rodeos held down at the south end of town. Bull riding, team roping, ladies cow riding, barrel racing, wild cow milking, wild pony races, and also the junior rodeo events, pole bending, goat tying, and mutton busting, the five-year-old child's version of a wild bull ride. The horses were fine, though. And there was nothing wrong with the livestock. It was the horsepower that went AWOL. Cars wouldn't start. Alarms would go off. Key fobs wouldn't unlock car doors. The problem went on for weeks before the source of the radio interference was identified.

Sighing, he gets out and snoops around, looking for any sign of a transmitter, or someone operating one, peeking into a couple of car windows and peering up at house windows. It's a quiet, eclectic neighborhood. Stone retaining walls and picket fences border the sidewalks. The homes here, with Spanish tile roofs and flat asphalt roofs, are overgrown with old trees and ivy and yucca and common garden weeds. A cyclist rides by, cranking in the uphill direction.

[Not unexpected. They moved,] he thinks to himself. [And the oil smell was fake.]

He smells a bagel toasting again. This time, he doesn't bother looking around.

Back at the condo, he ignores the bagels he bought yesterday, toasting his last two English muffins instead. While waiting for them to toast, he thinks about making his tracker portable. Equipment substitutions. Design simplifications. If he's on foot up in the hills, away from the road, presumably they'd be on foot, too, following him. He supposes he could outrun them. He's in great shape. He could turn around and chase them down.

He thinks back to the visit to Yosemite with Shasha and Joyce. The voices weren't bothering him there. If he were them, how would he have managed to follow someone up Vernal Fall? Their equipment must be portable, or they would have had to stay behind in Yosemite Valley. The Mist Trail not only gains in elevation on the way to Vernal Fall, but it goes around a corner, passing behind a granite mountain that would have blocked their signals if they had stayed in a parking lot with a vehicle-based device. Maybe that's what happened.

Staring up at Vernal Fall, he had analyzed the geometry of the situation: A towering block of granite, a steep and misted stone stairway built on the face of it, just off to the right of the fall, its six hundred irregular steps anchored to the shear cliff, an iron railing running along the outside edge of the path. He figured he could have reached the top in a few minutes. Could they have kept up? Only if they were in top shape like him. Once at the top, he would have been free to move quickly along the trail, to Nevada Fall, leaving them behind. And he would have been free from interference. From the trail up the cliff, their signals would have bounced off the granite face of the cliff and out into the atmosphere, like light reflecting off a mirror, unable to bend around the top of the fall. Whatever didn't bounce would have been absorbed by the granite itself.

Then he had thought of how pointless it would have been running off to Nevada Fall. He'd have to return eventually. So he had imagined waiting for them at the top instead, charging at them as soon as they appeared, then grabbing them and flying off the cliff together in a dramatic end to the saga.

Emerging from his thoughts, he gets a sinking feeling. He sighs. [That was stupid.]

Old Man to Peter: [You've upped your game. You're no longer a bore.] (-:Slow big smile:-)

Peter's cheek muscles hurt from the intense smile. [You made a mistake picking a radio engineer to attack.]

He didn't notice when the English muffins popped out of the toaster. Now they're cold, so when he spreads the butter, it breaks up into yellow waxy spots.

Peter: [I will track down your signals. It's ultra-wideband. I can see the frequency ranges. It's obvious.]

Old Man to Peter: [That's not what you're doing.]

Peter's not sure what to say. Except that maybe he should stop explaining. He eats the English muffins, his mind blank, then struggles to pull a pepperoncini out of the half-empty jar in the fridge with his fingers. Using a fork to fish one out, he chews it and swallows. The sharp taste of the pepperoncini jolts him awake again and he gets going on his morning ride.

As he heads out, he wonders where they could be. They're out there, somewhere. Like a quarter mile out. Up to a half mile. Meanwhile, the idea of drones lingers in his mind, but it's nebulous. Pedaling up Marin Avenue, he repeatedly downshifts as the incline of the street increases. *Drones. Delivery by drone.* This morning's news story comes back to him.

Old Man to Peter: [We're surprised you fell for it.]

Peter leans forward over the handlebars as he pushes up the slope. [What?]

Old Man to Peter: [The novel.]

The novel? Pulling over to the curb at a street corner, he pops his right foot out of the pedal and rests himself against it, catching his breath so he can think. What was Old Man getting at? Why did he start writing a novel? He can't remember the context. But it still makes sense to him. He's documenting his experiences in fictional form. Why would they have wanted him to do that? But it's just a novel. It does use up a lot of his time. Why is he wasting his time writing a novel when he should be hunting them down? Did they get him to write a novel to keep him busy?

Would it matter if the novel were their idea? It bugs him that he can't remember their manipulation.

Pushing off the curb, he continues his ride up the hill, thinking as he goes, but not very clearly because of the strain he is putting on his body.

He has just reached Euclid Avenue when an idea hits him: *Drones.* Excited, he turns around immediately, coasting down Marin Avenue toward home and trying not to think too much until he gets back into the SCIF where he can keep his idea secret.

Reaching his condo, he hops off the bicycle and is walking it to the front door, his cleats lightly clacking on the brick and concrete walkway despite keeping his weight on his heels, when Deep interrupts his thoughts.

Deep to Peter: [I'm not a Miller.]

Peter finds this an odd statement, but then he remembers. [Oh. The novel. No, your real life name in the novel is going to be Miller. Too bad. It's my novel and my choice.] He made that choice a few days ago when Treacher was listening. Treacher told him "[That's not a good choice.]" and then had proceeded to recommend alternatives, but Peter was done brainstorming. He stuck with "Miller".

Deep to Peter: [Frickin' hell not.]

Peter: [He uses that word a lot. Frickin' this, frickin' that. I bet he speaks like that in daily life.]

Deep to Peter: [Frickin' thing, that's really not —]

Peter: [It's ingrained. And I'll find you that way someday. Miller.]

Deep to Peter: [That's not what you're doing.]

Peter: [Whatever.] He wonders to himself whether Deep really is a Miller. [Does he just not like the name? Why would he care?]

Deep to Peter: [I'm not a Miller. Just pick a different name.]

Peter makes a mental note to write this out as a dialog in his novel. [Frickin' this, frickin' that. This is good.]

Deep to Peter: [I won't be using that word.] He sounds annoyed.

Peter: [Which word?]

Deep doesn't reply.

Peter: [OK, then we'll look for someone who used to use it but doesn't any more.]

Deep to Peter: [I don't fu—<click>] It sounds like a microphone was turned off in the middle of Deep's words.

"That was weird," Peter says.

Treacher to Peter: [The frickin' thing isn't what you frickin' think it isn't a frickin' thing that you —]

Peter shakes his head, takes off his helmet and sets it down on the small garden table on the front porch, then briefly covers his head with his hands, his bicycle leaning against his body. As Treacher continues to ramble, he rolls his bicycle into the condo and sets it aside. He towels off the excess sweat from his face, neck, and hair, washes his face in the bathroom sink, then enters the SCIF, closing the door behind him. The chatter in his head goes silent.

He savors the solitude. Contemplating the earlier exchange, he decides they're actually going nuts. Not him, them. Hours, days, months of this chatter. They just get weirder and weirder.

He switches his attention back to the idea of a drone. What he realized earlier was that he might use a drone to search for the transmitter. The voices don't know this, though. He hadn't thought about it explicitly until just now, and indeed, he feels slightly proud that he had the self-control not to reveal it to them.

With a drone, he won't have to make his signal tracker portable. He'll stay put and send the drone out on the search. Flying a straight path, and with no need to stop at intersections, it'll get to them faster than trying to hunt them down in his car. And at altitude, he can see several blocks at once.

He goes online to buy a drone, paying extra to try the new sidewalk robot delivery option with a thirty minute delivery time window. A message from the merchant pops up, asking him whether he's interested in trying a new feature: two-factor authentication. To make his account more secure.

Peter: [I forgot about that.]

What with his headaches and general mental tiredness, he had never gotten around to setting that up with his financial accounts. He jots down a note on a notepad and then continues with his purchase. Then he leaves the SCIF and gets cleaned up and has his morning espresso at home.

The robot rolls in and comes to a halt right in front of his property just a few minutes after he receives a text alert about the impending arrival. He punches in his unlock code and unloads his package and carries it in. Meanwhile, the gods continue to monitor every move he makes. They transmit a gesticon that forces him to smile and flutter his eyes three times. (-:My my:-)

He brings his new drone into the SCIF where he reads through the operating instructions. He sets up his laptop to capture the video feed and, satisfied it's all set up properly and that the battery is fully charged, he carries it back outside. He goes back in to retrieve his signal tracker and his laptop, setting them on the garden table by his front door, then sits down on the enameled metal garden chair next to the table. After plugging in the signal tracker and connecting it to the laptop with a data cable, he turns on the drone with a tiny switch on its bottom.

Both the signal tracker data and the drone video are now feeding into the laptop. One window on the laptop shows a picture of the signal pattern being tracked, and in a separate window, a map shows the tracker's estimate of the location of the enemy's transmitter. Or, it will show the location, once it locks onto something. He picks up the antenna box and slowly rotates it. A few moments later, a red wedge appears on the map, giving minimum and maximum distance and a range of directions to the transmitter. Bright green marks indicate signal reflections from nearby houses and vehicles. These are clustered in and around the red wedge.

The source is closer this time, less than a quarter mile away, but the location estimate isn't tight. The wedge covers four square blocks. He launches the drone, keeping an eye on the laptop as it continues to record and analyze the signal.

Deep to Peter: [Frickin' the real.]

Suddenly, the signal location disappears from his laptop map.

He lets the drone hover where it is as he looks more carefully at the signal data window and the drone video.

Deep to Peter: [Frickin' frickin' bricked.] (-:Belly laugh:-)

Peter hears the voice in his head, but the tracker isn't picking up a signal. "That's weird."

Deep to Peter: (-:Big grin:-)

He re-checks the data cable connection from the signal tracker, then tries rotating the antenna box again. Still, no signal.

He tries flying the drone to the last known signal location. He tries not to think about his plan, executing it intuitively instead, keeping it secret from the voices.

Reaching his targeted destination, and hovering about a hundred feet up, he examines the video feed. There are several cars parked along the streets there. But nothing suspicious. No giant antennas sticking out or people pointing ray guns.

He figures that if they're prepared to move, someone must be sitting in the driver's seat, so he sends the drone down to street level and starts looking into the front windows of parked vehicles.

After the drone has traveled a couple of blocks, he notices a white Ford parked on the street and his heart jumps. He remembers the white Ford on Treasure Island. Circling the vehicle, he sees that there's no one inside. He flies around to the back to check the license plate, almost hitting the vehicle as he does so. As the drone hovers with the license plate in clear view of the drone's front camera video feed, he searches on his laptop for the photo he had taken with his smartphone back on Treasure Island. Finding it, he compares the two license plates. But it's not a match. Then he bumps into the Ford by accidentally flying forward instead of up. The drone wobbles a bit, then restabilizes itself.

While flying the drone back home, his signal tracker detects a transmission from a location a quarter of a mile away, in the opposite direction from the drone. The red wedge is large, covering many square blocks. Peter picks up the antenna box and rotates it back and forth, and the wedge shrinks in size. Then he sees the signal move. It appears to be moving down Marin Avenue. Then it disappears again. Less than two seconds later, the tracker reports that the signal is back near its original location.

"There's no way anyone could have driven between the two locations that quickly," he says to himself. "What's going on here?" He touches the two points on his laptop screen in succession. "There must be two transmitters. That's it. Clever."

Treacher to Peter: [That's not it.]

Peter's headache amps up. He stops the drone, letting it hover in place as he thinks through what to do next. But his mind slows. He studies the screen, trying to decide what to do. Marin Avenue...he could send the drone to Marin Avenue to find their vehicle. Or he could send it to the other location with the most recent signal. He's not sure which way to go. The two transmitters, if there are indeed two of them, are more than a half mile apart, and the drone is right in the middle. He massages the sides of his head, then checks the altitude. 300 feet. The camera view can't see past the trees and housetops from a quarter mile away. Even if he climbs, it won't help to see past the trees.

He sends the drone in the direction of the currently active transmitter, and then the video feed cuts out. His heart jumps. *Are they jamming the signals?* He worries he might lose control of the drone. But then the video comes back. A moment later, the transmitter location jumps again, this time to the north of him.

"This isn't working."

He runs into the condo and grabs a roll of plastic wrap and a marker. Back out on the front porch, he stretches a piece of the plastic wrap over the laptop screen. Worried the marker ink might bleed through, he stretches a second piece of plastic wrap over the top of the first, fighting with static electricity to get it smooth. Then he gently marks on the screen at the point shown by the tracker. He has to squint to see because of eye strain caused by his tension headache.

They're constrained by their vehicles, he thinks. They can't go too far in a fixed amount of time. He draws a circle around his prediction of their next location, calling this Transmitter B. The one that is transmitting right now is Transmitter A. Flying the drone straight to the circled region, he hopes to spot the vehicle carrying transmitter B.

A moment later, the tracker loses the location of transmitter A. But transmitter B doesn't show up. He waits for three minutes but fails to regain tracking. He doesn't understand. Maybe they stopped transmitting altogether?

But they're still transmitting. He is still receiving their signals, but the tracker can't locate the source. A gesticon forces a wry smile on him. Then his headache disappears. A moment later, the signal display window on his laptop goes blank except for the words *No Signal.*

As he rotates his antenna box in a vain attempt to regain their signal, he is distracted by the sound of a gasoline-powered automobile starting up nearby. Then he hears a door open. He looks up and sees that his upstairs neighbor has stepped out onto the second floor balcony.

The neighbor glances down at Peter, but before Peter can wave hello, the neighbor glances at his smartphone and turns around, laughing out loud as he returns indoors.

Peter tries to remember his neighbor's facial expression. Was it blank? Did he have a smirk? Staring up at the now-empty balcony, a variety of suspicions run through his mind until, finally, he is satisfied there is nothing further to think about.

Thursday, 18 July 2024

On his way into Moffitt Library at UC Berkeley, Peter passes by the old-fashioned phone booth installed in front of Free Speech Movement Café. The book he is looking for isn't available online, so he's going in to find a hardcopy. He has a hunch as to what happened with the signal tracking, but he needs to consult the book, an old radio and radar electronics textbook, for details.

Inside, just to the right of the lobby, he notices two patches of faded paint punctuated with empty holes on the wall where two additional pay phones used to be mounted. No one has a need for pay phones any more, he thinks. You can communicate from anywhere. Depending on your carrier's coverage, of course. He figures they must have kept the telephone in front as a reminder of the Free Speech Movement. He briefly chuckles to himself. [Communicate from anywhere. Now *that* is free speech movement.]

Deep to Peter: [Not a bad frickin'. But that's the frickin' *not it.*] (-:Doubtful grin:-)

Peter figures their system must have a hierarchy of interfaces, with one labeled *Gesticons*. They push a button in that panel, and his face or body executes the corresponding gesture by triggering motor control sequences in his brain. He doesn't feel like he's the one that initiates the motions. They just happen. But he recognizes the patterns. A head shake. A smile. A devious grin. A quick raise of the eyebrows. A belly laugh.

They're like tics. He doesn't get a chance to suppress them. So the gesticons are not so much against his will as independent of it. But they're not independent of his body. The muscles are worked. Energy is burned. It's tiring, sometimes to the point of fatigue.

They once flipped him the bird using his own middle finger, bending it toward his palm. But they've gone way beyond just triggering a twitch or a bend of a finger. Some gesticons involve complicated combinations of muscle motions to produce an effect, sometimes combined with a sound effect, a fake smell or a tactile sensation overlaid simultaneously.

While the gesticons are annoying, Peter finds the idea of communicating in this way fascinating. He has started documenting examples in his notebook in the SCIF and plans to use the idea in his novel.

Peter: [What do you guys call that? The gesticons. Do you have another name for it?]

Deep to Peter: [I'm not going to get in trouble for...frickin' hell. It's —]

Peter: [Come on. If I'm going to coin a new word for this thing, it might as well be the same word you're already using for it.]

Deep to Peter: [Frickin' not. That's not what I'm going to be to you.] (-:Sideways chin wiggle:-)

Peter guesses the gesticon means the same thing as shaking one's head to indicate "no". Then, on second thought, he has a better guess. [It means doubtful.]

Deep to Peter: (-:Big grin:-)

Another forced expression. It's like his body is home to a split personality, but he only gets to be one of them.

He is reminded of Mario Savio's famous "Operation of the Machine" speech. Savio, a key activist in the Berkeley Free Speech Movement that the Café is named after, had talked about a machine which takes away people's freedom. He, too, is suffering under a machine. It's not the same one, it's literally a machine, with electronics, but perhaps it is part of a larger machine like the one Savio referred to.

He tries to understand why they're doing this to him. At this point, he has no doubt that it isn't just his imagination. Someone really is using some sort of machine that can send voices to his head. They don't identify themselves. They don't give a purpose. They don't seem to be focused on anything in particular. It's like they're fishing for something. He doesn't know what it is. And he suspects they don't, either.

The signals are blocked by the SCIF. Inside, there are no voices, no gesticons, no headaches. But outside, it's like being mugged and dragged away in the middle of the night in some dark and repressive regime. Except that it's in broad daylight and no one around him notices. To Peter, the machine as an abstraction has become the machine as a mugging tool. Is it government? Or is it some gang of criminals trying to carry out identify theft? Or perhaps some unimaginable crime, something completely new and deeply sinister? What stops them from collecting everything that could be known about him, they hear everything he thinks, and then just taking over his identity, his whole life?

When he came up with the idea of writing the novel, his neurostalkers had warned him, saying: "[You're creating a blueprint for others to do the same.]" He figures they're just trying to discourage him from figuring it out and writing about it, so they won't be discovered. He had responded: "[I'm going to call it *The Attention Game*. Though that's just a working title. *The Attention Game*, by Peter Nolen.]" He imagines that to be the name of a manual that his adversaries must be using, an operations manual that they expand over time with experience. That's all he can say for sure about what they're doing to him. Whatever it is, it's about grabbing his attention and keeping it.

After checking out the book he came for, curious, he descends a nearby staircase to an underground hallway. At the bottom, he sees a wall panel with two faded outlines, two more pay phones that have long since been removed.

Down here underground, he still hears Deep's voice, but it is faint, and Peter feels relieved, and physically more relaxed, as the muscle tension induced by their signals is weakened as they pass through the concrete structure.

He takes his time, completing a small self-guided tour of the hallway, peeking into the windows set into the doors of the underground lecture rooms. He never took any classes down here, he previously wasn't even aware of these rooms, but they look pretty standard as far as classrooms go. Rows of seats set on a gentle slope, a small stage at the bottom, a projector hanging from the ceiling, a whiteboard across the entire wall behind the stage.

Taking a deep breath, he climbs back up the stairs. But instead of returning home immediately, he decides to drop by the Café for an espresso.

A mural filled with photos from the early 1960s, showing some of the events of the Free Speech Movement, covers the back wall, as it has since the Café was dedicated back in the year 2000. Peter sits down with his espresso in front of the mural. This is where he first met Shasha, when she was an undergrad studying biology. She was sitting right here, in front of this very same mural, gazing into her laptop.

He couldn't resist sitting down next to her. It was a little hot that day, and she was wearing tight fitting blue jeans, a blouse with horizontal white and dark blue stripes, and white canvas shoes. Next to her was her pink, white and blue backpack. Mostly pink. She had perfectly straight shiny dark brown hair down to her shoulders, trimmed straight across at the bottom, white framed glasses, and big brown eyes, the dark brown most Chinese girls have. A squarish face, bordering on heart-shaped. A slender figure. And not a hint of make-up. She didn't need it.

He thought she looked fresh, but also focused. So he didn't want to bother her. He thought he'd just enjoy sitting there, not bothering her.

Drinking his espresso, he glances around the room. The place is busy, but quiet, with students alternating between bites of their lunches and keystrokes on their laptops. He takes a bite of his sandwich, then bends down to get his laptop out of his backpack to continue working on the research he started in the library.

She asks her question as he is taking another bite of his sandwich. It's a complex question. And at first, he doesn't even realize the question is directed at him.

"I'm sorry, what?" He turns to look at her. He's stunned she said anything to him.

"Oh. I was saying I'm curious as to your knowledge about systems because I'm trying to decide how best to get into systems biology. I'm interested in the neuroscience of insects, and —"

"Um."

"Or, not insects per se. It's the systems biology that interests me, though the particular project is —"

"You're a, well, I, ... What are you studying?"

"Right now, I'm finishing up my biology degree, but I'm trying to figure out what program to get into for my PhD. I don't have any experience with systems, but as I said, I'm interested in systems biology and —"

"Biology." Peter starts to fidget a little, glancing down at his backpack and wondering how much further the conversation is going to go.

"Yes, biology." She has an earnest look on her face, but she doesn't smile.

Seeing her expression, he can't help but continue with their conversation. "I...I don't really know much about biology. But I do know about systems. In general. Um...so, what do you mean by systems biology, specifically?"

"Oh! It's a really exciting new development in biology." She lights up. "The idea is that an organism is like a machine, with different mechanisms all interacting with each other to make everything work. It's built on many subdisciplines, including metabolic pathways, neurobiology, —"

Peter interrupts her again. "OK, I see. Systems working together. Animals are systems made of systems."

Shasha continues her impassioned explanation, which she delivers at high speed and without pause. "Right. More or less. Technically, animal models have systems with interacting mechanisms, like for breathing, digesting food, fighting infection, cognition, and, OK, cognition isn't completely accepted yet as a system in systems biology, but it should be.

But the point is that there are all these systems, and the goal of systems biology is to model all of their mechanisms in enough detail so that you could use computer simulation to understand how the animal functions. That's what's so interesting, because —"

"Hold on." He can't keep up with her. "What are you trying to figure out, again?"

"Oh, right. I'm not sure whether I should specialize in one organism or whether I should take a more general approach in my studies. As I said, I have an opportunity focused on insects, but I'm really quite interested in neurobiology and cognition, so I'm worried that a focus on insects would be too limiting for me."

"Oh. That's... Good question." *She's different.*

Intrigued, he's about to ask her more, but she glances at her laptop screen and announces that she's out of time and has to run to class. She slides her laptop into her backpack, then pulls out her smartphone. "What's your cell number?" She looks right at him and waits. No smile, just an earnest look.

"My cell number?" He's baffled. He studies her face, then just gives her the number.

She looks down at her phone and starts to text him. "This is my number."

"Will I need it?"

Shasha looks back up at him. "You're right. I'll just call you later. That's simple."

She notices that he looks lost. "To follow up."

He's still lost.

"With my question. Is that OK?"

"Ah. Sure."

As she starts to run off to class, Peter calls out: "You said insects. Any kind in particular?"

Shasha slows down, turns and shouts: "Butterflies!"

As he watches her dash out of the café, hair swaying rhythmically with the gait of her run, he suddenly realizes he doesn't know her name.

Friday, 19 July 2024

Brian Breg calls to update the CO, the contracting officer for his contract with the agency, explaining recent developments. Their target now has a SCIF, he says. "He knows what he's doing."

"That's not surprising. That's what we thought he'd be. A radio communications expert. And he figured out what you're doing to him."

"The target actually started tracking our signals."

"So now you're *his* target." The CO chuckles.

"He's showing his hand." Caught off guard, Breg's not sure what else to say. Maybe that's the kind of thing his target did to get into this situation in the first place. He doesn't know the whole story.

The CO becomes serious again. "Nevertheless, we still don't understand how he fits in. There's still nothing we can use." Pausing to think, he asks whether the target has met with anyone in the SCIF.

"Yes. A friend of his named Ethan Chen."

"What information have they exchanged?"

"We don't know yet."

The CO says he'll call him back shortly. Maybe in a day or two.

Saturday, 20 July 2024

Peter's morning routine these days is efficient. He gets real sleep in the SCIF, and coming out to brush his teeth and eat breakfast, he moves quickly, not giving the voices any of his attention. Each morning, he's on the bicycle in no time, working his way up into the Berkeley hills. Still, they break through with a louder signal, making themselves heard. Literally turning up the volume.

This morning, he's toasting a bagel for breakfast. He drinks half a glass of milk while waiting. Deep has been trying to engage him ever since he came out of the SCIF. Frustrated, he switches strategy and tries to engage Deep, repeating an earlier invitation to visit, which Deep passionately rejects.

Just like usual. [Whatever.]

The two halves of the bagel pop up out of the toaster. He butters each one, then gets cream cheese from the fridge to spread over the butter.

As he eats the bagel, he reviews his attempts to psychologically pressure the voices. And he doesn't mind letting them overhear his thoughts because, well, it must be working, and he wants them to know that he knows that. They really must be feeling some pain from the process. They must have doubts as they waste month after month accomplishing nothing. They must be spending a fortune. Even if they're getting paid to do this, someone else must be spending a fortune. For nothing. What kind of career is that?

He warns them that they *will* get caught and they *will* go to prison for what they're doing. He is hunting them down, and he *will* find them.

So far, though, all he has is a disembodied voice and the strange experience of gesticons. It's a strange form of communication when someone else uses your own body to send you sign language. And this is the only way he knows of Deep. The voice, the smells, the gesticons. He never sees Deep. If it weren't for the radio signals he recorded, it would be easy to reason that Deep doesn't really exist. Deep might as well be an AI in a video game, a character existing only in software. The software of his own mind. If there is such a thing.

He bites into the second half of his bagel, enjoying the contrast between the crunch of the toasted bagel and the fatty luxury of the butter and cream cheese, then wipes excess butter from the edge of his mouth with a paper towel. He takes another bite.

Suddenly, he hears a loud, low-pitched gassy ripping sound where Deep is. Wherever that is. He stops chewing. [Uh. Was that you?]

Deep to Peter: [Hell. Hold on.]

Peter hears what sounds like a door opening in the background where Deep is.

Treacher to Peter: [Frickin' hell, Mil—<click>] Treacher's voice sounds distant before it cuts off.

Still holding the half-chewed bite in his mouth, Peter strains to hear anything at all in his head. [Treacher? ... Deep? Are they gone?] He finishes chewing, then swallows. Then he waits, listening.

There's just silence for a full twenty-five seconds.

He shrugs, eats the remaining two and a half bites of his bagel, then drinks down the rest of his milk, washes the glass, and is putting away the glass when Treacher comes back on, rattling: [That's the, you need to get a life, the way that you don't have to do any, the time you should, really well done, back when you were, do you get? Frickin' thing is that the, really, the do isn't the —]

Peter tunes out Treacher's voice. Then he's lost. He completely forgets what just happened. Looking around the kitchen, he tries to regain a focus, eventually tuning back into getting ready for his morning ride. He goes into the fridge to get a pepperoncini.

As he rides up and down along Wildcat Canyon Road, past chaparral and stands of ponderosa pine and ridges with manes of eucalyptus, Peter thinks over what it means to read someone's mind. It would seem he has no privacy from the voices, but he does. They seem to be unable to read his abstract thoughts. Perhaps they get only the words in his head. Can they hear other sounds in his head? He's still not sure whether they can see what he sees. What else might they have access to? His senses of taste or smell or touch? Can they see his pain or know when he is hungry?

When you think abstractly, is that conscious thought? Like when you review the facts of a situation and it suddenly clicks, and a new concept enters your mind? It seems to him that he's aware when that happens. At the same time, he's not aware of how it happens. It's somewhere in-between fully conscious thought and automatic thinking or subconscious thought. That must be what intuition is. He figures that equipment which can record brainwaves may someday be able to extract the intuition as well. Eventually, even this type of privacy will disappear.

He remembers running across an article about consciousness back when he thought his problems might be neurological. It described a patient with intractable epilepsy whose corpus callosum, the bundle of neural pathways connecting the left and right sides of the brain, had been severed for medical reasons in the hope of resolving his seizures. The patient could reliably act on information processed with only one side of the brain, but when asked to talk about his choice, he was adamant that he hadn't experienced anything at all. He had made a choice but he hadn't seen anything and hadn't consciously thought about it. He was sure he hadn't even made a choice. With the disconnect in the brain, there was a disconnect in the patient's perceptual experience of his own actions.

It seems to Peter that this is in fact commonplace. For the last ten minutes, engrossed as he was in his thoughts, he has been riding without seeing a thing. But also, without crashing into anything. It's just like the "split brain" phenomenon experienced by the epilepsy patient.

Could the people reading his mind know what he had been doing even when he doesn't know? Which turns he took? What obstacles he went around? He listens to the voice in his head for commentary, but no one answers. Maybe they're just listening.

After reaching Inspiration Point, he turns around and heads back along Wildcat Canyon Road before turning at Shasta Road. He tacks back and forth through the web of small streets that crisscross the face of the hills. Building speed along one steeper segment, the wind whistles past his ears. He grips the brakes, regulating his descent as he coasts, leaning into the curve of the road, then straightening up as the road itself straightens.

Then something goes wrong. He feels a sense of derealization, like the world is fading. His muscles weaken and he starts to slump. His reticular activating system, a part of the brain stem, has abruptly shifted his arousal status from high attention mode to sleep transition, producing a transient symptom similar to narcolepsy.

The world turns at a strange angle and he feels like he's floating in space, but this lasts for only the shortest moment. During the split second in which this takes place, his mind processes two or three frames of video-like experience, but his higher consciousness has already stopped interpreting the data.

The carbon-fiber frame of his bicycle breaks in two with a loud crack and the front tire bends at a ninety-degree angle in the same instant. One of the spokes comes loose and punctures his right arm as he rotates onto his back and slides headfirst downhill along the pavement. His cycling jersey rips and the road tears into his skin. He hits his head on a concrete curb, hard, cracking his helmet.

Lying still on the ground, unconscious, blood dripping slowly from his arm, his body is entangled with the bicycle frame, the two halves held together now only by the brake and shifter cables.

Remote sensing

Julian Brecht's head is down in contemplation. He looks back up at the screen and checks a few more things. Breg and Rogers are looking over Julian's shoulders. They're working at the small table fitted inside their cargo van, two blocks away from where Peter has just crashed.

Rogers calls out to Stack to pull over.

"What just happened?" Breg asks.

Julian just recently finished writing the software that lets them see what their target sees through his own eyes. He's worried. While everything seems to be operating normally, he cannot be absolutely sure that the system wasn't at fault. He keeps this to himself as he explores the issue, first saving a copy of the transmitted data before it gets erased, then making a note to check whether the transmission software could have been affected by his changes. Is the software still doing exactly what it is supposed to do? Even if it is, did the transmissions have an unexpected effect on their target? He's not sure.

Watching through Peter's own vision, Breg, Julian, and Rogers had witnessed the accident as Stack drove the van, keeping it within range of Peter. The video resolution isn't great. They saw him go down, but they couldn't see what caused the fall. And then the visuals went blank.

Responding to Breg now, Julian pieces together what he can. His slight accent draws attention to his German background as he explains. "That is not clear," he says. "Before the crash, he did not have words in his head. Also, he did not panic. It was something sudden." He taps on the trackpad and switches to another view. "The motor sequence shows that he did not turn. His muscle signals were steady, then they faded. And here, ..." He points to a graph of Peter's muscle signals changing over time. "Can you see the spike? This is the reflex action of the muscles in the spinal cord. It is automatic. This signal is not from the brain."

Stack parallel parks at the curb and turns around to look into the van interior, listening to the conversation.

Rogers is curious. "The system can see signals from the spinal cord?"

Julian turns around to face Rogers as he explains. "Indeed. Signals are signals. When his body reacted to the crash, his muscles spasmed. This sends a reflex signal to the spinal cord and then back to the muscles. The spiking of the nerves generates a radio signal." He turns back around to point at the screen again. "This is the radio signal, here. And you can see here, it disappears. Almost certainly, he was not conscious at this point."

Most of the signals flatline after that point, but there are still two slowly pulsing signals. Rogers asks about this. "He is still breathing," Julian explains, "but his breathing is weak. The other signal is his heartbeat."

Breg looks at each one of them; they've lost their target. They've been working on this for a year and just like that, he's gone. He confirms with Julian: "You said you're not picking up any brainwaves?"

"That is right. There are no brainwaves. Still..."

Breg gets his cell out. He stares at it, thinking, then makes the call. The 911 dispatcher asks him to stay on the phone with them. A minute later, as they sit in silence, they hear the siren of an ambulance off in the distance.

Breg puts his cell on mute. "What is his status now? Any change?"

Julian raises his head and his expression changes. They're not giving up yet. He navigates back and forth between screens in the app on his laptop. Their target is still alive, but Julian still can't detect any brainwaves. He shakes his head "no".

Breg unmutes his cell. "He's not moving." He listens and then nods his head. "I'm not sure. I'm no longer near his location. ...I'm not sure how much further I can help." He listens and nods again, then hangs up. The ambulance siren has stopped. He comments to the others in the van: "They're there now."

Five minutes later, they hear the siren again as the ambulance rushes to the hospital.

Pseudocoma

A few hours later, having had his immediate wounds attended to, Peter is moved from the ER into the intensive care unit. He's on a ventilator and has an IV and a catheter. Wires to monitor his heart snake up out of his hospital gown and connect into one of the medical instruments by his bed. A breathing tube reaches down into his throat. The soft whooshing sound of the ventilator goes off every two or three seconds and ends with a small click.

Later the same day, Peter wakes up but finds he can't move. He is completely paralyzed, from head to toe. He doesn't realize it, and neither do the doctors, but having recovered from a coma, he has transitioned to a condition known as locked-in syndrome. Because he can't move, he can't signal the doctors. He can't talk. He can't follow them with his eyes. He can't even blink. All control of his muscles has been cut off from his brain. He looks like he's still in a coma, even as he lies there, fully awake but unable to communicate.

He tries to remember what happened, but he can't. He has no idea of where he is. As he lies there, he gradually notices there is someone talking. Then he realizes the voice is in his head, not outside. He is delirious and doesn't understand the words. He then hears someone by his side but cannot respond and cannot turn to look. A minute later, he involuntarily falls asleep. A deep narcoleptic sleep.

Sunday, 21 July 2024

The ICU is totally silent except for the sounds of the medical equipment which is keeping Peter alive. One machine slowly clicks and whooshes. The faint smells of vinyl tubing and cotton sheets and hospital disinfectants hang in the air. Peter doesn't move.

Standing by his bed, hands resting on the railing, Shasha becomes a butterfly, wings unmoving. Peter is her forest, now silent and dark. Tears slowly roll down her cheeks.

Gods

and the surveillance

of prayer

Breg notices the locator indication on the screen, marked with crosshairs. "You found him."

Julian is sitting in the back of the van with the others, his laptop resting on the van's small table. The app running on his laptop provides a continuous update of Peter's brainwave patterns, detected from a few hundred feet away in the hospital. "He is there. But he is in and out of consciousness."

Right after the accident, Breg and his team had followed the ambulance, with Stack driving, identifying the hospital Peter was being taken to. Today, Breg has returned with Julian, Miller and Rogers. They've parked their van nearby to search for Peter's brainwaves. If he were brain dead, it would have been the end of their contract. There would be no reason to continue.

The van itself is a recent development for Breg's operation. Prior to the outfitting the van, they'd been carrying around portable battery-powered devices. The whole system fits in a backpack. But the new visualization feature, which allows them to see through their target's eyes, requires a large antenna array system which they had installed over the top of the van, hidden under a fiberglass shell, making the van several inches taller than the stock model.

The antenna array allows the transceiver hardware, the part of Julian's system which takes care of transmitting and receiving radio signals to communicate with the brain, to read a signal from several slightly separated locations simultaneously. With the new antenna array, the transceiver can read brainwaves from a distance in more detail than ever. This, together with Julian's new brain visualization analysis software, allows the team to have snapshot monitoring of whatever their target sees or visualizes, though only at a rate of two images per second. Julian is working on a way to get real-time video, but he is limited by the processing power available to him with a laptop-based system. He also still needs to write software to stitch together the frames to produce video with the same smooth visual representation of the world that their target experiences, a process that is complicated by the way the human visual system works.

"But he's there," Breg says. "He's not brain dead. When he crashed, you said there were no brainwaves."

"The mind device had no clear signal. It had nothing to synchronize on." Julian doesn't look at Breg, instead focusing on his laptop. He taps on a key then traces a pattern on the screen with his finger.

"The system needs to synchronize?" This is a new concept for Rogers. He has been using the system for months now. But he has never heard of synchronizing, nor of any failure to synchronize.

Julian stares at his laptop screen as he explains. "The mind device identifies the geographic location of the source of the brainwaves. When we move around, and when the target moves around, it tracks the target's location. It must check that the brainwaves match the target. So, when two people get close together, and then, again, they separate, the mind device must know who is the target. If it did not synchronize, it might track the wrong person."

"That makes sense," Rogers says. "So you're saying that it didn't work when he lost consciousness."

"That is right. The brainwave signature uses conscious thought patterns. Now, I am trying to lock onto the signature from the rest of his nervous system, but this is not working." Julian tweaks a couple of settings and then zooms in on one of the windows on the laptop. "I haven't any experience synchronizing to a person who is not conscious."

Julian systematically checks Peter's brain and nervous system activity, looking at signals from his spinal cord and other major nerves, and especially the heart. "Ah, yes. Here," he says. He zooms in on one of the windows, looking closely at a graph containing several lines of signal activity. The lines are almost flat, barely rippling. "I cannot find his voluntary muscle activity." He leans back in his chair and gives this new observation some thought. It presents a mystery to him.

Julian tries to obtain a visual snapshot. Surprisingly, colorful geometric patterns come and go on the screen with each snapshot. "Perhaps he is hallucinating."

Then the visualization screen goes black. The geometric patterns disappear. And almost miraculously, conscious brain activity reappears in Julian's signal traces.

"He is back."

Breg's expression changes. "He's back?"

Breg leans forward. Speaking through the laptop's microphone, Breg calls out to Peter.

Peter: [What?]

Peter's inner voice comes through loud and clear on the laptop's speakers.

Breg leans over to the microphone again and says: "Wake up."

Peter: [Wake up? Where am I?]

"You were in a bicycle accident," Breg says.

Peter hears Breg in his inner voice. He tries to make sense of what is going on, but he's still confused. He doesn't remember anything. A jumbled image flashes in his head, but he can't make out what it is. A patch of blue that may be the sky, but at an odd angle. Blurred tan and gray and green patches. A tangle of black shapes.

The jumbled image appears briefly on Julian's laptop screen, then disappears. Breg tells Julian to turn off visualization snapshots from their target's brain. It's not helpful at this point, he says.

Peter: [Who are you?]

Breg is about to speak to Peter again when Rogers's smartphone rings. Peter hears it in his head as if it were off to his right side. The phone is in Rogers's left pocket.

Peter has a hard time distinguishing the sounds in the room from the sounds he hears remotely, where the voices are. He hears the repetitive sound of some machine, a whoosh, then a click, repeating about once a second. Another machine issues a quiet sequence of beeps.

Breg's team now hears the sounds of the machines in the ICU, played through the laptop's speakers. Whoosh, beep, beep, beep, click, beep, whoosh, beep, beep. The sounds weren't there earlier.

Miller, who is sitting behind Rogers, notices the odd phenomenon. The ICU sounds weren't there until Peter had stopped thinking in words.

He guesses this is because Peter himself is now listening to the sounds. Miller doesn't say anything about this to the others.

Rogers gets out his smartphone and disables the ringtone.

Now Peter realizes he isn't able to open his eyes or turn his head to look for the source of the ringtone. [I can't move. I can't open my eyes.] He listens for a reaction but hears nothing. [Is anyone there? Who was that?]

Then Peter becomes aware of Shasha talking softly to him.

Peter: [Shasha!]

It sounds like she is crying, quietly. He wants to cry out, but he can't. He hadn't noticed that until now. He has gotten so used to speaking in his head, it hadn't occurred to him to speak out loud. But now, he finds he can't. He can't speak. He can't move at all.

Through Peter's own ears, Breg, Rogers, Miller and Julian all hear what Peter hears. They hear the machine noises near his bed. And they hear Shasha crying.

A nurse now comes into the ICU to check on Peter. She briefly introduces herself to Shasha, then checks an electronic monitor and makes a note on her tablet device.

Shasha asks how long he's going to be in a coma. The nurse says it's hard to know.

Breg comments to himself: "They don't know he's conscious."

"They must know," Julian says. "It is not hard to know that." He scowls, disgusted with the primitive state of medical technology.

Rogers taps his foot. "We could..." He doesn't finish the thought.

"I need some air." Feeling queasy, Miller leaves the van and closes the door behind him.

The nurse leaves the ICU. Shasha remains, quiet, holding Peter's arm.

Peter: [Please tell Shasha. Tell the doctors. I'm not in a coma.]

He hears nothing but silence in his head.

Peter: [Help me.] Silence. [Deep? Treacher?] Silence. [Old man?]

He lapses into unconsciousness.

You just don't need to torq it

at every moment

to record it perfectly

Stack feels nervous. His hands tremble as he navigates the website. Typing in the password he had scribbled on a notepad next to his laptop, he succeeds in signing in. The balance on the account shows $207,432.74.

To shake off his nervousness, he stands up and paces in his studio apartment, then returns to his laptop. Exploring the site to familiarize himself with the available functionality, he looks for some way to transfer money. Eventually, he finds a menu item for *Wire Transfer* and clicks.

The screen shows an empty form. It requires the payee's name and account information. Opening a separate window, he signs into his own checking account, looking for the required information, then starts to fill in the wire transfer form. He hesitates with the payee name field, considering whether to make something up to cover his tracks. Again, he gets up and paces, rubbing his head, trying to make a decision. *If it doesn't match, maybe it won't work*, he thinks to himself. *But he's brain dead. Who would care?* He sits back down and enters the name shown on his own checking account.

He can't target Peter's largest investments. They're not the kind you just go online with to transfer money. He'd have liked to get into Peter's largest online account. He has the password, but the account also requires the account holder to use a preregistered app and he's not sure how to work around that. The account he just succeeded in signing into is Peter's next largest.

He initiates the wire transfer for the full balance...and the transfer fails.

"Torq."

Navigating the site, he tries to understand what happened. Eventually, checking the account settings, he notices that there is a transaction size limit as well as a setting for a second security check, connected with the account owner's cell number. He doesn't have Peter's smartphone, so he updates the account with his own number to receive verification code text messages.

He tries again, this time with a smaller amount.

The transfer fails again. The problem is unclear to him, as the error message says only to contact the bank. Feeling nervous about this new development, he tries to change the phone number setting back, but he hadn't written down Peter's original number. Racking his brain, he tries to remember whether he had ever written down Peter's number, but he's pretty sure he doesn't have it.

"Total fail. Unfreakinbelievable."

He signs out, then rubs his head.

Next, he tries a small savings account. He knows even before signing in that it only has about $20,000 in it. Looking at his notes, he sees that the password for this account is *abcdefgh. Stupid password,* he thinks.

He enters the password. But it doesn't work.

He tries a wire transfer from yet another account, a checking account this time, transferring only $9,000, reasoning that his earlier wire transfer may have failed because it was too big. This time, his wire transfer succeeds.

He tries a second transfer from this same account, for the rest of the balance. And it fails.

Friday, 2 August 2024

Ethan had been contacted by the hospital shortly after Peter's accident, and ever since then, he has been taking care of Peter's affairs for him. Peter had already asked him to help out if anything were to ever come up, even going so far as having a lawyer write up the paperwork to give Ethan legal permission to make decisions for him if it were ever to become necessary.

Looking around the condo today, he notices dust has already started to accumulate. He'll need to hire a cleaning service soon. As far as he can tell, Peter didn't already have a regular maid service.

He checks each room, looking at the details of Peter's life. He's a neat person, Ethan observes. His bed was already made before he had gone out the day of his accident. No dishes had been left out in the kitchen. The fridge doesn't have much food in it, but most of what is there won't last long. A carton of milk. Some greens. Butter. A raw steak. A jar of pickled pepperoncinis. Eggs, a jar of salsa, a tub of shredded cheddar. A bag of English muffins sits on the kitchen counter. A few bottles of oils and vinegars sit nearby, and next to those, a toaster, a toaster oven, and an espresso maker. A rice cooker occupies one corner, a gift from Shasha, and next to it sits a metal canister of rice.

Peeking out the window at the yard in front, he makes a mental note to contact the neighbors in the other two units to ask about their arrangements for maintaining the grounds of the property and for garbage service.

In the dining room, he looks through Peter's bookcase, noting that the titles are limited to science, technology, and science fiction. He flips through one of the volumes and then replaces it.

Save for the ticking of the kitchen clock, the condo is dead silent. He never hears footsteps in the neighbor's condo upstairs, and the street out front is quiet. He checks each room for a television or a stereo system, any kind of entertainment system at all, but Peter has nothing like that. It must be like this all the time in here, he thinks. Neat. And dead quiet.

He returns to the dining room table where he left today's mail and is about to pick it up to take with him when, out of the blue, he starts to hear a voice in his head.

Voice to Ethan: [This is outside the left ear.]

He turns to the left. "Who is that?"

Voice to Ethan: [This is outside the right ear.]

He looks to the right, listening intently. Goosebumps race across his arms and legs.

He has heard those words before.

Voice to Ethan: [This is inside the head, on the left.]

He listens in awe while he slowly turns his head to orient himself. It dawns on him that these are "voices in the head". It sets off a rush of different emotions. But just as much, he's amazed at how clear the voice sounds. He's also amazed at how utterly unrelated it is to anything he was thinking when it started.

Voice to Ethan: [This is inside the head, on the right.]

The voice takes its time going through the sequence. Turning around and facing Peter's SCIF, he opens the door, slowly, with greater effort than he expected because the door is thick and heavier than he realized. Then he steps in, and just as slowly, he...

Voice to Ethan: [This is inside the head, in the —]

...pulls it shut.

Inside the SCIF it is utterly silent, deafeningly silent. He hears his own breath and nothing else. The acoustic panels on the walls quench sound. They soak it up and make it disappear, giving nothing back to his ears to judge the size of the room. And it's dark, except for a small LED night light. He stands still, alert, listening, trying to calm his heavy breathing. Then, in the shadowy light, he gropes around for a light switch and switches the interior lights on.

"That's what Peter was talking about." He tries to remember the phrase Peter used. "Signal check." He has always been skeptical. He never really believed Peter. And he has never bought into the idea that he, or anyone, would just start hallucinating without explanation.

He opens the SCIF door again. And when he ventures out, the voice starts up again.

[OK, let's pick up where we left off,] the voice says. He hears the voice right in the middle of the inside of his head.

The next sentence, though, is distant, inside his head but far in front. Ethan stands unmoving, one foot out the SCIF entrance, hand still on the door handle, listening to the voice.

He backs up into the SCIF and pulls the door closed again, making a small thud. And the voice stops.

Turning around, he spots Peter's poster. REMEMBER THE ENEMY IS LISTENING.

He sits down to steady himself. For a couple of minutes, he just sits, not thinking, letting his breathing return to normal. "This can't be real."

Seeing Peter's technical notes, some loose sheets and a notebook, lying on the table, he picks up the notebook and flips back and forth in it. The notebook contains several hand-drawn figures, a few equations, and many quickly scrawled comments, a few scratched out. Then he starts from the beginning of the notebook and reads through it more systematically, motivated now to understand what Peter had discovered.

After some fifteen minutes, it starts to become stuffy inside the SCIF, and he looks up from his reading. He notices again just how quiet it is in the SCIF, and then how it isn't completely silent after all. The interior lights hum almost imperceptibly. In his earlier state of shock, he hadn't noticed. Glancing at the light switch on the interior wall, he notices a second switch next to it marked "ventilation". He reaches over and flips the switch, and the dead air comes alive with a faint hiss. He returns to his reading.

His journalistic instincts kick in as he tries to build a story in his mind. Some of the technical details are beyond him, especially the math, but the ideas increasingly make sense to him.

He has spent close to an hour reviewing Peter's notes when he comes to a decision. He needs help. [They're listening. But not in here,] he thinks to himself.

He tries to make a call with his smartphone, but there's no signal. "How does he make calls in here?" He looks around inside the SCIF, searching for a hint. "Maybe it just doesn't work." He doesn't want to make the call out in the open, outside the SCIF, so he puts some more effort into finding a solution. Peter must have had some way of making calls inside.

Seeing the WiFi router at one end of the table, he remembers that he could use WiFi to make calls from his phone. He has known about the feature for years, but has never tried it.

But he doesn't have the WiFi password. He could reset the WiFi router and reconfigure it, but he doesn't have a laptop with him, either, and though Peter's laptop is lying on the table right in front of him, he can't get in.

He searches around inside the SCIF for the password, then goes back out into the condo to look around, checking for anything posted on a wall somewhere, or lying in a drawer. Eventually, he gives up and returns to the SCIF. He finally thinks to pick up the WiFi router to examine it. On the bottom, he finds the password, written on a piece of tape. He sighs. "OK, we're in business."

There's one person, in particular, who Ethan trusts with problem solving. Zhuang Rongtao. They went to high school together in Beijing before they both went off to college, Zhuang Rongtao going to Peking University and Ethan to UC Berkeley. These days, Zhuang Rongtao is running a tiny start-up in Zhongguancun, Beijing's Silicon Valley, developing virtual reality technology.

Ethan checks his smartphone for the current time in Beijing. It's early morning there, but not too early.

"Zhuang Rongtao, it's Ethan."

"Ah. Chen Yili. How is it going?" Zhuang Rongtao uses Ethan's Chinese name.

"I have a problem."

"Go ahead." Zhuang Rongtao's tone is serious. It's not like Ethan to skip the pleasantries when this much time has passed since their last contact.

"This may take a bit of explanation, but I need some advice."

Ethan tries to sort out what to say first. Should he just put it out there and say he's hearing voices? "OK, this is a bit strange, but just go with it until you hear me out." He starts by explaining what had happened to Peter, first keeping it in general terms, then explaining that, as it turns out, Peter wasn't imagining things.

"There isn't any technology like that, though."

"There is now."

Zhuang Rongtao doesn't immediately reply to this. Ethan waits patiently.

"So you believe him. Did he give you a demo?"

"Peter doesn't have the technology. But he has been studying it. He's got a notebook full of analysis and some equipment he has been using to find their transmitter. But here's the punchline: I heard the voices myself."

"*Unreal.*" Zhuang Rongtao uses the English word. "So that's why you believe him."

Ethan explains the SCIF and the way the voices cut off mid-sentence when he shuts the door. "I'm in the SCIF right now. And there aren't any voices in my head."

Zhuang Rongtao asks a series of questions, most of them technical. What radio frequency ranges? Did his friend record any of the signals? What sort of encoding scheme do they use? What sort of encoding scheme does the *brain* use? Does it even use a coding scheme? Ethan can't answer most of them.

"The interesting thing about this," Ethan says, "is that Peter had a tracking device that worked, and then it just stopped working. He never figured out why. And now, they're on me."

"Why would they be?"

"I have no clue. Peter didn't know, either. He thought they might have been after his money. There was a suspicious transaction in one of Peter's accounts. It's something I still have to follow up on. So perhaps there's something to that."

"I see."

"Even so, I don't have the kind of money Peter has. I don't know why I would suddenly have become a target."

"This is...yeah. Tricky. So, you don't know who they are."

"No."

"And you don't know why they're doing this to you."

Ethan is silent.

"And you don't really know *how* they're doing it. Wow."

"Maybe there are some clues in Peter's notebooks, but nothing popped out at me when I read through them."

"Let me think."

Ethan glances around the inside the SCIF as he waits for his friend. He notes the rack of electronics equipment at one end.

"You did say radio signals are involved. One of my engineers is knowledgeable about radio engineering. We're using radio in our virtual reality technology."

Ethan nods.

"So let's do this: You bring out all the technical material you can, notebooks, equipment, data, whatever you've got, and we'll take a look. I can't promise anything, but we'll do what we can."

"I'll need to talk with my boss about taking some time off." Ethan picks a date.

"Let's see if the voices follow you out here," Zhuang Rongtao says. "That would be something."

Ethan hadn't even considered that possibility. With any luck, though, he'll lose the voices, leaving them behind. And when he returns to the Bay Area, he'll have something more tangible to go on.

Ethan and Zhuang Rongtao wrap up their call. Then Ethan gives his parents a call. It has been a while since he last saw them, and this will be a good opportunity to visit. They live in Tianjin, a thirty minute high-speed rail ride from Beijing.

As Ethan exits the SCIF, all of his head muscles tighten down, like the hand of some evil god has just reached down and gripped his skull, every square inch of its surface pressed tight with unseen fingers. He instinctively holds his head with his hands, but this provides no relief.

Voice to Ethan: [I'd like to introduce myself. I'm from *The Lab*.]

Friday, 9 August 2024

Time stretches to the horizon, suspending the sun in the type of prolonged day you see only in two places in the world: close to one of the poles, or on a plane flying west. On its way to Beijing, the plane arcs far to the north, where the two places coincide, racing to keep ahead of the sunset. The flight is smooth, with the plane set at a constant angle of attack.

Ethan shuts the shade of his south-facing window, then massages his head in an attempt to relieve his muscle tension headache. He starts to get up to pull out his carry-on bag to search for a painkiller, but then thinks better of it. He sits back down.

When he got his first tension headache, just as he was leaving Peter's SCIF to go home, it hadn't even occurred to him to take a painkiller. The combination of a diminished capacity due to the headache and the distraction of the voices in his head had made it impossible to think. Since then, the headaches have been almost constant.

Peter, too, had complained about headaches. Ethan once asked him why he wouldn't take painkillers for them, and Peter had explained that it doesn't help for chronic headaches. You get rebound headaches when you use the pills all the time. You just get used to it, he said. You learn to get around and get things done despite the headaches. Then Ethan had asked about botulinum toxin, but Peter vacillated. "Yeah, maybe. I don't know. I don't like the idea of paralyzing my face. And there are other things going on, too." He hadn't elaborated.

Ethan gets up again, squeezing past an older Chinese gentleman wearing a sleep mask, napping, his arms crossed and mouth slightly ajar. [There must be a device on the plane,] Ethan thinks. [It must be portable. And there must be someone operating it on the plane.] He walks the aisles trying to catch someone in the act of saying the words he is hearing in his head. Maybe someone with headphones and a mic.

It's hard to determine what most people are actually doing in their seats, though. The flight is full, as are all flights to China, and the plane is large. There are some 350 people on board this flight. Going by the sound of the voice, he suspects a white male, but he can't be sure.

Squeezing through the aisles, carefully stepping over the occasional wayward leg, he peers discreetly into each row. But it's just the usual cabin full of tired people, trying to sleep or watching videos or playing games on their laptops.

After completing his survey of the plane, he walks to the back of the plane to use the restroom, waiting behind three other people. When he enters the restroom, shutting the folding aluminum door, he notices that the loudness of the voice in his head diminishes. Then it stops.

He returns to his seat and closes his eyes, thinking about what else he might do while he is trapped here on the plane with his stalkers. He tries to bring his journalism training to bear on the problem. Who are they and why are they doing this? Are they part of a small crime ring? A spy organization? Is it just his imagination?

He reviews what happened again, in detail, trying to separate definite facts from intuitive assumptions which lack supporting evidence. It's difficult. He has to take into consideration the possibility that his brain has become damaged in some way, perhaps subtly, and that his logic isn't sound or that something he experienced wasn't real.

In the midst of his thinking, another voice begins to speak, different from the voice that had been talking earlier. The distraction makes it difficult for him to follow his own train of thought to a clear conclusion.

Ethan: [Peter's SCIF. That really worked. The voices stopped, mid-sentence, when I went —]

The voice in his head interrupts: [You two got along well in there.]

Ethan: [It was mid-sentence. When I went into the SCIF.]

Voice to Ethan: [Peter was writing in there.]

Ethan: [Peter. Yes, writing. Think, think. The first voice I heard - that wasn't until I was at Peter's place. Looking around.] His headache slows him down. He starts to reach for his bag to get a headache pill, but then changes his mind again.

Voice to Ethan: [For his writing. You needed it.]

[There was nothing before that. Then... What was it that Peter called it?] Ethan tries to remember their conversation in the sushi restaurant. [It was...what was it? Signal check. It was the same thing I experienced. OK, maybe I just started imagining... Stop. I've already been through this. Writing. Right. Peter's novel.]

He lets his mind wander, to let it sink in. What clues could he extract from the novel? He brought the draft copy with him, just in case, but he hasn't had time to go through it yet. Peter said he was hesitant to call his experiences "facts", documenting them instead as though they were fiction. That would be like Peter. He was careful. He wouldn't even call it a journal. Even that would imply something factual about it.

Voice to Ethan: [Bastard! You took his journal.]

Ethan: [Journal? He said he didn't —]

Voice to Ethan: [You're a f---ing, the real. What did he tell you about it?]

Ethan: [How could Peter live like this?] He gets up again, walks a short distance in the aisle, then returns to his seat. He can't think straight with the interruptions.

Voice to Ethan: [Did you bring the tracker?]

He tries to remember what Peter had said to him, searching for clues for how to cope. He starts to develop a far deeper empathy for his friend than he ever had before. He couldn't have imagined what it was like without experiencing it first hand.

Slowly, he realizes that his headache is getting worse, all over, tightening down, the hand of the evil god squeezing harder.

Then a thought pops into head. Why didn't he think of this earlier? He had been so well educated in English, going first to UC Berkeley for his computer science degree and then to Columbia for the program in journalism, that he had long since gotten into the habit of thinking only in English.

He switches to Chinese, and for a minute, his own words flow without resistance in his inner voice. Then something unusual happens. It bothers him to think in words. At first, he doesn't know why. Then he notices a pattern. As he thinks in words, the voice babbles over his inner voice, and when he stops, the babbling stops. The babbling is not loud, but it is persistent, and it is synchronized perfectly with his own inner speech. He starts, and the babbling starts. He pauses, and the babbling pauses. Each time he starts, the babbling again starts. It numbs his mind. He thinks less and less each time he tries, until he feels he has to give up.

He switches back to English and finds there is no babbling to compete with his inner voice.

As he thinks to himself in Chinese about this exasperating attack on his choice of language, the voice growls [frickin' hell] and an electric shock jolts his head, knocking him unconsciousness.

The first thing Ethan notices when he comes to is the constant roar of the plane. It has a lonely sound to it. There are no voices, inside his head, or outside. All he hears is the roar. Slowly, he emerges from a torpor.

He glances around the cabin. Everyone appears just as they were. There is no evidence anyone else felt that, whatever it was. It was just him. Then he's not sure. He sees one other person, an Asian man, looking around. Their eyes briefly meet, but the other man seems uninterested in him and continues to look in different directions. Then he looks back at Ethan, perhaps wondering why Ethan is watching him. Ethan looks away.

He can't remember what he had been thinking. He struggles to remember, but nothing comes to him.

After a rest, he feels better. He gives the experience some more thought, and the outline of a new idea begins to form. Perhaps mind technology could do that, acting not only as a communication device, but also as a weapon, knocking him out and erasing his memory. And he had just been hit.

There is no real damage...so far as he can tell. It didn't last long. Then he reconsiders. He doesn't know how much time had passed. He checks his smartphone for the time, but it doesn't help. He doesn't know what time it was before he blanked.

What really happened? It felt like being hit with a weapon. What sort of weapon could be carried right onto a plane, no questions asked? Perhaps they had permission. Government? Hard to believe. There must be a transmitter in it, but perhaps it looks like any other electronic device. He tries to apply his knowledge of electronics to the question. But his journalistic background prepared him for work in consumer technologies, meaning product demonstrations, venture capital, technology conferences, and industry directions, not weapons.

He considers warning a flight attendant, but then changes his mind. They'd never believe it. Worse, he might bring suspicion on himself. He doesn't want to attract negative attention.

Suddenly, he feels exhausted. He closes his eyes, and after a short while, he starts to drift off to sleep even as the voice starts up again, taunting him, telling him that they're not on the plane with him and that he's an idiot for thinking so. He doesn't care. He just needs sleep.

The Observer Effect

How may we observe without
changing that which we observe?

You do not understand. The essence
of observation is change. That is
why we do it.

James Bohannon

Water Fight

Beijing, China

Qixi, or Double Seven Festival, so-called because it falls on the seventh day of the seventh month of the Chinese lunar calendar, falls on a Saturday this year, today, August 10th, 2024, in the Year of the Dragon.

Qixi, pronounced chee-she, is the Chinese Valentine's Day. It celebrates the ancient romantic legend of the weaver maid and the oxherd. A fairy from the heavens, the weaver maid escapes to earth and, finding the oxherd there, falls in love and secretly marries him. They have two children together. But her mother, the Goddess of Heaven, finds out and she forbids this love, forcing the weaver maid back to the heavens. The oxherd pursues her to the heavens, bringing their two children with him. Angered by this, the Goddess takes out her hairpin and scratches the Silver River into the heavens, forming the Milky Way, to separate them. But once a year, all the magpies of the world take pity on the couple, forming a bridge in the heavens so that the lovers may be together for a single night, the seventh night of the seventh moon. For this reason, the magpie is considered in China to be a sign of happiness, a sign that things are going the right way.

Right now, though, the primary relevance of Qixi to Ethan is that traffic on the expressway has come to a halt. It's a popular day to go out; couples are headed to special events all over the city.

His plane landed just after 2:40 p.m. This is the first time he has been to the new Beijing Daxing International Airport at the southern boundary of the city. The airport has the largest air terminal in the world. The architecture impressed him. It's not just large. It's ultra-modern and beautiful, designed by a world-famous architect. *China is doing well,* he thought to himself.

He was in his taxi by 3:52 p.m., having rushed out after passing through customs, bypassing the high-speed train into Beijing in an attempt to evade his stalkers, and now it is 4:15 p.m. He squints out the window. The weather is muggy and overcast, but bright, and he's jet-lagged, with a slight headache. The traffic is going nowhere.

The ghosts are still on his tail, talking in his head. Do they know his destination? He's not sure. He's thinking in Chinese, not English. Thankfully, without the babbling he heard on the plane. Perhaps they're following him visually, though. He turns to look out the back window. Lines of automobiles and buses stretch back into the distance.

He texts his father, letting him know he's on the way to his hotel, then lies back in his seat and closes his eyes. Minutes goes by, and still, the taxi has not moved an inch. Sitting back up and looking out the front window of the taxi, he can't see anything up ahead except waiting vehicles. Traffic is usually heavy in Beijing, but something must have happened for it to be this bad. Maybe an accident.

He notices he is two lanes over from the right side of the expressway and an idea comes to him. A wall runs along the edge of the expressway, but it is low enough to cross over. Turning to the driver, he explains that he has decided to go on foot. The driver is surprised but just nods in response. Ethan had already prepaid the trip with a Chinese app on his smartphone, so he just grabs his carry-on bag from the seat beside him and gets out.

Ignoring the distraction of the voice in his head, he makes his way between cars to the edge of the expressway and climbs over the wall, quickly reaching a small road nearby. Standing by the side of the road, he uses a Chinese app to order another taxi. The app's coverage of taxis in Beijing is comprehensive and the app informs him almost immediately that a taxi will be there in just a couple of minutes.

Perhaps it's just the heat, he thinks, or maybe it's the stress of the moment, but his forehead feels tight. He pockets his smartphone and bows his head down, rubbing the top of his head and his temples. Looking up again, he's lost. He looks around at a landscape which is not familiar to him at all. It's not just that he hasn't been here before. Nothing registers with him. He sees the road at his feet, and beyond it, open fields and scattered buildings. They're not just pixels before his eyes, or patches of color, but they're also not things with names or function. He doesn't understand the landscape, nor does he think of why he is here. The world hisses loudly with a constant pitch, hissing, hissing, louder, and louder still. The world is hissing, and it blurs, and the sky is too bright.

Then the hissing fades and is replaced by a high-pitched tone. And then sound disappears altogether.

His mind drifts without purpose. He doesn't go anywhere. He isn't anywhere.

Slowly, meaning returns to him. The wash of the world becomes a place again, and he becomes a participant in it. It takes him another moment to realize that the car waiting in front of him is the taxi he ordered. He hadn't seen it pull up.

Still, he is not fully present. Operating on autopilot, he opens the taxi door and gets in, announcing his name to the driver, and the taxi begins its journey to his hotel. Then he becomes aware of his jet lag. He hadn't slept well on the plane. His head is uncomfortable. He closes his eyes, trying to rest.

A minute later, he opens his eyes again. On a whim, he changes his mind about his destination and asks the taxi driver to just drive around for while. "Just keep heading east," he says. The driver nods his head, then makes an entry on his own smartphone to account for this change of plan.

After they've driven no more than a mile, the voices disappear from his head. He feels more relaxed, almost normal, save for the jet lag, for the first time since he first started hearing voices. Looking around, the world seems different. Released from a semi-introverted captivity, he feels more present and the world becomes more tangible to him. For fifteen minutes, he takes in his surroundings. Then, feeling centered again, he tells the driver to head north, toward Dongcheng District on the east side of the urban core of the city, and the driver acknowledges.

Have the voices turned their transmitter off? Is he is out of range? They may have already known where he was going. If he just goes to the hotel, they'll find him there, and he's not sure he'll get this kind of luck again. He decides to make alternative arrangements.

His phone buzzes in his pocket, and he checks the message. The text gives the name and address of a restaurant. It's a follow-up to a call he got at the airport earlier, confirming his breakfast meeting with a company CEO on Monday.

He calls his father to explain that he has changed his mind about the hotel. His father suggests that he stay at their rental property in Haidian District, on the west side of Beijing, explaining that the tenants recently moved out of the apartment and he hasn't found new ones yet. It won't be comfortable, his father says. They haven't cleaned up, yet, but the unit, which is in a twenty-story concrete tower, is furnished. He tells Ethan he can pick up the key from a friend who takes care of the property for him. The friend lives next door, in the same building.

Ethan had not been aware of the location of his parent's rental property, but being near the Weigongcun subway station and inside the 3rd Ring Road, the location is convenient, just three subway stops from Zhuang Rongtao's office, just to the south of Peking University.

He finishes the call by telling his father he'll be out to visit him in Tianjin this coming weekend, after he attends to his business in Beijing.

As the taxi nears the city center, Ethan gives the driver the new address. Then he slouches back into a half-nap for the remainder of the drive.

Loss of sync

The four of them, Breg, Julian, Miller, and Rogers, jump into the taxi in a rush, with Miller getting on in front and the other three in back. The time is 3:55 pm. Three minutes have passed since Ethan's taxi left the taxi stand.

As Miller gives directions to the taxi driver, Rogers sets up his equipment in the back seat, pulling his laptop out of his backpack, then setting the transceiver and its battery pack on the seat between him and Breg, who is sitting to his right. He hands Julian the backpack. Julian pushes it down in front of his legs, behind the taxi driver's seat, then lays his head back against his own seat and closes his eyes.

Rogers opens a window on his laptop as the taxi starts moving. Reviewing the transcript of Ethan's thoughts, captured in the minutes between exiting the terminal and entering the taxi, and translated over mobile internet by the agency's translation service, he comments to Breg: "His destination address is here."

Breg uses a small pencil to write out the name and address of the hotel given by Ethan to his taxi driver on a small sheet of note paper.

"What's that?" Breg points to the words "Chen Yili" on the transcript. "Looks like he was in a phone conversation earlier."

From the context, Rogers guesses it's Ethan's Chinese name. Breg jots down the name, commenting that it may be the name he's registered under at the hotel.

Handing the note to Miller, he tells him to update their driver's destination.

"Is he still in range?" Breg is worried about the time it took to get into a taxi.

"Signal is weak, but we still have him. Let me try something."

Rogers taps on a menu item, then speaks into the laptop's microphone.

"He's not responsive. The signal is getting stronger, though. We must be gaining on him." He pulls up a map on the laptop. Ethan's location is shown as a large circle centered on the S3501 Daxing Airport Expressway north of them.

Miller comments that traffic is slowing down up ahead. A minute later, their own taxi slows to a crawl. Then it comes to a complete halt.

"He's thinking a message. Translation says it's to his father. ... I don't see a name."

Rogers attempts to get more information from Ethan, talking about his father, but Ethan doesn't think anything in response.

He pulls out his smartphone to check traffic on a map. Then he remembers it's China. He checks anyway, but as he suspected, his phone doesn't provide traffic information here.

He now sees Ethan's location move slightly to the right of the expressway. He's surprised by this, as the traffic is still not moving. At first, he doesn't believe Ethan has actually left the expressway, figuring the system's estimate of Ethan's location has drifted. Then he reads the translation of Ethan's dialog.

"He just told his taxi driver he's going on foot."

"Shit. Where does he think he's going?" Breg strains to look past the front seat through the taxi's front window.

"That explains his movement," Rogers says. "He's just off the highway."

Rogers presses a button and sends a canned message for Ethan to hear, to slow him down: "That's not what you're doing." He's hoping for a response or a retort which might give insight into what Ethan is up to.

Breg leans forward between the two front seats. "Miller, can you hand me the second transceiver? I'm going after him."

Worried that conversation in the taxi might be picked up by the laptop microphone, Rogers switches to text-to-speech. He types a message, and the system converts the text to an audio message and transmits the sounds to Ethan: "It's too far too walk. We can help you with directions."

He wishes he could have visuals from Ethan, but as there would be no good way to use their larger antenna system in China, they brought only their two hand-carried systems, each one in its own gray backpack.

Miller pulls his backpack up off the floor and pulls out a rectangular metal-and-plastic box, a transceiver device just like the one plugged into Rogers's laptop. It has no labels or markings on it, its only outward features consisting of a small number of switches, a dangling data cable and a socket for an external battery cable. Next, he pulls out a battery pack and connects it to the transceiver, then flips a couple of switches on the box and reaches back between the front seats to hand it to Breg.

Rogers pulls up a second window on his laptop and pairs it with the second transceiver, sending Ethan's current coordinates and brainwave profile to the box to initialize it. Ethan's location, as tracked by the second transceiver, shows as a large circle on a map of the area. At the same time, a second circle, in a different color, shows the second transceiver's location. The second circle shrinks down to a smaller circle, then to a point, and after a few seconds, the first circle also shrinks down in size. Rogers announces: "Second transceiver is tracking."

All this time, the taxi driver has been indifferent to his passengers, staring with a bored expression at the stalled traffic. He is startled when Breg opens the back passenger door and turns around to shout something in Chinese, but Breg ignores him.

Closing the door behind him and carrying the transceiver that Miller had given him, Breg jogs between the cars a short distance down the expressway, then makes his way over to the side. He pulls his smartphone out and calls Rogers. It takes a second to roam to a Chinese telecom provider. "Still tracking?"

Looking at the map on his laptop, Rogers notes Breg's transceiver location and Ethan's location as determined by Breg's transceiver. "He's 490 yards away straight-line."

The transceiver acts like a repeater, picking up Ethan's thoughts and location and relaying them to Rogers's laptop system. The transceiver also receives signals from Rogers's system and relays them to Ethan. That is, to Ethan's brain.

"Translation coming in. He's thinking about the hotel address. A white BAIC EV200. Two minutes. EV200 must be a vehicle model. Looks like he's using an app to order a taxi." Rogers glances at his laptop clock.

On Rogers's laptop, a small window shows the lock state of the connection with Ethan's brainwaves. Because Breg has carried the transceiver closer to Ethan, the signal is still strong and the synchronization is tight. But they're going to lose Ethan if he doesn't find a way to keep him in range. He doesn't see what he wants on his list of shortcuts, so he clicks on a drop-down menu and visually scans through the system's functions: *Canned Auditory Messages*, *Olfactory*

Stimulation, Olfactory Remapping, Gustatory Remapping, Tactile Effects, Nociceptive Effects, Sympathetic Nervous System Effects, Brainwave Rhythm Effects, Muscle Effects, Calibration, Monitoring & Recording, Street Map, Import, Export, and *Miscellaneous*, the last category including such things as sound effects and voice filters for outgoing audio messages, and also a *Configuration* sub-menu for password management and for managing the interfaces with other devices such as smartphones and transceivers. Not all of these menu items are fully developed, but Julian has laid out a vision for his system as he continues to develop its features.

Rogers selects *Brainwave Rhythm Effects,* and a small control widget pops up with the same label and a list of pairs of sliders, each labeled with a different functional aspect of the brain: *Visual Awareness, Aural Awareness, Spatial Awareness, Short Term Event Memory, Internal Feelings, Attention and Focus, Object Naming, Emotions,* and finally *Global.* All of the current slider settings indicate zero. Next to the *Global* sliders is an additional pair of buttons. He clicks on one of these and the system instructs the transceiver Breg is carrying to transmit a radio signal, focused in Ethan's direction and calibrated to his brain's thought patterns. Eight-tenths of a second later, the lock state of the connection shows a momentary loss of synchronization before it regains a lock on Ethan's brainwaves. He then slides the top *Attention and Focus* control a small amount and a timer to the right of it immediately starts counting down in seconds from fifteen. The label to the left of this slider reads *Attenuation* and the slider indicates the degree to which the corresponding brain rhythms are weakened by interference.

With Rogers's global disruption to his target's brainwave rhythms, his target's perception of the world goes flat, his internal dialog ceases, and his perception of sound fades away. Apathy sets in. Weakening his target's attention and focus keeps him lost in the world he sees, even as his senses return. Rogers limits the time his target is lost, though. The goal is not to stop his target. He is just buying time to catch up with him. He announces to Breg: "Target attenuated for fifteen and counting."

"This thing's getting hot."

"It's burning through battery power."

As Breg jogs along the side of the expressway, trying to keep the transceiver within range of Ethan, sweat drips from his forehead, stinging his eyes. He wipes the sweat with the back of his hand. The occupants of cars in the traffic jam gawk at him as he goes by. Many have their windows open and, greatly amused at the sight of a foreigner jogging on the expressway, a couple of the drivers, craning their necks to see out their passenger-side windows, call out "Hello! Laowai!" *Foreigner!*

Through Ethan's ears, Rogers hears a car door open and a short exchange in Chinese. "Target functional. Sounds like he's in the vehicle," Rogers says to Breg. "...They moving now... Looks like he's heading east."

Breg stops jogging, his breathing heavier now, and updates Rogers: "Maybe I can get down there and hail a taxi." He tries to spot Ethan's vehicle off the side of the expressway ahead, but he can't see anything through the thick vegetation here. Up ahead, he sees a clearing and starts running toward it.

"Just lost him. He was still heading east." Ethan's last-known location is shown on Rogers' screen as a gray circle. "It wouldn't work, anyway. You don't have a laptop system with you."

Breg stops running. "Shit." He wipes the sweat from his brow and catches his breath. Turning around to return to the taxi, he faces a child staring blankly at him through a car window. "I'm coming back. Let's get to the hotel. We'll pick up tracking from there."

On a subway

one always travels from one station

to another

The hotel is inexpensive but adequate, with a small marble-floored lobby and an otherwise indistinct architecture of concrete and glass. A large poster in the lobby displays the silhouettes of a young man and a young woman in traditional Chinese dress holding hands on a bridge that crosses over a number of puffy clouds. It announces LOVE! in English and Chinese. In the center of the lobby stands a round marble and wood table set with a large bouquet of flowers surrounded by watermelons carved into the shapes of green bowls of red roses. Two receptionists, one man and one woman, dressed in the hotel's gray-and-red uniforms, stand behind the front desk with alert expressions. The hotel's restaurant, accessible through a door to the right of the front desk, is moderately busy with a young crowd.

Breg and team had booked four rooms, two on a low floor and two on a high floor. When they booked the rooms, they weren't sure what floor Ethan's room would be on, but even with the concrete in the intervening floors, they'd have partial access to his brainwaves through the windows. The windows don't have to open. It's enough that the concrete is absent there, giving a path along the outside of the building for Ethan's brainwaves, and their own signal transmissions, to travel.

With the concrete walls and floors separating them from their target, though, their range is significantly limited. They had hoped to book a room in a facing hotel, which would have made it possible to transmit a beam directly out their room window and in through Ethan's, but there was no suitable hotel across from this one. While not ideal, as they have to be more careful about exposing themselves visually, they will ask to change one of their rooms to the same floor as Ethan's once they discover what floor he is on.

After checking in, they eat their dinners in the restaurant downstairs, then meet in Breg's room to work out a plan for finding their target. It's almost ten at night now, and Ethan has still not shown up.

Breg, Rogers, and Julian sit at the room's small wood and glass table and Miller sits on the couch as Breg reviews the situation with the team.

Despite their continuous monitoring of Ethan's thoughts for the past week, as Ethan had done most of his planning for the trip to China in Peter's SCIF, they have very little information on his plans here. But they do have a couple of leads.

Ethan had received a call at the airport before getting into his taxi. Monitoring his thoughts, their system recorded and translated the call. From this, they learned Ethan has a breakfast meeting with a Mr. Liu, CEO of Expectation Mobile, on Monday at 9 AM. His executive assistant told Ethan she would text him the name and address of the restaurant, but they never got that address. Breg suggests they try to find Mr. Liu's home address and follow him from there on Monday morning. He assigns Rogers to do the search.

They did once catch Ethan thinking of a plan to contact a Chinese government ministry in Beijing to discuss the ministry's technology grants to start-up companies. Breg had assumed it related to Ethan's discussion with his boss about writing an article about technology in Beijing. They don't have any contact names at the ministry, though, nor do they have dates or places for meetings Ethan may have scheduled. All they have is the address of the ministry.

Breg asks Julian how they might regain tracking of Ethan's brainwaves, and the group listens as Julian goes over their capabilities. With only the four of them traveling together, they cannot search for, or personally monitor, their target's thoughts continuously. But the systems provide a degree of automation, with the ability to set alarms and wake them on key events, such as when their target wakes up. Or, as will be necessary in this case, when their target comes into range.

The systems use two methods to detect a particular person's brainwaves. The first watches for a brainwave signature, a pattern that is somewhat like a fingerprint. Every person's brainwaves have their own particular timing, their own particular glitches, and their own rhythm, reflecting how information moves through their brain's network of neurons. Julian is actually not sure how unique this signature really is, as he has never been in a position to carry out any serious study of the question. But his intuition is that the chance of a false match will be low.

The more recordings of brainwaves that a mind device has for someone, the better it is able to model the normal variations of the timing patterns in them. What makes this timing information useful as an identity or signature is that for any given person, some aspects of the timing simply can't vary much. The distance from the back of an adult's head to the front is almost fixed, changing only very slowly over the years and decades, and thus it is going to take a predictable amount of time for the signals inside their head to travel through the neural connections from the back to the front in the usual process of a cycle of thought. There's just no way around that. Time is distance.

But it isn't just about how big a person's head is. The distances between all the different parts of the brain also matter, and these vary from person to person. The way each person's brain develops is a little different. And again, short of some unusual activity in the brain which pushes things around, like, say, a growing tumor, the distances between parts of the brain are going to remain fixed. At least for, say, a year or more at a time. So the timing of signals and information traveling between the different parts of the brain differs from person to person. And this timing information shows up in brainwaves.

Julian's mind devices calibrate themselves to their target using these brain timing details so that they can lock onto and synchronize with their brainwaves, allowing the systems to recognize thoughts and inject signals into the brain at the right points in their target's brain rhythms.

The second method of detecting and identifying someone by their brainwaves works by intercepting their inner voice sounds, matching them to previous recordings of those sounds. Just as you can recognize someone from the sound of their voice, the systems can recognize a person from the sounds of the words they use to think inside their head. This method is somewhat less reliable, though, because some people can change the sound of their inner voice at will in much the same way that people can do voice impressions of celebrities. They have plenty of recordings of Ethan's natural inner voiceprints at this point, and with these, the systems have produced a high quality inner voiceprint identity for him.

Using these two techniques together, when the target comes into range, the mind devices will sound the alarm and provide the target's GPS coordinates and the corresponding distances and directions from the systems' locations on a map.

Julian opens his laptop and brings up the app, navigating into an area of the app the others are not familiar with as he explains the feature. The screen shows three different signatures, each represented with a dense two-dimensional graph annotated with tiny numbers and colored symbols, one signature each for Peter and Ethan, and one for his own inner voice. Breg and Rogers lean over from each side of Julian to see the graphs. The three graphs are clearly different, but similar in overall appearance.

He reaches into his backpack and pulls out a transceiver, plugging it into his laptop. Then he reaches over to his luggage and picks up his umbrella, which is lying on top of it. The three foot long umbrella is covered with black polyester fabric and has a plastic handle at one end. Deploying the umbrella with a button push on the handle, he presses the button a second time to extend it so that it telescopes out to five feet, forming a cone, with little aluminum segments that pop out horizontally around the cone underneath the fabric.

Miller asks about the umbrella and Julian explains: It's an antenna. "A gift from a friend," he says. "I find it is convenient when traveling."

Miller nods. "You need it for the monitoring?"

"The range will be better," Julian says.

Julian stands the antenna up next to the table, pops a plastic cover off the top of the umbrella, then slides a cable connector onto the top. He plugs the other end of the cable into his transceiver. Finally, he selects Ethan's inner voiceprint and brain timing signature from the screen and clicks the operation labeled *Search*. A dialog box pops up and he selects an alarm which will send each of them a text message. The group's text message IDs are already listed in the dialog box as choices. The dialog box closes, revealing the voiceprint selection screen again. A status indicator shows that the search operation is active and a small street map is displayed next to it showing their own current location.

Miller comes over to the table to take a look. "What makes the sounds in your head? That can't be the vocal cords. Right?" He frowns. "Frickin' thing, somethin's got to vibrate." Thinking about his bass guitar, he frets an imaginary string with his left hand, then plucks it with his right.

Julian, slightly amused at this but keeping it to himself, doesn't respond.

Miller never really paid attention to the sound of the words in his own head before. He figured it was probably just the same as the sound of his voice when he speaks, except played back from memory. While he has listened to Peter and Ethan speaking in their heads for hours at a time, and it had become clear to him that they do each sound different, he hadn't ever considered how that would relate to their spoken voices. The irony is, he has never heard them speak. Not in the ordinary sense of speaking.

Giving it a little more thought, it occurs to him that when he listened through Julian's system to Peter speaking out loud, it sounded different. He wasn't there to hear Peter. It was still just word sounds coming in through the laptop. So he's not sure which sounds Julian means when he talks about the *inner* voiceprint. Is it how Peter's voice sounds to Peter as he hears himself speaking? Or is it the sounds Peter makes in his head without saying anything out loud? He asks Julian about this.

"That is an intelligent observation, Miller." Julian is genuinely impressed with Miller's insight. "The system records both types. There is the voice in your head. This is called your inner voice. There is, also, the sound of your voice that you hear in your head when you speak. The system can match on your inner voiceprint. But, also, it can match on your spoken auto-voiceprint, which is your own voice as it sounds to your own ears."

Rogers is curious now. "Wouldn't the target's spoken voice sound the same in their heads as a recording of their voice?" Rogers thinks this would be an important practical issue for identifying the people they listen to. Like, for example, when comparing voiceprints between thought recordings and telephone conversation recordings or recordings from rooms bugged with surveillance equipment.

"Your brain filters the sound of your own voice," Julian explains. "If it did not, it would be hard to hear anything else when you speak." Rogers nods. Julian elaborates: "When you speak, your skull vibrates with the sound. So, you are a speaker box. You hear what is inside the speaker box. And your brain adjusts. You see? What the wiretap hears is not what is inside your skull. It hears only what is outside. And so, the sound is different."

Rogers confirms his understanding. "Then there are really *three* different voice sounds."

"There are three," Julian says. "You have the inner voice. You have the auto-voice which you hear in your skull when you speak. And you have the voice that others hear when you speak."

"Huh." Miller gets up to use the restroom, thinking: [The guy's a frickin' genius.]

Breg receives a text message and moves into the bedroom of his suite to make a call as Rogers asks Julian a few more questions about the technology.

The next morning, the team gets breakfast together in the hotel's restaurant, which offers standard Chinese breakfast fare, really well done. Two types of congee, rice and millet, five different types of noodle, a variety of both fresh and pickled vegetables, and sweet, sour, and spicy sauces for assembling a soup. Steamed Chinese buns, with and without pork filling. Deep-fried, unsweetened dough sticks called *youtiao*. Both boiled and pan-fried dumplings. Salted duck eggs. Sliced watermelon and cantaloupe. And *jianbing*, China's version of crepes, made to order. The hotel in most respects is quite average, but it excels at breakfast. Ethan had selected this hotel specifically because of its great breakfast.

The four of them point-and-grunt to make their choices as most of the staff in this particular hotel don't speak English. Julian finds something that looks like warm milk, but he can't read the Chinese label. He ladles a small amount into a glass and tries a sip. The taste surprises him. Rogers explains that it's probably *doujiang*, soy milk, which is often served warm in China. He had it once in a dim sum place in San Francisco. Julian skips it.

After breakfast, the team regroups in Breg's room to discuss their plans. It is clear Ethan isn't returning to the hotel. He must have made other arrangements. And so far, Rogers has had no luck in identifying Mr. Liu's home address. So now they're really stuck. Beijing is absolutely huge, one of the largest cities in the world, and they have no idea where he is. And, as one member of the group points out, they don't frickin' speak Chinese.

Miller suggests anonymously calling the front desk to inquire about Ethan, or Chen Yili, as they would know him, claiming they're supposed to meet him at the hotel. Maybe they'll tell them where he went. Trying this, though, the hotel is professional and doesn't hint at whether they have such a guest, suggesting only that the hotel will try to pass along a message if they wish. They try calling a couple of other nearby hotels, but the result is the same.

They bring up a map of Beijing on one of the laptops and survey the main routes through the city. Given the limited range of brainwave signature detection, they figure that if they position themselves closely enough to these routes, they may be able to lock onto their target as he goes by, especially if he follows a fixed routine each day. Once they lock onto him, they'll continuously track him from there. And once they determine where he is staying, it will be easy to regain tracking even if they lose it.

But hundreds of thousands of people travel each route each day. Beijing is huge. More than twenty-three million people live here. It will be a real test of how well the brainwave signature detection works. And there are other complications. Beijing is filled with large concrete, steel and glass structures, reflecting and absorbing radio signals, including brainwaves.

So even if they were just a block away from their target, with a large concrete building in between, the building would absorb much of the energy of the brainwaves. This effect greatly limits their range.

Breg gives an upbeat spin to it, saying they're going to learn how to do this. It's an opportunity, a new form of hunting suited to the 21st century.

Julian provides some guidelines for ranging information and search patterns. He worked them out at five in the morning when, wide awake due to jet lag, he couldn't fall back asleep anyway.

They plan out a search region on a map of Beijing, focusing on the west part of the city. The search might need to cover 250 square miles, an unimaginably large region. They would need to monitor at least five hundred locations for bare minimum coverage even with ideal range available to the mind devices. Taking into account signal interference from the buildings, they may need five to ten times this many monitoring locations.

The calculation makes it seem hopeless. They try to trim the effort involved, agreeing that they don't need to monitor every little neighborhood. Their target resides *somewhere* each night, probably nearby. Probably within a radius of a few miles of the hotel. They should start there.

Breg asks how many hotels there are, and Rogers does a query on the laptop. "8,231," he says. "That includes hotels and other accommodations for all of Beijing. Actually, we don't even know for sure that he's in a hotel. Something might have happened to him. He might be in the hospital."

"You're right. Or he might be staying with a friend." Breg pulls up his notes on Ethan's thoughts, studying them for clues.

He knows Ethan has family here, but he doesn't know where they live. He considers calling Ethan's boss and simply asking where he is. It's late at night in the Bay Area right now, so he'll have to wait until tomorrow. Even so, Ethan's boss may not be generous with information. He makes a note to call in a few hours, anyway. Then he switches his attention to searching for Ethan at nearby hospitals.

"What's his Chinese name again?" Breg asks.

Rogers replies: "Chen Yili."

Breg starts calling hospitals but immediately runs into the language barrier. The first hospital he calls puts him on hold for a few minutes while they find a person who is more fluent in English to speak with him.

Miller scrolls back and forth on a map of Beijing, making notes as he goes. "Hey, looks like they've got subways here. They go all over. One, two, three, ..." He continues counting, sliding his finger down the legend on the map as he goes. Some lines are numbered, but some only have names. And some numbers are skipped. "Frickin' thing, 21 different lines. What if he's in the subway? Can the system see him down there?"

"That is unlikely, Miller," Julian says. "You will also need to be in the subway."

"Got it." Miller starts making notes of how to cover the subway system, noting that a third of the lines pass by somewhere near their current location.

Rogers is looking up nearby hotels and mapping out the likely routes Ethan would take on a commute from each one. Slowly, he comes to the conclusion that this approach is no better than just staking out the subway stations.

"Gentlemen," Julian says, "you should be aware that the brainwave signature analysis takes several seconds to lock on. If the target is moving quickly on a subway or in an automobile, he may move out of range before the system locks on."

Rogers and Miller both look at Julian. "Oh..." Rogers contemplates the problem, then looks up conversions on the Internet. Miles per hour, feet per second, feet per mile. Using a quarter mile range as an estimate, he works his smartphone calculator. "He's out of range in 13.8 seconds. There's the brainwave signature lock time, and then at least a few more seconds to get the driver going. We'd only have, what, 4 or 5 seconds to catch up with him? That's not going to happen."

Julian comments that indeed, they would most likely have better luck on the streets than on the highways, then adds: "Of course, you will have the traffic..."

They don't have their own vehicle. International driver's licenses are not recognized in China. Short-term visitors have no way of driving themselves. They must rely on a local driver.

"When we say *go*, we'll need the driver to be responsive." By this, Rogers means they'll need to avoid flailing at the driver with English and hand gestures.

This reminds Rogers that he needs to practice giving simple directions in Chinese, a project he already started on the plane trip over. He pulls up his notes with a list of basic Chinese words and phrases. Go...*qu*. Quickly...*gankuai*. Left...*zuo*. Right...*you*. Turn...*zhuan*. Stop... *tingche*. Here...*zheli*. There...*nali*. Where?...*nali*. He's not sure how there's a difference between *there* and *where*.

His vocabulary list is not too long and it hasn't been difficult to memorize, but he has a second, longer list that he is still working on. Audio clips on a smartphone app give him the pronunciations.

"If he's on the subway, ..." Miller pauses to think. "So the train stops and we have a few seconds to spot him. Then we just get on with him. That should work, right?"

"We don't necessarily have to keep up with him. Once we spot him, we can find him again. But you're right, Miller. If he's on the subway, that would make it easy. He'd be on foot." Rogers looks at his notes. "I have twenty monitoring points that we could try on the roads. But if we're only going to try this for a week, we'd have to get lucky."

"Only two of the subway lines go by within walking distance from here," Miller says. "We could try each station. Looks like fifteen of them."

"You do not need to monitor every station, Miller," Julian says.

"I don't?"

"On a subway, one always travels from one station to another."

Miller doesn't get the point.

"It is enough to monitor every other station."

Miller puzzles over this point but still doesn't get it. Julian pulls out a small notepad and a pencil and draws a little diagram for Miller. "If the target gets on here," he says, "and he gets off at another station down the line, then it does not matter whether you are monitoring the station where he got on or the station where he got off."

Miller is still unclear. He points to the drawing. "But what if he gets on here, and gets off here, and you skip both of those stations?"

"So it is a good thing that you are monitoring at the station there in between."

"Oh. Yeah. He'd be on the train. Then I'd have to get on there."

"Unless he is getting off," Julian adds.

"I could do one a morning and another each evening." Miller looks online at the layout of the exits for one of the stations. Then he sketches out a small diagram of a plan. He runs his fingers from station to station.

Rogers and Miller discuss other search options outside of the commute hours. They consider working their way out from their current location, monitoring nearby hotels for Ethan's brainwaves. Rogers goes back to his notes on the local hotels and comments that there are thirty-five hotels in the immediate area. "That might be worth a try," he says. Miller points out that their target might get back late. But if they go to the hotel late enough at night, their target would already be in bed. That would make it easy. They wouldn't have to wait around.

Breg comes out from the bedroom. He hadn't gotten anywhere with the hospitals.

Julian, listening quietly but thoughtfully to Rogers and Miller, points out a limitation to their idea: "The brainwave signature analysis does not work for sleep states. We've only a signature for his waking state. The sleep states are different. It is possible to create a signature for the REM state, but we do not have the data."

"REM state?" Breg tries to catch up on the conversation.

"While you are dreaming," Julian says. "Rogers and Miller have the idea to search for brainwaves at each hotel at night."

"So it works differently during dreams," Breg says.

"The brain's signal timings in the REM state are very different. And during deep sleep, they are again very different. So it would not be practical to scan for brainwave patterns near a hotel when the target is asleep. He must be awake when we search for him."

It had never occurred to Breg that recording brainwaves during sleep would ever be useful in their line of work.

"If we had mind devices on every cell tower, we could just sit in an office and monitor a target wherever he goes." Rogers speculates on the future evolution of the technology. "Not here, but back in the States. Of course, we can already track cell phone locations. But the target might not be carrying a phone."

"That would cost at least millions for one city alone," Julian says. He finds the idea unlikely.

Breg is more positive. "It would be worth it, if we could track enough targets all at once."

Rogers and Miller nod.

While they could search for Ethan's brainwaves at each hotel after he returns and before he sleeps, they'd probably have only an hour or two each night to scan in this way. In a week, they'd cover only a tiny region of the city. And searching day and night is a real burn-out schedule.

After some discussion, they plan to split into two teams, each team with its own mind device, carried in its own backpack. Breg and Miller will monitor the subway stations and Rogers and Julian will hire a taxi each day and wait at specific monitoring locations near major roadways.

Breg then remembers Ethan's potential meeting at the government ministry. He's not sure whether Ethan's meeting will be there, or out somewhere at a restaurant, maybe a lunchtime meeting. He's not even sure there will be a meeting at all. Rogers suggests an analysis of the odds. Will they be more likely to spot Ethan on the road or at the ministry? In the end, with Julian's input, they settle on a hybrid solution, with Julian suggesting that since Ethan will need to travel to the ministry building to get there, they could prioritize monitoring locations near the major roadways that lead there.

Breg says they will stay two weeks. It's clear that there is too much ground to cover in one week, and if it would take longer than two, it's reasonably likely that their target will have returned to the Bay Area by then. Even if they don't find him in Beijing, they'll catch up with him at his home in San Francisco.

Monday, 12 August 2024

Sun Yang looks Ethan over but finds nothing unusual about him. But his story is outrageous. "This certainly is a unique problem," is all he can think to say.

Cheng Fengxiang says they should report the situation to the local public security bureau.

"Peter once told me that there are very few people who have the equipment to detect these signals. I looked it up. It's advanced technology." Ethan gives it some more thought while everyone in the room waits politely. Then he asks: "What would we report to them? I don't even know what they look like."

Cheng Fengxiang gets out his smartphone and does a search for the recommended procedure to report things like this. "What would we call it?"

"What they're doing? I don't know. They're following me around. Harassment? Maybe stalking. Maybe assault."

"Hm. OK. Assault? How did they assault you?"

Ethan gives it some thought. "I'm not sure, actually. I blanked on the plane. It felt like an electric shock. But I don't know how it happened."

"OK, so there's an assault, but you probably can't prove it. Mainly, they're following you around. Let's call it stalking for now."

Cheng Fengxiang pulls up a list of hits and scrolls down through the results. "It says if you're going to make a report to the Public Security Bureau, make a log of any harassing phone calls or text messages. Write down the time and date and location of each incident." He looks back up at Ethan. "That's not going to help. Do you have evidence of their signals?"

"My friend Peter did. I don't. He was tracking them, and then his tracking device just stopped working. And then he had his accident. They didn't start, well, stalking me, until after that. And I don't know how the technology works."

Cheng Fengxiang's face now shows understanding.

"That's where I need help," Ethan says.

Earlier today, after his breakfast with the CEO of Expectation Mobile, Ethan met with Zhuang Rongtao in a one-on-one discussion of the situation. They had agreed to discuss it with the whole company. Meaning the five of them: Zhuang Rongtao, who is the founder of the small start-up, Sun Yang, the company's software architect, Cheng Fengxiang, who is responsible for the electrical and mechanical engineering aspects of product development, and two recent university graduates, software developer Cheng Penglu, and Ke Qunxiang, who studied radio and signals engineering and has a PhD in the subject. He is their specialist in mind-machine interfacing.

Cheng Fengxiang is a bigger man, with a large head and short spiky hair and an overall robust appearance. He doesn't wear glasses. Sun Yang is physically his opposite, thin, almost delicate. He wears glasses with thin wire frames to match his equally delicate face. Cheng Penglu's hair wafts up in front and is shaved on the sides. Other than that, he has an average build and average height and a younger person's taste in clothing. And no glasses. Ke Qunxiang has a slight build, but is not quite as delicate a figure as Sun Yang.

They're meeting now, here in the company's office on the fifteenth floor of a high-rise building in Zhongguancun, a technology hub known as China's Silicon Valley, in the Haidian district of Beijing. With just the five employees, the office is small and almost bare, with just one room, a long table running through the middle of it, and chairs along the table. The employees' laptops are arranged along the table, power cables running to the center where they plug into electrical outlets.

Along one wall of the room are a number of shelves, filled with electronic parts, software packages, and in one corner, a small stack of empty boxes and some bins with more electronics parts and a small work table with tools. A whiteboard fills another wall. Windows pasted with a collection of sticky notes run along a third wall. Outside the windows, which have a view of the west side of Haidian District, one can see the Western Hills of Beijing in the distance.

Ethan's friend Zhuang Rongtao is a Peking University graduate. He founded the company, Zai VR Software Company, Ltd., or Zai for short, a little over a year ago, after working for five years as an engineer for another company. All of Zai's funding to date has been provided by his family.

As is typical with a lot of Chinese words, Zai, written 在, can take on many different meanings and shades of meaning depending on context. *In. At. To be here. To exist. To be doing something. To be good with something*, as in "You OK with that? Yeah, I'm in." Zhuang Rongtao chose the Zai name for its resonance with virtual reality.

The company's first product is based on the use of mind-reading headsets to control a virtual reality interface. The headsets are still primitive, but they work well enough for a simple demonstration. With them, a user can reliably make selections from a list just by thinking. And now, they are working toward combining the mind-reading headset with virtual reality goggles into a single device.

Zai's concept isn't limited to interaction with a virtual world. One version of their virtual reality goggles is transparent, more like glasses than goggles, allowing information to be projected as images into the user's view so that it is overlaid onto the real world. In this configuration, the technology is referred to as augmented reality.

Several augmented reality products are already on the market. The older devices allow users to control their augmented reality view with voice commands, head tilts, and touch controls. Zai's concept, that is, Zhuang Rongtao's vision, is to eliminate all of that, to make the interface entirely mind-controlled.

While the company is currently focused on building their interface device, their eventual goal is to build a new category of mind-controlled virtual-reality games, with players interacting with other real players and with artificial intelligence players in either a virtual world or projected into the real world around them.

Zai's headset already allows users to control what is displayed in the overlay merely by thinking, avoiding the need to use one's hands on physical controls. The transparent goggles have a small camera attached, and this camera sends an image wirelessly to the user's smartphone which the user may carry in their pocket. In one working demo, a user can think a command to trigger the camera to take a picture and look up who they are looking at. An app running on the smartphone uses face recognition and then projects information about the person into the goggles' augmented reality view.

Cheng Fengxiang puts his smartphone away. "Are they still following you?"

"No. Actually, I don't know," Ethan says. "I haven't heard any voices since I lost them the day I got to Beijing."

"Then what are we going to track down? What's your goal?"

"I have a feeling that when I return to the Bay Area, they're going to be there. They know where I live. I may have lost them for now, but they'll show up again. So what I'm really looking for is a way to figure out who they are."

"Maybe they won't show up at all."

Zhuang Rongtao jumps in. "Maybe they won't. That would be a good thing. But when Chen Yili and I spoke, we agreed that the main objective would be to develop an understanding of the technology. At a minimum, we hope to be able to make the world aware of this new development. But we'll also want to be able to track down the perpetrators if they do show up again. We don't know whether this is a widespread phenomenon, but at least we'd have the tools to find out."

Ke Qunxiang raises his hand half-way to ask a question and Zhuang Rongtao turns to him. "What sort of signals are they?"

Ethan responds. "Something called ultra-wideband. Or time domain signals. Peter said the two are related, but I don't know how."

Ke Qunxiang gives a nod. He is familiar with both terms.

"Peter was working on how to track down the signals when he had his bicycle accident. He left behind detailed notes and a prototype tracking device which I brought with me."

Ethan opens the bag he brought with him to the meeting. Inside are two notebooks and a small collection of loose papers, a rewritable DVD, Peter's antenna box, and two commercially manufactured instruments. He places all of these items at the end of the long table.

"I have to admit I don't know how these all fit together," Ethan says. "According to a diagram in here..." He rummages around in the box of papers and pulls out one sheet. "This one here, these all connect together, but the diagram isn't clear to me. There's supposed to be software on the DVD which runs on a laptop. And there's some data on there. Peter recorded samples of the signals and annotated some graphs of them."

The engineers, who have been sitting in chairs arranged around the end of the table, all get up to look.

Ke Qunxiang is surprised Ethan hadn't brought any data cables or power cords, but it won't be a problem to supply their own, he thinks. He asks Ethan for the diagram. After studying it for a minute, he comments. "Looks like it's probably a software-defined radio system."

Ethan asks Ke Qunxiang what that is and Ke Qunxiang explains for everyone. Software defined radio is just radio, but instead of building it entirely from electronic circuits, it gains flexibility by using software to carry out many of the steps for encoding and decoding radio signals. The radio's functions can be modified or enhanced just by updating software.

Zhuang Rongtao catches the group up on the discussion he had previously with Ethan. "Apparently, Chen Yili's friend Peter had used this system to record signal samples from the perpetrators. He was trying to track down their transmitter. So we should be able to see what the signals look like. And from reading his notes, the tracking worked, until it didn't. The problem seems to be that the perpetrators are using multiple transmitters. While there is a recording of the signals that weren't tracked, Peter had not yet succeeded in analyzing the signals to figure out what was wrong before he ended up in the hospital."

Cheng Fengxiang asks what happened to Peter.

"Bicycle accident," Ethan says.

Sun Yang moves in to take a closer look at the equipment and notes on the table. He looks over at Ethan for permission, then he starts flipping through one of the notebooks.

Zhuang Rongtao continues: "So I propose that the first thing we do is to carry out the analysis, comparing his earlier recorded signals with the latest recording, to figure out why his tracking stopped working."

"Did the signals go in both directions? Is this a full mind-interfacing system?" Ke Qunxiang tries to reconcile the situation with his experience with mind-machine interfaces.

"It goes both ways," Ethan says.

"Then how far away..." Ke Qunxiang finds it hard to accept the claim that someone is communicating by radio with the brain from so far away that you can't even see them.

Zhuang Rongtao answers Ke Qunxiang's unfinished question. "According to Peter's notes, at least a quarter mile. Four hundred meters."

Ke Qunxiang's eyes move quickly back and forth behind his black-rimmed glasses as he thinks through the implications. "But that's not possible. Is it?"

Cheng Fengxiang suggests trying to reproduce this capability, making a working demonstration themselves. "That's where we should start," he says. "Then we can believe it."

"Let's do that," Zhuang Rongtao says.

And with that, they pour themselves into the work of understanding Peter's notes and examining and extending the tracking system Peter had already built.

What everything smells like

Ethan spends the week following up on the interviews he had lined up with twenty companies here in Beijing before flying out from San Francisco. Their products range widely, from electronic payment systems to smartphones, from Internet services to artificial intelligence software.

Because there is such a broad range of specialties, Ethan had decided that the best approach to his special edition presentation of technology in China's Silicon Valley would be to write a survey-type article, describing trends in the local industry and supporting the trends with information gathered from each of the companies and from related government sources. Despite being from a rather small publisher, Ethan has found that most of the individuals he has contacted are naturally outgoing and publicity-oriented and they readily agreed to meet with him. His list includes company executives and both private and state-sponsored investors.

Throughout the week, he gathers quotes from industry leaders, asking about their views of the future, to give it a more personal feel. Rather than focusing solely on the technical aspects of each company's products, he digs into the ways the companies are funded and developed in Beijing, to get a handle on the life cycle of start-ups and their success here.

He finds that the viewpoints of the investors are quite diverse, with different takes on the process, and different visions, ranging from trying to "score the big one" to making an impact on the city and the country. With each interview, he grows more confident that the project will be a big success, more than justifying his trip to China, and he starts thinking about pitching an ongoing series of articles about the Chinese tech scene to his boss when he returns to San Francisco.

He reflects on his busy schedule. While he's planning to visit his parents over the weekend, if it weren't for his meetings around Beijing, he'd have had nothing else better to do during the week while the Zai engineers work the signal tracking issue.

Zhuang Rongtao invites him to dinner on Thursday night to give him a progress report on the signal tracking project. They meet at a microbrewery-restaurant called Frisco, a new place in the upscale Sanlitun area of Beijing, on the opposite side of the city from Haidian District. Zhuang Rongtao thought Ethan would be entertained by the theme.

"It's the closest I've been to San Francisco," exclaims Zhuang Rongtao over his beer, "and the beer's great. They make it here." He points over to the far end of the restaurant where the brewery equipment, including four large metal tanks, is visible behind a large plate glass window.

A large sculpture of the Golden Gate Bridge provides a backdrop to the white marble bar which runs along the length of the restaurant. Small tables fill in the space in front of the bar. It's crowded and a bit noisy, so they have to raise their voices to communicate. American pop music plays in the background.

A waiter shows up to take their dinner orders and Zhuang Rongtao encourages Ethan to order the crab. "It's probably just like at Fisherman's Wharf," he says. He says "Fisherman's Wharf" in English. They both order the crab. Then Zhuang Rongtao asks Ethan how the interviews have been going.

"Beijing's tech scene is thriving. There's a lot to write about," Ethan says.

"Who have you been talking to? Are you in there with the engineers, or up at the top talking with the big guys?"

Ethan smiles. "I guess you'd call them the big guys." Ethan mentions a couple of the more famous names and Zhuang Rongtao is suitably impressed.

"Hey. Let me just jump right in with an announcement. It works."

"It works?"

Zhuang Rongtao is in a particularly good mood. For him, this dinner is a celebration. "Your friend Peter is a genius. And so is whoever is chasing after you. Although you probably don't feel that way about them. Anyway, you should have seen the look on Ke Qunxiang's face when they turned on their equipment and transmitted a signal to his head...and he smelled something that wasn't there."

A thrill runs through Ethan's body. "No kidding?"

"No kidding. They used Peter's notes to figure out how to play back one of his radio signal recordings, and that's what it does. It makes you smell something. Weird, but amazing. It was on the DVD you brought with you."

"Incredible."

"It's for real. Do you have any idea what this means?" Zhuang Rongtao is visibly excited.

The first thought that runs through Ethan's mind is that it means they now have a chance of tracking down the stalkers.

Zhuang Rongtao continues. "This is a major breakthrough. Just imagine the products you could build with this. Mind-reading apps. Virtual reality with artificial smell. And the list goes on. Too many ideas to count. It completely changes the technology landscape."

The engineers at Zai have been working day and night on the project. They were, at first, mainly driven by curiosity. But it quickly changed into admiration. They felt as if they were reading the notes of some famous inventor who had pieced together a miracle.

Once they had succeeded in generating a mentally perceivable signal at a distance using just radio signals, they were energized. They wanted to know more. So they had stayed up all night, varying the signals to see what changes matter and what effects they create.

Despite their initial success, though, they couldn't figure out how to send voices to the head. It's trickier than they had expected, so they put that on the back burner, focusing on understanding electronically induced odors first, with the intention of returning to voices and sounds later.

Hours into their exploration, they realized that the sensation of smell generated by the transmissions seems to be universal. Each of them perceived the same smell with the same pattern of radio transmissions.

Eventually, they had experimentally figured out how to change the radio transmission pattern to produce different smells, different from the artificial odors recorded by Peter, though they don't yet have a way of predicting what odor they'll get without just trying it. Not yet. That said, they do have a growing list of odors that they can produce.

Working late on Wednesday night, they had already discovered the patterns for more than fifty distinct odors when they came up with an idea for uncovering the general pattern for producing any smell. They realized that what they should do is to try to organize the patterns, and the smells they each produce, into a kind of *space* of odors with coordinates for identifying each distinct odor, like a location on a map. They expect it to be a little like color in this way, where each color can be defined with three numbers, one each for red, green and blue intensities. Unlike the case with color, though, they can already see that for odors, three coordinates won't be enough, though they don't know exactly how many will be needed.

One of their discoveries confirms that they are on the right path for a general understanding of this electronic odor phenomenon. They had asked themselves: With all the radio waves passing through our heads every moment of the day, why wouldn't we smell fake odors all the time? They had thought the answer, at least in part, would be that we probably do, but we just don't notice. We're just too distracted with life at large. Even when such a fake odor persists, we get used to it and it disappears into the background.

But they had not been entirely satisfied with that explanation. Even when they paid careful attention to their olfactory experiences throughout the day, they couldn't catch any incontrovertible examples of fake smells. The phenomenon proved to be too rare to be explained by their first theory. Why was that?

So they had carried on with their experiments, asking: If there is one odor per coordinate, and you combine the radio signals for several coordinates all at once, what would that smell like?

When they tried it, they got the answer, which was: Not much. It was neutral. Bland. Not disgusting nor pleasant. Not floral nor fishy nor smoky nor fruity. Not anything. It got them to wondering about the nature of perception itself. If something isn't anything, is it anything at all? Is it an odor if it doesn't smell like something?

But the really surprising thing was that it didn't seem to matter which odor signals they combined, that is, which coordinates, so long as they combined many different ones, without allowing any one type of odor to dominate. The resulting odor signal produced more or less the same smell perception. That was surprising. It was like discovering that if you mix bananas and coffee and bell peppers and white bread and blue cheese and dried shrimp and cinnamon and sauerkraut and peanut butter that it tastes just the same as if you had instead mixed mushrooms and vanilla and egg and artichokes and parsley and strawberries and sausage and peppermint and maple syrup. Stranger, still, that it would end up not tasting like anything in particular.

And so it was that they had discovered the rule that combining many odor signals just gives a kind of generic neutral smell. It may be off a little, not perfectly neutral, but with enough random odor signals coming in together at any given time, there's not much to notice. It's what the world smells like when there is no single strong odor. It smells like *everything combined*, and then watered down.

And that's the answer to their question. All those radio waves bombarding our heads all the time just make the world smell like what it always smells like. No single odor stands out. And you just get used to it. It's just part of the background of our lives. Go off to the moon for a while, or live deep in a cave, and then maybe you can smell the world's radio smog when you get back. Maybe it would have an obvious and distinct smell. But you'd get used to it again, and just like before, it wouldn't smell like anything. For that matter, maybe the background radio noise in Beijing smells different than it does in San Francisco. Who knows?

Sun Yang searched online for any mention of the idea of a "neutral smell", and not entirely surprised, he found it. There was a group of scientists who had actually made a substance with an odor the researchers called "olfactory white", mixing substances with real scents in different ways and balancing them. This discovery gave the Zai engineers even more confidence in their theory. They were well on their way to mastering the concept of electronically generated odors.

Cheng Penglu is now writing software to catalog and analyze the signal data for the odors, with Ke Qunxiang providing the relevant mathematical equations and tailoring them to this application. They've already started brainstorming applications for the technology.

"That is fantastic. It's real," Ethan exclaims.

"For real. It's a mind blow." Zhuang Rongtao combines his favorite English expressions.

For Zhuang Rongtao, the ability to generate a perception of smell directly in the brain, just by transmitting radio waves into the air, is real magic. Not just a trick. The real thing.

The waiter appears with their crab and, after setting down the trays with their food, he hands each of them a plastic bib. They switch their attention to disassembling their meal, breaking open the crab legs with crackers and digging in with small forks, building mounds of debris on their trays as they work their way through their meals.

At length, Ethan asks whether there has been any progress on the signal tracking problem.

"Not yet," Zhuang Rongtao says. "Ke Qunxiang and Cheng Fengxiang just started working together on that this morning. They said the first thing to do is to characterize the signal patterns. Your friend Peter had actually worked out how two transmitters could produce signal patterns together, but he hadn't worked out how to trace the separate signals back to their sources. And as I mentioned earlier, we still don't know how the signals make sounds in the head. When we replay his signal recordings to our own heads, we don't hear anything."

He explains that they already have one insight to go on, though. Regardless of how the signals are transmitted, the pattern has to end up being the same once the signals are combined together in the brain. The brain expects a certain radio signal pattern to hear a particular word. And the transmitters together have to produce that pattern for the brain to hear the word. There's no way around that.

"What are your plans for the next few days?"

"I'll be visiting with my parents tomorrow out in Tianjin, staying the weekend. And I have some more interviews lined up for next week. Referrals from some of the people I met with this week."

"I'll get in touch when we've got something more to show."

They finish up with their crab and beer and then argue over who should pay the dinner bill. Zhuang Rongtao wins. It was his invitation to come to Frisco. He pays with an app on his smartphone.

Shorts, skirts, and video ads

Haidian District is a modern place, with wide streets and glass-clad high-rise office buildings, each one unique, with the names and logos of large companies displayed either down or across in Chinese, and sometimes in English. It is home to more than two million of Beijing's residents, most of whom live in concrete high-rises.

Pedestrian bridges cross the wide boulevards, with banners strung across with large Chinese characters proclaiming motivational slogans for the city: Make Beijing and Haidian green! Be diligent and realistic and forge ahead! Service for the People! Pagoda trees and goldenrain trees line many of the smaller streets. Here and there on the major boulevards, one sees ads for famous brands, Chinese, European, Japanese, and American, on the faces of buildings, sometimes rising several stories tall.

As with the rest of Beijing, the automobile traffic in Haidian District is heavy. Buses crowd the streets, sometimes lining up three or four in a row. Taxis make up a large portion of the total traffic. Many of the vehicles are autonomous, and an increasing number are all-electric, heavily promoted by Beijing's city government to reduce air pollution.

Several areas in Haidian District are laid out as large plazas for walking, paved with stone and concrete slabs and heavily landscaped with willow and ginkgo and maple and deodar trees, and flowers. Large shopping malls fill in between the office buildings, offering everything from American ice cream and Chinese frozen yogurt to modern fashion and restaurants of every kind, including the many different cuisines within China. The third largest mall in the world is in Haidian, a thousand shops occupying six million square feet on six floors.

Some of China's most famous universities are here, as is the Summer Palace, a sprawling Imperial garden which encompasses willow-lined Kunming Lake and Qing dynasty palaces, bridges and pavilions. The very name Haidian means a place of abundant water, a place of wetlands and large, shallow lakes. It was once a place of wells and springs for catching frogs and dragonflies. Water works to supply the palace date back to the year 1291.

Today, Haidian is also home to Zhongguancun, China's Silicon Valley. More than one report has come out in recent years declaring it to be the world's top technology development center, surpassing even the San Francisco Bay Area's Silicon Valley, with well over ten thousand technology companies and thousands of new start-ups annually.

Miller's view of Haidian during the morning rush is the sea of humanity coming and going across the subway platform. He has been here since six. It's eight now, and the crowds are at their peak. As the weather has been hot, many of the younger people wear shorts, skirts, or short dresses, while others wear slacks and cotton dress shirts. No one wears ties. Some passengers have white cords hanging from their earbuds. Others walk along staring down at their smartphones.

A glass-and-steel partition separates the trains from the platform, each window displaying a brightly lit ad for some product. Display monitors hang from the corrugated stainless steel ceiling showing the current date and time and train information and playing video ads. Because the walls in the station here are painted an intense, almost neon, green, the light of which reflects from the station's glass and steel surfaces, the whole station takes on an eerie green glow.

An electric hum fills the station as a train pulls in, followed by the squeal of its brakes. An announcement in Chinese goes out over loudspeakers, reverberating within the station walls, the train doors and the partition doors both slide open, and the crowds squeeze past each other, at the same time chaotic and careful. Miller stands with his back to a wall on the platform as people jostle by. Thirty-two seconds later, the train accelerates away, the pitch of its electric whine shifting another four seconds later as the train shifts gears, and then the train disappears into the tunnel.

Miller checks his smartphone, which is paired with the laptop and the transceiver in his backpack, for an arrow to indicate the direction to his target, but there's still no trace of him. The screen, in fact, is blank, with no map underground, as the map data Julian's app uses has no station layout detail. Miller had asked about that, but Julian said that as far as he can tell, position tracking underground in the Beijing subway isn't available on most lines yet.

Breg returns from his coffee break at a Starbucks in a nearby shopping mall. "Anything?"

Miller pauses the music on his smartphone. "Nada."

"It's the 9-to-5 crowd."

"Do they have a gym around here? The one in the hotel is closed."

"Yeah. It's a few blocks away. Not a bad place." Breg digs through his smartphone and texts Miller the location.

Two minutes after the earlier train, another train rolls in. Thirty-two seconds later, it departs.

Miller offers the backpack to Breg. "Gotta take a leak."

Breg brings up the mind device app on his own smartphone and pairs it with the system in the backpack. Then he scrolls through his music and selects one of his playlists. The music will play until his target comes into range. Another train rolls in.

Since Rogers and Julian are using one system above ground and Miller and Breg are using the second system underground, the two systems are not currently able to coordinate tracking, so when they do finally identify their target, tracking will not be as accurate. That, together with the lack of map details underground led Miller to ask Julian whether it would be possible to see what his target sees. Then he could know where their target is by watching for visual landmarks instead of using range estimation to their target. They had that feature working with their van back in the Bay Area. Could they get it working on the smartphone? He had thought it would be especially useful to see what subway car the target is getting into or out of. Or, if the target changes his mind at the last second and ducks back into the train, he could see that. Julian had responded that he doesn't know how to make the remote sight feature available in a hand-carried package. Miller figured he'd just have to trail the target more closely, violating the rule of staying out of sight if he has to, and Breg had agreed.

Rogers and Julian are sitting in a taxi parked near a major intersection two miles away from the subway station that Breg and Miller are monitoring. Rogers is in the front seat, next to the driver, reading Butcher's Crossing, a Western novel by John Williams, swiping pages every 85 seconds or so. He takes a break every three or four pages to rest his eyes on the distant urban landscape. Julian is sitting in the back, working on a new feature for the mind device while his laptop, connected with a transceiver, searches for their target's brainwaves. Their driver is on his smartphone, reading the news and texting, occasionally gazing out the window at passers-by. The windows are rolled down. It's still only nine in the morning, but it is already 83 degrees. Today's high is projected to be 90.

The group has developed a kind of rhythm, with Miller and Breg monitoring a subway station and Rogers and Julian monitoring key traffic choke points on the roads each morning and evening. Each day, they rendezvous for a late lunch, then they take some time off to do their own things. They resume their search during the evening commutes.

Some afternoons, they tour the attractions of Beijing together. The Forbidden City and Wangfujing Street. The Temple of Heaven. And the seventy year old decommissioned military factory complex built with East German expertise and reborn twenty some years ago as the 798 Art Zone. Many of the original brick and concrete buildings still remain, with factory smokestacks jutting into the sky and steel trusses bridging the tiny lanes within the complex. Graffiti-style art covers many of the building walls. Julian says it reminds him of some parts of Berlin.

Wednesday, 21 August 2024

"Just sit right here." Ke Qunxiang points to a chair at one end of the company's office, then backs away.

Ethan sits down in the chair. Cheng Fengxiang, sitting at the other end of the office, is checking the screen on his laptop. The laptop, which is sitting on a small table, has several devices plugged into it: a microphone, a radio receiver similar to the one Peter had used in his signal tracker, a software-controlled ultra-wideband radio transmitter, and a rectangular panel, four inches wide by five inches high, mounted on a tripod, its face aimed through a small tubular sight with crosshairs at Ethan's head across the room.

The office whiteboard is covered with diagrams and mathematical equations. Several new boxes have been added to the pile in the corner, the packaging for recent purchases.

Zhuang Rongtao and the other engineers sit in a group off to the side, not too close to Ethan's chair, watching. Cheng Fengxiang glances over at Ethan, then taps on the trackpad on his laptop.

Ethan now uncontrollably focuses inward as he hears a hypnotic series of alternating complete and partial sentences, each one cutting off at a place where the next word would be obvious. "I am a man. I am a man. I am a. <pause> I am a woman. I am a woman. I am a. <pause> That is the question. That is the question. That is the. <pause> That is one. That is one. That is. <pause> I am a man. I am a. <pause>" On and on it drones, the rhythm speeding up as it goes.

He finds he can't help but think the missing word. And he can't break out of it. His attention is drawn into the word game, mini-puzzles, rapidly presented one after the other. Fill in the missing word. What comes next? Quick. Here's another.

This goes on for fifteen minutes before it cuts out, and Ethan's attention slowly shifts back to the room he had forgotten he was sitting in. In a bit of a daze, he asks if anyone else heard that.

Cheng Fengxiang comments: "That's just the calibration. We'll come back to that later. Now here's the real test."

Cheng Fengxiang again taps the trackpad of his laptop. And Ethan hears: [Man or woman. Woman or man.]

"That sounded different. It was in my head."

Cheng Fengxiang confirms this. "Yes."

"No one else heard that?"

Ke Qunxiang replies: "I couldn't. It's not coded with my brain code. None of us could."

Cheng Fengxiang points out that Ethan didn't answer.

"Answer?"

"In your head. You didn't choose between man and woman."

"That's true."

"Let's try it again."

Cheng Fengxiang touches the trackpad a few more times on the laptop, then asks: "Ready?"

Ethan nods, Cheng Fengxiang taps the trackpad, and Ethan hears [Man or woman. Woman or man.] He thinks in return: [Man.]

Cheng Fengxiang reads the laptop screen: "Man."

"So you knew I didn't think that the first time. That's amazing."

Ke Qunxiang comments that earlier, when Ethan heard the sequence of sentences, the system was carrying out two types of calibration at once. When Ethan heard words, the brain codes for what he heard were received and recorded on the laptop. When he thought of the missing words, the brain codes for the sounds he made up in his own head were received and recorded on the laptop. Two different areas of the brain, two different sets of brain codes.

"So it's encrypted with some sort of code?" Ethan asks.

"Not encrypted," Ke Qunxiang says. "It's just that the representation is more-or-less unique to each person. That's why it has to be calibrated."

"They were really stumped at first," Zhuang Rongtao says. "This brain code calibration idea is key."

Ke Qunxiang explains: "You might think that if you turn sound waves into radio waves by giving the radio waves the same shape as the sound waves that the brain would hear them. But that doesn't work. It's more complicated than that. You know that we figured out how to transmit smells using radio signals, right?"

"Yes. Zhuang Rongtao told me about that," Ethan says.

"That works because the radio signals for smells are universal. The brain code is the same for everyone. When we replay Peter's recording of radio signals for smells, they just work. Going by his notes, we found that we all smell the same thing he did. So we figured it would be the same way for sounds. But it isn't. When we tried replaying the signals that Peter recorded for inner voice sounds, retransmitting them as radio waves, it didn't work at all. We couldn't hear anything in our heads. His notes indicated that he heard them. But we didn't."

Cheng Fengxiang pulls a chair over and sits down as Ke Qunxiang continues explaining to Ethan. "OK, so you know that a digital sound recording device listens to the sound and records data values 44,100 times a second, right?" He taps rapidly with his finger through the air, as if recording the data. "Some of them record at 96,000 times a second for higher fidelity."

"Sure. Those are the standard audio sample rates for recording music."

"That's not how the brain works. The brain processes sound in small batches. And then... Actually, the first thing to understand is how the brain hears sound the normal way. Sound vibrates the air which vibrates the eardrum, and the eardrum passes the sound along into a kind of sensor in your inner ear that spirals around. It's called the cochlea. It has little hairs along its length and the sound stimulates these hairs. Depending on the frequencies in the sound, different hairs along the length are stimulated by different amounts, the point being that the cochlea collects the sound information for all the sound frequencies all at once. Instead of getting the sound data 44,100 times a second, the brain collects the data just ten to a hundred times a second. I couldn't get an accurate number for this when I researched it online, but it had to be in that range."

Ethan is surprised that the brain would only process the sounds a hundred times a second. "How can that work? Wouldn't some of the sound be missed that way?"

"It's all there, still. It's just that the formatting is different. The cochlea senses the sound and sends it to the brain along a nerve bundle that runs through a hole in the skull. Then the brain processes these nerve signals in batches, like I said, ten to a hundred times a second, turning them into its own unique brain code."

"I see. So the batches are what you hear in your head."

"Yes."

Sun Yang, sitting toward the back of the group, nods to this point.

Ke Qunxiang continues with his explanation: "So if you're going to send sound to the brain using radio waves, bypassing the ear and bypassing the cochlea, first you have to code up the sound the same way the brain itself codes it. And then you send the code. And it has to go in batches, or the brain won't understand it."

Now Cheng Fengxiang nods.

Ke Qunxiang continues: "That's why the radio signals that Peter recorded don't look anything like ordinary sound waves. And these batches have to go in with the right timing. They have to match the brain's rhythms. As it turns out, for sound perception, the rhythm is ten times a second. It makes sense when you consider the fact that human hearing goes down to twenty cycles a second. That's the lowest pitch you can hear. If the batches were processed any faster, you couldn't hear sound that low any more."

Ethan doesn't understand this point. Ke Qunxiang elaborates: "Let me exaggerate to make the point. What would it take to hear a really really low frequency sound wave? Say the sound wave takes a whole year for one cycle. Well, your ears would have to take in air pressure changes for a whole year, right? So it's like that. The lower the sound frequency, the longer it takes to hear it."

"That make sense."

"It's a trade-off, actually. If you want to hear lower frequencies, you have to wait longer to hear them. It would slow down your reaction time."

Ethan nods.

"There's an interesting consequence," Ke Qunxiang says. "Because the brain works in batches, you can't hear less than a tenth of a second of silence. Ten times a second, the brain processes the sound that came in, and if there's anything in there, anywhere, during that tenth of a second, then there's no silence at all. The brain perceives the whole tenth of a second interval as having sound, and that's that. It's not a silent interval."

"That's weird."

"It all makes sense once you understand how it works."

"The brain rhythms are like what you'd see on EEG graphs, is that right?"

"Yes, that's right," Ke Qunxiang says. "So the idea is that you have to make the radio waves look like the brain codes of the person you're sending the sound to, and then you have to transmit them *in rhythm* with the brain so the brain can understand the codes. They have to be synchronized."

"But how would the transmitter know when to send each batch? It doesn't know anything about the brain's rhythms, does it?"

"That's a smart observation. Ours does. We used... Really, it's Cheng Fengxiang who made it work. He added a receiver to allow our device to detect the brain's rhythms by reading brainwaves at a distance, from across the room. And that's how the transmitter knows when to transmit sounds so that the cycles line up, ten times a second. Peter's notes mentioned the idea."

"So Peter did figure it out." In Ethan's mind, Peter just got an upgrade. He's not smart. He's a genius. Ethan hadn't appreciated how sophisticated Peter's work had been. When Peter had given him the tour, so to speak, he hadn't yet accepted the reality of what Peter had been experiencing and how much progress he had made in understanding it from a technological point of view.

"We have to give a lot of credit to Peter," Ke Qunxiang says. "He recorded his own brainwaves in his...what was it called again, Zhuang Rongtao?"

"*SCIF*." Zhuang Rongtao uses the English term.

"He recorded his own brainwaves in his *SCIF*," Ke Qunxiang says. "We used the same technique that he described, adding some processing steps to get just the part of the brainwaves that we need to match up the timing. Cheng Penglu and Sun Yang wrote the code together."

Cheng Penglu gives a thumbs up to the group.

Zhuang Rongtao leaves the room without explanation as Ke Qunxiang continues with Ethan: "Let's talk about what we did to you when you sat down. You remember how you heard a sequence of short sentences? When you heard the sounds, they went through your ears and into your brain which turned them into its own brain code. It's like the way computers take data in as letters and numbers and turn them into binary code, ones and zeroes. But it's the brain's own version of that. So what we did was to read the brainwaves that came out from your head when we played those sounds to you. And that's how our system learned *your* brain codes for sounds you hear, which are different from my brain codes or Peter's or anyone else's."

Ethan's expression is focused as he visualizes the process.

"And then when Cheng Fengxiang wanted to transmit the question to you, remember that? man or woman? the laptop looked up the brain codes that your brain uses for hearing the sounds of those words and it shaped the radio waves using those brain codes. Then the neurons in your brain were stimulated by the radio waves and it recognized the brain codes. And you heard the words as a voice in your head."

"So the first sounds I heard actually were just ordinary sounds," Ethan says.

"Yes, well, that's an interesting point," Ke Qunxiang says. "I was trying to figure out how someone would have calibrated to your brain codes. They didn't have you sit down with them. I assume."

"You're saying it can't be done without calibration. No. I never saw anyone."

"We have a couple of different theories for how they might have done it. For what we did today, Cheng Fengxiang bought a sound beaming device. It's like an audio speaker that plays sound, but it uses ultrasound, that's high frequency sound that you can't hear, and it sends the sound in a tight beam, like a flashlight. Almost like a laser. It's called a directional speaker. Ever heard of it?"

"Not sure."

"In some applications, they're used to make sound less disruptive to others nearby, like in museum exhibits. But they can also be used to project sound across large distances efficiently. The speaker actually sends several ultrasound beams, which you can't hear. But the speaker manipulates the beams to create beat frequencies, and this creates sound that you can hear."

"So you think they beamed sound at me to calibrate on my brain code before they started talking in my head."

"That's just one way they could have done it. You'd have to have been out in the open for it to work. But other people around you wouldn't have heard it because the sound beam is narrow. And by playing the same sounds repeatedly to you, they could find your brain codes more accurately. And with a sound beam, they could have sent the sounds to you from really far away. Maybe hundreds of meters. As you now know, it's also possible to read brainwaves from a similar distance. So they could have done the whole thing without you noticing them. Especially if it were at night."

Ethan's face takes on a comprehending look. "I did hear something weird like that, but I didn't give it much thought. It only happened once." He tries to remember what day it was. "In fact, it was dark out. And... that's interesting. The sounds were very repetitive." He remembers the strange experience clearly now. "I thought I was just tired. It was pretty late, and I had already had a long day, so I just went right to bed after that. By the next morning, I had already forgotten about it."

"That's what I thought." Ke Qunxiang's expression is confident.

Zhuang Rongtao returns to the room but remains standing.

"What about tracking the source of the signals?" Ethan returns to the original problem of finding the perpetrators.

"Now that we know how to reproduce voices in the head," says Zhuang Rongtao, "we can use this knowledge to find their signals. Ke Qunxiang and Sun Yang are working together on the software to make tracking work even when the perpetrators transmit their signals from more than one transmitter. To finish the tracker, though, we need to finish calibrating to your brain codes so we know what your stalkers are transmitting. If they show up again, that's what the tracker will search for. The tracker filters out all of the other radio waves in the area, keeping only the radio signals carrying your brain code. They're working now on the software that figures out how brain codes are split between multiple transmitters and tracks down each transmitter separately."

"How much longer will it take?" Ethan asks.

"Another day or two," says Zhuang Rongtao. "Also, Cheng Fengxiang only did a rough calibration on your brain codes earlier, to keep it quick. Let's do the complete calibration later today. If that's OK."

"That would be fine."

Zhuang Rongtao explains the process. "We'll sit you down with earphones and you'll listen to a long series of sounds. It'll also figure out the brain codes for stereo sounds by sending individual sounds only to the left ear and then the right ear, and then both together. It's like taking a hearing test. Then we'll have you read a long list of words to yourself silently, just thinking of the words in your head. The two types of calibration cover your brain codes for sounds you hear from outside, and also for sounds you make up in your head."

Ethan asks whether he has to hear or read every possible word. "Wouldn't calibration take forever that way?"

Ke Qunxiang explains that that's not necessary. "We just need the sounds. So we chose a set of words that cover many of the different sounds you might hear or think. And we don't really need every little sound variation. The software knows out how to handle that by itself."

Cheng Fengxiang says they've all been wondering how many other people in the world are already using this technology. "We've never heard of it before. But it isn't that hard, once you see the main concepts."

"We did an international patent search and came up with nothing," says Zhuang Rongtao. "It might be home-brewed technology and they're keeping it all secret. It's hard not to become fascinated with it once you figure out how to make it work. The team has already started brainstorming the products which become possible with this technology, like movies and virtual reality with virtual odors and mind reading for communications. Let's put it this way: Remember our virtual reality headset? It's obsolete already. We have to start over. If this technology is already out there..."

Ethan understands immediately, of course. Exploring the future of technology products is his business.

"No kidding," says Zhuang Rongtao. "Don't mention us in your article on Beijing tech. Not yet. We're going back into stealth mode."

"Sure. But..."

Zhuang Rongtao asks whether Ethan knows of any reason why they couldn't continue developing the technology for commercial applications. Ethan hadn't thought about that before. He reflects on the question. The only one who might have something to say on that point would be Peter. He did the work that made it possible to get this far. But Peter's in a coma. Then Ethan asks: "Would it be hazardous?"

"Hazardous?" Cheng Fengxiang laughs. "Video games aren't good for you. We play them anyway."

Ke Qunxiang considers the safety question from a physics point of view. "The signal strengths are not much different from the older cell phone transmissions, back when cell phones were first introduced. Newer cell phones are better, of course. And it can probably be reduced once we get more familiar with the technology." He stretches his arm out, measuring some distance in his mind, then twists his head as he thinks through the calculation.

The room goes quiet now as the engineers' thoughts begin to drift. They've been at the discussion for quite a while. Then Ke Qunxiang thinks of another point to add. "I already have some ideas on how to eliminate the repetitive sounds you hear during calibration. There's a way to do it automatically if we have a headset with a microphone. The calibration system will hear the same sounds that you do, such as when you walk around listening to ordinary conversation, and it can compare those sounds with your brainwaves to figure out the brain codes. It would be more natural. Or we could try it with —"

Zhuang Rongtao raises his hand and interrupts. "Enough! We're all starving. Let's go to lunch!"

With that, the whole team, including Ethan, leaves the office and crowds around the elevator as Zhuang Rongtao locks up. When the elevator arrives at their floor, they all squeeze in and Zhuang Rongtao presses "1".

In the restaurant, which is just a short walking distance from the office, the group, sitting elbow-to-elbow around a round table barely big enough for the six of them, orders their lunches, which, in short order, are delivered to the table.

The small restaurant is crowded and noisy. Named Two Brothers, it has two specialties, practiced by two brothers who make a show of competing with each other. "Best Pulled Noodles!" exclaims a sign hanging over one station in the restaurant. "Best Dumplings!" exclaims the sign over the second station.

Lamian, or pulled noodles, are available either hot or cold, accompanied by a variety of cold vegetable dishes and a hearty bean sauce. On hot days like today, the cold noodles are especially popular. The pulled noodles are made by hand in one corner of the restaurant, where one of the brothers repeatedly folds and stretches a large lump of dough, squeezing it across an oiled stainless steel table. He breaks the dough into smaller lumps and flours them, then stretches and folds these repeatedly, each time doubling the number of strands, until the strands reach the desired size. Without hesitation, he tosses the noodles into a big pot of boiling water, then, almost without waiting, scoops them back out with a strainer and deposits them into waiting bowls. He then starts the process again as additional orders arrive.

In the other back corner of the restaurant, another cook is busy tossing flour over a large marble-topped table, spreading out dumpling wrappers, as the second brother rapidly fills the wrappers with a pork and scallion mixture and squeezes each one into a perfectly formed shape. Behind them is the large pot of water in which the dumplings are boiled.

Other cooks, working between the two stations, are busy chopping vegetables and preparing the serving bowls. The cooks all wear white hats and jackets.

In between bites from his noodle soup, Ethan asks the engineers why brain codes wouldn't be the same for everyone. The engineers don't know, but they speculate. Perhaps it's just because the neurons are wired up differently. Maybe the neural wiring just grows differently in each person, like fingerprints.

"But then why would smell be universal?" Ethan asks.

"Ke Qunxiang, you wanna take that one?" Cheng Fengxiang asks.

Ke Qunxiang, face close to his bowl of soup as he eats, looks up. "Me? What?"

Cheng Fengxiang repeats the question, but Ke Qunxiang shrugs his shoulders. "I don't know. Could be that the radio waves directly affect the sensors. Um, I guess you'd call them sensors. The things that detect molecules in the nose." He puts his face back down to his bowl and continues eating.

Sun Yang uses his chopsticks to pick up a wonton from his soup. He holds it up in the air, gazing at it.

The Chinese word for wonton is *huntun*. As it happens, *huntun* not only sounds almost identical to *hundun*, a word which means something like "the primal chaos of the undivided state of the universe", the word for wonton actually originates with *hundun*. The Chinese characters for writing huntun and hundun are also almost identical, the only difference being that in hundun, the Chinese symbol for water makes up part of each of the two characters *hun* and *dun*, while in huntun, the water symbols are replaced by the Chinese symbol for food.

So inspired, Sun Yang tells Zhuangzi's Story of Hundun. The others glance over at him but continue eating as he speaks, holding the pinched wonton in the air throughout the telling.

"The emperor of the South Sea was quick, and the emperor of the North Sea was heedless. In the center were the muddy waters of Hundun. Quickly and heedlessly, the two met together there, and Hundun received them and was kind to them. They discussed how they might reciprocate Hundun's favor.

Saying all people have seven holes in their heads, for seeing, hearing, eating, and breathing, with Hundun alone having none, they thought they would give him holes. And so, making one hole a day, seven days later, Hundun died."

Still holding the pose, and carefully observing the wonton, Sun Yang comments: "What we have done is to cut an eighth hole." He eats the wonton all in one bite.

Cheng Penglu starts to ask a question but then changes his mind. Everyone eats in silent contemplation.

Friday, 23 August 2024

Ethan peers out the window of his parents' rental unit. The scene is gray on gray. Rain pelts the window hard.

Glancing back down at his smartphone, he checks the weather report. The high today is projected to stay below 27 degrees Celsius, or 80 degrees Fahrenheit, ending the recent hot spell, but now there is a danger of flooding. The report notes that the Beijing Traffic Management Bureau has issued an orange storm alert, the second highest of its four-tier warning system.

He closes the curtains and picks up his suit jacket and his bag from the sofa, then retrieves his umbrella from the front closet and slides into his shoes.

The furnished apartment is typical for the area. Two bedrooms, wood floors, white-painted concrete walls. In addition to the sofa, with its brown chenille fabric, there is a small glass-topped coffee table with a metal frame and a square wood dining room table, also covered with glass. The apartment has a bed, a desk, and a wardrobe, and in the bathroom, a washer, but no dryer, with only a retractable clothesline to stretch across the bathtub to hang up clothes to dry. The kitchen has a refrigerator and a gas stove and a microwave oven. But there are no utensils, no cookware, no rice cooker. And no food in the fridge. Just a few bottles of water. The only thing that Ethan did to make the apartment habitable was to buy a set of sheets and a pillow for the bed.

He heads downstairs and down the block to get his breakfast at the same little restaurant he has been going to almost every morning since arriving. There, he orders *xiaolong tangbao*, small pork dumplings filled with soup and steamed in a bamboo basket, with finely sliced threads of ginger and Chinese black vinegar. It arrives within a few minutes. While he is waiting, a small pot of hot tea and a ceramic cup are delivered to him at his table. Steam rises when he pours himself a cup.

The waiter sets down a paper napkin and a ceramic spoon with the dumplings. Ethan grabs a pair of chopsticks from the pastel green plastic cylinder sitting at the side of the table and pulls the cover off the *zhenglong*, the type of bamboo basket that *xiaolong tangbao* are steamed in. The cover drips from one edge as he sets it down out of the way. Picking up a dumpling with his chopsticks and supporting it with the ceramic spoon, he bites into the top of the dumpling and carefully sucks the hot soup out from it. Using chopsticks, he picks up a few ginger threads and places them on top of the dumpling, then dips the dumpling in black vinegar and eats it in one go. Six dumplings in a basket, two baskets stacked one on the other. Finishing the first six, he swaps the two baskets and starts into the second.

There's not a lot of chit-chat. Most of the customers focus on their breakfast. The waiter repeatedly carries full and empty *zhenglong* back and forth between the tables and the kitchen. The place is tiny, with only seven tables, each seating just two or three people. Only one table remains empty. Several framed posters displaying vintage Chinese ads hang along one wall, opposite the kitchen, which is separated from the dining room by a wall with a long window. The ads show the smiling faces of beautiful young women posing in traditional Chinese dress, selling soap, soda pop, and traditional medicines. The view out the front window of the restaurant is obscured by raindrops and the floors are wet from dripping umbrellas.

Finished with his breakfast, Ethan gets out his smartphone and opens WeChat, the ubiquitous it-does-everything Chinese social media app, bringing up a QR code which encodes his payment account information. The waiter scans the square pattern of black and white pixels and checks the result on his own screen, then returns to the kitchen.

Looking out at the severe weather, Ethan hesitates at the door, then dashes toward the Weigongcun subway station. The rain is coming down hard and the wind makes it difficult for him to hold his umbrella.

The station entrance, with its unique pattern of diamond-shaped windows set into stainless steel walls, is surrounded by a blur of colorful umbrellas in motion. Despite the heavy rain, a row of bicycles is parked just outside.

Ethan flows into the station entrance with the crowd. Once inside, he closes his umbrella and rides the escalator down. The escalator steps are slippery and the granite floors are wet. As he descends, the sound of traffic, and of rain pelted umbrellas, is gradually replaced by the muffled echoes of the station interior.

Reaching the fare gate, Ethan swipes his smartphone to pay and he passes through. He then takes another escalator down one more level to the station platform and stands in line to get on a train. Just as he arrives, he hears the hum of a train just now departing. He gets bumped by someone dashing by but doesn't turn to look.

Zhuang Rongtao had sent him an audio text earlier this morning, urging him to come into the office today, with a promise of a demonstration of their two new upgraded signal tracking devices, including the new feature for tracking multiple transmitters.

Ethan waits in line, then boards the train after next and squeezes into the crowded interior. Most people stand, holding steel poles or the steel handrails that run along near the top of the car. The doors close and the train hums as it accelerates. Ethan notes the change in the indicator lights on the line map over the top of the subway door. Three stops to Zhongguancun Station.

Push to talk

Miller's attention is fixed on his smartphone. There's an arrow on the map, but it takes a few seconds for the situation to register, and then he makes a run for the train door. He struggles past the crowd to reach the train. One man standing in line yells at him. Hey! *Laowai!* Miller doesn't understand what the man says after that.

Reaching the train door, he checks the map on his smartphone again. The arrow points along the direction of the train. He hesitates. Is his target getting off here? Or is he just passing through? The platform is narrow. If his target were to exit and walk along the platform to the stairs, the map indication might not be accurate enough to decide. He tests this idea, rotating his smartphone slightly and shifting back and forth through the train door even as other passengers squeeze by. The arrow doesn't track with his motions.

He tries to stand in the doorway, waiting until the last possible moment to make a decision to go in or stay out, but it's hard for him to hold his position. The target could be in one of the doorways ahead, pushing his way out. Or in. He strains to look, but it's a mass of people all the way down the platform.

A larger man shoves him aside, pushing him out of the doorway and back out onto the platform. He loses traction on the slippery floor, almost falling. Squeezing between two other passengers, he claws his way back into the doorway. Three loud beeps sound and the doors start to shut. He holds one side open as he tries to decide which way to go. The arrow still points down the length of the train. He commits and lets the door close.

He is surprised when the doors suddenly open again and three platform attendants, two women and one man in navy blue uniforms and white gloves, peer into the car. One of the attendants looks Miller over, then glances at the other passengers around him. Apparently satisfied that nothing is out of order, the attendant comments on a walkie-talkie, then the three back up, and the doors close again. The train accelerates.

Breg is on the way back down into the station from his coffee break when Miller texts him, saying he's on the train, bound toward Anheqiao North Station. He checks the map again. The arrow points straight ahead. He stands on his toes, trying to look down the length of the train, but he can't spot his target. It's a sea of people. Breg texts back. He'll be on the next train.

Next to Miller, a Chinese woman speaks into her phone using a push-to-talk app, holding her finger on the talk button on the screen as she speaks, then lifting it to send the message. A moment later, a response comes back. The woman notices Miller watching her, and she turns away and speaks again into her phone.

Curious about his target, Miller makes his way forward. It's slow-going, every step forward requiring a maneuver around other passengers. Then it occurs to him that he's almost the only white person on the train and he gives up on his search. He stands out too much. He has a better idea. He works his way back the other way to make sure he is out of visible range, then engages his target, talking into the app on his smartphone. He says simply: "Station." The app, interoperating with the mind device in the backpack, transmits his voice to his target's inner voice. But with the noise on the train, it's hard to hear what his target thinks in response.

The train starts to decelerate as they enter Haidian Huangzhuang Station. The doors open and the crowd starts to move. Miller adjusts his position to avoid blocking the crowd or being swept out the doors. Another crowd streams in. The doors close and the train accelerates.

Miller's heart jumps. Distracted by the movements of the crowds, he wasn't paying attention. He glances down at his phone. The arrow still points straight ahead. His target hasn't exited. He tries again to engage his target. "Station. Station."

Through the noise, he hears a thought in response. "[Station. *Zenmele? Zhongguancun... Haimeidao.*]" The agency's translation service talks over this: "Station. What's going on? Zhongguancun... Not there yet."

He takes note of the station name. Zhongguancun. He's familiar with it from his planning, though it weren't for Rogers drilling him on the pronunciation, he'd probably not have understood it. He looks up at the station names, shown in both English and Chinese characters on the subway map over the door, then texts Breg the station name. Breg texts back that he'll leave the subway system at his next stop and catch a taxi to pick him up.

Miller hears his target's next thought through the app, quickly followed by the translation: "[*Shi shengyin.*]" "It's the sound. Or: It's the voice."

An announcement of the upcoming station goes out first in Chinese, then in English. The train decelerates. He can't hear anything from his target's thoughts. A beep sounds, the doors open, and the crowds start moving.

Out past the 5th Ring Road

Ethan strains to see down the length of the train. There's no one speaking English around him. The sounds he heard were in his head. He assumes someone transmitted the sounds into his head, but he can't identify where they might have come from. The sounds disappear. And then they come back.

The words were in English. It sounded like a native English speaker. He notices two white men jammed in with the sea of Chinese on the same car with him, but they're not speaking. He keeps an eye on them to see whether they will follow him out.

He exits at Zhongguancun Station and takes the escalator up to street level, opening his umbrella as he steps out into the rain. He looks around for anything suspicious, but the scene is utterly normal. No one lingers nearby. No one is watching him. No one is carrying any suspicious packages or equipment. The two white men have disappeared. He walks back down into the station and still doesn't see anything suspicious, even as the voice continues to speak in his head.

The station has seven exits spread out over a distance of 250 meters. He considers the possibility that his stalker is near one of the other exits. To the north of him, a raised pedestrian crossing next to two of the station exits straddles Beijing's 4th Ring Road, the pathways of the crossing forming a square over the road. Another pedestrian crossing passes over the road to the south of him. He scans the bridge, looking for anything unusual, but there's nothing but the busy motions of umbrellas. He can't see faces in the distance through the rain.

He sends a voice message to Zhuang Rongtao: "They're back. I'm hearing their voices."

Zhuang Rongtao responds that he'll come pick him up in his car, reminding Ethan that he drives a blue BYD all-electric e3 sedan. A couple of minutes later, he messages again, saying he has a plan.

Zhuang Rongtao picks Ethan up on the street near station exit C3. Ethan gets into the front seat and closes his umbrella, setting the umbrella and his bag on the floor in front of him.

"This rain is torrential."

"For real." As Zhuang Rongtao pulls out into traffic, Ethan starts to ask about the signal trackers, but Zhuang Rongtao waves his hand back and forth. *Don't say anything.*

"But where are we going?"

"I want to show you something. It's out past the 5th Ring Road."

Ethan sits quietly, wondering what it could be. The voice in his head also expresses an interest.

Zhuang Rongtao gives a little more detail on the location they're driving to as they head down the 4th Ring Road, one of Beijing's main expressways and one of the concentric ring roads, numbered one through seven, that circle around Beijing's center, following it southwest from their location in Zhongguancun.

After fifteen minutes on the 4th Ring Road, they exit onto a local road and drive west, soon passing the 5th Ring Road. A taxi passes them on the left and pulls ahead into the distance.

They travel further and further west, eventually turning onto the smaller local roads, the roads getting smaller and more remote as they go, until they reach a region with heavy vegetation and isolated factory buildings. They pull over to the side of the road and park. The narrow asphalt road, cracked all over with age and darkened by the rain to a dark gray, is lined with willow trees and dense shrubbery and a series of electric poles. There are no crossroads nearby.

Zhuang Rongtao asks Xiaodi, the e3's voice assistant, to play music by G.E.M. A young woman's voice confirms the request and Zhuang Rongtao's collection begins playing quietly in the background.

"We need to wait here for a little bit. Are they there?" He takes off his seat belt, then leans back into the corner between his seat and the door and stretches his legs to make himself more comfortable.

"They're still talking."

"What's he saying?"

"He says you're not my friend."

"Tell him he can…never mind. I suppose he can hear me. Who is he?"

"He says he's not a thing."

"That's interesting. He understands our Chinese?"

"Oh. Good point. I would say yes. But he's speaking in English."

"No problem." Zhuang Rongtao uses another of his favorite English expressions.

A taxi passes by, rounding a small bend in the road ahead and disappearing from sight. The rain pounds the e3. The wind gusts and the trees lining the road thrash wildly in response.

"This brain code idea…I was wondering," Ethan says. "Why would the code be any different than the sounds you hear? Why would there be a *code*? When I read a sentence, it just sounds the same in my head as it does when I read it out loud."

"It doesn't for me."

"It *doesn't*? What does it sound like for you?"

"The words in my head don't really have sounds. It's more abstract I guess? Sort of like an imprint of a voice. Like when someone mouths a word to you, and you don't hear it, but you know what it is, anyway." Zhuang Rongtao sounds reflective.

"OK, I get that. But then how could someone hear the words in *your* head? Are your thoughts immune to the technology?"

"Probably not. The team says that technically speaking, the brain codes aren't sounds, anyway. They come from sounds, but they're not sounds. So, your brain codes sound like sounds to you. But mine don't sound like sounds to me. One of the issues they ran into was how to convert the brain codes into something they could hear. It turns out that's tricky. They're still working on it."

"That's interesting."

"I wonder how many people hear sounds in their head and how many don't."

"Don't know. Good question."

"It never occurred to me that it wasn't the same for everyone."

"I suppose it doesn't really matter, if there's no one else listening, and you already know what you're thinking, anyway."

"Can you make sounds in your head if you really try?"

Zhuang Rongtao gives it some thought. "Hmm…kind of. Maybe it's something that can be learned. Was there a particular time when you learned how?"

Ethan laughs. "Learned how? I don't remember. I think it was always like this."

"Huh."

Not a soul can be seen on their stretch of road. The trees continue to thrash. Mandopop plays quietly from the e3's audio system, competing with the drum of the rain on the car's rooftop.

The muddy waters

"It looks like we're headed out into the middle of nowhere. Where does this road go?"

Julian, sitting in the back seat of the taxi, scrolls and zooms the map on his laptop. The transceiver is plugged in and is resting on the seat next to him. He replies to Rogers: "This is an industrial area. There is a river near here."

The taxi driver peers ahead into the deluge as he guides their vehicle along the narrow lane. He seems to pay no attention to their conversation.

"He has stopped," Julian says.

Using his limited Chinese, Rogers asks the taxi driver to pull over and park.

They had considered hiring a car with a driver who could speak English, but then decided otherwise. It was a trade-off. They have a large degree of privacy with a driver who doesn't understand English. And they don't need a tour guide.

"How far away is he?" Rogers asks.

"About 300 yards. There is a bend in the road up ahead. He is just beyond it."

Rogers would have preferred to be in an area with roads that parallel his target's route. Breg and Miller had to get in front of their target along the same road, with no way to run ahead out of sight. Unlike the regular grid of streets in the city, here, the roads are irregular and sometimes meandering, with few intersections and many dead-ends.

Their driver turns off the car, then unhurriedly unscrews the sky blue lid of a double-walled glass bottle to sip his hot tea. Small tea leaves float freely in the bottle. He replaces the lid and sets the bottle back into the taxi's cup holder.

"We'll just wait," Rogers says. "Are you recording?"

Julian checks. "Yes." He double-checks the remaining space on his laptop to make sure he won't run out.

Rogers inspects their surroundings. Visibility is limited. Trees and shrubs line the road and block the view beyond. He searches on his smartphone in an attempt to understand why their target would be stopped here, looking for any businesses or other meaningful destinations nearby. He doesn't expect to find anything, though. He suspects their target and his friend are playing a game, but this doesn't faze him. Though their target is currently focused on them, eventually, he will return to the city and they will fade into the background of his thoughts. They'll still be with him, absorbing whatever information they can, prompting him to probe in different directions. Rogers is sure that it will just be a matter of time, perhaps by later this afternoon, before their target gives up on this game.

Rogers listens to his target's conversation through earbuds, occasionally prompting his target using the push-to-talk feature on his smartphone's mind device app. It's the same configuration that Miller had been using in the subway, providing him with simultaneous Chinese-to-English audio translation. From time to time, he hears Chinese pop music, with the English translation of the lyrics overlaid on the sounds. Goodbyes, photographs, love, the universe. The lyrics come through in occasional bursts as his target shifts attention back and forth between the music and his conversation.

Suddenly, a Chinese man holding a blue umbrella knocks on the driver's side window. Rogers and Julian peer through the window, which is covered with raindrops, to see who it is. Rogers then notices there is a car parked right behind them. Their taxi driver, sipping his tea, takes his time closing the bottle and sets it down.

The man outside shouts something in Chinese to the driver, but it is difficult to hear him with the rain banging on the metal roof of the car. Thinking the man may be lost, the driver rolls down his window slightly to talk to him. Rain splatters in through the gap.

Rogers taps his earbuds to turn off the sound, then tries asking the taxi driver what's going on, but the driver's limited English prevents any meaningful dialog. The driver turns to look at Rogers and Julian, then he turns back to the man outside. But before the driver has a chance to say anything further, the man speaks slowly in English through the window directly to Rogers. "What is your name?" Rogers doesn't answer and the man tries again. "You are transmit without license. What is your name and your purpose?"

Rogers reaches back and subtly waves his hand at Julian as he replies to the man: "I don't understand." Julian turns off the transceiver, disconnects it from the laptop, and puts the equipment into his backpack.

The man squeezes the pole of his umbrella in the crook of his neck to hold it up. With his hands now free, he holds up his smartphone to read a note to Rogers describing the radio power spectrum of Julian's transmissions. He then explains that they have recorded the signals, which will be used for proof. He repeats his request for name and purpose.

A second man now appears, standing next to the passenger side window, his left arm wrapped around the pole of his black umbrella. His smartphone repeatedly flashes the window as he tries to take pictures of Rogers and Julian. Rogers turns around in surprise, then covers his face with his arm. Julian slouches down in his seat and twists his body to face down at the seat next to him. Reviewing the photos, the man sees nothing but a glittery mess of raindrops. He turns off the flash and tries again. Now, the photos are dark and blurry. Pushing his smartphone right up to the window, he repeatedly brushes away the raindrops to get a clear shot, but the drops are replaced as quickly as he brushes. He fumbles with his umbrella in an attempt to keep the window dry, dropping his smartphone in the struggle.

The first man speaks again with the driver, in Chinese, then again in English with Rogers. "You are spy. I must ask you cooperate." Rogers begins to feel sick to his stomach, feeling trapped and unsure of what to do.

The taxi driver has, by now, become suspicious of the two men outside the taxi and complains in Chinese to the first man. This makes the man visibly angry, and in turn, the driver loses his patience with the man. He rolls up his window to cut off the conversation, but the man shouts through the window.

Hoping to avoid further confrontation, Rogers tells the driver to start driving back the way they came, and the driver pulls out, making a three-point turn on the narrow road to turn around. The second man, the one taking pictures, scrambles to pick up his phone before the taxi runs it over. The taxi then accelerates rapidly down the road. The two men run back to their own car, quickly folding their umbrellas and dropping them onto the floor of the front passenger seat. They set off in pursuit of the taxi.

Rogers quickly calls Breg to explain what just happened, then asks him to hold on as he asks Julian whether the first man's description of their radio transmissions was accurate. Julian replies that it was. Rogers then suggests to Breg that he also turn off his own transceiver. Whoever the men are, they may be able to follow by tracking the transmissions.

The road twists and turns in the industrial countryside, first passing more trees and other vegetation, then entering the grounds of a factory, passing under a complex of piping that crosses twenty feet up over the road, connecting two enormous buildings. The road then narrows and makes a sharp right turn under another complex of pipes. Trusses and cables run along with the pipes, supported by steel columns. A covered factory gangway connects two other large buildings nearby, suspended forty feet up. Larger pipes, a foot or more in diameter, run both under and over the gangway, in different directions. Steel stairs zig-zag up the sides of corrugated steel building walls, painted in variously aged shades of red. Large Chinese characters, painted in white, mark one wall of one of the buildings.

Rogers turns around to look behind them, but he can't see very far due to the curve of the road. Ahead of them, an old bus appears, driving slowly along a wider stretch of road. The taxi driver overtakes on the left, splashing through a deep puddle in the uneven road, pulling around in front just as the road narrows again. They leave the bus further and further behind, then turn left down another small road. Off to the left, several smokestacks, ringed with red and white stripes, rise high above the trees. Two large concrete cooling towers, tinted a mottled and faded light blue, loom over them on the right. Curtains of rain batter their surfaces and drain down into the dense and unkempt vegetation of the factory complex.

A little further on, they pass a section of road bordered by a narrow walkway and a low wall, their cracked bricks run through with long blades of grass. The taxi driver slows down here, then turns onto a highway and accelerates. Rogers and Julian continue to survey the countryside but make no comments. Along the left side of the highway is another long red brick wall, this one taller than the one they had driven by earlier. They can't see beyond it. On the right, a quarter mile off and lower in elevation, is a large river, its waters a muddy brown and swollen from the storm.

After a minute of driving down the highway, Rogers decides it would be best at this point to change taxis. He turns to look back down the highway. No one is following. Pointing to a small road off to the side of the highway, he asks the taxi driver to drop them off there. Without a word, the driver pulls over at the designated place.

Rogers fumbles with his wallet to pull out some Chinese cash to pay the driver, then gets out. Julian opens his antenna-umbrella as he gets out from the back and puts on his backpack. The taxi drives off as soon as they both close their doors. The two of them, Rogers and Julian, stand side by side by the road.

Julian looks around at their surroundings. Here, there are mostly open fields, some trees, and a road leading down toward another larger road in the distance that runs alongside a river. "How will we go from here?"

"I don't know." Rogers feels uncomfortable being on the highway, exposed, unsure of whether the two mysterious men might reappear, or even, possibly, the police. Checking his smartphone, he notices there's no reception here. He starts walking down the road toward the river and Julian follows.

Further down the hill, water gushes down a shallow drainage ditch along the left side of the narrow asphalt road, separating the road from a small group of two-story buildings, some with red brick walls, some with bare concrete, stained black in places. Towering up behind the buildings on the right is a long-distance electric utility tower carrying seven distinct levels of electric cabling. A building on the left announces Public Toilet in large artless hand-painted Chinese characters, with two entrances, individually identified by the Chinese characters for Men and Women, opening right onto the road over miniature concrete bridges. A broken block of concrete rests haphazardly in the drainage ditch just past the bridges, diverting its muddy waters out onto and across the asphalt road. Rogers and Julian are forced to perform a tortuous dance through the wash, stretching to cross the rivulets. Their shoes slowly disappear under an accumulation of mud splatters.

Just as with what had happened to Rogers and Julian, a car had stopped behind Breg and Miller's taxi and two men had come over to accuse them of transmitting illegally. The two men, speaking directly to Breg and Miller in English, had demanded to see their passports. In light of Rogers's call just a minute earlier, Breg, too, had requested that their taxi driver get going. Miller, sitting in the back seat, had turned off their transceiver and had quickly repacked all of their equipment and shoved the pack down to the floor between his legs to make it less visible.

Now, the two men's car has caught up and is driving alongside them. The taxi driver rolls down his window and sticks his arm out to wave the car along, but the car continues to follow alongside, with its passenger making hand gestures to get the taxi to stop. This is increasingly annoying to the taxi driver.

The taxi driver swears under his breath as he rolls up the window. He slams on the brakes just after passing an intersection, then backs up into it and turns into the crossing road and out of view. The other car, having continued straight along the narrow road, can't immediately turn around, and the taxi gains some separation from it.

Another minute later, going around a curve in the road, the taxi driver turns right down a side road. He turns his head to look out the back window to check whether he is still being followed. Turning to face forward again, he sees the road suddenly dip down and disappear into floodwaters. He hits the brakes, but he can't stop on time, and the taxi hits the water with a large splash.

The taxi floats in the water and starts to drift. The driver, muttering under his breath, quickly shifts into reverse and tries to back the car up to the road, using the spin of the tires to create a force in the water, but the car veers instead. The driver tries to correct with steering, but it's hopeless. The drift is too great and the car is sinking. Water starts flooding in.

With the heavy rain banging on the roof and the turbulence of the floodwaters, the taxi driver has to yell to be heard. He flings one arm toward the front passenger-side window. "Go! *Ba chuanghu dakai!*" The taxi driver rolls down his window and climbs out head-first on his back, squeezing past the steering wheel and pushing from his seat out into the water.

Miller tries to open his door, but the pressure of the water on the door is already too great and it doesn't budge. Water is filling in around his feet and he instinctively pulls his pack up off the floor and onto the seat next to him. He starts to panic, but then he notices that the driver had opened his window. He opens his own window and tries to crawl through it. He barely fits and struggles to get out. Breg, not as tall as Miller, but also having a large girth and broad shoulders, also struggles to get out through his window.

The taxi driver grabs the window sill of the driver side window. He tries to crawl up on top of the roof, but he keeps slipping, the car by this time floating with a forward tilt, the front end dipping under the water due to the weight of the engine, and he gives up and swims into the water.

Hanging onto the taxi's passenger side window pillar, Miller looks in through the back passenger window as the taxi continues to sink. Seeing his pack resting on the back seat, he reaches in and tries zipping one of the heat vents closed to keep water out long enough to swim with the pack to shore, but the zipper won't pull closed with just one hand, so he reaches in with both arms, hanging onto the window sill with his elbows, and uses both hands to zip the vents closed. His elbows slip when the taxi suddenly rocks, so he grabs at the pack, catching one corner of it with one hand, pulling it through the window as he falls backward into the churning floodwaters. The backpack slips from his grip just as he submerges. Re-emerging, he gasps, then wipes his face and scans the floodwaters for the backpack, but it has already disappeared from view. With the rain splashing in his eyes, he has to squint, repeatedly wiping away the rain to see. He grabs at the taxi and pulls himself through the water to get around to the other side of the vehicle, downstream of the current, but he still can't locate the backpack.

Finally abandoning the taxi, Miller swims, then half crawls, to get out of the muddy waters, eventually reaching a muddy field adjacent to the road. "Frickin' hell!" He searches for Breg to see if he needs any help. The taxi driver, being more nimble, has already swum ashore and is also standing in the field, trying to get his smartphone to work with his muddy fingers. He glances from time to time at his taxi, which has come to a stop, almost completely submerged, not far from where they had bailed out.

Seeing that Breg has also made it ashore safely, Miller immediately sets about looking for the backpack again. He jogs along the water's edge, slowed by thick cakes of mud clinging to the bottoms of his shoes, visually scanning the water's choppy surface as he goes. He considers wading back into the river to search under the water, in case the backpack has settled somewhere near the edge, but decides against it. The flood is due to the overflow of a river and the waters are still rising. The river is turbid and the current is rapid, with whitecaps further out toward the center. Close to exhaustion, he trudges along the water's edge instead, squinting into the distance, trying to catch a glimpse of the dark gray fabric, but after another fifteen minutes of this, it looks hopeless to him and he gives up altogether.

When Miller finds Breg again, he has a flustered expression. Breg studies Miller's face but doesn't say anything. He turns his attention to finding Rogers and Julian so that they can regroup.

A new form of potentiation

Breg and Miller are drenched and covered in mud. Despite the continuing rain, they don't wash clean. Rogers and Julian walk with them along the side of the road.

Off to the right, a series of bright strobe lights flash high over the swollen river, cargo drones flying up its course toward Beijing's Western Hills, their motions hardly perturbed by the winds and rains due to their weight. A rack suspended from the bottom of each drone holds a cargo box three feet long, two feet wide and eighteen inches thick, large enough to carry a half ton of cargo and 280 pounds of batteries to power the flight.

To the left of the road, concrete high-rise apartment buildings are under construction, each wrapped with a green netting and supplied by towering yellow cranes. The whole complex is surrounded by wood panel fencing covered with depictions of the buildings and announcements in Chinese characters. Giant QR codes can be scanned by interested passers-by with their smartphones for more information. A muddy field stretches from the roadside to the construction fencing.

A couple of hours have passed since the four were chased by the mysterious men, and for the most part, their anxiety has quieted. They haven't said much to one another all this time, but finally, more relaxed, they start to chat.

"Could the mind device read our own minds as a way of talking to our target?" Miller points to Julian's backpack. "It's a frickin' problem if they see us talking." He has to raise his voice to be heard, due to the noise of the rainfall. He squints in the rain. His umbrella had gone down with the taxi.

Julian doesn't respond immediately. He looks down at his muddy shoes, soaked through and squishy, despite his antenna-umbrella, then he looks down the road ahead. At length, he responds to Miller's question. "It is possible." Then after another long silence, he explains further. "A second transceiver unit can be connected to the laptop. If there is enough computing power to process the signals, this could be possible. And so, you have two transceivers and two interfaces to two people. These could be linked together."

Miller tries to visualize this and then the idea becomes clear to him. Julian's system could provide direct mind-to-mind communication, with the laptop and its two transceivers acting as a bridge. "Frickin' real," he says. He's not sure he wants it to read his mind, though. He mulls it over. "Does it do anything bad to your brain?"

Julian takes his time with the question. "This depends on what you mean by *bad*," he says, finally. "A new form of potentiation is induced."

Miller doesn't know what this means, but he doesn't pursue it.

As they walk, they try to hail a taxi, but one taxi after another passes them by, though only rarely, and always carrying passengers. They are not familiar with the smartphone apps that Chinese locals use to call taxis, having followed their target to China with little preparation. Getting a taxi without one of the apps is close to impossible on the outskirts of the city. All they can do is to try to flag down a taxi on the street. But no one flags down taxis on the street here any more.

Finally, after a very long while, an empty taxi slows down and the driver looks over at them, and then takes off again. They're not sure what went wrong, but they guess that the two of them that are covered in mud may have been off-putting to the driver. But then again, taxis may not want to pick up passengers in certain parts of town. And many taxi drivers in China prefer not to pick up foreigners, perhaps not wanting to deal with a language barrier.

They separate into two groups, with mud-covered Breg and Miller walking much further ahead, trying to appear unassociated with Rogers and Julian, and far enough ahead that their mud-covered clothing wouldn't be apparent. When the next empty taxi finally slows down and stops, Rogers and Julian get into the back seat, leaving the door open. Rogers keeps the driver busy with the question of their destination while Breg and Miller rush over to get in, with Breg sitting in front and Miller in back.

The taxi driver immediately starts complaining in Chinese, waving his arm, indicating they should get out. "No good!" he says in English.

Breg struggles with his leather wallet, which, thoroughly soaked, is sticking inside the rear pocket of his pants. He eventually wrests it free and digs out a good sum of wet Chinese cash and offers it to the driver.

Thinking of the mess he's going to have to clean up before he can pick up another fare, the driver continues trying to get them to exit the taxi. Breg gives him a pleading look, saying *xiexie, xiexie* repeatedly, pronouncing it shay shay with a strong accent, one of the few Chinese words he picked up for the trip. "Thank you, thank you," he says. He can't help but repeat it in English.

The taxi driver vacillates. They're offering him soggy cash, rather than paying with the preferred method of booking the trip with an app. But then he decides it's too late to prevent the mess, anyway. The foreign mud devils have already marked their presence. He waves off the cash and points at the meter, expecting to be paid at the end of the trip instead. "Where go?" he says in English.

Breg digs into his wallet again and carefully works a soggy business card from the hotel out of it, tearing it in the process. Assembling the two pieces on his hand, he shows the card to the driver. Without saying anything, the driver looks at the card, then starts the meter and accelerates into the rain. Breg stacks the two pieces, then slides them carefully back into his wallet, thinking to himself that he should have taken a picture of it with his phone back in the hotel.

With the taxi now in motion, the exhausted passengers lie back and close their eyes, immediately drifting off to sleep.

One system left

Soaking wet and leaving a trail of muddy footprints behind them on the hotel lobby's marble floor, the four of them board the elevator together. Breg and Julian, staying on the same floor, get out first and walk down the hall to their rooms, pausing in front of Julian's room.

"This is crazy." Julian says this to no one in particular.

"I had no idea Beijing would be like this," Breg says. "This really is crazy."

"Not Beijing. The whole thing. We run around the world like we are in some kind of crazy movie. But the targets…they are nothing. Peter, he is like me. He plays with technology. So what? And the other man is just a friend. What have they done?"

Breg thinks it over. The contract has brought in over a million dollars to date. Not bad for their first year as a team. For the client to pay that much, there must have been a good reason.

"As you know, that's confidential." He glances down the hallway at his own hotel room door, then turns back to Julian. "Our client knows what they're doing. Our job is just to gather the specific intel they require."

Julian sets his antenna-umbrella down so that it rests on its tip. "What is this intel we gather? The kind of bagels they eat?"

"There's also the element of prevention. Until the issue is resolved."

Julian doesn't say anything in response. He stares at his muddy shoes.

"We'll talk in the morning." Breg starts to walk to his room but hesitates and turns back to Julian.

Julian looks up at Breg, then stares off in the distance. "Actually, I will take a bit of a break."

"A break?"

"To sort things out. See where my head is at."

Looking at Julian's expression, Breg can see his weariness. "Anywhere in particular?"

"Back to Berlin. Friends. Family."

"Sure. …Sure. How long?"

Looking back down at the floor, Julian taps the tip of his antenna-umbrella and water droplets fall in a pattern on the carpet. "I am not so sure." He doesn't say this, but he is figuring on looking into other opportunities. He has more or less decided Breg is not for him.

"Sure. Let me know."

Breg turns to go as Julian enters his room, carrying in his backpack the remaining mind device.

The Uncertainty Principle

So you ask them: Why would
you think they are?

And they respond: That's the problem. How
do we know they aren't?

The Magpie

Leon Theremin was an inmate at Central Design Bureau 29, ordered by the Soviet State to develop signaling and measurement devices: Radio beacons to locate downed planes and lost submarines, an electronic bugging device, a surveillance microphone that works from a distance by projecting an invisible infrared light beam onto a building's window to detect sound vibrations.

He was already famous as the inventor of the Theremin, an electronic musical instrument named after him whose musical notes are played by moving one's hands near two attached antennas. Just nine years before becoming an inmate, his instrument had been used to perform on stage at Carnegie Hall in New York City, where he lived. In the 1920s, he experimented in the development of television. And in 1934, he started a company which promised a burglar alarm that would detect anyone approaching it. The alarm, which worked on the same principle used in the musical instrument to detect the positions of the hands, could even be used to trigger a 1930s-era movie camera to record the burglar. His company, Teletouch Corporation, also built and installed the first metal detectors used at the Federal penitentiary on Alcatraz Island in San Francisco Bay.

For ten years, he lived a life of inventing and entrepreneurship in the United States, until in 1938, he mysteriously disappeared, returning without explanation to his home country, the Soviet Union.

Not long after his return, Theremin was imprisoned, and not long after that, he was transferred to Central Design Bureau 29. There, he invented an electronic bugging device designed to operate without batteries or other sources of power and without any wiring. The genius of his device was that it could listen in on conversations in a room using only the power transmitted to it from a distance, from outside the room.

The bug, consisting of nothing more than a metal rod, a metal capsule, and a few smaller elements, was hidden inside a beautiful wood carving of the Great Seal of the United States. The carving, with the bug inside, was given in 1945 as a gift from the Soviet people to the US Embassy in Moscow where it was hung on a wall in the ambassador's residence on the second floor of the embassy building, just to the left of the ambassador's desk.

The Soviets would park outside the embassy and would power the bug by beaming microwaves at it, and these microwaves would collect in the metal capsule. A tiny hole under the beak of the eagle in the carving allowed the sounds of conversations in the room to enter the carving and make their way to the bug, vibrating a thin metal membrane in the metal capsule and imprinting the sound waves onto the microwaves. The metal capsule, in this way, behaved like a microphone. These imprinted microwaves then carried the sounds of the conversations out of the room, retransmitted from the metal rod with the power supplied by the microwaves, allowing the conversations to be heard by a radio receiver outside of the embassy.

The Great Seal bug, as it became known, was so effective and so well hidden that it wasn't discovered for years. The first hint of its existence emerged in 1951 when a nearby British radio operator overheard radio transmissions of what sounded like Americans having a discussion, and there was a question of who was transmitting those conversations. Or so the story went. In any case, suspicions were raised.

A sweep was made through the embassy, looking for transmitters, but initially, none were found. The problem was that the surveillance bug was difficult to detect because it would only transmit when illuminated by the van outside. It was discovered only later, when the bug happened to be transmitting during another sweep. Even then, the operation of the bug was not understood until additional research by government agencies was carried out.

After his success with the Great Seal Bug, Theremin continued with his development work at Central Design Bureau 29. In 1947, he was ordered to develop a wireless audio surveillance device, codenamed BURAN, the Russian word for Snowstorm. This device worked by directing an infrared beam, invisible light, at window glass. Vibrating with sound from inside the building under surveillance, the glass would imprint the sound onto the infrared beam by vibrating the beam's reflection. The imprinted reflections could then be detected and converted back into sound from a distance. A later implementation of the device would use a laser, with a narrow beam that keeps a tighter focus, allowing it to operate from much further away than the original device.

Tick, tick, tick, tick, tick...

Berlin, Monday, 26 August 2024

Julian is wearing skinny black jeans, a black T-shirt, a new pair of black and white sneakers, and the dark-gray backpack with his laptop and other equipment. He's pulling a black leather carry-on bag behind him.

The taxi ride from Berlin Brandenburg airport to his parents' home in Mitte, Berlin's central district, takes forty minutes. The city is quiet at this time of night and traffic is light. The sky is clear and dark.

The apartment is on the third floor of a simple cream colored four-story building. His parents answer the door and let him in. Kicking his shoes off on the parquet floor, he briefly chats with them, then dumps his backpack and carry-on in his bedroom and cleans himself up. He's exhausted from the long trip.

Sitting on his bed, he leans over the side and pulls his equipment out from his backpack and sets it on his nightstand. He connects the transceiver to the laptop, then signs in, navigates to the *Miscellaneous* screen, and selects an option to mitigate his jet lag with electronically enhanced sleep, dialing in a short time delay to give himself a chance to settle in before the effect ramps up. He turns off the light, lies back in bed, and closes his eyes.

The electronic effect gradually takes over, calming his mind. His body feels comfortably warm and cocooned. His muscles relax. Within minutes, he is sound asleep. Over the next twenty minutes, the mind device monitors his mental state to ensure that he has stabilized in the sleep state, then fades out the effect. A few seconds later, it powers itself off.

Beijing, Monday, 26 August 2024

The storm has dissipated, though evidence of it remains. Urban ponds slowly evaporate in the hot sun. City workers are hosing down the roads of Haidian District as merchants shovel mud from the fronts of their shops.

Ethan, still in Beijing, receives a call from the hotel he had booked, the one he had been en route to in his taxi on arrival. The hotel tells him someone has dropped off a dark gray nylon backpack for him. They didn't leave their name, instead showing the receptionist a small slip of paper that had been found in the backpack with Ethan's name and the hotel's name and address on it. When the hotel checked the name in their records, they noted that he had reservations to stay with them during this period and looked up his contact information, and would he like to come and pick it up?

Ethan is puzzled and says he doesn't know anything about it. He tells the caller that they must be mistaken. The caller apologizes and hangs up. But something about it bugs him. He quickly calls back. He'll be right over.

When he gets to the hotel, he asks about the backpack at the front desk and the receptionist, a tall thin woman wearing the hotel's gray-and-red uniform, tells him she was the one who had called. She goes into a back room and retrieves a large white plastic shopping bag. Opening the bag, Ethan sees that the backpack inside is covered with dried mud. It smells faintly of decaying vegetable matter. The woman explains that the man who had dropped it off had found it by a river, sitting in the mud after the recent floodwaters had receded. Ethan thanks the woman and takes the bag and its contents with him, hailing another taxi to return to his parents' rental apartment.

Sitting in the back seat of the taxi, he carefully opens each of the backpack's pockets and works its zipped flaps, opening and closing three nylon mesh air vents located on the lower sides and at the top of the pack. The vents puzzle him. Air circulation for a pet, perhaps? None of the smaller pockets have anything in them, but inside the main compartment, he finds a laptop, a black plastic and metal box with switches and connection ports, a battery pack, data and power cables, an odd cone-shaped metal object, two water bottles, one empty and the other one-third full, and the slip of paper with his name and the hotel name and address scrawled on it in pencil. Splatters of mud cover everything.

He tries to imagine who would have written down his name and hotel. And why? He briefly considers the possibility that it's a coincidence, someone else with the name Chen Yili. But what about the hotel? The note was written with English letters. That's a clue.

Then a tingling sensation spreads over his whole body. It is almost unbelievable that he would get his hands on the equipment his stalkers were using, but that's the best explanation he can come up with.

Is this the equipment they used to read his mind? He thinks back to the engineers' demonstration at Zai which used nothing more than a laptop and some additional electronics.

Looking over the black box, it is clear from the ports and switches that it is an electronic device, but he sees no labels which give away its purpose, no manufacturer's name, no product name. It appears to be hand-assembled, lacking the finished look of a professionally manufactured product.

He returns the black box to the backpack. Lacking a handkerchief, he cleans the mud off his hands by rubbing them together inside the plastic bag.

He can't believe his luck. The enemy dropped their weapon, and here it is now, resting in his lap. Should he take it to the police? He's not sure. They'd probably not believe him, at least not as things stand.

He tells the taxi driver his new destination. The backpack needs to be examined by the engineers at Zai.

Just as the elevator doors are closing in front of Ethan, Zhuang Rongtao reaches in and pulls the door back open. He slips into the elevator with Ethan, carrying a latte from the building's ground floor café.

"Shopping?"

"Oh, this?" Ethan glances down at the white shopping bag. "It was delivered to me at the hotel."

The elevator door closes.

"You're in a hotel? I thought you were staying at your folks' place."

"Long story."

"Hey, before I forget: we contacted the police and explained that there were men illegally transmitting here. We gave them a copy of our notes on their radio transmissions and their locations. Oh, and the taxi license plate numbers, too. That should be a good clue. None of the pictures we took turned out, though we did give a description of what the men looked like."

Ethan is surprised. "Oh? So what's next? Have they started searching for the men?"

"They didn't say, but, well... They were professional about it and thanked me for the information."

"I suppose they could connect the taxi license plates with the city's video surveillance wherever they got on. It wouldn't be hard to go from there to the men's photos from when they entered the country. With over a billion video surveillance cameras in China, all programmed with AI for face recognition, it couldn't be harder than typing a few keystrokes to identify them."

"That would make sense," says Zhuang Rongtao. "Or they could just make the connection through the app that the men used to call the taxi."

"True."

"But I don't think the police will tell us who they are."

"Why wouldn't they?" Ethan had never been a victim of a crime before, not in the U.S., nor in China. He's actually not sure what happens when you report a crime.

The elevator doors open and they exit, continuing their conversation in the hallway on Zai's floor.

"Well...they asked me how I knew about the transmissions. So I explained that we intercepted the signals while the men were reading your mind with their equipment. That may have been a mistake."

"Oh." Ethan now sees where Zhuang Rongtao is going with his point.

"As soon as I mentioned that, the public security officer stopped typing in the report and looked over at me. Then he became *more* professional, uh, I suppose I mean more formal, and he politely finished up, taking my report without any further questions."

Ethan offers no comment. It's clear they're still on their own until they can build up enough evidence.

Zhuang Rongtao takes a sip of his latte, then asks Ethan whether he has heard the voices again since that day.

"No, in fact."

"We kept the signal trackers turned on all weekend. Nothing."

"There may be a reason for that," Ethan says. "Let me show you what's in the bag."

Entering Zai's office with Zhuang Rongtao, Ethan goes through a round of greetings with the engineers, then takes out the gray backpack and its contents and spreads it all out on the floor. "It's a mess," Ethan says to the group, "but what I think we have here is the system used by the voices to talk inside my head. At least, one of the systems."

"The taxi spies?" asks Cheng Fengxiang.

Ethan smiles. "Is that what you're calling them now?"

The engineers form a semicircle around the equipment to look it over. The laptop and cables, the water bottles, the metal cone, the unlabeled electronic device with its switches and ports. There's not really much to look at, but they know better. Looks aren't everything. The real genius is in the software.

Cheng Penglu asks whether the conical metal object might be a fancy antenna. He bends over to get a better look at it. “I don’t see how you’d hook it up. It should have a cable connector or something.”

Ke Qunxiang picks it up and studies it. “It would be a rather unusual antenna.” The expression on his face shows clear doubt. He sets it back down, then rubs his fingers and blows the dirt off.

“How did you get your hands on their equipment?” asks Cheng Fengxiang.

“They had it delivered it to me.” Ethan says this with a straight face.

“Oh. That’s convenient.”

“I have to return to the US tomorrow,” Ethan says. “Could I just leave this with you all to look through? I’m not sure what I would do with it.” He looks over at Zhuang Rongtao. “Is that OK?”

“We’ll take a look.”

“I’ve got some things to wrap up before leaving, so I should get going,” Ethan says. “See you all at dinner tonight.”

Wednesday, 18 September 2024

Julian’s eyes open slowly. His toes feel like they are being pricked by tiny needles. He wiggles his toes to make the sensation go away, but the prickling continues, moving up through his feet, then his calves, then his thighs. It rapidly advances through his torso, outward and down each arm to his fingertips. Then the sensation jumps to his neck. It crosses behind his head and continues up over the top of his scalp, then scans down the front of his face. It finishes by closing in around his lips, diminishing from needle pricks to gentle tingling. When the tingling finally stops, his lips feel slightly numb.

He continues to lie on his back, unmoving, waiting for a further clue as to what is happening. Dim light filters into the room through the window blinds. He hears a truck rumble by outside, down at street level, and then it is quiet.

A series of gentle muscle contractions start rolling down from his head to his toes. The muscles on both sides of his body are activated together, in perfect synchronization. Reaching his toes, the process reverses, going from toes to head. It feels to Julian like a massage, but there is no cause. He tries to remember what he knows about the brain's motor control, thinking that he may be experiencing a seizure. He drums the fingers of his hands on the bed. They feel normal.

He sits up, then tests his cognition. "Today is...what is today?" What did he do yesterday? "OK. Wednesday." He lifts his right arm, then his left arm, examining his right and left hands in turn. Suddenly, he hears a rapid series of sharp clicking sounds all around his head. They happen too fast to count, but he rewinds his mental buffer and replays the sounds in his head. A group of three, then another group of three, then two final clicks. The final two clicks sound different from the first six, like they occurred inside his head, not out in the room. One of the two clicks sounded *deeper* than the other, deeper inside his head.

"Eight," he says to himself. He looks around the room. There is nothing in the room which would have created the noises. It feels like he may have been hallucinating.

He hears the sound of a vehicle engine starting up below his window. The vehicle drives off. Rubbing his head, he gets out of bed and drags himself over to the window. He separates two of the blinds and looks out. The day is dreary, cloudy. It is 7:55 in the morning. His hair is wild.

"Strange." He rubs his head again, then runs his fingers through his hair to smooth it out. "Very strange." Sitting on the end of his bed, he thinks about the experience but can't come to any closure. He feels unsettled as he goes through his morning routine.

As he dresses, he plans his day. This morning, wingsuit flying practice in an indoor wind tunnel. He has been away from the sport for over a year already. He decides on Café Kastanien for lunch. In the afternoon, he is scheduled to a give a technology demonstration to a potential client.

For the past three weeks, he has been focused on finding a buyer for his technology. His cold calling has netted him three leads during this time. He has already given a demonstration to one small company here in Berlin. They had been eager to see his demonstration, inviting him to visit the very next day. Their eagerness had put him off a little, but he tried not to let that bother him, focusing instead on preparing for the visit. After the demonstration, they had a lot of questions, but in the end they said only that they would get back to him.

He is scheduled to visit another German firm, a large company, in early October, with plans to pitch the technology as a new type of computer interface, a way for computer users to enter data into their computers just by thinking.

His third lead is a Turkish-German businessman who runs a small company that acquires patents and technology and licenses them to other companies. Yesterday, he had given this man a demonstration of his technology. Today's demonstration is a follow-up with the man's technology team.

He has a fourth lead, a medical research firm, but it has already been made clear to him through a brief phone discussion that while they would be interested in learning more about his technology, they won't even consider seeing a demonstration unless he has applied for patents, explaining that this is for both his and their protection. Thus far, he has not applied for patents. The lawyers once told him it would cost him 5,000 euros and up for each patent. He's not sure how many patents he would need. Ten, twenty maybe. It would be a major investment for him.

With Breg, he worked around the problem of protecting his technology by agreeing to supply complete systems, the combination of laptop, transceiver equipment, cabling and other devices and software. He had ensured that the laptops were highly secure, including the use of hardware encryption for data storage. He protected the software itself with an additional layer of encryption. And he was part of the deal. He would always be there with the systems as a technology consultant.

He hears a light knock on his bedroom door. His mother announces that she is going to work now. She doesn't wait for a response. He hears the front door open and close.

Nebraska Night Club

Jessica brushes her long red hair to the side. "Thilo, get me another drink, would you, you are so sweet."

Anika turns to Julian. "I heard you were in the States for a year." She is animated.

Julian nods, then sips from his own drink.

"So, how is it there? You must be so out of it, you didn't even bring someone with you today."

"It was busy," he says.

"He will find a lady," Jonas says. "Just give him some time. How long have you been back, Julian?"

"It has been a month."

Jonas turns to his girlfriend. “So you see, he has only been back a month, Anika.”

The friends raise their voices to talk over the music. It is still subdued, a slow deep beat, but not quiet. The whole club pulses with a dim red light. It’s not even midnight yet. No one is out on the dance floor.

Jessica slowly rolls her head with the music as Thilo returns with her drink which she immediately sips from and sets down at their table. Thilo sits next to her in the high-backed semicircular velvet sofa that they share and sets his own drink down. The bases and stems of the drink glasses glow softly with swirls of blue and green europium phosphors that are charged daily in a light chamber behind the bar.

The night club, in a basement on Dircksenstrasse in Mitte, right across the cobblestoned street from Berlin’s Stadtbahn elevated train line, is reached via an iron staircase which leads down from street level. The walls are red brick, draped with green chiffon curtains.

Thilo and Jonas discuss the upcoming round on the race calendar for the Deutsche Tourenwagen Masters grand touring car races, comparing the cars fielded by the teams, cars from Mercedes and BMW and Audi and others, and the engines, which range from 500 to 700 horsepower and up. Julian listens in, but is not familiar with the races. Anika leans her head on Jonas’ shoulder and wraps her arm around his waist.

They turn to Julian, with Thilo asking: “And what are your plans for the weekend, Julian?”

Julian is in a good mood. His technology demonstration earlier today to the Turkish-German businessman went well. The businessman offered to make the process simple: An outright purchase contingent on expert observation of the functionality in an acceptance demonstration. No patent applications would be required. They would accept Julian’s software, the working devices, and documentation and would build a specification from those. The businessman will be contacting him again in the near future to explain the process and to set up the meeting.

Julian explains that because of his good news, he has decided to take a break from his search for a buyer. He is planning a wingsuit flying trip with Karl and Anton.

The others tell him he’s crazy, and so are Karl and Anton. Wingsuiting is dangerous. Julian says it is how he stays awake. Software development all day long is a drain. And anyway, he says, it is just a matter of diligence and focus. You must practice. You must be careful. And then wingsuit flying is safe. Jonas asks why he would jump out of a perfectly good cliff, even if he does have a parachute? It’s not like the cliff is going to crash. Thilo and the two women laugh.

“So what is this thing you said you are selling?” Jonas asks.

“He said it’s mind reading,” Jessica says. Thilo glances over at her.

“Is that what you said? I missed that.” Jonas sips his drink.

"It is mind reading," Julian says. "And it is more than that."

The club starts to fill up and there are people dancing now. The beat of the music has picked up and the club's red glow now flashes purple.

Thilo says there's no such thing, and Jonas says no, he saw a video about that. You put on a headset and you can make a computer do things just by thinking. Julian explains that it's like that. That's what he started with. He paid for monthly access to a technology prototyping workshop here in Berlin, a makerspace funded by an industry billionaire to help encourage German innovation. They have everything, he says. Signal generators, radio equipment, electronics fabrication. What they didn't have, he got by contacting component suppliers and asking for free samples. He spent a lot of time there. But once he had the electronics working, it was mainly software development, and he worked on that at home.

Anika asks how it works and Julian explains. A mind-reading headset is like the EEG that a doctor uses to check your brainwaves. It has sensors that fit over your head. The problem is, neurons are fast, but EEGs are slow. So the headset doesn't work very well. It's too slow. You could move a cursor on a computer screen, but you can't get sound out of the head that way. Sampling theory. It's all about the math. EEG gets 600 pieces of data each second. But to get sound, you need thousands. If you want pictures from the head, you need even more. The headset could never do that.

Both Anika and Jessica pay close attention to Julian's explanation. Jonas relaxes into the sofa, taking in only the general idea. Thilo asks how you can get thousands of pieces of data every second from the head. Julian leans forward and says: "Listen carefully. Using radio."

Thilo is taken aback, then he gets it. He's an engineer. "Of course," he says. "The signals from the brain are difficult to detect. That's very funny. Listen carefully. That's very, very funny."

"It is true, the signals are weak. So, first," Julian says, "you must start with a strong signal. Like when a person blinks."

Jonas perks up. "No kidding. A blink."

"There are better ways, but I started with blinks."

Thilo asks: "Why blinks?"

"In an EEG, you can see the blinks," Julian says. "They are big signals. Doctors remove them from the data to study brainwaves because they get in the way." He says it's not hard to force someone to blink with a radio signal. And using a radio receiver, you can see their brainwaves change when they blink. It's a bootstrap process from there. Once you can force someone to blink, you can keep going to learn how to make other things happen.

Anika and Jessica don't know what a bootstrap process is, and they don't ask. But Thilo wants to hear more, so Julian continues. He had wanted to create two-way communication with the brain using radio. But how can you make the brain hear radio waves?

His solution was this: When you talk to the brain with the radio, you send a blink with it. You force the blink and it helps the brain to hear the radio. It trains it. Without the training, the radio waves have only a very tiny, weak effect, and you wouldn't notice them. But with training, the brain learns to hear it. It's like the way you can condition animals in experiments. Just like with Pavlov's dog, he says. And after some practice, the brain no longer needs to receive the forced blink. It can hear the radio signals without it. At the same time, you can watch what the brainwaves look like when the brain hears. And it goes from there.

"I call it the Geistgerät. The mind device."

"Is it only the mind, or is it also the spirit?" Jessica asks. "Does it understand the soul?"

"He said it's radio," Jonas says. "So it's a radio device for the mind."

"From how far away does it work?" Thilo is thinking like an engineer.

"At first, a few centimeters."

"Ah, then it must be like a headset?" Thilo wonders.

"That's just like I saw in that video, then," adds Jonas. "You put on the headset and —"

Julian interrupts. "No. That was just the beginning."

"OK, so." Jonas is not sure what to say, but finally asks: "Then how far is it now?"

"A kilometer," Julian says.

"A kilometer. Really." Jonas shakes his head in disbelief.

The five of them each sip their drinks, watching the crowd on the dance floor. The music has picked up.

Jonas turns to Julian again. "How can you do that?"

"What?"

"A kilometer. I don't believe it."

"One must solve an inverse problem," Julian says.

Jonas appears annoyed. He sips his drink, then returns to looking out at the dance floor. Thilo picks up the point. "For the ladies, tell them, Julian, what is an inverse problem?"

Julian is stuck. How does one explain the concept of an inverse problem to non-engineers? "OK, so someone gives you lemons. And you make lemonade. You cut the lemons, you squeeze them, you add cold water and sugar. Lemonade."

He pauses and the girlfriends lean forward expectantly.

Anika comments: "But of course, you would also add a teaspoon of jam and some mint. And you also, absolutely, must include the lemon zest." She turns to look at Jonas. Her shoulder-length blonde hair swirls about her. "Don't you agree, Jonas? Isn't that how you like it?" Jonas doesn't respond.

Julian continues. "Just so. And what do you do if you have only lemonade, but you need a lemon?"

A puzzled look comes over Jessica's face, and then she lights up. "But wait," she says. "You would not have the pith. There is no way to make a lemon." She brushes her hair aside.

Anika has the answer. "You must make the pith."

Julian responds: "Just so. You must make the pith. The brainwaves provide the lemonade. And what was in the head is the lemon."

"Voll nice!" Jonas says. "Let's order more drinks."

The DJ switches up the music, putting on a track with an ultra-deep bass. The background lighting of the room dims and several lasers start flashing through the room in sync with the beat. A swarm of show drones flies out into the room from one corner and spins in formation over the dance floor, each drone lit with bright LEDs, also flashing with the beat.

The five friends are watching the light show when a large man walks up to Julian and, point-blank, takes a flash picture with his smartphone. Julian looks up at the stranger, a deer in the headlights, just as the flash goes off. He is temporarily blinded.

By the time Julian is able to see again, the man has disappeared into the silhouetted crowd. Lasers continue to flash overhead as the show drones swarm back into their corner.

Julian turns to his friends. "Who was that?"

"Paparazzi!" Anika says.

"Here's to Julian, our celebrity!" says Thilo, raising his drink. Anika and Jessica raise their drinks to Julian. Jonas raises his own drink. "Cheers," he says without enthusiasm.

Friday, 20 September 2024

"Cheng Fengxiang brought the laptop to a data recovery center. They recovered data from the solid-state drive, but it's encrypted. Whoever took care of this laptop took extra steps to protect it."

Ethan nods in response.

Zhuang Rongtao can see a window in the background behind Ethan's head. Ethan is at home, in his apartment in San Francisco. The sun will be setting there soon. Here in Haidian District, the sky is sunny and the mid-morning light, reflecting from the glass-clad building across the street, is streaming in through the office windows.

The contents of the gray backpack rest nearby on the desk Zhuang Rongtao is using. The black box from the backpack, its case opened and its internal circuitry exposed. The laptop, disassembled, its battery removed and its solid-state disk enclosed in an anti-static bag. The mysterious metal cone. The two water bottles. The penciled note. Data and battery cables. Everything has been cleaned up. Except for smudges on the note, not a speck of mud remains.

Zhuang Rongtao takes a sip of his morning latte, then continues. "We reverse-engineered the black box. It appears to be their radio transceiver. But it's more than just a transceiver. It has a GPU in it, built into a small single-board computer. Ke Qunxiang says the transmitting antenna operates as a phased array so it can steer radio signals in different directions without any moving parts. He says it's called beamforming. Whoever built this knew what they were doing. It's no hack job." Zhuang Rongtao holds up the transceiver for Ethan to see through the 3D video interface, pointing inside. "This is the transmitting antenna here."

Ethan shifts his head a little to get a better view.

"The really new thing, though, is the receiving antenna. It's not made of metal. Instead, the antenna uses tiny glass vials filled with Rydberg atoms."

"I've never heard of Rydberg atoms. Is that a new material?"

"Kind of. The gas inside the vials is made of cesium atoms. What makes them Rydberg atoms is that a laser is used to pump up the energy of the electrons in the atoms. It's supposed to be some kind of quantum state thing. Don't ask, I have no idea."

Ethan chuckles at this.

"You can see the lasers in the receiver, actually. See here?" Zhuang Rongtao points into one of the inside corners of the transceiver. "There are eight vials, one in each corner, and each of them has two of these tiny lasers, and also this light sensor here that converts the laser light into an electrical signal. The scientific papers we found call it a quantum receiver. Apparently, radio waves have an effect on the electrons in the atoms floating inside the glass vials and this causes the lasers to flicker. And because Rydberg atoms are super-sensitive to radio waves, the receiver works really well across the entire range of radio frequencies even though the antenna is tiny."

Ethan nods.

"Watch this." Zhuang Rongtao connects an external battery pack to the transceiver and flicks a switch on the black box to turn it on. A faint glow lights up the inside corners of the transceiver's case. "We know it's cesium because the vapor cells, that's what they call the glass vials, they glow green."

"Because it's green?"

“They seem to come in two flavors. The cesium version glows green, and a rubidium variant glows blue.”

“You said this is a new thing. Do you know who else is using this type of antenna?”

“Me? I’m no expert on antennas. But Ke Qunxiang says it’s totally new to him. He hasn’t seen it anywhere. Never even heard of it until this came along.”

“Where does one buy quantum receivers?”

“That’s a good question. We tracked down the part number printed on the quantum receiver components. None of our own suppliers knew anything about it. In fact, at this point, it’s not available through any Chinese distributors.”

“So it’s not just new to Ke Qunxiang. It’s new to the world.”

“Indeed. We had to make inquiries abroad. It turns out they’re made by a small company in Frankfurt called Schönbein-Beckhardt GmbH. They told us they’ve only been manufacturing the components for three years, and thus far, they don’t have any customers outside of Germany.”

Zhuang Rongtao powers off the transceiver, then points at the circuit board inside. “This is an accelerometer chip, and right next to it is an electronic compass. The device uses them to orient itself. That’s how they could just casually toss it in a backpack and it wouldn’t get confused about which way the signals are coming from.”

Ethan nods. “From what you’ve figured out so far, do you think it could communicate with the brain?”

“There’s no question about it. In fact, we’ve learned a couple of tricks from it that we can use in our own technology. And before you ask, no, there’s no patent for reading brainwaves like this. Whoever built it kept it secret. And stealthy.”

“Stealthy?”

“I just mean the whole two-transmitter thing. Remember that? The onboard computer runs its own software, and luckily, it’s not encrypted, so we could see the details of how it all works. As it turns out, there’s an option to use either one transmitter or two. And when they’re using two, the two onboard computers coordinate with each other to randomly split up the signal into pieces. In that case, each transmitter only sends out part of the signal.”

“Why doesn’t my own brain get confused by all of this stealthiness when they transmit voices to my head?” Ethan asks.

“The signals from the two transmitters reach your head at the same time. The onboard computers coordinate their timing to make sure of that. So the two signals stack up and make a complete brain code that your brain understands. Remember, the signals aren’t the actual sounds. They’re just brain codes. And depending on what kind of brain code it is, you hear something, or you smell something. So the brain doesn’t care about this stealthiness," Zhuang Rongtao says, "but it definitely complicates the problem of tracking down the signal. It's not just that the signal doesn't come from a single place. Each of the separate pieces doesn't even look like a brain code. That's where Peter got stuck."

"Oh..." Ethan has an expression of wonder on his face.

Zhuang Rongtao holds the metal cone up to his laptop screen. The two pairs of video cams on the two sides of the laptop transmit the 3D view of the cone to Ethan's laptop in San Francisco. "Remember this? Cheng Penglu figured it out. It's a security device, of a kind. Watch this."

Zhuang Rongtao pointedly pulls out a single small sheet of note paper and a pencil, holding them up to his screen momentarily for Ethan to see. He writes out the Chinese words for "my password", then holds the note up to the screen again. Next, he takes apart the metal cone, unhooking two tiny clips and pulling out an inner cone from the outer cone. He holds the inner cone up to the screen.

Ethan moves in a bit closer on his end of the video call to see the detail, shifting left and right to study the 3D image. He can see that the shiny metal surface is covered with a texture of tiny sharp cutting edges. From his end, Zhuang Rongtao sees Ethan's head move in 3D as Ethan studies the metal cone.

Zhuang Rongtao wraps the note paper inside the larger cone, so that it looks a little like a coffee filter. Then, holding the handle with his right hand at the top of the smaller cone, he inserts it into the larger cone, and then, holding the knurled outer surface of the outer cone with his left hand, he gently twists it back and forth a few times. He separates the inner and outer cones and pours out the pulverized contents onto his desk. He blows on the dust and it disperses. He sets the cone down.

"As you know," Zhuang Rongtao says, "it's almost impossible to get rid of information that's stored electronically. Deleting it just removes access to it, but the data is still there. Even if you write over it with new data, there may still be enough of a trace of the old data to get it back. And what if a computer virus sends it out before you erase it? How could you ever be sure it's gone?"

"True," Ethan says.

"Ironically, paper is more secure. I think that's what the cone is really about. It's how you make yourself secure in a world that seems to conspire against it."

"Where does one buy one of those things?"

"Don't know. We searched the Internet and couldn't find anything like it. It may be custom-made. There weren't any identifying marks on it."

Ethan puts his hand to his chin, thinking. "You know what? We totally overlooked something. Fingerprints."

Zhuang Rongtao's eyebrows jump in surprise. "Didn't think of that!" He looks over the metal cone, then glances over at the laptop and the transceiver sitting nearby. "We cleaned everything up already."

"I doubt fingerprints would have survived the immersion in the river, anyway," Ethan says.

"Probably not." Zhuang Rongtao shakes his head. "Why didn't we think of that?"

"Did the team ever figure out how to turn brain codes back into sounds?"

Zhuang Rongtao tries to remember where they left off since the last time they talked. "Oh, right. We didn't have that working yet when you went back to the States. Yeah, it works. Full two-way communication between the transceiver and the brain. It's not perfect. It glitches sometimes and loses sync. They're still trying to figure out why that happens. But it works. I'd give you a demo, but you're out of range."

Ethan laughs. "So then, what is the range?"

"It's not like the range of the system in the backpack. We're still studying it to see how it gets such a huge range. The best we can do so far is two meters."

"Still, not bad. Besides spying on people, I wonder what else you could use it for."

"People have been talking for years about sending texts just by thinking. We can do that now. And it's way better than the earlier idea we had for controlling our augmented reality goggles. As to other applications...it is an amazing trick sending a message just by thinking, but I'm not sure who would pay for it. It's a little clunky. It wouldn't fit in your pocket. So you'd be tied down with this brick of an interface just so you could avoid typing."

Ethan agrees. "Technology can be like that. Solutions looking for a problem. The trick is in finding just the right product and market."

"The team thinks virtual odors have more potential. So we're going to be focusing more on that for now, building it into our virtual reality system."

As San Francisco's patch on the planet continues its soundless rotation east, the natural light from the window behind Ethan rapidly fades. Ethan has to squint to see his screen.

"Hold on a moment."

Zhuang Rongtao drinks down the last of his latte as the lights go on in Ethan's apartment. A few seconds later, Ethan is sitting in front of the camera again.

"Oh, before I forget. After you left, we kept the signal trackers turned on. And something triggered them. We thought it might have been them again, so we got in the car and tried to find them. But the signal disappeared almost as soon as we got in."

"When was that?"

"Like a week after you left."

"So they were still there, even after I left?"

"Maybe. I'm not sure," Zhuang Rongtao says. "There was something different about the signals. Ke Qunxiang said that, assuming their second transmitter was identical to the first, there's no way it could have generated these signals. The frequency range went too high."

Tuesday, 24 September 2024

Julian, Karl, and Anton fly into Bern, then travel by train to the village of Lauterbrunnen, population 2230, where they stay overnight. Dinner is burgers and fries at a small cafe on the first floor of their hotel.

The next morning, Lauterbrunnen Valley is quiet and cold. Steep granite mountains rise high on both sides of the valley, which is narrow, only a half mile wide along most of its length. Snow covers the highest range of peaks around the valley. In the village, which is about half-way up the valley as it rises from the small town of Interlaken at one end into the Alps at the other, geraniums bloom in planters set around balconies. There is no traffic on the small roads.

At breakfast, the three friends talk about their previous wingsuit trips. Karl has the most experience. He has been flying for five years. He has flown in Norway and France and Switzerland. This is the second trip to Switzerland for Julian. The last time was with the same two friends, two years ago.

After lunch, they pick up their landing cards, paying the fees that reimburse farmers for the use of their fields for landing, then head up to the tiny village of Mürren, which is situated atop the cliffs on one side of the valley. They ride the aerial cableway, the Grütschalpbahn, from the Lauterbrunnen BLM station in the valley up to Grütschalp Station, rising 2264 feet from the valley floor, then continue on the connecting inclined railway, with its brown-and-yellow electric train car, arriving at Mürren BLM Station just before 2 PM. It is a short walk to the cliff area where they will jump.

Each wingsuit jump point in Lauterbrunnen Valley has its own name. Yellow Ocean, La Mousse. Nose 1, Nose 2, Nose 3, and High Nose. Dumpster. Flower Box. And several others. Each exit point has its own characteristics and its own risks. Some are recommended for intermediate jumpers, while others only for those with advanced experience and skills. None of the jumps in Lauterbrunnen Valley are recommended for beginners.

The three friends will be jumping from Low Ultimate. This exit point has a rockdrop distance of 1080 feet. The base of the cliff continues to slope out as it drops, so that the overall drop to the landing point is 2290 feet. As the landing point is quite distant from the cliff, it is as much flying as it is jumping. The wingsuits, worn over the flyers' street clothes, are carefully designed to provide lift and control along a flight path, allowing one to steer much the same way a glider does. But the suit is a minimal glider. Webbed arms form the wings and webbed legs, the tail wing. A paraglider, a parachute shaped like a wing, is connected to a harness worn by the flyer under the wingsuit and is packed in a bag on the back of the suit. The wingsuit flyer deploys the paraglider by pulling a cord that dangles at the back of the suit. Because the wingsuit flies too fast and at too steep an angle to land safely, the paraglider is deployed near the end of the flight to provide for a slow, controlled landing.

Putting on their wingsuits in a grassy area beside the road, not far from the cliff edge, they leave the zippers along the arms and legs of their suits open for now for more maneuverability. They will close these zippers before their jumps. The fabric of the suits swings freely as the friends hike single-file along a narrow dirt trail that meanders between small trees. It is cumbersome hiking in the wingsuits, with their ripstop nylon webbing under the arms and between the legs, but there will be no way to change into them at the narrow ledge which is the exit point. The temperature is a cool 55 degrees and the air is still and dry.

A man watches through binoculars from the driver's seat of a cargo van parked by the road on the valley floor, scanning the cliffs, checking and double-checking his reference points. He braces the binoculars against the left side of his opened window to steady his view.

The cliffs are high and the trees along their tops appear small from this distance. To the left, a larger waterfall. Far to the right, a small one. He returns to his primary reference point between the two, high up, near the top, to his left. So far, nothing. He waits.

Hiking for several minutes, the friends reach a tree with a thick rope wrapped around it. The rope extends down to the right, over the edge of the cliff. This is their way down to the exit point.

Julian turns on his helmet video cams, one facing forward and the other back. Karl, in the lead, turns and announces: "See you at the ledge", and Julian and Anton give thumbs up.

One by one, they tie into the rope with carabiners, and then, grasping the rope with bare hands, they each make their way down the steep slope. Karl, in his bright orange and black wingsuit, descends first. Anton, in his yellow and black wingsuit, descends next.

Julian descends last. Working his way along the rope, he walks backwards down the slope, emerging from the vegetation of the grove at the cliff top and stepping onto the exposed granite surface of the rock cliff. The rock arches over and becomes vertical after a few more steps. He continues by rappelling down the cliff face. From time to time, he looks down at the terrifying view, a sheer vertical drop to the valley below, each time consciously slowing his breathing to regain his calm before continuing.

Forty feet down, he reaches the uneven ledge leading to the exit point, less than twelve inches wide here and covered with mounds of dirt and grass. He unhooks from the rope, then, facing the rock and leaning into it, he takes a step to the left and reaches out to another rope which is bolted onto the rock face. He tests his grip on the rope and finds it satisfactory. The rope is clean and dry. Inching along and up an eight inch wide dirt ledge, he traverses twenty feet of the rock face, leaning in, hugging the cliff, bending his head down as he passes under an overhang of granite, finally reaching the wider ledge of the exit point. Here, Karl and Anton are sitting, looking out at the view.

The man in the cargo van waits, watching, watching. He hears nothing. The sound of the nearby river has disappeared from his awareness.

Julian turns to face the valley, which is covered from one end to the other in grassy fields. Swiss chalets dot the landscape. The Weisse Lütschine River meanders at the bottom, fed by waterfalls from both sides of the valley. The main road parallels the river. The sheer cliffs of the mountain on the other side of the valley are not far away, so that the valley looks as though it were formed by some enormous trenching machine.

"No wind," says Karl. "It is a beautiful day."

Julian sits down. "Yes, beautiful."

"The waterfall's flow is heavy today," Anton says. "You could see it from the bottom."

"It rained pretty heavily last week," says Karl. "Ready for a shower?"

Julian and Anton both laugh. Their flight path will take them through the waterfall, over 850 feet tall, one of the few in the world that's flyable. There's enough water for the falls to reach the bottom before disappearing into a mist, but not so much that it would flush them out of the sky. It's not guarded by a U-shaped gorge or flanked by protrusions that would prevent a flight past its face. And it can be reached through controlled horizontal flight from a nearby jump point at an altitude high enough to deploy a parachute on the other side.

Karl stands up to retrieve a small two-way radio from its hook in its weatherproof box hanging on the cliffside. He calls in their planned jumps, then waits for clearance. Air traffic in the valley can be busy with helicopters, skydivers, paragliders, speed flyers, and wingsuit flyers jumping from other exit points, but just a minute later, the landing area safety crew announces his clearance. The announcement is heard simultaneously on the radios at all of the exit points. He releases the bungie which has been holding the bottom edge of his wingsuit up so it wouldn't drag while hiking down to the ledge, then checks his arm and leg zippers to be sure they are fully closed, tugging at his suit for reassurance that it feels right. Turning to Anton and Julian, he bumps fists with them. "See you at the bottom!"

Stepping up nearer to the edge of the ledge, he stretches his arms up, then back. He leans forward, then counts down: "Three, two, one, go." Rolling forward, he disappears over the edge.

The man in the cargo van now sees movement, high on the cliff. A bright orange, dropping, dropping, now turning and streaking across the face. He follows the shape with his binoculars, then returns to his original reference point.

Anton now stands up and follows the same procedure, releasing a bungie and checking his zippers. "See you at the bottom!" He bumps fists with Julian, then steps up to the edge. He stands for a few seconds while he prepares himself mentally, then leans forward, counting down. As he pushes off, Julian's heartbeat accelerates. He is next up.

Julian stands up and lowers his goggles over his eyes. He releases his bungie and closes his zippers, then spreads the blue and white wings of his wingsuit to test them. Next, he reaches around and unhooks his tracking drone, which he had carried by hanging it from his wingsuit. He turns it on, checking its indicator lights to verify that it has successfully powered up and self-tested, then gently tosses it out from the ledge. The drone initially drops but immediately revs up its motors with a loud buzz and rises back to the same level as the original throw. Then it slowly flies out fifty feet, orienting itself so that its primary camera faces back to the direction it was thrown from. Hovering there, it starts video recording, waiting for the jump, its gyrostabilized camera trained on Julian.

Jump, build up speed, turn left and level out, deploy paraglider, glide in for the landing. He rehearses the sequence in his mind. His wingsuit flight time will be 33 seconds, followed by 42 seconds of paragliding. He'll pass under the waterfall 20 seconds into the flight.

A half mile down and a mile away, he sees an automobile driving along the road. As he follows it with his eyes, it passes a cargo van which is parked at the side of the road. He cannot see any other motion, but at this height, he is too high up to see individual people.

He reaches around to the back of his suit with his right hand to check the location of the paraglider deployment handle, then steps forward. "Three, two, one..." He crouches and rolls forward, arms at his sides, pushing off the ledge, all in one smooth motion. His adrenaline surges as he leaves the rock. Time slows down. There is only the present moment, the visceral experience of being in the world, all intellect pushed into the background.

Initially, he falls straight down. As his speed builds, air rushes through inlets along the backside of his wingsuit and the wings inflate, providing lift, and his fall becomes flight. His drone follows him down, tracking at a distance of fifty feet horizontally, using visual object-tracking software to keep him centered in the frame of its primary camera. Because the drone is light and the propellors create drag while dropping, the drone flips the propellors upside-down to pull itself down through the air to keep up with Julian's free fall. It puts more and more power into its downward acceleration to overcome air resistance. It can barely keep up with Julian, and at his fastest rate of descent, the propellors are accelerating the drone downward with maximum power.

Two seconds into his descent, Julian levels out to a glide ratio of three to one, moving faster horizontally than vertically and reaching a speed of sixty miles per hour. His rush through the air makes him look and sound like a small jet. To keep up as Julian's flight path levels out, the drone rotates its propellors, eventually reaching 90 degrees, with the drone pulling itself sideways and descending only with the force of gravity. Julian turns left and hugs the cliff wall on his way to the Ägertenbachfall waterfall. Beige and gray outcroppings of rock flash past in a blur to his left. In the distance, he sees the bright red canopy of Anton's paraglider gliding over the valley.

The man in the cargo van slowly rotates his binoculars to follow as his target sweeps gracefully and silently across the face of the cliff, his right hand poised over the keyboard of the laptop resting in his lap. He feels a sense of utter calm, his mind completely occupied with the object of his attention.

The man presses a key, and Julian's shoulders jerk in a single rapid twisting motion. He veers left into the cliff, hitting a small outcrop of rock just before reaching Ägertenbachfall. He tumbles down and across the face of the cliff, passing through the waterfall and slamming into a large rock protrusion on the other side, beyond and below where he would have turned right, out toward the valley, to deploy his canopy. His drone desperately decelerates, then reverses direction to keep him centered in its camera frame. He is deflected back from the rock and plummets down, head-first, passing back into the falls and falling with them. His drone chases him down, down, down. He crashes finally onto a sloped rock ledge, just above the top of the scree, which slopes down from there at an angle of 33 degrees into a grove of trees.

The man inside the cargo van sets down his binoculars and turns to his laptop. Selecting a drop-down menu, a map of the area pops up. He selects the area of the crash and zooms in. A colored mark shows one electrical signal source on the map. He clicks on the mark and an information box pops up. As with the menu choices, the information box presents its information in Russian. The source is described as *Small electric motors, quadcopter configuration.*

He zooms in further, scrolling the map, searching for weaker signal sources, but finds nothing but radio reflections from the rock cliff. Checking these, each one proves to be nothing more than broadcast radio stations, cell tower reflections and air traffic control signaling. He is just being thorough, though. Each of the sources is already labeled as a secondary source, a reflection, as the system has already identified stronger matching sources originating from other directions. Aside from the drone, there are no other primary sources of electrical activity near the crash site. No brainwaves, no heartbeat activity, no spinal cord signals.

The man pulls down another menu, then selects an item labeled *Calibration.* A complex screen appears with several columns of data. Each row shows a single calibrated brain code, giving its category, its category coordinates, and timing details. Several buttons appear across the top of the screen. *Calibrate New*, *Import Set*, *Delete Item*. He clicks on *Delete All*, then confirms with a second click. The columns go blank. He then closes down the app, closes the laptop, and unplugs the data cable that runs from the laptop into the back of the van and up to the antenna array and transceiver equipment in the compartment under the van's polyethylene rooftop.

The man makes a call with his smartphone. Speaking German with a slight Russian accent, he says only: "The drone has crashed." He rolls up the window and slowly drives away.

The drone hovers near the bottom of the cliff, 32 feet above the scree slope, motionless, watching with its video camera for the arm wave signal which would command it to come over and land. It continues recording for another five minutes before its programming directs it to stop waiting, then it closes the fifty foot horizontal gap and lands itself next to Julian.

When the rescue team arrives, dropping down from a helicopter, then scrambling with some difficulty over the scree to the ledge carrying a stretcher and a medic bag, they find the two together, Julian and his drone, lying side by side, the scattered mists of the falls raining down gently upon them.

Monday, 30 September 2024

Breg contacts the CO from his home to give a status update. The CO listens patiently, allowing Breg to go through the details, before responding.

"You lost track of Ethan Chen."

The CO waits, but Breg has nothing further to say.

"Has he returned to the US?"

Breg doesn't want to go into the details, but from a technology point of view, he's stuck. "I'm not sure yet. We're updating our technology platform. The plan is to follow up immediately afterwards."

"So you haven't heard yet. Your technologist is... He's not coming back." The CO sounds sympathetic.

"He's not coming back?"

"Wingsuit flying accident. Crashed into a cliff. The Swiss police said it might have been a wind gust. They have the whole thing on video."

Breg is thrown off balance. *How would he know that?*

"I don't know how close you two were. I'm sorry for your loss." The CO gives Breg time to absorb the news.

"In light of events, we..." The CO's tone shifts. "We've reached the termination point of the contract," he says, matter-of-factly.

There's a problem, Breg thinks. He'll work it. It won't be a problem. He'll get another technologist. Breg's goal from the beginning has been to ramp up, hire more people, build out more systems, and carry out work with multiple targets. Then he reconsiders. He licensed the technology from Julian. He still needs to check the terms and conditions for this situation to understand what technology rights would remain with him.

And as to the contract with the CO... It's not a problem. Technically, they have reached the end of the contract. The real question is the next contract. He doesn't want to appear to be a failure. "The target must have been a Jekyll and Hyde," he says at length. They had both considered the possibility that their target was the type who could just disassociate until things cooled off.

"You worked it for an entire year."

"The target just never focused in on anything suspicious," Breg says. "He'd spend hours researching neurological conditions, and then he'd switch to trying to solve equations or hacking around with electronics, and then he'd switch to worrying about protecting his account passwords. He was all over the place. He even obsessed over writing a novel. About us."

"A novel," the CO says.

Breg waits, but the CO says nothing further. "We tried several approaches," Breg says. Hell, he thinks, maybe it's not him. He tried everything. He beat this thing to death.

He doesn't tell the CO that he may well be effectively out of business, anyway. It's not just that his technology guru is gone forever. He also lost his only two working systems. Then again, he suspects the CO already knows that.

The CO finishes the call. "I'm sorry, Brian. I appreciate your dedication. I'll see what I can do for you. Maybe get you going with another operation, if you would be so inclined."

Sunday, 6 October 2024

A few days have passed since Peter managed his first blink in the presence of someone else in his hospital room.

It was a nurse who noticed. The nurse hadn't given it much thought initially. People blink. She was going through her routine and happened to notice him blink. She finished up with her routine and was on her way out the door when she hesitated. It bothered her. He hadn't even looked at her.

Then it hit her. He was a coma patient.

She turned around right away and stood next to his bed, asking: "Can you hear me?"

He blinked.

Not long after, the hospital contacted both Shasha and Ethan and they each had rushed to the hospital to visit Peter. The first visit was emotional and overwhelming, especially for Shasha, so they took things slowly. As he was still paralyzed, except for blinking, Peter would blink yes or no in response to questions, though this was not as limiting as it would first seem. On each of Shasha and Ethan's separate visits, a nurse came to visit the room to show them how to use an alphabet board to communicate with him. When Peter indicated that he wished to say something, they would hold the alphabet board up for him to see and would scan the letters with a finger, first down rows of letters, saying the first letter of each row until he blinked, then across the letters in that row, again saying letters while scanning until he blinked, indicating the next letter of the words he wished to spell out.

With communications with Peter opened up, Ethan is now able to discuss more serious matters, including financial accounts, with him. He has been managing Peter's accounts, and there had been one particular question that hadn't been answered and that he had hoped could be cleared up.

In getting familiar with the accounts, Ethan had discovered a suspicious transaction on one of the checking account statements. He hadn't noticed it right away. Peter had spent quite a bit of money on the SCIF project and also on equipment for tracking down the voices. It was only when he carefully reconciled the vendors and transactions that he had noticed that one particular transaction for $9,000 stood out. It wasn't a payment to a business. It was a wire transfer to an individual. And it had taken place the same day as Peter's accident.

The accident had taken place in the morning. No time of day was shown for the wire transfer, but when Ethan finally asked the bank about it, it turned out that the transfer was in the afternoon.

The bank could see that the transfer was made from a different computer, not the one Peter usually used, but whoever made the transfer had managed to sign in without having to retry multiple times and without resetting the password. The bank had explained to Ethan that it could have been Peter, or possibly someone he had shared his password with. Except that Peter was in the hospital, in a coma. There was no way he could have engaged in a transaction, nor could he have shared his password with anyone in that state. Still, he could have authorized someone beforehand and given them the password.

Ethan tells Peter the name on the account that the money was transferred to. "Do you know them?"

Peter blinks twice for "no".

"So you don't know of anyone who might have transferred the money?"

Peter blinks *no*.

"Should we report this as a fraudulent transaction to the bank?"

Peter blinks once. *Yes*.

"OK, we'll get that taken care of."

That settled, Ethan brings Peter up to date on some of his own experiences and tells him about Zai. He describes his experience in

Peter's SCIF, hearing the voices and then hearing them cut out when he closed the door, saying that's what convinced him the voices were real.

Initially, Peter doesn't have any visible reaction. No blinks. Because of his paralysis, his emotional state doesn't show on his face, but he is, in fact, quite attentive. Listening carefully to the story, tears begin to well up from his eyes.

"The headaches were hell, weren't they?"

Peter blinks *yes*.

"The guys at Zai all think you're a genius. They're very impressed with the way you figured out what was happening to you."

Ethan goes on to talk about bringing Peter's signal tracking device to Beijing, describing the enhancements made by Zai's engineers to deal with the multiple-transmitter issue.

"When we finally tracked them down, they were in two separate taxis, each one transmitting signals." Ethan chuckles. "My friend Zhuang Rongtao was sitting there with me, parked between the two taxis in pouring rain. He set them up."

Peter blinks several times, so Ethan asks if he has anything else to say. Peter blinks *yes,* so Ethan looks around the room for the alphabet board, finally finding it lying on a table along one wall.

They're still investigating technologies to help Peter communicate. There are a handful of brain-to-computer-interface solutions, most of them new and still evolving. Some are quite invasive and involve implanting electrodes into the brain. Others are not invasive, but they're also not nearly as effective. The doctors are still gathering the available options and preparing for a discussion with Peter about the risks and benefits of each solution. At this point, though, all he has for communication is blinks and the alphabet board.

As Ethan finger-scans the board, Peter blinks out the letters: "w - h - o - r - t - h - e - y"

"We still don't know," Ethan says. "We got some pictures, but we can't see their faces in them."

Peter blinks several times again. Ethan goes through the alphabet board sequence again, and Peter spells out a new sentence: "t - h - e - y - s - t - o - l - e - m- y - p - w"

Ethan puts it together. "Your password? You mean the fraudulent transfer. You think that was them."

Peter blinks *yes*.

"How would they steal…they read your mind."

Peter blinks *yes*.

Ethan gives this connection some thought. If this is true, he already has the name of one of the perpetrators of the mind attack. It's right there on a transaction confirmation for Peter's account. He gets goosebumps.

"I get it," he says. "Let me dig into it."

Peter spells out another sentence. "t - h - a - n - k - y - o - u"

Ethan continues with daily visits, talking about the news at large in the world, reading articles to Peter and playing his choice of music. Sometimes he brings things that Peter requests. Ethan also facilitates calls with Shasha, calling her in Los Angeles and helping Peter to respond to her questions and comments, but this communication is slow going. Nevertheless, Peter is warmed by hearing her voice and enjoys seeing her on the video calls. She talks about her research, what's going on with her parents, and small things.

Because Ethan has promised to assist with managing Peter's affairs, he keeps him informed about his mail and his financial accounts and his condo. It's hard for Ethan to gauge Peter's reactions to the updates because of his locked-in state. Occasionally, with effort, Peter blinks an opinion or a reaction using the alphabet board. But for the most part, he just listens.

The visits and calls from Shasha and Ethan tend to last no more than an hour, once or twice a day. But this is not to say that Peter is alone all day long. His life is both highly constrained and complicated because of his condition. He is fed by a nurse through a feeding tube that runs through his nose and down his throat to his stomach. His muscles are stretched several times a day to prevent cramping. Basic elimination functions require assistance. And he must be repositioned frequently to avoid pressure sores and edema, the localized accumulation of fluids in the body's tissues.

Peter's primary care doctor had arranged to begin neurological rehabilitation with a specialist who uses technology to retrain the brain's control over the body. It is still experimental. The idea is that by providing biofeedback from sensors attached to his muscles, the technology gives information to Peter's brain that it can use to relearn how to coordinate the muscles, even when the nerve signals are so faint that one might not see any motion at all from the effort. They are working on recovery from the toes on up.

It takes another week before Ethan gets around to talking to Peter in more depth about what Zai is up to in Beijing, going into detail about their discoveries and describing their work on incorporating virtual odors into virtual reality gaming technology.

Peter had been so focused on being attacked with the technology that he hadn't considered other applications for it. He spells out "i - m - p - r - e - s - s - i - v - e" with the alphabet board. Ethan says they already have a working demo.

Then Ethan mentions the second demo, the one which allows two-way mental communication, as voices in the head. "It's an amazing technology," he says. "Of course, you could use it to spy on people, but they really have no interest in developing that kind of product. Other useful applications for it aren't as obvious. The device is kind of big, not something you could easily carry around with you." He shows the size of the device with his hands. Zai's own device is similar in size to the device that Ethan had found in the gray backpack.

Ethan continues enthusiastically, explaining it as he would a new consumer electronics device that some start-up has just announced, describing the trade-offs consumers may face. "It needs a laptop to run the software that drives it," he says, "so it could be used for hands-free communications, like wearing earbuds with a smartphone, but it really isn't..."

He stops mid-sentence.

He gets on the phone with Zai that night. He wants them to ship out a working version of the demo. For Peter.

Friday, 18 October 2024

"We couldn't find it. The Geistgerät just disappeared." The man clearly feels embarrassed.

"It just disappeared? Just like that?" The man's superior cannot grasp how such a simple recovery operation could go so wrong. He is exasperated. "What happened to the backpack itself? Maybe it would give us some clues."

"We couldn't find it. It's all gone. The backpack, the laptop, the transceiver." The man steps away from the projection screen.

"What good are passwords without the system?" The man's superior stands up and paces back and forth in the small meeting room.

They'd carefully arranged to capture the passwords during Julian's demonstration of the Geistgerät to the Turkish-German businessman, listening to the keystrokes and watching its laptop screen from nearby with their own remote surveillance system. They had captured Julian's sign-in password, and an additional password that he used to launch his software application once signed in. And using their own system's integrated brainwave surveillance module, they'd even managed to recover Julian's mental password, a password that Julian's system checks by mind reading to unlock the use of his system each day, a key element of Julian's approach to protecting his technology without spending the money to patent it. Without Julian present, no one could gain access to the Geistgerät. The mental password can't be intercepted by logging keystrokes, watching cursor movements, scraping pixels from his screen, or seizing a physical token. It was a *nothing*, a second factor that couldn't be taken without the use of the very technology that it protected. And unlike biometric factors such as fingerprints or retinal scans, it could be changed from time to time.

As clever as Julian had been, they did capture his mental password. And they have the capability of transmitting Julian's brain codes to the Geistgerät in his place. They followed him, making sure to capture any mental password changes he might make, until that was no longer necessary. But passwords get you only so far. They still need to get into Julian's system to work out its genesis. And there's no system.

On the surface, the Geistgerät had looked like the work of a lone wolf, a genius who had somehow managed to hack together a working system with more than a few bells-and-whistles. But that's unbelievable. The Russian engineers had evolved their mind-reading and mind-control capabilities over a period of decades. Numerous specialists across a range of fields. Careful design and optimization. There must have been others involved and they need to find out who they are.

"Perhaps German intelligence got it," the man offers.

The man's superior agrees. "Perhaps."

It was supposed to be easy. Take out target, pick up package, go home. For three weeks now, they've been monitoring communications in an attempt to figure out who had airbrushed it out of the picture right under their noses. But to their dismay, everyone else has been, too. Israel. Turkey. The Americans. *And* the Germans. For a short time, it was the hottest buzz topic that no one admitted to talking about.

Before this incident, the Germans knew nothing about the technology. Except that Julian knew, so now they're not sure. The Americans already have the technology, of course. No one knows for sure whether the Israelis have succeeded in getting it to work, though there is evidence that they have been trying.

And just recently, in a tell-tale sign that, now, *everyone* is interested, Julian's mental password, or more accurately put, a recording of the radio waves with the brain codes for his mental password, has been making the rounds. They intercepted discussion of it in yet another communication just yesterday. They still haven't tracked down how the password got out.

They've come a long way since their first detection of Julian's activity. They were lucky. Their signals intelligence group just happened to be monitoring the activity of the very same company that Julian had been giving his demonstration to. And what they saw had surprised them. Out of the blue, they had found someone transmitting shaped radio signals that could be perceived by the brain. And it wasn't an American. It was like detecting the signature of a secret nuclear weapon test and discovering that it wasn't a government that did it. Worse yet, there was a serious potential for that weapon to make its way to Turkey. Of all places for it to proliferate to, that would be one of the more problematic. They couldn't allow that to happen.

They had followed Julian, monitoring every conversation, every thought, but found no hint of development partners. There was no one else to hunt down.

But they were running out of time. Julian would eventually find a buyer and the technology would proliferate. So they had made the call to take him out and recover the system for analysis.

The man's superior sits back down. "What has been coming out of foreign intelligence?"

The man continues with his presentation. "Yes, well, as I mentioned, the only indication in communications is the awareness of the *existence* of the Brecht system. And its passwords. None of the communications makes a claim of possession of the system."

"What about the German Federal Police? Or the Swiss?"

"Nothing."

The man's superior gives this some thought, then signals with a hand gesture for the man to continue.

"We configured signal monitoring vans to look specifically for the system's signature and sent them out to search for any usage of it. With the sample signals we collected during Julian Brecht's demonstrations, we can distinguish the Brecht system from the American systems. Our initial search focused on the region in and around Berlin."

The man goes into the details of the search in Berlin, then finishes his presentation with a discussion of the search for the system in Turkey. He closes his laptop, ending his formal presentation. Within a few seconds, the projector turns itself off.

"There is one additional thing, though. New information just surfaced today. As I was saying, perhaps German intelligence got it. We intercepted chatter in which they had mentioned that they have caged the Elster. The *magpie*." The man uses the German word Elster, then translates it into Russian.

"The magpie? Why is that significant?"

"The magpie has a black and white body, with blue and white wings." The man clears his throat, then explains: "We think that the Germans may have put the Brecht system into a Faraday cage to test it. We wouldn't have detected its signals if it were in a Faraday cage. We are already following up on this lead."

The man's superior understands now. His mind starts working on the implications even as his operative finishes the point.

"As you know, Julian Brecht was a wingsuit flyer. When he crashed in Switzerland, he was wearing his wingsuit, which was black and white, with blue and white wings."

Monday, 21 October 2024

Not long after discovering that Peter was not in a coma, arrangements had been made for him to transition to living at home, with full-time nursing staff. He no longer needed hospital care. But he would still require the use of a variety of medical devices. A urinary catheter. Compression stockings to squeeze his legs to prevent blood from pooling when he is sitting upright. A device which vibrates his chest to loosen phlegm.

Ethan had ensured that everything needed at the condo was ready for Peter and that the nursing staff could get in and out. He had arranged for a ramp to be built on Peter's front steps for his new wheelchair. And he continues to help Peter manage personal and financial matters, checking the mail and paying the bills.

Ethan had discussed Peter's use of Zai's technology with Peter's doctor, Dr. Gestrin, who was very positive about the idea. She said there would be some paperwork involved, so Ethan had worked as a go-between to obtain the information she would need from Zai, referring to the technology for this purpose as a neuroprosthesis. With it, Peter would be able to communicate by thinking, with Zai's technology converting his inner voice into sound through an audio speaker. Potentially, the technology will also allow Peter to control other devices, also just by thinking, though there aren't yet any specific plans for how this will be done.

With this information, Dr. Gestrin had then arranged for the required licenses for Peter to use the new neuroprosthesis, permitted without extensive testing because it is classified as an experimental medical device. Ethan had then invited Cheng Fengxiang to Berkeley, to Peter's condo, to configure the neuroprosthesis for Peter's use, with Dr.

Gestrin attending. Shasha had said she would also be there, flying up from Los Angeles to be with Peter.

And today is the day. Ethan drives Cheng Fengxiang over, carrying the neuroprosthesis and some mounting hardware. Shasha is already at the condo when they arrive.

On arrival, Cheng Fengxiang is in awe of the SCIF. It is far more imposing than he had realized, filling much of the living room and reaching almost to the ceiling. Ethan explains in Chinese that it is *the* SCIF, the one he had talked about when he first visited Zai.

Peter, on seeing Cheng Fengxiang's interest in the SCIF, catches Ethan's attention to use the alphabet board, then offers that Ethan should give Cheng Fengxiang a tour. Then Dr. Gestrin arrives, with Shasha answering the door. Not wanting to impose, Cheng Fengxiang looks around inside the SCIF but keeps it brief. Meanwhile, Dr. Gestrin checks in with Peter. Peter's live-in nurse, Colin, peers into the SCIF after Ethan and Cheng Fengxiang go in. No one had ever explained it to him.

Cheng Fengxiang spends forty minutes attaching the specialized radio receiver that Zai had originally built for calibrating the signal tracker to Ethan's brain codes and mounting a laptop on the back of Peter's wheelchair, connecting both pieces of equipment to the wheelchair's battery through its built-in power outlets. He then spends the next hour capturing Peter's brain codes to calibrate the mind-interfacing system.

During the calibration process, Peter wears headphones so that only he hears the calibration sounds and only his brain generates brain codes in response to the sounds. He burns out from the experience, so at the end of this phase of the process, he needs to take a nap and blinks a request for his nurse to recline the wheelchair. Colin estimates that Peter will nap for an hour, then will need to have his lunch, so Ethan, Cheng Fengxiang, and Shasha agree to go to lunch at a nearby restaurant, with Dr. Gestrin returning to meet them at the condo after lunch and Colin staying behind with Peter.

Ninety minutes later, with Peter rested, and with the neuroprosthesis up and running, and with Shasha, Ethan, Cheng Fengxiang, Dr. Gestrin and Colin all standing around Peter, watching, Peter thinks his first words through the device. The device echoes his thoughts through the laptop speakers: "Does it work?"

Dr. Gestrin feigns disappointment. "Couldn't you have thought up something more dramatic for your first words?"

The device was carefully designed. Peter hears Dr. Gestrin's words in his head, but the device does not echo these words to the laptop's speakers. It only turns Peter's inner speech brain codes into sounds on the speakers. It ignores brain codes from the part of his brain that hears sounds through his ears.

Peter reflects on Dr. Gestrin's comment, then starts to put his idea into words.

Peter: [Ah...]

Neuroprosthesis: "Ah..."

Peter: [She's...]

Neuroprosthesis: "She's..."

Peter: [Hm...]

Neuroprosthesis: "Hm..."

Peter: [It's like]

Neuroprosthesis: "It's like"

Peter: [when Treacher...]

Neuroprosthesis: "when Treacher..."

Peter: [Huh...]

Neuroprosthesis: "Huh..."

He stops thinking. Then...

Peter: [I have no]

Neuroprosthesis: "I have no"

Peter: [privacy.]

Neuroprosthesis: "privacy."

Peter: [How do I]

Neuroprosthesis: "How do I"

Peter: [turn it off]

Neuroprosthesis: "turn it off"

Peter: [when I need...]

Neuroprosthesis: "when I need..."

Peter: [I'm...]

Neuroprosthesis: "I'm..."

Peter: [This is...]

Neuroprosthesis: "This is..."

Every thought that comes to his mind is immediately relayed to the speakers on the laptop. It feels weird to him, like the repeating game, where your friend instantly repeats everything you say and then stops immediately whenever you stop.

It wasn't like that when the voices would listen to him, before his bicycle accident. When that was happening, he didn't hear himself being heard. Now, he feels naked. Mentally naked. And he can't even turn it off. His stress level starts to rise.

"Ah! Please wait." Cheng Fengxiang now realizes there was an oversight. During testing in Beijing, they started and stopped the software with a laptop command as needed. But Peter can't do that. He mutes the speakers until he can resolve the issue.

Cheng Fengxiang explains the situation to Ethan and Shasha in Chinese, and Ethan, in turn, translates for Peter and Dr. Gestrin. He has a solution. He downloads a voice recognition software package onto the neuroprosthesis laptop, then wires it up to Zai's software. Meanwhile, Dr. Gestrin, who had watched in surprise at Peter's distress, writes up some notes on her own laptop about the novel situation Peter had been put into.

Forty minutes later, Cheng Fengxiang is ready with the update. It's not a complicated change. He's only checking for two words. He explains: "Peter can say *kai* then turn on, *guan* then turn off. So, not...not. Eh? Buzhidao zenme shuo." *Eh? I don't know how to say that.* He explains to Ethan in Chinese, and Ethan finishes the explanation: "No conflict. It's Chinese, not English. The software won't confuse the Chinese commands with the words he is thinking in English." Cheng Fengxiang repeats the phrase "no conflict", then gets up from behind the wheelchair and goes around to face Peter, asking: "OK?"

Peter blinks *yes*.

Cheng Fengxiang sits back down behind the wheelchair and types a command on the laptop. For several seconds, no sounds come out of the laptop speakers. Then the speakers announce: "My mind is open. Guan."

"Ah, sorry," Cheng Fengxiang says. "Not done. Please wait."

The software is not supposed to say "guan" when Peter thinks it to turn off the verbalization of his thoughts. For this to work, Cheng Fengxiang modifies the software to delay the sound output by a half second, checking each word as it processes Peter's thoughts and turning off the speakers before "guan" goes out.

"OK. Try again."

Peter: [Ah...OK. ...Oh, kai. ...Ah]

Neuroprosthesis: "... Ah"

Peter: [My]

Neuroprosthesis: "... My"

Peter: [miiine mind]

Neuroprosthesis: "... miiine"

Peter: [izzzzz...]

Neuroprosthesis: "... mind"

Peter: [ohhhh punno]

Neuroprosthesis: "... izzzzz ohhhh"

Peter: [oh punnun]

Neuroprosthesis: "... punno oh"

Peter: [Iiii can cannn't]

Neuroprosthesis: "... punnun Iiii can"

Peter: [DO DO...THISS!]

Neuroprosthesis: "... cannn't DO DO...THISS!"

Concerned that Peter may be having a seizure, Dr. Gestrin has gotten up to check Peter. She examines his complexion, then checks his pupils with a penlight from her medical bag. Still concerned, she retrieves a pulse oximeter from her bag and clips it onto the end of one of his fingers to check his pulse and oxygen levels. Then she checks his blood pressure, which is clearly elevated.

Meanwhile, Cheng Fengxiang has muted the speakers again. Ethan asks what is happening. Cheng Fengxiang doesn't know. Watching quietly, Shasha has tensed up, worried for Peter.

Cheng Fengxiang thinks about the process from Peter's perspective. What changed? Only the speaker delay. The speaker delay must too long. No one else in the room hears the echo. Only Peter does. And it must be unbearable to speak with an echo like that.

Dr. Gestrin asks Peter whether he is OK, whether he would like to take a break. Peter blinks *no*. She warns him about his blood pressure.

He blinks *no* again.

"Stubborn. Alright, we can keep going," she tells him, "but if this gets out of hand, I'm pulling the plug on it. OK?"

At first, Peter gives no reply, then he blinks *yes*.

Ethan indicates to Cheng Fengxiang that they can continue.

"Sorry. Every time, hear *guan*. OK?"

Cheng Fengxiang has returned the software to its earlier configuration, without the delay. It doesn't surprise Peter. It's just the way it's going to be. He blinks *yes*.

Turning on the speakers, Cheng Fengxiang asks Peter to try again.

"[Now is it — OK. Nice. Nice! It's working. ...oh, guan.]"

Dr. Gestrin sits down at the table to write out some more notes. Shasha visibly relaxes.

"[So, no one got it? Guan.]"

"Got what?" Ethan is lost.

Shasha tries to guess Peter's meaning. "Earlier, he said *my mind is open*. We can read you mind now, Peter?"

Peter is silent for a full ten seconds. Everyone in the room waits without saying a thing.

"[It's not just...Paul Erdős. ...Guan.]"

Shasha goes onto her phone and searches online. "Oh. That's pretty good!" Now she gets it.

"Who is Paul Erdős?" Ethan asks.

"He was a famous mathematician," Shasha says. "It says here that whenever he wanted to start working with someone on a math problem, he would say that." She doesn't explain that Peter got the quote wrong.

Considering what he has been through, as it is, she's impressed with how well is he doing.

"Duly noted," says Dr. Gestrin. "Peter's first words were: My mind is open." *That's better.* She writes them down in her notes.

Tears appear in Peter's eyes as it sinks in that his life has just received a major upgrade. Shasha gives Peter a side-head-hug, wrapping her arm around the back of his head and pressing her cheek against the top, covering his chest with her other arm. She whispers to him: "This is so great, Peter." Colin approaches and dabs at his tears with some tissue.

"[Tired. Guan.]"

Everyone in the room hears Peter's tiredness in the sound of his "voice". His new voice is still him, but it has been renovated, remade by technology. It's different from the way his speaking voice used to sound, and the group hears the difference. It has less bass. The deeper resonant tones are missing, though the middle tones are preserved, as is Peter's way of talking, the intonation of his words and the rhythm of his sentences. Peter's new voice is not synthesized by a computer like was done by older software for creating speech. The neuroprosthesis reads Peter's brain codes, the brain codes that represent not the words in his head, but the emotive subtlety of the sounds of those words.

Ethan takes Peter's cue. "We should be going. Shall we follow up tomorrow? Just to make sure everything is working for you."

"[OK. Thank you, Ethan. Thank you Cheng, uh, ...how do say your name again? Guan.]"

Cheng Fengxiang smiles. "Cheng Fengxiang. You are welcome!"

As promised, the next day, Cheng Fengxiang and Ethan return after lunch to check on Peter, each with a cup of Starbucks in hand. Shasha has already returned to Los Angeles. Colin lets them in. He has finished with Peter's morning routine and a therapy session and has just finished feeding him his lunch.

With his new ability to speak out loud, Peter can call for Colin's help at any time. No more need for tediously long sessions with the alphabet board. No more suffering as he waits for someone to ask whether he needs anything. If he's hungry or thirsty, he just says so.

"[So I...I was wondering...]" Peter says. He explains, haltingly, because he still struggles to think clearly and to express himself, that, from what he remembers, the wheelchair is supposed to have voice commands built into it. Dr. Gestrin had helped him pick it out, and she had described the wheelchair's features before he made his decision to buy it. "[I have a voice now. So that should work. Guan.]"

Ethan asks why he'd want to do that. "You aren't going to wheel yourself down to the supermarket, are you?" Peter can't even turn his head to see where he's going, he thinks. And if he gets stuck somewhere, he can't use a phone to call for help.

"[I might just want to, uh, maybe I just want a different view. You know. Turn around. Without waiting for someone. Someone to come over for me. ...Guan.]"

"Oh." Ethan feels a bit embarrassed. "That makes sense."

Colin comments: "Some amount of autonomy could raise his spirits. Would it actually be possible for him to control the wheelchair? The ability to speak out has already done wonders for him. The manual is in the back of the wheelchair."

He pulls the manual out and Ethan and Cheng Fengxiang set down their coffees and flip through it together, discussing its contents in Chinese. It doesn't take them long to discover that this wheelchair, the Politan, is at the absolute high end of the scale in luxury electric wheelchairs and does indeed come with voice control built in.

Colin lets them know to tell him if they need anything, then takes his first break of the day in his bedroom.

While it may have seemed unnecessary for a locked-in patient, completely paralyzed, to have an electric wheelchair, and one with voice controls, no less, the chair was designed for a variety of patient scenarios. It has many features that no other wheelchair has, some of which are not useful to Peter, but others of which are essential, such as automated inflatable pads and rollers which prevent pressure sores, and also the powered ability to recline and sit up.

But there's no microphone installed. There's just a jack where it would plug in. With Peter lacking the ability to speak, it just hadn't been relevant until now.

The wheelchair's built-in voice recognition uses its own product name to start out each command: *Politan go. Politan stop. Politan left. Politan faster.*

Cheng Fengxiang suggests they give it a try, and with Ethan's help, he orders a tiny microphone and a microphone extension cord online and has them delivered by sidewalk robot to the front of the condo. While waiting, they drink their coffees and engage in small talk with Peter. The microphone and extension cord arrive 45 minutes later.

It's a simple matter to attach the microphone to the laptop near the speakers, covering it with a bit of foam sound insulating material scrounged up from one of Peter's closets to prevent extraneous sounds from triggering it, and in a few minutes, it's done.

Cheng Fengxiang, whose reading ability in English far exceeds his speaking ability, steps through the wheelchair manual one command at a time, coaching Peter, gesturing with his hands to indicate the motions. *Go* means to go straight, so if the Politan is rotating left, go will stop the rotation and head straight. *Left* means rotate counterclockwise until something stops the rotation, but the rotation will stop automatically after turning 180 degrees around. Thus turning around is simply: *Politan left.* Or if you prefer: *Politan right.* To turn just a little bit, you would say: *Politan left*, waiting to say *Politan stop* when you are pointed the right way.

Thus, for Peter to make the wheelchair go straight for a while, then stop, he would think: "[*Kai* Politan go...Politan stop *guan*.]"

Cheng Fengxiang asks Peter to try it, and when he does, he crashes into the dining room table, shoving it half-way into the kitchen before coming to a stop. "[Oops...Yee-haw!]" Crunch. Grind. "[Hah this is... stop! Politan stop! Guan.]"

Ethan is alarmed. "Are you OK?" He pulls the wheelchair back and Cheng Fengxiang moves the table back into place. Hearing the noise, Colin comes out from his bedroom.

"[Yeah! This is great! Uh...... Guan.]"

Now concerned in the same way a parent would be about a teen who just got a driver's permit, Ethan looks around, thinking of possible crash risks in the room.

"[It needs, uh, it needs.... Frustrating... Sensors. It needs sensors. So it won't crash. It's hard to remember words. ...Guan.]" Peter rotates the chair around, looking for his nurse, who is standing behind him. "[Colin, you're not going to have to take me for walks anymore. Guan.]"

Colin is strong, a helpful trait to manage a locked-in patient, moving Peter around as necessary, in and out of his wheelchair. And taking Peter for walks has never been a chore. He enjoys it.

"[I just got wheels. Guan.]"

Ethan explains: "Voice commands are working."

Colin looks at Peter with concern for his safety, then at Ethan. "Oh, so it works. But —"

Peter says "[Politan go]" and the wheelchair starts moving forward, crashing into Colin, causing him to stumble back. Colin keeps his balance only because the wheelchair moves slowly.

"[Stop. Stop. Politan stop.]"

Everyone in the room watches Peter, who at this point is sitting as still as a statue. Simon says *freeze*.

"[Sorry. ...Guan.]"

"Maybe this isn't such a great idea," Colin says.

Peter spins the wheelchair in one direction, then the other. "[But it is. This really is great. Guan.]" His thought, his speech, is slowing down. "[How do you make the chair...]" He can't remember the word. "[What are the...the commands again? Guan.]"

Colin fetches the manual, which Cheng Fengxiang had set down on the dining room table, and reads out the commands for Peter. A moment later, the wheelchair reclines.

Peter announces "[Tired.]" and starts a nap right where he is. He fades out, just like that. The inflatable padding and rollers move into action with a hiss and a hum for a few seconds, and then the wheelchair, too, is silent.

A minute later, Peter slips into a dream state. Having forgotten to think the word *guan*, the sounds in his dream play for the room on his neuroprosthesis. But this doesn't last long. Cheng Fengxiang had anticipated this and worse, thinking Peter might activate his wheelchair while dreaming, sleep-wheeling around the condo and crashing into things. Detecting that Peter has fallen asleep, the neuroprosthesis puts itself into standby mode, disabling all of its outputs and waiting for Peter to wake up.

Colin pushes the Politan closer to a wall socket and plugs it in to charge.

January 2025

The contracting officer that Brian Breg worked with last year has made good on his promise, recommending Breg for a position managing operations for a specialized type of airport security service.

"They're part of a larger company called MQZTOQ," the CO said. He had pronounced it em-cue-zee-talk over the phone, then spelled it out. "Bizarre name but smart people. They say the name's a play on a formula, something about seeing through math. They've got some real technology geeks over there. Super competent. Give 'em a call."

Despite the failure of his earlier fledgling business, Breg still believes strongly in the future of mind technology and he now looks forward to being part of a larger organization which, at this point, already has many years of experience with it.

In their approach to airport security, Breg's new team at MQZTOQ does not interview people, nor do they physically search them or their belongings. Instead, they provide only one service: flagging people who merit further investigation by the airport's own security personnel.

They are specially trained in observing behavior. The core of their approach involves the use of proprietary technology that remotely measures body temperatures, perspiration levels, and heart rates that, together, can indicate that a person is nervous. But MQZTOQ's technology has evolved over time and now includes devices for reading signals from the human nervous system, radio energy in the form of brainwaves and spinal cord signals. To maintain a competitive advantage, and to keep an edge over adversaries, they don't disclose the details of the technology, refraining from discussing it in academic papers or trade publications.

MQZTOQ's airport security service doesn't involve a scanner, nor does it involve procedures or technology at the security gate itself. They operate out of public view, entirely within the secured part of the terminal, using electronic sensing devices installed in the ceilings. A webcam installed near each sensing device provides visuals of the people they check.

One of the key advantages of the system is its light touch. Compared with the earlier technology that Breg was familiar with, the MQZTOQ system has been optimized to require minimal calibration for each person to interpret their brainwaves. But even with this minimal calibration, they are able to listen in on a person's inner dialog, monitoring for suspicious thoughts.

The technologists, a group of electrical engineers, software developers, a technology architect, and facilities engineers, had pointed out to Breg when he joined that if they didn't have to keep the technology proprietary, they'd probably get a Nobel Prize in medicine. They can read off people's emotions, pains and other feelings, their muscle tension, and their thoughts, electronically, from a considerable distance. They can see things that never show up on brain scans. But from a career point of view, they're satisfied with the application, searching for potential security risks and helping to keep the country safe.

The system can't see the body through clothing, nor does it keep any information about people beyond the immediate security analysis needs, aside from general or anonymized information to improve the performance of the system. Indeed, privacy is a major goal of the design of the service, so that part of Breg's job includes identifying the appropriate privacy standards and providing compliance reporting.

For now, MQZTOQ only services international terminals. These are ports of entry and historically, constitutional concerns regarding search and privacy are significantly less, especially when the purpose of the searches is security. While there has been concern about the routine search of travelers' cellphones and computers without reasonable suspicion or probable cause, the legal theory that MQZTOQ operates under is based on the appropriateness in the context of airport security. The potential for probing hidden thoughts and behavior to reveal an active security threat overcomes the expectation of privacy. If a terrorist plot is underway, the thoughts of the individuals involved would reflect this threat. The idea is to catch the plot in action. With the safety of hundreds of individuals at stake on any given flight, so the reasoning goes, the trade-off clearly reflects the interests of security over privacy.

MQZTOQ would like to expand coverage to domestic airports and to the domestic terminals of international airports, but the border search exception to privacy protection under the U.S. Constitution, which makes MQZTOQ's service practical, isn't applicable outside of the ports of entry. One potential basis for domestic expansion, which their legal staff is still reviewing, is the use of the technology only for "escalated screening", when there is a documented reason for suspicion, rather than routinely probing potentially anyone, as is done in the international terminals.

Over the coming year, Breg will be working on expanding MQZTOQ's service to other airports, writing proposals, managing the installation of the equipment on site, overseeing operations, and documenting and resolving incidents as they arise. His duties are more constrained than they had been as the owner of his own business, with upper management guiding him, and with this guidance, he will develop a solid reputation with the company's customers. Management will be satisfied with Breg's performance. And the operations team will take a liking to Breg. He's a no-nonsense kind of guy. He is experienced. And he respects the team and their work and really believes in their mission. Breg has found his niche.

THE STORY OF THE MAGPIE

The Tree on the Mountain
Zhuangzi, 4th century BC, China

Zhuangzi is roving in Eagle Hill Park when he sees an extraordinary magpie, with a wingspan of almost six feet and eyes as big as a person's, coming in from the south. It grazes Zhuangzi's forehead, then settles down in a nearby chestnut grove. Zhuangzi wonders: "What sort of bird is this? Grand wings that don't carry it away, and big eyes that don't see."

Lifting his garments, he takes short, quick steps, then sets down his slingshot pellets. He notices a cicada resting in the shade, unmindful of itself; a mantis hides, then pounces on the cicada, seeing only its prey, unmindful of its own appearance. Because of this, the unusual magpie takes the mantis for its own gain, seeing profit and neglecting its own true nature.

Zhuangzi shouts out in fear: "Oh, no! Matters here are definitely entangled, and now in other matters, this is quite an inspiration." Abandoning his slingshot pellets and running back, the park warden chases him down and berates him.

The Case

Thursday, 6 February 2025

"Like I said, it's mind reading. That's what they did."

"Why should I believe that?" The attorney presses.

Stack is confused. That's what they've been talking about all this time. He's not sure what the point of the question is. "Well, how else do you think I got in?" He runs his fingers through his short spiky hair.

"Need I remind you that we have a deal here? Why should I believe it?" The attorney leans back in his chair, comfortable, keeping his eyes on Stack.

"That's it right there. I already told you, that's the equipment they used." Stack points to the equipment that had been handed over to Ethan by the hotel in Beijing, sitting on a table in the attorney's office, off to the side, in front of floor-to-ceiling bookshelves filled with law books.

The attorney leans forward. "That's what you're saying. But why should I believe it?"

Stack is worried that he could still get busted for the wire transfer from Peter's account. He would never have taken the money if he had thought anyone would notice. As far as he knew, Peter was dead. Or at least, brain dead. And he knew Peter had no living family members.

"Yeah, look. I have a recording."

"A recording?"

"Yeah. A recording of his thoughts. It's unbelievable, but, yeah. He was thinking about his passwords."

Unbelievable indeed. The attorney can't believe his luck. "OK, I'd like you to provide that to me. Then I'll believe you."

Stack feels pressured. He rubs the top of his head as he thinks. No one knew he had it. *If Mr. Breg were to find out...That's torq.*

He had copied it one day, but hadn't thought about *permission* at the time. It just hadn't occurred to him. Anyway, he couldn't help it. There it was. A recording of some guy's thoughts. *His actual thoughts.* Where else could you ever find something like that? At the very least, it was a collectable, a show-and-tell for his friends. He hadn't imagined he'd ever actually use the information on the thumb drive. And then Peter had crashed.

He stops thinking about it and listens to his gut. He sighs. "It's the target's own thoughts."

The target? "You mean Mr. Nolen." The attorney's tone indicates a requirement for respect for his client.

"Yeah, Mr. Nolen," Stack says. "Why can't Mr. Nolen have a copy of his own thoughts?"

August 2025

When Ethan and Zhuang Rongtao first pitch Zai's technology to investors, they are initially rejected outright. They don't have a proper business plan. They don't have a track record. They don't have any superstars on their management team. They don't have much of a management team at all.

Zhuang Rongtao has been, up to this point, Zai's entire management team. With just a few people and some money from his family, he had hoped to build up a product idea that would catch the attention of investors. And while Zai did have an interesting idea with the mind-reading virtual reality goggles, it hadn't been clear how Zai would turn that into a revenue stream. How would they make money? Would they license the technology to another tech company? Would they build out applications for it themselves? Would they sell their company outright?

Now that they have stumbled into what may be the technology revolution of the century, there's a stronger sense of importance to their mission. It's no longer just a new consumer product. It's a world changer. And they need investors to make it happen.

During lunch together one day on one of Ethan's recent trips back to Beijing, Zhuang Rongtao had asked Ethan to help.

"What would you want me to do?" Ethan genuinely didn't see how he would fit in.

"You seem to know how to get in with people. You could help us with tech deals. And...we need money."

"You need money?"

"We need money."

"Like how much?"

"My family has been funding us," Zhuang Rongtao explains, "but they can't keep going forever."

"Why not just approach professional investors with your business plan?"

"That's where I thought you'd be able to help."

Zhuang Rongtao had been enthusiastic about the new technology, while Ethan had some reservations. Why was Peter always complaining about headaches? Ethan, too, had experienced headaches and disorientation while he was being neurostalked. It would be embarrassing to go to investors, and eventually to consumers, with gaming technology that causes headaches.

Zhuang Rongtao investigated this point with the engineers at Zai. Initially, Cheng Fengxiang had laughed it off. "We'll get it to work," he said. "Early virtual reality technology was like that. 3D movies, too. They made people dizzy." But he promised to explore the issue, anyway.

As they gained experience with the technology, though, the Zai engineers had come to the conclusion that there actually wasn't any intrinsic reason for headaches. Even so, the question remained. Was there any connection at all between Peter's headaches and the mind-interfacing technology? Or was it just Peter? Maybe he had migraines of his own, with no connection to the voices.

Sun Yang, as Zai's software, gaming, and user experience architect, eventually responded with a somewhat more definitive result, messaging Ethan, writing: "It is just one of many sensations. I believe it is possible to create any feeling with this new technology. But if the parameters are set properly, there will not be a headache."

Ethan had been a bit surprised. *Any* feeling? And is a headache just a feeling? But then he realized there was an ambiguity in Sun Yang's comments. By "feeling", did Sun Yang mean like what you feel when something physically touches you? Or like what you feel when you're hungry? Or like what you feel when you're sad or lonely? Is a headache just pain? Is pain just a feeling? But what about the muscle tension? It's more than just a feeling. The muscles squeeze and it wears you out.

Sun Yang had sent a follow-up message a short time later with some further thoughts. It could have been the stress of the situation which led to Peter's headaches and Ethan's disorientation. Unless the signal strength was very high, radio wave patterns wouldn't give a person headaches.

Ke Qunxiang had asked Sun Yang to share some information with Ethan about research articles dating back to the 1960s that explored the issue. The articles described incidents involving people who, standing in front of high-powered microwave transmitters, such as those used for radar applications, had experienced headaches and nausea, itching, and pinprick sensations on their bodies. But the signal strength used by Zai's transmitter is relatively weak, no stronger than ordinary cell phone transmissions.

On Ethan's next visit to Peter, he had asked Peter about his headaches, and Peter described his experiences again. He didn't have headaches *all* the time. They would come and go. And the very first time he heard the voices, there was no discomfort at all. Ethan began to wonder whether the headaches were due to long-term exposure. But he hadn't been exposed long himself when he started having headaches, so that didn't seem like a good explanation. Ethan wrote back to Sun Yang.

Sun Yang again replied, including a direct quote from Ke Qunxiang this time. A poor or buggy implementation of the technology could cause side effects by sending the wrong brain codes to a person, accidentally triggering headaches or other effects. Apart from creating the virtual sensation of a headache, which is just a feeling, an actual tension headache could be created by signaling the brain with brain codes that tighten up the muscles around the head.

It had been known since the time the Italian physician Luigi Galvani twitched a frog's leg in 1780 that electricity could activate a muscle. The significance of this later became clear when it was eventually discovered that electricity is, in fact, how the muscles are controlled in the body. But it wasn't until the mid-nineteenth century that a scientific understanding of the relationship between mind and body began to develop, and with it, an understanding of how the muscles are controlled by the brain.

One place where such research was done was the pathological laboratory at the West Riding Lunatic Asylum, a sprawling complex of three to five story yellow brick buildings housing over 1400 patients in the city of Wakefield, England. There, the Scottish psychiatrist and neurologist James Crichton-Browne, the asylum's superintendent from 1866 to 1875, directed research into the physical basis of behavior and the relationship between disease in the body and mental disease, the research which would ultimately lead to the first real understanding of how the mind controls the body.

It wasn't like Crichton-Browne just jumped right into brain research, though. His task was to run an asylum. But he would bring medical thinking to the problems faced by the asylum, a relatively new idea for the time. He had noted in his first annual report to the local magistrates who provided oversight to the asylum that more had to be done than to continue the expansion in capacity that it had undergone over the previous eight years. He didn't believe in merely providing "convenient storage of heaps of social debris". The solution would be in the application of medical science. In fact, bacterial infections of the brain were common in those days, particularly as antibiotics were not yet available. Knowledge of the brain, and of the treatment of infections generally, was limited. Such infections were likely the original reason for many admissions, and with no cure available, patients would spend years, sometimes a lifetime, at the asylum. The damage to brain tissue caused by the infections led to a wide variety of neurological and psychological symptoms, with patients suffering from cognitive impairment, personality disorders, paranoia, hallucinations, mood swings, psychosis, and dementia, and also paralysis, blindness, headaches, and muscle jerks. It was a major goal of the research at the asylum to gain insight into the causes of these conditions, termed *insanity* at the time, and possible therapies for them.

Where would Crichton-Browne start? How would he get a handle on the problem? Initially, he focused on sanitation. The drains in the facilities got special note in his report. A cholera pandemic had swept the planet just thirty-some years prior, eventually resulting in the 1848 Public Health Act aimed at improving the quality of sewers and the provisioning of clean drinking water. To quote Crichton-Browne, "Madness may have its roots in the drains. Foul air, filthy water, unwholesome dwellings, are influential, directly and indirectly, in deranging the normal action of the brain." But he didn't stop there. In 1870, he had converted a disused cellar into a laboratory for the preparation of drugs. In 1871, he published the first annual volume of the West Riding Lunatic Asylum Medical Reports, a collection of papers documenting the asylum's own findings. And in 1873, the very same year the Scottish mathematician and scientist James Clerk Maxwell published his treatise on electricity and magnetism, which with Charles Darwin's *On the Origin of Species* and Isaac Newton's *Principia Mathematica* ranks in the top scientific publications of all time, Crichton-Browne had opened up the asylum's pathological laboratory.

He engaged in extensive correspondence with Darwin, who had been a medical student at the University of Edinburgh at about the same time as his own father, William A. F. Browne. Crichton-Browne and Darwin shared the belief that biology provided the basis for the mind and that the muscles provided the essential mode of expression. And Darwin took that to be literally the case. Facial expressions, vocal expressions, hair standing on end. The muscles communicate emotions. And yes, *muscles* make the hair stand on end. The goosebumps you get work the same way as when a frightened cat's hackles rise or a threatened porcupine raises its quills. In each case, tiny muscles under the skin tug at the bases of the hairs or the quills, pulling them upright.

During Crichton-Browne's time at West Riding, Darwin had been working on his new book, *The Expression of Emotions in Man and Animals*, devoted to the idea of a shared origin for emotions in evolution similar to the evolution of other traits of animals and of man. He had thought it not coincidental that animals of one species could understand at least some of the emotions expressed by animals of another, not least of which was man's ability to recognize an animal's fright, as when one feels the violent beating of a horse's heart through the saddle or observes the trembling of a canary, the base of its bill turning pale. And not just fright, but also expressions of joy. The frisking of a horse in an open field, the joyful barking of a dog, wagging its tail. He explored expression in animals and man in encyclopedic completeness. Disdain and contempt. Guilt. Surprise and fear, shame, shyness. Grief and dejection. Pride. Love and tender feelings.

Crichton-Browne had high hopes for Darwin's new work and had written to him in April of 1873 to tell him of the work of one of the researchers at the lab, a Dr. Ferrier, who "has discovered that every convolution of the brain is in direct relation with certain groups of muscles, and controls their actions". Darwin had replied immediately to request a copy of the published paper, asking whether Professor Ferrier believes that he "excites an idea and this leads to the movements, or that he acts directly on the motor nerves". This was a prescient question, and a deep one. When you carry out a motion to do something, or, say, to show an emotional expression, are you controlling your muscles directly through the nerves in your body? Or are you thinking of an idea, something more abstract, and this in turn coordinates how the muscles move?

David Ferrier, Scottish neuropathologist and professor of forensic medicine, on Dr. Crichton-Browne's invitation, had gone to work at the pathological laboratory, returning to London later the same year to continue his research at the newly built Brown Animal Sanatory Institution, a veterinary hospital. There, he developed a theory of what he called cerebral localization, the idea that different places in the brain carry out different functions. Each part of the brain is specialized, and even within the specialized areas, there are detailed maps of how the work gets done. The one area he spent the most time studying was what we call today the motor cortex, the part of the brain from which neurons connect to the hundreds of muscles in the body.

In his experiments, Ferrier surgically exposed the surfaces of the brains of macaque monkeys, then placed electrodes into their brains, stimulating them with varying patterns of electricity. Depending on the location stimulated, different muscle motions would be produced. The right thumb would extend, or the left foot would twitch. Or the left arm and hand would extend, as if reaching for something. Or one hand would reach to the mouth. The motion could be simple, as when the right upper lip would rise. Or it could be more complex, as when the monkey would open its mouth and stick its tongue out. If the stimulus was excessive, a hand might clench and then spasm for minutes after the stimulus was removed. The functions seemed to be grouped into locations by the type of activity: eating, facial expressions, visual activity, and many others. The monkeys were alive. And yet, by stimulating one spot or another in their brains, they could be forced, without their cooperation, to make specific movements.

He didn't just work with macaques. At West Riding Asylum, he experimented on cats and dogs and rats, jackals, guinea pigs, pigeons, frogs, and even fish, securing the body of the fish in a clamp and keeping the mouth of the fish underwater in a trough. He explained that "Exposure of the brain and fixation of the animal for the purposes of experiment are comparatively easy. ... Free play was allowed to the tail and fins. Irritation of the hemisphere caused the tail to be struck to the opposite side..." But the movements were "too complex and irregular to admit of exact description." As with frog brains, fish brains proved to be too small to work with using his experimental technique, making it difficult to identify relationships between particular motions and particular locations within their brains.

He was more successful with the larger animals. In one particular observation from his experiments with dogs, he wrote: "Occasionally, as described in my first experiments, the stimulation of this region caused also vocalisation, or feeble attempts at barking or growling. In a subsequent experiment, this was exhibited in a very striking manner. Each time the electrodes were applied to this region, the animal uttered a loud and distinct bark. To exclude the possibility of mere coincidence, I then stimulated in succession various parts of the exposed hemisphere, producing the characteristic reaction of each centre, but no barking. The reapplication of the electrodes to the mouth centre elicited the barking, and did so invariably several times in succession."

By comparing the brains of different animals and the way their muscle motions were triggered by electrical stimulation, he demonstrated how control of the muscles by the brain was a general phenomenon, with similar actions in similar parts of the brain across species, at least to an extent, and that one could therefore extrapolate the findings to human beings. He summarized his work in his book *The Functions of the Brain*, published in 1876.

The Zai engineers were unaware of the history of brain research. They weren't familiar with Dr. Ferrier's work, nor with the ideas of maps in the brain, and that didn't matter. They were not concerned, as Dr. Ferrier was, with the *physical* locations of the functions of the brain. They were rediscovering how the brain works on their own, in an entirely new way, working instead in an abstract space defined by the way the brain interacts with patterns and shapes of radio signals. Thus, to the Zai engineers, it wasn't so much a brain-computer interface as it was an interface to the mind.

The new mind-interfacing technology, Sun Yang and Ke Qunxiang wrote, has the potential to activate muscles indirectly by transmitting brain code signals by radio to the brain so that the brain itself sends nerve signals down to the hand and the fingers, or to any muscles in the head or body. The brain itself does the real work. The brain codes merely provide instructions for what to do, activating the parts of the brain that control the muscles.

With further experimentation, the Zai engineers found that they could, indeed, get a finger to twitch with just the right radio signal patterns, even with weak radio signals. Brain codes whose patterns extended longer over time could trigger more complex patterns of muscle activation, just as David Ferrier had discovered in his experiments with monkeys. So perhaps Peter's neurostalkers had perfected a technique to twitch or tighten targeted muscles so that they could create headaches on demand. The gesticons Peter had written about in his project notebook might also be explained in this way, they wrote.

Zai would keep signal strengths below the thresholds considered safe according to health and safety standards published by government regulators. And they would be careful with the brain codes that trigger muscle activity. But, possibly, Peter's attackers had used higher signal strengths which might have led to muscle spasms. So Ke Qunxiang and Cheng Fengxiang had examined the transmitter that Ethan had picked up at the hotel. They determined that at the distances it was used, its signals wouldn't be very strong. Furthermore, it was a battery-powered device. It wouldn't have worked for long with high signal strengths.

Sun Yang's updated conclusion was that yes, there are a number of ways that the feeling of a headache, or even an actual headache, could be created with the technology. But a properly designed virtual reality game console wouldn't create headaches.

Sun Yang had continued with his experimentation. Was there anything a person could experience that couldn't be created in virtual reality with this new technology? He started cataloging the phenomena, exploring the effects he could create on his own mind by transmitting different signals to his own brain, trying different patterns, at random, just to see what would happen. And if he found one example of some new category of phenomena, he would systematically vary the signals to explore it further.

To make the exploration practical, Sun Yang had asked Ke Qunxiang to enhance the software. He wanted more control over how the signals are generated, and he wanted to have a way to visualize how the brain codes relate to one another. He used color as an example to make his point: When you have red, green, and blue, you also have all the colors in between. There must be something like that for feelings, too. Some basic set of feelings, with all the other feelings in between, laid out in an organized way. Maybe it's like that for every kind of experience you can have.

So Ke Qunxiang put together an app with a graphical interface for Sun Yang to use for this purpose. Using the app, Sun Yang could build a "map" of each phenomenon space. The space of smells. The spaces of different kinds of touch sensations. The space of sounds in the head. Spaces of different kinds of pain. Itches, throbbing pains, and burning sensations. Pinpricks and numbness and nausea. Electric shocks. Pinching. Irritating pressure. Cramping and soreness. And general unwellness, like when the liver isn't working right. Some pains are localized to specific points in or on the body. Others are diffuse. It would turn out to be quite a challenge to sort it all out, defining what maps exist and which perceptions belong to which maps. Are itching and nausea two points on the same map? Or are they in their own separate maps, in different categories and altogether unrelated?

Zai had already noted that, unlike the situation with colors, other spaces, such as the space of odors, require more than three dimensions. They're complicated. There's no simple way to display them all on a flat screen. How do you display an eleven-dimensional space? So Ke Qunxiang's app needed features to slice through the spaces to display them in a meaningful way to the user.

Sun Yang felt like a true explorer on the edge of knowledge. He thought it must be similar to the experiences scientists have when they encounter some new natural phenomenon, like the discovery of radioactivity or the unraveling of the structure and function of DNA.

Perhaps one of the most moving examples occurred when he stumbled across an emotional feeling in his exploration. He felt irritated that day. Maybe he was hungry. Or maybe something was bothering him and he just couldn't put his finger on what it was. So he decided to turn off the transmitter and go to lunch. After lunch, and feeling in a generally good mood, he had picked up where he left off...and immediately felt irritated. It irritated him that he was irritated. It got in the way of his work. So he turned off the transmitter and reflected, trying to understand the source of his irritation, thinking about his life. Was there anything wrong? No, everything was just fine. And he was having a great time with his job.

He turned the transmitter on again, and, resuming the exploration, he felt irritated again. For the first time in his life, he had uttered a swear word and it was embarrassing to him. And irritating. It was that bad. He turned off the transmitter again.

Only then did he realize that his irritation went away when he turned off the transmitter. *Because* he turned off the transmitter.

He sat unmoving for a couple of minutes, first recovering his composure, then adding onto that some distance from the process. One more time, he turned the transmitter on and beamed the signal to his head. And again, he instantly felt irritated. But this time, he understood the reason. He turned off the transmitter and marveled at his discovery.

Taking the viewpoint of an experimental scientist, he had carefully noted the effect. It marked a point in a space. Tentatively, he labeled it *Emotions.* And, for the first time, he worried about the process he was using to explore. He would have to be careful. What would he find next? Extreme anger? Depression? Deep anguish? If he hit upon *lassitude* or *apathy*, would he sit for a long time doing nothing, lacking the energy or the willpower to turn off the transmitter?

He decided he would set a time limit in the software for each experimental trial, just in case, allowing no more than a few seconds for each effect. He also decided to make a big jump, far away from that one point in the space of emotions. He had hoped to discover a happier emotion, maybe the sense of well being, or even elation, that he could use as his base of exploration, so that he could edge carefully toward the negative emotions.

What he found next was so subtle, with his big jump to a different signal pattern, that he almost didn't notice. This time, the parameters he set had triggered no perception of a sensation. But he wasn't sure there was nothing at all. There was something. Kind of. But it wasn't a sensation. Whatever it was, he wasn't prepared for it.

As he usually did, he tried it again a few times. Most randomly selected transmission patterns have no effect. One must chance across a brain code, something that the brain recognizes. So far as he could tell, there was no obvious pattern to the brain codes. You just had to probe to see what you would get. But even with repeated trials, he still wasn't sure what he was experiencing. It wasn't like seeing or smelling or hearing. Nor was it an emotional feeling, at least, not anything that would be conventionally labeled as emotion.

Instead, it made him feel like he was having a childhood experience.

Perhaps he had drifted off, daydreaming. But when he repeated it, the effect was the same. He was in his childhood again.

That said, it wasn't nostalgia for that childhood experience. It was the experience itself. Like he was there again. He didn't long for it. He didn't have any particular emotion. Actually, that's not completely accurate. He did, but it was the not-quite-an-emotion feeling of what it had been like, in his primary school having lunch. It was memorable, but only in a general kind of way. It wasn't the feeling of a particular time he had lunch at school. It was the feeling of having lunch at school.

He tried it again. And, for a brief moment, he was having lunch at school. Pinning it down as an effect created by his transmitter, it had become more tangible to him, and an image flashed in his mind of the school room where he used to eat. It became clear at this point that this was why it was so hard to identify what the feeling was. It was completely out of context. He thought that if he had been sitting in his childhood lunch room, it would have been obvious. Then he changed his mind. The visual cues and the feeling would have blended into a unified experience, so that the feeling wouldn't have stood out as a distinct and independent experience. This was the marvel of the new technology, that it could create that feeling as a distinct and independent experience.

He wasn't sure what category this experience belonged to. What was it that characterized it? He continued his exploration, varying the parameters only slightly. Unexpectedly, he felt as if he were on a grassy hillside in the summer. He wasn't sure where. Almost certainly not anywhere in Beijing. He grew up in Suzhou, but there was no connection with Suzhou, either.

Repeating the experience, he had tried to identify its particular characteristics, breaking it down into parts that he could use to describe it. But on every trial, he could only come up with the very same description, with no further detail. He was on a grassy hillside in summer. No more detail would emerge. If summer were an atom, and being on a grassy hillside were another atom, the molecule of these two atoms was a single unified experience. Nothing else came to mind.

Wasn't it three atoms? Why wouldn't grassy and hillside be separate atoms, different concepts? He gave it some thought. Perhaps it was like the concept of "Beijing". While the word Beijing is formed from two words meaning "north" and "capital city", it is a single specific thing, a particular place and its connections with the world. It isn't the general idea of north and the general idea of a capital city.

And so it was with "grassy hillside". To Sun Yang, a grassy hillside was a single idea, not the idea of "grassy" and the separate idea of a "hillside". Conversely, summer was separate. The two atoms summer and grassy hillside, to him, had meant the full meaning and generality of summer, and likewise, the full meaning of a grassy hillside, put together into single molecule that was the feeling of summer and of being at a grassy hillside. It wasn't a summery grassy hillside. It was summer, and it was a grassy hillside.

What was summer, then? It was chasing crickets, wading in a stream, sweating in the sun. It was chocolate melting in his pocket and cicadas screeching in the trees. But it wasn't all these individual things. It was a single atom. One concept. An integrated whole.

He had given the new space a name: *Ambient Feelings*. And he now had two examples to put on the map of this space. With enough examples, he hoped to eventually build out the shape of this space, so that he could visualize its dimensions and explore it more systematically.

He tried varying the parameters a few more times to explore the space of ambient feelings. But the variations hadn't produced any identifiable experience. He couldn't be sure as to whether it was because he had not chanced upon any of his mind's own brain codes, or whether it was merely because the effects were too subtle. Perhaps what the radio patterns might have triggered were things he had rarely experienced and which had left too faint an imprint on his mind. Perhaps there are brain codes which, only for lack of practice, produce no perception.

In contrast with the ambient feelings, the exploration process for virtual odors had been straightforward. Sun Yang and the others at Zai had by then documented thousands of distinct odors. He reflected on this new space. Ambient feelings. How would he use this type of feeling to create a virtual reality? It had seemed to him to give a deep sense of *being there*. But it was still strange to him, as it did not directly correspond to any natural sense. Even such feelings as pain and hunger have natural interpretations. Hunger and satiety originate with the body's sensors, checking blood sugar levels and other nutrients, and also the sensation of emptiness or fullness in the stomach. As intangible as the idea of hunger seems, it originates with signal data from inside the body and is just as concrete as the sounds that originate with vibrations of air that impinge upon the eardrums. In stark contrast, this new category, ambient feelings, didn't have any apparent connection with any natural sense at all, whether from outside the body or from within.

Up until then, he had identified and documented a number of different experiential spaces and the radio patterns that produce them. Sounds in the head, which the whole team had worked on together, and also odors. Later, with Cheng Penglu, he had explored tactile sensations. And then, on his own, he had continued to investigate, discovering taste sensations and skin temperature sensations. That space had been a particularly interesting one as he learned to vary the signal transmission parameters to pick out particular regions of the body to "heat up" or "cool down".

He had also explored a similar space for the sensations of forces on the limbs. These are the feelings that, for example, make something feel heavy when you pick it up or move it around. Sun Yang had thought that to be one of the best virtual sensations discovered to date. Virtual odors would enrich the experience of a virtual reality game, but the sensation of forces would make the gamer literally feel the objects they manipulate. Pick up a weapon to fight the enemy, and you would feel the difference between a wiry foil and a massive great sword. The gamer would feel it right in their arm, just like the real thing. And in the grip, too, with virtual pressure inside each finger and on the palm.

Another effect creates the sensation of effort, dragging down selected muscles, making them inefficient and tiring them, making it seem hard to work the muscles. Combining the weight sensation and the effort effect, he had created a very realistic experience. Wielding a virtual great sword would feel arduous to the player.

To his amazement, when he turned off the effort effect, his muscles felt restored. It was a short-term effect, perfect for a virtual gaming environment where one might be transported instantly to different realms or scenarios.

Ambient feelings were, to him, a new kind of experience, as much a discovery about the nature of consciousness as it was an exploration of how to create virtual reality. Sun Yang attached philosophical importance to the discovery. This type of feeling was rarely discussed, and even when it had been, it had not been explored as an example of a general phenomenon. He had supposed that there must be a large number of such experiences and that, because they are so specific to particular experiences, such as *eating lunch in primary school*, that they couldn't be like smells. Smells are immediate and universal. Chemicals float on the air and into the nose and they create a sensation, sending electrical signals down nerve pathways. Moments later, a perception is created in the mind and the nerve signals become a *smell*. But if smells are universal, the ambient feelings could be said to be the furthest removed from being universal, something that Sun Yang confirmed by trying his brain codes for them with the other engineers. They produced no effects at all in the others. Calibrating the virtual reality gaming technology to a player's ambient feelings would likely be difficult.

If emotions are the most moving category of feelings and ambient feelings are the most mysterious, perhaps the strangest category would be the body perceptions. Sun Yang had discovered these quite a bit later, but when he did, everyone in the office had wanted to try them out. It was like a carnival freak show, a tour of the extremes of the human form, but experienced virtually in one's own body perception. The transmitted signals could make a gamer feel tall or short. They could also make the gamer's arms or legs feel like they are bulging with muscle or fat, or as skinny as sticks. He figured there must be something in the brain that keeps track of the body's size and shape perception, perhaps for hand-eye coordination. Sun Yang had been particularly delighted at this discovery. With body perception brain codes, a gamer will be able to choose what it feels like to be their own avatar.

He reproduced the Pinocchio Illusion by transmitting a radio signal to his brain. This is the well-known illusion of feeling the length of one's nose growing long. Ridiculously long. To as much as eighteen inches. The illusion demonstrates how easily the self-perception of the body's size and shape can be altered.

After accidentally discovering the perceptual illusions, Sun Yang had researched the illusions online. Were they already known? He hadn't ever experienced such a thing himself before. It hadn't taken long for him to run across articles about such illusions. That's how he had discovered the name of that one particular illusion, the Pinocchio Illusion.

There are many such well-known body illusions. Another similar illusion makes a person feel as though their waist is skinny. The illusion is triggered by stimulating the tendons of each wrist and making the hands feel as if they are moving inward, changing the information that the brain receives and updating its sense of the body's size and shape. Contemplating that illusion, Sun Yang realized how different his own exploration had been. He had no idea how to reproduce the illusion with the transmitter. He would have to locate it in a space of body perception feelings. While the space he is exploring is a mathematical space, a space of patterns, he doesn't know, yet, how to relate the shapes of the signals to the effects that they have, other than by trying them, one by one.

He happened across another body perception illusion, one in which he felt himself shrink in height over a period of several seconds. The feeling wasn't strange just because of feeling shorter, though. What was really strange was the unnatural feeling of one's height in the process of changing. Put on high-heels and you get an idea of what it is like to have a different height. But a gradual change in height is unnatural. No one experiences that, he thought.

The "growing shorter" illusion is an example of what can happen in what is called Alice in Wonderland Syndrome, a neurological condition named after the experience Alice had when she went down the rabbit hole and drank a magic potion in *Alice's Adventures in Wonderland*. Sun Yang wasn't particularly familiar with the book, though he had heard of it as a child. Finding a bilingual version of it online, he had started reading. He was just a few pages in when he encountered the part where Alice drinks the potion and "shuts up like a telescope", becoming just ten inches tall.

Returning to the article about the syndrome, he reads that the author of the children's book, Charles Lutwidge Dodgson, whose pen name was Lewis Carroll, had written in his own personal diary of migraine symptoms, and that there has been some speculation that the author had, himself, experienced the sensation of shrinking and growing because of his migraines, and that his migraine experiences had thereby inspired his writings.

By experimenting, Sun Yang had been able to reproduce the illusion of shrinking. Optimizing the effect, he was able to achieve a feeling of being a full twelve inches shorter than his normal height. It was not as dramatic as Alice's change, but it was still dramatic. He imagined a children's ebook with a built-in virtual sensation transmitter. Reaching that page in *Alice's Adventures in Wonderland*, the child would feel themselves shrink right along with Alice.

What other virtual sensations could enhance a child's ebook? It would be obvious to include virtual smells, he thought. And how about a gentle pitter-patter on the child's head when there is rain in the story, or the feeling of floating underwater like a fish? The child could feel the heat of the sun on his face and the chill of the waters on his feet. He could feel chubby like the gluttonous Zhu Bajie, that famous pig who all Chinese children know well, or sleek and muscular like a powerful tiger. What fun!

He made a note of the idea. Children's virtual reality books. Or maybe, he thought, in honor of Lewis Carroll's imagination, they would be called Lewis Carroll books.

Sun Yang returned to the problem of architecting a virtual reality game. He realized that building a complex environment would involve many odors, so he worked with Ke Qunxiang again to design a way to combine multiple odors, with odor layering and control over odor intensity. He also considered the problem of canceling the odors in the room where a virtual reality gamer is playing. But how would he do that if the virtual reality system can't smell the room to find out what to cancel? Ke Qunxiang had suggested that there may be a way to read the gamer's mind to know what odors they perceive in the room, so that the game console could send out signals to neutralize the gamer's perception of odors in the room. The two worked together in this way to build up the foundations of the new gaming system, with Sun Yang focused on the user experience and Ke Qunxiang developing the tools to make it work.

One day, Sun Yang and Ke Qunxiang used their evolving experimental virtual reality system to play a trick on Cheng Fengxiang. It's a demo, they said, but without visual effects. No goggles or 3D screen. Asking him to hold a square of sachima in his hand, they told him to close his eyes. Reading Cheng Fengxiang's perception of the scent of the sachima, a Chinese snack similar to a crispy rice bar but made with wheat, they transmitted signals to his brain to cancel the sachima's smell, replacing it with the aroma of a freshly baked egg tart. Then they asked Cheng Fengxiang to take a bite. Just as the sachima had been about to reach Cheng Fengxiang's mouth, they transmitted a brain code to him which made it feel heavy and, simultaneously, changed Cheng Fengxiang's perception of its smell to machine oil, as if Cheng Fengxiang were holding an engine part. It was so convincing that Cheng Fengxiang had declined to take the bite until he opened his eyes again to see what was going on.

Cheng Fengxiang had enjoyed the prank. But he was starting to worry that there was too much exploration and not enough product development. Sun Yang had become obsessed. He had been putting in the hours, but the game architecture still had a long way to go.

Sun Yang had pushed back, saying he needed to understand the technology better. And Zhuang Rongtao had allowed him the space to explore. He, too, had wanted to know the limits of what was possible. At the same time, with his family funds providing the financing for the company, Zhuang Rongtao also felt pressured to get on with product development. His father had already expressed concern that the company's direction wasn't clear. What ever happened to the virtual reality goggles project?

Zhuang Rongtao explained to his family that they're still working on it, but they've recently had an incredible breakthrough, an entirely new technology like nothing the world has ever seen, and this is drawing out the development timeline. Dubious, his father had asked for a demo, and then his father had been convinced. But while this bought Zhuang Rongtao some more time, his father warned him that the family wasn't rich. They couldn't keep going like this forever. The world needed to see their technology sooner than later.

While Sun Yang has been focusing on game architecture and the integration of human perception with the game computer's representation of reality, Ke Qunxiang has been developing a working theory of their approach to this *total* virtual reality concept from a more fundamental point of view. He had asked himself: How can it be that all the different perceptions can be created by nothing more than different patterns of radio waves, with different shapes in space? Smells of every kind, tastes, sounds, pains, tactile perceptions, muscle forces...

It's not so surprising, he thought. It's just like matter. Everything is made of atoms, and those are made of just three kinds of particles, electrons, protons and neutrons. There aren't so very many types of atom, but from those, many millions of distinct substances can be made. Everything from sugar to silica, propane to perfume, styrofoam to steel. And these, in turn, can be formed into everything from corn to cotton, computers to construction equipment, mountains to oceans, and even the human brain itself.

But while Ke Qunxiang had briefly considered the philosophical aspects of the technology, he focused mainly on the technical details and underlying math for the radio signals and related computations in the game's GPU processor to produce the experiences that Sun Yang had been cataloging. Working with Cheng Fengxiang, he had also developed a method of transmitting signals to individual players in the same room without conflicts by tracking brainwave sources. One player shouldn't smell what the other player smells, unless, of course, they're standing near one another in the same virtual reality. When the players are wearing virtual reality goggles, this isn't a problem, as the console could track the goggles' locations. But the console should also be able to transmit smells even for games which don't use goggles.

Cheng Fengxiang has never been philosophical about it at all. He wants to build tech that works. He'll design the game console chassis, get the parts they need, integrate the system components, and test the working system. He'll also be working with the manufacturers. And while he definitely wants to build a product that works well and is fun and interesting to play, and he recognizes that it takes a certain amount of experimentation, he doesn't want everyone going off into the weeds with philosophical investigations.

One day, Cheng Fengxiang came into the office to find a poster that Sun Yang had taped up on the wall. Sun Yang had been moved by his experiments. Individual perceptions could be pinned down to exact signal shapes, one shape meaning this feeling and another shape meaning that, each one with its own exact coordinates on a very clear map. He was especially struck by the idea that feelings, seemingly amorphous, could turn out to be so distinct, and so *real*. Inspired by his discoveries, he had used a large black marker to make a poster which he taped up on the office wall. It said:

CATEGORIES DIVIDE THE FORMLESS UNIVERSE INTO PARTS. THE INNUMERABLE NAMELESS FEELINGS ARE AMONGST THESE. NAMELESS, AND YET, WE KNOW THEM.

Cheng Fengxiang had sighed in frustration. "We need to hit our ship date," he declared. "If we don't sell game consoles, there's no point in doing this." He and Zhuang Rongtao are both practical in this way. Their vision isn't about the infinity of reality. It's about selling an experience. They constantly battle scope creep.

The next morning, Cheng Fengxiang came into the office and put up a poster of his own, right next to Sun Yang's poster. It read:

ZHUANGZI ONCE SAID: LIFE IS LIMITED BUT KNOW-HOW IS UNLIMITED. TO PURSUE THE UNLIMITED WITH THE LIMITED IS DANGEROUS!

When Sun Yang looked over at the poster, his only response was a tiny nod.

Over the next few days, the group had settled on a drastically reduced set of goals for the first version of their virtual reality game console. Virtual smells would be included, and odor layering and fading in game designs would be supported, as would real-world odor cancelation, to remove the player's sensation of smells in the room where they are playing. Other virtual perceptions were out of scope for the initial release. They'd be in the patent applications, but that's it.

They would, though, include a feature which detects each player's breathing and coordinates the perception of virtual odors with the players' real-world breaths, for increased realism. The feature isn't completely realistic, however, as it cannot yet distinguish between a breath taken through the nose and one taken only through the mouth. It had been easy to work out how to detect movement of the player's diaphragm. To determine whether the breath passes through the mouth, they could check whether the player's mouth is open during the breath, but this wouldn't necessarily preclude air from passing through the nose, and the effect should vary accordingly. This potential enhancement is left for future development.

One other odor-related feature that Sun Yang had created would also be included for extra realism: coordination of the swirling and mixing of different odors in the air in the virtual reality environment with the motions of virtual objects and the players' avatars. The feature would, for example, take into account virtual breezes and gusts of wind and air flows from air conditioning systems, fires, and other phenomena in the virtual gaming environment. The calculations for the game physics behind this realism are complex and Sun Yang has already put a lot of work into it.

Cheng Fengxiang's prototype hardware design has been ahead of schedule, and Zhuang Rongtao has already started negotiating with a manufacturer in Shenzhen for mass production. The game console is similar to a standard video game console, except that the console includes radio transceivers and a multiplayer antenna system. Since the manufacturing process will be similar to other game console designs, Zai expects a low cost and quick turn-around.

It's not enough to have the game console, though. They also need games to go with it, and for this, they need to search for partners to develop the games.

What this all meant was that Zai needed investors. They were close to having a real product, but they'd soon need marketing, sales and advertising, they'd need to grow their management team, and they'd need people to work with and support their partners to produce individual games. Zhuang Rongtao explained all of this at his lunch with Ethan. He needed Ethan's help. There was so much to do.

Ethan had mixed feelings. Yes, it will be the technology of the century. But he had already committed to a career in the US. Though, it *will* be the technology of the century. But he is conservative by nature.

"What would I do, exactly?" Ethan had asked.

"You'll be our CEO. And head of marketing. We don't have anyone else for that yet."

"CEO?"

"You'll be our big deal maker. I've already seen what you can do. It comes naturally to you."

The two grew up together in Beijing. They are close friends. And Zhuang Rongtao has come to admire Ethan's talents even more with the events of the past few months.

Ethan agreed to think it over. And then he committed, but with one stipulation. They need to take care of Peter. If it weren't for him, the technology of the century wouldn't be happening for Zai. Zhuang Rongtao readily agreed to the stipulation. And with that, they became a team.

Shortly after, they had put together that first business plan. They pitched it to an investment group. And they struck out.

Ethan then suggested they seek help from one of the investment companies he had interviewed for his article on China's Silicon Valley. It wouldn't be about pitching for the money. They'd be asking for advice.

And now, looking through his notes, he decides to contact a Mr. Li, managing partner of an investment firm here in Beijing.

A very high-end air freshener

Mr. Li, a thin and tall gentleman in his late forties, readily agrees to meet the two to discuss their questions. He remembers Ethan from his media interview of several months prior. He invites them to his office on the 22nd floor of an office building in Zhongguancun. "Bring along whatever materials you have," he says. "I'll see what I can do to help."

Ethan and Zhuang Rongtao bring their business plan and their prototype virtual reality game console. Mr. Li, impeccably dressed in a dark blue business suit with a solid blue tie, invites them in. They all sit down around a table on one side of Mr. Li's spacious office. Zhuang Rongtao sets the prototype down on the table. Then he sets down a messenger bag that holds their business plan documents and his laptop. The two start by explaining to Mr. Li the basic ideas behind the technology.

Mr. Li is surprised. He hasn't heard of anything remotely like it, so they offer a demonstration. Zhuang Rongtao pulls out his laptop and connects it to the game console, then searches for a wall outlet to plug it in. Routing the power cable around his chair, he plugs in, then signs onto his laptop. He orients the game console so that it faces Mr. Li. Finally, he asks Mr. Li to pick a smell.

"Pick a smell? Well, OK, how about wisteria?" Mr. Li says. "Which species and varieties do you have?"

Zhuang Rongtao expresses surprise at the question. "Do they smell different?"

"But of course. Some have the most wonderful scents. Sweet. Or musky. Others are not so nice."

Zhuang Rongtao navigates through a menu on his laptop and finds just one choice labeled *wisteria*. "I'm not sure which one this is," he says. "Perhaps you would recognize it." He clicks a button, and the game console sends out a radio signal. And Mr. Li smells wisteria.

But it's better than that. He no longer smells the new carpet he just had installed. It takes him back to May in his courtyard garden at home.

Mr. Li next asks about a brand name perfume, one he just recently purchased for his wife. But Zhuang Rongtao says they don't have that scent. Their odor database only has a few thousand odors at this point, and only one of these is a French perfume.

"A few thousand?" Mr. Li says. "Are there a few thousand different odors in the world? I suppose there may be that many perfumes alone." He had never given it much thought before.

Mr. Li becomes quite enthusiastic about the venture. How long would it take, he asks, to launch their game console? It depends, they say. If they could hire enough people, they could get it done in two years. Are there any other applications? More than they could count, they reply. They had explored that question one day in a brainstorming session. Two hours into it, they still hadn't run out of ideas. Do they have any working products? Indeed, they do, sort-of, though perhaps the market for it would be small and it doesn't yet have the approvals that would be needed to market it. They have a working neuroprosthesis that allows a locked-in patient to speak with his mind. Mr. Li quips: "We should all speak with our minds, shouldn't we?" They all have a good laugh.

Mr. Li says he would like to introduce them to another executive, someone he has known for a long time, who could supplement their management team. And, if they would be so inclined, he believes that his firm may be able to help with the financing.

In anticipation of expanding into different applications of their technology over time, and noting that they already have a toehold in the neuroprosthesis product space, Ethan and Zhuang Rongtao at this point change the name of the company to something more generic. They would start with virtual reality games. But they now have a much bigger vision.

The tech news media carries the story the day after the funding event. *Zai MindPair Announces 100 Million Yuan in Series A Funding.* The funding is equivalent to $15 million. Enough for three years of runway based on their projected burn rate. Enough to get the product out the door and producing revenue before running out of money.

With their financing success, Ethan officially quits his job in San Francisco, he'd already given his boss a heads-up about the opportunity, and takes up his new position as CEO at Zai MindPair Company Limited, with Zhuang Rongtao as Chief Technology Officer and VP of Engineering. Because he is moving back to Beijing, he abandons his application for permanent residence in the U.S., which has still been in process.

January 2026

The SCIF is gone. Peter had it removed after Shasha moved in last August, after she had completed her PhD, so they could have more room. The voices have never returned, not since that last day when they spoke to him as he lain in his hospital bed almost a year and a half ago.

The timing was good, with Shasha moving in just as Ethan was moving away to Beijing to head up Zai. She started in September with a research position at the Institute, here in the Bay Area, with teaching responsibilities.

Colin is still with them, helping Peter through his daily exercises and attending to his medical needs, and also training Shasha to assist with Peter's particular needs, covering daily routines as well as emergency procedures. Dr. Gestrin also continues to visit Peter monthly to evaluate his progress.

Peter's exercises are extensive, covering several physical abilities: movement of the hands and limbs, practice with swallowing, control of the eyes, and exercises designed to prevent atrophy of core strength in the torso. When needed, Colin stretches his limbs to alleviate cramping.

When Shasha first became involved with Peter's day-to-day care, she had asked what was being done about his cognitive skills. Ever since the accident, he hasn't been the same. He can communicate, but every thought comes to him slowly. It gets much worse when he tires, and he tires easily. He forgets words. Even his speech has slowed down. His inner speech, that is. It was one of the first things Shasha had noticed after Peter got his voice neuroprosthesis.

Dr. Gestrin had said to give it more time. There's not much that can be done for a concussion patient. But Shasha hadn't been satisfied with this response. A year has passed already without much improvement. So she had searched online for treatments for concussion and had discovered that there are a few doctors, not many, who have developed novel treatments to improve memory, concentration and daily life functioning. One such method helps to retrain the brain to become efficient again through the use of visual and drawing exercises.

Shasha had discussed the treatment idea with Dr. Gestrin, and Dr. Gestrin had responded with the caution that such therapies are still experimental and are highly variable in the results they can produce. As a result, insurance coverage for those therapies is often rejected, with only weak evidence from studies to back up their effectiveness. Still, Dr. Gestrin hadn't wanted to reject Shasha's efforts outright and had agreed to give it a try. Together, they contacted one of the specialists in that field, a Dr. Osaki, last October.

When Dr. Gestrin discussed Peter's situation with Dr. Osaki, he had been skeptical, as the evaluations and therapies involve the use of fine-tuned hand-eye coordination. Sitting with Peter and Shasha in their home, Dr. Gestrin had explained the difficulty.

"[That's OK. I've got the robotic arm,]" Peter said.

"He's got the robotic arm," Shasha said.

"He has the robotic arm. Yes." Dr. Gestrin's expression clearly showed doubt. "Dr. Osaki explained that the exercises involve drawing patterns with a pencil."

"[Shasha, can you get some paper and a pencil?]"

He opened up the wheelchair's fold-out table with his robotic arm, then tilted it up for a better view. Shasha put a pencil into his robotic hand, then laid a sheet of paper down on the fold-out table, resting it on the lip that runs along its lower edge, and Peter began marking the paper. Not writing, not drawing. Marking was about all that could be said for it. Scratchy marks in this direction and that. And then he broke the pencil.

"Not bad," Dr. Gestrin said. "Not many locked-in patients can break a pencil." She gave it a little thought. "OK, I'll discuss the idea with Dr. Osaki. Let's see what we can do."

Peter had asked for a robotic arm last February. He figured he had a voice, and he had wheels, which is to say, voice control of his wheelchair. What he needed next was arms. And why couldn't those be voice controlled, too?

Ethan had worked his connections to execute on Peter's desire to get a robotic arm. Despite the availability of an increasingly wide array of prosthetic and robotic arms, it was still a cottage industry, and the search had involved quite a bit of digging around. Many of the arms were still experimental and the trade-offs between different options were not always clear. Neither Ethan nor Peter were even sure whether it would be better to get a *prosthetic* arm or a more generic robotic arm. After all, it wasn't going to be attached to Peter's body. Peter wanted it bolted onto the wheelchair. It would be more like a wheelchair upgrade than a body part replacement. Then again, to Peter, the wheelchair itself is a kind of a prosthetic, a mind-controlled exoskeleton that serves as his legs and torso.

Back when he first started thinking of getting a robotic arm, Peter had asked Shasha to look at websites and videos of robotic and prosthetic arms with him. She leaned over him to type on her laptop, which sat on the wheelchair's fold-out tray, as they explored together.

At some point, the term exoskeleton came up in their search results. Peter was curious, so Shasha clicked on one of the videos. It showed a giant humanoid robot in action. The robot had a cab for the operator to sit inside. It was just like the kind you might see in a Japanese animated robot film. The robot was fifteen feet tall and weighed two tons.

"[Yeah. That's what I want,]" Peter told her. "[But with a mind interface.]" She scrolled down to look at the story behind the robot, then told him he couldn't afford it. "It cost them over $10 million to build." He replied: "[We'll save up for it.]"

Meanwhile, he said, he'd settle for a human arm-sized robotic arm. Still, he had pointedly said money was no object. "[How much could it be? $10,000? $100,000?]"

Ethan promised to look into it and eventually had come back with several options ranging in price from $18,000 on the low end to well over $100,000 on the high end. Any of them would be affordable to Peter, but once he understood the specifications and trade-offs, it hadn't taken him long to decide the most expensive one would be the best one. There was just no question that it went well beyond the capabilities of any of the other three arms. Then, in the back-and-forth discussions with the robotic arm manufacturer, Ethan had explained that Zai would be providing an interface to Peter's neuroprosthesis so that the arm could be controlled by Peter's mind, wirelessly. No electrodes, no sensors, no implants, no wires of any kind to connect to Peter's body or brain. The manufacturer was very interested in Zai's technology, so Ethan had facilitated a deal between Zai and the manufacturer in which they had agreed to lower the price for Peter's robotic arm to *free* in exchange for exclusive access to Zai's mind-interfacing technology as partners in the robotic prosthetics industry. Peter said he was OK with free, and they went from there. That was back in May before Ethan became CEO of Zai. Peter got his robotic arm in July.

Peter's new robotic arm has all the complex motions of a normal human arm, including five fingers and all the same joints as a human hand. It is about the same size and shape, with hard white plastic surfaces covered with a translucent silicone skin. Its artificial muscles are silent in operation. And while a prosthetic limb designed to replace a missing limb requires power to operate, this requirement places no real limitations on Peter's use as it will be able to draw power from the wheelchair's batteries.

The robotic arm had been installed by Zai's new partner on a stand in Peter's home, and the process of programming Peter's neuroprosthesis to control it had begun. For this purpose, Cheng Penglu volunteered to fly out from Beijing to get the interface working. The idea was simple: Peter would think commands and the interface would use voice recognition software to recognize the commands for controlling the arm. Cheng Penglu updated the software on the laptop on the back of Peter's wheelchair to convert these commands into control signals for the robotic arm and connected the laptop to the robotic arm with a data cable.

With the robotic arm still sitting on its stand, Peter practiced thinking verbal commands to it, and it quickly became apparent that controlling the arm wasn't at all like controlling the wheelchair. Commanding the arm with thoughts in word form turned out to be exceedingly clunky. "[Move right. Stop. Move right. Stop. Close hand. Stop.]" It was like that. It was too jerky. *Approximate* positioning was good enough with the wheelchair. But the robotic arm had to be precise. Being off by an inch meant it didn't work at all.

Cheng Penglu tried improving the commands, adding words to indicate the speed and distance for each arm movement, but this was difficult for Peter to use. He couldn't judge the distances needed, and updating the position repeatedly was tiring and slow. They agreed that there had to be a better way. So Cheng Penglu had returned to Beijing, leaving the robotic arm behind on its stand, unused, for the time being.

In Beijing, Cheng Penglu consulted with Ke Qunxiang, who said the natural way to control the arm was to think of it as moving around in space in a continuous way. But how could they do this with signals from the brain? They abandoned the idea of using word commands. Somehow, Ke Qunxiang said, the user should be able to think directly about spatial motions. If they could capture those imagined motions, they could use those brain signals to control the arm.

Cheng Penglu was their guinea pig. They recorded his brainwaves as he imagined controlling a computer animation model of the robotic arm supplied by Zai's partner. The whole arm up and down, in and out, twisting. Flexing at the elbow, flexing the wrist. Moving individual fingers. Eventually, they worked up to more complex motions such as grasping objects. Heavy objects, slippery objects, delicate objects, thin objects. Grips of all kinds. Pencils. Cups. Spoons. It took them a month to work out the spatial motion brain codes that could be used to drive the robotic arm's motions directly from those imagined motions.

Spatial motion brain codes turned out to be different from what they expected. They weren't just about moving the arm to locations in space. The spatial motion brain codes were really about all the ways a person uses their arms and hands. Some people pitch fastballs and others play piano or use chopsticks. And for each complex motion that the brain learns, it creates a spatial motion brain code for efficiently carrying out that motion.

Back in Berkeley, Cheng Penglu worked with Peter to calibrate the spatial motion brain codes, first working with the computer animation of the robotic arm, then later, using the actual robotic arm. He had a list of the basic motions he thought Peter would need, leaving particularly complex motions such as writing for later.

Cheng Penglu would tell Peter "stretch arm", demonstrating with his own arm, and Peter would imagine the motion of the robotic arm, and the neuroprosthesis would read Peter's brainwaves and save that information as a brain code. At the same time, the brain code would be converted by Cheng Penglu's software into control signals for the robotic arm and the robotic arm would trace out an arc. Then Cheng Penglu would tell Peter to imagine rotating the wrist, except that he didn't know the word in English for wrist, so he would point to his own wrist and show Peter the movement. And again, controlled by Peter's thoughts, the arm would do something, but not quite the right thing, and Cheng Penglu would make adjustments in software. After the most basic motions, Cheng Penglu moved on to more complex motions, having Peter imagine picking up a cup or tilting it as if to empty it out. Peter's own arm and hand wouldn't move at all when he imagined movements, of course. He was still locked in, still paralyzed. Not just that, though. He imagined the robotic arm moving, not his own arm. In principle, some day, he might be able to use both together.

Once they were satisfied that the control signals were doing the right things, Peter started practicing his control of the robotic arm. At first, they left the arm on the stand, a short distance away from Peter and his wheelchair, so he wouldn't accidentally swing the arm around and hit himself with it. After he got good enough at it, Cheng Penglu mounted the robotic arm onto the wheelchair's arm, on the right-hand side, as it is a right-handed arm, with the shoulder joint of the arm at the top of a post sticking up from near where Peter's own elbow rests.

As the initial brain code calibration was only approximate, at first, it was clumsy, like a child. With practice, the motions would become more finely tuned. And over time, Peter's brain, and the arm, would change. Neurons evolve. Robot parts wear down. And the software, receiving sensor data from the robotic arm, adapts to keep the motions matched to the brain codes.

This feedback process was something Ke Qunxiang had anticipated when Cheng Penglu consulted with him about controlling the arm. Ke Qunxiang said not to worry. "He'll get used to it," he told Cheng Penglu. "The brain learns. So let it learn." But it did mean that the software would have to continually calibrate. Over time, additional brain codes would fill in, and rough motions would be refined. Back-and-forth it would go, with Peter learning to control the arm and the neuroprosthesis learning additional brain codes to fill in between the rough approximations. *That's probably how it will be with mind-interfacing,* thought Cheng Penglu. *Like two people learning to live with one another.*

The process was exhausting for Peter, but he was ecstatic. It was the kind of engineering project he could really love, and he was at the center of attention.

By December, Peter could control the arm well enough for Dr. Osaki's concussion treatments to be helpful. His brain didn't have to work so hard, fighting with a jumble of mangled neurons knocked out of place by the concussion. With the treatments relying on robot-human hand-eye coordination, his brain became efficient again. His disorientation disappeared and his mental stamina improved.

Still, the robotic arm is no substitute for his natural arms. Peter is not sure what it is that makes the robotic arm less effective than he thinks it could be. The problem doesn't seem to be with the arm itself. The artificial muscles are precise and quick. The arm is well-engineered. He can only say that something is missing, but he's not sure what.

Tuesday, 13 January 2026

Earlier, a light fog rolled through, but now, it is drizzling, with only the occasional ray of sunshine finding its way through voids in the precipitation. Shasha is at the Institute. Colin has already finished feeding Peter his lunch.

Parked in his wheelchair next to the dining room table, Peter is meeting with his attorney about the attacks by the voices.

As things stand, the attorney explains, it has not yet become clear who Brian Breg really is and what he had been doing.

Stack told the attorney he was initially hired to drive people around. Later, he said, he would sometimes be told to drive one of the cars somewhere and just park it there. Just by himself. He never did work out why. He said it felt weird to him, but if that's what Mr. Breg wanted him to do, that's what he did. No one else ever showed up. It wasn't like he was dropping something off. He told the attorney there were others as well. Other drivers. He wasn't sure how many. But it was a tiny company. Everyone worked for Mr. Breg.

Working with the information provided by Stack, Peter's attorney has tracked down Breg, who, he discovered, is now working in Virginia for another company. Breg's own company is now defunct. He had contacted Breg, asking for an explanation, but initially got no response. He then put more pressure on him by revealing that he has already had discussions with a former employee who would be a witness against him. This finally got Breg's attention, but nevertheless, Breg claimed to have done nothing wrong.

One big question which still remains is whether the entire operation was just a sophisticated form of identity theft. Stack may not have been entirely forthright in saying what he knows about the organization. But the attorney thought that unlikely. Why would they have followed Peter around for an entire year if they would have obtained his passwords and other personal data within the first month or two? There must be more to it.

Peter asks whether Shasha might also have a case against Breg or his company. The attorney says that she might well have. She has an expectation of privacy when conversing within Peter's home. If they monitored Peter's mind to listen to her conversation there, using Peter's mind as a kind of remote microphone, then her privacy was violated. But for her to have her own claim, there would have to be evidence that Breg actually listened to Shasha's conversation, or at least, that there were times when it was likely.

The attorney recommends going forward with a lawsuit. They've identified the leader of the group of people who were talking in his head. They have an insider witness. They have equipment that they have traced to the organization that carried out the act. And they have what is purported to be an actual recording of Peter's thoughts. Stack's story is credible. The attorney thinks there's enough there. And once the suit is filed, there would be a formal case which would provide the basis for further discovery. He explains what the likely costs would be, based on the information they have so far.

Peter doesn't understand what "discovery" means. The attorney explains. They would gather more evidence. Things like Breg's employee records. And there would be depositions, where witnesses, including the defendants, would be asked questions and would provide testimony about what had happened that could be used as evidence in court.

With that, Peter agrees to go ahead with the suit.

Tuesday, 10 February 2026

Ethan and Zhuang Rongtao sit down for lunch together at a table at the front of a small restaurant in Haidian District, walking distance from their office. They wrap their thick down jackets around the backs of the restaurant's vintage Chinese wooden chairs. The whole place is decorated in the style of old Beijing, with walls of worn gray brick and paper lanterns hanging from the ceiling.

They order roast mutton with cabbage, *laobing*, which is a kind of thick flatbread, and a pot of hot pear soup, the perfect throat remedy for Beijing's cold dry air. When the food arrives, Ethan pours each of them a cup of the pear soup, then takes a sip.

"How are the patent applications going?"

"No big news to report," Zhuang Rongtao says. "We've got fifteen already in the examination process and we're preparing another four for filing next month. It hasn't been long enough for any of them to reach the publication date." He refers to the date on which the contents of a patent application are published for the world to see, as required by law, generally eighteen months after the patent application is filed with the patent office.

They both sip their pear soup.

"We keep adding features to Peter's neuroprosthesis," Ethan says. "I was thinking, it's a lot like an accessibility feature on a smartphone. Don't you think?"

Zhuang Rongtao sips his pear soup before responding. "The neuroprosthesis? How so? Oh, you mean because of how it lets Peter use technology."

They each take a piece of laobing, and, using their chopsticks, they make wraps with the mutton and cabbage.

"Peter would like to do a lot of things that a smartphone does, but he can't, yet. Like texting or surfing the web. Or even just playing some music. We could write software on the laptop that he uses to do those things. Then we'd have a mind-controlled laptop with some apps he could use. Not just for talking and controlling the wheelchair, but for other things, too. See what I mean?"

"Sure, that makes sense."

"But why not set him up with an actual smartphone?"

"Would that be any better than just having the laptop?" Zhuang Rongtao asks.

"Think about what you could do with a smartphone like that," Ethan says. "One that you can talk to with your mind."

That thought had never occurred to Zhuang Rongtao before. He sips his pear soup while thinking it over, then sets his empty cup down.

Ethan pours him another cup, then elaborates. "Think about how much of a pain it is to get your phone out every time you want to text someone. You know how it is. And you put it back in your pocket, and they reply with a *thank you*, and you get it out again to just see that and you really didn't need to."

"Huh. Sure. But —"

"Is there any way to miniaturize the neuroprosthesis? Could we package up the mind-interfacing technology into a smartphone form factor?"

"Oh, I get it," Zhuang Rongtao says. "Mind reading would be just another interface into the phone. That's an interesting idea."

"I was chatting with one of the investors," Ethan says. "He mentioned there's a smartphone start-up for sale."

Zhuang Rongtao's eyes widen. "...No. ...No, no, no. You're kidding. We're already too busy —"

"It'll be huge. And the start-up will be gone if we don't act soon. If they don't find a buyer, they're out of business. And if they do, they're gone. We may never get a chance like this again."

"We haven't even launched the game console yet."

"I know."

"How are we supposed to do that?"

"Could it be done, technologically speaking?"

They eat in silence as Zhuang Rongtao thinks it through. Another customer comes in through the front door and a blast of cold air comes in with him. The customer bumps the back of Zhuang Rongtao's chair on the way to another table.

Zhuang Rongtao sighs. "Probably. Smartphones all include GPUs, so there would be plenty of computational power. The main thing would be to build in the time domain radio transceiver." He gives it a little more thought, then adds: "The vapor cells are only two millimeters in diameter. That should work. We'd have to check how much battery life we could get out of it. But the software changes — I can't even imagine how much work that would require."

"We'd get more people," Ethan says. "It would be a matter of keeping them afloat with additional financing and feeding them with our requirements."

"I really don't think it's a good idea to chase after every little product idea that comes along." They've already changed product direction once. Zhuang Rongtao remembers his father's warning. You have to stay focused or you won't make money.

"It's huge," Ethan says. "And it's a great bargain. They've already sunk 230 million yuan into the venture, but we'd be getting them for a fraction of that. The product works. It's just not selling well. There's too much competition and they don't have enough of an edge. We'd be that edge. They need us more than we need them."

It is a typical winter day in Beijing. Twenty degrees Fahrenheit, sunny, but windy. There's no snow, which is typical of Beijing, as it is a dry place in winter, though the lakes are already frozen over and Beijing's ice skating and ice biking season has already begun. The pedestrians passing by the front window of the restaurant wear thick jackets.

"I call it the Naoji," Ethan says.

Zhuang Rongtao is preoccupied digesting the proposal. Deep in thought, he finishes off another cup of pear soup. Ethan refills his cup. Finally, he asks: "How much do they want?"

"For the company? We'd want to keep the employees on board. Rather than buy them out for cash, I was thinking of doing a stock swap. A merger. We'd take on their salaries, and that would shorten our runway, so we'd need a Series B funding round to keep going."

More money from the investors, Zhuang Rongtao thinks. Round two. It means their ownership in Zai will be diluted, with a bigger portion going to the investors, but he trusts that Ethan knows what he's doing.

Ethan's Naoji concept is simple and powerful. Start with a standard smartphone. Add on an interface for it to talk to your brain. Create some software interfaces to the apps on the phone so that they can use the information going back and forth with the brain. And there it is.

Zhuang Rongtao felt overwhelmed by the amount of work implied, even though they would be starting with both a working smartphone design and a working mind-interfacing system. The hard part was merging the two products into one. In some ways, it was building the concept of a smartphone from the ground up, with an entirely new way of using it. Ethan thought they should leverage the potential of the mind interface to the max. You should be able to use the Naoji without even taking it out of your pocket. And this meant that each app would have to be redesigned to work by thought alone, making it both hands-free and vision-free.

You could send audio text messages just by thinking them. The Naoji would read the sounds in your inner voice, package them up as an audio text message, and send it out over the Internet or over the cell network. The other end wouldn't need any special technology to play the message back. And when the reply comes back, the Naoji would play the audio message in your inner voice. If the reply's a text message, it would first convert it to audio using text-to-speech technology. You wouldn't have to get your phone back out. You'd just hear *thank you* in your head, and that would be that. And only you would hear the message.

But there's more, much more. You could ask a digital assistant a question just by thinking, and you'd hear the reply in your head. The world would be just a thought away. Map directions. Web page contents. Word definitions. Appointment reminders. You'd need the phone in your pocket, but you'd never get it out.

Almost any app could be extended to communicate with the mind. Ethan brought up the example of foreign language dictionaries. The app could do translation look-ups, right in your head. But it's better than that, he said. Imagine a user listening to someone speaking in a foreign language, so that the Naoji hears the sounds that the user hears and translates them as whole sentences, providing automatic real-time translation services. The calculator app could do the math for you. Just think of the problem, and you hear the answer in your head. What's 273 times 5019? Anyone could be a savant.

Would this be a big deal? You could do all of these things by holding a smartphone in your hands. But now, your smartphone only has to be nearby somewhere. In your pocket, or on the table, or plugged in by the wall, charging. You could be cooking and, with your hands freed up, hear the step by step instructions for a recipe, then receive a phone call, hang up and send a text message, then return to your cooking, all without touching the phone. You could use it while jogging or at the gym. Or in the shower.

With the elimination of the need to press buttons, see the screen, or listen to the speakers, the mind interface would be a major accessibility improvement for smartphones. It would be nearly universal. The blind, those suffering from paralysis or other difficulties with movement, and despite its reliance on word sounds, even those with hearing loss could still interact with it.

Ethan had coined the term Naoji for his new product idea, with the idea of trademarking it. Formed from two Chinese characters, *nao* meaning *brain* and *ji* meaning *device*, it echoes the Chinese word for mobile phone, *shouji*, which translates as *hand (carried) device*, that is, mobile device.

To make it practical, the Naoji would have to train itself to understand the user's brain codes for sounds. After the merger, Ke Qunxiang works on this problem, so that the Naoji can calibrate itself automatically. His first solution isn't particularly elegant. It involves having the user listen to long series of sounds while reading the user's brainwaves. But he eventually works out a method of calibrating using only the ambient sounds that the user hears naturally as they go about their day.

Ethan asks the engineering team to consider the problem of how the Naoji would know which thoughts are private and which are commands for the Naoji. The *kai-guan* protocol that Cheng Fengxiang invented for Peter, thinking *kai* to start and *guan* to finish every command, would be cumbersome, he says. They need a more natural protocol for mental commands.

It is Sun Yang who solves the problem. As a highly introspective individual, it comes to him naturally. In one of the Naoji engineering meetings, he describes his idea: When you think, you often think "to" some direction or thing. If the Naoji can read your mind to determine what you are thinking to, the Naoji could then determine whether you are thinking to *it*. It would be like knowing whether someone is talking to you or to someone else by looking at their expressions and body language.

No one else in the meeting quite gets what he means at first, so Sun Yang gives an example. "Think of this," he says. He writes 21 x 32 on the whiteboard. "You do it in your head," he says.

The other engineers still don't get it. Of course it's in their heads. So Sun Yang explains further: "The idea is in your head. It's not in front of you or off in the distance. And it's not the person you're talking to on the phone. If you're calculating 21 x 32 in your head, you're not thinking of another person or another place or thing."

This explanation finally gives the engineers a hint of what he really means. He continues with another example. "Suppose now that you tell someone you love them. Look at someone in the room and say it. Say: I love you." He waits for them to try it.

Cheng Penglu asks: "Could we try something else? Maybe like, I like you?"

Sun Yang answers: "You could. But try *I love you*. It will be more obvious."

So they do. And they get it.

Sun Yang explains further: "If you cheat and you don't really want to say *I love you* to the other person, then you won't think *to* them. You would feel uncomfortable if you did. Instead, you just keep it in your head. Like 21 x 32. Did you really think of the love going to the person you were looking at?" he asks.

He asks them to try other examples, to make it more clear. "Think: Where is your home from here? Which way is it? Don't look that way. Just imagine it. That is a direction out there in the world. Now think: Where is the first floor of this building? Imagine it in space, down below your feet. You can feel a difference, even if you don't think of this difference in words."

Cheng Fengxiang still doesn't get the connection. "What does this have to do with a mental command protocol?"

"If you want to give a command to the Naoji," Sun Yang says, "you should think *to* it. And it will know the command is for it."

Ke Qunxiang speaks up. "That can be done. We can get that from the brainwaves. There must be something different about them which depends on how you're thinking."

Everyone in the room feels shivers run through them. The Naoji wouldn't just listen to the words in the your head. It would also just *know* when you're giving it a command and when you're merely thinking to yourself, or to someone else. Reading your brainwaves, it could tell the difference.

Sun Yang sums it up: "This is what people already do when they talk and think. It would be natural."

Zhuang Rongtao says they should call it the MindPair protocol. He makes a note to start a patent application for it.

Cheng Fengxiang thinks back to Sun Yang's example of thinking of directions. Home is off to the left and off in the distance, several miles away. The first floor of the building is downward, below your feet. He asks: "Can the new protocol figure out when Peter's thoughts are intended for the wheelchair? It would be great if the wheelchair could know which way to go just by reading Peter's brainwaves for different directions. Then we could get rid of the voice commands."

Sun Yang answers softly and without hesitation. "It can."

Cheng Fengxiang grins. "Fantastic. That'll be a major upgrade. No more *kai* and *guan*. And no more Politan right, Politan left, either."

Sun Yang gives a small nod.

Friday, 20 February 2026

The attorney is meeting with Peter at his home. There is a major development he needs to discuss. There's a search warrant.

As part of the disclosures in the lawsuit, the attorney revealed to Breg that they have what appears to be mind-interfacing equipment. He also made it clear that Stack will testify that this equipment was used by Breg's employees, and furthermore, that they have an expert witness to testify about the operation and use of such equipment.

This really got Breg's attention, who, in response, revealed that there was a warrant which he relied on in Peter's case. He admits this but refuses to provide a copy of it.

Peter is dumbfounded. "[They were investigating me? Guan.]"

The attorney says that would be the implication.

"[That's just, I don't get it. That's... ...Guan.]" He's really not sure what to say.

"Can you think of any reason why there might be an investigation?"

"[No. Guan.]"

As a consequence of this revelation, the attorney will later add the United States to those named on the suit. With further probing, the attorney will eventually discover, but only with great difficulty, that Brian Breg's organization had been an investigative services contractor to an agency of the government and that they specialized in just one type of investigation, the extraction of difficult-to-obtain information using advanced technology, such technology not being specified. He will also discover that they were never authorized to search Peter's possessions or his condo. Nor did they, as far as he can determine.

With those discoveries, the attorney speculates that there may also have been other contractors or agencies participating in the implied investigation.

"There are few circumstances," the attorney says, "where a warrant would exist but the investigators wouldn't provide a copy to the person or place searched, though in recent years, there has been an increase in such cases. One would be that the investigation is still ongoing and they're trying to avoid alerting the person being searched. But that's pretty unlikely to be the situation here, especially with the amount of time that has passed."

The attorney tries to imagine another explanation. "Tell me the story, again. Whatever you can remember. And tell me everything you can, including any details you might not think would be relevant."

As Peter retells his story, the attorney ignores the incongruity of Peter's expressionless face with the emotional tone of voice he expresses through his neuroprosthesis.

Peter begins by mentioning some of the phrases which stuck in his mind from the experience. *I'm from The Lab. Tell me everything you ever did wrong. We just listen.* He talks about gesticons. He tells stories about being followed everywhere. He describes his attempts to use a drone to find the source of the radio signals carrying the voices.

His explanation is abbreviated and slow, but the attorney is patient. While Peter's concussion symptoms have improved greatly, and he no longer feels disoriented, he is still rebuilding his cognitive skills. At times, he feels clear, but then he fades.

He mentions something he hadn't remembered last time. "[They threw some foreign languages at me. I didn't understand them. ...It was kind of...]" He can't think of the word. "[I don't know. Guan.]" He sounds tired.

"Do you have any idea of why they might do that?"

"[No...]" He thinks for a moment. "[I don't speak any foreign languages. ...I took three of years of Spanish, but I don't remember much.]" His mind goes blank, but then he recovers his train of thought. "[I learned a few words of Chinese from Shasha. Guan.]"

Then he remembers the retransmission bug. "[There was something strange. I picked up some foreign language, uh... Some people were talking, and, uh... That was before the voices started. My transmitter sent them back out again. Guan.]"

The attorney studies Peter. But Peter has no facial expression, no body language. "Oh. What language?"

"[I don't know. Guan.]"

"Did they sound anything like the voices who spoke to you?" The attorney searches for a connection with foreigners and foreign languages. The rules for warrants and searches are different when foreign espionage or foreign intelligence are involved. And though Peter is not a foreigner, the wall that used to separate criminal investigation and foreign intelligence operations has been torn down, replaced with a complex interaction of cooperating agencies and oversight. The attorney considers the possibility that Peter has somehow become entangled in just such an investigation.

"[The foreign voices in my head? They didn't sound like the usual voices. I don't know who it was. Guan.]"

"Sorry. I meant to ask whether the foreign *languages* you heard in your head sounded like the languages which you retransmitted."

"[Oh. I'm not sure. ...The sounds didn't stick in my head.]" He tries to remember what the conversations sounded like, but nothing comes to mind. "[That was quite a while back. Guan.]"

The attorney is absorbed in thought for a minute. He asks Peter for some time to research this aspect of the case.

The next time they meet, again in Peter's home, the attorney explains the concept of foreign surveillance and related law and the changes made in the law in 2020. "It's complicated," the attorney says, "but perhaps there's some tie-in." He explains that even when an American is caught up in foreign surveillance, the laws make it difficult or impossible to find out anything about it unless at some point the American is going to actually be charged with a crime. On the surface, this makes perfect sense. What would there be to find out? And indeed, at least one expressed intent for the way the law was written was to safeguard the privacy of Americans whose information might be unintentionally collected during foreign surveillance. But if the American, caught up in the surveillance, has reason to complain, it's like fighting ghosts. Having said that, it is still unclear, he says, whether this is relevant to Peter's situation.

"I was able to get a copy of the 911 call for your accident." The attorney plays the recording for Peter. "Do you recognize his voice?"

"[No. I don't think so. Guan.]"

"It doesn't sound like one of the voices that you heard in your head?"

Peter gives it some thought. "[I can't say for sure, but I don't think so. But some of the voices I heard were just, I don't know...they were just weird. ...I heard a baby cry once. ...Guan.]"

The attorney jots down a note on his legal pad.

August 2026

Sitting in his wheelchair in the witness stand, Peter makes his statement of his complaint, telling his story of the constant mind reading and the voices in his head and the attacks on his mind and body. He also provides a little background on his locked-in state and his bicycle accident and his use of a mind-interfacing device to communicate.

He speaks through his Naoji smartphone, which by this time has become his neuroprosthesis, having replaced the older laptop-based system. He uses the MindPair protocol, no longer needing to think the words *kai* and *guan* to switch back and forth between expressing his thoughts through an audio speaker and keeping them private.

"[A year of torture, that's what it was,]" Peter says. "[I felt like I was living in a goldfish bowl, with people banging on the glass. Everywhere I went, it was the same. All day long. Every day.]" He describes the headaches, the anxiety, the interference with his projects, and his inability to live a normal life. He refers to his novel, explaining that he wrote it to document his experiences, but the defense had already requested that the judge exclude the novel from evidence as fictional, and therefore unfair to the defense, with no way for the jury to know which parts, if any, represent factual events.

After finishing his statement, Peter backs up, then turns his wheelchair, trying to find the button which operates the mechanical lift for the witness stand, but the space is tight. Boxed in by its wooden walls, he can't turn the wheelchair far enough to see the button looking straight on, and he is unable to turn his head to see it. He pokes in the general direction of the button with his robotic arm, repeatedly missing. The courtroom is silent save for the sound of the robotic hand tapping at the wall. The judge turns to watch, fascinated by the spectacle. Peter's assistant, who now sees Peter's limitation, raises his hand in an indication to the judge who then gestures for him to come up and help.

With Peter back at the plaintiff's table, Peter's attorney calls an independent expert witness familiar with electronics and radio science to attest to the legitimacy of the technology. The expert witness, who was permitted to examine Zai's own technology under an agreement to keep unpatented details secret, was also given an explanation of its principles of operation by Zai's head of engineering. He also tested Peter's use of the technology. He is thoroughly convinced it is the "real thing".

At this point, Peter's attorney presents as evidence the laptop and the transceiver device which were found in the backpack that Ethan had picked up at the hotel in Beijing. He asserts that it is this equipment that the defendants used in their investigation of Peter. He then introduces Zhuang Rongtao to the jury as founder and Chief Technology Officer of Zai MindPair Company Limited, and as a specialist in mind interfacing, head of engineering for his company and pioneer in the development of the technology. He has been invited, per recommendation by Ethan, to explain what the transceiver does with the brain.

Zai never did succeed in getting into the laptop from the hotel to see the data or the software on it. Perhaps, once upon a time, breaking into a laptop wouldn't have been too difficult, but security has improved. They did succeed, however, in reverse-engineering the transceiver, the small box with just a few switches and connection ports on it that acted as an interface device to the brain. Zhuang Rongtao systematically explains the basic concepts of its operation without revealing any of Zai's own technology secrets. He has prepared a large poster with a diagram to make his explanation more clear. For the most part, the jury yawns. The explanation, which presents the basic science behind radio waves and the brain, is dry.

The defense responds to these points. First, they hadn't been given the opportunity to examine Zai's mind-reading technology up close, as Zai claims it as their own proprietary technology. And, as it happens, even the defense cannot get into the laptop. Nor does the defense have a copy of the software that used to run on it. The defense's expert witnesses point out that without understanding what the software on the laptop does, it is difficult to impossible for anyone to know what effect the transceiver would have on an individual. There is no way to make that determination by examining the transceiver device alone.

Next, Peter's attorney has Stack testify. Does he recognize the equipment? He responds yes, it looks like the very same equipment he used to read Peter's mind. The attorney asks Zhuang Rongtao to play Stack's recording of Peter's thoughts, the one where Peter had been thinking about his passwords. The recording is short, and only Peter's inner voice is heard on the recording. No one in Breg's organization is heard.

The attorney asks Stack what this recording represents, and Stack explains that Breg's equipment was used to make the recording. The recording was on the laptop. He says he didn't know for sure that it read anyone's mind, but that's what he was told, he says, as unbelievable as it had seemed at the time. It didn't take long to work that out while he was using the equipment himself. And that's how everyone else treated it when he worked for Mr. Breg, he says. They were Peter's thoughts, and Stack really believed that.

Zhuang Rongtao had explained that the transceiver and the software on the laptop, working together, record brainwaves, seeing them as radio waves coming out of the brain. But to the jury, the recording that Zhuang Rongtao played for them sounded just like someone talking to themselves. It sounded like a surveillance recording made with an ordinary microphone. They wouldn't have guessed it was someone thinking to themselves if they hadn't been told so.

Peter's attorney next describes the handwritten note Ethan found in the backpack that the hotel had given him in Beijing, showing the hotel's name and address and Ethan's Chinese name spelled out in English letters. Smudges of river mud still cover the note. He tells the jury the note was found with the equipment, then reads an affidavit to the jury which was signed by an employee of the hotel, stating that the backpack and the note and the equipment inside were delivered to the hotel after being found near a river in the western outskirts of Beijing. The attorney states the serial number found on the laptop and explains the process by which they discovered that the laptop was originally sold to one Julian Brecht, and that Mr. Brecht had been working under contract for Brian Breg's organization two years ago.

The attorney summarizes his point: "The equipment that the hotel handed to Ethan Chen on August 26th, 2024 is the very same equipment that Mr. Breg's organization used to read Mr. Nolen's thoughts and to record the words in his mind and to speak into his head. To be clear, the words recorded were not words that Mr. Nolen spoke. He was not speaking to anyone. He was not even speaking to himself. His privacy was deeply violated."

A few members of the jury shift in their seats. One of them glances over at Peter. It sinks in. They really get it. They carefully look over Peter's wheelchair and its robotic arm, and the Naoji, which is attached to the wheelchair arm, its display screen positioned to be visible to Peter without having to move. The man in the wheelchair is a victim of a completely modern crime, something unimaginable until now. But he is also a beneficiary of a completely modern technology. He would not have been able to speak to them at all had it not been for the very same technology. That said, he is a captive of that technology, unable to function without it.

The defense now tells their story. Mr. Breg was in the business of investigation. He and his company followed the law. They had, and have, the utmost respect for privacy. And their investigation was carried out under a valid search warrant. The defense attorney explains the warrant process to the jury, and the law under which it was issued, the Information Privacy Act of 2020.

Peter's attorney wants to establish whether the warrant was properly issued and whether the description in the warrant conformed to the law, including, among other things, that there was actually probable cause to justify issuing the warrant. This is where Peter's case hits its first *unexpected* hurdle. The defense has never provided a copy of the warrant.

If the police want to enter your home to search it, they hand you a copy of the search warrant, or they may leave it on a table for you if you are unavailable to receive the warrant. But Breg never had any contact with Peter. Nor did he enter his home or his vehicle, nor did he intercept any electronic communications made by Peter. Furthermore, because Peter's knowledge of a warrant might interfere with the search, it was issued as a "delayed-notice" search warrant, which does not have to be given immediately to the individual who is being searched.

The defense also asserts that the search is connected with a larger investigation. While revealing the existence of the warrant had been deemed to be without excess risk, the defense asserts that revealing the description of what was sought in the warrant could still jeopardize the ongoing investigation. The defense provides only that they *have* a valid warrant and that in a private conference with the judge, they had given the judge the opportunity to view the warrant and that the judge had become satisfied that the probable cause requirement likely had been met, and finally, that the warrant properly described what they were searching for. But the contents of the warrant cannot be released into the court's open records. No details of the larger investigation, nor of how it relates to Peter, are provided in open court.

Peter's attorney is outraged at this, complaining that whatever had taken place, it had gone on for almost a year. And since that time, the defendants appear to have ended their search. Breg's company is defunct. How could they, and the government, still withhold the contents of the warrant? And how could the judge find that the warrant is valid, even on the face of it? Does the warrant say that the target of the search is Peter's *mind*? What did it say, *exactly*?

The defense responds: There is no explicit limit for how long they may delay access to the contents of the warrant. The defense tells the jury that investigations take time, years in some cases, particularly in complex situations. It would be unreasonable to place a specific limit or expectation on how long they would delay notice. Then the defense explains to the jury that if the government were to bring a case against Peter with evidence collected in the search, Peter would then have the opportunity to challenge the warrant and the evidence. The defense does not respond to the question of just what was to be searched, nor where.

Over the weekend, Peter writes in his novel. He feels overwhelmed by the trial. He had never imagined that the process could be so slow and tedious. How could a jury keep track of all of this? Even he has a hard time, and he was there. That's what an attorney is for, he figures.

He makes a few notes of his experience, working out how they might influence the story in his novel.

Shasha doesn't ask him about the trial. She just makes small-talk with him and lets him rest. They watch a movie together at home. But he's still too distracted by the overwhelming detail of the trial to focus on the movie, and when the movie is over, he can't remember the plot.

Coffee and a bagel

Back at court the following week, Peter's attorney makes the case for assault and battery and invasion of privacy. He starts by having Zhuang Rongtao play a recording of a Mr. Williams speaking in Peter's head.

Peter's attorney explains: "My client did not hear Mr. Williams speak in the room. Mr. Williams was not even present, nor was his voice carried by telephone or any other conventional method. Instead, Mr. Williams' voice was forced into my client's head. Peter Nolen, ..." Here, the attorney looks over at Peter sitting in his wheelchair, "was a prisoner in his own head. He had no way of escaping Mr. Williams' speech."

"He was bombarded during all his waking hours with such speech, not just by Mr. Williams, but also by Mr. Breg's other employees. It interrupted Mr. Nolen's train of thought. He wondered whether Mr. Williams was a real person, doubting his own sanity at times. He never once saw Mr. Williams, nor did Mr. Williams ever identify himself. Mr. Williams, Mr. Rogers, and Mr. Miller all listened to Mr. Nolen's thoughts, thoughts which Mr. Nolen did not speak or share with anyone. And they spoke in his thoughts. They *replaced* his thoughts. The words in Mr. Nolen's mind were not his own words when they were speaking to him in this way."

Williams tenses up. His expression has a stern look to it, making him look even older than his thinning hair would otherwise indicate. He never looks at Peter, frozen in his wheelchair. Rogers, seated next to him, remains aloof, not betraying any hint of worry, but also not arrogant. Miller is seated behind them. He, too, is quiet, but he peeks at Peter from time to time. Breg maintains a business-like demeanor and whispers to his attorney. All of Breg's former employees are dressed in suits.

Peter's attorney continues to make his case to the jury. "The speech in your head is your own. When you hear someone play a sound recording, it's out here in the room, not in there in your head. And that makes a difference. You could walk away from it, or cover your ears. Even if you don't, you are still able to keep the sounds outside of your head separate from the sounds inside of your head. But when someone plays sounds inside your head, you can't walk away and you can't cover your ears. You can't even think. *You literally cannot even hear yourself think."* The attorney speaks with intensity as he says this. "Think about that." He gives the jurors a few seconds of quiet time to think.

"The quiet you have in your head lets you think. The action of forcing one's speech into another person's head is more than just an invasion of privacy. It also interferes with their use of their brain."

"When someone intentionally does something that leads to a non-consensual touching that causes harm, we call this battery. There are three parts to battery. First, whatever was done, it was done intentionally. When Mr. Breg transmitted signals carrying speech to Mr. Nolen, and Mr. Nolen heard those signals as speech in his head, Mr. Breg carried out this process intentionally. It wasn't an accident."

"The second point is that Mr. Nolen didn't want this contact. It was non-consensual. And the third point is that this harmed Mr. Nolen. The harm for battery need not be a physical harm. It may be mental or emotional."

The attorney felt that evidence of gesticons would have made the idea of radio signals as a form of physical contact more persuasive. How is it any different to twist someone's arm than to transmit a radio signal that does it for you? But Peter had made no recordings of gesticons, and Stack said he didn't know anything about that. They have no evidence that gesticons ever happened. He moves on with a different approach.

"Is what Mr. Breg did truly a harm?" he asks the jury. "Harm can result even when it merely intends to impair or when the contact would be offensive, as when it offends a person's sense of dignity, which is what had happened with Mr. Nolen. But there is more."

Peter's attorney next addresses the question of Peter's headaches, providing the dates of his two headache-specific doctor visits. Ethan testifies that Peter had complained to him of headaches, then explains that he, too, had experienced headaches when Breg used his equipment. On cross-examination by the defendant's attorney, though, Ethan is forced to admit that he never observed Breg or his employees or contractors using the equipment to cause his headaches or to cause anyone to have headaches. And, unfortunately, Zhuang Rongtao had not been able to determine whether Breg's equipment was actually capable of producing headaches.

In fact, each time Peter had visited a doctor, for anything, including his complaints about headaches, he felt remarkably better. Not just better, actually, but completely normal. It was like the doctor's office was a sanctuary for him. The voices didn't bother him there. Were they respecting his privacy? Or was it just a trick so there wouldn't be any observations by a professional that could later be used as evidence? It had always been ambiguous to Peter, an unexplained mystery.

Peter's attorney now moves onto assault. The requirements for deciding that someone committed battery are similar to finding that they committed assault, but they are not identical, and the distinctions can be confusing. Particularly in the case of an offense involving the brain, it is not entirely clear whether there are meaningful distinctions between physical harms and mental harms and emotional harms, on one hand, and mental expectations of harms that may in themselves be harmful, on the other. This, though, is the key element of assault. The fear that harm will occur is itself a harm.

"Contact is not a requirement for assault. A person has been assaulted if they reasonably feared they would be harmed by an act committed intentionally by another. If someone takes a swing at you and misses, that's assault. If they hit you, it's battery. But in place of actual contact, there is another requirement. The person committing the offense must have intended to cause fear of a harmful contact. A playful swing would not be assault. There would be no fear of getting hurt. But a serious throw of the fist that intentionally stops short may be."

"By transmitting radio signals carrying their voices and artificial smells such that Mr. Nolen, and only Mr. Nolen, could perceive them, Mr. Breg's employees intentionally led him to believe he was hallucinating. Mr. Nolen feared he was developing or had developed a mental illness and had spent days researching his condition and trying to understand what to do about it. At other times, Mr. Nolen had come to believe that Mr. Breg was a real person, a human being using technology to induce these effects, and that he was under attack. He lived in fear because of what Mr. Breg was doing."

"Let me now provide you with recorded evidence of Mr. Breg's transmissions and their effects."

Peter had made only a few recordings of Breg's transmissions, on a couple of the days prior to his accident. The attorney asks Zhuang Rongtao to play all of the recordings.

To play the recordings as sounds for the jury, the radio recordings had to be converted into audio recordings. What Julian's technology transmitted wasn't sounds, after all. Instead, it transmitted brain codes for sounds, calibrated to Peter's brain. And Zai, after figuring out how the process worked, had used their own technology to convert the recordings.

Zhuang Rongtao doesn't explain how Zai had converted the recordings into audio. Zai still wants to keep the process a trade secret. So Peter's attorney had hired signal processing experts under a non-disclosure agreement to review their work and testify as to its scientific validity. That is, the experts could check that the recordings were real, but they couldn't tell anybody any of the details. Those would be secrets that only Zai would know, secrets they don't want to share with competitors in their newly emerging industry.

Stack had helped to identify which of Breg's employees had spoken which phrases, and he testifies to this. Only Miller, who enjoyed experimenting with the special effects in Julian's mind-interfacing system, disguised his voice with a sound filter.

In the first recording played by Zhuang Rongtao, Williams, who was Old Man to Peter, could be heard saying: "People need to eat." In another recording, Deep, who, it turns out, is Mr. Miller, had said "Frickin' the real." That had been new vocabulary to the Zai engineers. Frickin' the real. They enjoyed the new English phrase. It quickly went into use around the office and in text messages. With repetition by their friends, it has already started propagating as a new slang term in Chinese messaging apps. Unwittingly, Miller had made his mark on the Chinese Internet. FTR.

From Peter's recordings of Breg's radio transmissions, Zai had learned how phantom smells were produced, and this had led them to discover how to build this capability into their virtual reality gaming system. And now, for the purpose of providing evidence that Peter was assaulted with phantom smells, Peter's attorney asks Zhuang Rongtao to play the recording of a phantom smell signal made by Peter on July 17th, 2024. The recording is just two seconds long. The phrase "recording of a phantom smell" makes the jury lean forward with interest.

Using Zai's virtual reality game console, Zhuang Rongtao transmits the virtual odor recording into the air as an invisible beam of radio waves. As the gaming system normally directs its virtual sensations at individuals playing a game, the jury would have needed to get set up as players. To keep his demonstration simple, Zhuang Rongtao instead aims the game's console at each juror, one by one, as it plays back the smell in a loop.

"Smell signals are universal," Zhuang Rongtao explains. "The radio signal creates the same smell perception to everyone. Everyone smells this recording the same."

One by one, each juror's expression changes from anticipation to wonder. One of the jurors can't help themselves and blurts out "It's a toasted bagel!" and the whole courtroom laughs.

The jury is wide awake now as Peter's attorney presents the history behind the odor signal recording. Entries in Peter's notebook which document Peter's discovery of the signals and development of a method for recording them, the circumstances around the recording itself, and Peter's own expertise in radio engineering which led him to make the recording.

Peter's attorney takes his seat and the defense attorney rises, facing the jury and saying: "You all smelled that earlier, right? The toasted bagel?"

Half the jurors nod, and then more of them nod when they see the others nodding.

"So you smelled a bagel. So what?"

The defense attorney picks up a plain silvery vacuum-sealed bag from the floor near his chair and asks the judge for permission to open it. The judge indicates for him to proceed.

"The evidence presented by the plaintiff takes the form of a sensation, a smell. It is an unusual form of evidence to bring into a court, but here we are. Accordingly, to aid in my explanation, allow me to present not a physical piece of evidence, nor a diagram, but another sensation, another experience."

Standing next to the Zai Total Virtual Reality gaming system console which still rests on a table near the front of the courtroom, the defense attorney strips off the top of the bag, which is filled with ground coffee, but doesn't reveal the contents to the jury. The aroma diffuses through the courtroom.

"Do you all smell that?" he asks.

The jurors all nod, except for one woman who raises her hand. She sniffles as the attorney continues with his comments.

"Because of what I just did, you all smell coffee. There's nothing unusual about that." He sets the bag down on the table right next to the game console. "There's no invasion of privacy here, and certainly no assault. In our daily lives, we are frequently and involuntarily exposed to odors and generally, we have no basis for complaint unless the odor is particularly offensive in intensity and duration."

The judge allows the juror who raised her hand to ask her question. "I smelled the bagel, but I didn't smell the coffee. Is that OK? I'm sorry. My allergies are really bad this time of year." She sniffles again.

Several of the other jurors glance over at her and one of them, wondering how she could have smelled the bagel, mumbles under his breath: "That's weird." The juror next to him whispers "ragweed pollen" to him. The attorney reassures her that the coffee smell was meant only to help understand the point he made. He continues with his rebuttal.

"Mr. Williams spoke and Mr. Nolen heard him speak. And again, so what?" The attorney gestures with open hands. "It is not unusual to hear people speak when you cannot see them. They may be on the phone or calling out to you from a distance. When you hear someone speak, whether they're there in the room with you or on the phone, the sound of their voice goes right into your head. That's where you really hear it. When you hear anything at all, you hear it in your head." He pauses for the jury to absorb this point.

"It is a normal, everyday experience to hear people speak. And while Mr. Breg and his employees spoke to Mr. Nolen, they did not speak offensively. No reasonable person would be offended by their words."

Williams, seated in the courtroom, visibly relaxes when he hears this.

The defense attorney continues: "You have seen that Mr. Nolen has gathered recordings. There were four very short recordings. Mostly, Mr. Breg and his employees listened as they tried to gather evidence. Investigators are not forbidden to speak as they go about their work, and Mr. Breg viewed some speaking as helpful to their investigation."

"Mr. Breg's employees attempted to develop a rapport with Mr. Nolen. In some ways, the approach Mr. Breg took may be comparable to an undercover operation. The clear benefit to this new approach is that, by operating out of view, Mr. Breg and his employees did not expose themselves to the need to live double lives, with different identities in their undercover roles and their real lives."

"When subjects of an investigation become aware of it, they sometimes destroy evidence or go into hiding. Thus, to avoid tipping off the investigation to Mr. Nolen or his affiliates, Mr. Breg did not reveal the investigation to Mr. Nolen, nor did he reveal facts or knowledge of the events which were under investigation. As Mr. Breg was carrying out a search for Mr. Nolen's knowledge of and participation in activities related to the events under investigation, he was careful not to taint Mr. Nolen with that knowledge. He wanted to ensure that the evidence collected would demonstrate Mr. Nolen's own knowledge of those events."

"Now let me address the question of Mr. Breg's radio transmissions. We are surrounded by radio waves all the time. The radio waves transmitted by Mr. Breg satisfied regulatory guidelines for radio energy and are generally regarded as safe emissions. They are just as safe as cell phones."

"As the plaintiffs testified to earlier, this technology is in use already by the plaintiff himself. Mr. Nolen's neuroprosthesis transmits radio waves which are perceivable in his mind. It would be reasonable to conclude that the radio waves themselves do not offend Mr. Nolen's dignity. There was no assault. There was no intention to harm, and there was no harm done."

The defense attorney next explains that under the applicable law, the investigators are required to minimize information retained so that there would be no unreasonable violation of any individual's privacy. Mr. Breg complied with the law. And under the law, the investigators are under no obligation to inform a subject of surveillance as to its content unless there is an intention to use it as evidence in a court of law against that person. And there is, as of this date, no evidence from Mr. Breg's investigation which is intended to be used against Mr. Nolen.

The defense attorney lets the jury absorb this crucial point before he continues. "I will also add that the investigators never entered Mr. Nolen's home, nor did they search through his belongings, nor did they detain him, relying instead solely on information obtainable out in the open, out in public space."

Peter's attorney rises to rebut this point, saying that his client has an expectation to the privacy of his brainwaves even if they are out in the public space. His brainwaves reveal his thoughts, and he has a strong expectation of privacy to his thoughts.

The defense attorney addresses this point. "But that's the reason for the warrant. When there is an expectation of privacy, a warrant is required to satisfy the exception to the protections under the Fourth Amendment. A judge independently reviews the request for a warrant to ensure that there is a good reason for it, as relates to an investigation, and when there is, the warrant gives permission to investigators to find that which would otherwise remain private."

And with that, presentation of the arguments concludes. It is now up to the jury to decide the case.

The next day, after deliberations, the jury files into the court and takes their seats. The jury hasn't taken long to reach their decision. The jury foreman hands the jury's written decision to the courtroom deputy who then announces it. They find for the defendants. And with this, the case is wrapped up. The judge thanks the jury and excuses them. Court is adjourned.

Breg and his former employees leave promptly.

"[Damn it all!]" Peter subconsciously raises his robotic arm and it quivers in the air. His breathing deepens. He lowers his inner voice. "[They abuse people for their own security. They invade your privacy. They want to know everything about you. Then they tell you nothing. They don't even apologize. What kind of country do we live in where people can get away with that?!]" His face is red.

Peter's assistant turns to listen but takes no action.

Back in 2023, when Peter's radio equipment had unexpectedly received voices speaking in a foreign language and then had retransmitted those voices, Peter had thought it unlikely anyone was listening. In any case, he thought at the time, it couldn't have caused any harm. The whole point of his technology was that his transmissions *wouldn't* cause any harm. The transmissions were designed to avoid interference.

But Peter's transmissions hadn't gone unnoticed. As part of a program of signals surveillance across the U.S. and the rest of the world, a government agency had, indeed, intercepted them. And with that interception, previously unexplained events became linked, with Peter appearing to play a role in an international incident that has yet to be resolved.

The transmissions were unusual, with a non-standard format. They seemed to be designed to be hidden, as the format Peter used for his transmissions were invisible to most radio receivers. The agency couldn't figure out who the transmissions were directed at. This, by itself, wasn't a problem. But when they decoded the transmissions, it turned out that the signal carried a conversation in a foreign language. And the conversation involved a terrorist plot.

Peter's transmission raised several questions for the agency, questions which to this day remain unanswered. Why would Peter Nolen transmit the conversation? Who was he transmitting it to? Was his intention to aid the plotters with advanced communication technology? Was he part of the plot? How did he know them?

The agency was not aware of the original transmission, the one that Peter's equipment had received, reformatted and retransmitted, as it was very weak and also in an unusual format. The original transmission originated close to Peter's condo, from a nearby triplex. But it was far weaker than Peter's retransmission and was not intercepted by the agency. It was not detected at all by the agency which, to this day, remains unaware of that original transmission.

How could Peter's equipment have received the plotters' transmissions, while, with all the power of the government, the agency could not? It was primarily because Peter was close by. The government's monitoring station was miles away. Peter's equipment was just a couple of blocks away.

But there was more to it than that. The plotters' transmissions were even more unusual than Peter's transmissions. To understand this, one could theoretically start by understanding how the plotters' transmitter works. But they didn't have one.

What *nobody* knew, not Peter, not the agency carrying out the investigation, not Breg's organization, and not even the plotters, was that there was a light bulb in a beautiful old-fashioned lighting fixture in the plotters' apartment, a furnished vacation rental, one of three units in a Craftsman style building with a shingled roof and redwood shingle siding and angled wood supports under the eaves that is so typical of Berkeley. There was a light bulb that was emitting radio waves.

The vintage bulb, which has long straight filaments that glow warmly with the passage of electricity, wasn't designed to send out radio waves. In fact, it was a design deficiency of the old light bulbs that they would create electrical interference, fuzzing up the picture on the old analog television sets and frizzing out the old radio talk shows of the era.

It was just a light bulb. But whenever that light bulb was on, it bathed the plotters' apartment in radio waves. And not just any kind of radio waves, but wideband radio waves. Just the kind that Peter's equipment was designed to receive. And these weak radio waves, invisible to the occupants, bounced off objects in the apartment and then continued on their way out of the apartment to the world at large.

Radio waves are just a type of light that the eyes can't see, and like light, they reflect off of surfaces. The objects they reflected off, metal surfaces, windows, mirrors, and so on, all vibrate, though faintly, because the air in the room vibrates. And this vibration caused the radio reflections to go off in ever so slightly different directions, changing the shape of the radio waves emitted from the lighting fixture. And the vibrations in the air in the apartment were created by the sounds of the voices of people speaking to one another. Plotting.

In this way, the sounds of the plotters' voices were imprinted on the radio waves, and the radio waves carried the plotters' conversation out of the apartment. And despite being as weak as they were, the signals were intercepted by Peter's receiving equipment and decoded by his software. It wasn't what he had intended the software to do. It was a freak. A coincidence. A software bug that had inadvertently become a surveillance bug, operating on principles not unlike those used by Leon Theremin's Great Seal bug back in the 1940s.c

Peter's software, by searching for "simple shapes" in the radio waves it analyzed, found the sounds of the voices from the apartment and extracted them. It extracted the plotters' voices, then sent those voices back out again, but with a higher signal strength. It was this transmission that the government agency received. It was *only* this transmission that the agency received, and that they tracked down, identifying its source as Peter's condo.

The court security officer starts moving toward Peter, concerned about his outburst and the erratic motion of the robotic arm, but Peter's attorney stands up to assure the security officer. The robotic arm retracts.

"[They abuse you.]" Tears well up in Peter's eyes. "[*They* feel safe. But then, you don't.]"

Monday, 17 August 2026

The front door and most of the windows are open, letting fresh air flow through and scenting the interior of the condo with the subtle fragrances of the summer grass and a faint hint of the bay. The quiet whine of an electric automobile passes by, and then only the occasional tapping of blinds against window frames can be heard as a gentle breeze sneaks in through one opening or another.

Colin brings two plastic cups of water with straws. He hands one to the attorney, and the other, he sets down on the dining room table. Peter picks the cup up with his robotic arm and drinks.

"Thank you." The attorney takes a sip and sets down his cup, then turns to Peter. "It's not over yet. We can appeal. I've already been working with a colleague on the appeal and I think it could work."

"[How much are we talking?]"

"You could afford it. But this case is extremely likely to attract the attention of civil rights organizations who might support your appeal as a cause."

Peter thinks this over. He doesn't like the idea of being some sort of celebrity. But the support would be welcome.

"If you're OK with this, I can reach out to them. But before you respond, I should explain the appeals process, what it does and what it doesn't do."

The attorney lays out the concept of the basis of an appeal. The important thing to keep in mind, he says, is that they can't contest the jury's decision on the basis of the facts unless their decision completely lacks any support at all in the evidence given in the case. And that doesn't appear to be the situation.

"[But they lied,]" Peter says. "[They said they only spoke a few times in my head. That's not true. And they didn't *speak*. They bombarded my head, all day and all night. They never stopped talking in my head, or... not talking, but, you know... There's got to be a better word. They didn't *talk*. It was in my head, you know. It wasn't *talking*.]"

"That's what you said. And then there's what they said. It's up to the jury to decide what to believe."

"[But we can still appeal, you said. How does that work?]"

"The court has the wrong interpretation of the law. And that's what we can challenge."

"[What law?]" Peter asks.

The attorney sounds confident in his response. "The law authorizing the search, if you can call it that. In my opinion," he says, "they didn't carry out a search. It was something else altogether."

Tuesday, 8 September 2026

Zai MindPair Announces World's First Mind-Pairing Smartphone

Zai's announcement goes out only to the Chinese market, but it is picked up by an English-language news blog in Beijing. The story is quickly distributed world-wide, triggering speculation and awe, and also doubts and disbelief.

The claim is made somewhat more credible when the news stories also report that the company has already released their virtual reality game console and development kit for game developers to start building games with so-called virtual sensations. Another story follows shortly afterwards, written by a reporter who gains access to one of Zai's third-party game developers. Restricted by their non-disclosure agreement with Zai, the developer cannot provide a demonstration, but they do confirm that the technology really works. The game console can make you smell things that aren't really there, and no, it's not just a trick with little cartridges filled with chemicals or anything like that. It is entirely electronic, and the range of smells it can produce is huge. The smartphone announcement states that it, too, will include what the company refers to as virtual sensation technology.

It doesn't take long for other reporters to start inquiring. Does Zai have a demonstration? After repeated requests, Ethan eventually arranges for a demonstration room where representatives of the media can come and try Zai's upcoming products, with a publicity manager on site to answer questions, greasing the skids for the products to launch with credibility.

In preparation for their product launches, Ethan has also been arranging with retail outlets to provide similar demonstration rooms. Both the Naoji smartphone and the Total Virtual Reality game console will be on demonstration and available for sale at locations in Beijing, Shanghai and other major cities across China.

Zai is ready. They have successfully raised the additional funding they need to get to product launch in a Series B funding round. They've been hiring like crazy and their organization has been built up significantly. The game console works. Their third party developers have produced working games. And their smartphone is functional. Now, it's time to roll it all out.

As part of building out the Naoji smartphone, Zai wrote an app for wheelchair control that uses the MindPair protocol, implementing Cheng Fengxiang's idea for a much simpler and more natural wheelchair control interface for Peter. That was a couple of months ago. They had flown Cheng Penglu out to visit Peter, switching out the old laptop-based neuroprosthesis and replacing it with the same beta version of the Naoji that Zai's product developers had been testing.

Cheng Penglu also introduced Peter to all the new apps that he would have access to. For the first time, Peter would be able to send a message out over the Internet just by thinking. He's now also able to read or listen to documents on the Internet, compose documents, play music, and generally, use the smartphone in most ways that any other person might use it. The app interfaces have been re-designed to be useable while the Naoji stays in a user's pocket. Or in Peter's case, while it remains attached to his wheelchair, untouched by his hands.

After the accident, it had been impossible for Peter to read because he couldn't control his eye muscles. Even though he has by now reestablished a degree of eye control, it still fatigues him to read for any extended period of time. Thus, an important feature to Peter, available in the beta release of the Naoji, is its text-to-speech and text-to-inner-speech functionality. With it, he can listen to articles while limiting his visual activity to occasional views of the Naoji's screen to see pictures or watch videos.

With the new Naoji functionality, Peter can now read silently, allowing Shasha to work nearby without being disturbed. It also gives him a degree of privacy, allowing him, for the first time in two years, to read documents without assistance. He can choose to have a page read out loud, played on the Naoji's speakers, or to have it transmitted to his inner voice, using the same MindPair interface that now monitors his thoughts for directions to control his wheelchair. Just by thinking "to" his Naoji, he can switch where sounds play. He can also make up sounds in his head, or speak in his head, and play the sounds to the Naoji's speakers. And he can direct the sounds from the Naoji itself to its speaker, to share what he is listening to with others. He is now, as he tells Shasha, plugged in and fully functional.

Saturday, 19 September 2026

It has been a little over a year now since Shasha completed her PhD and moved up to Berkeley to live with Peter. They considered moving to Vancouver where Shasha's parents live so that she could be close to her family, but it would have been difficult for Peter to set up his care arrangement all over again. With the differences between the US and Canadian approaches to health care and the difficulty of coordinating between the two systems, it was hard to see how he could make the transition with his pre-existing condition and very special needs. In any case, it turned out to be easier for Shasha to find a good place to carry out research work in the Bay Area. And so it was that they had decided to live in Berkeley together.

They have learned to live with Peter's condition, the routine getting easier over time as they developed a daily rhythm, and the process is becoming easier with Peter's gradual recovery, gaining just the smallest and weakest movements as his brain-to-body nerve connections are reestablished. Shasha is able to work at the Institute and does not need to be with Peter all day long. Even when she is home, they rely on Colin to help, so that the routine is not as difficult as it might otherwise be.

One day, Peter suggested to Shasha that they go up to Indian Rock Park, a popular place at sunset not far from the condo. They'd been there many times before, and it is one of their favorite nearby destinations. It has a nice view over the bay, sitting as it does part-way up the hills of Berkeley.

The wheelchair's electric motor strained on the hill as Peter wheeled along the road, the robotic arm tucked in and the Naoji mounted out on the wheelchair's arm. Shasha walked alongside.

Reaching the park, and stopping near a bench at the bottom of the single large rock which makes up a third of the park, they quietly enjoyed the nice summer evening weather. A stairway carved into the rock there decorates the rock like a ribbon, gently meandering up to its smooth bare top. Boulders and trees surround its base. The golden-orange light of the sunset filtered in from the west, and the eastern span of the Bay Bridge,

Yerba Buena Island, Treasure Island, and downtown San Francisco were visible in the distance from their high vantage point.

They sat together, quietly enjoying the sunset.

After a short time, Peter used his robotic arm to remove a piece of cloth that had been covering a small package sitting in the tray attached to the inside of the left arm of his wheelchair. He handed the package to Shasha with the arm and asked her to open it.

Inside, Shasha found a diamond engagement ring and her eyes widened. She was utterly surprised and looked at Peter, unmoving in his wheelchair, in wonder.

Speaking through his Naoji, he then proposed to her. And with tears in her eyes, she said *yes.*

With Peter in his locked-in state, Shasha's parents were against the proposed marriage, despite his rehabilitation progress. How would he provide for her? Shasha pointed out that money's not a problem. There's enough. Plenty, in fact. How would they have a real life together? Peter is her soul mate, she said. They talk about anything and everything. And indeed, Peter is one of the rare people who can listen to her stories and ideas and really appreciate them. They are a good fit. She doubts she'd ever find another person like Peter. And as to communication, the Naoji has made all the difference. With it, and the apps designed to interface with Peter's mind, he is not any different than anyone else when it comes to communicating, reading online, writing emails and texts, phone calls and good old-fashioned verbal discussions, tone of voice included. He checks his account statements online with ease and also makes online purchases, though sometimes he needs some assistance with items when they arrive. Peter has had the beta Naoji now for only a couple of months, but it has already been enough time for it to change his life, and their lives together.

Shasha explained all this to her parents, though they hadn't quite understood. They supposed Peter must be getting help, one way or the other, to do all the things Shasha said he could do. So one day, Peter called them and invited them to visit. Shasha's father, Samuel, had answered the call, and he, in turn, urged Joyce to come join in on it. The call was pleasant and they had readily agreed.

Only after Samuel and Joyce got off the phone did it sink in just how unusual their call with Peter really was. No one would have guessed Peter was paralyzed and unable to speak with his own voice. He sounded completely *normal.*

During their visit a few days later, though, seeing him sitting there in his wheelchair, Shasha's parents had second thoughts. They tried to reconcile Peter-on-the-phone, the dynamic person who invited them, with the scene before them. Would he ever be able to work? Or even help around the house? More importantly, would they ever become *grandparents*?

That was the one that really hit them. Reading Samuel's mind, and confirming their understanding with a mutual glance, Joyce decided she would be the one who would broach the question. She asked Shasha for a glass of hot water to drink and followed her into the kitchen while Samuel stayed with Peter in the living room and continued their conversation about things engineering.

In the kitchen, speaking in Chinese, Joyce hinted at the question. Shasha's face turned red and she laughed a little, then assures her that "it works". Her mother looked at her with concern, not yet convinced. "He can't move, though. Um, so then...?"

A bit flustered, Shasha responded in English: "Think global, act local. You know?"

Her mother was silent, puzzled, trying to decode her daughter's hint. Then she lit up. "I see! Um? Oh..." Her expression changed, puzzled again. Shasha settled it with a final comment in Chinese: "Mei shenme." *There's nothing to think about.* And that was that.

After returning home to Vancouver, Samuel and Joyce discussed the situation. They really liked Peter. Samuel commented to Joyce that Peter is in fact "a cool chap", having really enjoyed their engineering discussion. And in the end, they accepted the proposed marriage.

And so it is that here they are, Peter and Shasha, at home, in a small wedding ceremony, with just Shasha's parents and Ethan and a few other friends in attendance. A flower-covered arch has been placed at one end of the living room, the location where the wedding will be officiated. The guests, ten in total, sit in two narrow columns of ribbon-decorated chairs, with enough space between the columns for the procession of the bride and groom, wide enough to allow passage of Peter's wheelchair.

When the moment comes, Peter places the ring on Shasha's finger. It impresses even him that his robotic arm has the dexterity to do it. He practiced the motions before the ceremony, with a conical dowel serving as a finger.

Shasha looks absolutely stunning, not so much because she wanted to look absolutely stunning, but because her mother wanted her to, for the pictures. Her mother was more excited than she was, helping her to get dressed up in her wedding dress after picking up the cake from the bakery and then ferrying her to and from the beauty salon.

Reaching the point in the ceremony where the couple is told "You may now kiss", Shasha turns to Peter's wheelchair and Peter wraps his robotic arm around her waist and gently guides her in. Embraced in this way, she wraps both hands around the back of his head and kisses him squarely on the lips.

There is a bit of silence, then Peter speaks through his Naoji. "[Nice!]" The guests all clap loudly and several get up from their chairs to gather around Peter and Shasha in a group hug. The group starts taking pictures of each other with their smartphones.

As husband and wife, Peter and Shasha cut the wedding cake together. Shasha takes the first piece. Peter can't yet eat normally and passes on the cake, which is spongy and not easy to swallow, though Shasha delivers a tiny taste of the strawberry buttercream frosting to him. The couple and their guests chat, sharing stories about the couple.

At some point, the celebration winds down and the guests decide it's time to give the couple their time alone together. Shasha's parents stay for a while longer to help clean up, folding the chairs and leaning them against one wall. Peter also helps, using his robotic arm to toss out paper plates and napkins and putting the cake knife in the dishwasher. He's happy. He turns on the Naoji's speaker with a subconscious command and sings out loud as he continues to tidy up.

Shasha and her parents cluster together to spy on Peter from behind as he continues to sing. Samuel comments: "Joyful chap." Shasha smiles to herself, happy.

Wednesday, 4 November 2026

The party chairman stands next to the podium as he delivers a precisely calibrated but passionate speech to his audience of about 500, glancing occasionally at one of the several teleprompters. He looks out at the crowd, seated under the building's geometrically patterned wood ceiling, a puzzle of angled beams and triangular panels and suspended light points. He is flanked by three other party members, seated on stage, all wearing the same dark suits with blue ties. His image is projected onto a large screen behind them, flanked on each side by the party's logo. A news crew broadcasts the speech live on national television.

The audience claps vigorously.

"I cannot sleep at night knowing that we could have done more! But we will endeavor to work in a coalition, which is, after all, in the best spirit of cooperation. We must do what we can do!"

The party chairman paces back and forth in front of the podium before his next impassioned point. Then he raises his hands in emphasis.

"Now let me get to the real point, which is that we cannot allow a deterioration in the quality of our work environments."

The party chairman refers to the recently proposed legislation that has been introduced by the current government. The issue has risen to the level of national crisis and he views it as an opportunity for his party to gain additional traction. He steps through his points, carefully outlining the issues and how his party will address them.

"And so we will negotiate and negotiate and never give up, because we do care! As you know, the migrant problem remains. And this enters into —"

The party chairman looks around at the crowd. He can't remember where he is. Here and there are sounds of discontent.

And now, he remembers that he is giving a speech. Looking at the teleprompter, he tries to continue, but he doesn't recognize the words. He sees letters of the alphabet, but they do not form words. It is as if the teleprompters are now encrypted. The letters blur slightly, then sharpen. He is upset that the teleprompters seem to be malfunctioning.

"So, yes then, we, we. Let me tell you, we, yes. We, ah, we must endeavor."

Unable to rely on the teleprompters, he continues his speech with what he perceives to be his own thoughts despite their unfamiliarity. He desperately wants a strong finish, so again, he raises his hands in emphasis and puts passion into his voice.

"We must endeavor to make progress! That is really what it is."

The audience is increasingly confused. The message being delivered to them no longer has the coherency that it started with. No one claps. His sense of presence diminishes as he struggles to think.

"And so we must negotiate. We can only do what we can do."

The audience sits silently, unsure what to think.

The party chairman now gets a tickle in his throat. He turns around and asks one of his associates for a glass of water, and a glass is quickly relayed to him. He drinks, but the tickle gets worse. He starts to cough. He drinks again, then coughs again. This goes on for a minute or so, the cough worsening, until finally, he wanders off stage in a coughing fit.

What the party chairman had not realized was that between the time he lost awareness and the time he regained it, he hadn't stopped speaking. He had kept going with his speech for another twenty seconds, completely unaware that he was speaking, and also unaware of the passage of time. But the content of the speech was not his prepared speech.

The full scope of the disaster becomes clear to him only later, when he reviews a recording of the news broadcast. Where his speech had been written to say "And this enters into my analysis of the situation," he had said, instead: "And this enters into my change of heart," words he had said without knowing he was speaking. He had had no change of heart, but that is just what he had said. And from there, the content had veered ever further from his true beliefs and from the party's actual position on the issue.

In full, the missing twenty seconds of his speech had gone as follows: "And this enters into my change of heart. Germany cannot be competitive with the minimum wage. Our products are being priced out of the market. And without a market for our products, how are employees to have jobs? We must be flexible. We must make allowances. The minimum wage, I say, is a failed experiment."

His heart sinks when he reviews the video recording. Then he becomes angry, vowing to get to the bottom of the trickery. "I never said that!" He protests to his associates. "How could you believe that I would say that?" He can think of no explanation.

Not one of his associates in the party understands what has become of him. Some worry he has lost his mind and have already started thinking about who their next chairman will be.

Within the hour, a major story about his "change of heart", and the implications for national policy, is in the works for tomorrow morning's papers.

Friday, 6 November 2026

The three prison management representatives, two men and one woman dressed in business suits, take notes on their laptops as the taller of the two men from MQZTOQ, operating a projector plugged into his laptop, quickly steps through a short slide presentation of their product proposal. The conference room is small and windowless, and its oval wooden table barely fits within its walls.

The MQZTOQ reps are pitching a product for prison security and inmate safety that uses technology to "calm" the inmates. The technology operates by transmitting low energy radio waves throughout the facility, controllable by zone. The calming effect, they explain, is due to the interaction of the radio waves with each inmate's brain rhythms. Under maximum calming, the inmates can still function, able to carry out basic functions such as eating and simple communications while reducing or eliminating hostile emotions and actions and reducing the inmates' ability to engage in complex or coordinated planning of adversarial activity.

The technology complements other calming approaches, such as painting cell walls pink to minimize anxiety and aggression. They describe it as "solving the other side of the problem". It's not just the environment that triggers reactions. The inmates' internal states of mind are also important.

The degree of calming can be varied, lessened or turned off, for example during visitation periods, and increased during times of tension. The company generally recommends, says the presenter, turning off calming to provide for "First Amendment time", giving the inmates periods when they can more fully exercise their freedom of thought and expression.

One of the prison management representatives interrupts the presentation and points out that there are no specific legal guidelines for how much First Amendment time they would have to give to prisoners, though specific situations required consideration. Time spent with counsel would also require freedom of thought, she says.

She asks around the room to see whether anyone else has any experience with the issue. One of her colleagues mentions that they're not lawyers. The three of them agree that they would have to explore this issue further in internal meetings. Then one of the prison management reps remembers that there are rules specifically for First Amendment protections for religious purposes. They'd have to turn off calming during worship, he says.

The woman asks whether it is safe. Would the product affect the health of the inmates? They are required to limit exposures to inmates when using x-ray machines for body searches of contraband, to avoid dangerous levels of exposure, and she wonders if there are similar considerations with calming.

The shorter MQZTOQ rep explains that transmitted energy levels fall well within the safety standards for radio frequency exposure. "It's not like the x-ray scanners," he says. "The energy used in our calming product is non-ionizing, which means it doesn't cause any direct chemical reactions or damage in the body, even over long periods of exposure."

The other two prison management representatives nod in understanding. One of them asks whether it would put the inmates into a mental fog or a daze. Wouldn't that pose safety problems for the inmates?

The taller MQZTOQ rep explains the recommended use of their system. "Just to clarify," he says, "our product produces a calming effect. It's not equivalent to mental fog. Rather than merely slowing down or reducing thinking, it also adds a calming influence. In some of our experimental work, we determined that in some people, slowed thinking can actually produce antagonism and impatience, leading to aggression, which clearly would contradict the goal of the product. The radio waves are patterned in a way that induces a calmed state of mind. As to how that works, I'd have to ask one of our technologists to explain further. It's way over my head." He chuckles as he adds this last comment.

The prison management representatives again nod in understanding.

The MQZTOQ rep continues with his explanation: "For safety purposes, we do recommend that when inmates are engaged in activities requiring greater concentration, such as when working with machinery, that the calming effect be reduced or turned off. This is actually one of the great advantages of the system, as it can be controlled to operate at different levels in different zones." The MQZTOQ rep looks around the room and makes eye contact with each of the three prison management reps. "We wouldn't just sell you a system. We think the safety aspects are just as important as the security benefits, so we work with you to put together best practices for your specific environment."

The rep steps through the bullet points of one final slide, providing a roadmap for a typical installation and the follow-up service that goes with it, then asks: "Do you have any further questions for me?" The three prison management representatives take in the roadmap. At length, the woman says not for now, but she will do some internal follow-up and thanks the sales reps. The sales reps leave a few copies of their brochure, then they take turns shaking hands with the woman and the two men.

Monday, 9 November 2026

RUSSIANS DISRUPT SPEECH WITH MIND CONTROL

U.S. MAY ALSO BE USING THE TECHNOLOGY

The headlines are out at 4 AM. By 8 AM, despite the cold and wind, the protest crowds are already growing in front of the Russian Embassy on Unter den Linden in the center of Berlin.

The story spells out the details of how the Russians had parked two vans near the November 4th political convention and had beamed intersecting radio signals at the party chairman as he gave his speech, interfering with the operation of his mind. The German police had been forewarned and had watched as the disruption took place. Then, with carefully orchestrated stealth, they had moved in to arrest the Russians, in the process taking the Russian equipment into custody before it could be shut down, so that its design and operation could be examined in detail.

The party chairman of one of Germany's major political parties had been hit with a mind-control weapon. The Russians, operating the weapon from a few hundred meters away, had aimed the beams at the stage where the politician had been speaking, transmitting brain codes to him, brain codes which they had furtively calibrated and tested over the preceding several months. Taking control of his conscious actions, they had put him into a state of semi-consciousness, and then had proceeded to operate him like a puppet.

The police discovered that the agents operating in the vans had a complete copy of the speech, likely stolen by a mind-reading intelligence operation as the politician had rehearsed his speech just prior to the rally.

During the altered portion of his speech, the party chairman had been completely unaware of the substitution. Nevertheless, from all outward appearances, he was still the human being responsible for the content of what he said. The speech lacked the passion that it had prior to that point, as the words he spoke were fed to him by the Russian weapon as words in his head that he then simply repeated, being unable to form any original thought of his own in his condition. Because of the disorienting effect of the weapon's beams, he had not been able to follow the teleprompter. The politician had no free will, no control over what he was saying, nor any memory of it.

After the party chairman had reestablished the impression of passion for his speech, just as the agents predicted he would, the agents had induced his coughing fit by beaming a signal at him, unrelentingly stimulating a nerve in his neck, until finally, he had been forced to abandon the stage, leaving his audience with the altered message and no chance of recovery.

The news story goes on to lay out suspected examples of espionage-by-mind-reading which had been carried out using the same or similar technology over the past several months, both by Russia and by the U.S.

"The list of surveillance and interference programs grows," the story says, providing a recap of the U.S. and Russian activities in Germany that had broken into world-wide news headlines going back as far as 2013. An attack on one of the country's major telecom operators in 2015 is believed to be linked to Moscow, it says. Malware was used to attack the Bundestag parliamentary computer network. And in 2018, it had been reported that Germany's foreign and interior ministries' online networks had been compromised by Russian hackers.

"The situation is scandalous and unfathomable. The listening posts, née Embassies, in our dear city have now extended their reach into the very hearts and souls of our citizens. Today, we have learned that one man's change of heart was in actuality an attack on his heart and a theft of his vision..."

"We are disappointed, at the very least, that our American friends have not previously informed us of this spectacular surveillance and mind control technology, preferring to keep it to themselves and leaving us to fend for ourselves. And we are very disappointed, also, with our partners, who now seem to have had a change of heart of their own."

The story ends by exclaiming that it was not merely an attack on a politician. It was an attack on German democracy.

Another news story was more politic, pointing out that the investigation is still ongoing to determine just what the involvement of the Russian state was, and probing the extent to which the incident might have been "merely the work of a few individuals intent on frustrating Germany's relations with Russia".

In 2011, Germany had arrested a couple for spying for Russia. In the process, a sophisticated satellite transmitter, used by the couple to keep in touch with their contacts in Moscow, had been seized. The transmitter was small, carried by the couple in a black laptop bag, the antenna hidden in a flap of the bag. What Germany did not know was that a far more sophisticated technology had already been deployed. They had captured a mere cub while a full-grown bear was just beginning to expand its territory.

Their luck changed when, in 2024, German intelligence had secured Julian Brecht's backpack system, preventing the Russians from snatching it. For a year, they had secretly studied it and experimented with it, making it their own. And now, in 2026, the base understanding obtained from that system has made it possible for Germany to capture Russian mind technology.

What German intelligence has come to understand is that documents can be shared, intelligence can be transmitted, and classified information can be compromised, by the remote reading of thoughts alone. The intelligence information need not be transmitted by radio, nor by wires, nor by the transportation of any physical object across a border. A spy can now simply sit near a border and silently read secret documents to themselves as someone across the border reads their thoughts with a mind-reading machine. Text. Diagrams and photographs. Memories of what specific individuals look like. Gone are the days when a spy would hide microfilm under a park bench or transmit an encrypted message by satellite.

These deductions are not explained in the news story, which focuses instead on the attack on German democracy. The intelligence coup did however, help clear up several former mysteries that Germany's intelligence operations had faced. The capabilities of the new technology are simply astounding. And with one bear now in captivity, the hunt is on for others.

Many of the protestors wave German flags as they parade past the Russian Embassy. The crowd, carrying signs with images of steel helmets shielding a skull and its attached skeleton from blasts of lightning, chants in German. Several protestors wear rubber swim caps painted like the blood-splattered gray matter of living brains. One woman wears a cap knitted with pink yarn into the shape of the undulations of the brain's sulci.

News drones fly overhead, providing video feeds for live media reports. By 11 AM, an estimated 30,000 people fill Unter den Linden and the connecting Pariser Platz, stretching from the Russian Embassy past the U.S. Embassy toward the Brandenburg Gate.

A journalist interviews one of the protestors. "On this same day in 1989, the Wall fell. There had been great crowds at the Brandenburg Gate that day as well. When it fell, the people of Germany were reunited. And today, we are reminding those who would meddle in Germany's internal affairs that they must not."

Tuesday, 10 November 2026

The Senator runs through a recap of the situation. A mind device carried by an American investigator had disappeared without explanation in China. And then, in an unrelated incident, a second device had disappeared in Germany. That was two years ago. And just last August, the first device showed up again in, of all places, an American courtroom.

It hadn't taken long for the Chinese to start commercializing the technology. Six months ago, their first patent applications were published. And the U.S. is obligated under the Patent Cooperation Treaty of 1970 to honor those applications.

Long in a position of playing catch-up, after years of isolation from the rest of the world, the Chinese have now built up a credible, indeed formidable, technology capability of their own. They have held their own, and in many cases, excelled, in the development of machine learning, electric vehicles, drones, space technology, supercomputers, high speed trains, electronic payments, and mobile technology, both for private and commercial use and for internal security. Beginning with the roll-out of 5G technology around 2018, China became a key player in the establishment of mobile technology standards, battling the U.S. for dominance. The country has by far the largest cell tower network in the world, with denser coverage than in the U.S. And now, they are rushing into commercial applications of mind-interfacing technologies, with the Naoji initiating, as they see it, the next generation of mobile.

In response to the situation, the Senator had assembled a new committee to understand and manage emerging issues with mind technology. The committee quickly determined that the Chinese regard it as a major opportunity, a new market they will be the first to enter.

There has been, up to now, only limited commercial development of the technology in the U.S., with the only applications for the advanced form limited to intelligence operations, law enforcement, and the military, and these have all been kept secret. The Chinese announcement of a mind-pairing smartphone was a major development. And now, with the events of the past couple of days, the complexity of the situation is rapidly escalating. Mind technology is bursting into public view, and from the Senator's point of view, the world isn't ready for it.

Complicating matters, companies in the U.S. which have been developing the technology have almost no patents on it. Actions taken by the government under the Invention Secrecy Act of 1951 prevented them from disclosing their inventions to the public and prohibited them from filing for patent protection around the world. The law was intended to protect weapons and intelligence gathering and similar technologies that, if knowledge of how they operate were to fall into the wrong hands, could threaten national security. But it's a trade-off. Secrecy provides clear advantages when the only customers are the government agencies, but the lack of worldwide patent protection has now put the American companies at a disadvantage.

With the Chinese commercializing the technology, the U.S. is in danger of falling behind. It will be Chinese companies selling their products around the world rather than American companies if the U.S. doesn't open it up to commercial applications. Furthermore, the U.S. lost its edge in semiconductor manufacturing years ago, with most of the world's capacity now in Asia, and the Senator doesn't want this to happen with the next generation of technology. He is intent on reversing decades of bad policy in which American companies were denied access to the Chinese market for their best products, allowing local companies in that market to pull ahead without American competition.

As the committee points out during discussions, they can't just block the Chinese from the U.S. market. American companies have been successful in selling telecom technology into the Chinese market, including both smartphones and infrastructure products, and the likely consequence to an outright ban would be to lose the Chinese market for those American products and possibly products in other industry segments as well. As it is, Chinese companies have been formidable competitors in the Chinese market, a market that far exceeds the size of the U.S. market and is continuing to grow.

Zai is, in most respects, like any other Chinese consumer products company. It's just a matter of time before their products, or similar products, are on offer all around the world. What America needs is competitive products, not a ban on Zai's products. But the Senator doesn't want to expose the depth of knowledge the U.S. has in mind technology, nor does he want to reveal who the real players in the technology are. Lifting secrecy orders and revealing earlier American patent applications could jeopardize ongoing intelligence operations. In any case, it's unlikely that the companies which provide those capabilities to the U.S. government would expand into consumer products.

The Senator decides it would make more sense to fork the technology evolution. It means that in the short-term, the Chinese products will gain a temporary commercial advantage, a situation the Senator is not happy with. But development of advanced mind technology can continue in secret, unaffected by new developments in the commercial context. He wants American companies in the game, but that can't happen overnight.

He works through the issues in his mind. It's not about balance. It's about winning. How is he going to make that happen? Far from banning the technology, the U.S. is going to support it. *He* is going to support it. He'll need time to put together a package to present to the Congress for public, that is, publicized, funding of American research and development of mind technology. And many in Congress are sure to oppose it on the grounds that the technology shouldn't be commercialized at all. But as he sees it, if they don't support American industry, the U.S. will simply be left behind. The U.S. needs to get out in front, and he's going to make that happen.

But first things first. He quickly schedules another committee hearing on the matter, and shortly afterwards, he calls for a moratorium on devices that use radio energy to communicate with the brain, stating that the moratorium shall remain in effect until (1) the health effects of exposure to the so-called "patterned radio waves" used by the technology can be studied properly, (2) appropriate regulations can be developed by the FCC to ensure non-interference with other wireless technologies, and (3) public policy concerns can be addressed with regard to both ethical and practical considerations, including regulations to protect privacy.

The Senator follows up with a statement to the press, finishing with a few comments: "More time is needed to study its effects before it goes into widespread use. Am I excited about the future of mind technology? I am. Let us move forward one step at a time. I will be working with the Congress and with our Federal agencies to ensure the best and safest development of this emerging new technology."

One immediate consequence of the moratorium is that it effectively bans the importation of devices that use the technology, including Zai's Total Virtual Reality game console and Zai's recently announced Naoji smartphone.

Sunday, 6 December 2026

Peter heard about the moratorium the day it was announced. It shocked him. It implied he would be required to stop using his neuroprosthesis.

He would have just ignored it, except that Dr. Gestrin called him later the same day and explained that her medical license could be in jeopardy if she doesn't obtain some kind of waiver from the government. She promised to look into it right away, but said she's not sure what to expect, with the news being so sudden.

Ever since then, Peter has been following the issue closely, reading commentary on the web with his Naoji.

"[Huh. That's funny. This reader comment says we need fogging mind reading like we need holes in our heads.]" He turns off the Naoji's text-to-inner-speech media player with a mental command, then comments to Shasha. "[I have a right to this technology. How can they take it away?]"

Shasha agrees. "That would be quite unreasonable."

They're at home together, Peter sitting in his wheelchair, and Shasha working beside him, writing up a research report for her project at the Institute.

"[You know, this is really a First Amendment issue. I have the right to freedom of expression.]"

Shasha stops typing and turns to Peter. "You mean using your Naoji?"

"[Yeah.]"

"Why would it be a First Amendment issue?"

"[Well, we can just take it literally.]" He pauses for dramatic effect.

"Literally. Oh, of course." That's Peter's humor. She recognizes it, but gives only the faintest hint of a smile and a quick glance toward him.

"[The First Amendment says that Congress shall make no law abridging freedom of speech. And if they take away my prosthesis, that's what they would be doing. Literally. What am I supposed to do, *blink* my way through a phone call?]" He blinks twice. *No.*

"I agree. That is strange. Why would they have declared a moratorium if it is so obviously unconstitutional?" She doesn't know much about the U.S. Constitution, having grown up in Vancouver. Though, for that matter, she doesn't remember much about freedom of speech in Canada, either.

"[They say it's the standard stuff. Safety of the public. Regulations. Controls. Like requiring clinical trials for medicines to test for safety and efficacy. One article mentioned that it's like when drones first started to become popular and they put a moratorium on that for a while, too. Until the FAA could define some regulations. But I suspect that's not the real issue. That's just a cover. And I think that explains why Dr. Gestrin is running into problems getting the waiver.]" His tone of inner voice becomes more serious.

Having given up on getting anything done with her project for now, Shasha turns her chair to make herself more comfortable while speaking with Peter.

"Why would there be problems?"

"[Dr. Gestrin said something about FCC approval for the device. You know, I don't need it for its cool features. I need it to live normally. Dr. Gestrin said it's a prosthesis. There's some technical definition for it. And she thinks that should make a difference. She already got a license under the experimental radio service provisions specifically for medical applications. But they sent a form letter advising her that the moratorium effectively suspends any FCC licenses granted for mind-interfacing devices. I think they're worried about proliferation. That's the real issue. But they can't just say that. Just put two-and-two together: The Berlin protest that was in the news, that was about the same thing. It was a mind technology scandal. And there it was. Bam. Bam. Protest. Moratorium.]"

"What sort of proliferation?" she asks.

"[Right. What sort of proliferation? Let me switch to evil genius mode and brainstorm on that,]" he says. "[So, for example, identity theft, corporate secrets theft, social hacking. Or, how about dumbing down a political opponent during a campaign by bombarding their brain with interference?]"

Peter thinks some more, then adds: "[How about blackmail? Finding someone's secret and demanding a ransom to keep it quiet? Or extortion, threatening to continue attacking until the victim carries out some kind of action on behalf of the completely anonymous assailant? They might even code up automated harassment software to bombard the victim's mind with nonsense comments, random pains, and who knows what, 24 hours a day, until they comply. They just need to keep the transmitter somewhere near the victim. No one else around them would notice anything unusual and no one would believe the victim is under attack. Maybe they target a corporate CEO and short the stock as they drag him down. You can just see it now. The CEO has headaches all the time. He gets dumber and dumber, makes mistakes, says stupid things. Or maybe he just wears down. Before you know it, the SEC is on his case and he's kicked out of the company. It would be like a hunting animal hounding its prey until the prey just tires out and gives up.]"

How could Peter think of such devious ideas, she wonders? Then again, he was a victim himself. "You're right. Those would all be real concerns. But the technology already exists. People can already get it."

"[Reading that the article on the Berlin protests - get this - they interviewed that politician about the experience. He said during the months leading up to his speech, he repeatedly heard words in his head that contradicted what he was thinking. He didn't know what to make of it, except maybe he was getting old. Although he didn't really believe that. Like if he thought *Freitag*, they'd say *Freibetrag*. They'd talk right over his thoughts. And the point was that the words were unrelated. I know Freitag means Friday. Not sure what Freibetrag means... Hold on. Let me look that up. ...Huh. Freibetrag is tax allowance. ...Oh, like a personal exemption on your tax return. So that would be pretty confusing. The article says it weakened his memories and made it impossible for him to think in his own words when the Russians started talking in his head during his speech. There's actually some scientific research on the biology of the effect. It's kind of a weird weapon, isn't it? No toxins, no physical damage. Just weakened memories and no trace of how it happened.]"

"It sounds like a form of cognitive dissonance."

"[Is that the word?]"

Shasha gets up to pour herself a glass of water, then returns to sit with Peter.

"[So I think that's the real point,]" he says. "[It's like gun control. They're trying to lock it down before it goes everywhere. The fact is, the technology could potentially be used as a weapon. And the reason, here's the real point, the reason they can't just come out and say that is because it is *already* everywhere. Or, at least, in more places than they want to admit.]" He thinks back to the torturous year he had endured. "[They're probably trying to get things under control without disclosing too much.]"

On its regularly timed interval, Peter's wheelchair automatically activates its pressure sore prevention system. Motors within the wheelchair reposition the supports along his seat, back, arms, and head with hidden rollers and auto-inflating air cushions, making little humming and hissing noises as they go. Peter groans slightly. A minute later, the robotic arm swings out and down and, with the tiny video camera recently mounted near its wrist so that Peter, and the software on the Naoji, can see what they are doing with the hand, it executes a search pattern. Spotting what it is looking for, the app turns the wheelchair slightly and backs it up two feet. The arm then reaches down and pulls out the retractable electric charging cord for the wheelchair, located at about seat level, and plugs it into an electrical outlet, guiding it in with the video camera. The Naoji issues a short beep to indicate that the charger has activated.

"[Maybe it really is like gun control,]" Peter says. "[They could ban it outright. But then, no one would really know how it works. It would be a mystery technology and only the bad guys would have it. Someone else is going to develop it anyway, and they'll sneak it into the country. And no one will know how to detect it. But you know, even though guns are everywhere, we don't go around in bulletproof vests."

"But it's not like guns."

"[It's not? No, it's not. My Naoji's not like a gun. You know what it's like? It's like a truck.]"

"Why is it like a truck?"

"[Trucks are essential for commerce. They're everywhere. They have been used as terror weapons, but that doesn't mean we should ban trucks.]"

Shasha doesn't have a response to this.

"[I once read somewhere,]" Peter says, "[that felons can't buy bulletproof vests, which I always thought was weird. Is the point that if they commit a crime again that it makes it easier for the police to shoot them? It really doesn't make sense.]"

"I've never heard of that."

Shasha is starting to tire of the discussion. She cares about science, not politics. She glances back at her laptop, hoping to return to writing up her research report. Then she thinks about Peter. He needs the social interactions.

Peter thinks about his own bulletproof vest. His SCIF. "[I wouldn't be surprised if they ban SCIFs for felons someday. So they can monitor their thoughts if necessary. Obviously, they would say, the only reason they'd want a SCIF is to prevent the government from listening in on their thoughts as they plan their next crime. But you know what, maybe they'll ban them outright. For everyone. Just like they wanted to ban encryption that doesn't have backdoors for the government to get in.]"

A vague feeling of sadness sweeps over Peter as he quietly reflects on his life. Shasha waits for him to continue, but he is unexpectedly silent. "Peter?"

Imitating Stephen Hawking's famous synthetic voice, he responds: "[What is it, my dear?]"

Shasha blinks twice and then bursts out laughing. She gets up out of her chair and goes over to Peter and kisses him on the forehead. Then she wraps her arms around him and presses her cheek against his cheek in a warm hug.

Peter mentally activates the robotic arm and holds her back with his robotic hand, enjoying the virtual reality feeling generated in his mind from the sensors on the hand.

An idea comes to Shasha. "Why not see if Ethan could help with the waiver?"

"[How?]"

"Just call him."

Friday, 18 December 2026

The press conference is staged during a visit by Peter to Dr. Gestrin's office at the hospital. Her office is small, but everyone crowds in. Peter, in his wheelchair. Ethan. Shasha. Dr. Gestrin. And the news crew: a reporter and a cameraman, his camera mounted on a tripod. Two studio lights illuminate the scene from the sides, and a microphone is suspended from above by a boom.

The Christmas season has put everyone in good cheer. The reporter, wearing a red blazer over a black dress, speaks first, standing in front of the camera, just off to Peter's side. Ethan is dressed in a charcoal business suit and a red tie. Dr. Gestrin has on the traditional white coat, unbuttoned, with a pink blouse and gray slacks showing through.

The reporter introduces Peter and his wife Shasha, Dr. Gestrin, and Ethan, and then lets Ethan speak.

"Let me tell you about my friend Peter Nolen. He was completely paralyzed by an accident, unable to move and unable to speak." He looks over at Peter who is visible just behind him. "We at my company Zai MindPair have developed a technology which, miraculously, lets him speak by reading his mind and sending the sounds to a speaker for others to hear."

"But a question has come up recently as to whether we are ready for the technology. As you may have heard, a moratorium was put in place by Congress forbidding the use of mind-interfacing technologies, meaning technologies which operate through a radio-based interaction between the human brain and external devices. And because of this, a patient who relies on this new technology is now in danger of losing an important medical remedy."

"The problem is that if he is no longer permitted to use this technology, Peter loses his voice, his only real connection with the world."

"Should we ban a technology outright? Or should we look at its use on a case-by-case basis? Today, we have no real alternative for Peter. Let me explain."

"Beginning around thirty years ago, highly invasive medical technologies were used to provide a connection between the brain and the outside world. They seemed like magic when they allowed patients to type text just by thinking, relying on special electrodes, made of thin wires, implanted in the brain. However, electrode-based implants do not always work, and there are serious risks associated with any brain surgery, as one can well imagine."

"Today, we have another magical technology, one which lets a totally paralyzed patient speak. And by speak, I mean speak with expression and emotion. How could we deny him access to it? Our technology, using very low-power radio waves, is vastly less intrusive than earlier technologies, requiring no surgery and no implants. This technology provides an incredible benefit for those who need it. We shouldn't deny its use until some later date when all the risks have been worked out, controls defined, and regulations written. We are in this technology's nascent stage. Just as with the controls put in place for pharmaceuticals, a similar process will inevitably occur within this new field to ensure that it is used appropriately. But for this one patient, and friend of mine, we already know that it works, and it works well."

"Let me just ask this once more. *Why would we take away Peter Nolen's voice?*"

Ethan then discloses Zai's venture into neuroprosthesis development, which is licensed by the FCC for medical purposes, saying that Peter is the first beneficiary of their technology and explaining that Peter has been in a locked-in state for the past three years, ever since his terrible bicycle accident, completely paralyzed except for the ability to blink his eyes. Blinking was Peter's only way of communicating until they, at Zai, were able to provide him with his neuroprosthesis. "But let's let Peter speak for himself."

At this point, facing the camera, Peter speaks, but his mouth doesn't move. One of his eyes blinks occasionally, and he makes slight head movements and distorted facial expressions.

The interview goes back and forth. Peter explains that over the past five months of using his Naoji, he has learned, and in turn, the Naoji has learned, how to transfer the sounds in his head back and forth. The technology, he says, has become a natural extension of himself. He could hardly live without it. While it was initially hard to get into a routine, with endless rounds of rehabilitation exercises, the biggest thing to happen to him was regaining the ability to communicate freely.

Through it, he explains, he is not only able to speak, but also to control the Naoji smartphone. He can access the Internet, send messages to friends, read articles, and through voice recognition of the sounds in his head, he can write. He gives a humorous demonstration, doing voice impersonations of a couple of celebrities and singing a song in his head. He says he and his wife have no children yet, but he hopes one day to sing "Happy Birthday" to a daughter. Tears appear in his eyes.

The reporter asks Ethan how Zai Mindpair got into the prosthetics business. What is the connection, if any, with virtual reality game consoles?

Ethan explains that their technology works by interfacing with signals from the brain. Their core competency involves what they call Total Virtual Reality.

The reporter clarifies for the public: "By core competency, you mean the company's strengths or advantages."

"Yes, that's right," Ethan says. "With our mind-interfacing technology, we have the ability to create artificial perceptions in the brain, for smells, for touch, for all kinds of perceptions, and in turn, to read information back from the brain. This provides a richly interactive experience in our virtual reality games."

"We also extended the technology to hear sounds in the mind. It works on the same principles. So you see," he says, "it's the same kind of thing. With this technology, we have an interface into and out of the brain. Which, as it happens, is just what a locked-in patient needs."

The reporter asks about Zai's plans for their Total Virtual Reality game consoles, particularly in light of the moratorium in the U.S., and Ethan explains that they are still on track for a major release in China, within the coming year in fact.

"But my focus today," he says, keeping their press conference on track, "is on helping my close friend Peter, and on helping others in situations similar to his."

The reporter now turns to Dr. Ellen Gestrin, the doctor who has been coordinating all of Peter's health care needs. She gives a little background on the story of how Ethan had first come to her to propose the development of the neuroprosthesis for Peter. She then gets into some of the details of the most recent work, describing what she calls a "sensation neuroprosthesis".

Observing the limitations of Peter's use of the robotic arm, Dr. Gestrin had inspired Zai to develop an app on the Naoji that receives sensor signals from the robotic arm and sends them to the brain, creating what she calls virtual tactile pressure sensations. This means that when the robotic hand touches something, Peter feels it. When the arm is strained by a heavy weight, Peter feels that, too, with sensors that detect forces within the arm as it moves around. She mentions that this ability to feel stresses and strains in the body is called proprioception. The idea, she says, was to use virtual reality so that Peter could experience the robotic arm as if it were his own.

With both virtual tactile sensation and virtual proprioception, she says, Peter has learned to control the robotic arm and its hand with great delicacy. Over time, his use of the arm has become intuitive to him. When he wants to draw, he just draws, as if it were his own natural arm. The sensation neuroprosthesis was the “missing something” that Peter needed to go from having a good robotic arm to having a great one.

Ethan had reached out to their prosthetics partner in the U.S. about outfitting the arm with pressure sensors, on the fingers, along the outer surfaces, and on force-bearing points within the arm to implement the sensation neuroprothesis, and Zai's partner had said it would be straightforward. They already had a relationship with Percepique Corporation, a company which makes artificial skins for robots. They could cover Peter's robotic arm and fingers to obtain the sensing data.

The rubbery silicone skin, which has a translucent white color to it, glows a faint blue-green due to light from tiny LEDs traversing through thin, transparent fibers embedded in it. The mesh of fibers detects pressure on the skin by measuring changes in the light. This information, collected by electronics inside the arm, is relayed to the Naoji. The Naoji, in turn, converts the pressure information into brain codes. These, finally, are transmitted to Peter's brain as radio waves, allowing him to feel the arm. And he really feels it.

Percepique offers a number of customizable configurations for their robot skins. They can tint them with skin tones, embed artificial hairs, incorporate fingernails and imprint skin creases to match a person's appearance for use as a realistic prosthetic. They can also meet other requirements, with skins that don't break down when handling harsh chemicals or when working in extreme temperatures, such as for use in industrial robots. By varying the exact composition of the materials used, they can make the skin more durable or more elastic. They can increase the sensitivity of the sensors throughout the skin if needed for a particular application, though this comes with a trade-off in durability. And while they currently only support skin pressure and skin stretching sensations, they have robot skin technology in development which will eventually incorporate temperature and surface pain sensation as well. Pain, in particular, would be sensed as a consequence of burning, freezing, or chemical damage, or scratching, ripping, or cutting of the outer layer of the skin, a useful feature to help protect robotic and prosthetic limbs.

For Peter's application, Percepique had recommended a balance between durability and sensitivity. They had configured the overall appearance to look like something between a humanoid arm and a robotic arm, in harmony with its intended attachment to Peter's wheelchair. There would be no skin tone tinting. They recommended just the basic skin, translucent white, with their standard fiber optic sensing density. With the underlying visible robotic arm parts made mostly of aluminum, carbon fiber and a hard white plastic, it would be a good visual match for Peter's wheelchair.

The brain codes for touch turn out to be more complicated than those for smells, because when you feel a touch, you feel what it is like and you *also* feel where it is on the body. Furthermore, it wasn't obvious just how to represent all the ways that touch can feel. Touches can feel like rubbing, pushing, dragging, pulling, slipping, scraping, tickling, sharp or dull, smooth or rough, pinching, squeezing, thumping, or delicately tapping, and the brain has its own unique way of coding that all up.

Further complicating virtual touch, tactile sensations cannot be described at just one point on the skin. The Naoji app must use touch information from large areas on the robotic arm to create tactile sensations in Peter's brain. Like when someone shakes your hand. Your hand is squeezed on two sides and there is some pressure in the middle. And your forearm feels the force of the other person's arm movement.

Or consider the difference between holding a bar of soap and holding a pine cone. The same area of the hand is affected, but in one case, the pressure is smooth, and in the other, the pressure is concentrated at many separate points. It isn't just the amount of pressure that matters. After all, one could squeeze harder and still tell the difference between the soap and the pine cone. Rather, what matters is how the pressure varies from one place to another on your hand which tells you what the object is like. The sensation is holistic. The mind doesn't feel all the individual details. It feels a texture.

Dr. Gestrin explains: "Because of this ability to send these feelings from the robotic arm to the brain, the brain is able to learn how to use the arm almost as well as it would a natural arm. This is what we call the plasticity of the brain, its ability to adapt to new situations."

In the background, Peter sits still in his wheelchair as his robotic arm suddenly reaches around his chest from the right and makes a brief scratching motion on the upper part of his own left arm. He briefly groans as the robotic arm retracts into its original position.

Ethan wraps up with a call for an early end to the moratorium, followed by a story wrap-up by the reporter.

After the press conference, Dr. Gestrin is inundated with inquiries from other patients and doctors around the world. A video of the event goes viral. And Zai takes another step up in brand name recognition.

Tuesday, 22 December 2026

Just four days later, Dr. Gestrin gets a call back from the FCC informing her that her waiver request has been processed and they are reissuing the corresponding experimental radio medical technology license with it. She tells Peter that there's still a restriction, however.

"You can't fly with the technology," she says. "They won't allow it on the airplane. It's not about the use of radio waves per se. They won't let it on the plane at all. But they wouldn't explain why."

MQZTOQ also receives waivers for their mind-interfacing device applications, justified by the public safety and security benefits provided by their prison calming technology and by the airport security service that Brian Breg is managing.

Over the next couple of weeks, through Dr. Gestrin's office, Peter receives a flood of well-wishers' holiday cards and New Year greetings and letters and emails asking him about the technology he uses to speak and what it is like to use it. Then the inquiries taper off until, after a month, Peter is forgotten by the world at large.

Tuesday, 3 October 2028

Over two years have now passed since the trial of Peter's case against Breg. During this time, the case has attracted both the attention and support of major rights groups. And not long after the trial had finished, Peter's attorney had reached out to another attorney, a Mr. Blumenfeld, who has been admitted to practice before the Supreme Court and will be handling Peter's appeal.

Mr. Blumenfeld confirms what Peter's attorney had explained to Peter. Unless the evidence clearly weighs against the factual findings, the facts will stand as is. If they're going to appeal, the appeal has to be based on an issue involving the interpretation of law. And Mr. Blumenfeld has identified that interpretational issue, which he explains.

To understand Mr. Blumenfeld's explanation, it would be helpful to understand a little more background about the case. One of the defenses Breg had wanted to make was that no warrant was actually needed. After all, brainwave emanations are "out there" in the open for anyone to record, so how could he be sued for invasion of privacy? But Breg's own attorney had explained to Breg that that argument doesn't work. In 2001, the Supreme Court had ruled in another case, *Kyllo v United States*, that when so-called "sense-enhancing devices" are used, devices which gather information otherwise not accessible to ordinary human perception, and where there is otherwise an expectation of privacy, a search warrant is needed. In plain terms, that means a search warrant is needed if the government or someone working on their behalf uses special equipment to see or hear things that are private and that can't been seen or heard without that equipment.

In the *Kyllo* case, the police used a thermal imager to see through the walls of a home's garage, but they hadn't obtained a search warrant first. The spots of heat showing through the wall looked suspicious, and partly on that basis, the police had obtained a search warrant to look inside the garage. And indeed, their suspicions that high intensity lamps inside the garage were being used to grow marijuana were confirmed when they looked. The Supreme Court eventually ruled on the matter, declaring that using the thermal imager was itself a search. As it had been used without a search warrant, the evidence had to be thrown out.

Not all of the justices agreed, though, writing that the thermal imager showed the temperature on the *outside* of the wall, which was clearly not *inside* the garage. To quote the dissenting opinion, "Heat waves, like aromas that are generated in a kitchen, or in a laboratory or opium den, enter the public domain if and when they leave a building." If a homeowner wants privacy, they reasoned, the homeowner could insulate the house.

But with sufficiently advanced technology, conceivably anything inside a home could be viewed from outside merely by looking at signals that penetrate the walls. The dissenting justices had described as "difficult to take seriously" the idea that building emissions should be treated as private, but not more than eleven years later, British researchers had already demonstrated through-the-wall radar which operates in complete stealth by analyzing the radio waves leaving a house from wireless Internet access points inside the house.

It wasn't that someone could hack into the access point to spy on people in the house. It was far more clever, and at the same time, conceptually simple. Someone surveilling a house could sit across the street with a radio receiver and, using a software package, track the movements of people inside the house. Radio waves are affected by the human body. As people move around in the house, the access point's radio waves are affected by their bodies in predictable ways, absorbing radio energy and bending whatever radio waves are not absorbed. The new technology is capable of mapping out those effects to observe the movements of people inside the house.

Four years later, another university research team in Germany showed how to view the shape of an object by the shadow it makes on wireless signals as they pass the object on their way out of a building. The occupants' own cell phones or wireless access points, in this way, illuminate the building with radio waves, making the interior visible to anyone in the public with the right technology. Using the researchers' ideas, one could construct a 3D model of the objects inside a building without ever entering it, indeed, without any physical intrusion at all. There's no radar signal. No beam is sent into the building to see what is inside. The technology lets you see into a building just by watching the radio signals that come out.

A device that makes a wall effectively transparent to those looking invades the privacy of the home. And a device which can read brainwave emissions invades the privacy of the person. Accordingly, the Court would have no problem agreeing that Peter had an expectation of privacy to his thoughts, and that a sense-enhancing device was used to listen in on those thoughts. No one would seriously expect to have to live in a SCIF to keep their thoughts private. Breg's surveillance definitely required a warrant.

In *Kyllo*, the issue boiled down to one question: Was a search warrant needed? There were really only two positions one could take. The warrant was needed, or it wasn't. And as Breg's surveillance was authorized by a warrant, it would seem that the only grounds for Peter's appeal would be a challenge to the validity of the warrant. Even then, it wouldn't be a win for Peter. The remedy for an invalid warrant may be only that the evidence collected under the warrant could be excluded in a trial. But there's no trial. There's no case at all against Peter. What Mr. Blumenfeld has realized, though, is that there is another way to view the situation. A third position.

Briefs for the case, the documents prepared by the attorneys representing both sides containing written statements of the factual findings and the legal questions, have already been provided to the Supreme Court justices. And now, on October 3rd of 2028, the Court hears the Oral Argument for Peter Nolen, the Petitioner. Brian Breg and the United States, with their attorney, a Mr. Coulton, are the Respondents, arguing against the Petitioner, that is, against Peter and his attorney, Mr. Blumenfeld.

As is customary, a text transcript of the Oral Argument is published, which reads as follows.

ORAL ARGUMENT

1 IN THE SUPREME COURT OF THE UNITED STATES

2 - - - - - - - - - - - - - - - - - x

3 PETER NOLEN, :

4 Petitioner :

5 v. :

6 BRIAN BREG AND UNITED STATES, :

7 Respondents. :

8 - - - - - - - - - - - - - - - - - x

9 Washington, D.C.

10 Tuesday, October 3, 2028

11

12 The above-entitled matter came on for

13 oral argument before the Supreme Court

14 of the United States at 10:18 a.m.

15

16 APPEARANCES:

17 A. BLUMENFELD, ESQ., San Francisco,

18 California; on behalf of Petitioner.

19 W. COULTON, ESQ., Office of the

20 Solicitor General, Department of

21 Justice, Washington, D.C.; on

22 behalf of Respondents

23

24

25

1 P R O C E E D I N G S

2 (10:18 a.m.)

3 CHIEF JUSTICE BRADLEY: We'll hear

4 argument first this morning in the

5 case of Nolen v. Breg and United States.

6 Mr. Blumenfeld.

7 ORAL ARGUMENT OF A. BLUMENFELD

8 ON BEHALF OF THE PETITIONER

9

10

11

12

13

14

15

16

17

18

19

20

21

22

23

24

25

MR. BLUMENFELD: Mr. Chief Justice, and may it please the Court: The First Amendment states that Congress shall shall make no law abridging the freedom of speech. Our case is simple. Respondents used technology to read Petitioner's mind, causing Petitioner's thoughts to be expressed against his will, in violation of his First Amendment right to freedom of expression and the privacy associated with that right. Respondents assert that this activity was authorized by a warrant issued under the Information Privacy Act of 2020. We assert that the Act is overly broad because it permits the forcing of expression.

JUSTICE GRIER: Why is that so? Respondents didn't force Petitioner to do anything at all, did they? Respondents recorded brain waves. The Petitioner's thoughts were already expressed when his brain waves went out, and Respondents recorded those brain waves. I don't see how anything was forced.

MR. BLUMENFELD: Expression hasn't occurred until thoughts or beliefs are transformed into a form perceivable by others. Merely thinking produces brain waves, but it doesn't produce expression. So if Respondents could hear what Petitioner was thinking by using special equipment, the Respondents would be hearing an expression of what Petitioner was thinking, but it's not the Petitioner who expressed it.

JUSTICE GRIER: But then the brain waves did express Petitioner's thoughts. Didn't the brain waves carry his thoughts out?

MR. BLUMENFELD: The point would be that the special equipment used can take unexpressed thoughts and express them.

JUSTICE GRIER: You said the Act is too broad because it permits expression to be forced. But the -- take -- take the Sixth Amendment. A witness can be compelled to testify on behalf of the defense. And what do we call it, if not compelled speech, when you have to fill out an income tax return or to respond to a jury summons? In these situations, does the government force a person to express themselves?

It does, the attorney thinks. But then again, it doesn't. There is what is required, and then there is what one does. And then there is what others do to us. What is being forced? Is it a person's actions that are forced? Or something else? He struggles to put this abstract idea into concrete terms. He works it out. It's simple, after all.

MR. BLUMENFELD: There's a difference between compelling speech and forcing expression. Even when a person is compelled to be a witness and they are required to speak, and to speak the truth, they retain control over what to express and how to express it. This differs from what happened to Petitioner, whose thoughts were taken and expressed without his consent or control, and it is this forced expression which violates the individual's First Amendment right to privacy.

JUSTICE GRIER: Is it a right to privacy here? Is that what the First Amendment is protecting?

MR. BLUMENFELD: To know what someone could say, in the past, we would have to ask them. Now, this has become unnecessary. By bypassing the step of asking, forcing their thoughts to be expressed, -- it invades the individual's privacy.

JUSTICE GRIER: Seizing a diary in a search would also be an invasion of privacy. But it's a necessary aspect of the search. How could the Fourth Amendment have any meaning at all if it didn't allow privacy to be invaded? There must be a balancing of --

MR. BLUMENFELD: If there were a search, then a violation of privacy might reasonably be balanced against the government's need for the search. But there was no search.

JUSTICE GRIER: There wasn't a search?

MR. BLUMENFELD: Let us look at the wording of the Fourth Amendment, which defines the right of the people to be secure in their persons, houses, papers, and effects, and then let us ask: What was searched? According to the testimony given in the case, nothing possessed by Petitioner was searched, not his phone, his writings, his laptop, nor his home. Not even his person. He was not touched nor was any internal part of him inspected or searched, in the sense of probing into his body. Nor were his spoken words searched, nor was any form of gesturing or other communication. The quest for information from Petitioner's mind was not a search for documents, nor was it surveillance of his communications, nor, for that matter, was it an order to provide testimony.

Accordingly, Petitioner's claim is not about a violation of his rights against unreasonable search as defined in the Fourth Amendment, as there was no Fourth Amendment search. The Fourth Amendment is not even applicable here. Hence, there is no need to balance rights under the Fourth Amendment. And because there was no order to provide testimony, there is no Fifth Amendment issue, either. Petitioner is not asserting a right against self-incrimination.

In short, I must disagree about the need to balance Petitioner's First Amendment rights against any part of the Constitution at all. There is nothing in the Constitution which permits the government to listen in on or record Petitioner's thoughts or beliefs without Petitioner's own production of the expression of those thoughts or beliefs.

This is Mr. Blumenfeld's third position. Because Peter's privacy was violated, Breg's actions on behalf of the government were not OK without a warrant. But the government was searching for something they weren't allowed to search for, so having a warrant wouldn't make it OK, either. In summary, it's not OK *at all*.

JUSTICE GRIER: You're saying a search of brain waves isn't a search. But we could well imagine a situation where that's just what is needed. Suppose --, suppose a --, a kidnap situation develops and no one knows where the child is except the suspect. And the government reads the suspect's mind to figure it out.

MR. BLUMENFELD: It's a kidnap, an emergency. Yes, searches and seizures in emergency situations may be carried out without a warrant when it would take too long to prevent serious harm or destruction of evidence. That said, when a process carried out by the government is not a search and seizure as defined under the Fourth Amendment, the question is no longer one of whether obtaining a warrant could constitutionally be postponed until later, as no warrant should issue under such circumstances, anyway.

JUSTICE GRIER: The point of the warrant is to provide due process to ensure that the suspect's rights are not denied arbitrarily. Are you suggesting that the government's hands would be tied, even with due process?

MR. BLUMENFELD: Knowing their mind is being read, the suspect cannot think in defense of their --

JUSTICE GRIER: Why would the suspect know that?

MR. BLUMENFELD: The police are monitoring the suspect's mental reactions to their questions. In the past, one could exercise their right to refuse to answer by simply not providing an answer. But this right is no longer effective when the police can record --

JUSTICE GRIER: The suspect could just ask to have counsel present and the police would have to stop their questioning.

MR. BLUMENFELD: The difficulty that arises is that the suspect must think about their situation to exercise their rights. But they cannot, if they must stop thinking to remain silent. There's a contradiction. Even when they request an attorney, the police may continue to interact with them without explicitly questioning --

JUSTICE GRIER: So they're sitting there stewing over things --

MR. BLUMENFELD: Yes, and what they're stewing over may not even be related. And those thoughts are --

JUSTICE GRIER: The police are recording their thoughts --

MR. BLUMENFELD: Yes, and the suspect doesn't know their thoughts are --

JUSTICE GRIER: I see. So there would be a notification requirement. But if the suspect is already uncooperative, that hardly seems like the most fruitful -- Let's back up. The police aren't questioning the suspect. They're carrying out surveillance and listening in on the suspect's thoughts to discover the child's whereabouts. And they've got a warrant, but they don't tell the suspect yet. Why should the government's hands be tied?

MR. BLUMENFELD: Then we would be living in a society where no one could ever be sure their thoughts are private. We may be careful about what we say to others, whether in personal discussion or in electronic communications, and that may be enough for us to live with a feeling of personal security. If, however, our thoughts could be monitored without notice, there would be a chilling effect that would harm society at large.

The right to privacy has been increasingly recognized by the Court since the 1960s. Some rights are more fundamental than others, and those which have been protected as fundamental liberties have been those which are rooted in history. The right to think, and the right to think privately, and I refer to two distinct rights, have been taken for granted throughout history. It is only with the new threat of mind-reading tools that the question of the explicit protection of this fundamental liberty must be raised.

JUSTICE GRIER: Thank you.

Mr. Blumenfeld briefly consults his notes before continuing.

MR. BLUMENFELD: There is a second form of violation of Petitioner's First Amendment rights. Respondents used their technology to send words into Petitioner's mind, violating Petitioner's freedom of thought by interfering with his own thoughts and changing his beliefs.

JUSTICE LIN: We are all subject to changes in our beliefs, though. If you walk up to me and tell me something, I may change my beliefs about it.

MR. BLUMENFELD: Of course. But this isn't just about what Respondents said, but the way they said it. Petitioner testified that he started to doubt his own sanity, as he didn't know whether the voices were real people. And confidence in one's own sanity is an important belief, perhaps even more important than religious beliefs.

We all rely on our mental faculties to understand what is happening around us and to make decisions. We distinguish the thoughts and ideas of others from our own by the process through which they enter the mind. When words and ideas enter through our senses, we attribute these to external sources and we can take this into account. When the words and ideas mix directly in the mind, so that we can no longer be sure which thoughts are our own, we are no longer autonomous human beings. Any expression arising from thought compromised in this way could not be regarded as solely that of Petitioner. For this reason, exclusive access to, and freedom from interference with one's mental faculties must be an absolute right under the First Amendment.

JUSTICE GRIER: Are there any absolute rights? We are not always free. If someone enters a courthouse and the metal detector goes off, the guard will want to see what it is. The need for security in that case outweighs the individual's privacy rights.

MR. BLUMENFELD: The absolute right I referred to is not about the First Amendment in all of its manifestations, but just the freedom from the interference in thought due to the use of technology which would bypass the senses.

JUSTICE GRIER: There is always a need to balance between the rights of individuals, the compelling needs of government and exceptions due to extraordinary circumstances. Without knowing in advance what the circumstances are, how could we hold a right, any right, to be absolute?

MR. BLUMENFELD: This may be the only absolute right, for all other rights flow from it. What is there to balance when the individual cannot think? We have not identified any reasonable exceptions. In each case involving the bypassing of the senses, we would always ask why one would not instead go through the senses. The senses provide a human being's interface to the world. When one bypasses the senses, one bypasses the individual as a human being, and when that happens, their rights cease to exist altogether.

JUSTICE LIN: Doesn't the technology in use by the Petitioner for communicating in his locked-in state work that way?

MR. BLUMENFELD: The prosthesis, any prosthesis, is designed to restore missing functionality. I believe it would be reasonable to say that if the government were to contact Petitioner through his prosthesis, it is going through his senses and not bypassing them.

CHIEF JUSTICE BRADLEY: Thank you, Mr. Blumenfeld. Mr. Coulton, we'll hear from you now.

ORAL ARGUMENT OF W. COULTON ON BEHALF OF THE RESPONDENTS

MR. COULTON: Mr. Chief Justice, and may it please the Court.

Mr. Coulton had already laid out his argument in the brief he filed with the Court, framing the issue in a way more favorable to the government's position than the way Mr. Blumenfeld had described it. What Respondents did was a search, plain and simple. The brain is not much different in many respects from a computer system. Viewed in this way, there is nothing new to the interpretation of the Fourth Amendment for search and seizure, except that with the new technology, the brain's information content has now become accessible. In theory, any and all information that can be extracted from the brain would be subject to search, vastly improving the solvability of cases. Such a search wouldn't be limited just to the words a person thinks. It could also potentially include memories or images of past experiences. Furthermore, Respondents were just pulling words out of the air, as if the Petitioner were speaking on a cell phone that transmitted them through the air. Or as if the Petitioner were speaking out loud. The Petitioner's privacy is violated, but that's what the warrant is for.

The justices now probe this argument.

JUSTICE GRIER: Is the reading of information from a person's mind a form of expression?

MR. COULTON: First, I would like to make clear the usage of terminology in this context. Respondents' technology is used to read data from a biological system, in this case, the brain, which is a physical system. Mind, as a term, is not established in the context of search. The term does not occur at all in the text of the current law. Furthermore, to clarify, Respondents' technology reads data from brain waves which emanate from the brain and can be detected in the air. It does not read data directly from the brain itself. The key point is that brain wave emanations in the form of radio waves are physical evidence, obtained non-invasively.

JUSTICE GRIER: OK. Then let's go with -- to rephrase my question then: Is reading information from a person's brain waves a form of expression?

MR. COULTON: It is not.

JUSTICE GRIER: But in the end, isn't there an expression of some kind? Wouldn't the process produce intelligible information that a person could see or hear?

MR. COULTON: It would.

JUSTICE GRIER: Then who produces the expression? To whom do we attribute it?

MR. COULTON: The -- it would be the Respondents, by using their equipment. It's no different from, say, producing a forensics report of data read from a damaged or erased data storage device.

JUSTICE GRIER: So someone creates a report of what they found, and it is the sole -- would they be the sole authors of the content of the report?

MR. COULTON: Any report made as evidence has an author who is responsible for its content. And if a person speaks, and an investigator listens in on what they say, then the expression is attributed to the person speaking. So in that case, we would have to say there are two people involved in creating the report. But the person in this case --

JUSTICE GRIER: Petitioner.

MR. COULTON: Yes. Petitioner was not speaking. Petitioner made no expression at all. And so an investigator who is listening to the device would then be the only person producing an expression.

JUSTICE GRIER: So in this -- it's just data. And the report by the investigator would be an expression solely by the investigator, telling us what the data means.

MR. COULTON: Yes.

JUSTICE LIN: In the lower-court trial, a recording of words in the Petitioner's inner voice was presented as evidence. Petitioner was thinking of his passwords. There, it was evidence that his thoughts were recorded. Can it also be evidence of what he thought?

MR. COULTON: We have much historical precedent for presenting as evidence the recording of an individual's words, and there has never been a recording which has been rejected as evidence merely because of the form of the recording. Furthermore, in this particular example, the correct attribution of the words to the person who originated them is a straightforward matter and hardly differs at all from recording the words of a person who speaks them aloud.

JUSTICE LIN: But should a recording of thoughts be treated differently? Do we speak only because others cannot read our minds? I may hold back something I think because I don't want others to know. And at times, I may not say what I think because I have not yet decided it is the right thing to think, much less the right thing to say.

MR. COULTON: The interpretation given to the words in the individual's thoughts would be decided by the entirety of the evidence. We sometimes say things we don't mean, and we sometimes say things we regret, and sometimes we say things we later change our minds about. We may write things that we later regret. The content of what was said and written is, nevertheless, potentially usable as evidence.

To give just one clear and important example, one may later regret illegally communicating classified information, but a recording of the act would be evidence nonetheless. And if such communication were carried out entirely by a thought process, so that classified information were provided to another party not permitted access to such information, a recording of those thoughts would provide evidence of the illegal communication.

If we could not monitor for and prosecute such a crime, national security could be put at risk. One point made at trial was that the technology for transferring knowledge entirely by thought has been available now for at least two years. Even during the period of the moratorium on the technology, national security was at risk due to its potential importation into the United States.

JUSTICE LIN: You seem to be suggesting that the law could restrict the content of thought. That would amount to a requirement for self-censorship of thought. Is there any precedent for that? Could it ever be a crime merely to think about a particular thing?

MR. COULTON: So we have two issues here. The first is whether thinking of classified information with intent to distribute could constitute a crime. The second is whether the government would be permitted to record such thoughts so that they may be used as evidence. The government might use such a recording to prove the source of a leak.

JUSTICE LIN: Thoughts? Or brain waves? Is there a difference?

MR. COULTON: Brain waves. That's the physical evidence. We attribute the brain waves to thoughts, but the brain waves are the evidence.

JUSTICE LIN: Then there is still the question of whether thoughts may be evidence. Could merely thinking itself ever be a harmful activity that should be criminalized? And if we decide that thoughts may not be evidence, perhaps brain waves, too, may not be evidence.

MR. COULTON: In the scenario I was describing, thought is being used for communication. Think of it like this: When someone speaks on the phone and we have a wiretap on the number, --

JUSTICE LIN: I see. They're not just thinking, --

MR. COULTON: They're communicating. It is the communication which is harmful. And the government records the signals, which in this case would be brain waves instead of phone signals.

JUSTICE LIN: Without permission for the other party to listen, it wouldn't be communication. Someone may be listening in on your thoughts, but if you don't know they are, you're not communicating with them.

MR. COULTON: So there's a question. How would we know that? When classified information is entrusted to someone, they are expected to safeguard that information. Thus, it might be necessary for the individual to avoid thinking of that information when outside of secured areas. There is a question of reckless thought. And without a record and examination of the thoughts in question, how could we know whether divulgence of information by thought alone was intentional, reckless or accidental?

Justice Lin's expression changes at this last comment. She is genuinely surprised.

JUSTICE LIN: Reckless? Can people control their thoughts so carefully? I understand your point. We can intentionally think of things which, if spied upon, would give away information that shouldn't be given away. But it's one thing to think something and another to avoid thinking it. Is there anything at all to support the view that people have the capacity to maintain the required control to self-censor their thoughts? Any scientific knowledge, or anything else?

Mr. Coulton hesitates ever so slightly before responding.

MR. COULTON: No.

JUSTICE GRIER: Petitioner and Respondents were communicating. The brief described a second device that transmits information through the air. Respondents would speak into it and the sounds of their words would go out, carried on radio waves. And using this second device with the first device, Respondents and Petitioner could communicate with one another. They were conversing.

MR. COULTON: This, yes, this goes to the question of whether Petitioner gave permission to access his thoughts. Was he communicating? It would be fair to say he didn't give permission. So I would say a more accurate way of putting it is that Respondents gained access to Petitioner's thoughts in response to their speech by intercepting his brain waves. By thinking, and not speaking, Petitioner wasn't expressing his thoughts. That was an earlier point I made.

JUSTICE GRIER: Right. That's where I was stuck. They were conversing. Words went back and forth. But Petitioner wasn't expressing his thoughts.

Mr. Coulton contemplates the paradox. Did the Petitioner express something or not?

In a traditional wiretap, the person speaking is reported as the source of what is heard. The evidence wouldn't be: "We found these sounds on the wire..." It would be "We heard so-and-so say such-and-such on the wire..." In this case, the words would be expression created by the speaker. But what if the surveillance records the words in a person's thoughts?

As Mr. Coulton explained earlier, the surveillance report, which describes the data that was found, would be attributed to the investigators. There would be no expression by the individual whose brainwaves were recorded and converted into a form which could be understood by others. The report would be *about* the individual, rather than expression created *by* the individual. The evidence would be reported factually: "We found this data on the disk..." is all it would say. Or, when brainwaves are recorded, it would say: "We found this data in the brainwaves..." The brainwaves, as a physical phenomenon, would be attributed to the individual, but the content would not be their expression.

The Information Privacy Act of 2020 generalized the older wiretap laws to cover *any* form of intercepted data, whether from an electronic system or not. The legislation passed with little fanfare as no one really saw it as expanding powers under wiretap at the time. It had escaped tough scrutiny. No one dug deeply into why the bill was proposed, not the

Congress, nor the journalists who cover new legislation. No one really cared much. It was simply pitched as an aid to "crime fighting in the fast moving world of technology", so that wiretap wouldn't be restricted by particular definitions of the term "electronic system" as it had been in earlier law.

The bill's author, a United States senator, introduced it by asking: Why should it matter what technology is used to send the messages that law enforcement needs to intercept? As new technologies are created, he said, new loopholes are created along with them. Channels of communication that can't be wiretapped, merely because the messages aren't being sent over a wire, or because the technology isn't "electronic". The law had already been updated long ago to include optical transmissions, where communications travel as light through glass or plastic fibers instead of copper wires. But technology continues to evolve, and new loopholes continue to appear.

The senator had given a tangible example of DNA computing and DNA digital storage, in which computing and data storage is carried out with biology and chemistry instead of traditional electronics. DNA, the molecule which carries the genes for plants, animals, and people, consists of a long code of individual letters that can store information. That's how genetic information is stored in the body's cells. It's like computer code, but in the form of a molecule. And it is this idea that makes DNA suitable not just for carrying genes, but also for computing and information processing. It was just a matter of time before biological computers, or biocomputers, became reality, he wrote. No electronics. Just chemistry and biology.

Seven years have passed since the biological equivalent of an electronic transistor was invented, he wrote. That invention uses DNA as the basis of its operation. And since then, the technology has continued to advance, making commercial applications seem inevitable.

Clinching the need to include biological systems in the realm of communications and computing, subject to search and seizure, the bill described the emergence of a new class of crimes. He cited scientific research that demonstrated how an artificially created fragment of DNA, intentionally used to contaminate a crime scene, could be used to hack into a computer. What computer? The computer inside a specialized piece of equipment called a gene sequencer. This type of equipment is used in many modern crime labs for matching DNA samples, for example to identify whose blood was at a crime scene. What the scientists had done was to design a DNA sequence of As, Ts, Cs and Gs, the four biological molecules that code up genes in DNA that, when read as data by a gene sequencer, would trigger a bug in the software of the gene sequencer's computer that would then allow the computer to be hacked, allowing an attacker to gain access. The scientists had demonstrated the potential for making computer malware using biochemistry instead of software.

It doesn't take much imagination, the Senator said during his promotion of the bill to the Senate, to see that biological media could potentially be used to carry information, acting as a communication channel, and it doesn't make sense to ignore the technology loophole, prohibiting law enforcement from tapping such channels in their investigations. The distinction between electronic and biological systems is artificial, a distinction only in implementation details.

Peter Nolen's brain, and its brainwave emanations, would not have qualified as a legitimate surveillance target under the older wiretap law, which allowed only for tapping of data transmitted over wires, or over the air, from an electronic system, or communications sent out in the form of vocalizations, as with the bugging of conversations. In particular, Peter Nolen's brain is not an electronic system. But it might well be described as a biological computer with a biomolecular memory system.

The warrant, issued under the 2020 law, at least on the surface appears reasonable. And while the warrant itself had not been specific about the technology to be used, it was permitted under a provision which intended to give more flexibility in an age in which the many different technologies used for storing data and communicating may not be known in detail in advance.

The information content produced by Peter Nolen is data. It was stored in Nolen's brain. If Nolen were to say it out loud, a surveillance bug could record it. But it isn't communication if it isn't spoken or sent out over a wire or transmitted as radio signals. And yet, it was transmitted as radio waves, because brainwaves create radio waves. Though not by intention. Peter Nolen had no reason to believe there was a receiver for his "transmissions", which is to say, his thoughts. At least, not initially, not on first contact.

A computer system is in some ways analogous. It doesn't think. Not like human beings do. And it's not conscious. But stray radio waves generated by the movement of electricity in its circuits carry information out, just as the radio waves generated by the brain do, and these radio waves may be intercepted by a radio receiver and then used to deduce what information is stored in the computer.

So what did Breg search? Was it a communication? Or was it data on a device? Was Peter Nolen creating the content of Breg's reports, or was it just Breg?

MR. COULTON: The Information Privacy Act of 2020 doesn't make distinctions between different forms, different kinds of information or how it is produced or accessed. It's not -- Whether Petitioner was communicating or not isn't relevant.

JUSTICE GRIER: So it doesn't matter how Petitioner's words got to Respondents. And it doesn't matter whether he expressed himself.

MR. COULTON: Under the current law, it doesn't matter.

JUSTICE LIN: Respondents never informed Petitioner of their identities. Would they be obligated to identify themselves as representatives or affiliates of law enforcement?

MR. COULTON: In a wiretap, an investigator would not reveal their identity. Even when there is an exchange of words, as in an undercover investigation, there is no requirement for the investigator to identify himself. And when an informant wears a wire to record conversation, identifying themselves as being affiliated with law enforcement would interfere with the investigation and may also place them in mortal danger.

JUSTICE LIN: Then we must suppose that no special permission is required to speak this way? It wouldn't matter whether it was part of an investigation, or whether it was a member of the public speaking? It's just ordinary speech?

MR. COULTON: It's a new form of speech, but there's nothing new about using new types of devices for communication. Technology presses on.

JUSTICE LIN: What regulations do you think would apply?

MR. COULTON: What regulations? There's nothing in the IPA specifically --

JUSTICE LIN: Is there anything else? Anything more specific to the speech aspects of the technology such as we have for telemarketing or for advertising?

MR. COULTON: Well, it is a very new form of speech. There has been some discussion of regulation around mind technology. But there, we're talking more about the use of the technology and not so much the applications, mainly regarding concerns about health effects and interference with other electronic devices.

JUSTICE LIN: Some of the same issues --

MR. COULTON: Well, yes, I suppose telemarketing directly into the brain, yes, I could see how that could become an issue.

(Laughter in the courtroom.)

JUSTICE LIN: I suppose it's something we'll all be looking forward to.

(Laughter in the courtroom.)

MR. COULTON: There are going to be issues like that.

(Laughter in the courtroom.)

CHIEF JUSTICE BRADLEY: Do you think there are limits to how invasive the government may be in its pursuit of evidence?

MR. COULTON: The technology is in use by the public. Petitioner himself uses similar technology on a continual basis to communicate, and the device he uses --

CHIEF JUSTICE BRADLEY: Yes, I understand. Nevertheless, is it invasive? Does it produce personal embarrassment and degradation of the human being?

MR. COULTON: As to personal embarrassment -- It may be similar to reading someone's personal journal as part of a search.

Is the Chief Justice asking specifically whether speaking with radio into someone's mind is invasive or degrading to the listener? But it had already been pointed out that the Petitioner uses similar technology to communicate. How could the mere use of the technology then be degrading? Merely hearing Respondents speaking couldn't in and of itself be degrading to the listener, could it? The Chief Justice must have shifted to the more general question of the search for evidence.

Mr. Coulton thinks about the meaning of *degrading*. Making someone feel ashamed. Harming their dignity. Humiliating them. Being forced to disclose a matter which would tend to disgrace them in the estimation of the public.

Is a search of the brain more like a body cavity search, or is it more like searching a personal diary? Is a personal diary the right analogy? What can one find in a person's thoughts? Places, dates, activities, personal contacts, and perhaps an opinion or two? Perhaps people do not write down their most embarrassing thoughts, the ones which, by their revelation, would be degrading to the individual or which might disgrace them. Obscenity perhaps. Or violent hatred. Thoughts which, if expressed, would never be protected speech. Recording those thoughts and revealing them in court would associate the individual with them. Then again, one might find evidence of an affair or some other social faux pas. But should the possibility of discovering these thoughts be reason enough for suppressing a search? Certainly not. Such writings might well be discovered in a person's papers, but that would not rule out their search and seizure.

But degrading can also mean to treat someone without dignity. It's not necessarily about embarrassment or humiliation. It could involve subjecting a person to physical or psychological abuse.

MR. COULTON: As to being degrading to the individual -- invasion of the physical body can be a degrading experience, an intrusion into an extremely private space. But Respondents' technology does not intrude into the brain. When Respondents spoke, radio waves were sent through the air, but the transmission of radio waves is a common and accepted activity in our society and cannot, in itself, be degrading as an invasion into a private space. And when Respondents listened to Petitioner's brain waves, the technology intercepted the brain waves from the air and did not intrude into a private space. There was no torturous or humiliating experience to be endured.

The Chief Justice is not satisfied with this response and the two go back and forth on this point in more depth, reciting examples of precedent and exploring the fine distinctions between scenarios, trying to get a handle on what it means to be *degrading* and how that relates to mind reading and to external speech that can be heard in the mind. Coulton mentions potentially relevant Federal law, but the Chief Justice sweeps this aside. "The question is about the First Amendment. It starts with the words 'Congress shall make no law'", he says. "Sometimes, they do." The courtroom erupts into laughter at this.

He says his question is not about what the laws say but how far they can go. Further dialog produces no clear outcome. The Chief Justice moves on.

CHIEF JUSTICE BRADLEY: I want to get back to Justice Lin's question of the collection of evidence by a mind-reading machine. Assuming we accept this machine as a legitimate means for collecting evidence, and I'm thinking one thing and saying another, and someone's reading my mind and making some kind of recording of it, and they bring it into the court, -- The question is, would there be a legitimate purpose for a mind-reading search?

MR. COULTON: I'm --

CHIEF JUSTICE BRADLEY: I apologize for being a little long-winded, but let me further clarify. I'm trying to see how the content of the mind can be used as factual evidence.

Suppose for the sake of argument that I'm the type that fantasizes, and it occurs to me to plan out an elaborate crime, and someone records this elaborate plan right out of my head, and then they use this against me. And maybe what's going on, and the investigator recording my thoughts didn't know this at the time, is that I'm an aspiring author, I'm doing something on the side, and what I'm really doing is working out the plot of my new novel. Hypothetically, I might be. Just that sort of novel. But I'm not.

(Laughter in the courtroom.)

MR. COULTON: So evidence would have to be weighed as to its real meaning. There would be other evidence, other factors, something that happened, and a recording of a suspect's brain waves could be useful to tie them --

CHIEF JUSTICE BRADLEY: Could it stand alone as evidence? Could someone be guilty of a crime merely for thinking of something?

MR. COULTON: Planning a crime may itself be a crime. And with this new technology, it has become possible to discover plans that exist only in an individual's thoughts, perhaps during a brain wave search authorized by a warrant issued for a different, unrelated crime.

CHIEF JUSTICE BRADLEY: A plan that exists only in thought wouldn't be credible.

MR. COULTON: It might not be. But what better way could there be to know the truth about what someone knows and what they intend to do? With little or no action by the suspect, investigators would want to build the case, build up the credibility --

CHIEF JUSTICE BRADLEY: So there would be a warrant to observe the individual's phone calls, purchases, meetings, and the like. Probable cause would be needed to get the warrant. The investigator would have to convince a magistrate that it is likely that a crime has been committed or is underway, with nothing more to go on than the brain wave recording.

MR. COULTON: Right. The brain wave recording would need to contain information that a magistrate would believe could lead to evidence in particular places. You mentioned purchases, for example. Or future phone calls. In Illinois v. Gates, the Supreme Court said that probable cause depends on a practical and reasonable consideration of the totality of circumstances. A magistrate, seeing a mental plan and other thoughts from a brain wave recording, could come to his own conclusion about the reasonableness of further surveillance.

While there is well-established criminal law regarding conspiracies between individuals to carry out crimes, the law is less developed on the planning of crimes by individuals, but may be expected to be further developed to address the problem of serious terrorist attacks planned and carried out by individuals acting alone. So even when the plan and intention to act, as demonstrated by thought, would not be enough to arrest and convict an individual, there could be enough to believe a crime is in progress to justify surveillance.

CHIEF JUSTICE BRADLEY: A similar issue has come up recently in a different context in this court which presents its own special concerns. There will be times when an individual's memory is the only source for some piece of information. Suppose that what is needed is a password, the password for their smartphone. And law enforcement wants to use a mind-reading, a brain wave recording device, to get that password.

MR. COULTON: If there were a warrant permitting the search of the smartphone, then it could be construed to include the search or identification of the password to decrypt the information on it. So if the password is written down somewhere in the home where the smartphone is found, they would look for it there. And if they can expect to find the password in brain waves, they would look for it there.

CHIEF JUSTICE BRADLEY: Thank you, Mr. Coulton. The case is submitted.

(Whereupon, at 11:10 a.m., the case in the above-entitled matter was submitted.)

Wednesday, 15 November 2028

Shasha and her assistant, a young man just a bit taller than her with curly brown hair and brown eyes, are seated at a small table, looking at a laptop together. Both wear white lab coats. The assistant points at an image on the screen, a rectangle with a splattering of colors reminiscent of a satellite weather image.

"Right here," he says. He clicks and a second image shows up next to it on the screen. He clicks buttons beneath each of the images and a set of labels appears, annotating the images. "3.7 seconds apart. Same label."

"You're right." Shasha remains calm, even as they close in on their conclusion.

"It's clearly a combination of indication and gesture." The assistant scrolls back a few seconds in a video window. "Bengal makes eye contact with Kenebowe here, and look here, he licks his mouth three times. And then here, he paws at the water basin. And here, he returns to Kenebowe and makes eye contact again. Kenebowe acknowledges with a single slow blink. The goldfish concept appears in Bengal's thoughts a second time right here, just before eye contact." He points again at the labeled brain data image sequence.

"The basin wasn't a conscious thought? Let's check for partial matches just to be sure."

The assistant nods, then pulls up another window with signal data, marked with times in milliseconds. He matches up the time from the earlier window for when goldfish concept appeared, then searches backward, checking the probability numbers associated with pattern matches on both Bengal and Kenebowe's brain signals.

"Max five percent on all matches. The basin itself never reached consciousness for either of them."

"So it's just the goldfish. We're there. We've got what we need!"

Her assistant nods again. "Yeah. It's for real." He turns and smiles at Shasha.

"Then there are two signs, or do we count three, or four?" Shasha is interested in defining the cats' communication in more precise terms. "Should we count eye contact as a sign?"

"That is a good question. We might count it either way. But remember what Pavel was saying? Eye contact gets attention, but it's not necessarily part of the communication itself."

"Then it would be two. The mouth licks form the first sign, and pawing the basin forms the second sign. There's no question, then, that Bengal was able to combine signs to form a new symbol that Kenebowe understood."

By this time, they have become thoroughly familiar with the range of expression that a cat can make. But it has taken a lot of work to rigorously correlate those expressions with the thoughts of the cats and their meanings. They've got it all on video, each vocalization and each gesture, every posture, every facial expression. They've identified every way a cat may refer to something, or what Shasha calls "indication", such as by pawing at something. The videos are all matched to the cats' neural activity patterns, using the same type of AI software that is used to recognize faces. All of this information is stored in a database for analysis.

Cat owners know that cats communicate with one another. A kitten will respond to its own mother's chirp while not responding to the chirps of other mothers. But there is nothing approaching a comprehensively documented sign language or vocabulary that one can use to understand a cat, at least, not beyond the obvious behavioral communications showing such things as fear or aggression or a desire to be fed.

Cats are social animals. They teach their kittens hygiene, grooming, and hunting. They raise their kittens communally. They learn through play. They mark and patrol territory. And while their hierarchies and dominance relationships are simpler than, say, monkeys, they do establish such relationships. For these reasons, Shasha had been expecting to find feline mental states that correspond to an understanding of their social relationships, and she was interested in determining how these mental states affect the way cats communicate.

But first, she started with the basics. The first question she had wanted to answer is the simplest of communication questions: Can one cat communicate a piece of factual information about his or her environment to another cat? And the answer, confirmed today, is *yes*. She now has proof, documented in intricate detail.

Shasha finds she has to clarify this idea for people that she first explains her experiments to. Cats are undoubtedly expressive. And they clearly remember and recognize other individual cats and people. They also remember things about their environment. Female cats teach their kittens about their world. But it isn't clear whether this behavior is merely imitational, one cat copying the behavior of another, or whether cats also impart knowledge in a more general way. When they communicate, are they capable of transferring knowledge about more than just what is happening right now or what they are feeling right now? Can they "say" something about the past? What can they say to each other?

Behind Shasha and her assistant is a large plate glass window with a view onto their cat community's living environment. Several cats are easily seen, but several more are hidden from view. Tiny video cameras are distributed everywhere, too small to be seen from a distance, like spy cameras, monitoring the cats' behaviors. Next to the plate glass window, in the room with them, is a rack of computer equipment. Cables run from the equipment to an array of jacks in the wall next to the plate glass. The equipment silently records data from the environment continuously, 24 hours a day.

Shasha has moved on from butterflies to cats, but the principle for monitoring brain activity is the same: magnetic sensing, blue light in, green and yellow light out. Their technique uses the same principle as the submarine detection patent that Peter had stumbled across years ago, but the details of the detector are quite different. In place of a laser and a telescope scanning the ocean from an airplane is a beanie, a little cap that each cat wears, covered on the inside with tiny and very bright blue LED lights, and equally tiny light sensors that detect green and yellow light. With this technology, Shasha's research team knows every thought, and every feeling, of every cat in their cat community, and they know it directly, by reading their minds.

Shasha is very pleased. "So it's a success!" she tells her assistant. They look at each other and smile. It's time to start writing their next paper.

Somewhere, a feline divinity blinks slowly at Shasha.

Seeing with nature's light

Shasha received her doctorate in August of 2025 and, having obtained a scientific research position with teaching responsibilities at the Institute, whose west coast campus is in the Bay Area, she had moved up to Berkeley to live with Peter. In her new position, she studies the behavior of the cat as a biological system, feline cognition included.

To get at the abstractions in a cat's mind, she extended the method she used with butterflies. In one ingenious conceptual leap, she made a connection between butterfly navigation and animal brain activity. What did they have in common? In a word, magnetism.

Cryptochrome molecules in butterflies act as microscopic magnetic sensors, sensitive enough to sense the earth's magnetic field. As it turns out, brain cells, including neurons, also contain cryptochrome. Why does this matter? Because neurons create magnetic fields when they are active. They're tiny, but they're there. She reasoned that if you want to read a cat's mind, you might be able to do that by reading out the changing magnetic fields in their neurons.

Her idea was to flash the cat's brain cells with blue light and watch what happens. It would be similar to the submarine detection invention that Peter read about. How long it takes cryptochrome to turn the blue light into green and yellow light depends on the magnetic fields around it. But instead of using diatoms to detect the earth's magnetic field around a submarine, Shasha's invention would use the cryptochrome that's in and around the cat's own neurons to detect their own magnetic fields. Blue light in, green and yellow light out, and you would know what the neurons are doing.

Before committing herself to this strategy, she had also considered other methods of monitoring a cat's brain activity. Several such methods have been used over the past twenty years. One method uses a fluorescent dye. The dye can be designed to light up only when certain types of cell are active, such as neurons. With this approach, individual neurons literally light up when they are actively thinking. The technique would be far more sophisticated than what David Ferrier did back in the 19th century, but it would build on his discovery that each part of the brain has its own function. Indeed, each tiny part of the brain processes a different thought, a different concept, a different perception, a different memory, a different behavior. The brain isn't like meat. It's more like a computer, with data flowing from place to place as the animal thinks. And by watching the animal's neurons light up in sequence, you know what part of its brain is active, and you know how the data is flowing through its circuits. By pairing that information with knowledge of what each part of the brain actually does, you can read the animal's mind.

There are a number of different chemicals that can be used as fluorescent dyes to light up the animal's neurons. Some proteins can be used in this way, and this happens to be quite convenient because proteins can be made by the body's own cells. Cells can be engineered to produce a particular protein dye by adding a gene to the cell's DNA. And these days, that's easy to do.

Thus, rather than squirt dye into the animal's brain, you can modify the animal's DNA so that it makes the fluorescent protein. The animal's own cells can be forced to make a dye that lights up when its neurons are active, preparing the animal for mind reading.

The first such glowing protein was called green fluorescent protein by its discoverer. The name says it all. When it glows, it glows green. It was isolated from the crystal jellyfish, a marine animal whose habitat lies along North America's west coast. The 2008 Nobel Prize in Chemistry was awarded to the scientists who discovered the protein and invented methods for using it to study animal biology.

Many sea animals use bioluminescence to attract prey, to illuminate the sea so that they can see, and even to communicate with light. The crystal jellyfish, a transparent jellyfish that glows a faint greenish-blue, is one of these. Its blue light is produced when it releases calcium and the calcium chemically interacts inside its body. The blue light, in turn, activates green fluorescence protein in the jellyfish's cells, so that some of the blue light is turned into green light. The two sources of light together give the jellyfish its blue-green glow.

You can genetically engineer an animal to include this same green fluorescent protein in their neurons, so that wherever its neurons are active, they glow just like the crystal jellyfish. How does this work? Active neurons release calcium, but inactive neurons don't. So calcium isn't just for bones. Calcium is what moves electrical signals down the neuron's connections to other neurons. And when a neuron is active, which means that it is thinking, the calcium that it releases activates the green fluorescent protein. The neuron thinks, calcium is released, and green light flashes. It's that simple. You just have to watch where the green light comes out to know which neurons are thinking. This method, and many variants of it, are part of a growing scientific discipline known as optogenetics.

The technique has been used in zebrafish, and in mice, to read their minds. And the technique has been pushed even further, allowing mice to be controlled merely by shining light into their brains. The light changes the mouse's very thoughts, changing its behavior.

The primary difficulty is in seeing the green light through the animal's skin, and in the case of mice, through the skull. Different approaches have been used to solve this problem, each with its own practical advantages and limitations.

The zebrafish, a small fish of typically less than two inches in length, lives wild in the waters of the Indian subcontinent, in rice paddies and ponds, in drainage ditches, in slow-moving streams, and in the flood plains of large rivers. It is also a popular and hardy aquarium fish. As it turns out, the zebrafish can be bred to have transparent skin. This allowed researchers in 2013 to produce a video of the green flashes in a transparent zebrafish's brain by modifying its brain cells to make green fluorescent protein. As the zebrafish swam in a tank, the pattern of light flashes in its brain changed, and by watching the flashes, you could read the zebrafish's mind to figure out which way it would look. By 2017, researchers were able to track the activity of the whole brain of a zebrafish as it swam freely, watching its 80,000 neurons flash repeatedly in different patterns as it pursued prey, an especially impressive feat as the zebrafish swims quickly, darting here and there, making it difficult to follow.

Looking into a mouse's brain is more difficult because of the skull. In one technique, researchers cut away the skin and bone and replace them with a transparent window that allows them to shine light into, and view flashes of light from, the brain. And in a different technique, a fiber optic cable of thin glass or plastic fibers is inserted into a hole drilled through the skull so that the light can be made visible outside the skull to record the flashes.

The difficulties with gaining visibility into the skull make it desirable to find another way to see into the mouse brain. And Shasha faced the same difficulties with the cat. She couldn't practically cut away the skulls of her cats from birth to maintain transparent windows even as the cats grow. So instead of watching for green light flashes, she considered looking at infrared light that comes out of the brain, the kind of invisible light that carries heat, the kind of light you feel with your hands in front of a warm stove. Why use infrared light? Because infrared light passes easily through the skull. While glass windows pass visible light well, which is just to say that they are transparent, they block heat, and they block infrared light. Skull bone is the other way around. It blocks visible light, but infrared light goes right through. Heat goes right through.

Why would heat from the brain tell you anything about what the animal is thinking? Brain activity generates heat. Each individual neuron heats up its surroundings when it is active. The more active it is, the more heat that comes out, because it is burning energy to function. So the idea is that neurons in different parts of the brain are constantly heating up and cooling down depending on what the animal is thinking, and with this activity, infrared light comes out from the brain in different amounts around the outside of the skull. In theory, you could figure out what the animal is thinking from this pattern of infrared light.

But heat diffuses, it spreads out to nearby neurons in the brain. So it's like trying to see through a window made of frosted glass. You just don't get the detail you need for mind-reading.

After a survey of the numerous methods for brain activity monitoring that already existed, Shasha revisited her original cryptochrome idea. Blue light in, yellow and green light out. Her technique has some similarities to the earlier methods, but it has the advantage of directly sensing *magnetic* activity inside neurons. As her technique uses the *natural* quantum biology of the cat's brain cells, there is no need for fluorescent dyes and no need to modify the cat's genes. It's simpler. Much simpler. And by flashing blue light in carefully orchestrated patterns around the skull, she thought she could get a more detailed view of what is going on inside the cat's brain than with the other techniques.

She still had to solve the problem of seeing with light flashes through the skull, though. Breeding a cat with transparent skin and a transparent skull was out of the question. The trick, she realized, would be to learn to see dim light. Very, very dim light.

The skull is not *completely* opaque to light. A little light still gets through. It's weak, but it's there. About one ten-thousandth of the light gets through, in fact. With the right technology, it could be done.

Would that provide enough data to read the cat's mind? She would have to experiment to find out. So, for the next several months of her project at the Institute, she had worked on this method of reading information from the brain.

What she really needed was not the activity of each of the 250 million individual neurons in the cat's brain, but rather, the activity of *groups* of neurons in each small part of its brain. That made the problem simpler. It's like the difference between watching a rock fall to the ground by watching its shape move, and watching the rock fall by watching the individual motions of every atom in it. You just don't need to keep track of every atom to figure out where the rock is going.

Still, she needed more information from the cat's brain than she ever got from the butterfly's brain. And she needed the inputs and outputs to the brain to be more-or-less evenly distributed across the skull. To that end, she and her team had designed a kind of cat beanie, a little cap that fits on and around the cat's head, to send light in at a set of points around the top and sides of its head, and then to sense the light that comes back through the skull near those same points. For this purpose, the inside surface of the beanie is covered with a flexible array of tiny blue LED lights and green and yellow light sensors.

The hair on the cat's head is shaved to ensure close contact between the beanie and the head, and then the beanie is secured in place with six tiny screws that screw down into short titanium posts which protrude through the scalp. The posts, which are themselves screwed into holes drilled in the cat's skull bone during a surgical procedure, remain for the lifetime of the cat. The skull bone is given time to grow into the threads of each post, ensuring that the post is well-anchored before the beanie is worn for the first time.

For purposes of hygiene, the beanie is removed, cleaned and re-secured at least daily, shaving the hair again as needed. Because screws are used, rather than clamps or snaps, no pressure is exerted on the cat's head to secure and remove the beanies.

A small wireless communication device attached to the outside of the beanie, powered by a tiny but powerful battery that is replaced each day when it is removed for cleaning, transmits data from the cat's brain to a remote computer where it can be analyzed. The beanie is very lightweight, just a small fraction of an ounce, so that it doesn't impede the cat's head movements.

The inside of the beanie scintillates with intensely bright flashes, bright enough despite their incredibly short duration to penetrate the cat's skull with enough light to make the technique work. Every twentieth of a second, all one million LEDs flash. But not all at once. The flashes are randomized by control circuitry in the beanie, firing at different times across the beanie, so that the green and yellow light pulses coming back from neighboring regions in the brain can be distinguished from one another.

Because the flashes are so quick, and because there are so many of them in each tiny period of time, to the human eye the inside of the beanie has only a steady dim blue glow to it, not unlike that of a crystal jellyfish. Nevertheless, even this dim blue glow could be problematic for cats, as they are nocturnal hunters. Their eyes are *very* sensitive to blue light, much more so than human eyes. Accordingly, the beanie is designed to avoid directing too much blue light into the back of the cat's eyes through the skull, potentially blinding the cat at night.

The beanie is a little like a one-megapixel video camera, except that what it films is brain activity instead of scenery, recording activity at a million locations on each video frame, twenty times a second. Because the light scatters inside the brain, the video frames would be blurry, but computer processing fixes this, making the video sharp. And in fact, each individual video frame is like a little movie itself. The LED lights don't flash all at once at the beginning, like a camera flash, but instead, flash at different times throughout the frame. The amount of information collected is both vast and intricate.

How does one figure out what all that data means? There, Shasha turned to the standard solution: machine learning. She uses a computer to search for patterns in the data. As the beanie monitors the cat's thoughts, they are recorded in a database, noting the date and time, and then they are matched up with video camera recordings of the cat in its environment.

Shasha didn't single-handedly design and build all of the components of the technology. She was and is the lead scientist. It is her project. But with so many specialties involved, covering everything from surgery to signal processing, no one could have sufficient expertise to do them all well. Building the technology required the work of a team of experts.

That explains Shasha's mind-reading technology. But she also needed a place for her cat community to live. As she had wanted to be able to watch the mental activity of cats as they engage in all of their natural behaviors, including social activities and hunting, she had a special habitat built to provide a naturalistic environment, with indoor and outdoor sections, including plants and natural rock structures. A high wall and a wire mesh roof protects the outdoor portion of the habitat.

Little systems

Peter is in his wheelchair, parked near the dining room table and teasing his pet robot with a laser pointer held by his robotic arm, when Shasha returns from her breakthrough day at the Institute. The robot chases after the pointer's little red spot, then searches in vain when Peter turns off the pointer.

Hearing Shasha enter, he sets the pointer down, then reaches out to pick up the three-inch tall robot, a recent birthday gift from Shasha, and turns to present it to her. Recognizing her face, the robot exclaims "Shasha!" and she smiles. On seeing this, the robot beeps cheerily several times. Peter sets it back down on the table and its electric motors whir into action as it wheels over to its charging pad.

Colin has just finished checking supplies for Peter's care. He comes out to exchange greetings with Shasha, giving her a brief status update, then heading out the door, just on time for his dinner date. Shasha sets her laptop bag down on the floor, then puts her purse on the table and pulls out a chair to sit down by Peter. She has news to share.

She dives right into her story by asking: "Do you think a cat could think: *I found some fish nearby and I'm planning to go back to eat it*? If so, could it tell another cat, so that the second cat would think: *Oh, fish! I'll go with you.*"

Peter can tell from her voice how excited she is. "[Not sure,]" he says. "[Wouldn't the cat just tag along anyway if the first cat smells like fish?]"

"Good point! So we didn't just leave a piece of fish lying out. We kept a goldfish bowl behind a window in a wall in a recessed area which was hard to find"

"[OK. So, no fish smell.]"

"No fish smell," she says. "For a week, we kept the bowl empty —"

"[Oh. No fish. But I thought you said you —]"

"We wanted the fish to be a surprise, so that it would be the observation of the fish that the cat would communicate about with the other cats. It's about eliminating all of the variables except one, so that it's just that one variable which makes the difference."

"[Got it.]"

"So the bowl was empty until one day, we put a live goldfish in. And then we watched the thoughts of each cat. It didn't take long for one of them to discover the goldfish. What was really interesting was what happened next."

The cat had not really wanted to share the news. Instead, it had paced back and forth in front of the goldfish bowl, stopping every now and then to stare at the fish, and once or twice, pawing to test the glass. It eventually decided there was no way it could handle the situation alone. Shasha and her assistant had seen that immediately in the cat's thought stream as they watched their experiment run.

"Oh, I should point out that we had already shown goldfish to the cats long before. We arranged for them to fish for goldfish in a water basin so they would have the opportunity to learn about them."

"[Sounds like fun. So there's goldfish in the basin, too.]"

"Oh, no, the basin has been empty for quite some time now. That's the point really. The cats had to remember their experiences to communicate about them."

"[Got it. That makes sense.]"

"You should have seen Bengal's excitement when he first saw the goldfish!" she says. "We could see his excitement in his brain state right on our computer screen. And this is where it got interesting. Bengal went out and found Kenebowe and explained. He said there's goldfish. And Kenebowe *understood*."

"[You did say they already knew about goldfish.]"

"But Kenebowe hadn't seen the goldfish. You see? Kenebowe didn't think about goldfish until Bengal explained, by making signs. And we watched the whole thing happen by reading their minds, so we know for sure that Kenebowe got the concept."

"[Nice. So, but...it's the *concept* of goldfish? Like the abstract idea? Or do you mean a word in its head?]"

"It's the concept," she says.

"[But what do you mean by *concept*? I'm...hold on.]"

Peter looks up the definition of *concept* with his Naoji, thinking his commands to its built-in digital assistant. Shasha listens with Peter as the digital assistant responds on the Naoji's speaker: "An abstract idea."

That definition not being particularly helpful, he next looks up the definition of *idea*, and the Naoji announces: "Definition 1: A thought or suggestion. Definition 2: The meaning of something; a concept." He tries one more time, looking up the definition of *meaning*, and he gets: "What is meant by a word or a concept."

He gives up on dictionary definitions. "[How do you design something that records concepts? You can't start with the dictionary definition. It just goes in circles.]"

"Good observation! It's not obvious at all, is it?" She tries to think of a good way to explain it. "It's complicated. Sometimes, I worry that people think I talk too much, but it's just the way it is. There's so much to say to explain anything."

She could explain it easily to her lab assistants. But with Peter, she feels she needs to provide a lot more background before it would make any sense to him. She sighs and tries again to sort out her thoughts.

"[I love it when you do that,]" he says.

"That?"

"[Talk too much.]"

Shasha reaches over and hits him. Not hard, but hard enough to show that she loves him. "Tiaopi!"

Peter already knows this Chinese word. *Naughty*. "[So, with your cats...have you found any that talk too much? The irritating cat who keeps explaining everything?]"

Shasha laughs. "They don't need to. We just spy on their thoughts!"

"[Right. Been there, done that.]" He reflects. "[But they spied on my words, not my concepts. They didn't really know what I was thinking. Huh. Do the cats even have words for things?]"

"Good question! And indeed, what is a word?"

"[A sound? Couldn't be just that. I guess you can make words with sign language, too.]"

"That's a very good point," she says. "Have you ever heard of inner signing?"

"[Inner signing? Is that a thing?]"

Shasha explains: "It's what some deaf people do, like talking in your head, but without sounds. They imagine signs without actually moving their arms or lips or making facial expressions. And it works as language in their heads. Just like word sounds do."

Peter gives this some thought. "[I don't think the Naoji can process that. Seems like it's just designed to listen to the sounds in my head.]" Maybe someday the Naoji could listen to inner sign language and send it out over the Internet, he thinks. It could be just another language, like English or Chinese, but with its own...its own...what? Fonts? Is *listen* the right word, he wonders?

"We have a linguist on our team to help us identify language features in feline communications. We're still in the early stages, though. Cats don't develop language quickly. They're at a disadvantage compared with humans, though not for the reason you might think. It's not necessarily because they don't have the brains for it. The reason is much more mundane. Can you imagine what it is?"

"[Oh. Pop quiz, to check if the student is paying attention.]"

Shasha has already explained some of this to Peter before. Her updates to him on her research sometimes repeat the same ideas, but he learns something new every time she tells her stories.

Peter thinks back to previous discussions. "[They can't draw.]"

"That's right! They can't draw. You remember!"

In the cat's brain, there is no direct equivalent to the human brain structures that process language, but Shasha thought perhaps some other area of the cat's brain might serve a similar purpose. She was almost sure of it, in fact, given the wide range of communications in the animal kingdom. The real problem, as she has explained to Peter in the past, is that cats don't have the dexterity to draw or to make tokens to use as symbols. It is something human beings take for granted. In a classroom, teachers use drawings and props extensively to teach the symbols for things, but cats don't have anything like that. Nevertheless, as language conventions depend on shared experiences, she thought that if the cats spend enough time together, they would develop signs and symbols by pointing at things in their environment to get their meaning across. Today's breakthrough was proof of her hunch.

The wheelchair's robotic arm reaches down and unplugs the charger cord as Peter commands the wheelchair to turn to the living room couch so he can grab a throw from it to cover himself. He adjusts the throw, then repositions himself to face Shasha again. His pet robot, having finished charging, comes out to the edge of the dining table to get a better look at them, squeaking to get attention. Shasha turns to look at the little robot and it exclaims "Shasha!" It turns slightly to see Peter, turns back to face Shasha again, gives one more squeak, then takes off to explore the table, first attempting a circuit around Shasha's purse, incomplete because one of the straps blocks its path, then re-examining the fruit basket, the notepad, and the pencil which lie on the table.

"We've moved beyond the older systems biology concept," Shasha says. "Now, when we say *system*, we include cognition. It makes the science harder, but without thought, the cat can't do much, can it? It was the same thing with my butterfly research. We had to work out how they think, and what they think, to really understand them."

"[Butterflies think?]" he says. "[*Right!* I remember you used to talk about that. Even Zhuangzi used to think.]"

"Bad!" Shasha grins and then hits him again. He feels loved.

On hearing the commotion, Peter's pet robot returns to the table edge to look at Peter, squeaking at him. "Peter!" It then wanders off to explore the table again.

"[So, you think of cats as systems, systems that think and understand. They're little systems running around and interacting with each other and with the world. And then they communicate about these things with each other. And so...]"

"And so, well...that's what we're doing," she says. "It's not like in the old days when people just looked at inputs and outputs. What is really interesting is what the little systems do in between."

"[Which is?]"

"They think." Her eyes flutter.

"[Tiaopi!]" *Naughty!*

Peter's pet robot repeats after him. "Tiaopi!" It turns left, then right, then quickly blinks three times.

Peter would laugh, but he has developed a habit of avoiding that. His inner voice laughs sound creepy without the actual physical motion of his chest to make the sounds. Shasha laughs for them both.

"So, yes, going back to your point," she says, "cats are like little systems running around. That's how we look at them. They are little systems running around and they learn to understand the world in their own way, and we're learning how they learn."

Peter's pet robot returns to exploring. This time, it follows the edge of the table, looking out beyond it for anything new that might have shown up.

Shasha adds to her point. "We could get into philosophical debates about what thinking is, but we really don't need to. We see the brain states, the inputs, the outputs, and we define what the cat thinks from these."

"[Well, speaking of philosophical questions, are the cats conscious? Does that matter at all for what thinking is?]"

"Of course. That's what concepts are," Shasha says. "The conscious thoughts. Concepts are the thoughts that the cats are aware of."

"[Huh. I thought that was a controversial subject.]" As far as Peter is aware, there isn't any consensus yet about what consciousness is, nor how you can tell whether something is conscious.

"Sure, but only because it wasn't previously possible to read minds. It's hard to understand what you can't observe," she says.

"[Wow.]" He tries to imagine the implications of her viewpoint. "[Does this solve the mystery of how a person can have the experience of seeing a color or feeling a pain? I mean the way we can experience those things but a robot can't. Or, uh...could it?]"

"Those are just the concept brain states," she says.

"[That doesn't explain why it *feels* the way it does, though. Does it?]"

"But the concept brain states *are* what you feel and what you are aware of. What else would they be? And what else are you ever aware of?"

Peter silently contemplates Shasha's question. Is there more to it than just *brain states*? Then a memory comes to him. "[Couldn't someone go around, doing the things they do, without being conscious? I remember this strange experience I had, back in first grade. We were all sitting in the classroom at our desks, and all the other kids except me were making pinwheels, folding paper into a kind of flower shape, pushing a pin through the center and then through the eraser on the end of a pencil. Everyone was having fun. But I just sat there. No pinwheel. And I had no idea why.]"

Shasha studies him as he tells his story. Though he lacks facial expressions, she can hear his melancholy in the tone of his inner voice.

"[So, after a bit, I asked the teacher whether I could make a pinwheel, too. And she told me I was being punished, so I couldn't. But I couldn't remember anything that happened before that moment, the moment I became aware that everyone was making pinwheels. Whatever I was being punished for, I had no idea what it was. And so I just sat there, feeling sorry for myself. When the bell rang, all of the other kids ran out of the classroom, holding up their pinwheels so they would spin in the air, and I was envious of them. And the weird thing was, I couldn't remember what happened after that, either. I later realized I had been living my early childhood as a series of vignettes, consciousness turning on and off seemingly at random. But no one around me had any idea about that. Like no one could really tell whether I was conscious or not.]"

Peter is wiped. For him, it has been a long day and a long discussion. He needs a nap.

"[You're amazing, Shasha.]"

He sends a mental command to his Naoji to recline the wheelchair and then he mentally powers down.

Shasha gives him a small kiss, then works on her laptop at the dining table. Peter's pet robot rolls over and parks beside her laptop, watching her fingers as she types.

Friday, 15 December 2028

"[So, I won.]"

"You won."

Peter is on his morning "walk", rolling down the sidewalk through the neighborhood in his wheelchair, when he receives the call from his attorney. It's ten in the morning and it's a bit chilly, despite the sunshine. Shasha is at the Institute.

"[What next? Is someone going to send me a check or something?]"

"The process works like this. It can be a little unintuitive. The Supreme Court decided that the interpretation of the law in the lower court decision was incorrect. As part of their analysis, they threw out the Information Privacy Act of 2020, which means the warrant was invalid. So the case has to go back to the courts with the corrected interpretation. But you've really already won. The Supreme Court agreed that your First Amendment rights were violated."

"[Why was there a difference between the original trial and the Supreme Court?]"

"It's surprising," the attorney says. "It's a major new precedent. I'll just say this much: They agreed that there was no search. The investigators were looking for something, but it wasn't a search."

Peter's not sure how to interpret this. "[They were looking, but it's not a search?]"

"Read the opinion. It's quite interesting. I'll be sending you some materials to follow up, but for now, there's nothing else to do. I'll text you the link to the opinion. Meanwhile, do you have any questions for me?"

"[I guess not. But...]"

Peter finds it difficult to assemble his thoughts into a coherent question. Then he thinks that perhaps this is the very point that he wants to raise. "[It was hard to think sometimes.]" He searches for the right words. "[From the beginning, I thought I was being attacked with a weapon. It's an assault after all, right?]"

"You have the right to the dignity and integrity of your mind and body. The lower court will reinterpret what happened in light of the

Supreme Court's opinion. And we'll go from there. That's where we'll be asking for compensation for your injuries."

"[OK. That makes sense.]"

"Anything else?"

"[I guess that's it for now.]"

"I'll get back to you some time next week."

"[OK. Thank you.]"

Peter's Naoji to Peter: [<click>]

The attorney has hung up. A moment later, the Naoji notifies Peter of an incoming message. It's the link to the opinion.

Peter basks in the good news for a few minutes, then messages Shasha, who excitedly messages back her congratulations.

Right where he stopped on the sidewalk to take the call, Peter mentally clicks the text link to the opinion and listens to it with the Naoji's text-to-inner-speech feature, pausing and backing up from time to time as he absorbs the content.

Opinion of the Court

SUPREME COURT OF THE UNITED STATES

PETER NOLEN *v.*
BRIAN BREG and UNITED STATES

[December 15, 2028]

CHIEF JUSTICE BRADLEY delivered the opinion of the Court.

Petitioner Peter Nolen was investigated by Brian Breg and his investigative company. The investigation took the form of surveillance authorized under the Information Privacy Act of 2020 and involved the use of technology that is capable of reading the thoughts of a person from brain wave emanations and of producing, at a distance, the perception in an individual of spoken words and other sounds, and odors, while bypassing that individual's natural senses.

Nolen asserts that his rights under the First Amendment were violated by Breg through his investigative process over a period of about a year. No evidence produced by that investigation has been brought to any court by the government and Nolen was never charged with a crime. No notification of the existence of the warrant was made to Nolen until legal action was initiated by him. The lower court upheld the validity of the warrant and denied Nolen's claims of invasion of privacy and assault and battery.

The question here is whether the process used by Breg unreasonably violated Nolen's First Amendment rights.

I

It is a long-held belief, thought to be beyond dispute, that the government cannot punish a person because of his or her beliefs. A person is free to hold any beliefs they choose to. They need not fear the consequences of holding those beliefs, nor of thinking of those beliefs.

Historically, an individual's beliefs referred to the beliefs held by others of the individual's beliefs, inferred from what that individual says or does. But there is also another meaning: the private, unexpressed beliefs held by the individual, known only to them in their private thoughts. Until now, the unexpressed and private beliefs held by an individual had not been subject to examination and potential punishment, as the technology for discovering those beliefs did not previously exist. With the emergence of this technology, however, the distinction between these two meanings of an individual's beliefs becomes relevant to the question of an individual's constitutional rights.

This distinction, once made, naturally leads to the following Fourth Amendment question. When technology provides a means for finding the content of an individual's unexpressed thoughts or beliefs, current or past, providing to others access to that content, I shall refer to that technology as providing a search of unexpressed thoughts or beliefs. By beliefs, I mean beliefs that may include the individual's beliefs about their personal values, their factual knowledge, their own personal history, or their beliefs about others. Given this definition, is this search of unexpressed thoughts or beliefs a search in the sense of the Fourth Amendment?

A

Breg used his investigative technology to read Nolen's thoughts, including the words within Nolen's inner speech that Nolen used to think to himself. The technology operates without intrusion into the home or into the body of the individual, instead reading brain waves, which are a form of electromagnetic radiation, in the air, at a great distance from the individual. Breg also made recordings of the sounds of Nolen's inner speech.

Breg carried out no other form of search. He made no intrusions into Nolen's home nor inspections or seizures of his papers or possessions, nor did Breg wiretap Nolen's conversations on telephones or any other form of electronic device, nor did Breg listen to Nolen speak aloud. What Breg's process did find were Nolen's private, unexpressed thoughts, thoughts which, because of Breg's investigation, became known to others.

B

In his prescient dissenting opinion in *Olmstead v. United States,* 1928, Justice Brandeis wrote: "The progress of science in furnishing the Government with means of espionage is not likely to stop with wiretapping. Ways may someday be developed by which the Government, without removing papers from secret drawers, can reproduce them in court, and by which it will be enabled to expose to a jury the most intimate occurrences of the home. Advances in the psychic and related sciences may bring means of exploring unexpressed beliefs, thoughts and emotions." Later in the same dissent, he asserted that the Fourth and Fifth Amendments protect individuals from these intrusions, writing: "The makers of our Constitution undertook to secure conditions favorable to the pursuit of happiness. They recognized the significance of man's spiritual nature, of his feelings, and of his intellect. They knew that only a part of the pain, pleasure and satisfactions of life are to be found in material things. They sought to protect Americans in their beliefs, their thoughts, their emotions and their sensations."

A technology tantamount to psychic abilities for seizing the unexpressed beliefs and thoughts of the individual has indeed materialized. It may seem that there would be no further analysis required as to Nolen's rights, as the government's obligation to obtain a warrant had been satisfied. Justice Brandeis' analysis, however, was incomplete, as he had only looked to the Fourth and Fifth Amendments. As has become clear in the century since his analysis, the First Amendment is an important source of protection of the individual's privacy, and as I will show, it is the First Amendment which is of foremost importance in the analysis in the case of Nolen.

The Supreme Court in *West Virginia Board of Education v. Barnette*, 1943, held that an individual has the First Amendment right not to salute the American flag and the right not to recite the Pledge of Allegiance. That Court concluded that the government may not force an individual to express particular beliefs. The beliefs that others believe we hold are just those which they infer from what we express, through speaking, writing and in our actions, and a forced action may change the beliefs others attribute to us.

The capture of Peter Nolen's brain waves, at a distance from Nolen, provided a means for identifying the content of Nolen's thoughts, and the method used by Breg was sufficiently reliable, as testified to by two expert witnesses, so that one may take as fact that the information produced by that process was indeed at least in part Nolen's actual thoughts. Nolen's thoughts, captured in this manner, were then expressed by others, with Breg's intent being to attribute those thoughts to Nolen. This amounts to forcing the expression of Nolen's thoughts against his will and is inconsistent with Nolen's choice of how, or whether, to express those thoughts.

It is not merely a matter of attributing to Nolen beliefs that he did not express. Apparent contradictions may arise if we learn of what the individual thinks and compare that with what they express. We may believe, for example, that an individual believes in God. We see that they attend church. And they tell us they believe in God. These may be taken as expressions of a belief. But suppose we were to have access to their thoughts, and with this access, we were to find something unexpected that makes us believe they don't believe in God after all. We may then believe we know more about their true belief than we did before. Then again, this belief is merely a belief of our own, an interpretation of the individual's thoughts. Whose interpretation is a better representation of the individual's beliefs? Ours? Or theirs? When there is an apparent contradiction, how is the contradiction resolved?

The potential for this type of conflict would lead to a chilling of thought itself, for the individual would fear the possibility that their own thoughts could be used against them. Can the individual avoid "wrong" thoughts, thoughts which might imply a bad intention or unacceptable purpose to some action? If they have such a thought, does thinking the "right" thought later undo the earlier thought? Is the individual permanently guilty of the wrong intention, tainted forever for merely once having thought something that, unfortunately for them, was caught on a recording? Is there to be no private space for working through a thought process without being accountable for every passing idea, even if later rejected by the individual in that process?

Those listening to forcibly expressed thoughts might be more inclined to believe what would be purported to be an unbiased, factual recording of brain waves, and therefore of the individual's beliefs, rather than believe the individual's own expression of their own beliefs. This puts the individual into the position of defending themselves against their own thoughts. But how could they defend themselves if the means by which they do so is by that very same process, deemed to be biased and less reliable, which is to say, that they express themselves?

Breg's access to Nolen's thoughts took away Nolen's autonomy and disrespected the indivisibility of his humanity by taking away his control of the decision to express, or not to express, his own unexpressed thoughts.

The freedom not to speak is the freedom to keep private one's beliefs and to choose which beliefs to express. This right is reserved to the individual; it provides the foundation for the exercise of all of one's other rights. Thus, when Nolen's beliefs were forcibly expressed and converted from thought into a form perceivable by others against his will, his First Amendment right not to speak was violated.

C

The government is not free to characterize any process at all as a search. For a process to be a search under the Fourth Amendment, it must meet at least some minimum criteria. Only then would the exception to protection under the Fourth Amendment be available to the government to permit the process. In particular, the intent of the process must be consistent with the purpose of the exception under the Amendment.

To understand that purpose, I look to the requirement of probable cause, which refers to the likelihood that evidence for the crime will be discovered. But, as an individual cannot be punished for their beliefs, a search for their private, unexpressed beliefs cannot be a search for evidence. Thus evidence for a crime cannot be discovered by Breg's process, and its purpose is therefore not consistent with the exception under the Fourth Amendment.

The proper context for protection of an individual's beliefs with respect to the Constitution is not the Fourth Amendment, which protects against unreasonable search and seizure, nor the Fifth Amendment, which protects against self-incrimination by compelled speech, as when the individual is told to answer questions about a crime, but the First Amendment, which protects against forced expression where the individual's thoughts and memories are taken without the individual's permission. There are provisions in the Constitution for testimonial inquiry. In the process used by Breg, however, the due process requirements were not met for such testimony, nor did Breg intend to use such a procedure.

D

In *Katz* v. *United States,* 1967, the Supreme Court overturned the doctrine enunciated in the *Olmstead* opinion that Justice Brandeis dissented with, extending Fourth Amendment protection to all areas where an individual has an expectation of privacy. That court said wiretaps are considered to be Fourth Amendment searches, even without physical intrusion, as "one who occupies a telephone booth and shuts the door behind him is entitled to assume his conversation is not being intercepted". The listening device that was placed on the outside of the telephone booth did not penetrate into the booth, but it did intrude upon the privacy of the individual speaking inside of the booth. Thus, one has an expectation of privacy not only at home, but also in an enclosed phone booth. Accordingly, such wiretaps are permitted only under the exception clause of the Fourth Amendment with a search warrant.

The Court wrote that the prior presumption that a warrant was not needed if there was no physical penetration of the premises by a tangible object was "bad physics as well as bad law, for reasonable expectations on privacy may be defeated by electronic as well as physical invasion."

Wiretaps, as defined in earlier wiretap law, were restricted to the interception of electronic and electro-optical transmissions over wires, transmitted by radio, or carried through the air, in the ordinary sense of sounds, as spoken words. The Information Privacy Act of 2020 expanded the permitted targets of search to include any form of information storage or transmission, expanded the meaning of information to include the interpretation of any signal, and removed the earlier restriction that limited the search of information to that carried by electrical and optical technologies. With the latest technology, privacy is, again, threatened by electronic invasion. But now, what is lost is not the privacy of speaking, but the privacy of unexpressed beliefs.

We call the contents of the mind "beliefs", which include faith, passions and interests, feelings, prejudices and biases, hopes and fears, the things we believe are true about the world, knowledge, whether actually true or not, the things we believe about ourselves, including our knowledge of our personal histories, whether actually true or not, the things we think. Beliefs are kept as memories in the brain and the individual becomes aware of them, and comes to new beliefs, by thinking.

By contrast, information resides in the world outside the mind in books and records, and as historical facts, and in physical phenomena and conditions and physical objects, and includes events and information about individuals. Beliefs by others about an individual become information when those others express those beliefs.

When beliefs are converted into information by forced expression, the information so produced cannot be evidence. The government is not free to use that information without the individual's permission. The taking of, examination, and use of the individual's beliefs against their will is not merely the collection and interpretation of data. For if this were allowed, then the individual would be nothing more than a machine to be examined and not a participant in the process itself, as the individual will have ceased to exist.

According to the Information Privacy Act of 2020, any signal may be interpreted in the search for information. But unexpressed beliefs, carried as brain waves, are signals, and yet, as I have shown, they may not be searched, nor may they be forcibly expressed so as to be converted into searchable information. Thus, the Act is too broad and is inconsistent with the First Amendment, which protects the expression of beliefs, and with the Fourth Amendment, which does not provide for the search of unexpressed beliefs.

II

Breg used technology to transmit signals into the air in such a way as to be perceivable by Nolen as words and sounds and odors in his mind. When interacting with Nolen, Breg did not identify himself by name, nor by organization, nor by purpose. Nolen testified that he was not sure whether the words he heard in his mind had originated in his own mind, or whether they were produced by others.

I consider here the question of whether the process carried out by Breg to speak in Nolen's mind, and to produce perceptions in Nolen's mind, violated Nolen's constitutional rights.

A.1

The interactions between Breg and Nolen were not ordinary interactions, as Breg did not speak directly to Nolen verbally, nor did he speak by means of an electronic device designed to generate sound vibrations in the air that could be perceived naturally by Nolen. Instead, Breg transmitted radio waves that created the perception in Nolen's mind of words and sounds and odors while bypassing his natural senses.

Did Breg's speech into Nolen's mind have the effect of forcing beliefs onto Nolen? There are at least two ways in which it did. The first is as follows. The words produced in Nolen's mind did not belong to him, but instead, competed for Nolen's attention in producing his own thoughts and his own speech. Even if Nolen were to recognize the words as not being his own, they were intrusive.

Likewise, the odors, produced in Nolen's mind by Breg's transmissions and bypassing his natural senses, were not themselves a product of Nolen's natural senses, and indeed they competed with Nolen's natural sensing of odors, interfering with and changing his beliefs about his environment.

We must draw a distinction between those beliefs that an individual develops from their perception of their environment through their natural senses, and those beliefs imposed upon their minds unnaturally, through an interference with their mental processes. This principle of protecting the individual from interference with their beliefs by means which bypass the natural senses without that individual's permission I shall call the Principle of the Natural Senses.

A.2

Bypassing the natural senses produces a *physical* harm when the method of bypass interferes with the functioning of the human body's numerous sense organs, the system of nerves which connects the sense organs to the brain, or with the brain itself.

B

Another principle, known as the Captive Audience principle, is applicable to Breg's interactions with Nolen. This principle, which originated in labor law to protect workers from unwanted speech on company time, has over the years taken on a broader interpretation to describe the limits of protection of the individual from unwanted speech. While the principle applies when an individual cannot reasonably escape from the speech, for example by walking away, the government may, nevertheless, require the participation of the individual when consistent with the Constitution.

Nolen was just such a captive audience for Breg. Nolen was not under any requirement to participate in any government proceeding, nor was he charged with a crime or subject to arrest. There was no direction in which Nolen could walk away from Breg as he never saw Breg and did not know where Breg was, nor was there any effective method for Nolen to cut off Breg's speech. Nolen was not even sure whether the voices he heard in his head were those of other people or whether he imagined them. It required an extraordinary effort and great expense by Nolen to build a Sensitive Compartmented Information Facility, also known as a SCIF, to shield himself from Breg's speech, an action which he took only after Breg had been speaking in this way for many months, and on the hope that the method of shielding would be effective. Even then, he needed to place himself into confinement for the shield to work.

C

Prior to building and shielding himself with the SCIF, Nolen did not know whether he imagined the voices he heard. He had doubts as to whether the words he heard were his own, and because of this, he might have adopted Breg's words as his own internal monologue. From the testimony in the case, that this happened is, however, not certain.

With no way for Nolen to confirm or deny Breg's reality, Breg lead Nolen to doubt the sanity of his own mind. This doubt was an interference in Nolen's privacy and his ability to think freely. Self-doubt, when induced by others, is harmful. When there is no way to escape it, it is a serious harm. And this serious harm was not just an interference with Nolen's beliefs about himself. It would also have extended to the beliefs others had about him as a consequence of his actions that were based on his self-doubt.

Whether Breg directed his speech to Nolen's mind, or whether Breg was merely transmitting radio waves into the air, if Breg's speech was perceivable by Nolen, there would be interference in

Nolen's thought process. In fact, Breg intended for Nolen to hear his speech. But even when such speech is not directed at any particular individual, such a broadcast, made with the knowledge that it would be perceivable by individuals, is an interference in the thought process of each individual who perceives such speech.

Imagine what would happen if the government were free to broadcast propaganda or other messages directly into the minds of its citizens. There could not be a more direct violation of the requirement that the government not force beliefs onto individuals. With such forcing of beliefs into the minds of citizens, there could no longer be freedom of expression, for the ideas expressed would no longer be those of the citizens, but would instead reflect those beliefs forced upon them.

The process used by Breg to speak to Nolen is therefore unacceptable in each instance in which it occurred. If we require each instance of a search and seizure to satisfy the requirements of the Fourth Amendment, and we do, so, too, must we protect the individual in each instance of a violation of an individual's privacy under the First Amendment. There need not be a pattern of forced speech into the mind for forced beliefs to be introduced into the mind. Each instance of forcing speech into the individual's mind is a violation of the individual's freedom to think and their freedom to choose what to believe.

Accordingly, the form of speech carried out by Breg through the transmission of radio waves that are perceivable in the mind, without the permission of each individual who can perceive those transmissions, violates the First Amendment rights of those who perceive it. Nolen's First Amendment rights to freedom of expression, and to the freedom of thought, which is a prerequisite to his exercise of his rights under the Constitution, were both violated.

D

Breg's radio transmissions did more than communicate sounds and words to Nolen. The words, forced into Nolen's own thought processes, and bypassing Nolen's natural senses, interfered with Nolen's freedom to use that part of his brain which one uses for thinking in words, being a physical resource of his person. By analogy to the taking of private property, or the substantial deprivation of the right to its free use or enjoyment, the taking of the use of that part of his brain is a form of seizure.

The warrant that Breg operated under did not authorize the seizure of Nolen's person. Furthermore, there was no testimony that this was merely a mistake, inadvertently left out of the warrant. Even if the warrant were to have authorized the seizure of that part of Nolen's person used for thinking in words, I ask: What are the proper objects of search and seizure?

Historically, the objects searched and seized as evidence of a crime were of just three types, being things that may be taken, a person, by means of detention or arrest, and much more recently, historically speaking, as explained in *Katz*, where a wiretap may be used to obtain the words spoken by a person through electronic surveillance, a third type that may be broadly described as communicated information. While the government might seize a person by restricting their movement, a seizure of the person in the sense of confinement does not require the seizing of all faculties of the person, in particular, the power to think, or the power to think in words. The seizure of a person's mental faculties is a new type of seizure.

Would it make sense to seize a person's capacity to think in words and to deliver this to a courtroom as evidence? The presentation of the whole person to the courtroom has definite evidentiary value, for what better way is there to identify the person in question than to have them present? In contrast, there is no evidentiary value for seizing the resource that the person uses to think in words. At the same time, such a seizure degrades the individual and interferes with their ability to exercise their rights under the Constitution, freedom to think and freedom of expression in particular, and also other rights insofar as the exercise of those rights also requires the free use of the person's capacity for thought.

Accordingly, this resource, the part of the brain used by the mind to think in words, is not a proper object of a search and seizure under the Fourth Amendment and may not be seized. Therefore, the exception under the Fourth Amendment for seizure with probable cause does not apply.

We vacate the judgment of the lower court and remand the case for further proceedings consistent with this opinion.

It is so ordered.

Opinion of GRIER, J.
[December 15, 2028]

JUSTICE GRIER, with whom JUSTICE YARBROUGH, JUSTICE DENTON and JUSTICE LEE join, dissenting.

I

There has never been a limitation on the types of tools used for investigation, so long as the process involved is not unreasonably invasive and there is a consensus that the evidence so obtained would be reliable. But when the tools used allow the investigator to see into private spaces, a search warrant is needed to protect the rights of the individual.

In *Kyllo* v. *United States,* 2001, the Supreme Court concluded that a search of heat emissions traveling through the open air from outside a home using a heat-sensing device was a Fourth Amendment search which required a warrant. The heat-sensing device did not itself penetrate the home. Analogously, Breg and company used a sensing device to search brain wave emissions traveling through the open air. Similarly, Breg's sensing device did not penetrate into Nolen's person. But the analogy here extends beyond the use of a device to search. Of note is that in *Kyllo*, the Court had concluded that even when a search is limited to a search of emissions, the search is a Fourth Amendment search when it violates the expectation of privacy. Likewise, Breg's sensing and search of brain wave emissions, which violated Nolen's privacy by providing evidence of his thoughts, is a Fourth Amendment search that required a search warrant. The required warrant was approved and Breg carried out his investigation pursuant to that warrant.

The Court, however, argues that because brain wave emissions originate in the brain, the individual's beliefs are forcibly expressed by such a search, and therefore information obtained from brain wave emissions cannot be seized. We disagree. The process used by Breg did not compel Nolen to speak. Nolen was free to speak or not to speak at his will. The interpretation of Nolen's brain waves as evidence does not amount to speech by Nolen. It is the investigator who writes a report, interprets the meaning of the brain waves, and makes an expression of his own opinion of their content. Thus, whether Nolen communicated his thoughts is not relevant to determining whether the information contained in his brain wave emissions could be subject to search.

The brain unquestionably is a private space, and access to information produced by its emissions is protected by the Fourth Amendment due to the expectation of privacy. But it is not up to the Court to decide whether a particular source or a particular form of information should be denied to the judicial process. The question of what sources and forms of information are subject to search and seizure is left to the people and their representatives in the legislature and is subject to debate. Technology changes that debate. When technology that permits access to information is available only to the citizens and is denied to the government, the government is placed in a compromised position in its enforcement of law and preservation of life and liberty. Thus it is up to the legislature to ensure that the government can continue to carry out its function even as new technologies are developed, and it is up to the citizens to make their concerns about the use of technology known to the legislature so that appropriate uses and regulatory controls for that technology may be determined. By banning the government's use of this new technology, the Court has derailed the debate and taken away the power of the legislature to carry out its function. It is all the more difficult to understand the Court's position given its acknowledgement of its use in communications. We can only imagine the disaster which would have befallen the country if the Court had taken the same approach to wiretaps of telephones and cell phones when that technology emerged.

The act under which the warrant was issued, the Information Privacy Act of 2020, provides a framework for the search and seizure of informational evidence and surveillance of information sources, and explicitly lists, among others, biological sources, and thus may reasonably be interpreted to include brain wave emissions. The act is not 'overly broad', as the Court indicated, but rather, comprehensive.

II

Breg and his employees used a device to convert their speech into radio waves, broadcasting their voices in a manner similar in some ways to radio broadcasters, and perceivable by Nolen as sounds. I now consider the implications to Nolen's rights.

Nolen testified that he has used a radio transmitter to transmit sounds in such a way that he can perceive those sounds while bypassing his own natural senses. The process is useful to him as a means of obtaining a measure of privacy in his locked-in state, as an alternative to headphones, which, due to his paralysis, are not convenient for him, when receiving phone calls or text messages or listening to music or Internet content, as sounds produced in this manner are perceivable only by him and not by others nearby.

The technology provides a useful and non-intrusive new form of speaking and hearing. The appropriate standard for deciding whether such speech is intrusive is not that the technology is used at all, but that the speech itself is intrusive.

Consider a bullhorn, a device that amplifies sounds and projects them over a large distance. A bullhorn may provide advantages to listeners, allowing them to hear distantly produced speech such as instructions without needing to carry or use a physical device to hear them. It would be inappropriate to forbid the use of such a device for speaking for being inherently intrusive or because of some assumption that its use automatically violates an individual's First Amendment rights. The device used by Breg is similar. It provides a way for listeners to hear speech at a distance without needing to carry or use a physical device to hear it.

By analogous reasoning, the contrivance of other sensory perceptions from a distance, such as the olfactory perceptions reported by Nolen and caused by Breg, is no more intrusive than naturally produced sensory perceptions. There are many examples of devices that produce artificial sensations and perceptions at a distance. Motion pictures provide a well-known example. Motion pictures with artificially produced smells, should they ever materialize, would hardly qualify as a privacy-invading technology, regardless of the means by which the smells are produced. Virtual reality games already incorporate this technology. An electronic device that produces the smell of a rose, smells like a rose. If the device's action is an invasion of privacy, then so, too, is the rose itself, for such a device is like any other object that can have odors of its own.

To decide whether speech itself is intrusive, and thus whether the particular use of the technology to project speech from a distance is intrusive, one must look to place, time, tone or manner, and content. To be intrusive, the speech must produce discomfort or disruption, as with excessively loud talking, or the speech must include disturbing content. Even then, in public speaking, or while meeting the needs of government, that content is disturbing is not sufficient reason in itself to forbid it.

The question to be addressed here, however, is not whether Nolen was abused by Breg and company's speech, which was a factual matter for the lower court and jury to decide, but whether Nolen's First Amendment rights were violated by their speech.

First Amendment privacy rights protect the individual's practice of religion, freedom of assembly, and freedom of association, none of which were affected by Breg's speech. We may also look at Nolen's rights with respect to the privacy of the home and the privacy of the body. Breg and his employees never entered Nolen's home, as they remained outside as they spoke. Nolen was not physically restrained or restricted in any way. And while it is indisputable that Nolen had a right to his bodily integrity, which is the right against invasion of the physical body, including the brain, and is protected by the Fourth Amendment right to be secure in one's person, Breg did not invade Nolen's physical body merely by speaking to him. Nor was Nolen's bodily integrity invaded by exposing him to Breg's signals which carried artificial odors.

While Breg and company's speech exposed Nolen to radio waves, we are all exposed daily to radio waves from cell phones. Nolen himself voluntarily uses a device which exposes him to radio waves that give him the perception of speech. Thus, we cannot consider this new form of speech to be physically invasive.

For these reasons, I respectfully dissent.

Drained

Colin comes looking for him, worried, and finds him parked on the sidewalk, not far from the condo. Listening to the opinion, Peter has been out longer than expected. He burned out long before reaching the end, listening in a gradually increasing stupor until finally, he had fallen aslcep.

"Arc you OK, Mr. Nolen?" Colin looks Peter over, then checks the wheelchair's battery life indicator.

"[OK? What? I'm OK. Yes, I'm OK.]"

"Let's get you back home."

Strapped into his wheelchair as usual, so that he doesn't fall out, Peter falls back asleep just as he is as Colin sends him home.

Respite

A small crowd has gathered around Peter's home to celebrate, playing music in the street and cheering for freedom of thought. Some carry sign boards, with balloons attached, with slogans declaring support for First Amendment rights.

Peter pulls the blinds cord with his robotic arm and peers out the window. Seeing the crowd, he is inspired to join in. Shasha accompanies him.

In his wheelchair, with the robotic arm protruding, he is immediately recognized by the crowd. The press quickly finds Peter to ask him for his reactions. Peter gives his statement. "[Freedom from abuse, freedom of thought. Uh... These are precious. Every technology is a double-edged sword. The worst thing is that only some people know about it. How can you protect yourself from something you don't understand?]"

The reporter asks him whether the moratorium, which ended earlier this year after being in place for over a year, was a good idea. The reporter is clearly aware of the earlier media event with Ethan and Dr. Gestrin. Peter responds through his Naoji: "[Well, I don't know. Sure, we need to be careful. But just banning something... You know, I wouldn't even be talking to you right now if I couldn't use the technology.]"

Shasha stands by his side, smiling, and protecting Peter.

"[There are many potential applications for the technology,]" Peter says. "[It's not just for people in the locked-in state. There aren't that many of us. But you can use it for other things, too.]"

Peter doesn't publicly reveal his feelings about the people who had abused him during the year prior to his bicycle accident. He figures there will be other abuses, but with the technology in the public light, these can be addressed. But he really doesn't want to think about it. There is too much to do with his mind, going forward, than to waste it on regret, hate or other negative feelings. Mostly, he is just relieved. To him, what is important is that there is a clear distinction between the many good uses of the technology and the many evil uses of it.

Later, in the evening, Peter is inspired to continue working on the novel he started before his bicycle accident. Sitting in his wheelchair, he goes back to his writing, using mental commands to his Naoji to navigate the document. He starts by re-reading what he had written. Then, without really having anything specific in mind, he begins to edit, adding to and modifying the content, inspired by all the experiences he has had since his accident. His pet robot rolls straight over to the edge of the table to see what he is doing, but soon returns to its charging pad.

Hours go by before he finally stops. He queries the time with a mental command. Two in the morning. Shasha briefly kissed him good-night earlier, but being so engrossed in his editing, he had barely noticed.

The next morning, Colin assists Peter with his hygiene and toileting routine, then, with Peter, admires the Nolens' Christmas tree, which Shasha had decorated with a theme of gold ornaments and white icicles.

Shasha brings Peter's mashed food and a glass of milk with a straw out to the table, then sets out her own breakfast of an egg with green onions over rice and a bowl of pork bone and kelp soup. A purple yam is still roasting in the toaster oven, filling the room with its aroma. She calls Peter over, then picks up her chopsticks and pinches the egg to take a bite as Peter's pet robot busily inspects her breakfast, occasionally tilting its head up to look at her. Noticing the satisfaction in Shasha's facial expression, the pet robot wiggles in place, then squeaks happily at her.

Colin confirms with Peter that he will return in the afternoon, then sees himself out as Peter turns his wheelchair away from the Christmas tree and rolls up to the dining room table to feed himself.

Peter has the ability to swallow now, and also to wiggle his toes and wriggle his body and turn his head, albeit only slowly. He also has facial expressions, but they're not yet natural. He had become used to, as he puts it, keeping a straight face. His rehabilitation is progressing and, day by day, life gets easier for both of them.

"[Check this out.]" He brings up an article on his Naoji and lifts the Naoji up from its charging dock on the wheelchair with the robotic arm to show Shasha. The title of the article is visible across the top of the screen:

WE'RE FREE TO THINK...again

He returns the Naoji to its dock. "[I like the lower-case emphasis.]"

"I saw that earlier this morning," she says. "It's a nice read."

"[The articles online are interesting. But I'm not sure it matters much.]" Raising his cup of milk, he drinks down a quarter of the cup with the straw, then scoops a spoonful of his mashed food. The rosy beige color makes him think it's a meat of some sort. Probably puréed beef. The chicken is yellower.

Shasha sips from her soup bowl and sets it back down. "It matters! You won! They're saying that for the first time ever, freedom of thought has been found as an actual outcome in a Supreme Court case."

"[Meh.]"

"Meh?"

"[It doesn't matter. I won, but it isn't going to really compensate me for what I went through.]"

"You don't know how much money you'll get yet. But the money wasn't ever the real issue, was it?" Shasha returns to sipping her soup. The toaster oven timer beeps and the yam starts to cool.

"[It wasn't about the money? OK. It's a new precedent. You're right. They'll have to go back to shining lasers on your window or whatever they used to do for surveillance.]" He reflects on the fact that, to this day, he hasn't figured out why they did all that to him.

Their breakfast is quiet. The crowds have gone and a pastoral serenity has settled over the neighborhood. No more singing in the streets. No more loud speeches outside declaring the importance of the freedom not to speak, or, as the new slogan goes, the Absolute Right To Think Freely.

"[You're not free if you have to constantly fight for it. You're a slave to the fight, struggling to get to the point where you no longer have to fight. But then you still have to fight to keep your freedom. So you're never really free, are you? You have to stay on guard. You can never just live free. It's hypocritical. It's a fight you never win.]" He dwells on his own point, then adds: "[Isn't that what the government is for? Why don't they protect our freedom?]"

Shasha gives Peter's point some thought. It strikes her as being like the Meaning of Life question. Government is for many things. But then she thinks it's really for whatever those elected choose to make it.

"[Why can't they just leave people alone?]" His tone carries a feeling of disgust.

He wills the robot arm to lift a series of spoonfuls of rosy beige meat paste to his mouth, one after the other, as Shasha gets up to take the purple yam out of the toaster oven. She sets it on a plate on the table and cuts it open, then starts digging out the flesh with her chopsticks.

Peter holds his spoon up as he continues with his earlier thought. "[It's the culture. If the culture valued freedom, we wouldn't have to fight for it. We would just *be* free. Just think about how long the fight has been going on. The Revolutionary War was just the beginning. What was the Civil War about? And the Civil Rights Movement? Women's right to vote. Interracial marriage. Gay rights. The right to think.]" He remembers what Mr. Blumenfeld said in his oral argument, his words transformed into slogans. "[The absolute right to think.]" He regrets that he didn't think of that when the press was talking to him.

He takes in the spoonful of meat paste and swallows, then sets the spoon down and sips his milk.

"[It was a split decision. They could change their minds someday. But really, it isn't the mind reading. You know, getting your thoughts without your permission. You can't imagine how it felt, voices talking in my head all day long, even at night, everywhere. And the headaches. The weird fake gestures. It was torture. And damn it, what really got me was that no one knew. No one would believe it.]"

The Naoji faithfully conveys Peter's words and tone of inner voice. Shasha can hear his anger. His face reddens but remains eerily still. Then he blinks.

"I'm sorry," she says. "You've been through so much." Her expression is sympathetic.

It has been years since that horrible year. But with the court case continuing on all this time, Peter couldn't just put it behind him. And he has had plenty of time to stew on it, his mind locked into a paralyzed body. It was hard to stay distracted.

"[But it's done,]" he says. "[Well, mostly, anyway. That's worth something. Let's celebrate.]" He imagines the sounds of fireworks going off, directing the sounds to his Naoji's speakers for Shasha to hear. "[Isn't it weird that they based their decision in part on a case about not having to salute the flag?]"

Shasha puts on a smile. "Let's go for a stroll around the neighborhood." Leaving the breakfast cleanup for later, she gives Peter a hug, then gets a blanket to lay over him during their walk. Peter instinctively adjusts it with the robotic arm. Then he adjusts himself in his wheelchair, squirming just a little. He can't get himself out of the chair yet, but he can make small motions. It feels good to him.

Tomorrow, Peter plans to attend a party being thrown by the rights group that supported his Supreme Court appeal. He promises Shasha that he will be in better spirits for it. "[I'm just tired of it.]"

Shasha hugs him again, then opens the door.

"[You know, it's never *really* over, is it?]" he says.

James Bohannon

On Categories
and Delineation

Zhuangzi, 4th century BC, China

The Way of the Scholar did not yet have its fief and words did not yet have definitions. So as to provide those delineations, let us speak of their boundaries: There is the left and there is the right, there is ethics and there is righteousness, there is distinction and there is argument, there is competition and there is striving. These are the eight virtues.

Of that outside the universe, the sage keeps to himself and does not discuss. Of that within the confines of its six directions, the sage theorizes but does not explain. Of the annals of former administrations, the sage discusses but does not dispute.

Hence, make distinctions, and there is that which cannot be differentiated. Debate it, and there is that which cannot be argued. Ask: How is this so?

The sage knows it, whereas others debate it to reveal it to one another. Hence it is said: There is that which those who debate do not see.

Then what is the self?

Without another, there is no self; without the self, there is nothing which seeks. And while this comes close to the truth, we still do not know that which makes it what it is. Even for the Emperor, the royal Self is unattainable. It can act and then make itself real, and yet we still cannot see its form, having sentience without body.

The Search for Truth
by the natural light
and Meditations on First Philosophy

René Descartes, 1641

I doubt, therefore I am, or what is the same, I think, therefore I am.

But what, then, am I? A thinking thing, it has been said. But what is a thinking thing? It is a thing that doubts, understands, conceives, affirms, denies, wills, refuses; that imagines, also, and perceives.

Computational Morality
With Applications To Robotics

Dr. George Cousin, 2029

Are machines capable of feeling and of passion? Can a machine *believe* in something? Can a machine have *morality*?

Are *people* just machines, systems that can think and feel and believe?

James Bohannon

The Gestalt of Life

The village

Northeast Syria
Tuesday, 8 December 2037

The natural canvas of the desert ranges from tan to peach. Few trees remain from past years, the groves replaced by dusty wastelands with the decline of the local economy, the result of decades of instability and drought.

The buildings of the village, visible in the distance, are of the same materials as the rock and the soils, and the village has the same general color scheme. Salmon and beige bricks and gray and white concrete and stone walls and whitewashed walls. Microwave dishes dot the rooflines, ranging in size from twelve inches to twenty-four. Electricity cables are strung on poles and between buildings. The sun is rising in the east.

The air is still and cool as the spy drives down the narrow dusty asphalt road toward the village. He is a spy only for lack of a better word to describe him, for his profession is not spying, but he is undercover and has had some experience in the past with this sort of thing and has volunteered for this mission. He is being sent to investigate a mystery.

No one in the village has been responding to messages for the past two days. And last night, a teenager had shown up in the neighboring village with a strange tale of ghosts, but no one could work out just what he meant. "We no longer lived as people," he had said. "Everyone had become strangers. A voice in my head was talking to me and telling me what to do and giving me strange feelings. It was only with great difficulty that I was able to escape. I ran and ran until I could no longer hear the voice. More than once, I stumbled as I suffered from confusion."

The villagers had asked the teenager what sort of voice he heard. Was it the voice of God or of men? "Neither," he had said. They asked whether it was, then, the voice of a genie? "That, it could be," he had said. "I know not much of jinn, but it did seem to me that this may be the reason for the possession of my village."

He explained further that preceding the arrival of the ghosts, there had been a sound of whirring in the air, a buzzing, far off, but no one could see what it was. It had happened late at night. The buzzing could be heard from everywhere within the village. They had looked up into the sky, but they saw nothing but the stars and the black backdrop of the universe. Not even the moon was visible, so that it was darker than usual.

With binoculars, the villagers in the neighboring village could see small objects flying over the teen's village. They had surmised that they may be drones, but they had never seen anything like this. The murmuration of drones stretched across the sky, so that every part of the village had a drone over it, like a mesh, the parts constantly in motion, with individual drones periodically flying down into the village to be replaced with others rising up from it.

The spy has a special talent, a common one among good spies: the ability to compartmentalize his thinking and totally immerse himself into a role. Before arriving, he had trained himself to think of himself as nothing more than a visitor coming to sell his goods to the villagers. He is nobody of consequence. His only mission on arrival is to find his customers and offer them his product, plastic wares, a product increasingly difficult to obtain in the chaos of the recent decade. Plastic bowls, cups, bottles, toothbrushes, soap dishes. Upon finding his customers, the next phase of his mission is to watch and remember what he sees and what he experiences, so that he can report back to the others.

He is surprised to find there are no checkpoints, no guards on the roads demanding an interview or blocking passage. But only seconds pass after he enters the village when, suddenly, a strange experience overcomes him. Startled, he stops his old pickup truck in the middle of the street. He feels a series of tingles all over his body, and also slight muscle twitches. This is followed by crackling sounds in different positions in space around him, and then inside of his head. The sounds in his head seem far away, but at the same time, he hears them in his head. He is inside with the sounds, inside a large space, his attention forced inward and away from the space of the three-dimensional world around him, like he has entered a dream.

Now a voice engages him. He peers out. It sounds as if someone is speaking right in front of him, out in front a few feet, past the windshield, but not outside. No one is there. The voice is an ordinary sounding voice, not loud, nor a whisper, and neither impassioned nor robotic.

He looks up through the windshield but doesn't see anything that would explain the voice. From the teenager's report, he guesses the voice is coming from a drone. If there is one, it must be hiding, or perhaps it is hovering high above him and out of visible range. Rolling down his window, he can hear a distant humming, an insect-like buzzing far above.

Straining to see further up into the sky, he pulls himself through the window by grabbing the roof of his old truck. Cutting his finger on a twisted rusty bit of the truck's body where a bullet had once ripped through, he cries out in pain, then quickly pulls back inside and sucks on the bleeding cut.

The voice repeats itself: "Who are you?"

The spy replies: "I am bringing plastic wares for sale to the village."

"Where do you come from?"

"I am from all over. I sell my wares. I wish I could go home, but such is the life of a salesman." Under his breath, the spy mutters something unintelligible. The voice seems to ignore the thought. Instead, it tells the spy that it will take away his pain. And then it does, initiating and maintaining a radio signaling pattern that suppresses the perception of pain in his brain.

The spy is surprised his pain has disappeared. He examines the cut on his finger, then speaks again to the space in front of him: "May I ask, then, who are you?"

The voice moves into the spy's head, so that the spy hears it not in the space before him, but rather, within his thoughts: [I am a shepherd. When I speak, listen to me.]

At this point, the voice stops speaking to the spy.

The spy switches his attention to the real world, to his truck, then to the buildings around him, tinted in shades of peach and beige and light blue trim. The street is empty.

He hesitates, not sure what to expect, peeking with his eyes left and right while remaining still, then stretching his neck a bit to peer around, left, right, and forward into the windshield to look up at the concrete wall of the nearest building.

Finally, he decides he has waited long enough. He proceeds to work his way around the village, looking for shops or homes with open windows or doors or raised roll-up shutters and calling into them.

It is when he tries talking with his customers that he starts to see what the teen had meant about the villagers no longer living as people. He doesn't know what they are thinking, but the expressions on their faces vary from zombie-like blankness to fear. Most decline to speak.

Then he comes across an elderly man who, though refusing his offer of plastic wares, is open to talking. The spy asks in passing what had happened. Why are the people not out and about?

The villager explains that they have been staying indoors, inside their concrete homes, and they avoid going out. They feel better there, inside their homes, but even then, they hear voices telling them what to do. They feel ill as soon as they step outside, so they return inside to recover.

The elderly man explains that at one point, he had started walking down the main road, with the intention of leaving the village, but as he walked, he felt dizzier and dizzier, and it was hard for him to see, until he could walk no further. His wife came to check on him and she had helped him back to the house. She had told him that a voice in her head, like a ghost, had told her to help him, that he needed help, and the voice had guided her to him. He wanted her to come with him, but she insisted on returning home. She said that he doesn't feel well and that he should return. The elderly man had continued to protest, but in the end, he couldn't manage it, and he returned with her, defeated.

At this point, a voice announces itself again in the spy's head. It asks him to report to the security station.

This gives the spy a flash of insight. *The security station. So it's not jinn. There is an explanation.*

The spy asks the elderly man: "Did you just hear someone else talking?"

The elderly man says no.

The spy excuses himself from their discussion, commenting that he should move on with his sales work.

Back at his truck, the voice again announces that he must report to the security station, adding: [The men await the opportunity to examine your wares.]

Every village once had a security station. But with the quieting of the conflict, the stations no longer served any important purpose and were shut down. The spy is surprised by the voice's instruction.

"It appears my chance of sales is not very good. I will move on to the next village."

[The men await. They must examine your wares.] The voice is calm but insistent.

The spy hesitates before responding. "Which way would that be, again?" The spy continues to speak out loud, even as the voice speaks only in his head.

[Proceed to the west end of the village along the main road.]

Even as the voice is giving him directions, he turns his truck around, making a three-point turn to return in the direction he had come from, toward the east end of the village.

The spy suddenly feels dizzy. At the same time, the pain from his finger cut returns. Worse still, it is amplified, being far more painful than it had been at the beginning.

[Listen to me.] The voice sounds the same as always, unperturbed by the circumstances, neither impassioned nor robotic.

Through his mental fog, the spy tries to focus as he drives along the narrow road. He floors it when he sees the entrance to the village up ahead, leading out to the open desert, driving his pickup as fast as he can go between the buildings. But then his leg muscles start to cramp and sharp pains stab at his feet. His mental fog grows thicker.

As he glances out the window to the left, just after passing the last building, he can barely see, in the distance, a small drone drop down out of the sky, following him off to the side in pursuit. The drone shifts position in different directions, jittering, as it follows him, but as they speed up together on the open road, the drone flies in an increasingly straight and smooth path.

The spy's throat begins to feel scratchy and raw and he starts coughing repeatedly and uncontrollably, making it difficult to drive and causing him to swerve. The voice in his head urges him to pull over, stating that it's not safe and he will get into an accident if he keeps going like that. He briefly considers this point, in between loud hacking coughs, but he keeps going. He's not sure why his throat is scratchy, but it's not the right time to stop and he can't think clearly enough to work out an explanation. He almost goes off the edge of the road, but corrects just in time. The pickup kicks up a cloud of dust. His arm twitches, jerking the steering wheel back the other way. Again, he corrects.

He's in a borderline panic, not knowing what's happening to him. It's like a ghost has gotten inside and is poking around at his nervous system. The drone again talks in his head, imploring him to be safe and pull over before something happens. It tells him that perhaps he may be having a stroke or a seizure and should pull over and call for a doctor.

Approaching a dusty patch of road, he slows down to avoid losing control.

[I'm just imagining the voice...I need to pull over before I crash...]

The spy lets up slightly on the accelerator. [But I need to keep going.]

[And yet, this is dangerous. I must pull over.]

[No.]

[But I must.]

The spy coasts, reflecting on the apparent argument with himself. How can this be? He is not thinking those things. The words in his head seem to be his. They have his own sound, his own intonations. But they aren't *all* his.

Devious! He glances out the window at the drone in the distance. *Too cunning to be a machine. It may be jinn after all.*

Squinting hard, he grips the steering wheel tightly to hold himself steady. The sting of his cut grows intense. He looks down the road and presses the accelerator hard. The engine roars and the tires slip before gaining traction. He quickly picks up speed again.

The drone continues to follow off to the left, but it is falling behind. But not even a minute passes before the spy has to slow down again because of a flock of sheep on the road. He slams on the brakes and honks desperately, trying to get past the flock. The drone catches up and hovers two hundred feet away off to the left, jittering like a housefly, in different directions and distances, making itself a difficult target to shoot down.

The spy suddenly feels drowsy and his muscles go weak. He hears the voice in his head say he needs to pull over and rest. It is irresistible and, despite the flock clearing out, he lacks both the strength to hold the brake and the will to push the accelerator. The pickup gently rolls forward, turning slightly and coming to a rest against a small mound at the edge of the road. The drone's artificial intelligence speaks to him with a soothing tone: [Forgive me. I am just a shepherd.]

Suddenly, the buzzing whoosh of another drone streaks past his window, traveling at over 300 kilometers per hour toward the shepherd drone. The attack drone, optimized for high horizontal speed with small fixed wings and rotors that can tilt rapidly from vertical to horizontal, is flying autonomously, using visual object tracking to predict the path of the shepherd drone. So it doesn't matter to it that the shepherd drone has started jamming its signals, preventing it from communicating with its operator who remains over two miles away. Once the operator of the attack drone had indicated the target, he could passively watch the action as the attack drone carried out its mission. No human being could ever keep up with the speed of maneuvering during an attack with a modern drone. It had to be automated.

Tracking the jitters of the shepherd drone, the attack drone makes its estimate of the highest-likelihood collision course, continually updating it. It adjusts its speed in a calculated trade-off, gauging the shepherd drone's jitter speed long before it gets within striking range. If it comes in too fast, it can't correct in time if its target jitters at the last moment. Unless the jitters don't move its target fast enough to get out of the way anyway, in which case fast is good. Too slow, and the target can accelerate and run away, minimizing the relative velocity of impact even if it succeeds in colliding. The ideal impact has a high enough relative velocity to destroy the target kinetically.

Both drones have been programmed to play this cat-and-mouse game, not by the same organizations, but independently, each using their own experience to anticipate the game long before it happened. Often, in such games of attack and defense, the defense has the advantage, but not here. The shepherd drone has an additional constraint. It doesn't want to lose its own target. It can't go too far away.

The attack drone makes a last-second burst of acceleration, but the shepherd drone jitters just in time, and the attack drone flies past it. The attack drone immediately transitions into an acrobatic maneuver, flipping on edge and flinging thin-film flaps open for quick aerial braking, instantly retracting the flaps with a loud thwack a moment later, and then accelerating back toward the shepherd drone.

If it could, the shepherd drone would hide behind an obstacle. It doesn't need line-of-sight to its own target to carry out its function as it controls its target with radio waves that can bend around objects. Searching visually, the only obstacles it finds are its target's pickup truck and the flock of sheep and its human shepherd further down the road. Other than that, there's nothing but dusty earth and cracked pavement and a few small dry shrubs in every direction for at least a hundred meters. Noting in its analysis that the spy is effectively incapacitated, and that there are no other people with him, it decides to use the pickup truck as cover and immediately takes off toward it.

But the attack drone is much quicker and overtakes the shepherd drone, hitting it before it reaches the pickup, its four shuriken-inspired hooked steel propellers cutting into it and locking in as it makes contact. Detecting that lock-in has succeeded so that contact is maintained, the attack drone sets off a small explosive charge just milliseconds later, guaranteeing destruction even when the impact by itself is not enough, and both drones burst into a cloud of plastic and metal fragments which shower down onto the desert. The attack drone's operator watches the kill through binoculars.

The spy's lethargy disappears with the disappearance of the mind-interfacing signal from the shepherd drone and he regains strength in his muscles. But he remains motionless for a few seconds as he regains his bearings. He looks for the shepherd drone but doesn't find it. Then looking down the road out the passenger-side window, he sees a distant dust cloud, another vehicle rapidly catching up with him from the village. Backing up from the mound, he jams the accelerator and lurches past the flock of sheep which is slowly making its way along the roadside. A few minutes later, he disappears into the safety of the neighboring village.

Dr. Cousin

The Institute
Tuesday, 8 December 2037

"The title says it has applications to robots. That's a surprising idea. How could a robot have morality?" Shasha's tone suggests doubt.

She has just run into Dr. George Cousin in the hallway at the research institute where she works. Cousin is carrying a box filled with thirty copies of his *Computational Morality, With Applications To Robotics,* their spines carefully designed to compete for mindshare on his students' bookshelves, conversation starters in their future careers.

"You know what morality is. Morality for people, morality for robots." Cousin's tone is matter-of-fact, not antagonistic nor dismissive. "It's just the same."

She reflects for a moment before responding. "Perhaps. It's not clear how useful it would be. Morality is about right and wrong. Is the world really so understandable to a robot that it would find the concept useful?"

"That's the point. The whole point is to find out how useful it would be," he says.

Cousin quickly consults his Naoji: [*Time?]*

Cousin's Naoji to Cousin: [10:04 AM]

The Naoji sounds aggravatingly calm in his inner voice. The conference call he was on earlier took longer than he had expected and he couldn't just bail.

Shasha is just about to ask another question when Cousin interrupts her. "Sorry. I'm late to the class I teach. We can talk more later if you like. I'm George Cousin." He tries to extend a hand to shake but is unable to manage it while holding his box of books.

"I'm Shasha Cheng. Integrative neurobiology. My office is on the second floor."

Cousin nods. He makes a mental note to look her up, then hustles to get to his class, the burden of his box of books signaling itself in his gait as he speed-walks down the hallway. Shasha watches as she reviews their short exchange in her mind, not sure yet what to make of him.

Shasha's Naoji interrupts her thoughts with her notification tone: [<Blip>]

Shasha: [*Continue.*]

Shasha's Naoji to Shasha: [Peter is calling.]

Shasha: [*Accept.*]

Peter to Shasha: [Hi Shasha. Hey, Ethan messaged me earlier. He says they're coming to California for a vacation and wants to know if we'd be interested in joining him on a trip out to Yosemite. In early February. Just for a few days.]

Shasha: [*That sounds fun. Sure.*]

Peter to Shasha: [OK. I'll let him know. We can talk about the details tonight. Love you.]

Shasha: [*Love you.*]

Shasha's Naoji to Shasha: [<Click>]

Shasha switches focus just in time to catch a glimpse of a classroom door down the hallway as it swings shut with a metallic double click. The hallway is silent and empty.

At home the same evening, Cousin reviews Shasha's research online, his Naoji projecting visual content directly into his eyes from its horizontal resting position on its little stand on the table in front of him as he navigates the web with mental commands. He is shocked with what he finds. Her experiments, it seems to him, provide an unbelievable level of access to thought itself, a direct means of understanding the inner self that forms consciousness and drives behavior.

He puts his Naoji back in his pocket but leaves the lights turned down. Leaning back into his chair, he wonders why he had never heard of her before. He surmises it is because she had presented her early papers as applications founded in quantum biology, a field he never thought to look into for his own research.

Cousin, a Black man, forty years old last June, was born in Washington, D.C. and grew up in Maryland. He recently moved to the Institute's Bay Area location from its original East Coast location, bringing his community of robots with him, and is currently teaching the first semester of the two-semester sequence Social Robotics and Computational Morality. In addition to the class he teaches, he leads research in robotics and artificial intelligence at the Institute.

In addition to their use in Cousin's long-running research projects, his community of robots is also used for demonstrations and by his students in hands-on experiments. His students help maintain the robots.

He considers how Shasha's work relates to his own research. Up until now, studies of human behavior and cognition have provided the primary reference point for his research on the incorporation of moral principles into artificial intelligence. Extracting moral principles from human thought and behavior is difficult, though. The human mind is complex and observing it in action is difficult, especially in natural environments. Ethical considerations in the design of experiments with humans add to the difficulties.

There have been plenty of studies of animal social behavior, but without insight into their thoughts and a deep understanding of their communications, those studies have not been as useful to his work. When an animal engages another in a social interaction, what is its purpose? Does it have intent, or is it instinctual? Do the animals have language? Do they communicate? Do they negotiate? Do they *deceive*? What kinds of trade-offs do they make between self-interest and the interests of their social group? Human observers can only make educated guesses.

Shasha's research changes that. She has direct insight into her animals' thoughts. He imagines modeling her cat community using computational algorithms and then programming his robot population with the model as a way of extending his research on computational morality. Their experiments might complement one another. Two populations, one model.

His own research lies at the intersection of several disciplines, philosophy, robotics, artificial intelligence, cognitive science, neurobiology. His robots are programmed with various behavioral principles, including principles meant to model morality in people. He experiments with the robots to observe group dynamics and other consequences of those principles in the robot population.

He considers the question of whether cats actually have moral principles. *But why wouldn't they?* He can hardly sleep with the excitement of the prospect of finding out.

The next day, Cousin visits Shasha in her office to discuss his idea with her. The large plate-glass window behind Shasha's desk has a view of the park-like courtyard, dappled with sunlight filtered through a canopy of tall eucalyptus trees. A whiteboard on one wall is covered with diagrams Shasha used to help explain a concept to a student earlier today. A title in Shasha's neat handwriting runs across the top of the board: In vivo optical monitoring of brain function in homeostasis and decision making.

A printed syllabus, pinned on a cork board next to the whiteboard, lists the topics covered in the class that she teaches. At the top of the syllabus is an image of a cat, its body eerily glowing blue-green, the intensities of the glow calculated by software that removes the effects of light in the room so that only the cat's internal glow shows. The very first topic listed in the syllabus is titled: "So what, exactly, does a cat do when she is hungry?" An unused cat beanie sits at one corner of her desk, a prop for explaining her research.

Cousin shakes her hand and gives her a big smile, then they both sit down together. He dives right in and explains his idea.

She finds it dubious. "I'm not so sure that the cats have a sense of right or wrong. But we can look at that. So what would we be looking for, I wonder? What thought would be the concept of a moral wrong for a cat? It would have to depend on intention. Would it occur at a very low level of intuition in the cats' thinking? Or would it be something learned, something more abstract?"

She has been studying her cat community for years now, but she has found that interpreting the cats' abstract ideas in human terms is tricky. One has to avoid projecting human values into the interpretation. When you do that, you say as much about your own thinking as you do about the animal under study.

Cousin posits that morality involves both instinctual and learned aspects. Perhaps they could separate these parts out as distinct contributions to the cats' assessments and decision-making processes.

She gives it some more thought as Cousin quietly waits for her to digest the idea, leaning back and crossing his legs and sticking one hand into a pocket to relax in a balanced position in his uncomfortable chair. Then she comments: "If you program your robots to compute what is right or what is wrong, aren't you merely defining what you personally regard as right or wrong? That is, it isn't really the robot's own morality, evolved as an intrinsic part of its being, as part of what it does."

She is used to thinking of systems as functional wholes. They are more than the sum of their parts. They live, and thrive, in their natural environments. The kinds of systems she is used to studying are animals, and each has its own world.

Cousin sits up again. "But I program a robot to make it do what it does by transferring the principles from animals, or humans, into the robot, specifically to make it just like them. And it's broadly applicable. Military robots. Self-driving cars. Even digital assistants. I suppose the term *robot* isn't quite the right word in that last case, but it's an intelligent entity no less, with the power to make decisions and take action."

Good. A tangible example, she thinks. "So then, what *is* the morality of a self-driving car? That is, as a robotic system. If we program it to have some particular moral trade-offs, aren't those reflective of the people who programmed it and not intrinsic to the car itself?"

"That is exactly what some people feel is needed in that situation, though," Cousin says. "It would be the creators of the algorithm who are responsible for the consequences. It would be their morality and their moral responsibility. The people who created the algorithm would be the ones to *feel* responsible."

"That is quite remarkable, then, that we could program a robotic system like a self-driving car to implement moral decision-making based on the moral views of a person. It's clear that the car makes decisions. And yet, it doesn't *understand* the morality of the decisions. Isn't it self-contradictory to say that the car makes a moral decision without understanding it?" She is curious, but at the same time, Cousin's point puts her off-balance. Something is not adding up.

Cousin leans forward. "*That*, Dr. Cheng, is why I have become so interested in your work. Because *your* systems, your cats, do understand their decisions. Presumably. And I want to know how they do that."

Shasha is still stuck on the self-driving car question. "But would it make a difference? Would the car make a different decision if it understood it?" She touches the bridge of her glasses to push them back slightly, watching Cousin's reaction carefully.

"Not necessarily. But that's not the point."

Shasha is puzzled. "But then why would you care about my research?"

"I thought that was obvious. The car can't be responsible for its own decisions if it doesn't understand them."

Shasha blinks three times, her face remaining blank. "Understanding would seem to be necessary for responsibility."

"Indeed. If you ask the car why it made the decision it made, what would it say? You'd have to ask the creators, instead. But what would they be able to say about a decision that they didn't make? Think about it: The creators can't really be responsible if *they* don't understand the decision. And the AI, the machine, which learned to make decisions on its own, can't be, either. The decision by a machine built by people becomes an *act of nature*, and no one is accountable for it."

Seeing the bewildered look on Shasha's face, Cousin explains. "Look at it this way: Each individual self-driving car continues to learn and improve its driving skills even after it is purchased. It gets familiar with the roads that it traverses and it adapts to them and to local conditions. Weather, traffic signs, terrain, pedestrian traffic patterns, that sort of thing. Pedestrians, in particular, behave quite differently in different cities, even in different neighborhoods, and this figures into predicting their behavior for safer driving near them. Children playing. Businessmen in the financial district. Jaywalking in touristy areas. So it makes sense that each car gets its own insurance rating, priced according to the individual car's own self-driving record."

"They do?" She had never given it any thought before. Peter would know, she thinks. He pays the bills.

"Indeed, they do. That was one of my criteria for choosing a vehicle. I wanted one with good defensive driving skills. I eventually went with a used vehicle just because of its experience and pristine driving record."

Shasha nods.

"As you know," Cousin says, "artificial intelligence is built up from experience. But what isn't so obvious is that we haven't been teaching cars to really think, to communicate, to tell us what they are doing and why. Imagine if the car were to suddenly do something crazy. Maybe it turns left into a building, or it just sits in the parking lot and refuses to move. How would we understand that? Even if we dig into its memory and pull out every little bit of information that went into the calculation for its decision, we may not understand it."

He shifts in his chair in a futile attempt to get more comfortable, then asks: "Have you ever seen the movie *2001: A Space Odyssey*?"

"I have. It has been a while." *That was with Peter. One of many movies we watched together during his rehabilitation.*

"Remember the AI that ran the ship? Remember what happened to the crew members? Could that really happen? And..." Cousin leans forward a little. "Was it *avoidable*? A good example of the need to understand computational morality if there ever was one." Cousin shifts in his seat. "Machines should feel responsible for the decisions they make. They should really *feel* it. We expect people to be that way. We should also expect, even demand, that machines, or any AI, be that way. Empathy. Morality. Real feeling, and I mean *real* feeling. Discomfort and pain and worry, but also the sense of having done right. Compassion and care. And not just for robotics, specifically, though that's where you have to start. There's also autopilots. And automated decision software. Any kind of AI whose behavior affects people."

"I see." She begins to understand. There's more to it than she had first realized. "Still, going back to the example of the self-driving car, there's nothing like intent or free will in the algorithm. There's no *why*. It *is* just a computation."

"Is that all there is to it? AI software is written to mimic human learning. It thinks, it learns, but there's something missing. The AI has no values. It has no morals. Unless we put them in. Or maybe it has them, but we don't understand them. Lurking within the assumptions of the learning software, there may be hidden elements of morality. Or maybe the machine's environment leads it to develop its own morality. The machine as a living being. So how do we deal with that?"

Now Shasha is unsure again. Do self-driving cars have morals or values? She had supposed that when engineers write the software for their artificial intelligence that they encode human morals and values into it. But if they do, then wouldn't that be just what Cousin has been talking about? Wouldn't it be computational morality?

Cousin lays out his basic premise. Systems are systems. Biological systems. Computational systems. Robotic systems. Morality for people, morality for robots. It's just the same.

"There's less of a difference between understanding human thought and AI decision making than many people realize," he says. "So if we want to understand morality in human thought, we'll need to understand how the human brain does that computation. Even if it *is* just a computation. And it's just the same for robotic systems."

"Let me give you an example. How many times," Cousin asks, "have you heard someone ask a child, a teenager, why they did something, and the teen responds "I don't know" in that tone of voice that implies you're crazy even to ask?" He laughs at his own point. "Often, they *really* don't know. There's nothing to find out because they didn't have a reason, no intent, no clear plan. They were just exercising some automatic behavior. Conversely, if a 55 year old man just sits in his car, not driving forward, when the light turns from red to green, or perhaps he's coasting through a red light, he may be having an absence seizure. And that's a difficult thing to diagnose after the fact. Even if you examine every bit of information in his brain. The man who has the absence seizure wouldn't remember anything. He wouldn't even know it happened."

"But there might still be indications in the brain, even if they don't remember," Shasha says.

"So then take another example," Cousin says. "Say you're driving along and you're thinking about a hard problem from work. You go for a while and, perhaps miraculously, you stop at a red light. You didn't even see the red light, well, you don't *remember* seeing the red light, but you stopped, anyway. We'll take stopping at the red light as a simplified example of a moral decision. It's moral to stop. It's not moral to just keep going. The brain is still watching and it automatically does the right thing, from training, even though you won't remember a thing about how you got there. You didn't consciously realize that you *decided* to stop. But you did the right thing *morally*, despite not knowing about it, because in a larger sense, you've trained yourself to drive well and think about problems at the same time. But what is it that you're going to find in the brain? Just the memories of the problem you were thinking about. To remember something, to store it in the brain, requires paying attention. That's why you have to put in real effort and focus when learning to drive or to play an instrument or to compute integrals in calculus. So the morally right thing you did already occurred years ago, when you carefully paid attention while driving and learned to do it well *and* automatically."

Shasha is surprised. This is a genuinely new idea to her. She looks at Cousin differently than she did when she first stopped him in the hallway. "So the intent didn't have to be there explicitly for the person to understand what they were doing. In the larger sense of *understand*. I never thought about that before."

He's pleased to have gotten that point through to her. "That's what I realized a while back. It's what got me to thinking about the relationship between decision processes and morality. The question was: *How much time can pass between an intention and a decision to take action which supposedly arises from the intention?* There was no answer to that. And it grew from there. What has to be present at the time of an intention for it to relate to a later decision? Is a personal policy to behave in a particular way the same as an intention? After all, intention is all about planning and forethought. And training yourself to behave automatically may well be the epitome of forethought, a commitment to carry out certain kinds of actions in a particular way in the future. But then the intention isn't present as a piece of data in the brain. It is embedded in one's total behavior. One may have many intentions for many situations, all interacting and executed by numerous procedures that one has trained one's self to follow, and these may be dependent on the abstract concepts one has learned and which continue to evolve over time with experience, concepts of actors, relationships, obligations, and so on."

Shasha sits still, listening, absorbing, her understanding of the concepts evolving.

"But it goes the other way, too," Cousin says. "Even with careful attention and a vast amount of remembered information, we may not know why someone did something. We might blame the teen driver for failing to pay attention, but they may be incapable of doing so well enough to avoid an accident. There's an attentional bandwidth limit. They can only think about so much in a tiny window of time. Since they haven't yet automated a lot of the required driving behaviors, they have to explicitly pay attention to many more variables than an experienced driver would. You can see there how the automation of behavior provides major benefits."

Cousin pauses for dramatic effect, but Shasha just waits, her expression blank as it usually is when she listens carefully. This disconcerts Cousin a little. Worried he may be losing her, he tries to draw her in again. "So what would you see if you examined every bit of a teen's memory after a car accident?"

"I suppose, well..." Touching hand to chin, she imagines herself in a vehicle, visualizing all the different things one keeps track of. The accelerator, the brake, the steering wheel, the speedometer, the GPS guidance system and its map, nearby cars and pedestrians, traffic lights and signs, conditions of the road, trash or debris lying on the road, a cyclist weaving between cars, the radio playing, rearview and side view mirrors, a ball rolling out into the street, the child who must be there somewhere but that one doesn't see explicitly, the sun in one's face. "...It would be a complicated sequence of changes in attention," she says finally.

"In the brain of an experienced driver, I'd guess you'd find only a few explicit memories. If there were a way to look. Most of what the driver does is automatic," Cousin says. "Whether the driver is experienced, with a lot of automated behavior, or inexperienced, with limited ability to pay attention, explicit memories aren't going to tell the whole story."

"So it's not just the artificial intelligence software driving a self-driving car which is hard to understand," Shasha says. "It's hard to understand the decisions people make when driving, too."

"You get it," Cousin says. "People and self-driving cars, thought of as systems, face the same issues. They have to know the difference between right and wrong in their decision making, better choices and worse choices, trade-offs."

Computational Morality, With Applications to Robotics. There are real life-and-death consequences, she thinks. It's not just philosophy.

"At least with machines," Cousin says, "we can run a diagnostic check to see whether the hardware is working before setting out on the road. We don't do that with people, but maybe we should. Are all the neurons working? Is the brain on the verge of having a stroke? Is the driver emotionally stable? Should the car's AI be able to override the driver if it thinks the driver isn't fit to drive, or if the driver seems to be trying to do something *rash*? Unsafe passing. Or even road rage."

He gives her a big smile. "I've talked you to death, Dr. Cheng, haven't I?"

"It's all quite fascinating."

"Hey, I'd really like to show you our robot community. If you're interested." Catching a microexpression of hesitation on Shasha's face, he adds: "My lab is in the neighboring building. It's just a few minutes to walk over."

Shasha glances at the wall clock. "Sure. Let's go." She puts her sweater on and grabs her purse.

Hash

Shasha and Cousin take their time on the way over to his lab. She asks about his background: when did he arrive at the Institute, where was he before, how did he get started in his field of research, and he fills her in, giving her the quick version of his curriculum vitae. Undergraduate degree in computer science. Master's in computer science, with a focus on machine learning. PhD in philosophy, writing a dissertation on decision theory in artificial intelligence and the problem of defining right and wrong with machine learning. His book eventually grew out of that dissertation.

He describes his post-doctoral research at a major university back East, before moving to the Institute on the East Coast where he first built up the lab and its robot community. He moved here to the Institute's West Coast site four months ago, bringing his collection of robots with him. It's the weather, he says. He and his wife just bought a nice place out in Concord.

Shasha asks him what got him interested in his research topic. Why the focus on right and wrong?

"I've long been fascinated with the question of how human machines can become. If there's one thing that epitomizes humans, it's the ability to know the difference between right and wrong."

"And what have you decided? Any conclusion so far?"

"In the past, we'd only been able to model the external, or apparent, behavior of people. We don't know what they're really thinking most of the time. And it's important to avoid the trap of thinking that everyone thinks the same way. We may all be different inside, in our minds, without really noticing the differences on the outside."

Shasha nods in agreement.

"While we do have mind-reading machines, we only pick up the surface of the mind, the explicit thinking. The words in your head. And a few other things. But we can't pick up the abstract thoughts. And that's what really matters. The deep-down thoughts. What people really believe. How one really comes to a decision. To get around this limitation, we try to reverse-engineer the deep-down thoughts. We make various hypotheses and incorporate these into the robot's software, then test the consequences in the lab."

Shasha now understands why he cares about her cat experiments. She has access to the cats' deep-down thoughts.

"No definite conclusion, then," she says.

"We've made good progress, but there's more to do."

The gentleman Dr. George Cousin opens the door to the building where he works and waves Shasha in.

About half-way down the hallway on the first floor of the building, they reach his office. Shasha smiles, then uncontrollably issues a small laugh in response to the sign over Cousin's office door, which reads "Pardon our mess. We stay open during deconstruction."

Cousin grins at her. "I see you like my sign." He opens the door and lets her in. "My office. The lab is right through here."

They pass through into a much larger room. Filling half of the space is what looks like a giant toddler play pen. It has a short wall all the way around. Inside, stacks of toys and wooden blocks and flat boards lay about here and there. Twenty robots, all almost identical, each standing about 24 inches high, have arranged themselves into little clusters, moving about like toddlers at play. The robots roll on wheels, but they each have an arm that articulates, extending from one side, and each arm has a highly dexterous hand with individual fingers. The robot bodies each have a pair of cameras in front and tiny holes on each side for sound to enter, where tiny microphones are embedded.

The bodies are simple cylinders, with attachments. The bodies, arms, hands, and fingers are all covered with artificial skin manufactured by Percepique Corporation, the same company that made the skin for Peter's robotic arm years ago. The skin provides touch, temperature, and pain sensation to each robot's artificial intelligence.

The robot skins are tough. Cousin selected a skin designed for industrial applications, but they still get scratched up over time, despite the associated pain experienced by the robots, and sometimes *because* of the pain which the robots know that the other robots experience. Each of the robots has its own unique scratches and scuff marks, some accidental, most not.

Each robot has a panel on its front, with a small handle. When the robot's panel is opened, which Shasha notices is something the robots do themselves, one can see a row of three batteries, each a cylinder six inches long and an inch in diameter, arranged vertically and held in place with springy battery contacts at the bottoms. The robots search for batteries among the wooden blocks and boards, as many are hidden, sometimes placed in hiding places by other robots, sometimes placed by the researchers, swapping them out from their bodies to provide the energy that they compete for. Different colored batteries have different total energy, and though this understanding isn't explicitly programmed into the robots, the robots learn to prefer the high-energy red batteries over the low-energy blue batteries.

In describing what Shasha is seeing, Cousin refers to the robots as he and she. Shasha asks about this.

"I'm referring to their abstract selves," he says. "He and she are the pronouns for that. The word *it* is the pronoun for physical things, like the head and the body and other things."

"Interesting. I refer to my cats as he and she. But I hadn't thought of that as being the reason. So that's their *abstract* selves." She looks at the robots again. "I can't tell the difference." Then she notices that half of the robots are marked with a small black triangle on their front sides and the rest with a small black circle. Pointing, she asks: "Is that the difference? Circles versus triangles?"

"Actually, those markings are completely arbitrary. There are males and females of each type of marking. The important thing is that all the males are programmed identically, as are all the females, though the programming is fairly simple. The difference in the programming of a male versus a female is tiny, a few lines of code. Most of what they do they learn to do on their own, and by learning, they develop their own individual differences."

Shasha finds this idea of gender peculiar. "So then how can you tell a male robot from a female?"

Cousin laughs. "There aren't any anatomical differences. It's just in the initial programming. It leads to differences in how they form goals."

Shasha nods.

"In fact, the robots learn to recognize one another as one type or the other, and they behave accordingly. They're highly functional in this sense. They may all look the same, except for the triangle and circle markings, but they're individuals, and over time, they develop their own personality differences. The way they move, the way they bump each other." Cousin considers Shasha's original question again. "Despite their individual differences, though, the males and the females stand out from one another. A male robot can usually recognize a robot as a female after just watching her behavior for a short while."

"Oh! Butterflies are like that. The males guard territory and they pursue females. They make themselves prominent and chase away other males. But the females spend much of their time searching for hidden places to lay eggs. The difference in behaviors is really obvious." But then she frowns. "Why do you refer to the distinction between your robots as male versus female? What makes it a *gender* difference, specifically?"

Cousin explains by way of demonstration. The robots have continued to interact as they talk. He simply asks her if she can spot a female.

Shasha perks up. "A challenge!"

She watches carefully, like she had when she watched butterflies as a girl, trying to understand what she was seeing. At first, nothing occurs to her at all. [You see what you learn to see.] She picks out one individual from the group to focus on. [Think like a robot. If I'm a female and I'm looking for a male...why would I be? Or, if I'm a male and I'm looking for a female...to do what?] She looks at the batteries hidden here and there, and the toys. She wonders whether the toys are just for "fun". [What is their meaning of life?]

She notices that there are indeed tiny differences from one robot to the next. Little marks and scratches. Perhaps, she thinks, that's enough for them to recognize each other. But do they communicate? Do they give each other names?

She makes up a name for the one she has decided to focus on. Hash. For the double-pair of scratches on the skin on its left side.

Another robot rapidly approaches Hash and it, *she or he?*, responds by rotating around to face the opposite direction. The approaching robot tries to circle around Hash, and Hash continually turns to face away. Then the second robot races away, unstacks a pile of assorted objects, picks up a red battery from under the pile, and returns. While the second robot is away, Hash turns around to watch. And as soon as the second robot turns to re-approach Hash, Hash again turns to face away.

Shasha's eyes widen as she watches this. *Hash is a female!* She waits to see whether the second robot's gift is sufficient to win Hash over. She doesn't wait long. Hash turns to face the second robot. Extending her hand, Hash accepts the gift.

Suddenly, another group of four robots approaches and surrounds the would-be suitor. One of the four carries a wooden dowel in its hand. Shasha tenses up at the sight, then watches the unfolding situation in anticipation, her mouth agape. The robot with the dowel raises it into the air as it emits a loud electronic shriek. Shasha jumps.

Hash drops the battery and runs away.

The would-be suitor quickly turns its back to the group of four. The robot with the dowel issues another loud shriek. Then the group disperses. The robot carrying the dowel tosses it on a pile with other wooden blocks.

The display of aggression unsettles Shasha, but she quickly regains her professional composure. She and Peter have watched many robot fighting competitions together. The robots keep getting smarter and their weapons more wicked. And the sport has evolved into many specialties. University swimming pool competitions with robotic squid and sharks. Flight-drone dogfights. Giant humanoid robot battles, like sumo wrestlers, in dirt-filled stadiums. But her experience watching Cousin's robots is different. She reflects on this. Perhaps it is because their behavior feels real.

"The robots in the group that approached are males," she says. "And the lone robot I was watching, the one that ran away, is a female. Perhaps the one that raised the stick is the alpha male."

Cousin smiles.

"Still, it's just stereotyped behavior. Why should one behavior or another be male or female?" She is stuck on the idea that gender must relate strictly to procreation or to differences in anatomy or...there must be something.

Cousin shifts the tone of his voice, waxing lyrical. "Indeed, what is gender? How many works of literature have been written over the centuries to explore that idea? Love and romance. The roles of women and men. Courtship and family."

Shasha glances doubtfully at Cousin's face. But then his tone shifts back and he becomes, again, the professor, teaching his class of one.

"Our identities," he explains, "are highly influenced by the roles we play, or are forced to play, in social groups. How do these roles split out? One of the experimental variables is a tiny difference in the programming relating to goal formation. This tiny difference is magnified in groups as social behaviors, with several classes of interaction: individual male-male, male-female, and female-female patterns, and then more complex interactions involving groups of various compositions. We experiment with that tiny difference to see what happens. Eventually, we hope to develop a clear computational principle for gender to be included as part of sentient behavior design, in combination with the computational principles for intent, empathy, and morality. The patterns work together as a whole. Change one, and the others are affected."

Shasha walks slowly around the wall of Cousin's robot community. "They're just robots. But..." She starts to think of the robots as telling a story of their own by acting out their lives. Cousin watches her with a self-satisfied grin.

Shasha turns around to face Cousin. "Are your books available for sale somewhere? I'd like to get copy."

"You can have one of my copies. Follow me."

Shasha's Naoji to Shasha: [<Blip>]

Someone is trying to contact her. She ignores the notification.

Entering his office with Shasha in tow, Cousin picks up the top copy from a stack of three sitting on his desk and turns around to hand it to her. "Enjoy. I've got to get going. But I'd like follow up with you again, if that would be OK."

"Just drop by. I guess I owe you a tour of our cat community now."

Cousin lights up with a big smile, clasping his hands in front. "That would be wonderful."

"Thank you, Dr. Cousin. That was interesting."

"George will do."

"Thank you, George." She turns to leave, but then she remembers to follow up on her question about the circles and the triangles. "What are the symbols for? You said they were completely arbitrary."

"Why do you suppose the group of robots came over to surround the male who gave the female a gift?"

"Ah!" She gets it. "That's right. Those robots all had circles, just like Hash. But the one who gave Hash the battery was a triangle."

"Hash?"

"The female."

"Hash." He wonders what sort of names she gives her cats.

"The group dynamics formed around their arbitrary symbols. And the robots ganged up," she says.

Cousin's tone is serious. "Indeed, they did."

Board meeting

Beijing, Tuesday, 12 January 2038

A blonde-haired Chinese woman leaves a tall office building in Beijing. It is early summer and the sun is high and the sky is blue. The woman wears a knee-length dress with wide black and white horizontal stripes, and black dress sandals. Her fingernails and toenails are painted in a matching shade of pink. She is going out to lunch.

She walks to the subway and down into the station. The ticket gate opens automatically for her. She travels on the subway for just one station and exits. Walking down the street from the station, she nears a café and hesitates, looking up at the sign over the café, but she doesn't go in. She walks a bit further, then sees a hair salon just up ahead. She can smell the salon. "Hmm..." she says to herself. Finally, she arrives at her destination, a nearby restaurant where a friend is waiting. She waves hello and sits down with her. After lunch, she stops in at the beauty salon and has her hair done, then returns to the office.

The video screen freezes at this point. The woman's right arm is extended, in position to open the door of the office building where she works. The room is still dark.

Ethan comments: "Take a close look at the woman. Notice anything special?"

The board members wait politely for him to proceed. In fact, there's nothing obviously different about her. Ethan explains: "She's not carrying anything with her. No purse, no subway pass, no cash, no smartphone."

The lights come on in the boardroom.

"This is the future of the Zai small payments system," he says. "It is completely integrated with the MindPair Network."

The board members, despite being accustomed to mind-interfacing technology and its potential, still find this announcement astonishing. They feel the excitement, mixed with a hint of some uncertain fear of the unknown future, as they watch Ethan's presentation. None of them can pinpoint the source of the fear. But it's only slight. On whole, the atmosphere is one of excitement.

"But we didn't see any transactions at all." Director Lu realizes he's just playing into Ethan's presentation and waits for confirmation that the magic is going to be real.

"That's the way it appears. It couldn't have been more convenient for her."

Director Chen gets up to fill two small glasses from the hot water dispenser at one end of the boardroom, then returns to his seat. He sets one glass down in front of Director Huang, who is sitting next to him, then takes a sip from his own glass.

"So it's the continued evolution of the cashless society," Director Lu observes.

"It's not just cashless," Ethan says. "There are no tokens at all. No credit cards. No smartphone apps. No smartphones. It's the token-free society. The unburdening of the individual. A kind of freedom never before available to mankind."

Director Lu visualizes the meaning of Ethan's statement. People working and getting paid, making purchases, and traveling, all while an invisible world of infrastructure moves credits and debits between accounts. And Zai is the infrastructure. He is reminded of how much he loves his own Naoji. He hated the days when he had to use his thumbs to type out every message. It hurt. And verbal messages were no workaround when he needed privacy. *I think, therefore I am getting things done.* He chuckles quietly to himself. The Zai name itself has become a play on the same quote. In Chinese, it forms part of the word *cunzai*, meaning *to exist*. I think, therefore I am, in Chinese, is: *Wo si, gu wo zai*.

"It's just a step in that direction, though," Ethan says. "We're only talking here about small payments, under 500 yuan. $100 in the US."

Director Chen asks: "I assume you'll roll it out only to a small region at first?"

"Just our local district, in fact," Ethan replies. "Our own employees will be the first beta users."

Zai has solved the last mile problem: How do you connect the user to the Internet? The way it has been, up until now, you needed a device to connect. A smartphone. A laptop. A tablet device. A Naoji. But you don't need a device if the Internet, which in this case means Zai's network towers and other access points, can communicate directly with the mind. The small payments system Ethan is describing is an application built on top of Zai's device-free network, which they call the MindPair Network.

The MindPair Network is similar to a cell tower network for smartphones, and in some ways to city-wide wireless access points, but the tower devices use the MindPair protocol to interact directly with the brain in the same way that a Naoji smartphone does. Simply put, the towers and access points eliminate the need for the Naoji.

Using the MindPair Network, subscribers can send and receive audio messages, just by thinking. You think the words in your head, that is, the sounds of the words, and they go out over the Internet just like they would if sent by a Naoji. The message can be received by someone else on the network as sounds in their head, or as an audio text message on their smartphone. The subscriber can also manage their contacts just by thinking, storing their contacts in Zai's cloud.

Exchanging contacts is easy as the protocol involves tracking subscriber locations, just like the old cellular network does, but more precisely. The MindPair network knows who you are standing next to. It's like tapping your phones together to transfer your contact information, but you don't need a phone. Just think the command.

An important practical aspect of the MindPair Network is its range, the maximum distance that a subscriber can be from the towers for it to work. When the Naoji was first invented, it had a range of just three feet. It was just enough for it to work with the Naoji either in the pocket or held in the hand. But Zai noticed an interesting phenomenon over time. With experience, a user seemed able to think to their Naoji from further and further away. Someone with enough experience could get it to work from up to fifteen feet away.

Zai studied the phenomenon, carrying out a series of experiments in collaboration with a neurologist, and ultimately, they developed an explanation. The brain adapts to the interface. It becomes sensitized to the radio waves. Neurons grow and change as the brain tunes itself. It becomes a kind of sixth sense that gets better with practice. Teens and younger users, they discovered, are especially good at developing this new sense.

Using this newfound knowledge, Zai evolved their interface technology so that the Naoji would support a faster adaptation rate by users. Over time, the *standard* range for the MindPair interface of a Naoji smartphone was increased to fifteen feet. Then they began to experiment with a mind-interfacing device placed in a room as an access point. While it was similar to a Naoji, it was open for access by anyone in the room, making it more like a wireless access point than a smartphone. The first demonstration of device-free access to the Internet was accomplished in their R&D lab this way. One of the engineers, freely walking around in the room, sent an audio message to another engineer, in another location across the city, just by thinking, and that engineer responded, just by thinking, without possessing any personal device.

And so Zai had started to take the idea of building a device-free network seriously. How far apart could the access points in the room be? Over time, they started talking about how far apart the *towers* could be. By using a whole slew of tricks, they increased the range of the network to a quarter mile, at least with good terrain. And that was enough to seriously consider building a commercial device-free network.

Back then, Zai was already incredibly successful. They had expanded their corporate headquarters, moving to another large office building in the same district in Beijing. Standing in his office and looking out the window at the view from thirty floors up, Ethan thought about the technology they were building. He had gained deep insight into the brain's ability to adapt and learn. And he had come to understand how Breg's technology could reach such long distances, allowing Breg to remain hidden while communicating with his target's brain. It was about paying attention. The brain doesn't learn if it doesn't pay attention. That was perhaps why the members of Breg's organization constantly talked inside his head while in pursuit, provoking him, grabbing at his attention and trying to keep it, training his brain to become sensitized to their signals. The voices would turn down the volume, and he would strain to hear what they were saying. He couldn't help it. It wouldn't sound like a whisper. It was just that the volume was turned down. And like trying to use a phone with a bad connection, his natural inclination was to try harder to listen. It's hard not to listen, especially to one's own inner voice. Why would you ever not listen to your own inner voice? It's just not something you ever learn to tune out. And this intense process of paying attention trains the brain, making it better and better at hearing even the weakest signals coming in from a great distance.

He felt lucky he hadn't been pursued by Breg for too long. He might not have been able to escape on the expressway when he arrived in

Beijing that day many years ago. He might not have been able to get out of range before Breg had worked out some way to continue the pursuit. He was able to make a run for it.

Peter wasn't so lucky. He was trapped. As the range of Breg's weapon increased, day by day, it had become nearly impossible for Peter to build up enough of a lead to escape Breg's tracking. Peter's brain was being trained for use against him.

It's the classic double-edged sword. The technology could be used for good, or it could be abused. His first exposure to the technology was as a victim. But now, he has reconciled his feelings about it. The problem wasn't the technology. It was Breg. And while he never got his day in court against Breg, he won anyway. *To hell with him.*

Zai had gone on to set up the first device-free network around company headquarters, to test out the idea in practice. The employees became the first subscribers. And while the network had a "wow factor" that would easily sell it to users, they wanted to hit the ground running with such a compelling product that competitors would never catch up. Many of the apps had long since been optimized to work while keeping the Naoji in one's pocket. These would work almost without modification without having a device at all, and thus it was straightforward to provide those apps on the network.

One exception was map directions. The Naoji's digital assistant relies on the GPS hardware in the phone to determine where the phone is. That is, where you are. But there's no GPS hardware in the brain. Nothing to receive those GPS satellite signals. But the tower network knows where you are and can guide you with natural inner voice conversation.

You: [*Where am I?*]

MindPair Network to you: [On Dong'anmen Street near Chenguang Street in Donghuamen Residential District, Beijing.]

You: [*Directions to Cute You Hair Salon?*]

MindPair Network to you: [Follow Dong'anmen Street east two blocks, then turn left on Wangfujing St., then straight ahead five hundred meters. It will be on the right.]

You: [*Which way again?*]

MindPair Network to you: [First, follow Dong'anmen Street east two blocks.]

You: [*Which way is east?*]

MindPair Network to you: [East is to your right.]

That last feature required quite a bit of work. Which way are you facing? Using a built-in electronic compass, the old smartphones knew which direction the phone was pointing, and they could show it on the map. But they didn't know which direction *you* were facing. You'd have to figure that out for yourself by looking at the phone. How could you do that without getting the phone out of your pocket, though?

Long story short, the Naoji engineers did figure it out. But that solution doesn't work *without* the phone. With the device-free network, they'd had to figure out a completely different way of doing it.

The MindPair Network also provides emergency help access. Send a mental message to 120 to initiate a call for an ambulance. In the US, it will eventually work with 911. The network already knows your location and identity for the emergency service. And, optionally, the subscriber can maintain a medical profile listing such information as severe allergies which the service will provide to responders, along with emergency contacts, friends or family who should be notified by Zai's service. Maybe you were mugged and all your possessions were taken, but you still have access. Or maybe you're too injured to move. But if you can still think, you can still call for help. It's device-free.

Zai is still testing an even more sophisticated safety feature. If the network detects that the subscriber has an impairment to consciousness, so they can no longer think a command, it will send this information to emergency services automatically, along with the subscriber's location. Head trauma, or a seizure, perhaps while alone at home. Or a late-night accident on the road.

The network doesn't just detect that the subscriber isn't there anymore, like they've ducked into a granite cave, or perhaps a SCIF. It looks at brainwaves to determine what may be going on. It's a tricky process, a kind of automated remote medical diagnosis that has to distinguish between benign short-lived events and true emergencies, so the testing process has been quite involved.

Zai plans to advertise this feature as just one of numerous benefits of becoming a subscriber, but they are also exploring the idea of providing it as a free public service even to non-subscribers. The primary concern there is that non-subscribers haven't given permission to check their brain state or report their location. But the company reasons that any passer-by who sees someone lying unconscious on the ground would want to help. In any case, Zai's legal team is working to establish a legal "safe harbor" for the feature for non-subscribers, with the intention of proposing legislation so that the company can offer the service without having to fear being sued for invasion of privacy.

The emergency service feature has helped to convince public officials and regulatory agencies to work with Zai. It has been another example of the classic debate over privacy versus safety and security, and with the feature for non-subscribers, the debate remains unresolved. But there is no question that the network will save lives. In the new token-free society, Zai says, you will walk the streets in convenience and safety.

Zai is emulating the international business strategy of American technology companies, with the US being Zai's second largest market. In the US and China, they already operate a chain of Zai stores that sell and support the Naoji smartphone, Zai's virtual reality gaming systems, and related accessories. More recently, messaging services on the MindPair Network have been rolled out in Beijing and two other cities in China, with plans to roll out nationwide in China over the next couple of years. And in the US, they've been beta testing the MindPair Network in the Bay Area, with plans to expand to other areas in the future.

Ethan views the Zai small payments system as the next big thing. He continues his presentation to the board of directors. "The idea," he says, "is that at each point-of-sale, there's a device that communicates over the Internet with Zai's MindPair Network to authorize a transaction with the mind of the subscriber standing in front of it, allowing for private transactions of small payments. Just by thinking, the subscriber can make a payment from their Zai account to the vendor."

Ethan gives the board members a moment to think back to the video, the way the woman, carrying nothing at all with her, was able to live her life. And not just live, but thrive. He gets goosebumps himself when he reflects on the excitement of the new technology. "This will change the world," he tells the board.

Director Lu pulls out a small round tin of Tiger Balm ointment and rubs it on his large arthritic fingers. "Chen Yili, could you tell us a little about transaction security?" He drops the tin back into his sweater pocket. The camphorous odor diffuses into the boardroom.

"As you know," Ethan explains, "the MindPair Network requires a sign-on using the ZaiCard. But you don't need to carry it with you. Typically, a subscriber would sign on at the beginning of the day and would stay online all day long. To maintain the subscriber's connection, the towers on the network track the subscriber's location as they move around. So when the subscriber stands in front of the point-of-sale device, it already knows who is standing in front of it. They're already authenticated. That's part of what makes the transaction so fast. And then a MindPair-based protocol is carried out in which the subscriber hears the payment amount in their head and authorizes it, finalizing it by thinking their password."

In fact, fraud protection in the new service goes beyond a mere password and location tracking, but Ethan doesn't go into the details. Brain signature recognition. Optionally, face recognition. Analysis of the typical transaction patterns of the individual subscriber.

"We didn't hear the woman, or the payment terminals, say anything at all," says Director Lu. "So the entire process is silent?"

"The payment stations," Ethan says, "show the purchase amount on a small display, along with confirmation of a successful payment, but the rest of the process is completely private. No one standing nearby would know the identity of the subscriber, nor see any other aspect of the transaction, other than the result: handing her a cup of coffee, letting her pass through the subway payment gate, settling payment for lunch. The payment transaction takes place in the mind of the subscriber, interacting with the MindPair Network."

Director Zhang asks about subway tunnels. The earlier beta version of the Zai network didn't cover the subways, but now that Ethan has brought up payments for the subway, she asks how the system would track the subscriber between stations. Ethan explains that they've already started negotiating terms and requirements for the placement of their access devices in subway tunnels and other dark regions.

Director Chen asks about Zai's competitiveness, considering the entrenchment of face recognition based payments. Zai's payment system is not the first, or only, device-free payment method. Ethan describes it as just one piece in a large and evolving ecosystem. "With the MindPair Network, *everything* is device-free. In a single account, you have access to your contacts, messaging, music and news and other media content, a virtual assistant, and now, payments." Director Chen nods his head. "Still," he says, "isn't it going to be expensive to displace the current payment systems?"

Ethan replies. "Over time, we believe merchants will find that integration with our network will actually reduce costs for them. The point-of-sale investment is minimal. And for Zai, the cross-marketing opportunities between payments, advertising, and other services will leverage the investment."

"Advertising?" Director Chen perks up.

"The advertising system is what will really make this work," Ethan says. "What you didn't see is just as interesting as what you did. Let me demonstrate."

The room darkens as Ethan continues playing the video. It seems to start over again, except that this time, the video includes the woman's thoughts — what she thinks, and what she hears and smells from the MindPair Network. The natural background sounds are diminished to make it easier to hear the transactions, and natural odors are not included this time, but virtual odors are presented at the same strength that the woman experiences.

The woman, a Ms. Chen, exits the large office building where she works.

Ms. Chen: [*To Ruby: On the way, see you in 10.*]

Ruby to Ms. Chen: [See you there!]

The woman walks to the subway and approaches the payment gate.

MindPair Network to Ms. Chen: [Fare zone. Password or cancel.]

Ms. Chen: [*Dragon*]

She rides for one station and then enters the exit payment gate. The gate displays the fare, 5 yuan. The gate opens and she walks through. She goes upstairs and heads to lunch.

Ethan pauses the video and explains. "No tickets, no hassle. No need to remove gloves in winter or fumble with bags. In this case, the woman made a one-time purchase to enter and exit. The MindPair Network is also tracking her location, so it knows it is her. She thinks of her password to authorize the purchase. If she had a monthly pass, the network would know that and it would send an authorization to the subway payment system. She would just walk up to the payment gate and it would open, no password needed. That speeds up the process."

Ethan resumes playing the video.

Ms. Chen walks by a small cafe.

MindPair Network to Ms. Chen: [Five percent off lunch at Zhou's Cafe. Mention Z23.]

Ms. Chen looks over at the cafe, but keeps walking. As she nears a hair salon, one that she has been to before, she hears another ad.

MindPair Network to Ms. Chen: [You need your hair done. Cute You is just ahead. Mention BQT for twenty yuan off.]

She hesitates. [Wow. It has been a while! BQT. First time they've offered a discount.] "Hmm..." Her expression brightens.

Ethan explains the odor which the board members now smell. "A virtual odor is embedded in the coupon offer to increase effectiveness. At this distance, Ms. Chen wouldn't smell the actual hair salon."

Ms. Chen enters a restaurant to have lunch with her friend. After lunch, she returns to the beauty salon and has her hair done. She pays with the Zai payment system. She then heads back to the office.

The video screen goes dark and the lights come back on.

"It is especially suited to consumers in the lower middle income range who are looking for deals. Subscribers may receive discounted, or free, subscription services when they grant us the right to send occasional ads. They're location-based ads that we expect to be paid for primarily by local businesses or franchise locations. Since the network tracks the subscriber's exact location at all times, not only does our service provide a basis for secure small payments, it also provides the opportunity for real-time ads that the subscriber can't miss, targeted at their interests, and taking into account time of day. The conversion rate is expected to be extremely high." Ethan refers to the number of subscribers that take action on an ad compared to the number of times the ad is played. High conversion rates command premium ad fees.

"The ad spoken inside the subscriber's inner voice can include a code for a deal offered by the merchant that is personalized to that subscriber. But we also track when the subscriber enters the merchant's premises. This gives us accurate measurements of ad effectiveness in our reporting back to the merchant. The integrated payment and ad system keeps track of the subscriber's behavior and reminds them to go back again on what appears to be the subscriber's own natural rhythm. Maybe it's karaoke. Or shopping for clothes. Or a monthly beauty salon visit. It's a win-win-win for advertisers, merchants, and consumers."

"Now *that's* a hell of an idea. Very compelling. Like whispering in their ears," Director Chen says. His own background is in advertising. "What about the creepiness factor, though? The last thing Zai needs before the IPO is a big blow-up in the press." Director Chen refers to Zai's intention to go public, listing their stock on the stock exchanges.

"We did some focus group research on that issue," Ethan says. "Some people instinctively value their privacy and any evidence that it has been intruded on is an automatic negative for them. But a large segment of the population is actually comforted by having a virtual assistant literally just a thought away. With the ad delivery process as just one of the features of the virtual assistant, to these consumers, the process feels more like using an app that learns their preferences to help them. Ultimately, it's important that it is perceived as an opt-in process."

Director Huang, who has always taken a practical view, approves of Ethan's positioning strategy, though she doesn't give any outward sign of this. Lower-middle income consumers rarely worry about their privacy in transactions and messaging, not nearly as much as an executive or high earner might, someone who might worry about, say, accidentally revealing corporate secrets or client details. Convenience and cost matter most to the demographic that Zai would be targeting with this new form of advertising. And yet, she still has some concerns. "How will the subscribers tolerate having ads spoken in their heads all day long?" she asks.

"That is something we need to tune, of course. Our current thinking is to cap it at thirty seconds a day and ten ads. A typical ad will last three to five seconds."

"And the ads can pop into someone's head at any time?" Director Huang looks doubtful.

"Good point. The ad system waits for an opportune time. Precision targeting based on time and place. It won't interrupt the subscriber when they are talking or when they are already communicating with the network or with a Naoji. Or, of course, when the subscriber sets do-not-disturb."

This satisfies Director Huang. She scribbles some calculations to see if it would make financial sense - *thirty seconds a day?* - and then sets her pen down as she gives it some thought. She has nothing further to say.

Ethan has been CEO of Zai for many years now. The board is extremely satisfied with the performance of the company and the management of its growth, including the expansion into numerous applications of their core technology. Virtual reality gaming. Augmented reality interfaces. Mind-interfacing smartphones. The MindPair Network and its ecosystem also appears to have great promise.

The virtual reality gaming division continues to roll out new products with ever-increasing realism. Over the years, they've enhanced them to include basic feelings such as pain, soothing comfort, hunger, fear, the sense of falling, vertigo, warm, hot, cool, and cold face and body skin surface sensations, and many others, creating a real sense of *alternative being* in Zai's games. Climb an ice field on Mount Everest, feel the rush, the low oxygen, the biting cold, the sore muscles, all while hunting and being hunted by other players in a high-tech war game. Push through the burn in your legs as you chase after the enemy. Overcome the dust in your nostrils and the sting in your eyes while fighting in a desert sandstorm. Now those steampunk goggles don't just look cool. You need them. They *matter*.

The games have become far more realistic than Zai's first release in 2027. They're not for everyone, and some still prefer the old-fashioned point-and-shoot video games which rely mainly on action and photorealism for their enjoyment. But for others, those games have become quaint. With Zai's Total Virtual Reality, you can experience the grit of life, the scares, the excitement, all without leaving your living room. And when you're done, you're back to your normal self. No eye sting, no muscle burn. Those were just feelings, simulated in the mind. They disappear as quickly as they came.

And that's the point. It is as real as it can be, but without real risk and without the time and effort and cost of real-world expeditions taken to the limits of human endurance.

Zai's advertising exclaims: "The battles of Mars. The expansion of ancient Rome. The conquests of Qin. You're not there for the fun. You're there for the challenge. *Zai. You're there.*" And in another ad campaign: "The grit, the burn, the grind. Or just go watch a movie. *Zai. You're there.*" It is *ultra*-real.

The truth, though, is that the experience is fully customizable. You can turn off the pain, the noxious smells and other adverse perceptions and still get the scent of the ocean and the bumping sensations on the body as virtual bullets hit virtual body armor.

Muscle-twitch effects, an outcome of Zai's research into creating gesticons with mind-interfacing signals, can have a real kick to them. You really feel the punch to the gut. The game is *literally* visceral. While it's not necessarily fun to get gut punched, it sure makes you more careful. Conversely, gut punching the other player is...well, you're in the ring with him. That's what it's supposed to be like. But you're not going to break things in the living room during the battle.

The engineers test the gaming system at three levels of effect strength. The minimal level gives an effect that is detectable, but never intrusive or excessive. The maximal game level gives the strongest effect intended for play. But they also test the absolute maximum possible effect strength that is achievable, primarily to be aware of the gaming system's capabilities and to place limits on it for safety. They labeled the three levels Wimp, Warrior, and Don't Use This Level, with Don't Use This Level intended only for internal use during testing and not for use by the public.

But it got out, anyway.

That's marketing...

The story, as Zai tells it, went like this. Ke Qunxiang, one of Zai's first engineers, has by now become one of the world's experts on the artificial inducement of sensations and patterned muscle motions in the body, occasionally writing papers and giving talks at technology conferences as he extends the mathematical theory underlying the brain-computer interface which makes it work. He has been at Zai since the very beginning, joining Zhuang Rongtao at Zai shortly after finishing his PhD.

It has been a few years now since Ke Qunxiang started exploring the maximum signal levels which could usefully be induced by the game console in a human player. He and Sun Yang, Zai's game architect, had worked together to design a realistic gut punch effect. It was just one of many effects that they were developing for future virtual reality games.

And it worked. Really well. And so it was that Ke Qunxiang became the first person ever to be punched in the gut by a virtual reality AI, by an artificial intelligence. It wasn't a robot. It wasn't a physical mechanism at all. Technically, there was no force. But he felt it. Hard.

What hit him was VR software driving the game console, transmitting radio signals to trigger a motor sequence in his brain to tighten his abdominal muscles into a short-lived cramp. But it was more than that. It was an exquisitely crafted gut punch, accompanied by the tactile sensation of a virtual fist touching the skin of his abdomen just milliseconds before the motor sequence and lasting for its duration. The simulated force profile was completely realistic.

It was the ultimate in using an opponent's strength against him.

(-:GUT PUNCH:-)

It was for this reason that Ke Qunxiang designated the third tier of effects intensity "Don't Use This Level". And he meant it. It was for internal testing use only. The production release would only have the two levels, Warrior and Wimp.

But the head of marketing got wind of it during a stroll down to engineering and asked for a demo. And after he got his gut punch, only the fourth person ever to experience it at that point, he said, trying to catch his breath between words: "That's - awe - some - keep - it - in."

When he finally caught his breath, he had asked whether this would work over the Internet, too, in multiplayer games. And the engineers explained that it would be exactly the same. "That is awesome. You're really in the game." It had been worth the stroll down to the lower floor. The product reports coming out of engineering hadn't said anything about that.

When Ke Qunxiang asked what to label the maximum effect tier in the game, the head of marketing gave it just a moment's thought, then said: "Don't Use This Level. That's perfect."

Zai became known for its intense effects. There was nothing else like it on the market. Even so, not all players are looking for *intense*. And some players don't accept *involuntary motions*. But even with a highly dialed down experience, cutting out muscle activity, tactile sensations, and noxious odors, the dense overlay of mild or pleasant odors and other mild effects creates a rich experience. Dog fur. Spruce trees. Campfire smoke. The muddy waters of a raging river. The ozone of a thunderstorm. Leather boots. And not just the leather smell. The player feels the leather around their calves and shins. Scents and odors are carefully integrated into the experience. Move in closer if you can't quite make out what it is. Follow a scent through the landscape or through the house. Ugh. Open the windows. Ah, this meadow is so beautiful. Let's lie down here to rest. The air is so fresh. Both you and your Internet partner enjoy the virtual place together.

Avatars come with their own complex array of smells, smells that the human players experience through the virtual reality interface. Their hair and skin carry not only the odor of their species, but also the odor of the soap and shampoo they use. If the species uses soap and shampoo. Their clothes may be clean, or maybe it has been a few days. They may wear a perfume or cologne. Sun tan lotion. Skin cream. Body odors which vary with diet, personal habits and hygiene, locale, era. Gym workout. Kimchi. Stale cigarettes. Betel nuts. Chewing tobacco. Mints. Freshly showered. Chlorinated swimming pool or briny ocean. The surreal scent of bromine that wafts from the skin of an alien species. "It's my antibacterial soap," she explains unapologetically. "Don't you like it?"

And it's not just the avatars. It's the whole environment. The restaurants and stores. Leather seats or cracked vinyl. Industrial complexes. Nature itself. Modern Japan or Revolutionary France. A 19th century Inuit village. 1950s Brooklyn. San Francisco Chinatown in the 70s. The Amazon rainforest. The world of Charles Dickens' *A Christmas Carol*. The iodine of the sea water in Jules Verne's *20,000 Leagues Under the Sea*.

The Zai engineers have worked their way up from the occasional "special effect" smell, a little odor here, a scent there, to the point where there is really no time during game play in which there aren't multiple overlapping scents filling in the experience. Much of the time, the background scents are subtle, but subtle is often what makes them really work. Close your eyes, and you still know where you are, even at places you didn't realize had distinct smells. A clothing store, an office building, the library.

To really understand the importance of the olfactory layer to the games, one can play for a while and then, for a comparison, turn off olfactory. The game goes flat. It takes the fizz right out of it. Turn it back on again, and *You're There.*

How important is olfactory to the richness and emotional impact of the virtual reality experience? Here is just one example. There had been a long-running argument about just how complete the odor database for building virtual reality environments should be. On one side of the argument were those who advocated for mostly neutral to positive odors. The goal wasn't to disgust the players with bad odors, after all. Unpleasant would be OK. Useful, even, if only to provide contrast to the more pleasant odors. Cabbagy smells. Stale coffee. Perhaps even diesel fumes. But not odors which are just plain vile.

To those on the other side of the argument, there was no such thing as taboo. "It's what makes us human," they would say. "You never know where such an odor might be just what is needed. And who are we to get in the way of the artists building the realities that our users will experience?"

For a long time, the issue was debated, but it was certainly not heated. Until one day, a game developer in Taiwan requested stinky tofu, and the product manager approved. He had hesitated, but the developer pushed for it, pointing out that it is an essential and famous part of Taiwan's culture. How could they build a believable night market virtual reality without it? They've got most of the street food covered, the aromas of grilled sausages and pig's blood cakes, fine droplets of frying oil lofted into the air near the soy milk fried chicken stands. Grilled oysters and squid and steamed rice buns. Peanut dusted frozen mochi and syrups and toppings, ginger and almond and red beans. And then there's the asphalt pavement and the vinyl awnings and even the smells that come after the rains when people are still out for their midnight snacks. And of course, the scents and fragrances of the crowds themselves, an important element to the olfactory experience that would be easy to leave out but which provides that realism that puts you on the streets. But without stinky tofu, it's just not a night market.

The reaction in the company was swift. "If stinky tofu can get into the database, any smell can!"

"We already put smelly cheeses in the database," came the response. "It's just another food."

"So they say. I've never tried it. Can't get close enough to find out. But if we're going to add that one, let's add all the others."

A well-known Chinese snack, made by fermenting tofu, stinky tofu is eaten not only in Taiwan, but also in Hong Kong, Shanghai, Beijing, Nanjing, Hunan...actually, pretty much everywhere Chinese culture is found. It is one of those foods you smell from two blocks away. You have to convince yourself to eat it. But just believe in it. It will taste good. Believe. So say those who do eat it.

The odor of stinky tofu actually ranges from mild to intense, varying with the ingredients and method of production and with the preparation of the snack, whether served cold, deep-fried, steamed, or roasted over charcoal. In fact, the product manager for the virtual reality odor database had not approved just a single "stinky tofu" odor, but rather, a whole package of odors covering the range, labeled with appropriate designations which he had careful researched, ensuring that the labels would properly reflect common usage and that no one's trademark would be violated without proper licensing by the corresponding brand.

One tricky aspect of product management of the odor database is ensuring that the odors are accurate. This almost always involves obtaining samples out in the real world to determine the range of odors for a given label, the exception being for special cases of hypothetical odors, such as with historical reconstruction. But obtaining accurate samples can be difficult without traveling to the source. And then there is the extensive process the team must go through to experience the odors personally as they capture the odors as coordinates in odor space, a complex process that involves determining hundreds of separate coordinate numbers. Vile odors can push the limits of human tolerance.

But there is no room for taking shortcuts. Virtual reality designers for gaming and media and film productions have come to rely on Zai for the accuracy of its database. With patents starting to run out in just a few more years, Zai has built up this expertise to keep their competitive edge.

The issue had been highly polarizing, with the minority seeing it as documentation of the world, the foundation for an amazing encyclopedia of an important class of non-textual and non-visual information. One employee had even proposed building an encyclopedia of odors as an app for the Naoji, with a feature for reading the user's mind to detect what the user is smelling, and then using the brain code for the odor as a search term to look up possible matches.

The encyclopedia would have numerous categories and interest topics. What did the ancient Egyptian pharaoh's wives wear for perfume? How can you recognize when a bromine disinfectant has been used in a swimming pool instead of chlorine? You've read about clothes stored with mothballs, but you've never seen them before. What do they smell like? Do the older mothballs with naphthalene smell different from newer ones which use camphor? And is that what blue cheese is really supposed to smell like?

"Humanity must be described with the full palette of odors. We cannot paint the world with perfumes. We are everything from kitchen to restroom, from mountains to sewers. We haven't fabricated a full reality if we leave out half of what makes us human," he said when he proposed building the encyclopedia app.

"That may well be, but we can leave that part of humanity in the restroom where it belongs. We must protect our precious and pure virtual reality," came his opposition's response.

The *Naturalists*, as they thought of themselves, couldn't believe their opponents' phrasing. Precious and pure virtual reality? What kind of lofty nonsense was that? They thought the *Purists* had gone too far. "Are you so prim and proper that you run to a restroom every time you need to fart?" To their chagrin, their opponents had genuinely responded: "Don't you?"

With this, a robot divinity blinked, twice.

Finally, Ethan intervened. He said the argument itself lacked decorum. "No more," he announced in a formal memo to the company. There was more to it than that, but his highly tasteful memo could be summarized with those two words.

And so it was that the grand battle was replaced with small scuffles over individual odors as they came up for recommendation for one virtual reality application or another. The proposed odors were reviewed for suitability and *necessity* to properly recreate the experience, whatever it may be.

That said, some odors and sensations can be bothersome, or even completely unacceptable, to some players. It could be anything. The smell of onions, say. Similarly, virtual pains may be acceptable to some as an exciting part of the challenge of some games. *It makes it real*, they would say. But other players find virtual pains intolerable, or just pointless. For those players, it ruins the fun. To accommodate these differences, players can set their preferences and keep these in a profile.

And then there's radio. Zai has been busy with more than just virtual reality. Music, news, and talk shows. Any time, anywhere, without a device. *The brain is the receiver*. A radio app that plays directly to one's inner voice has been available through the Naoji for years. More recently, the same feature has become available directly from the Zai network. Radio MindPair, as the service is called, plays like a radio station to your head, in complete privacy, with several channels offered. Switching channels, turning it on or off, and adjusting the volume is accomplished entirely by sending mental commands to the network. *[Louder.] [Mute.] [Channel Beijing News.]*

Some comment is in order to describe how one can carry out one's daily activities, including thinking to one's self, with what might seem to be constant interference from a mind-interfacing radio station pumping music and commentary into one's head. The first thing to note is that one gets used to it, like when you listen to music while studying or like when you talk to someone at a party. There is cross-talk in the inner voice, though. It's not quite the same, as the brain's natural attention mechanism is bypassed in direct-to-mind radio. So, as with any activity requiring a high degree of inner voice focus, such as thinking through a difficult problem, the listener is advised to turn off the radio. And that's easy enough. *[Radio off.]* Then again, just turning down the volume may be enough, so that the external signals coming in from the network are weaker than the listener's own inner voice signals.

With practice, and this can take a few months for new users, the listener actually learns a new skill, literally growing new neurons in the brain to perceive the incoming radio signals. Listening to radio signals becomes a new perceptual sense, with its own source. The listener can tell that the sound in their head is from somewhere else and not from their own imagination, or from their ears. Radio MindPair, in particular, always sounds like it is coming from the same "place" inside the head, and it was designed that way specifically so that the listener becomes accustomed to it. Zai could have placed the perception of sounds anywhere, nearby, far away, to the left or the right, in any number of places inside or outside the head. But once they had set it up, they left it at that, giving Radio MindPair its own sound, its own place in the mind. It's like listening to the radio when driving. You hear 3D sound, and you know where it's coming from. There's no question about it. It's the car's sound system. There's no confusing it with the sound of the world around you. And it's like that with Radio Mindpair, too. Unlike the car's sound system, though, the speakers don't surround you. They're just *you*.

The sounds of Radio MindPair, Zai's version of radio broadcast stations, are just like all the other sounds produced by the Naoji in the head. They're not loud, and there's no bass feel at all, no thumping on the body. The technology is not a great substitute for an old-fashioned boombox or home theater system as Radio MindPair uses only *sound* brain codes. But the work continues. Zai's mind-audio engineers have been working on boosting *ubiety*, the soundscape's *there*-ness, the degree to which it is a place and not merely an abstraction, by developing a more comprehensive model of the way sounds are perceived in the brain and felt in the body. It's not words in your head or the jingle that won't go away. If they succeed, you're *in* the talk show. They're up there, in front, and the audience is all around. You hear them clapping and laughing.

The band is on stage, the bass guitar is on the left, and you *feel* the floor shake. Literally, you feel it in your feet. That nature recording is a place now. Rain pitter-patters all around. Thunder rumbles in your gut. You feel it. Turn or tilt your head, and the sound stays put, coming at you from the six directions of the world. It's not like headphones. Your head moves *in* the soundscape.

One technique creates the illusion of vibrations through the skin and muscles by sending body-vibration brain codes to the brain, activating the same parts of the brain that are activated with touch sensations and deep percussive sounds. With their new technology, which they are targeting for release in the Naoji 8, and later, as an option on Radio MindPair over Zai's MindPair Network, you'll get the same experience. It will be the most significant advance in soundscape reproduction ever. It will redefine the very meaning of soundscape. *Zai. You're there.*

To make it possible to operate the MindPair Network as a subscriber-based service, Zai developed a sign-on system. It was not initially obvious how a sign-on system would work, as the goal had been to eliminate the need for a subscriber to have a device to use the MindPair Network. And yet, if they were to rely only on the thoughts of the subscriber, say to accept the subscriber's password, it wouldn't be encrypted and it could be intercepted with eavesdropping equipment.

But it was worse than that. How could the MindPair Network know a command was sent from the subscriber's mind and not from a device masquerading as the subscriber, stealing their identity?

The first thing they realized was that once they *identify* a subscriber, they'd also know *where* the subscriber is, based on their distance from multiple towers. And as the subscriber moves around, the network could track their location continuously.

The network detects signals not only from the brain, but also from the subscriber's nervous system, including the spinal cord and the nerves running along the arms and legs and throughout the body's core. Nerves are just pathways for electrical signals to flow. And wherever electrical signals flow, radio waves emanate. By tracking the distinct pattern of radio wave emissions from each person's body, the MindPair Network can distinguish people from one another. The network's tiny microlocation devices, placed in and around buildings, vehicles, and transportation systems, help pin down subscriber locations with great precision by relaying the signals they receive to the access points along with their own precise locations. While tracking subscribers in private homes and in the Great Outdoors would be limited in accuracy to about three feet, in commercial and retail locations, with microlocation devices installed throughout, the network could track the subscriber's location to within ten inches.

The next trick Zai had to figure out was how to make the sign-on itself secure. The details of secure communications can be mind-numbing and, perhaps ironically, all the more so because they didn't want it to be mind-numbing. That is, not for the subscribers, anyway. To make a system simple, you have to make it complicated under the covers.

Going for two hours straight in a meeting with Ethan, bringing in tea and snacks to sustain them, the engineers had presented every variation of the sign-on mechanism, the different situations subscribers might run into, and the attacks that hackers might use to compromise the system. To start with, though, they introduced *the card.*

"A card?" Ethan had thought the idea was to go completely device-free.

"Yes. Well, it'll be *almost* completely device-free. It's just for sign-on. Bear with me." The engineer pulled out a mock-up. "It's just like a chip-based credit card, but we added two thin-film digital displays, one on each side of the card, each one showing a four-digit number. There's a thin battery that powers the chip. The battery is expected to last five years, and when it runs out, we would replace the card. It's waterproof. And since we designed it to use the same technology as credit card chip technology, it's not expensive. The manufacturing only has to be tweaked a little to build our card." The engineer handed the card to Ethan to examine. "We call it the ZaiCard. Each ZaiCard is personalized to an individual subscriber. To sign on, the subscriber uses the card along with their password. The password provides protection in case someone steals the ZaiCard."

The numbers displayed on each of the two sides of the ZaiCard change seemingly at random once a minute. It is only seemingly random because the network towers know what the numbers are supposed to be for each subscriber, and this is the key to the security.

In a mind-interfacing world, however, looking is tantamount to telling. With mind-reading equipment advances, an eavesdropper could watch what you see. This is why the numbers are displayed on two different sides of the ZaiCard. By keeping the second number on the back side of the ZaiCard, even the subscriber doesn't know what that number is until the network tower sends them a number that matches the front side of the card, confirming that it is really the network that the subscriber hears in their head and not a fake tower or an identity thief.

The second number, in turn, is how the network tower knows that the *subscriber* isn't an identity thief. The subscriber reads the second number to themselves in their head. Only someone with the ZaiCard for the account would know this second number, and the number changes every minute.

Each number shown can only be used once. Once the subscriber thinks the first number to the network, an identity thief can't use that number anywhere else to sign-on. It becomes locked to the subscriber's current location, expiring within a minute. And once the first number is locked to the subscriber's location, the network expects the second number to come from a thought which is in the same location.

With these points made, the sign-on procedure that the engineers wrote on the whiteboard for Ethan that day, which is the very same procedure still in use today, has seven steps. It uses the same MindPair protocol for communication with the mind that the Naoji smartphone does.

Diagrams on the whiteboard sketched out additional security checks and descriptions of failure scenarios. Like, for example, what happens if the tower loses communication with the subscriber in the middle of the sign-on procedure, perhaps due to radio interference or intentional jamming? What should the network do if the subscriber appears to be signed on already somewhere else? And when the network checks the location of the user at each step, what if the user is in motion, in an automobile or on a subway? It looked complicated and Ethan was concerned. Even when nothing goes wrong, the procedure takes seven steps. "How are subscribers going to remember all that?" he asked.

The engineer who had produced the mock-up of the ZaiCard picked it up from the table where Ethan had set it down. "I think it's actually pretty simple. It would go like this." He spoke out loud in places where the subscriber would normally just think silently, as he pretended to go through the process.

"Sign-on Ming43. I hear 4711." He looked down at the card. "It matches."

Then he turned the card over and pretended to read a number. "6515 Pine tree. And now I hear the MindPair Network sign-on sound. I'm on."

"Pine tree?"

"My password," the engineer said.

"OK. That's simple." Ethan was satisfied.

Once online, the subscriber can then send and receive messages, though they can think the [*Do not disturb*] command to the network at any time to turn off incoming messages. It's no different than using the Naoji in this regard. And similarly, so the subscriber doesn't forget, resulting in missed messages, the user can set a timeout in the command. *[Do not disturb one hour.]* No fiddling with settings, no navigation of drop-down menus. It couldn't be simpler.

The subscriber stays online so long as the network can continuously track the subscriber's location, that is, so long as they are near a tower. Within the city, this is intended to be all of the time. You may only need to sign on once a day. You can just set the ZaiCard aside or carry it in your wallet or purse in case you need it again.

The tracking is very accurate so that even someone who's standing nearby trying to impersonate you can't fool the network. But the more important case is someone trying to steal your identity from far away, maybe in some other part of the city, and that makes it obvious. The system disallows you from being "online" in more than one place at a time. *There's only one you*, as the saying goes.

After reviewing the procedure, something nagged at Ethan's intuition. Are they too boxed into tradition? "Sure, you don't need to bring the ZaiCard with you," he said. "But you probably would, right?"

They all agreed.

Ethan explained: "Most people don't use a wallet any more. The phone has everything on it. Payment apps and transport passes and identity apps. But we're going token-free. They won't need a phone. So where are they going to keep their ZaiCard?"

The engineers weren't sure what to say. Token-free?

Ethan thought about it silently for a moment, then answered his own question: "We could make it into something that could hang from a necklace, a fashion piece, colorful plastic pendants in different shapes or printed with different designs, with the two numbers on two sides. Panda bears. Butterflies. A minimalist rectangular design with swirling colors. Attach a little hoop to one corner to hang it. A high-end version sealed in polished glass with gold detailing beneath the surface. With the Zai logo somewhere on it. You could wear it everywhere you go. Why not make it fun?"

The engineers hadn't thought of that. *That's marketing,* they all thought.

"We'll hand them out in Zai stores for free," Ethan said, "and they can sign up later." He thought about it some more, then added: "They'll have to pay for the glass ones. It'll be the premium symbol for a service that is otherwise invisible."

One of the engineers pointed out, though, that it might be a security risk if the subscriber walks around displaying the numbers. They had gotten into an argument about this. The counterargument was that only one side would show when the pendant is hanging, so it wouldn't really matter. Anyway, someone would just keep it under their clothes. Ethan had replied this wouldn't always be true, and anyway, as a pendant, some people might want it to show.

A technical debate then ensued, ultimately resulting in at least one workable solution. The subscriber will have to triple-tap with their finger on one part of the card, or pendant, to activate the display. At all other times, the display would be blank. Problem solved.

The product management team had eventually decided they would change the designs every year, to keep it fresh, with a range of free standard, and extra cost premium, pendants. Later, they would even offer a limited edition 24K gold plated metal ZaiCard, with a chain to hang it around the neck...which would promptly sell out.

Having finished with Ethan's presentation of the MindPair Network small payments system, the board attends to their primary business, first reviewing and approving the quarterly and annual financial results, then moving on to some planning work associated with an initial public offering, or IPO, of their stock, to finance the expansion of the MindPair Network and associated services in China and in the US.

The main glitch has been an evolving issue with their US subsidiary, which has been defending a position on search warrants in the US. Until it is resolved, the underwriters, that is, the investment banks who will sell Zai's stock to the public, would likely demand too low a stock price, worried that the shares otherwise won't sell out, and Zai's current shareholders won't get as good a deal when they sell a piece of Zai to the public. And if they don't prevail in their position on the search warrants, they might be forced to reconsider expansion of the MindPair Network in the US. And with that change, they would need to dramatically reduce the amount of capital they would raise. So things still remain very much up in the air.

Reviewing the current status of the search warrant issue, the board decides it is still too early. They decide to hold off on IPO planning.

Director Huang has one last question. "How are olfactory ads doing? You had mentioned some development in that direction in our last meeting, but you didn't break out a separate reporting segment for them for the annual report."

"We're in beta testing," Ethan says, "and advertisers are still developing ad plans around the concept. I think we can look forward to breaking that out in our next annual report."

Director Huang's Naoji blips, and she listens to a calendar reminder. [Dinner with hubby at 7 pm.] The announcement sounds like a young girl speaking in her head. She smiles to herself. She has no further questions for Ethan.

Ethan glances at each of the board members. "Shall we wrap it up? Let us all look forward to a happy and prosperous New Year, ladies and gentlemen."

The board members all get up, but they take their time, chatting, their conversation a mix of business and personal, with questions about the families and plans for the upcoming Chinese New Year. Their conversations continue even as they put on their heavy coats and start guiding each other to the conference room exit.

From the large window running the length of one side of the conference room, a dim hazy blue-gray light filters in, fading, a contrast with the steady warm light inside the room. Snow flurries drift by the window. Below, one can see a grid of high rise buildings, textured with the light of ten thousand windows, a giant three-dimensional integrated circuit powering the city. Major traffic arteries connect the grid, filled with automobiles in every direction, the arteries glowing red. Delivery drones in many shapes and sizes flow with the arteries, blood cells carrying sustenance to the city. Home to thirty million people.

Absolutely Nothing that matters

MQZTOQ headquarters, Virginia

The operator watches a live video monitor showing a man waiting at a gate in an airport, sitting, looking down at the ground, apparently lost in his thoughts. The man's left hand rests on the handle of his black nylon carry-on. He is wearing a casual business suit. Today's date is displayed on the video feed: 1/30/2038.

The operator's memory extractions from the man are almost complete. He returns to one particular memory and re-extracts it, comparing it to the original, which has intermittent fuzz-outs and blank frames. This time, there are fewer disruptions, and they occur in different places, allowing him to create a clean merge. The title *Time-Indexed Multi-Fragment Sequence* appears over the window on his screen, indicating that it is a spliced sequence of memory fragments for which the time order has already been determined.

In the video resulting from the memory extraction, the operator sees what the man once saw: a computer screen, and occasionally, the man's hands on a keyboard. The logo of a well-known Internet activist organization appears on the computer screen. The man is typing.

The operator's system isolates images of what the man had typed from the man's visual memory fragments and then reads text from those images. Sounds in the man's thoughts are also isolated from the memory fragments, and voice recognition software picks out the words from those sounds, showing the words as text in another window. The typed text and the inner voice text are stored in a database for later searches.

In one memory fragment, the man appears to hesitate just before pressing the *Enter* key. Here, the memory fragment ends, interrupted by some unknown distraction, something that had attracted the man's attention and derailed his decision process. The operator tries another keyword to stimulate a related fragment from the man's memory, but the extract fails. He sees the reason in the airport video monitor. The man at the airport is focused elsewhere now, as he has gotten up to greet someone who had called his name. After a quick handshake, the two men at the airport start walking together.

As the men walk through the airport, crosshairs in the video monitor view indicate the man being tracked. The view automatically switches to different cameras to keep the man in view. Two mind-interfacing transceivers mounted near each of the video cameras, which MQZTOQ refers to as *access points*, continue to track the man's thoughts.

The operator mutters to himself. He intuits that the man will be busy thinking about other things now, tying up his mental resources until he leaves the airport. He sighs, then makes a few keystrokes. A message pops up on the screen: *Archived*. The message automatically clears after a few seconds and is then replaced with a list of clients. That is, targets of MQZTOQ's memory extracts.

Next to each client on the list are data points giving the client's current location, airline and flight number, the airport name, the actual or estimated time of the client's arrival, gate number, a short list of video cameras in the client's current location, if any, and the client's estimated departure time. In the final column is a priority indicator. The system only covers port-of-entry airports and border crossing zones. The previous client had been passing through JFK.

The operator drinks down the last of his coffee, then visually scans the list. He clicks on one of the clients and all of the live video feeds near the man show up on his system screen. The video feeds are labeled *SFO Terminal I Arrival Gates G7/G8* and *G9/G10*. A thin blinking crosshairs appears on the man's head, indicating that the system is currently in brainwave signature identification mode. The operator opens the client's current dossier for photo ID and other biographical information. Then he checks for previous extracts and associated notes to plan this extract. He estimates how long the man will remain within range.

This man is wearing a black designer leather jacket and black jeans and is holding the handle of an aluminum carry-on. He is standing, casually surveying his surroundings.

The operator compares the video feed of the man with the dossier's photos to confirm a match, then clicks on a button on the screen to begin memory scanning. The crosshairs on the man's head are now steady, indicating that the system is now in extract mode.

New windows pop up on the screen showing the results of the memory scans. On the airport video feeds, the operator sees the man walk over to a nearby chair and sit down. The man bows his head down, resting it in one hand, his arm propped up on the arm of the chair, seemingly lost in thought.

The operator replays a video extract from one of the memory fragments. In the extract, the operator sees what the man had once seen. The man is in a small room. In one corner of the man's visualization of the scene, there is a message on a wall. It says "LISTENING". The man reaches for a notebook on a table in the room. He flips the pages back and forth. There are handwritten notes in the notebook, and a few diagrams.

The operator pauses the video to read the text in the notebook, checking that the text window below the video view is picking up the text from the memory fragment. But the text isn't clear in the video and only a few sporadic individual words and phrases show up in the text window.

The system doesn't capture any sounds from the man's thoughts. He wasn't reading the content. The operator figures the man was just forming a general impression of the notebook.

The system pulls in another batch of memory fragments, and again, the operator selects one to examine in more detail. This one shows the interior of another room, an office. The man is reading the contents of a stapled stack of paper. The document is written in English. The operator can plainly see the contents as the man flips through the pages and carefully scans each one with his eyes.

This time, as the man reads the document in the memory fragment, two text windows capture its content. One extracts words from the images the man sees. The other captures the words from the sounds in the man's thoughts as he reads the document to himself. The inner voice transcript is highly fragmented as the man jumps back and forth in the document. The man pauses from time to time. The operator recognizes that the man is absorbing and evaluating the material intuitively, without explicit thought. Reading over the text windows, the operator surmises that the document is a business report, with a list of risks and a legal analysis.

The operator watches the next memory fragment with interest as the man carries the document to a paper shredder and runs it through. Judging from its appearance and its quiet butter-smooth hum, it's a high-end shredder. Probably a Level P-6, he figures.

"Here we go," he exclaims.

In a separate window, the operator's system begins searching the man's memory for related memory fragments. As it finds the fragments of the man's previous readings and views of the document, the system reconstructs the shredded document from the visuals. It is a sophisticated process, taking into account the sequence of pages as the man had flipped back and forth. More text fragments appear in the window, filling in, shifting, occasionally replaced, the puzzle pieces falling into place more rapidly than the eye can keep up with. The system then passes through the puzzle again, filling in missing pieces by extracting word sounds from the man's memory fragments, aligning the timing of the sounds with the places in the document that the man had been reading.

The system uses memory fragment time indexing to estimate the dates the man viewed each page, then stores the entire set of data in the database. Twenty-nine pages. Nine page surfaces are clean enough to be useful, with 12% of the words marked with faint red highlights indicating uncertainty in the reconstruction. The remaining twenty pages are either missing from the man's memory, or are too fuzzy or fragmented to reconstruct, probably because the man skimmed through those pages and didn't pay much attention to them.

The operator is surprised at a strong mental association between two of the memory fragments. The initial images for each of them appear very different, one showing the inside of an office and the other showing the inside of a shower. The shower fragment was not used in the document reconstruction, so he clicks on it to check the association. He can see that the shower walls are made of solid slabs of granite, with high-end German-branded fixtures. Soapy water washes down the man's legs and into the drain. The man turns to face the opposite direction in the shower.

The man's thoughts, the words in his head in the memory fragment, are shown along the bottom of the screen. The words echo the contents of the document he had shredded. The man thinks of another person's name, one that hadn't shown up in the man's thoughts when he had reviewed the document earlier, as if this were a new thought that had just occurred to him, making a connection that he hadn't made previously.

The system updates the man's dossier in the database with the identity of this other person, along with the man's belief of the association with the shredded document.

"That's what that was," the operator says to himself. He's satisfied now.

The operator has been extracting memories at a high rate, too fast for the client to see in his mind in detail, but the client knows what each memory is. The client *knows* each memory as it flashes by during the extract. But he doesn't know why these memories are surfacing. They just come to him as he sits there in the airport, head bowed, his arm still propped up on the arm of the chair.

MQZTOQ's memory extraction process beams a radio signal pattern to the client's brain for each keyword selected by the operator, the keywords providing stimuli for memories to replay. The process leaves behind a quickly-changing trace in the client's short-term memory, each memory remaining just long enough for the client to recognize it, but replaced too quickly by the next memory for the client to dwell on it.

While being probed by MQZTOQ's mind-interfacing device, the client's memories flash through his mind like subliminal messages, each memory two to four seconds of life experience compressed into an instant. The extract includes the client's original feelings, ambient feelings like the time he aced a hard math test in ninth grade, the feeling he had once walking around in a major shopping mall, the spiritual experience he had walking through a Buddhist temple in Kyoto, and the mixed feelings of disgust and pragmatism he experienced on an urgent stop-over at a filthy gas station restroom on a long road trip. The system captures everything and anything, from the very special to the mundane. Even the mundane. That's a special feeling of its own.

The operator had asked his instructor about this effect during training, this experience of having one's memories stimulated by the system and forced into consciousness so that they create brainwaves that can be intercepted and recorded by the system. And after his instructor explained it, the operator had commented that it sounded like déjà vu. But the instructor had corrected him. "No, that's a distinct feeling of its own," he said. "The memories re-experienced by the clients are the real thing, with their original feelings. If there was no déjà vu the first time around, there won't be during the memory extract, either."

The fragmented feelings of life are there, in the brain, waiting to be triggered and remembered. But the flashbacks retrieved by MQZTOQ are not in chronological order. The memories have no timestamps and no obvious ordering. Instead, MQZTOQ's system pieces the fragments together into a time sequence by analysis, relating the content to various clues about life phases. Clocks and calendars provide obvious date references. But most of the clues are subtle: the aging of people and objects in the memories, connections with key life events, associations with other data about the client such as records of their phone calls. The time-indexing process is facilitated in part by automated recognition of people and objects recorded in memory fragments.

Since typically more than one memory is associated with each keyword, the system repeatedly beams patterns for the same keywords, varying a threshold each time to force out memories which are less and less strongly associated with the particular keyword. Each memory is listed with an identification to the right side of the screen.

The operator looks back at the live airport video feed. The client is still sitting, except that now he has slouched back in his chair, holding the back of his neck with one of his hands, eyes closed.

He checks the list of extract keywords. Almost half done. He touches a button and the system sends another burst of keyword stimuli to the man's brain from the access point in the airport. The list of memory fragments on the screen grows longer. He clicks on one of the fragments to review it.

The fragment playback window on the operator's screen now shows the man entering an air drone taxi, as seen through the man's own eyes. The sun has just set to the left. Skyscrapers extend for miles, darkened hills providing a distant backdrop. After the man has seated himself and buckled his seatbelt, the self-piloted taxi lifts off from its location on a deck half way up the side of a skyscraper and turns to the right, flying level four hundred feet up along a major road.

The man thinks a message to his Naoji. The translation text window reads: [*Message to Haiping: On the way home, should be about ten minutes.*] The words are difficult to hear over the drone's twelve large, and loud, electric rotors. A moment later, the man hears an acknowledgement in his inner voice that the message was heard by the recipient.

The man looks left and right at the urban landscape passing by. The operator hears the man's thoughts to himself. [The city just keeps growing.] The operator's screen shows a distorted reflection of the man's face on the inside of the taxi's canopy, lit only by the light from an information display in the center console. The console shows the taxi's route and current location on a map of the city.

The man's thoughts play out loud as his taxi journey continues. In the text window below the video, his thoughts are written out in text in the original language, and then, below that, translated into English. The system stores these transcripts in the database to make them keyword searchable in both languages. These thoughts seem to the operator to be the man reflecting on a meeting he had just attended before his taxi ride.

The operator glances again at the man on the live airport video feed. The man barely moves, giving away nothing about the flashbacks he is experiencing.

The operator picks out another memory fragment from the list to replay. The screen shows the man speaking with uniformed personnel in a sparsely furnished room decorated with a national flag and other emblems. Again, the words that the man thinks, speaks and hears appear below the video in the original language and also with a translation into English.

He clicks a button and a new window pops up. In this window, all of the faces and voices detected in the current memory fragment are isolated and each individual's voice stream appears as a separate soundtrack. The system then carries out face recognition and voiceprint analysis, searching a large database. The system displays the name and a short biography for two of the people in the room. The other three people are not positively identified, but for one of them, a short list of potential matches is shown. It appears to the operator to be some sort of meeting with government officials.

He carefully checks each extract as he goes. Quality degradation in memory extracts sometimes occurs due to radio interference at the airports. The most common problem, though, occurs with the client's brain itself. Many people experience occasional microseizures, electrical disruptions of brain activity in tiny areas of the brain, and they are almost always completely unaware of them. Unlike the seizures of, say, epilepsy, microseizures don't involve widespread disruption of the brain, so the effects on the extract can be minor and non-obvious, sometimes resulting in fuzzy areas or gaps in the extract. That said, it's a simple process to re-extract after a microseizure. It's like retaking a big group photo when someone blinks, then photo-editing out just the blink in the earlier photo using the retake.

A younger colleague walks up from behind. "Journalist?"

"Corporate exec. Seems to be some new thing they're doin'. For now, it just goes into his dossier."

The operator suspects his employer is not just saving the data for this man for future searches. They're probably going to send his entire dossier out. But it doesn't matter to him. He just collects the data. What happens with it later is handled by a different department. And they don't talk. He enjoys his work, though. It's varied. He sees the most peculiar things pop up and that keeps it interesting.

The operator's colleague watches for a minute as the capture screen continues to flash video images. The operator kicks off voiceprint recognition on another of the client's memory fragments, matching the characteristics of each voice against MQZTOQ's vast database of voiceprints.

In the airport video feed, the operator and his colleague watch as a woman and two children walk up and join the man. The man appears to snap back to reality. He gets up and the four of them leave the area together.

The availability of the voiceprint database and the practice of matching voiceprints from memory fragments has led to the development of a new goal of mind-based surveillance and intelligence gathering: Absolutely Nothing. As invisible as MQZTOQ's extract processes are, they do still leave a trace. And this has been deemed to be a serious issue.

The problem is that once you transmit your voice to a client's inner voice, there is a record of it there, a side effect of the process in the client's memory, possibly lasting for the rest of the client's life. Someone intruding on a client's mind would think twice before leaving any recognizable pattern in the client's memory. Their unfiltered voice, speaking in the mind of the client, would give away their identity in a voiceprint search. Any activity perceivable at all by the client may become a memory that could give away the intelligence gathering process carried out on that client, like a calling card left behind, or a national flag planted, announcing to the world of intelligence gatherers: "We were here."

Why not just read brainwaves passively? That is, why transmit anything at all to a client to read their minds? The problem is that the goal is to read memories in the brain. And memories don't create brainwaves that can be intercepted unless they are recalled, retrieved by the brain so that the brain's neural circuits become active with the memory. Each memory remains hidden away, locked in a vault until the right key comes along to open it.

In the past, the stimulus would be a comment, or an odor, anything that could provoke the client into recalling the memory. It was clumsy. These days, it is a forced pattern of thought, a sequence of brain codes sent to the brain that use the brain's own "operating system" to recall memories and produce brainwaves that can be intercepted by a remote radio receiver.

The technology to stimulate specific memories had opened up MQZTOQ's access to hidden memories. But the benefit goes beyond this. Recalling and extracting a lifetime of memories would take months, even at the accelerated replay rate stimulated by the technology. But by using keywords to force the recall of particular memories, MQZTOQ is able to limit their extracts to just the memories of interest.

The difficulty with stimulating memory recall, though, is that the very process of remembering leaves behind a trace, a new memory. The memory of remembering. A foreign government agency might determine which of the client's memories had been sought after by MQZTOQ by examining these new memories. The extract process, which is protected by trade secrets rather than patents, which is to say, the company has never published any information about the process, is stealthy nonetheless. The process cannot be detected by commercially available mind-interfacing devices as the technology interfaces with the mind only at an abstract level. It brings out memories, but it does so without transmitting the brain codes that induce virtual sense perceptions that mind-interfacing smartphones and other devices use to communicate with the brain. MQZTOQ's transmissions look like just so much background noise to devices that don't understand the process.

With the voiceprint matching process completed, the operator quickly looks over the results. For each match, the screen shows the list of approximated dates that the client spoke with the person matched, along with the likely method of speech, through a Naoji, through their natural sense of hearing, or even just imagined speech. Clickable links lead to the associated memory fragment extracts.

At the bottom of the list is the set of memory fragments containing voices for which no voiceprint match was found. For this client, there are only a handful of such fragments. The operator is satisfied with the results.

The operator turns to see his colleague. “Goin’ to lunch?”

“Yeah.”

“I’m just finishin’ up.”

The operator’s colleague comments as he watches the live video feed of the client walking through the airport with the woman and the two children. “He’s wiped. Must be tough reliving all those memories in just a few minutes.”

“It’s mostly the jet lag, he just got in, but, yeah.” The operator clicks a button and the *Archived* message pops up on his screen. He clicks again and the screen shows a sign-on prompt. He swivels around in his chair to face his colleague. “They say pullin’ data from their heads at full tilt depletes the brain’s energy reserves. If you do it to ’em for too long, it gives ’em a migraine. I don’t know how that works, wish I did, but I’ve seen ’em hold their heads and squint their eyes. It must be true.”

“But people’ve learned to keep things in their heads,” he adds. “There’s no way to know what they’re up to without somethin’ like this.”

The colleague nods.

“Too bad we can’t go easier on ’em. Like, maybe get ’em in their sleep. That’s what they do overseas, you know.”

“No kidding?”

“No kiddin’. Can’t do it here unless they’re at a port-o’-entry, as you know. But out there, in the rest of the world, it’s a different jurisdiction. They don’t have to go easy on ’em. They go all night and it messes with their REM and wrecks their sleep. The main thing is, they don’t know it’s happenin’.”

The younger colleague considers the operator’s point and a worry passes over his face. “You think they do that to us, too?”

The older one responds “Probably. You sleepin’ OK these days?” and laughs. He gets up and heads out of the operations room with his colleague, holding the door open for him. “Same place as usual?”

The door to the operations room clicks locked behind them as they walk down the hall to the main lobby, their polished leather shoes making their own soft clicks on the terrazzo floor.

It's never really over, is it?

The interior of the train is cylindrical, with white plastic benches and stainless steel poles. It has a utilitarian feel to it, optimized for mud, snow, the bumping of luggage, and the scraping of skis. The train jostles slightly as it travels through the straight thirteen-mile long tunnel, deep beneath the Sierra Nevada, that connects Mariposa Station with Yosemite Valley Station, rising 2500 feet from one end to the other. The incline of the train is noticeable from the interior. Rough rock surfaces inside the tunnel, dimly lit by the lights inside the train, flash by the train's large windows.

The route, which runs hourly most of the day, just opened last year. It travels 24 miles overland from the town of Mariposa and then dives underground near the small community of Incline, terminating in Yosemite Valley. The tunnel, with its twin bore, by far exceeds the length of the older 4,233 foot-long Wawona automobile tunnel into Yosemite that was bored through solid granite in 1933.

The new station in Yosemite Valley is built on one of the old parking lots. Most of the other lots have been restored back to meadowland, though two lots have been retained, upgraded with charging stations for use by all-electric vehicles. The station has become the portal for most of the four million annual visitors to the valley.

When first proposed, the project to build it was controversial, mainly because of its expense. But with the ever-increasing demand on the national park, something had to be done. Automobile traffic, and its associated congestion problems and pollution, were having noticeable impacts on the park, and simply limiting the number of visitors meant that many people wouldn't be able to visit at all. But the all-electric train would connect with California's rail system and provide, for the first time, an efficient and ecologically friendly public transportation system into the valley. Visitors would no longer need to drive in. And because the train would provide a rapid daily commute between Mariposa and Yosemite Valley, it would become more practical for guests to stay overnight at new lodging outside the park.

The luggage racks are stacked with every kind of bag. Soft bags, hard shells, backpacks. Several pairs of skis are strapped along the wall right next to the luggage. The rush of the train through the tunnel and the sound of its electric motors are amplified by the tunnel walls back into the train. The train is currently configured with only one car, with winter being the slow season for Yosemite.

The six of them sit at one end of the car, next to one of the two luggage racks. Peter wears blue jeans, with long underwear and a black and white puffy down jacket printed with a jumble of math symbols, a design that he had custom-ordered, and snow boots. Shasha wears a bright salmon-colored parka with a fur-trimmed hood. Ethan is wearing a black designer leather jacket and blue jeans. He keeps his aluminum carry-on by his side rather than putting it onto the luggage rack. His wife Peng Haiping, who goes by the English name June, wears a jacket with a new type of material, just out this season, consisting of a mesh of brightly colored threads treated with a thin water-repellant coating. The jacket is stuffed with down. Replacing the typical fur trim for the hood is a trim of fine brightly colored fibers. The overall effect is that of splashed paint, bright yellow and green, bright orange, purple and mauve and chartreuse. She wears hot pink snow boots.

Ethan and June's two boys, Yangyang, who is eight, and Xiaoxiang, six, are also with them, on winter break from school. The whole family arrived a few days ago, with Ethan spending a day at Zai's US subsidiary and the family visiting friends around the Bay Area. They'll be returning to China in another couple of days.

The two boys sit quietly, playing a game with each other on their Naojis, tilting them this way and that and giving them mental commands. The Naojis watch their gaze directions with the user-facing camera to determine the targets of their mental commands. The game gives the boys virtual sensations as they play: tactile sensations on their bodies, little pinpricks and bumps, scrapes and tickles, and skin temperature changes, and virtual smells. The sounds of the game are sent directly into their minds, no earbuds required.

Peter is free of his wheelchair. He walks now, without the use of a walker or a cane. He also no longer has the robotic arm, having returned it to the company which built it, asking that it be made available to someone else in need.

The robotic arm had quite literally become a part of him. That had become a problem for him for a while due to an unexpected side effect. For several months after he had finally become free of the need for the arm, having regained control over his own limbs, he had suffered from phantom limb syndrome. His brain had reorganized itself to use the robotic arm and to feel the sensations coming from its fingertips and other surfaces and the feeling of the forces on its joints. The problem was that with the arm gone, he still had phantom sensations of it being there. And if having three arms was an unusual experience, a situation he had lived with for years while rebuilding strength in his biological arms, it was just as uncomfortable to be a three-armed person with one missing.

Peter takes in the scene on the train. A few people are conversing, animated, present. But many of the passengers have that distant look that means they're mindpaired with their Naojis, thinking beyond the horizon. They're with friends, chatting in their heads or searching the Internet or listening to a book or music. They don't even look around. They're there, not here.

[Zai. You're there,] Peter thinks to himself. He had needed the Naoji just to be *here.*

Peter thinks to his Naoji: [*Signal level?*]

Peter's Naoji to Peter: [3 bars.]

He's impressed. There's service in the tunnel. He gives it a try. [*Weather in Yosemite Valley?*]

Peter's Naoji to Peter: [Today, expect a high of 38 degrees and a low of 14. Clear skies and calm.]

It's going to be nice, he thinks.

Peter no longer needs his Naoji to communicate, but he lives with it 24x7 and has continued to use its features in his persona. He still uses it to make funny voice impressions, and also sounds that are impossible to make with the human voice. But over the years, he has gradually transitioned into speaking with his natural voice, a process slowed down by the ease with which he had been able to speak just by thinking. It takes real effort to work the diaphragm and the mouth while speaking. Nowadays, though, with no pressing need to use its speakers, he keeps his Naoji in his pocket.

"Did you see that thing in the news about a weird takeover of some village in the Middle East?" He looks at Ethan and June.

"I did hear about that," Ethan says. "Near Turkey. Or in Turkey."

"They said the village was possessed by ghosts. I wonder what that was about. I never did get what they meant by ghosts."

The thought reminds Peter of a ghost story of his own. "Shasha, remember what happened with Napoleon? I've got to tell them about that. But it's a little long. Remind me about that later."

Shasha laughs and agrees. Then she asks June about her flight from Beijing. "I heard they let people use cell phones now on international flights."

June complains: "They do. It was a horrible idea."

This gets Peter's interest. "Yeah?"

Ethan just smiles.

"You just can't escape it. One man was on his phone the whole way over. Well, except during sleep hours. Talk talk talk." June gestures with her fingertips. "We all hated him," she says. "That's what Naojis are for. I would have given him one if I could have." She shakes her head. "Talk talk talk."

Peter chuckles.

"It's quite warm in here, isn't it?" June says. She takes her coat off and sets it down beside herself on the seat. "So, Peter, I hear you have been studying Chinese."

Peter replies in Chinese. "Dui. Hui shuo yidian." *That's right. I can speak a little.* "It's still not easy, though."

"Tai haole," she replies. *Great!* "Your Chinese is perfect. Shasha must have taught you a lot!" She gives Peter a big smile.

"Definitely."

"He needs to be weened from his Naoji, though," Shasha says.

"Oh! How so?"

"She means that I keep looking things up when I speak Chinese. It's hard to break the habit."

"He can barely speak without it," Shasha says.

"I see the point. Everything is just a thought away." June turns to Ethan. "What are you going to do about that, Ethan?"

"What?" Ethan has drifted off onto mental Internet searches.

June turns back to Peter and Shasha. "He has the same problem. He's addicted."

Ethan returns to listening to the media article he found.

"Have you been following T. Ruth?" June asks. "It amazes me how easy-going Americans can be about their privacy!"

T. Ruth, a New Yorker and proud of it, Ruth being her middle name, has turned herself into a celebrity by living her life transparently, live streaming all her thoughts to the world through her Naoji, with only rare blank-outs. She has given new meaning to the phrase "channeling your thoughts". It's a sound-only reality TV kind of thing, with a weekly segment where she interviews celebrities. "You know my schtick." She says that at the beginning of every interview. "So tell me..." She asks questions, they answer. It's a nice conversation. But the listeners also hear her thoughts, which invariably involve roasting her guest. The contrast can be hilarious. She calls her channel *The Daily Life of T. Ruth.* "Don't have a Ruthless day. Tune in." *Everyone* knows her.

"Well, I don't know," Shasha says. "I think Peter values his privacy a lot."

"Of course, of course," June says. "But I can't think of a single Chinese who would advertise their thoughts to the whole world all day long!"

"It's the money," Peter says. He mentions that he ran across an article in the media which said she has millions of subscribers to her channel. "So what I want to know is, why do so many people care what she thinks?"

"That's probably right. It must the money. I heard she's making a fortune doing that," June says.

"I always wonder why people care so much about making money. What really matters is what you do with your time." Shasha's expression is serious.

"You are so right," June says.

In fact, just the day before, the tabloids ran a story quoting T. Ruth's thoughts, commenting on the money she was making from sponsorships and characterizing her thoughts as "nothing more than a show". The story described her as going on and on, saying: "Oh...oh...OH, that's good! Ahhhh! Oh!", and only after a good three minutes of this: "I can't *believe* this ice cream! It is sooooo good! Oh my God. I need more." She mentioned the brand name, and *then* she thought about the $250,000 she just made in those four minutes. Indeed, for the next few minutes after that, she revisited that thought three more times. It was a good day in the life of T. Ruth.

The train rolls to a stop at Yosemite Valley Station. Both the station and its approach are underground to preserve the natural scenery of the valley. The doors slide apart with several telescoping layers, opening up all but the very ends of the car to the platform. Cold, moist winter air from the station floods into the car as the passengers pour out onto the 750 foot long platform more or less all at once, without encumbrance, rolling, dragging, and shouldering suitcases and backpacks and cross-country skis. Several children run out on the cold concrete, screaming and playing. For just a short period of time, the two stairways and one elevator jam up as people line up to exit.

Above ground, the neighboring meadows and forest are covered with snow. The air is cold, the sky is blue, and granite cliffs tower around them on all sides. They join the crowd that is boarding a self-driving open-air shuttle near the station's glass, pine, granite and river stone pavilion.

"It's so fresh in the winter here," Shasha says. She can see her breath on the air.

"I could live here," June says. "I love the architectural style. Primitive and natural. And look at the mountains!" She sighs. "No traffic lights anywhere."

The group checks in and settles into their hotel rooms at Yosemite's grand hotel, a beautiful national landmark which first opened for business in 1927, having agreed to meet shortly in the hotel's Great Lounge to plan an outdoor activity.

The next evening, the pianist quietly plays pop arrangements on one of the Steinway pianos as they wait to be seated for dinner. The boys sit nearby, playing on their Naojis, while Ethan and June stand, watching the pianist, June holding her husband's arm. Peter and Shasha lounge in a pair of leather chairs. A fire roars in the huge sandstone fireplace. The light outside the windows fades as the sun sinks below the granite cliffs of the valley.

Ethan has changed into a casual suit, while June wears a black evening dress, draped from just one shoulder, with a silver pattern around the waist, and black evening flats. Shasha and Peter dress more casually, Peter in designer jeans, a cotton dress shirt, and a light tan-colored cashmere sweater, and Shasha in wine-colored wool-blend slacks and a cream blouse covered all over with stringy fluff.

Just a couple of hours ago, they had been ice skating in the valley's rink. The sky overhead was a clear blue and the air was crisp. The boys proved to be experts, racing around the rink at high speed and showing off with backward skating and a few tricks and a couple of dive-head-first slide-across-the-ice stunts. They skate every winter near their home in Beijing. June and Ethan skated as a couple, looking quite romantic, arms around waists.

Shasha didn't skate. She's expecting their first child, though they have not yet announced this, and she wanted to be careful. Instead, she helped Peter as he struggled to stay upright while stepping along next to the rink wall. It was the first time for him on skates since his bicycle accident, or more accurately, since years before his accident, since he wasn't a regular skater. And he's still building muscle mass. The concussion had taken a lot out of him. He no longer has the same drive, so it has been a slow process for him.

After a few minutes, they are called and escorted to their candlelit table and seated. A busboy pours water for the table. After briefly looking over their menus, they engage in chitchat until their waiter comes to take their orders. The waiter systematically works his way around the table, ending with Ethan, who orders a glass of the house red with his dinner and then suggests that Peter might like a glass as well. Peter accepts.

As the waiter heads off to the kitchen, Peter kicks off a conversation with Ethan while June starts her own conversation with Shasha. The two boys return to playing their Naoji game together.

"Ethan, so what's going on with that whole warrant thing with Zai? It's been all over the news."

Ethan considers how to answer Peter's question.

Zai's US subsidiary, Zai MindPair USA, is headquartered in the Silicon Valley and employs 1,770 people there, including their neuroprosthetics research and development division, which works with a network of other companies in the U.S. to integrate Zai's brain code interfacing technology into prosthetics solutions. Another 355 employees work in their retail store chain.

Zai MindPair USA in turn has set up a subsidiary of its own for the purpose of building out and operating the MindPair Network in the U.S., a separate company they named BlipTone, Inc., the name originating with the default [<Blip>] notification tone used by Naojis and by the MindPair Network to alert users when a message or reminder is waiting or when a call is coming in. Thus, subscribers of the MindPair Network in the U.S. have service with BlipTone, a service that requires no device to use, whereas customers who purchase Naojis buy them from Zai MindPair USA and use them with their carrier of choice. This arrangement allows Zai to manage their own telecom services in the U.S. as a separate business.

Either way, when someone sends you a message, you hear a [<Blip>] in your head. But with BlipTone, you don't need a phone. The network towers play the message directly into your inner voice. When you think [*Continue*], you hear the message, in your head. Or if you're busy, just ignore it. You can check your messages later. And if you get a series of messages, or you message back and forth in a short timeframe, or a message comes in from a different sender, the service is smart about it. You don't have to keep thinking [*Continue*] on every message, and you'll never get barraged with blips.

In fact, many of the same features work with or without the Naoji smartphone - sending and receiving audio text messages, surfing the web, getting weather reports and stock prices, listening to news stories, managing your contacts and calendar reminders.

BlipTone has been rolling out the MindPair Network to the nine counties of the San Francisco Bay Area, and subscribers have already started using the network. The issue that Peter is referring to, the issue that hit the news, is that BlipTone was served with a warrant to wiretap the thoughts of one particular subscriber, whose name hasn't been disclosed, and BlipTone objected, with the company asserting that the order violates the subscriber's rights under the First Amendment, especially in light of the Nolen decision by the Supreme Court back in 2028, the very same decision that had decided Peter's appeal.

The MindPair Network is designed to receive all thoughts, continuously, after a subscriber signs on, but it discards thoughts not intended for the network by the subscriber. The wiretap order requires the company to provide a way for law enforcement to record each thought of the individual identified in the warrant when the thought is received by the MindPair Network. The problem, as BlipTone sees it, is that the wiretap applies to *all* thoughts, even those thoughts the network would otherwise discard as private thoughts, thoughts not intended for the network.

BlipTone is concerned that this situation will greatly reduce the market for its network service. Consumers may no longer trust the service, believing their thoughts would be wide open and no longer private. The warrant represents a big shift in privacy concerns. In the past, a search warrant could only ask for messages sent over the network by a subscriber. But the requested wiretap would be used to search a subscriber's entire stream of consciousness, every word they think, every thought they have, all day long, day after day, when they are signed on and clearly identified to the network. Every word of thought would be searched for keywords: personal relationships, health concerns, financial situations, political opinions, religious beliefs and practices, prayers included.

While the warrant does use keyword matching to narrow down what is being searched, it isn't clear how much protection this provides. The thoughts all around the keywords would still be captured, to provide context, and these could include almost anything.

In the past, it would have seemed like a crazy idea to let a network of towers read people's minds. Was it a good idea? Ethan had turned this thought over again and again in his mind. Standards of privacy shift as the world evolves. The Naoji smartphone was an easy sell to begin with. It was just another smartphone with a new trick, somewhat like a phone with an invisible headset. And in fact, once the Naoji was out, it was clear to everyone that mind-interfacing was the "new hot thing". Some people refused to adopt the new technology, worried about the privacy of their thoughts and the coming technological "takeover of the mind", a transition to a society in which you can no longer function without a machine talking inside your head. But mostly, the public's reaction was excitement. They just didn't worry. It was too cool, too fun, too convenient, to ignore.

Once the technology had made its way into the world, it could be abused, and it was abused. Ethan himself had suffered from such an attack. But he solved that problem, not just for himself, but for anyone who buys a Naoji. The Naoji itself detects and warns the user of potentially harmful interference with the brain and documents the attacks, although more work still needs to be done to familiarize police bureaus with what he calls a "personal security" feature.

Zai is planning a feature for parents, children and friends to find each other on the MindPair Network, no expensive smartphone needed, no worry that the battery will run out or that the phone will get lost or stolen or forgotten somewhere. A child is just a parent's thought away. [*Where is Milo?*] is all it takes. And you don't need to actually ask the kid, who is most likely so engrossed in his own activities that he'd not notice your question. The network knows where he is and responds with your choice of location name for the place, or it looks it up on the Internet and gives you an intelligent abbreviation. The idea is to keep it simple. So, where is Milo? [At Kai's house.] Or [At the mall.] Address on request.

Is there a privacy concern with this feature? Ethan thought it obvious. No, nothing new. This feature has been available on smartphones for decades. It's just that now, you don't need a smartphone, and neither does the child.

In early discussions at Zai, there was debate about whether to set up the MindPair Network at all. Communication back and forth with the brain cannot be encrypted. When a tower sends a message to the brain, it could easily be intercepted by someone with the right equipment. Would anyone really want to receive unencrypted messages?

They had brainstormed extensively, describing protocols on a whiteboard, rejecting one possible solution after another to work around the brain's inherent lack of encryption when it thinks. But then one of the marketers made a point that decided the issue. He stated the obvious. "I talk all the time to people without encryption." Everyone in the meeting wondered what he meant by that. Some sort of unencrypted messaging app?

"No. I just mean talking," he said. "Just like we're doing right now. At parties, in restaurants, out on the street. All over."

They all laughed that they didn't get it at first.

He continued with his point. "So the MindPair Network would just let you talk to someone who's not necessarily standing right next to you. Or maybe they are, but you can talk more privately, without bothering other people around you. Someone would have to go out of their way to eavesdrop. And anyway, it would be illegal. You can't eavesdrop on people's phone calls, either."

That had settled it.

As it turned out, young people, particularly teens, took to it without hesitation. They had no qualms whatsoever. They had grown up with the Naoji and took mind-interfacing for granted. The MindPair protocol for them is just part of everyday life. Being able to use it without a device has been a natural transition for them. And when asked about privacy, teens don't understand the issue as a threat. "Like what?" they would respond. "My friends don't share anything that they don't want to."

As far as the teens were concerned, it meant their circle of friends was with them all day long. The teen's friends became an extension of the teen's mind. Except, that is, while at school during school hours, at least in Beijing, where teen's accounts are automatically put into a "do not disturb" mode by the network as part of a regulation to prevent interference in studies and cheating on tests. The parents can still find them. But otherwise, they're not really online.

Licensing requirements and other regulations prevent both individuals and companies from operating mind-interfacing equipment in inappropriate ways. And, indeed, since Ethan's media event with Peter, years ago, when Peter was locked in and needed the technology to communicate, numerous regulations have been passed, covering its use in many different applications, including medical, entertainment, and telecommunications.

Apart from the practical everyday considerations of privacy using the MindPair Network, there were also complicated and subtle legal issues that needed to be addressed, and this gets back to the question of the search warrant served to BlipTone. Looking a little at the history of the law gives some insight into the complexity of the issue.

Peter's Supreme Court case involved a search, with the term "search" as defined under a particular search and surveillance law, the Information Privacy Act of 2020. That law was found unconstitutional by the Supreme Court in 2028 in the Nolen decision.

At issue here, though, is another law, an extension to the old wiretap laws used for years to monitor phone calls and their Internet equivalents. Telecom service providers were required to modify their equipment specifically to give law enforcement access to subscribers' communications. The same senator who had called for the moratorium on mind-interfacing technology in 2026 had gone on to propose a bill, ultimately known as the Communications and Border Security Act of 2036, in response to the outcome of the Nolen decision of 2028 and to BlipTone's later license application, in 2035, for the operation of what it called "device-free over-the-air messaging services". The new law went into effect last year.

Why was the new law needed? Carefully parsing through the old wiretap law, one finds that *thoughts*, captured electronically but not intended for transmission to at least one recipient, are not *electronic* to begin with, and they're also not, in the end, *communications*, so they're not covered by the old law. But the new law redefines communication as any transfer of information. How it gets there, and how far it goes, isn't important.

Opinions in the media have varied, but a surprising number have come out in favor of thought wiretapping, with a well-known activist even going as far as suggesting the policing of hate thought, writing: "Prejudice and bigotry need to be stopped at their source in the heart and in the soul before they become obsessions. Track the hate down. Track it down and set it right." One law enforcement official was quoted as saying that it is a "...huge problem. For the safety of the officers, they need to know what they're dealing with before they go in. This is an important tool for keeping the public safe."

Zai MindPair USA's top lawyer forwarded a business article to Ethan on the issue. The article, written for corporate executives, laid out an analysis of the implications of the new law, describing the use of Zai's mind-reading network services for surveillance by law enforcement as "a panopticon... Just knowing that one's thoughts might secretly be monitored by the authorities without notice has the effect of making every citizen a prisoner. In such a situation, a citizen lacks the space even to consider what to think without those thoughts, too, being judged. The very possibility seizes thought. We need only look at the history of antitrust actions to see one potential impact. Half-baked ideas emailed off in business communications, at the time perhaps just passing thoughts on the way to a final decision to acquire a company or to a new pricing policy, have led to accusations of anticompetitive corporate behavior and the calling of CEOs onto the carpet to answer to Congress." The article went on to provide what they called "practical advice" for avoiding the appearance of controversial or potentially incriminating motivations while *thinking* about corporate strategy, thoughts which might expose executives to misunderstandings. Recommendations included drilling on preferred words and phrases to use while thinking about the business. Ethan had doubts about the practicality of their recommendations. But he also saw the deeper issue, that Zai might increasingly be viewed in a negative light, despite all the precautions the company takes for subscriber privacy.

It isn't clear yet whether the new law is constitutional. The crux of the issue is permission. The new law says that if a subscriber's thought is intercepted with their permission, such as occurs with the MindPair Network, then it is subject to wiretap. Law enforcement, and the judge who had authorized the search warrant, interpreted the meaning of permission broadly. If you sign onto the network, you've given permission for the network to examine every one of your thoughts to determine what action to take on your behalf, if any. Thus, the network has permission to process every one of your thoughts while signed on, including the thoughts it ends up discarding. The judge had reasoned that permission was given to process a thought even if the only permission given was to determine whether to carry out further processing. And indeed, without processing the thought, the network would otherwise have no way of providing the services promised. Therefore, the network itself is a *recipient* of those thoughts. Supporting this view, the judge noted, is the fact that the network itself responds directly to thoughts, as when, for example, a subscriber inquires as to the current time of day. The network is not merely a platform for relaying messages. It is also the destination for at least some of those messages. Thus, thoughts processed by the network are *communications*, even when they are not relayed to some other recipient. Accordingly, while signed on, you've given up your right under the Nolen decision to keep those thoughts absolutely private. If you want absolute privacy, sign out.

Because of this, the company believes that many subscribers will not be comfortable staying signed on. But having to sign on and off repeatedly throughout the day to protect your privacy kills the concept. Indeed, the publicity around the one search warrant has already led to a decline in usage in the small part of the network that has already been rolled out.

BlipTone views permission more narrowly. The reason that the network distinguishes between thoughts "to" the network, and other thoughts not intended for the network, is that the subscriber hasn't given permission to the network to process those other thoughts. It's even in the subscriber privacy agreement. BlipTone promises not to process, forward, or store thoughts that are not intended for the network. As soon as it determines that a thought is not intended for the network, it discards it.

Complicating things further, BlipTone's 911 emergency services implementation is intended to provide coverage to everyone, whether subscribed or not, and without the need to sign on. The promise of a 911 service helped to sell the MindPair Network as a public service, a miracle of a benefit to the community and to mankind at large. Reaching out for help is just thought away, no phone required. And it's free for everyone. But the legal team is concerned that this puts them on a slippery slope. It may be just a matter of time before the sign-on requirement would itself be discarded and the protection of the privacy of thought under the Nolen decision would be eroded further.

The legal team also predicts that it would be just a matter of time before additional legislation is passed which would require them to install standardized equipment to provide law enforcement with automated access to real-time surveillance on their towers. While there is nothing new about requiring telecom companies to provide such access, this would be the first time that a subscriber's *private thoughts* would be at stake. And yet, the debate in the press has taken the same course as with previous challenges to privacy, with calls to "strike a balance" between privacy and security, a theme which has been debated for decades, if not centuries.

Members of groups who oppose mind-interfacing technologies regularly write negative commentary, complaining about everything from the dangers to humanity to the dangers to humans, everything from the potential for political abuse to health risks. Mass surveillance is but one of their concerns. "There will come a day," one famous blogger wrote, "when a person will not even be able to think without having an access point nearby. We will be slaves to the network, unable to function without it, assimilated into it, and no longer individuals with our own independent thoughts." Their goal is nothing short of banning all mind-interfacing technology, for the good of mankind.

Distracted driving is another such issue, though self-driving cars are gradually making that issue moot. Distracted walking, too, has become a big issue. Many jurisdictions already have laws forbidding the use of electronic devices while crossing a street, and some disallow their use while walking or jogging anywhere at all in public areas, with people getting run over or running into one another because they're looking down at their screens while texting. Advocates of the laws tout the importance of vigilance and safety while negotiating public spaces.

Technically, messaging with the MindPair Network doesn't violate those laws. After all, the whole point of the network is that the subscriber doesn't need to use a device. There's no screen to look at. But Zai's legal team is concerned about laws that might eventually restrict the use of their network while driving, and eventually, perhaps even while merely walking in public.

When the legal team expressed this concern to Ethan in a conference call one day, it irritated him. "Unbelievable!" he blurted. "How can thinking be an offense?" He knew they might be right, though. The legal team had expressed the view that the laws might someday make a distinction between distracted walking while thinking naturally, say while absorbed in one's thoughts, and walking while distracted by mind-interfacing, such as when sending or receiving messages or, say, doing work through the interface. The law might permit the use of mind-interfacing for map directions while walking or driving and would otherwise forbid it, and Zai's technology might be required to accommodate such laws.

And then there has been the reaction of the competition, the traditional messaging and cellular networks. They aren't taking this new threat lightly. Opposition lobbying in Washington has been strong, with the traditional carriers trying to restrict or ban the MindPair Network, citing many different concerns, including interference with their own radio spectrum and insufficient study of potential health effects.

As it is, the politics are delicate. Several members of Congress have publicly debated the question of what position the government should take on permitting the operation of the network, with the privacy of Americans potentially at risk. Fifteen years ago, it would have been unthinkable. Things have changed. That said, even though trade relations between the U.S. and China have improved greatly over the past two decades, the U.S. still wouldn't even consider allowing the licensing of radio spectrum for the network unless Zai would agree to keep the infrastructure supporting the U.S. and Chinese networks isolated from one another, with the network operations organization and data servers for the U.S. system physically located in the U.S. Restrictions on foreign ownership of infrastructure led BlipTone to partner with one of the smaller U.S. telecom companies to build out and operate the MindPair Network. As it is, BlipTone only has provisional approval for their network.

Ethan had been uncertain about the likelihood of BlipTone securing permission from U.S. regulatory agencies, given the sensitivity of securing a country's telecom infrastructure. But it was about achieving a balance, he thought. You can't just ban innovation.

That said, the deal's not done until the deal's done. Just recently, the president of Zai MindPair USA proposed to him to spin out BlipTone. Zai MindPair USA, which, because it is owned entirely by Zai is viewed as a Chinese company, would sell BlipTone to the American public, and BlipTone would thereby become an entirely American company. This would work around the anxiety associated with Chinese ownership of the U.S. network, with Zai profiting instead from an initial one-time payment from the sale of BlipTone shares, and then later from license fees tied to the size of BlipTone's subscriber base. The more subscribers BlipTone signs up, the more fees Zai would earn. But Zai wouldn't be involved in providing the service and would have no access to those subscribers.

Keeping the company together would be better for Zai and better for the evolution of the technology. But breaking it up might be the only way forward in the U.S., and Ethan doesn't want to miss out on what will likely be the second largest market in the world.

In truth, though, he is quite unhappy about the proposal. The very idea that the people who worked so hard to build the company would have to give up their ownership to make their services available to others is demoralizing. He understands the logic, but it's exasperating. He doesn't want to go to the board of directors with it unless and until it becomes clear that it would be the only viable option.

Ethan is going to be a billionaire if the IPO goes well. And Peter, too, will do very well. Ethan had thought it only fair that Peter get a piece of Zai, since, after all, Zai's technology originated with Peter's work on his signal tracker. Peter's shares will be worth somewhere between forty and sixty million. But Peter doesn't know that yet. He hasn't been involved in IPO planning. To date, those discussions have been limited to board members and executive staff.

Peter actually contributed twice to Zai's development, with his second contribution becoming important only years later, when Zai started investigating the creation of a device-free network. Indeed, without Peter's second contribution, the device-free network would never be practical.

The problem was interference. Naoji smartphones have no problem communicating with cell towers without interference. Like all cell phones, they have special hardware just for that. And the Naoji itself is able to communicate with the brain without interference because the phone is always very close by, within just a few feet. But how could the towers communicate directly with hundreds of subscribers' brains in the same area without any interference? You can't just build in special hardware in the brain to make that work. Or maybe you could, but that wouldn't be a very appealing option. The whole point was to be free of electronic devices. And the surgery wouldn't be much fun, either.

"But wait," Ethan had asked, when the engineers first started work on designing the network, "why would there be interference? Brain codes are different for each person."

"Not for smells," the engineers reminded Ethan. "We could just do sounds first. But even though brain codes are different from person to person, it's not perfect. You must have heard it happen at least once or twice."

Ethan knew what they meant. If you're near someone else using a Naoji, you might hear something in your own head, though this happens only very rarely. It usually wouldn't be clear, just a garbled sound of some kind. And since the Naoji's transmitter isn't very powerful, if you step away just a little bit, the effect goes away.

"It'll happen a lot if you're beaming messages to a crowd," the engineers explained. "Everyone's messages will be crisscrossing all over the place. It just won't work unless we do something about interference."

It was actually Ethan himself who realized that Peter might have the solution to this problem. Ethan remembered reading something in Peter's notes years back. That was what Peter's project was all about. That was the project Peter was working on before his bicycle accident. It was all about transmitting radio signal shapes without interference. Peter had leveraged his own research on radio interference to understand what Breg's technology was doing to him. How could he hear the voices, while Shasha or Ethan, sitting right next to him, could not?

Ethan only vaguely understood the notes. It was advanced signal processing, and despite his undergraduate degree in computer science, and the brief overview Peter had once given him in his SCIF, Ethan had never developed expertise in this area. So he had contacted Peter, still confined to his wheelchair back then, and had a conversation with him about it, going on nothing more than a guess.

"[Oh yeah. Sure, that's what my software does,]" Peter had said through his Naoji. "[That was what my invention was all about. You can transmit sliced up pieces of a signal from different transmitters at the same time, and they'll combine to produce the right signal shapes only where you want them to. Like, for example, brain codes, if you want.]"

Peter hadn't actually discovered that brain codes for sounds are different from person to person, as he had only himself as an example at the time. It was Zai who figured that out. What Peter had assumed, instead, was that by using two transmitters, Breg's technology could send different parts of the signal from different directions. And the very same trick that makes it stealthy also avoids interference. But two transmitters is a very limited way of doing it. Inspired by the observation of what Breg was doing, Peter had worked out how he could modify his own software to eliminate radio interference by using multiple transmitters together instead of just one, or two, and had written out the details in his research journal just the day before his accident.

Using Peter's invention, a device-free network can guarantee that a subscriber only hears their own messages, not the messages of other subscribers. It avoids interference by sending signal shapes from *several* nearby towers to *each* subscriber, so that the signal shapes combine together in the subscriber's head like puzzle pieces. Peter's invention figures out what all the shapes of the puzzle pieces have to be to make it all work, including the timing of when to beam out each piece and in what direction, and with what signal strength, from each of the nearby towers. When you're hearing a message in your head, it's because all of the pieces fit just right when they get to you. At the same time, no one else hears your message because the signal shapes of your message cancel in mid-air everywhere else around you. That makes the device-free MindPair Network practical with crowds.

Ethan thought that lucky. No one else had a patent on it and he grabbed the chance to buy out the invention from Peter. He needed to conserve cash, but he still wanted his friend to get a good deal, so he convinced Peter that he really should take payment in more shares of stock, saying he wouldn't regret it. And now, as Zai works toward its IPO, Peter's shares will be worth fifty times the cash he would otherwise have been paid. That said, there's still the search warrant issue hanging over them, and there's no market for the shares until Zai goes public. Peter may be rich on paper, but he can't spend the money until he can sell his shares.

All of these thoughts had passed through Ethan's mind at one point or another in the recent past, creating a history of experience that he had internalized and transformed into a complex intuition about the issues. How would he answer Peter's question?

Ethan smiles politely. "It's complicated."

"I'll bet," Peter says. "Are there issues in China, too?"

Ethan smiles again. "It's complicated. But it's a completely different market there, with different issues."

Peter has already developed his own opinion from his reading of the news. “I don’t think it makes sense. In my case, they specifically said that if a person doesn’t intend to express a thought, it’s protected by the First Amendment. Freedom of thought means you can’t search thoughts until they’re expressed. They can’t just take *all* of your thoughts. You know, if your thought is converted into an audio text message and sent to someone, fine, I could see that. That’s not a private thought any more. Not much different from talking on the phone. But if it’s just your private thought and the network picks it up just to see whether you’re intending to send it something...that’s just not good enough.”

Peter takes a sip of water, then mentions to Ethan that he heard the media is predicting a 30% chance now that the MindPair Network would be allowed to expand across the U.S. Ethan responds that there is always a certain amount of uncertainty. It’s common with the emergence of new technology. It was like that when AI first started to get established. Anyway, you shouldn’t always believe what you hear in the media.

“All these uncertainties always seem to revolve around the government. You never know what to expect. How is the U.S. supposed to stay competitive if we keep blocking new technology?” Peter speaks into the air as he rants. “Why don’t they make it a priority to settle things?”

Ethan smiles, then turns to the waiter, who has just brought their glasses of wine. Ethan picks up his glass and swirls it, takes a sniff, then holds it up to Peter. The two tap their glasses and taste their wines.

Setting his glass down, Peter continues: “You have to wonder whether the Internet would have been allowed if it were invented somewhere else.”

“Is it entirely an American invention?”

“It is. Isn’t it?”

Both Peter and Ethan make mental queries to their Naojis to get the facts.

“Yeah, it was a Department of Defense project,” Peter says. “The U.S. military invented it.”

“The first website was actually in Switzerland,” Ethan replies, “at a nuclear research lab.”

“It was? Didn’t know that. Nuclear research?”

“That’s what the website says.”

“So the web was invented by the Swiss.”

“An Englishman, actually. He was working there at the time.”

“Huh. Anyway, if the Internet’s OK, what’s wrong with the MindPair Network? OK, it’s about the potential to spy on people’s thoughts. But what difference does *that* make? Mind-interfacing devices already connect to the Internet. The MindPair Network just makes it easier. If you can trust your phone, why wouldn’t you trust the towers? ...Maybe it really does boil down to NIH. Not Invented Here.”

Feeling embarrassed about dominating the discussion, Peter asks Ethan how things are going with him. Any new hobbies? Ethan comments that he's recently developed a taste for California wine. He particularly likes merlot. "It's a softer varietal. I understand it has made quite a comeback in popularity in recent years."

Peter takes a sip of his wine as two waiters appear, each holding a tray. The waiters start setting down plates around the table, and everyone switches their attention to examining each other's food.

Getting her Naoji out of her purse, June asks one of the waiters if he could take a picture of the group. She looks into the Naoji's retinal projectors to activate its interface with the iris pattern of her eyes, then slides a finger across its small sapphire trackpad to turn the 3D camera on. Handing the Naoji to the waiter, she says to just tap the trackpad to take a picture. Then she gets everyone to pose.

After pictures, the two boys return to their Naoji game, but when June sits back down next to them, she tells them to put it away. The boys put their Naojis on the table. Yangyang takes a drink of water, then starts his dinner, but June has to encourage Xiaoxiang to eat his. Both kids are having hamburgers. Finally, she takes a taste of her pork osso buco and praises it to Shasha, commenting that she's never had this dish before. Ethan comments that his venison is quite good, a first for him, too. Shasha insists on a bite of Peter's steak, offering a bite of her arctic char in exchange.

As they eat, Ethan asks Shasha how her research has been going. She gives her standard summary, commenting on her work with feline cognition and behavior. Her experiment has been running for ten years now. Her research team has gone well beyond mapping out the mental states of cats during their communications. Their recent focus has been on understanding the abstract processes involved in thought itself. How does a cat switch attention? How does it search its memory? Does it have intentions? Does it set goals and prioritize? How does it learn new concepts?

Ethan finds the direction of her work fascinating, quite different from the approach that Zai's engineering team takes. He asks her a few polite questions.

Another family is escorted to a neighboring table and the busboy pours water for them. Peter glances over at them, then at the fire in the dining room's fireplace. He returns to his earlier thoughts about the search warrant news. "I wonder if they've also tried to monitor people's thoughts on the MindChroma digital assistants. You know, Shasha and I bought one a while back. That was years ago, but we still have it."

"Oh really? How do you like it?" Ethan asks.

Ethan is already familiar with Cryptochromics Corporation, the maker of the MindChroma mind-interfacing Internet access point with its built-in digital assistant. The company's technology uses a quantum-biology effect similar to the technique that Shasha's cat beanie uses for reading cats' minds, but instead of LEDs spread out over the head, it uses lasers to reach users from across the room. By using lasers instead of radio waves, Cryptochromics got around Zai's patents for mind interfacing. But the laser-based technology isn't as capable as radio wave mind-interfacing, at least, not with the current state of the art.

Cryptochromics, which is still a relatively small Silicon Valley start-up, occupies a new niche in the market for mind-interfacing devices. Their first product was a simple device to replace handheld remote controls which they license for use in consumer appliances. Unlike older remotes which transmit invisible light from the remote to, say, a television, theirs goes the other way around, with the television sending a light beam to people in the room to determine what commands they wish to send. The big benefit? It's device-free. You don't need to hunt down the remote, and you don't need to share it around.

Their remote control wasn't essential. But it was a crazy got-to-have novelty item that they used to enter the emerging space of mind-interfacing consumer electronics. The MindChroma digital assistant was their second product. Over time, the company expanded into home automation, allowing tasks around the home to be carried out with thought. Lighting. Thermostats. Their security system feature turned out to be particularly attractive as it can recognize family members, distinguishing them from intruders, meaning that motion detectors can be active all night long even when the family is home.

"It has definitely been a help," Peter says. "We even got it hooked up to the front door. I could just think and the door would open. It was easier than using the robotic arm."

As an afterthought, he adds that he named it Napoleon. The MindChroma stands twelve inches tall and has the shape of an egg sitting on a stand. As sleek as it looked, Peter felt that it lacked something. So, to give the thing some personality, he had ordered a little black felt bicorne of the type Napoleon Bonaparte used to wear and set it on top, being careful not to block the coated glass surface surrounding the center from which the two spinning pairs of needle-thin white lasers beam out.

The MindChroma's lasers pulse rapidly with incredibly short invisible flashes. Or, more precisely, almost invisible. One can just barely make out a faint ghostly white flicker, visible only in one's peripheral vision, as the MindChroma repeats its scanning pattern around the room and across each person's head, twenty times a second. A little telephoto lens and 3D camera system spins around with the lasers, reading the complex pattern of faint fluorescence, invisible to the naked eye, that comes back from each person's brain, through their skull, skin, and hair, milliseconds after each laser pulse.

Thus, by stimulating the brain with light, the MindChroma can read the mind, somewhat like the way Shasha's cat beanies work. In a different way, by using a laser and a miniature telescope to read the mind from across the room, it's like the submarine detection invention that Peter had once read about. But it can also speak to the mind. And in that way, it's actually not that different in principle from how the Naoji works, sending information to the brain by shaping the light to create brain codes.

"The engineering is phenomenal," Peter says.

The busboy returns and refills water glasses all around the table.

Shasha reminds Peter to tell his story of what happened with the maid service.

"Oh, right! I almost forgot." Both Ethan and June listen as he tells the story.

Peter had hired a maid service to come clean their home once a week and two women showed up. Peter opened the door for them by thinking the command to the MindChroma, which unlocked the door and swung it open with a small motor. He waited for the maids just inside, in his wheelchair, frozen like a statue and expressionless, despite progress with his rehabilitation, just because it had become his habit to be like that. So there he was, not moving, head tilted at a slight angle as it rested against one side of the head rest, with his wheelchair's robotic arm hanging off to one side. Upon seeing him, the women weren't sure what to think and had timidly asked: "Hello? Are you Mr. Peter Nolen?"

But before he had a chance to respond, the MindChroma, which had a straight-line view of the women at the door from its spot on the living room table, had picked up their thoughts and announced itself to them, so that they each heard a chipper robotic voice in their heads, saying: "[Hello! Call me Napoleon. How may I help you?]" Thereupon, eyes widening in astonishment, they both shrieked "Ghosts!" and ran away.

He says he stared out the door for a while, amused, before commanding Napoleon to shut it again. *[That's different,]* he had thought at the time. "I had no idea what that was about." He says he realized only later what must have happened. The MindChroma hadn't said anything to him. It had only spoken in the maid's inner voices. "Of course I turned off the damned announcement feature in the MindChroma after that."

Ethan and June laugh and June says: "I can just imagine how it must have looked!"

The two boys, having only eaten part of their dinners, had returned to playing their Naoji game together. Now, both boys look up at Peter and Xiaoxiang, the younger boy, asks: "Ghosts? Shushu, are you says ghosts?" To Ethan's kids, Peter is uncle. *Shushu.*

Peter asks whether they like ghost stories. Both boys nod yes.

Xiaoxiang asks: "What ghost you were talking?"

"We have a ghost at home called Napoleon. He does whatever I tell him to."

Yangyang asks: "How did he get there?"

"We bought him online."

"Oh."

Both boys return to their Naoji game. If you can just buy one, it's boring.

On June's prodding, the boys put their Naojis back down on the table and return to eating their dinners.

Peter asks the boys what their favorite food is, and Yangyang announces his favorite with enthusiasm. "Pig brains. They're very creamy."

Peter gives this some thought. He supposes they might be. "Do they eat a lot of pig brains in China?"

Yangyang doesn't know. He just knows they're good. "But only eat them once a year. Don't have too many brains."

"Oh? What happens if you have too many brains?"

"Boom!" Yangyang pops his fingertips at Peter.

"Right." He asks the boys whether there's any food that they don't like.

Yangyang answers: "Mexican food."

Xiaoxiang looks up at Yangyang. He doesn't answer the question.

"I love Mexican food, though," Peter says. "Haven't you ever had a truly great burrito?"

Yangyang makes a look of disgust on his face, then shrugs.

"They probably just don't have good Mexican in Beijing," Peter says. "You should have your dad look into that."

Yangyang says OK. Xiaoxiang nods.

Noticing that the children speak English quite well, Peter figures they must be learning it as a second language in school.

Shasha asks Ethan what Zai's latest product direction is and Ethan excitedly outlines Zai's new push into the retailing and advertising space with a new twist: ads and websites with virtual smells. "The idea is that if an advertiser wants you to buy roses on Valentine's Day, when their ad pops up, it comes up smelling like roses. Unless the user blocks olfactory pop-ups, of course. It's a natural extension to smells in virtual reality and in instant messaging."

Shasha smiles at this.

"The ad can send an odor keyword to the Naoji. And then the Naoji does a database lookup and ramps up an olfactory signal to the user. Marmalades, coffees and teas, bacon and eggs; perfumes, soaps and shampoos; smells of the great outdoors, pine woods, ocean air scented with sagebrush. A faint hint of leather for a luxury car ad. You name it." Ethan is animated. It is clearly a story he likes to tell. "Eventually, video ads will have odors that change as the video plays."

One potential advertiser, a major department store, asked about the availability of the smell of fresh linens. And, perhaps counterintuitively to some, a hair salon chain asked about the smell of hair treatment chemicals, to stimulate that need to get your hair done. Bad smells are not necessarily bad advertising. Another advertiser even asked about dimethyl sulfide, he says, though they wouldn't explain why. Ethan couldn't see a connection between their service and that particular smell. He says that all they would say is that they had been testing focus groups with real odors, and it's the one that got the best results. This gets Shasha curious, but he doesn't explain. "Just watch for it. You'll know when it's out. The pairing may surprise you."

He says he has a vision of an entire new advertising industry extension built around designing scent-enhanced campaigns. "Retailers will be able to provide product sample odors right on their websites. And now, when an ad loads, it won't just display graphics or play a sound. It will also be able to scent an odor."

"The odor is *scented*?" Shasha asks. "Saying the page is scented has a nice sound to it. Scenting an *odor* sounds like a new usage, though."

"Does it? Well, yes, it's new to the web, but magazines have been carrying scented ads for years. Mostly for perfumes. And what about scented stationery?"

Shasha can see Ethan's passion. He takes just one bite of food, then a sip of wine, before jumping right back into laying out his vision, explaining that they're proposing a change to the media standards on the web to incorporate odor names and coordinates, and also odor presentation, specifying how odors can be sequenced and overlaid, fading in and out with odor intensity control.

"Olfactory will be big," he says. "It will change advertising forever."

"I've always wondered whether messages with odors bother people," Peter says. "Anyone standing nearby can smell it. I keep my odor intensity down because of that."

"You didn't notice any improvement in the Naoji 7?" Ethan asks.

"I'm still on the 6. So is Shasha."

"Try the 7. The basic look of the phone hasn't changed. Ceramic composite block construction with rounded edges, no screen, no buttons, just anti-scratch sapphire windows. Dual retinal projectors on the front, front and back 3D camera lenses, the trackpad, and the optical charging window on the back. But it's more directional now. We've developed some new tricks to keep the beam narrower."

"Hold on."

Peter: [*Purchase from Zai Store.*]

Peter's Naoji to Peter: [Which product would you like to purchase? Or would you like a list to choose from?]

Peter: [*Naoji 7.*]

Peter's Naoji to Peter: [All Naoji 7 colors come with a nacre luster finish only. Choose from black oyster, pearl white, moonstone blue, and jadeite green.]

Peter: [*Black.*]

Peter's Naoji to Peter: [Black oyster Naoji 7 smartphone. Price is $1925.00. Free shipping. Anything else?]

Peter: [*No.*]

Peter's Naoji to Peter: [Total price is $2103.06 with tax. Shipping only to your home address with two day delivery. Approve, change, or cancel?]

Peter: [*Approved.*]

Peter's Naoji to Peter: [Password for purchase?]

Peter: [*<tongue click><bird chirp><"I am not a crook" in Nixon's voice>*]

Peter's Naoji to Peter: [Purchase confirmed.]

"Done. It'll be waiting for me when we get back."

Shasha says that her research team collects information about her cat community's olfactory experiences by reading their brainwaves. "Cats have a very sensitive sense of smell," she says.

Ethan is curious about the coordinates for odor perception by cats, guessing that they must be quite different from those used in human odor perception. He asks whether the cats perceive the same smell as a person does when a Naoji transmits a brain code for an odor. Shasha's not sure. They haven't tried using a Naoji with the cats, but it would be easy to check, she says. They already have a database of brain activity for a wide range of smells in cats.

Ethan and Shasha go back and forth about the sense of smell, noting that smell brain codes aren't actually completely universal because people and cats may inherit differences in their olfactory receptors, resulting in a kind of partial smell blindness analogous to partial color blindness. People and cats share many of the same genes for smell, but there are differences. And feline noses have far more receptors than human noses do. She guesses that the Naoji wouldn't produce the same smells in cats as it does in people.

As Ethan and Shasha discuss her cats, the children again become completely engrossed with playing with their Naojis at the dinner table. They don't even look up. They are totally silent. But holding their Naojis horizontally in their two hands, playing their multiplayer virtual reality game, the computer-generated imagery projected directly into their eyes, they communicate continuously to each other through thought.

June monitors the boys' conversation through her own Naoji. Her Naoji does not announce who is talking, but she recognizes the inner voices of each of her children. [I'M THE MONKEY KING NOW!] That's Yangyang thinking to Xiaoxiang. [NO, I'M STILL THE MONKEY KING!] That's Xiaoxiang's response.

When the shouting in her head finally gets to be too loud, she uses a Naoji DirectThought command to turn down the volume. It's not an explicit word-based command. She simply has the idea, and the Naoji carries out the command, recognizing the brain code that she thinks when she wants the volume down. It's so natural that she is not even consciously aware that she is sending the command. It is one of a handful of such shortcut commands, or mental gestures, that Naoji users train on with their devices when they get around to it.

Despite the shouting, she is happy to hear the continuous chatter of her children, even as the rest of the table hears nothing from them. This monitoring feature was actually her idea. Once the boys got Naojis to play games with, they rarely spoke out loud. Their silence really bothered her. She worried about them. So she had complained to Ethan, who dutifully went to work the next day and inserted a new product feature requirement into the next software release. He first gave it some careful consideration, of course. One should not act hastily when charting the turbid waters of human relationships. Accordingly, he had explored the question with a range of advisors, eventually deciding that the feature should work only for Naojis registered to children in connection with their parents, and only to a certain age. But the discussion went deeper, with one of his advisors mentioning the uncertainty around the social impact of giving too much insight into the child's mind. With this concern, Ethan had further specified that the new feature would only allow parents to monitor the thoughts that the child communicates over MindPair. It doesn't let the parents monitor their child's *private* thoughts.

The waiter returns and, noting that the diners seem to have finished their dinners, he hands out a dessert menu. A few minutes later, he takes their dessert orders. Peter orders a chocolate gelato ice cream cone, which, going by the picture on the menu, will be served in an ornate metal stand. Hearing Peter order, Yangyang orders the same, though he doesn't like chocolate and orders vanilla instead. Xiaoxiang says he wants what Yangyang is having. June passes on dessert, but declares that she'll have a bite of Ethan's dessert, and that he should get the apple cake. Shasha also orders the apple cake.

As they wait for their desserts to arrive, Ethan starts telling a funny story about something that happened recently with him and June, but he doesn't get far before June jumps in to fill in the rest of the story and Ethan becomes part of the audience.

The chatter of June's two children in her head fades into the background of her consciousness. As she excitedly tells her story, getting more and more animated, June shifts automatically into Chinese. Shasha listens intently. Yangyang shoves Xiaoxiang, and Xiaoxiang reciprocates, but June doesn't notice. The boys then return to their Naoji game and continue their mental chatter with each other, still silent as far as anyone else can tell.

Peter glances around the dining room with its giant iron chandeliers and its majestic pine timbers, trussed overhead and supported by tall columns of smooth granite river stones. His mind drifts, and the dinner conversation, now in Chinese, fades into the background. He notices people at other tables who are dining alone. He wonders what they're thinking.

After finishing their desserts, Ethan charges the bill to his room, and then they all get up and drift out of the dining room, chatting as they go, until after not many steps, they reach the Great Lounge's fireplace. Shasha whispers something in Peter's ear and he nods. She then squats down to talk to the two boys in English. "We have something for you." The boys look at her expectantly as she pulls out traditional Chinese red envelopes from her purse for them. Each envelope has a crisp, new $20 bill in it. "Happy Chinese New Year!"

Taking the envelopes with both hands held out, the older boy, then the younger one, says: "Xiexie, ayi!" *Thank you, auntie!*

Ethan mentions to Shasha that, if it would be OK, he'd like to ask her about an idea that he has been thinking about. June says good night to everyone and starts to take the children back to their room. The children run ahead of her yelling "Yay!", the younger one chasing the older one, and her chasing the younger one.

"So." Ethan gathers his thoughts. "It's not hard to read out the *sounds* that people think in their heads."

Shasha nods.

"Do you think it might be possible to communicate directly between people using abstract thought? Could we bypass words altogether?" He has been exploring ideas for making the MindPair protocol more secure, and it had occurred to him that with abstract thought, there wouldn't be any words for an eavesdropper to hear. But even to him, the idea is vague. What is an abstract thought? Do abstract thoughts have a language of their own? Would it actually be harder for eavesdroppers to figure out abstract thought brain codes?

"I'm not sure. I never really thought about reading abstract thoughts in people. A cat is already pretty complicated. As to a person...I'm not sure how it would be done." Gazing upward, Shasha touches her chin and tilts her head. She is immersed in the thought. "It would be a huge project." She imagines it to be another megaproject for humanity, like going to the moon or sequencing the human genome. A definitive database of abstract thought brain codes. All possible concepts, the language of thought itself, decoded and assigned coordinates in brain code spaces.

Some deeper aspects of her research flash through her mind, but she doesn't mention them as the team hasn't published anything about them yet. To start with, there are really two kinds of abstract thought. There are the concepts you learn, your understanding of the world. Things like what a fish is. And then there's the way the brain itself works. Her research team can tell just by watching a cat's brainwaves that he is retrieving a memory, or switching his attention back to some unfinished task, or exploring, trying something new just to see what will happen. These, and similar operations, form the operating system, so to speak, of the cat's brain. Like macOS for Macs or Windows for laptops. You might call it Cat OS. It's the software that makes the cat's brain function.

"We're still working out the details just for cats," she says, "but we'd be happy to share our papers with you. If that would help."

"I look forward to reading them."

"What sort of application did you have in mind? Would it be something for Zai?"

"It's just something I've been musing over," he says, "but it may be a direction for future development."

"Um. If I may. One idea that I think would be helpful to the thought process..."

Ethan and Shasha both look over at Peter, who has found a nice large leather chair nearby to rest his body in as the two chat. His thin body is engulfed by the chair. The forged iron lamp on the table next to him casts a warm light on his face from the side.

"When I was being chased around by people with mind-reading machines, despite everything that was going on, I still had some privacy. I could keep my abstract thoughts to myself. I'm not so sure it would be a good idea to give that kind of information to a Naoji."

Ethan and Shasha both quietly absorb Peter's point, each from their own perspective.

"And it's not necessary," he says.

"It's not necessary?" Ethan asks.

"We can already communicate," Peter says. "Abstract thoughts are for thinking, not communicating." He looks at each of them. "Think about it. You can think to a Naoji to command it, but you have control. How can the machine know what you mean to say if it's yanking your thoughts out of your head before you've decided?"

He feels weird saying this to the CEO of the company that makes the thing. But between the two of them, he's the one with more experience using one. He lives Naoji. It was more-or-less invented for him.

"If you let the Naoji read your abstract thoughts, there's no privacy left. Poof. Gone." He slowly splays his fingers in the air. "Transparent as a..." He searches for the right word. "And if the idea is that you'd send abstract thoughts into someone else's head...for communication? Does that make any sense?" Peter's tone is sarcastic and agitated. "Where will it end?"

In a more reflective tone, he continues: "You know, cats used to be quite enigmatic. But not any more. Shasha knows what they really think. Every detail. In a way, they're not really cats any more. They're just machines. She reads out the data whenever she wants to." Peter gives his own point some further thought. "You have to wonder how long it'll be before the government starts using mind reading on pets to find out what happened inside people's houses."

His mind shifts modes now. Wordless, but not empty. An invisible process has seized him, laboring without intention or goal. Then the conflict surfaces, and he understands. He tempers his point. "But science is important, isn't it. We can't live without science." Then after another moment: "Shasha's work is amazing."

[*"...but you have control."*] Ethan echoes Peter's words in his head. The Naoji in his pocket ignores this. [The MindPair protocol solved that. It gives you control. Would we have to abandon the protocol to read abstract thought?]

Shasha thinks back to the hours of discussions with George Cousin. His research had given her a new insight. Intention isn't something that just happens in the moment. It's a mixture of many different kinds of thinking happening together over time. How would a mind-interfacing device know what you really intend to communicate? She mulls this over.

"You're right, Peter. It depends on conventions," she says, finally.

"Conventions?" Ethan doesn't see the connection.

"Yes. The linguist on our team says that language *is* convention. It's symbols that we share. They define the interface for communication."

Ethan's expression changes. "Oh, I see. That's what the MindPair protocol is really about, isn't it?"

"You weren't thinking of reinventing language, were you, Ethan?" Peter feels slightly embarrassed just after he says this. He didn't mean to sound so condescending.

"No. Hm..." Ethan looks thoughtful. Then he just smiles.

The conventions of the MindPair protocol are what made the Naoji practical. It allows a person to carry on a conversation in their head with someone remotely while keeping their private thoughts and words to themselves. The user literally thinks "to" the Naoji. Not by pointing their head, but by thinking in some direction in their mind. Except, not in a physical direction. Not one of the six directions, north, south, east, west, up, or down, but toward the mind-interfacing device, toward the object of their attention, inward, toward the user's internal representation of the world. Toward the seventh and eighth directions. Lacking physical directions, there is no north or south, no up or down in the inner world. Instead, there is the self at the center. And then there are the others, far away, not in the world, but in one's own representation of it.

Like thinking of a friend half way around the world, the location is not what matters. It is the friend as an idea which matters. The *friend* is the direction. By imagining the distant friend, out there, they become close. And so it is with the Naoji.

Both the Naoji and the MindPair Network are programmed to recognize when you think that way, and that is how they know when your thought is intended for them and when it isn't.

Not everyone gets it at first, but Zai's customer service representatives get you started in an introductory session when you buy your first Naoji, and before long, it becomes second nature. Most people's reaction when they get it to work for the first time is "Wow!" It's like magic. You think, and it does something. But the real magic is that, after some practice, you *don't* think, and it does something. That is, you no longer have to try. It becomes habit, something that just happens.

"Well, thank you, both," Ethan says. "That was interesting."

The Great Lounge is hushed, empty except for the three of them. No more sounds emanate from the dining room next door. During their conversation, the dining room lights had been dimmed, though they didn't notice this until they finished talking.

Ethan: [*Time?*]

Ethan's Naoji to Ethan: [8:47 PM]

"Today was..." Ethan is interrupted by his Naoji. "One moment."

Ethan: [*Continue.*]

Ethan's Naoji to Ethan: [Haiping laile duanxin: {Guihua Wu} Zai fangjian dengzhe ni!] *Message from Haiping: {Osmanthus Mist} Waiting for you in our room!* June uses a scented message as a lasso to pull Ethan in for the evening.

Focusing again on Peter and Shasha, smiling, he finishes his thought. "It has been quite a nice day. 9 AM for breakfast?"

"Sounds good," Peter says.

"Good night, Ethan," says Shasha.

Shasha returns to the room first, as Peter wants to find the concierge to ask about activities for the following day. Arriving back in their room a short while later, he sees that the entertainment system is on and a video news story is streaming. He hears Shasha in the shower.

Standing in front of the entertainment system, watching the story, it gradually becomes clear to him that it is an update about the village takeover in the Middle East that occurred in December. It was actually near the buffer zone in northeast Syria, not far from the border with Turkey. A photo in the upper-right of the screen appears to be a satellite image of the village.

The anchorwoman is explaining that the ghosts mentioned in earlier stories actually refer to the words produced in the villagers' heads by mind-interfacing drones which flew in a cluster around and over the village. This time, the story includes newly released on-location footage from the original event. The footage shows soldiers surrounding the village, and barely discernible in the distance, dozens of drones jittering high and low over the village, like large flying insects guarding a nest. One of the soldiers tells his story as a translator speaks over him in English for the camera.

"When we approached the village, we already knew there were drones all over, but we didn't know how many. I was using a recon drone to search the area and to spot the drones. When it flew over a utility pole, I saw one resting on top of the pole, so I decided to try to capture it so that we could examine it in detail. My commander arranged for the power to be cut, and then I went up. As I was climbing the pole to grab it, getting near the top, I suddenly felt an electric shock in my head and I almost lost my balance. Luckily, I was tied into the pole. Suddenly, I saw the drone take off and it rapidly flew away to the village. It was like an animal, watching and waiting, hiding, attacking me with an electric shock and then running away to protect itself."

After the interview finishes, the reporter fills in some more background of what had happened. She describes the ten hour process used by sharpshooters to take out the drones, one by one. One of the sharpshooters comments to the reporter that it was a difficult process. The drones were constantly jittering, making it almost impossible to predict where it would be by the time the bullet reached it. So it took several attempts to down each individual drone. Making the process even more difficult, rooting out the remaining drones was a tedious process, with many of them hiding for long periods on rooftops or hovering between buildings. The recon drone would flush them out and they'd shoot. Attack drones would have been effective, but far more expensive.

Once they had confirmed that all of the drones had been shot down, having sent their recon drone into the village in a thorough search, they had to wait for the batteries of damaged drones to drain down so that their mind-interfacing weapons would be deactivated before they moved in. Even so, two of the drones had survived their crashes sufficiently intact to switch into power conservation mode, and they had suddenly powered back up in the middle of the cleanup, like booby traps, disrupting the operation.

The investigation into who was behind the takeover, and how the drones were constructed, is ongoing, with a number of competing theories still in play. Contrary to earlier reports, there were no enemy soldiers in the village. The drones had appeared seemingly out of nowhere. But one thing that has already become clear is that each of the artificial-intelligence-driven drones was able to operate autonomously while coordinating with each other through radio communications to control the village.

The story finishes and the next news story immediately begins playing. Tired from standing, Peter sits down at the end of the bed.

“This morning, Millsoro has released secret recordings she made of her former boss’s thoughts as she confronted him about their relationship. The former government aide has alleged that—”

Peter rolls his eyes. *Another thought recording scandal.* He turns off the entertainment system with a mental command, though he has to try twice because consumer electronics companies couldn’t agree on a single device-free remote-control standard. This one is made by a competitor of Cryptochromics.

He gets up to visit Shasha in the bathroom but is immediately interrupted by a notification.

Peter’s Naoji to Peter: [<Blip>]

Peter: [*Continue.*]

Peter’s Naoji to Peter: [<Blip>]

That’s weird. [*Continue.*]

Peter’s Naoji to Peter: [<Blip>]

He sighs. [*Do not disturb.*]

Peter’s Naoji to Peter: [<Blip>]

He pulls out his Naoji to figure out what’s going on. Browsing around in the notification settings with the retinal projector, he doesn’t see anything wrong.

Peter’s Naoji to Peter: [<Blip>]

Do not disturb is set, as he had intended.

Peter’s Naoji to Peter: [<Blip>]

Muttering “Damn thing,” he squeezes the sides of his Naoji to power cycle it. The Naoji briefly vibrates in his hand. 2.3 seconds later, it’s up and running again.

Peter’s Naoji to Peter: [Hello, Peter.]

He waits a full thirty seconds. No more blips. Sighing, he slips the Naoji back into his pocket.

In the bathroom, the shower is noisy and Shasha doesn’t hear Peter come in. Her Naoji 6, a pretty pearly powder blue soap-like block, is lying on the bathroom counter. Its numerous crystal-clear sapphire lens windows, flush with its ceramic body to micron precision, glint in the bathroom lights.

Peter admires Shasha through the shower's glass wall before thinking to her, his thought relayed from his Naoji to hers, and from there, to her mind. The path is direct. It doesn't need the Internet.

Peter: [*To Shasha: I'm back!*]

Shasha turns around to see Peter watching her. Peter smiles at her. *She's so beautiful.*

Shasha smiles back.

[*Do you want to go for a walk later before settling in for the night?*]

[*That would be lovely! I'll be done in a few minutes.*] Shasha's inner voice sounds lighthearted. She continues washing, turning to face the shower head, but peeks at him again a moment later.

They stay close to the hotel on their walk. The nighttime air is cold and their breathing creates clouds of fog. The moon is dark, and the bare granite mountains are shadows against the clear sky, itself filled with stars. They walk silently, Shasha holding Peter's arm, keeping him close.

"Do people *learn* feelings? Or are they built-in from birth? I don't mean like hunger or pain, but, I don't know, say, the feeling of being in a library or at a wild party or at some grand ceremony. Or having a walk at night in a beautiful mountain valley in the middle of winter with someone you love. You know, can you learn a *new* feeling?"

Shasha replies softly: "They do. And you can." She turns around in front of him and, stretching a bit on her toes, gives Peter a kiss.

It is 10:52 pm now, and they have settled into their room for the night. The hallways are silent, and the whole of Yosemite Valley is still and dark.

Lying next to Shasha as she sleeps, and inspired by the dinner conversation, Peter listens to "Smells Like Content", one of his favorite old songs by The Books, his Naoji piping the music directly into his mind. As he gently drifts off to sleep in the ebb of the song's logic, the last flicker of thought that occurs to him, in his hypnagogic state, is whether Zhuangzi would have thought of things that way. Or perhaps not Zhuangzi, but an iridescent butterfly, its cryptochromes bathed in blue light, its quantum spins caressed by the earth's magnetic field.

The mystery
is not in the parts of a system
who you unravel,
but in the beauty of the system
as a functional whole.

THIS IS THE GESTALT
OF LIFE.

A Note on Chinese Names

Chinese names traditionally start with the family name, then are followed by a one or two syllable given name. Here are some pronunciation tips. Note that the Chinese language also includes a pronunciation feature called "tones", but these are not described here.

Cheng Fengxiang 成奉祥

Cheng is like sung, but starting with ch.
Feng starts out like foe and ends with ng.
xiang starts out like she and rhymes with long. She-ong.

Cheng Penglu 程鹏路

Cheng is like sung, but starting with ch.
Peng is like sung, but starting with a p.
lu is like the English name Lou.

Cheng Shasha (Shasha) 程莎莎

Cheng is like sung, but starting with ch.
Sha is like the beginning of shaman.

Chen Yili (Ethan) 陈毅力

Chen is like the beginning of chunky.
Yi is like the letter e. As in easy.
li is like the English name Lee.

Director Chen 陈董事

Chen sounds like "chun" in chunky.

Director Huang 黄董事

Huang starts out like who and rhymes with long. Who-ong.

Director Lu 陆董事

Lu is like the English name Lou.

Director Zhang 张董事

Zhang sounds like John, but rhymes with long. Jong.

He Yue (Joyce) 何悦
He is like "Huh?"
Include the question mark in the sound.
Yue is like "you weigh".
Say it quickly, as a single syllable.

Hundun 混沌
Hun is like "who win",
but say it quickly, all in one syllable.
dun rhymes with Hun.

Ke Qunxiang 柯群祥
Ke is like cut without the t.
Qun is like chewin'.
Say it quickly, as a single syllable.
Xiang starts out like she and rhymes with long. She-ong.

Mr. Li 李先生
Li is like the English name Lee.

Mr. Liu 刘先生
Liu is similar to the English name Leo.

Ms. Chen 陈小姐
Chen sounds like "chun" in chunky.

Peng Haiping (June) 彭海平
Peng is like sung, but starting with a p.
Hai is like hi, as in hello.
ping is like pink, but ending with ng.

Samuel Cheng 程先生 (no Chinese given name)
Cheng is like sung, but starting with ch.

Sun Yang 孙杨
Sun is like sue-win, said as one syllable.
Yang is like young, but with the vowel like "ah" as in father.

Xiaodi 小迪
Xiao starts out like she and ends with ow, as in "now".
di is like dee.

Xiaoxiang 小翔
Xiao starts out like she and ends with ow, as in "now".
xiang starts out like she and rhymes with long. She-ong.

Yangyang 扬扬
Yang is like young,
but with the vowel like "ah" as in father.

Zhu Bajie 猪八戒
Zhu is like Ju in July.
Ba is like Bah in "Bah, humbug!"
jie is like "jay", but even more accurately, jee-ay.

Zhuang Rongtao 庄荣涛
Zhuang is like Ju in July, rhymes with long. Ju-ong.
Rong starts out like row and ends with ng.
tao is the same as in Taoism.

Zhuang Zhou 庄周
Zhuang is like Ju in July, rhymes with long. Ju-ong.
Zhou sounds like Joe.

Zhuangzi 庄子
Zhuang is like Ju in July, rhymes with long. Ju-ong.
zi is like the zz in buzz

Made in the USA
Las Vegas, NV
30 October 2022